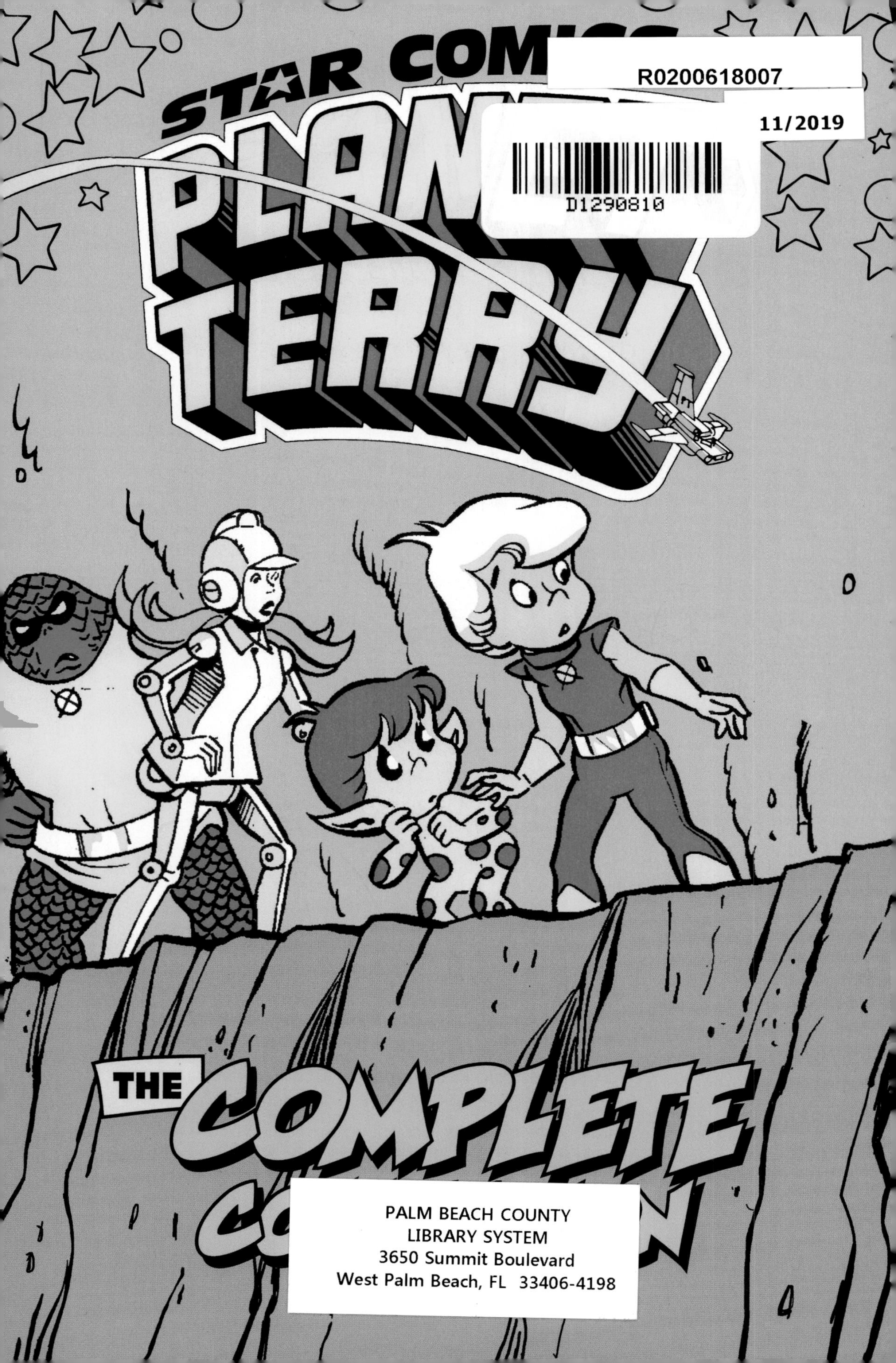
STAR
TERRY
THE COMPLETE

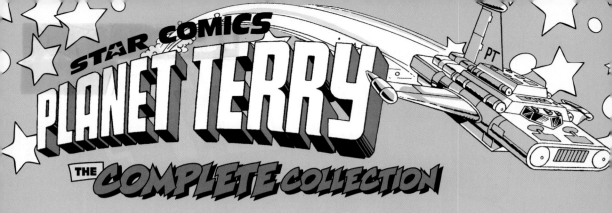

STAR COMICS PLANET TERRY

THE COMPLETE COLLECTION

LENNIE HERMAN, STAN KAY & DAVE MANAK
WRITERS

WARREN KREMER
PENCILER

VINCE COLLETTA, JON D'AGOSTINO & JACQUELINE ROETTCHER
INKERS

PETER KREMER & GEORGE ROUSSOS
COLORISTS

GRACE KREMER & JOE ROSEN
LETTERERS

LAURA HITCHCOCK & NANCY BROWN
ASSISTANT EDITORS

SID JACOBSON
EDITOR

TOM DEFALCO
EXECUTIVE EDITOR

WARREN KREMER & VERONICA GANDINI
FRONT COVER ARTISTS

WARREN KREMER
BACK COVER ARTIST

COLLECTION EDITOR **MARK D. BEAZLEY** ★ ASSISTANT EDITOR **CAITLIN O'CONNELL**
ASSOCIATE MANAGING EDITOR **KATERI WOODY** ★ ASSOCIATE MANAGER, DIGITAL ASSETS **JOE HOCHSTEIN**
SENIOR EDITOR, SPECIAL PROJECTS **JENNIFER GRÜNWALD** ★ VP PRODUCTION & SPECIAL PROJECTS **JEFF YOUNGQUIST**
RESEARCH & LAYOUT **JEPH YORK** ★ PRODUCTION **COLORTEK & JOE FRONTIRRE**
BOOK DESIGNER **JAY BOWEN**

SVP PRINT, SALES & MARKETING **DAVID GABRIEL** ★ DIRECTOR, LICENSED PUBLISHING **SVEN LARSEN**
EDITOR IN CHIEF **C.B. CEBULSKI** ★ CHIEF CREATIVE OFFICER **JOE QUESADA**
PRESIDENT **DAN BUCKLEY** ★ EXECUTIVE PRODUCER **ALAN FINE**

Special Thanks to **MIKE HANSEN** & **MARC RIEMER**

STAR COMICS: PLANET TERRY — THE COMPLETE COLLECTION. Contains material originally published in magazine form as PLANET TERRY #1-12. First printing 2019. ISBN 978-1-302-91864-4. Published by MARVEL WORLDWIDE, INC., a subsidiary of MARVEL ENTERTAINMENT, LLC. OFFICE OF PUBLICATION: 135 West 50th Street, New York, NY 10020. **Printed in the U.S.A.** DAN BUCKLEY, President, Marvel Entertainment; JOHN NEE, Publisher; JOE QUESADA, Chief Creative Officer; TOM BREVOORT, SVP of Publishing; DAVID BOGART, Associate Publisher & SVP of Talent Affairs; DAVID GABRIEL, SVP of Sales & Marketing, Publishing; JEFF YOUNGQUIST, VP of Production & Special Projects; DAN CARR, Executive Director of Publishing Technology; ALEX MORALES, Director of Publishing Operations; DAN EDINGTON, Managing Editor; SUSAN CRESPI, Production Manager; STAN LEE, Chairman Emeritus. For information regarding advertising in Marvel Comics or on Marvel.com, please contact Vit DeBellis, Custom Solutions & Integrated Advertising Manager, at vdebellis@marvel.com. For Marvel subscription inquiries, please call 888-511-5480. **Manufactured between 3/29/2019 and 4/30/2019 by LSC COMMUNICATIONS INC., KENDALLVILLE, IN, USA.**

10 9 8 7 6 5 4 3 2 1

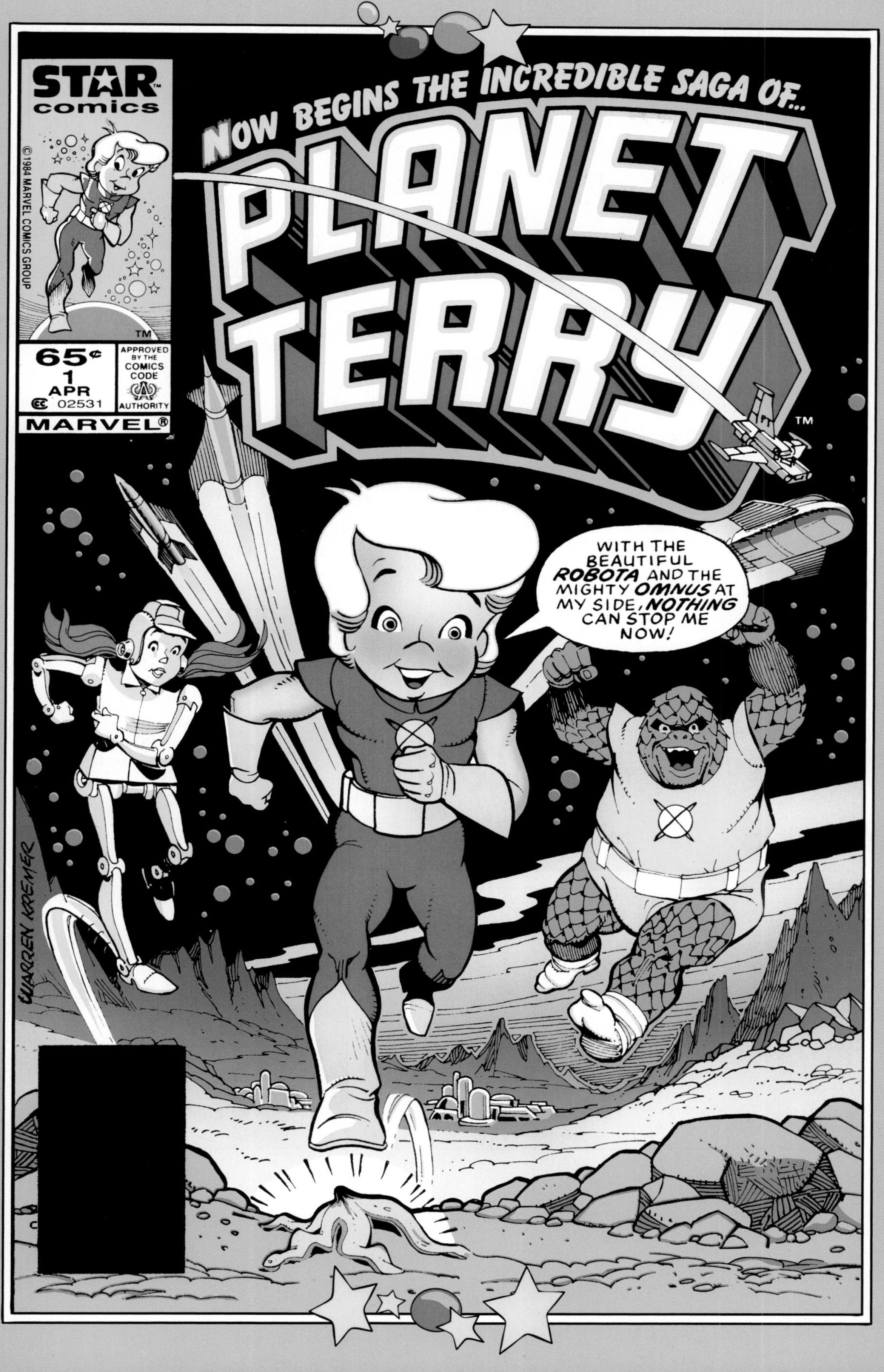
STAR™ comics
© 1984 MARVEL COMICS GROUP
65¢
1
APR
02531
APPROVED BY THE COMICS CODE AUTHORITY
MARVEL®
NOW BEGINS THE INCREDIBLE SAGA OF...
PLANET TERRY™
WITH THE BEAUTIFUL ROBOTA AND THE MIGHTY OMNUS AT MY SIDE, NOTHING CAN STOP ME NOW!
WARREN KREMER

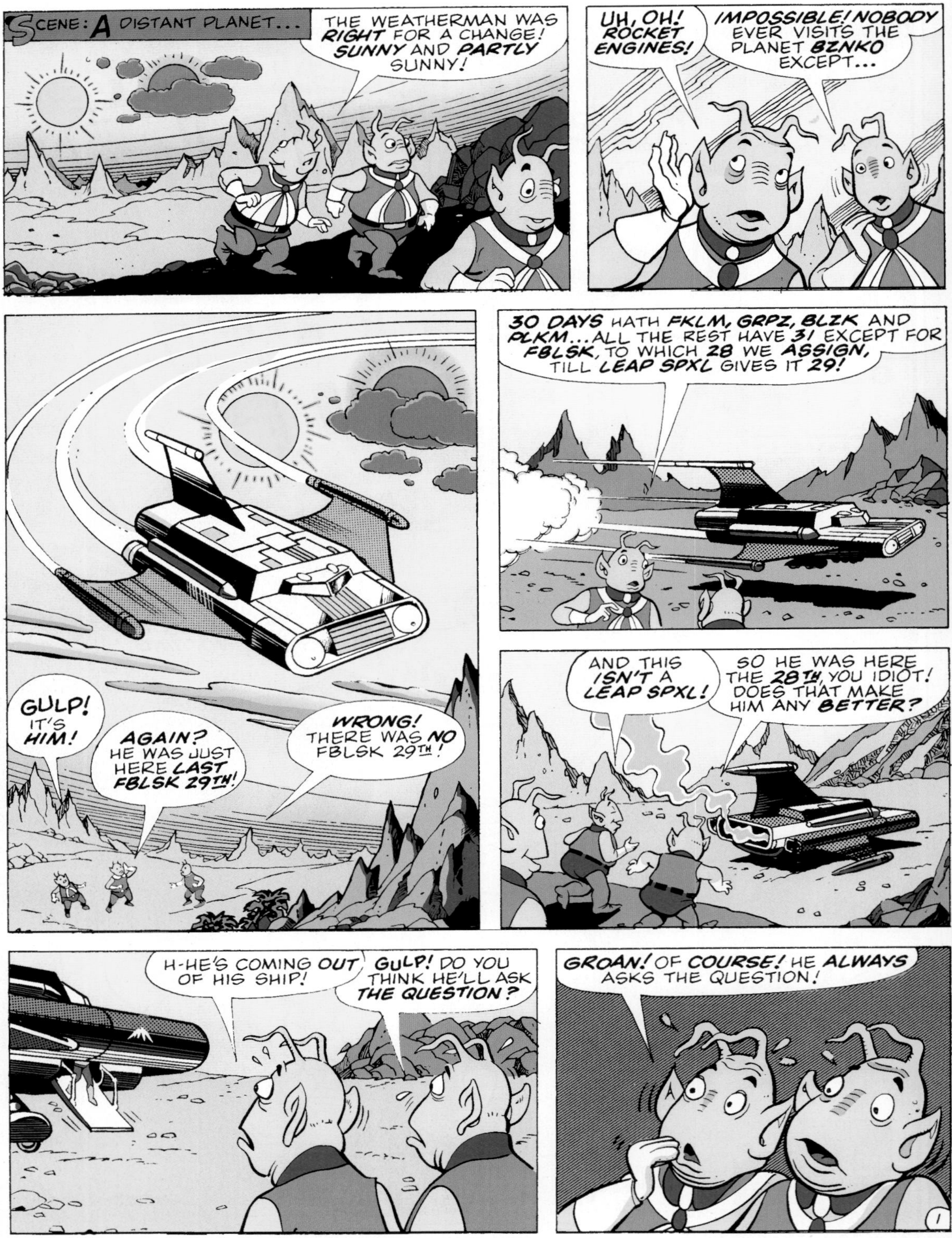
SCENE: A DISTANT PLANET...
THE WEATHERMAN WAS RIGHT FOR A CHANGE! SUNNY AND PARTLY SUNNY!
UH, OH! ROCKET ENGINES!
IMPOSSIBLE! NOBODY EVER VISITS THE PLANET BZNKO EXCEPT...
GULP! IT'S HIM!
AGAIN? HE WAS JUST HERE LAST FBLSK 29TH!
WRONG! THERE WAS NO FBLSK 29TH!
30 DAYS HATH FKLM, GRPZ, BLZK AND PLKM...ALL THE REST HAVE 31 EXCEPT FOR FBLSK, TO WHICH 28 WE ASSIGN, TILL LEAP SPXL GIVES IT 29!
AND THIS ISN'T A LEAP SPXL!
SO HE WAS HERE THE 28TH, YOU IDIOT! DOES THAT MAKE HIM ANY BETTER?
H-HE'S COMING OUT OF HIS SHIP!
GULP! DO YOU THINK HE'LL ASK THE QUESTION?
GROAN! OF COURSE! HE ALWAYS ASKS THE QUESTION!
1

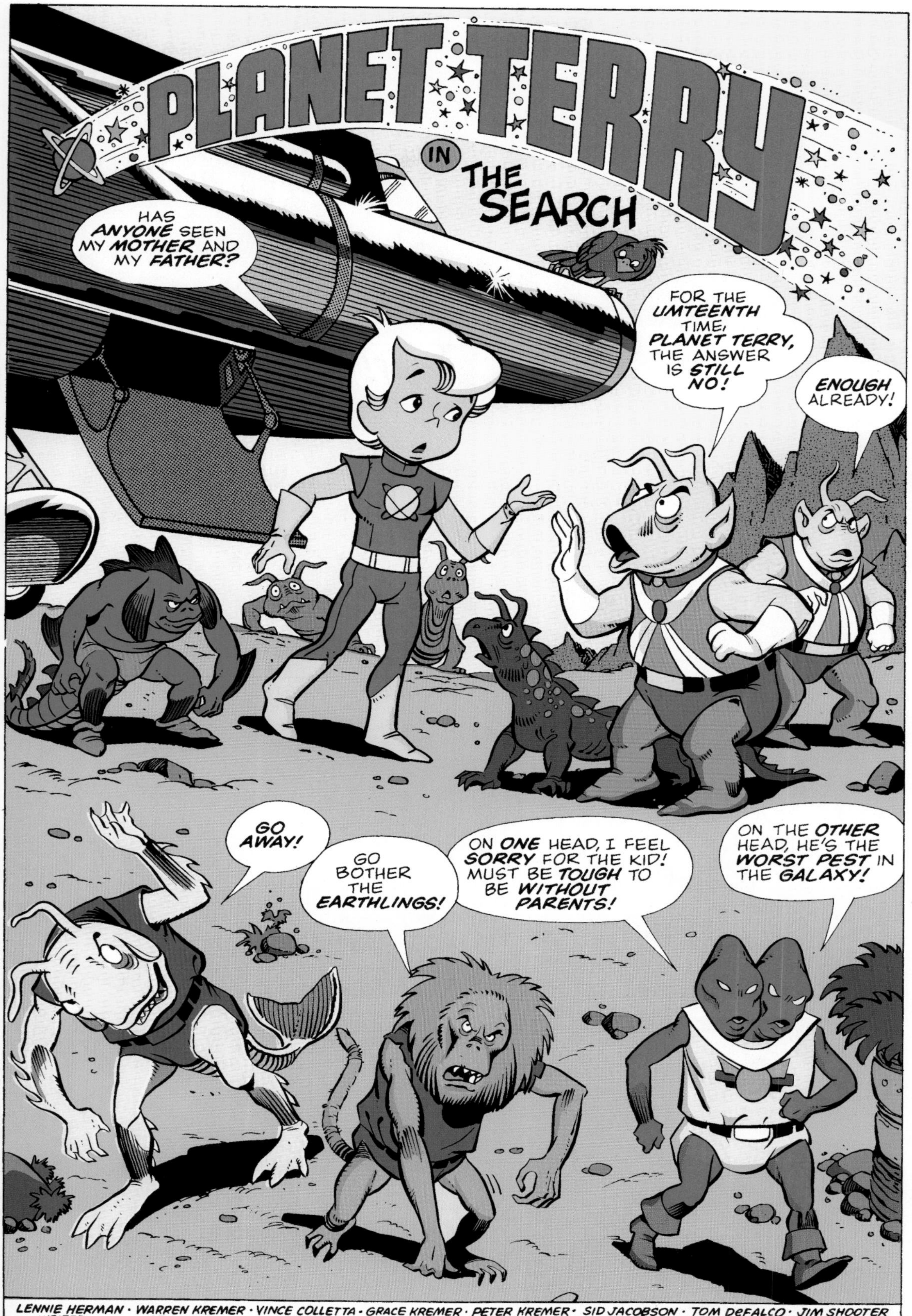
PLANET TERRY
IN THE SEARCH
HAS ANYONE SEEN MY MOTHER AND MY FATHER?
FOR THE UMTEENTH TIME, PLANET TERRY, THE ANSWER IS STILL NO!
ENOUGH ALREADY!
GO AWAY!
GO BOTHER THE EARTHLINGS!
ON ONE HEAD, I FEEL SORRY FOR THE KID! MUST BE TOUGH TO BE WITHOUT PARENTS!
ON THE OTHER HEAD, HE'S THE WORST PEST IN THE GALAXY!

LENNIE HERMAN · WARREN KREMER · VINCE COLLETTA · GRACE KREMER · PETER KREMER · SID JACOBSON · TOM DeFALCO · JIM SHOOTER
WRITER · PENCILER · INKER · LETTERER · COLORIST · EDITOR · EXECUTIVE EDITOR · EDITOR IN CHIEF

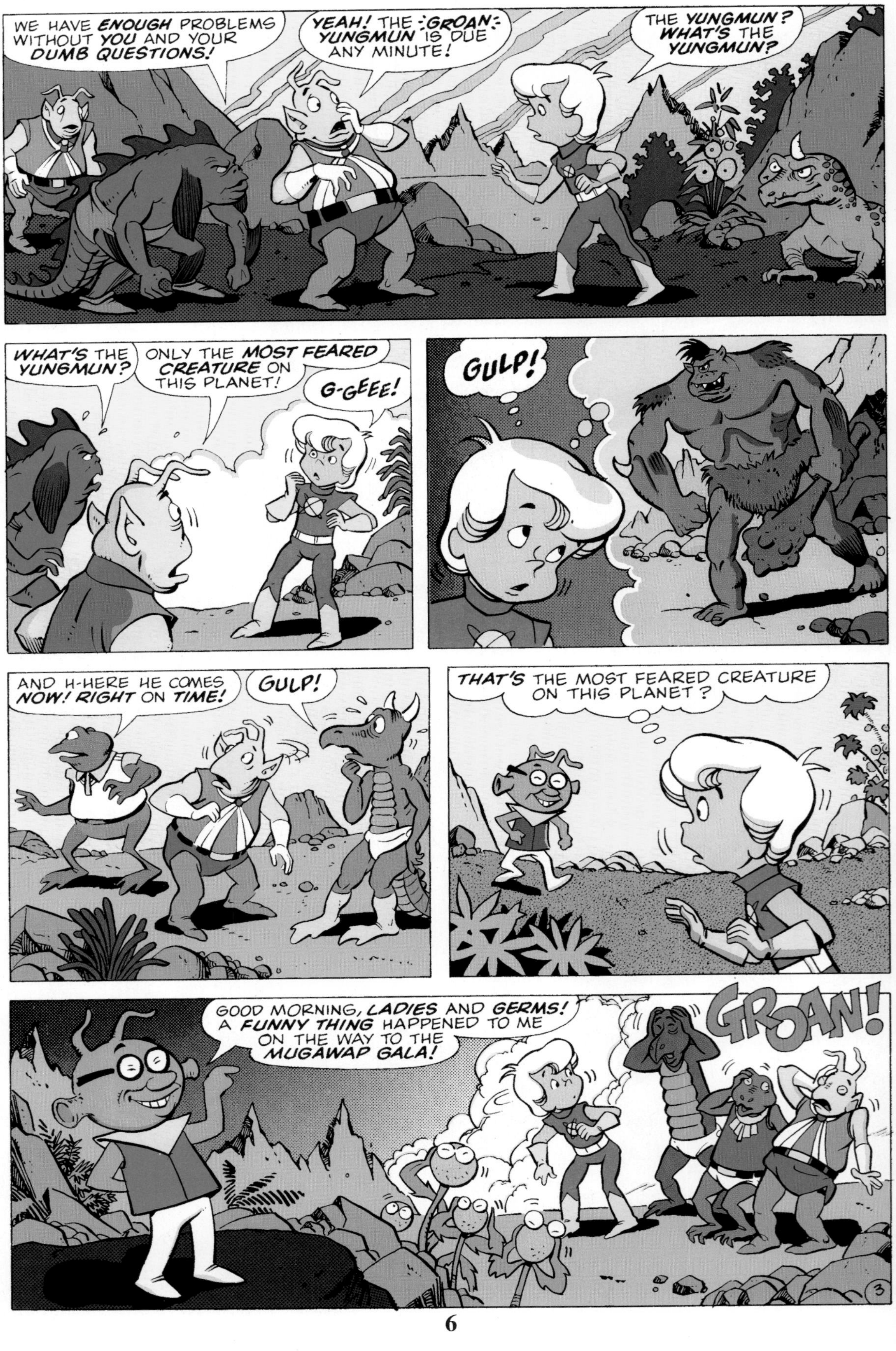
WE HAVE ENOUGH PROBLEMS WITHOUT YOU AND YOUR DUMB QUESTIONS!
YEAH! THE GROAN YUNGMUN IS DUE ANY MINUTE!
THE YUNGMUN? WHAT'S THE YUNGMUN?
WHAT'S THE YUNGMUN?
ONLY THE MOST FEARED CREATURE ON THIS PLANET!
G-GEEE!
GULP!
AND H-HERE HE COMES NOW! RIGHT ON TIME!
GULP!
THAT'S THE MOST FEARED CREATURE ON THIS PLANET?
GOOD MORNING, LADIES AND GERMS! A FUNNY THING HAPPENED TO ME ON THE WAY TO THE MUGAWAP GALA!
GROAN!
3

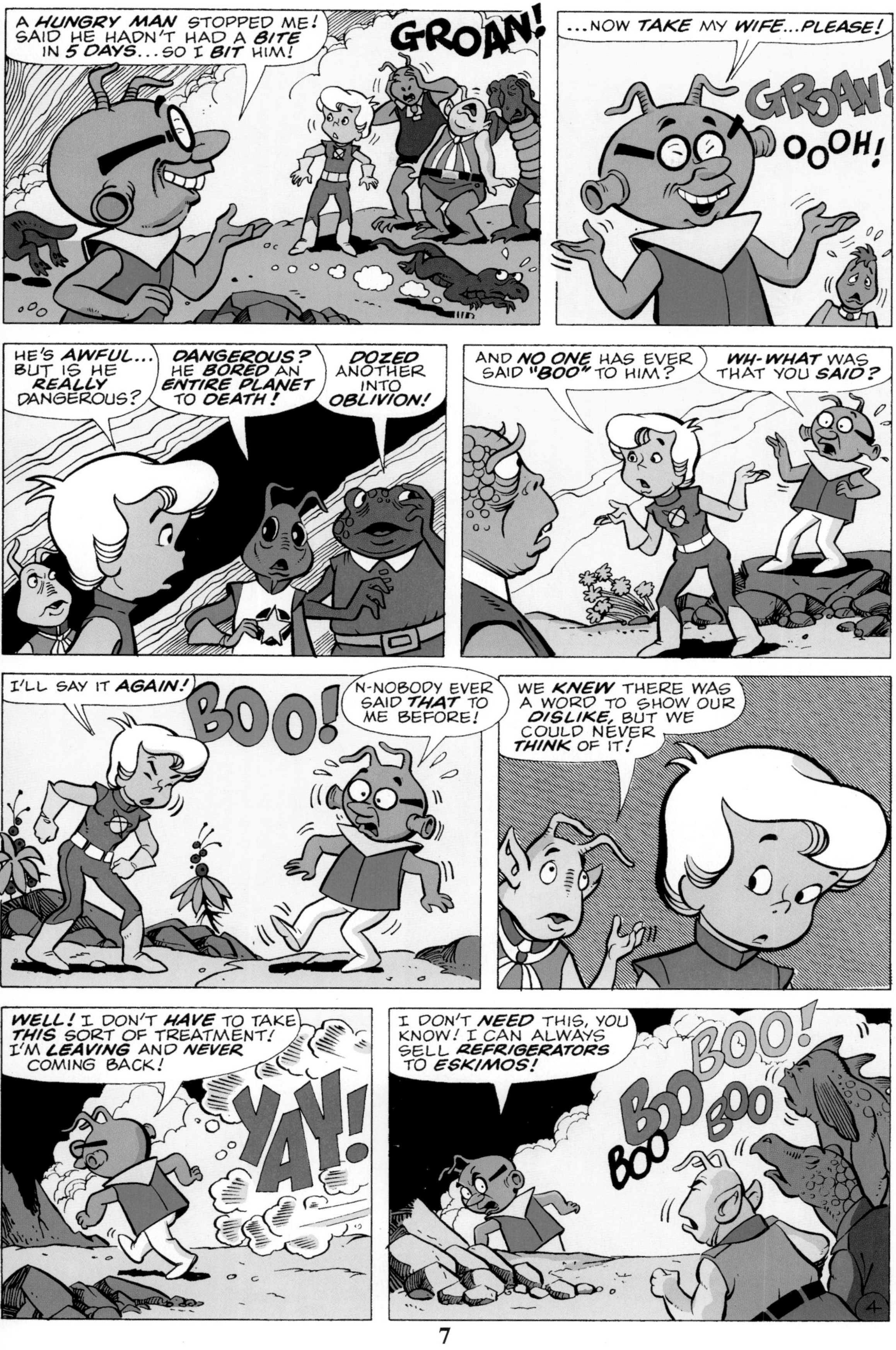
A HUNGRY MAN STOPPED ME! SAID HE HADN'T HAD A BITE IN 5 DAYS... SO I BIT HIM!
GROAN!
...NOW TAKE MY WIFE...PLEASE!
GROAN!
OOOH!
HE'S AWFUL... BUT IS HE REALLY DANGEROUS?
DANGEROUS? HE BORED AN ENTIRE PLANET TO DEATH!
DOZED ANOTHER INTO OBLIVION!
AND NO ONE HAS EVER SAID "BOO" TO HIM?
WH-WHAT WAS THAT YOU SAID?
I'LL SAY IT AGAIN!
BOO!
N-NOBODY EVER SAID THAT TO ME BEFORE!
WE KNEW THERE WAS A WORD TO SHOW OUR DISLIKE, BUT WE COULD NEVER THINK OF IT!
WELL! I DON'T HAVE TO TAKE THIS SORT OF TREATMENT! I'M LEAVING AND NEVER COMING BACK!
YAY!
I DON'T NEED THIS, YOU KNOW! I CAN ALWAYS SELL REFRIGERATORS TO ESKIMOS!
BOO BOO BOO BOO BOO!
4

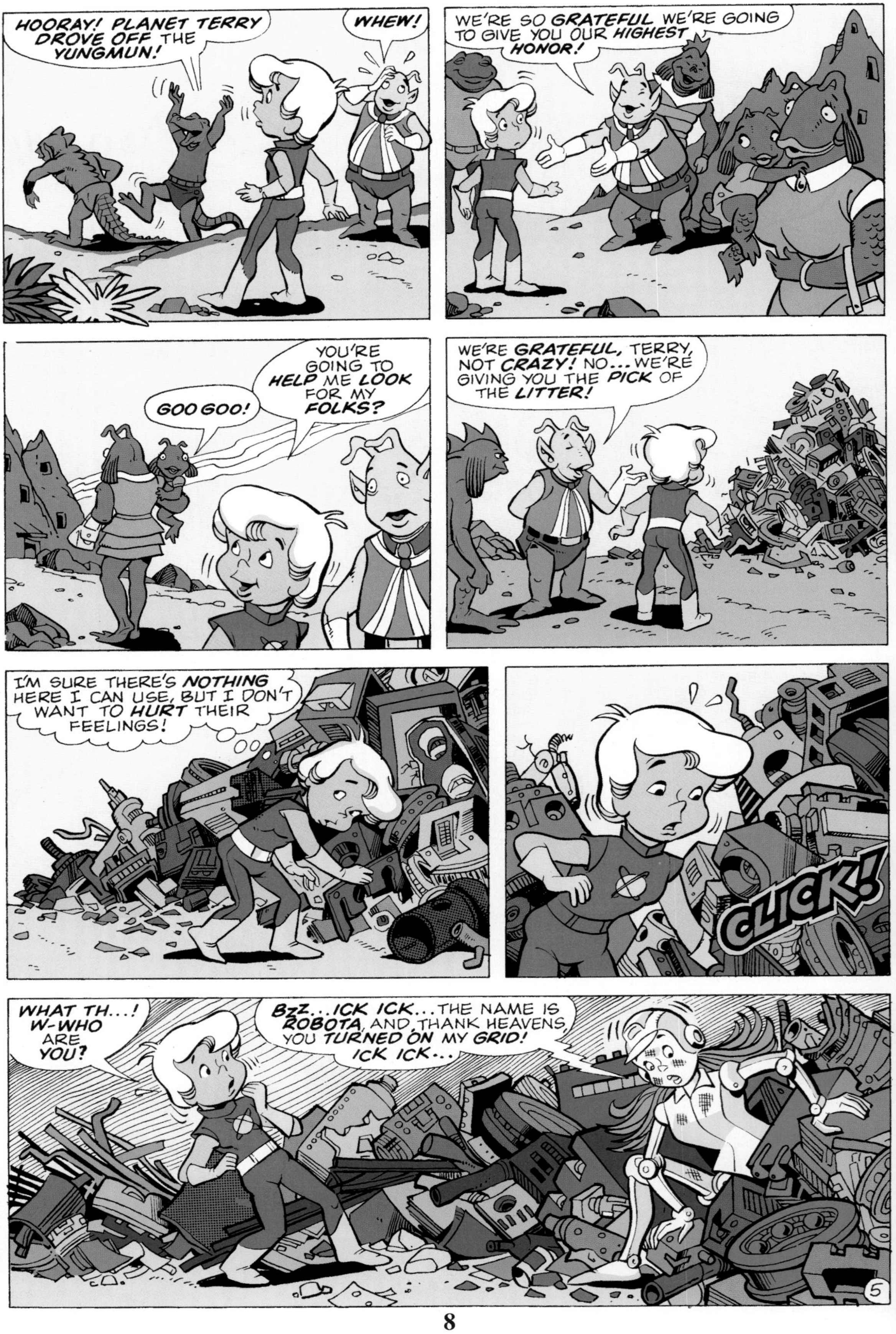
HOORAY! PLANET TERRY DROVE OFF THE YUNGMUN!
WHEW!
WE'RE SO GRATEFUL WE'RE GOING TO GIVE YOU OUR HIGHEST HONOR!
GOO GOO!
YOU'RE GOING TO HELP ME LOOK FOR MY FOLKS?
WE'RE GRATEFUL, TERRY, NOT CRAZY! NO... WE'RE GIVING YOU THE PICK OF THE LITTER!
I'M SURE THERE'S NOTHING HERE I CAN USE, BUT I DON'T WANT TO HURT THEIR FEELINGS!
CLICK!
WHAT TH...! W-WHO ARE YOU?
BZZ... ICK ICK... THE NAME IS ROBOTA, AND THANK HEAVENS, YOU TURNED ON MY GRID! ICK ICK...
5

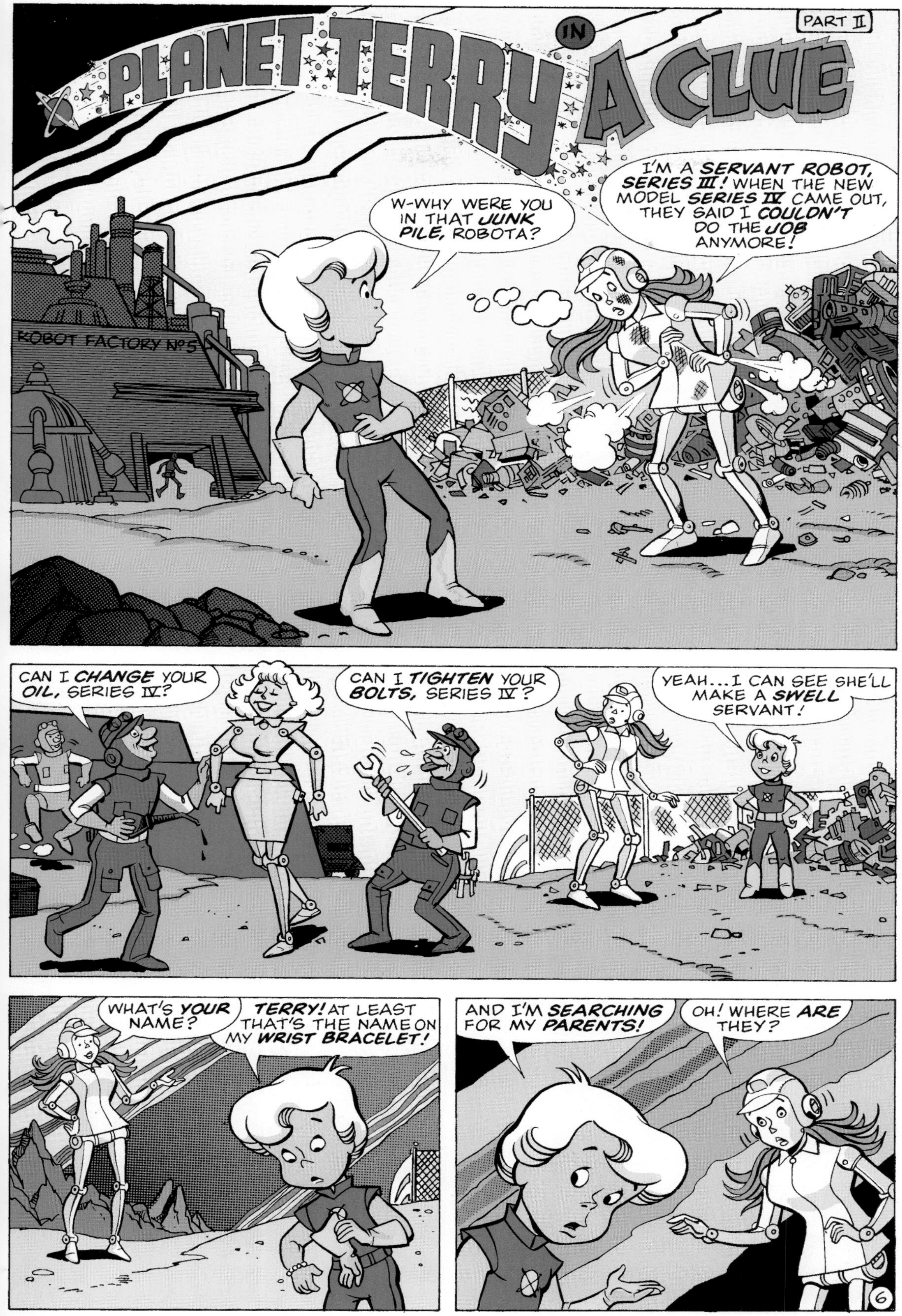
PART II
PLANET TERRY IN A CLUE
W-WHY WERE YOU IN THAT JUNK PILE, ROBOTA?
I'M A SERVANT ROBOT, SERIES III! WHEN THE NEW MODEL SERIES IV CAME OUT, THEY SAID I COULDN'T DO THE JOB ANYMORE!
ROBOT FACTORY Nº5
CAN I CHANGE YOUR OIL, SERIES IV?
CAN I TIGHTEN YOUR BOLTS, SERIES IV?
YEAH...I CAN SEE SHE'LL MAKE A SWELL SERVANT!
WHAT'S YOUR NAME?
TERRY! AT LEAST THAT'S THE NAME ON MY WRIST BRACELET!
AND I'M SEARCHING FOR MY PARENTS!
OH! WHERE ARE THEY?
6

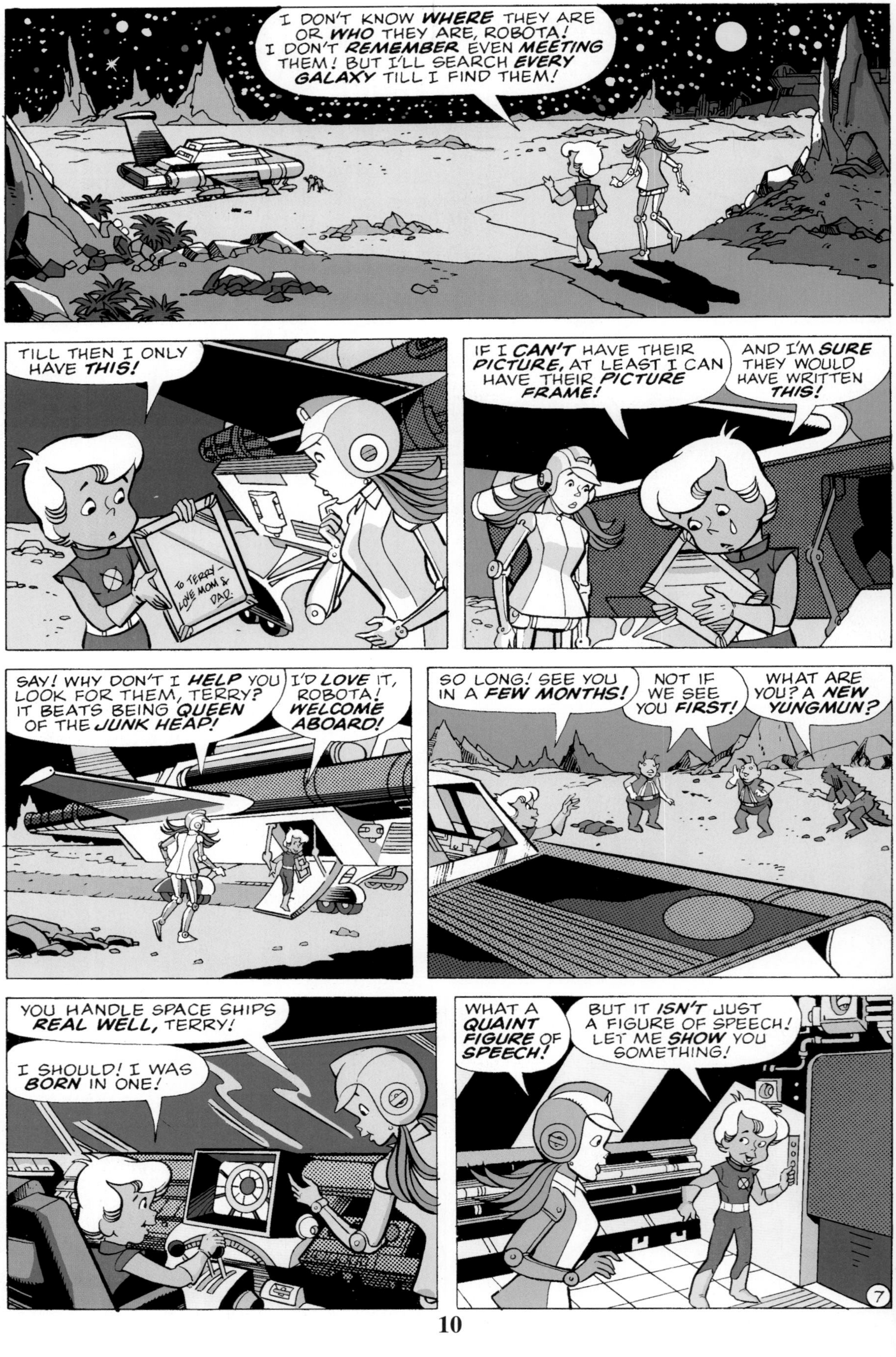
I DON'T KNOW WHERE THEY ARE OR WHO THEY ARE, ROBOTA! I DON'T REMEMBER EVEN MEETING THEM! BUT I'LL SEARCH EVERY GALAXY TILL I FIND THEM!
TILL THEN I ONLY HAVE THIS!
TO TERRY - LOVE MOM & DAD.
IF I CAN'T HAVE THEIR PICTURE, AT LEAST I CAN HAVE THEIR PICTURE FRAME!
AND I'M SURE THEY WOULD HAVE WRITTEN THIS!
SAY! WHY DON'T I HELP YOU LOOK FOR THEM, TERRY? IT BEATS BEING QUEEN OF THE JUNK HEAP!
I'D LOVE IT, ROBOTA! WELCOME ABOARD!
SO LONG! SEE YOU IN A FEW MONTHS!
NOT IF WE SEE YOU FIRST!
WHAT ARE YOU? A NEW YUNGMUN?
YOU HANDLE SPACE SHIPS REAL WELL, TERRY!
I SHOULD! I WAS BORN IN ONE!
WHAT A QUAINT FIGURE OF SPEECH!
BUT IT ISN'T JUST A FIGURE OF SPEECH! LET ME SHOW YOU SOMETHING!
7

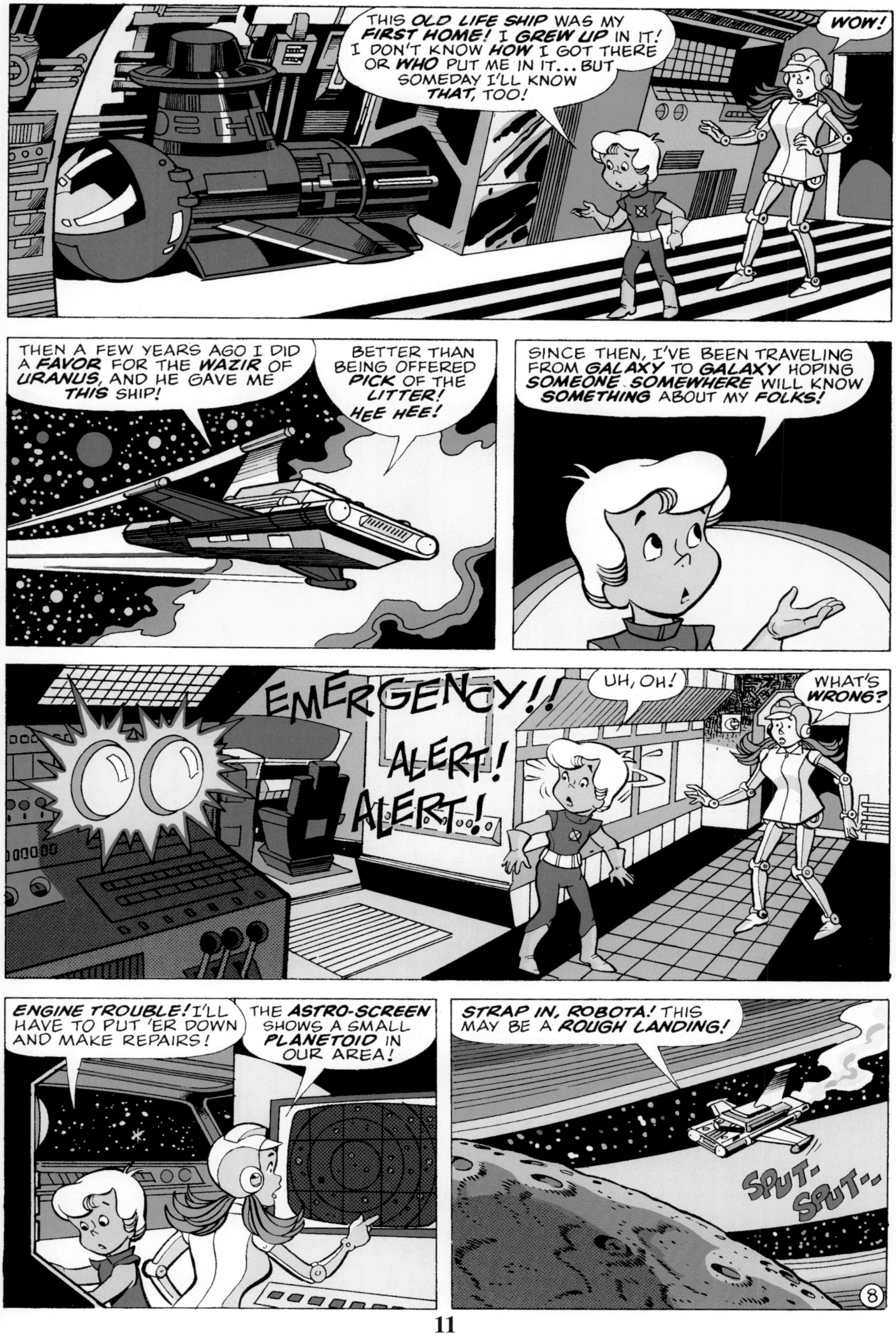
THIS OLD LIFE SHIP WAS MY FIRST HOME! I GREW UP IN IT! I DON'T KNOW HOW I GOT THERE OR WHO PUT ME IN IT... BUT SOMEDAY I'LL KNOW THAT, TOO!
WOW!
THEN A FEW YEARS AGO I DID A FAVOR FOR THE WAZIR OF URANUS, AND HE GAVE ME THIS SHIP!
BETTER THAN BEING OFFERED PICK OF THE LITTER! HEE HEE!
SINCE THEN, I'VE BEEN TRAVELING FROM GALAXY TO GALAXY HOPING SOMEONE SOMEWHERE WILL KNOW SOMETHING ABOUT MY FOLKS!
EMERGENCY!!
ALERT!
ALERT!
UH, OH!
WHAT'S WRONG?
ENGINE TROUBLE! I'LL HAVE TO PUT 'ER DOWN AND MAKE REPAIRS!
THE ASTRO-SCREEN SHOWS A SMALL PLANETOID IN OUR AREA!
STRAP IN, ROBOTA! THIS MAY BE A ROUGH LANDING!
SPUT-
SPUT-.
8

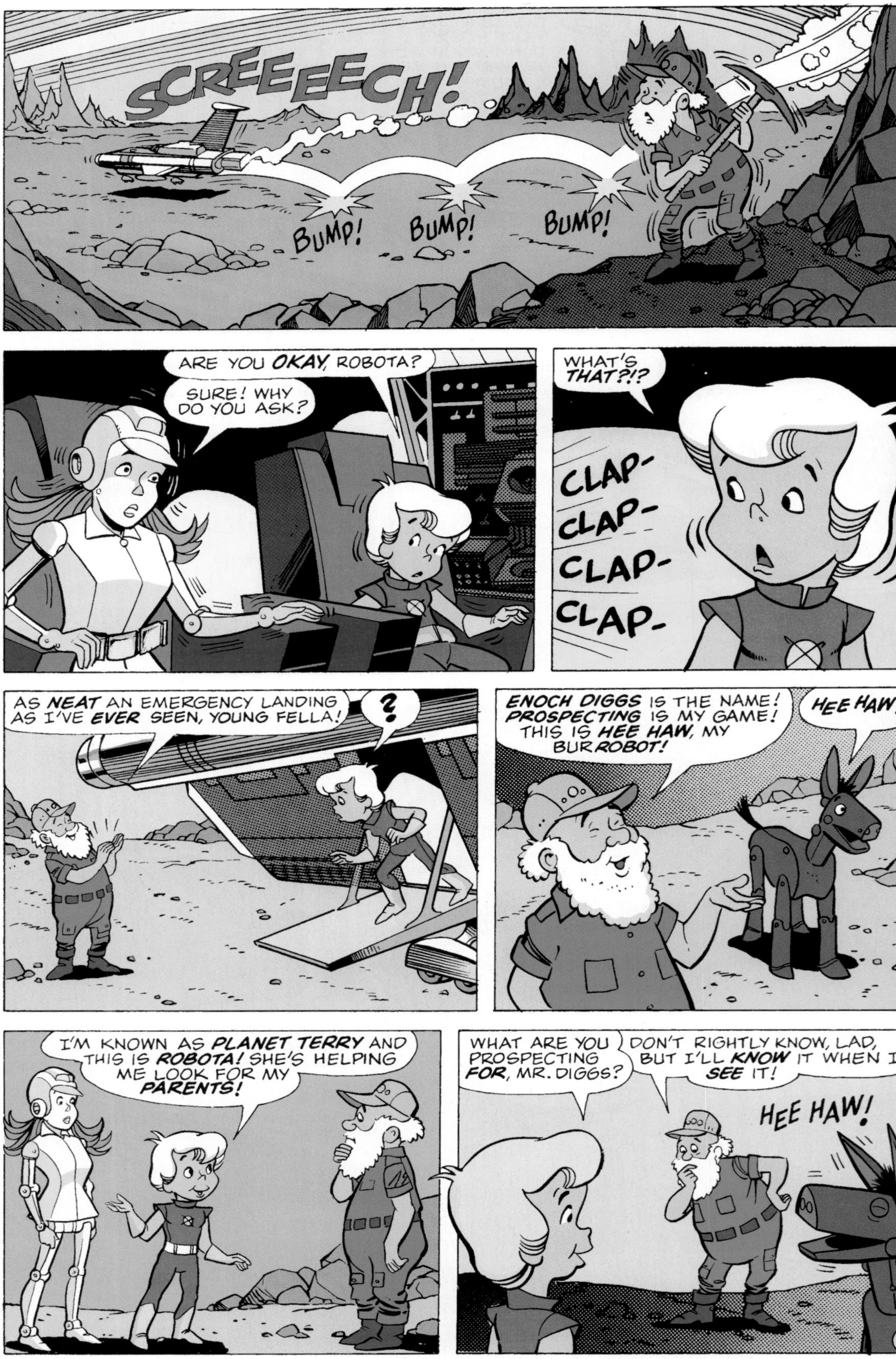
SCREEEEECH!
BUMP! BUMP! BUMP!
ARE YOU OKAY, ROBOTA?
SURE! WHY DO YOU ASK?
WHAT'S THAT?!?
CLAP-
CLAP-
CLAP-
CLAP-
AS NEAT AN EMERGENCY LANDING AS I'VE EVER SEEN, YOUNG FELLA!
?
ENOCH DIGGS IS THE NAME! PROSPECTING IS MY GAME! THIS IS HEE HAW, MY BURROBOT!
HEE HAW!
I'M KNOWN AS PLANET TERRY AND THIS IS ROBOTA! SHE'S HELPING ME LOOK FOR MY PARENTS!
WHAT ARE YOU PROSPECTING FOR, MR. DIGGS?
DON'T RIGHTLY KNOW, LAD, BUT I'LL KNOW IT WHEN I SEE IT!
HEE HAW!
9

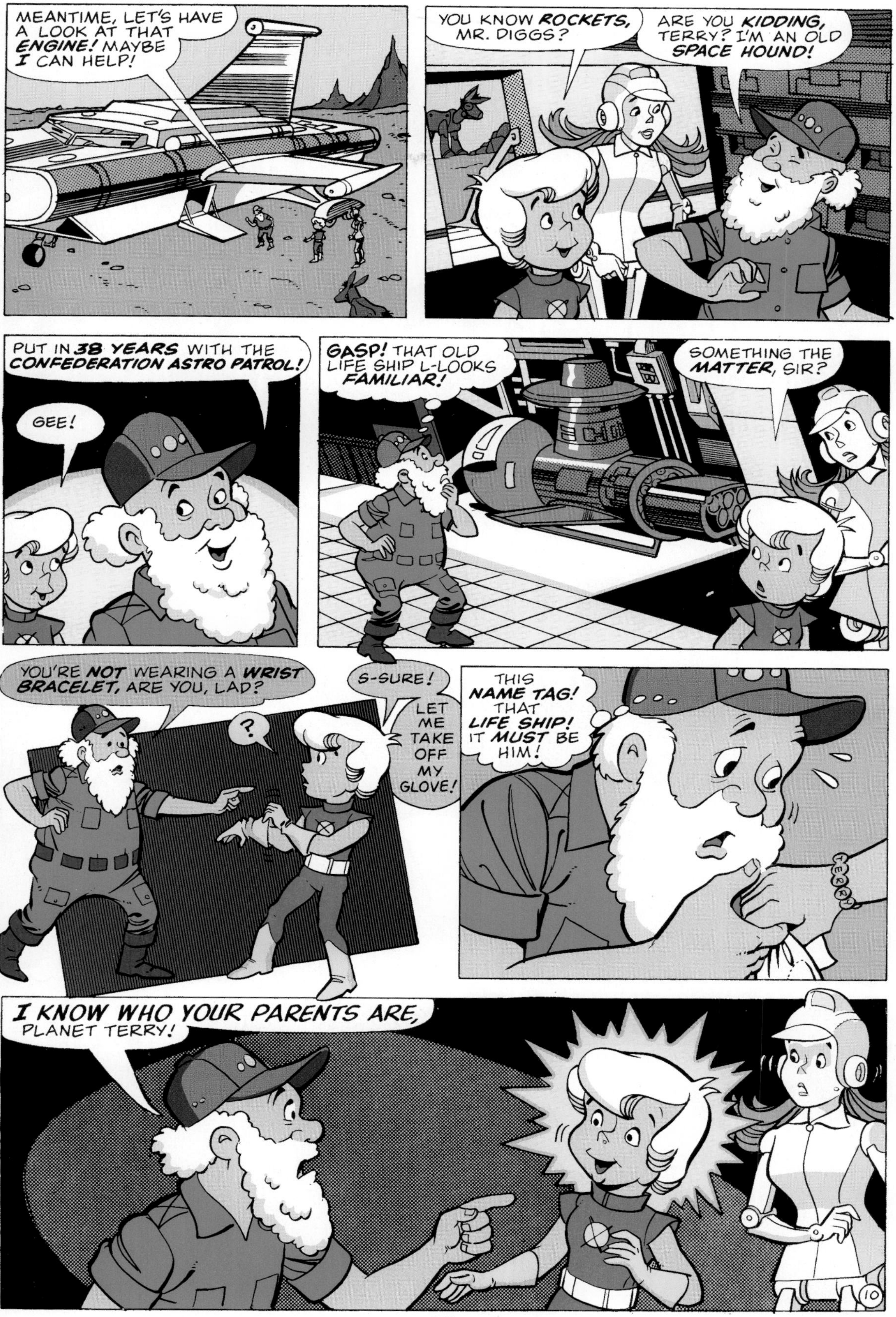
MEANTIME, LET'S HAVE A LOOK AT THAT ENGINE! MAYBE I CAN HELP!
YOU KNOW ROCKETS, MR. DIGGS?
ARE YOU KIDDING, TERRY? I'M AN OLD SPACE HOUND!
PUT IN 38 YEARS WITH THE CONFEDERATION ASTRO PATROL!
GEE!
GASP! THAT OLD LIFE SHIP L-LOOKS FAMILIAR!
SOMETHING THE MATTER, SIR?
YOU'RE NOT WEARING A WRIST BRACELET, ARE YOU, LAD?
?
S-SURE!
LET ME TAKE OFF MY GLOVE!
THIS NAME TAG! THAT LIFE SHIP! IT MUST BE HIM!
I KNOW WHO YOUR PARENTS ARE, PLANET TERRY!

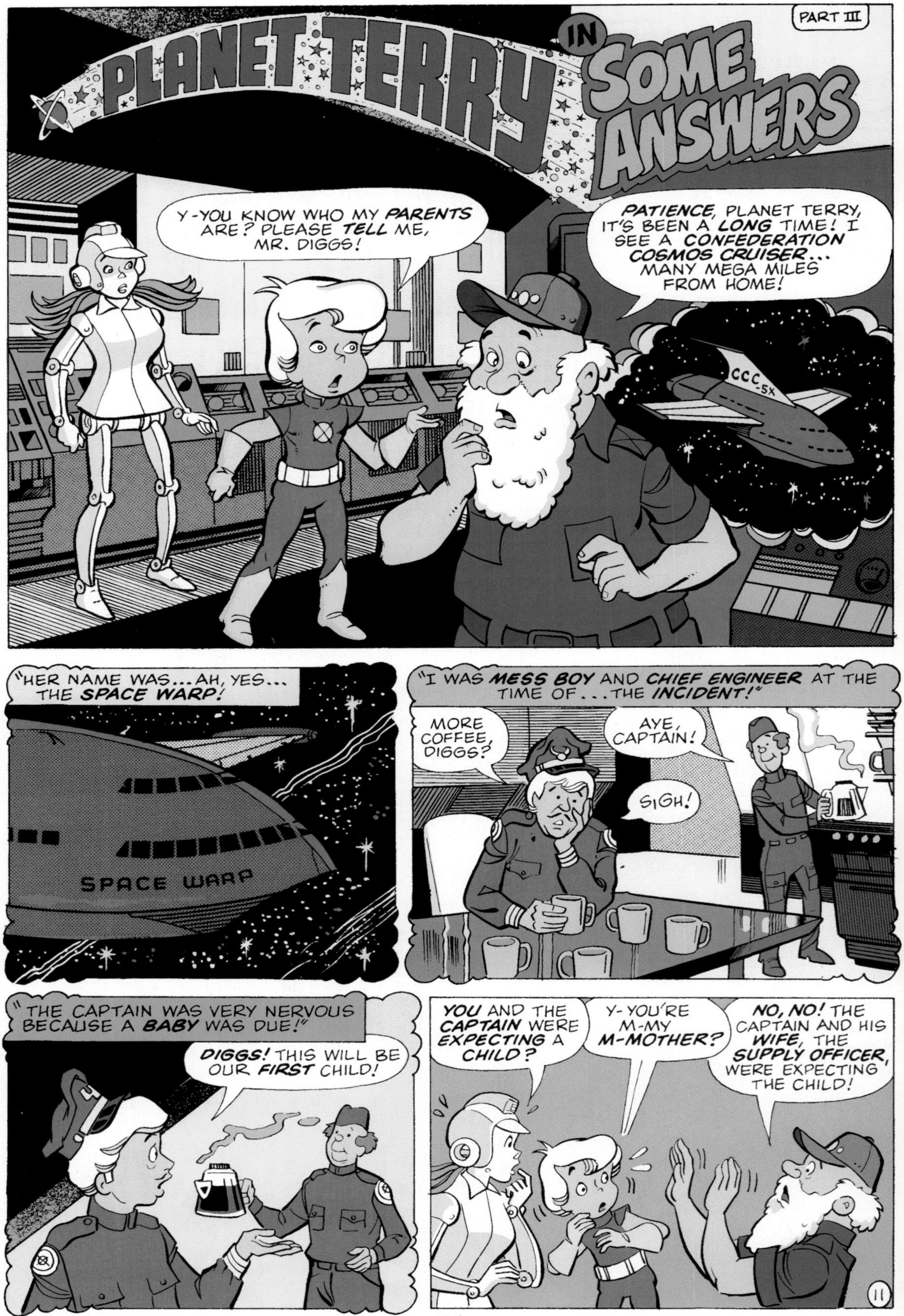

PART III
PLANET TERRY IN SOME ANSWERS
Y-YOU KNOW WHO MY PARENTS ARE? PLEASE TELL ME, MR. DIGGS!
PATIENCE, PLANET TERRY, IT'S BEEN A LONG TIME! I SEE A CONFEDERATION COSMOS CRUISER... MANY MEGA MILES FROM HOME!
CCC-5X
"HER NAME WAS...AH, YES... THE SPACE WARP!
SPACE WARP
"I WAS MESS BOY AND CHIEF ENGINEER AT THE TIME OF...THE INCIDENT!"
MORE COFFEE, DIGGS?
AYE, CAPTAIN!
SIGH!
"THE CAPTAIN WAS VERY NERVOUS BECAUSE A BABY WAS DUE!"
DIGGS! THIS WILL BE OUR FIRST CHILD!
YOU AND THE CAPTAIN WERE EXPECTING A CHILD?
Y-YOU'RE M-MY M-MOTHER?
NO, NO! THE CAPTAIN AND HIS WIFE, THE SUPPLY OFFICER, WERE EXPECTING THE CHILD!
11

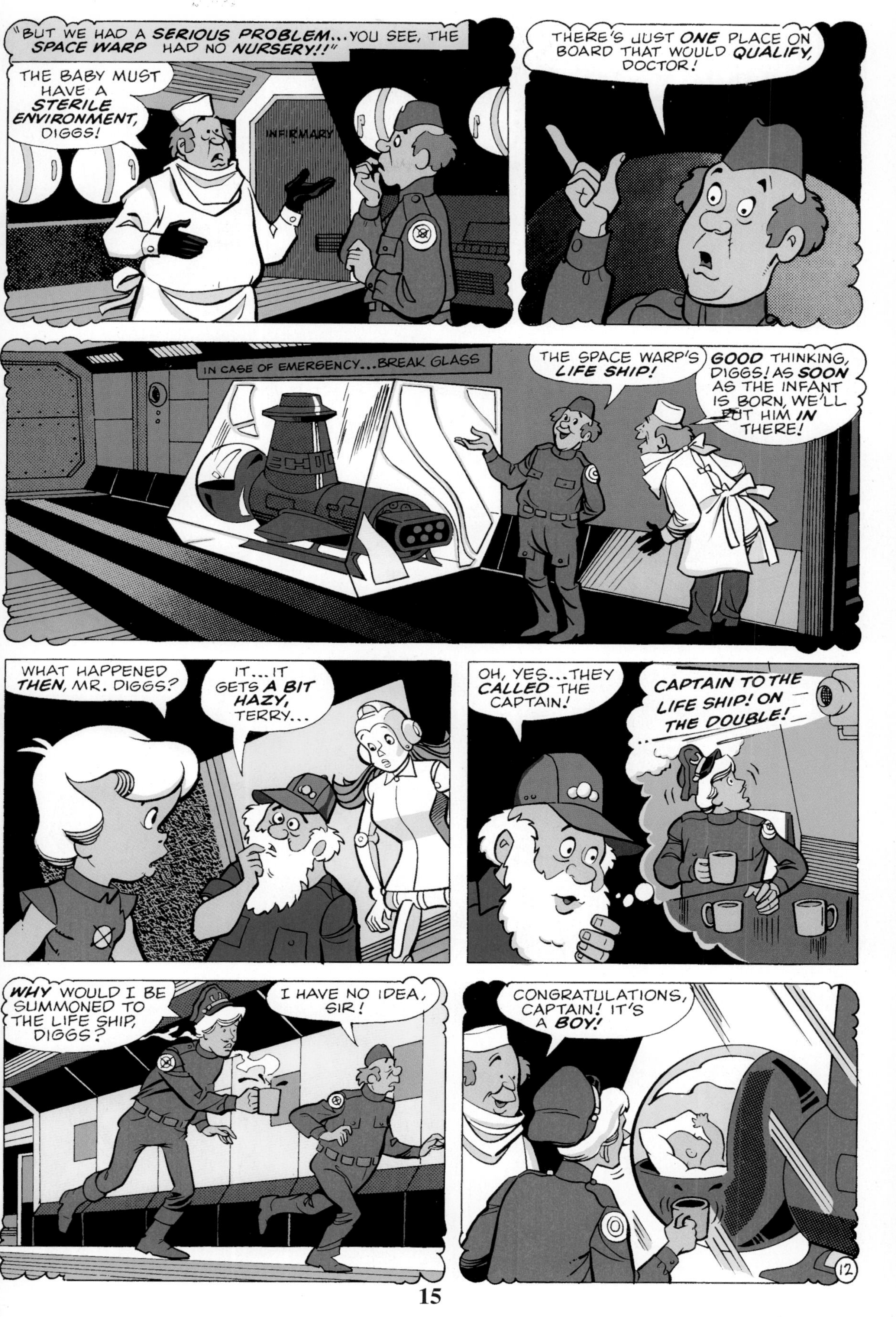
"BUT WE HAD A SERIOUS PROBLEM... YOU SEE, THE SPACE WARP HAD NO NURSERY!!"
THE BABY MUST HAVE A STERILE ENVIRONMENT, DIGGS!
INFIRMARY
THERE'S JUST ONE PLACE ON BOARD THAT WOULD QUALIFY, DOCTOR!
IN CASE OF EMERGENCY...BREAK GLASS
THE SPACE WARP'S LIFE SHIP!
GOOD THINKING, DIGGS! AS SOON AS THE INFANT IS BORN, WE'LL PUT HIM IN THERE!
WHAT HAPPENED THEN, MR. DIGGS?
IT...IT GETS A BIT HAZY, TERRY...
OH, YES...THEY CALLED THE CAPTAIN!
CAPTAIN TO THE LIFE SHIP! ON THE DOUBLE!
WHY WOULD I BE SUMMONED TO THE LIFE SHIP, DIGGS?
I HAVE NO IDEA, SIR!
CONGRATULATIONS, CAPTAIN! IT'S A BOY!
12

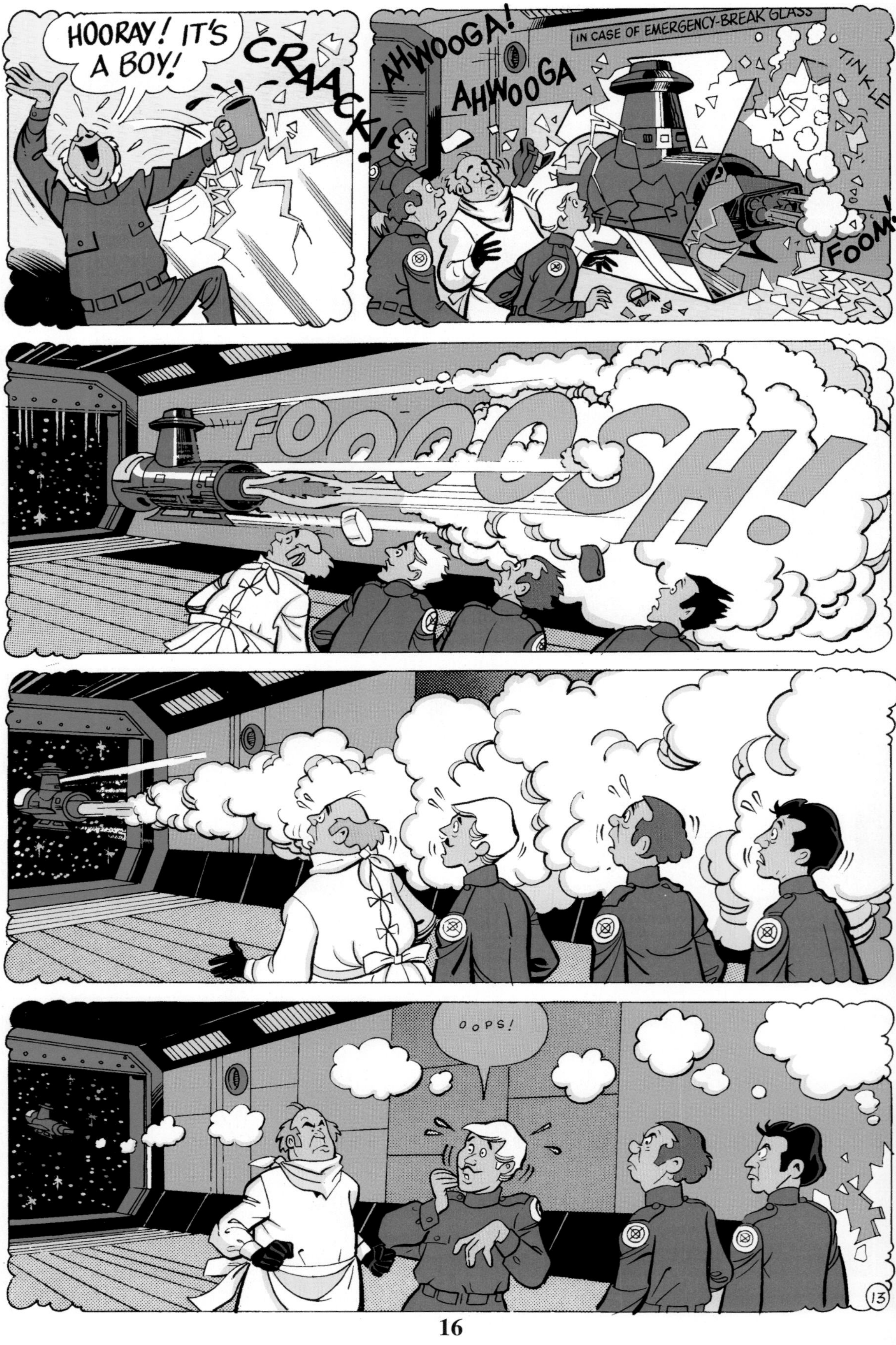
HOORAY! IT'S A BOY!
CRAACK!
AHWOOGA!
AHWOOGA
IN CASE OF EMERGENCY-BREAK GLASS
TINKLE
FOOM!
FOOOOOSH!
OOPS!
13

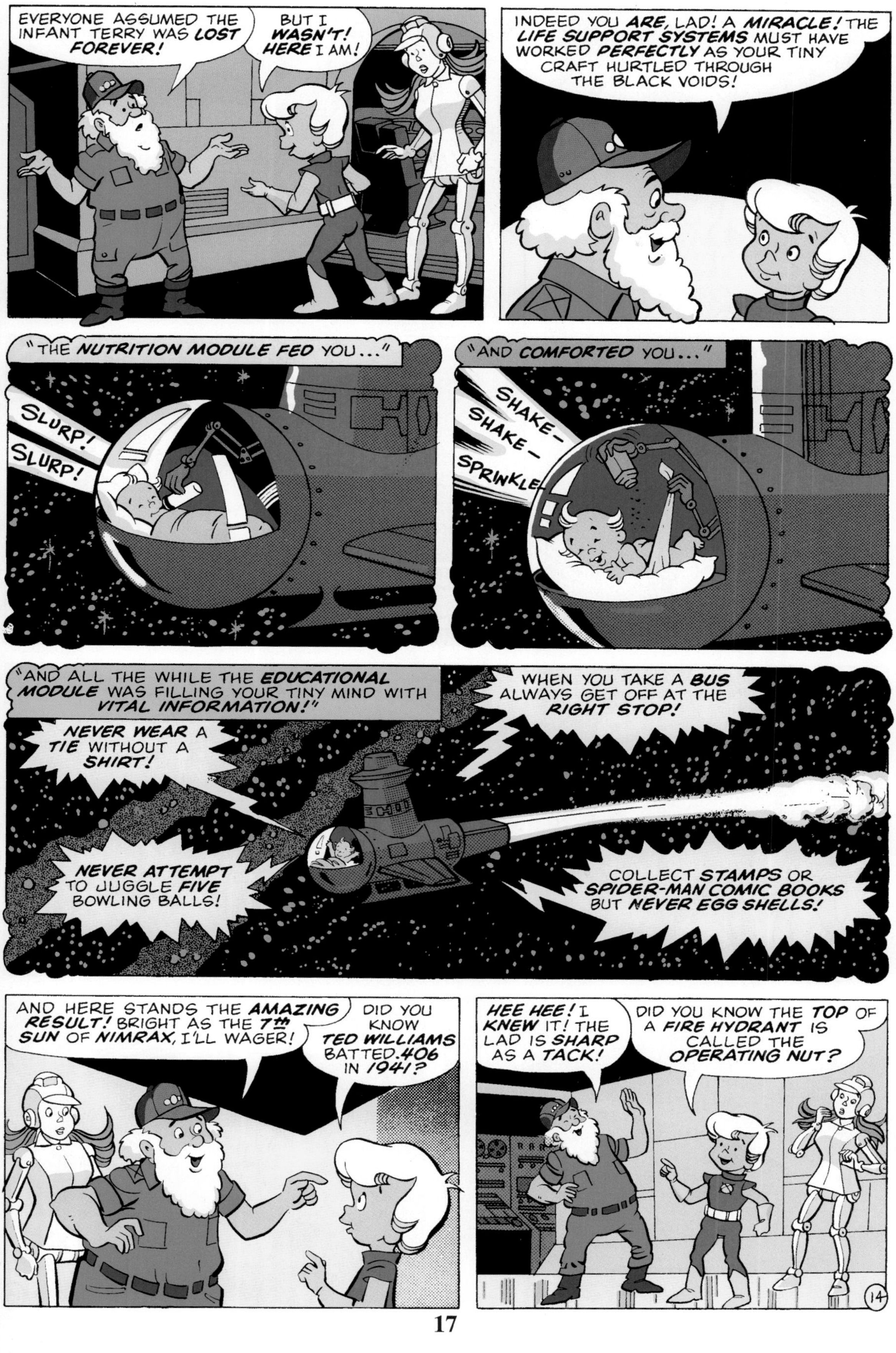
EVERYONE ASSUMED THE INFANT TERRY WAS LOST FOREVER!
BUT I WASN'T! HERE I AM!
INDEED YOU ARE, LAD! A MIRACLE! THE LIFE SUPPORT SYSTEMS MUST HAVE WORKED PERFECTLY AS YOUR TINY CRAFT HURTLED THROUGH THE BLACK VOIDS!
"THE NUTRITION MODULE FED YOU..."
SLURP! SLURP!
"AND COMFORTED YOU..."
SHAKE- SHAKE- SPRINKLE
"AND ALL THE WHILE THE EDUCATIONAL MODULE WAS FILLING YOUR TINY MIND WITH VITAL INFORMATION!"
NEVER WEAR A TIE WITHOUT A SHIRT!
WHEN YOU TAKE A BUS ALWAYS GET OFF AT THE RIGHT STOP!
NEVER ATTEMPT TO JUGGLE FIVE BOWLING BALLS!
COLLECT STAMPS OR SPIDER-MAN COMIC BOOKS BUT NEVER EGG SHELLS!
AND HERE STANDS THE AMAZING RESULT! BRIGHT AS THE 7th SUN OF NIMRAX, I'LL WAGER!
DID YOU KNOW TED WILLIAMS BATTED .406 IN 1941?
HEE HEE! I KNEW IT! THE LAD IS SHARP AS A TACK!
DID YOU KNOW THE TOP OF A FIRE HYDRANT IS CALLED THE OPERATING NUT?
14

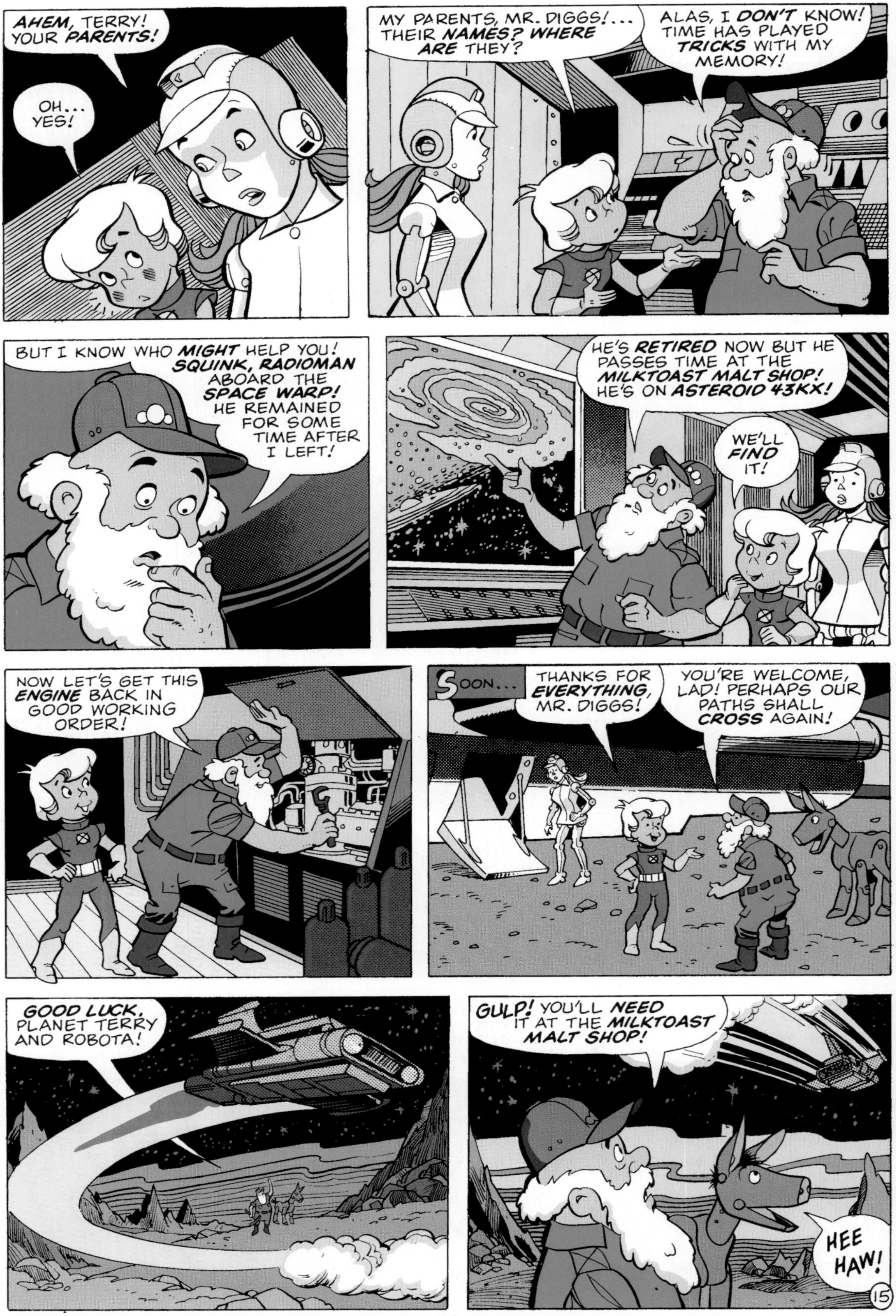
AHEM, TERRY! YOUR PARENTS!
OH... YES!
MY PARENTS, MR. DIGGS!... THEIR NAMES? WHERE ARE THEY?
ALAS, I DON'T KNOW! TIME HAS PLAYED TRICKS WITH MY MEMORY!
BUT I KNOW WHO MIGHT HELP YOU! SQUINK, RADIOMAN ABOARD THE SPACE WARP! HE REMAINED FOR SOME TIME AFTER I LEFT!
HE'S RETIRED NOW BUT HE PASSES TIME AT THE MILKTOAST MALT SHOP! HE'S ON ASTEROID 43KX!
WE'LL FIND IT!
NOW LET'S GET THIS ENGINE BACK IN GOOD WORKING ORDER!
SOON...
THANKS FOR EVERYTHING, MR. DIGGS!
YOU'RE WELCOME, LAD! PERHAPS OUR PATHS SHALL CROSS AGAIN!
GOOD LUCK, PLANET TERRY AND ROBOTA!
GULP! YOU'LL NEED IT AT THE MILKTOAST MALT SHOP!
HEE HAW!
15

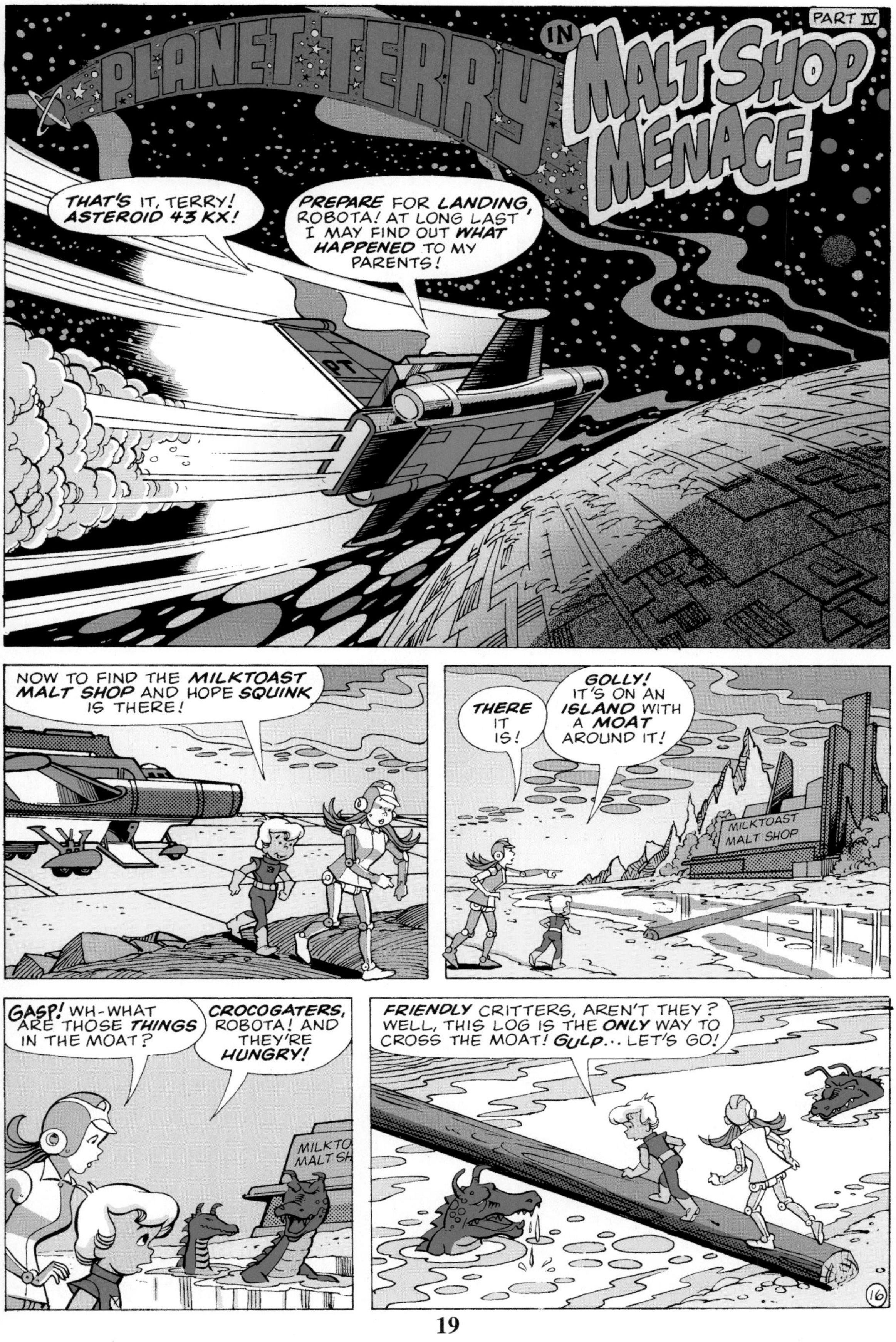
PLANET TERRY IN
MALT SHOP MENACE
PART IV
THAT'S IT, TERRY! ASTEROID 43 KX!
PREPARE FOR LANDING, ROBOTA! AT LONG LAST I MAY FIND OUT WHAT HAPPENED TO MY PARENTS!
PT
NOW TO FIND THE MILKTOAST MALT SHOP AND HOPE SQUINK IS THERE!
THERE IT IS!
GOLLY! IT'S ON AN ISLAND WITH A MOAT AROUND IT!
MILKTOAST MALT SHOP
GASP! WH-WHAT ARE THOSE THINGS IN THE MOAT?
CROCOGATERS, ROBOTA! AND THEY'RE HUNGRY!
FRIENDLY CRITTERS, AREN'T THEY? WELL, THIS LOG IS THE ONLY WAY TO CROSS THE MOAT! GULP.. LET'S GO!
16

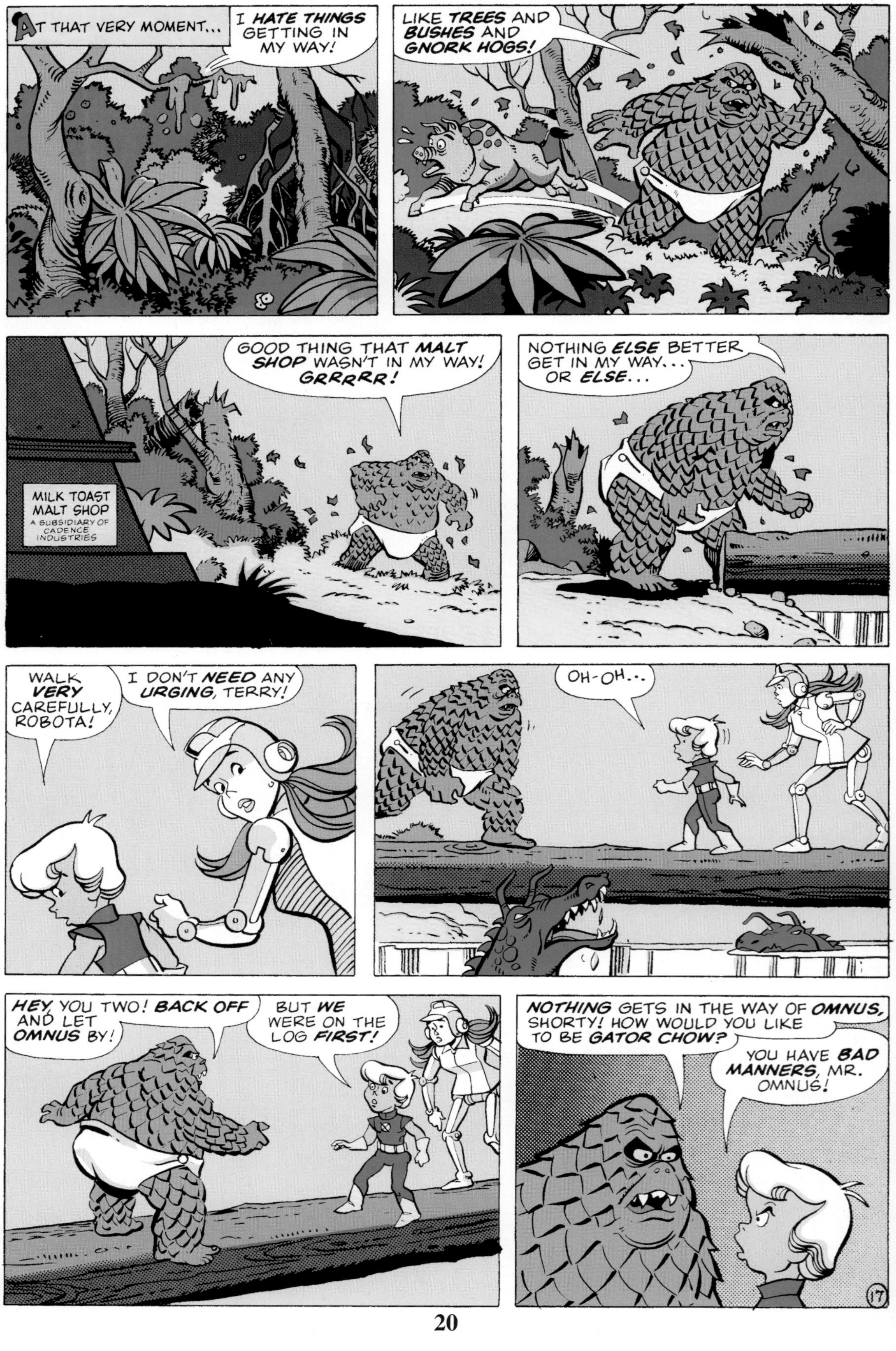
AT THAT VERY MOMENT...
I HATE THINGS GETTING IN MY WAY!
LIKE TREES AND BUSHES AND GNORK HOGS!
GOOD THING THAT MALT SHOP WASN'T IN MY WAY! GRRRRR!
MILK TOAST MALT SHOP A SUBSIDIARY OF CADENCE INDUSTRIES
NOTHING ELSE BETTER GET IN MY WAY... OR ELSE...
WALK VERY CAREFULLY, ROBOTA!
I DON'T NEED ANY URGING, TERRY!
OH-OH...
HEY, YOU TWO! BACK OFF AND LET OMNUS BY!
BUT WE WERE ON THE LOG FIRST!
NOTHING GETS IN THE WAY OF OMNUS, SHORTY! HOW WOULD YOU LIKE TO BE GATOR CHOW?
YOU HAVE BAD MANNERS, MR. OMNUS!
17

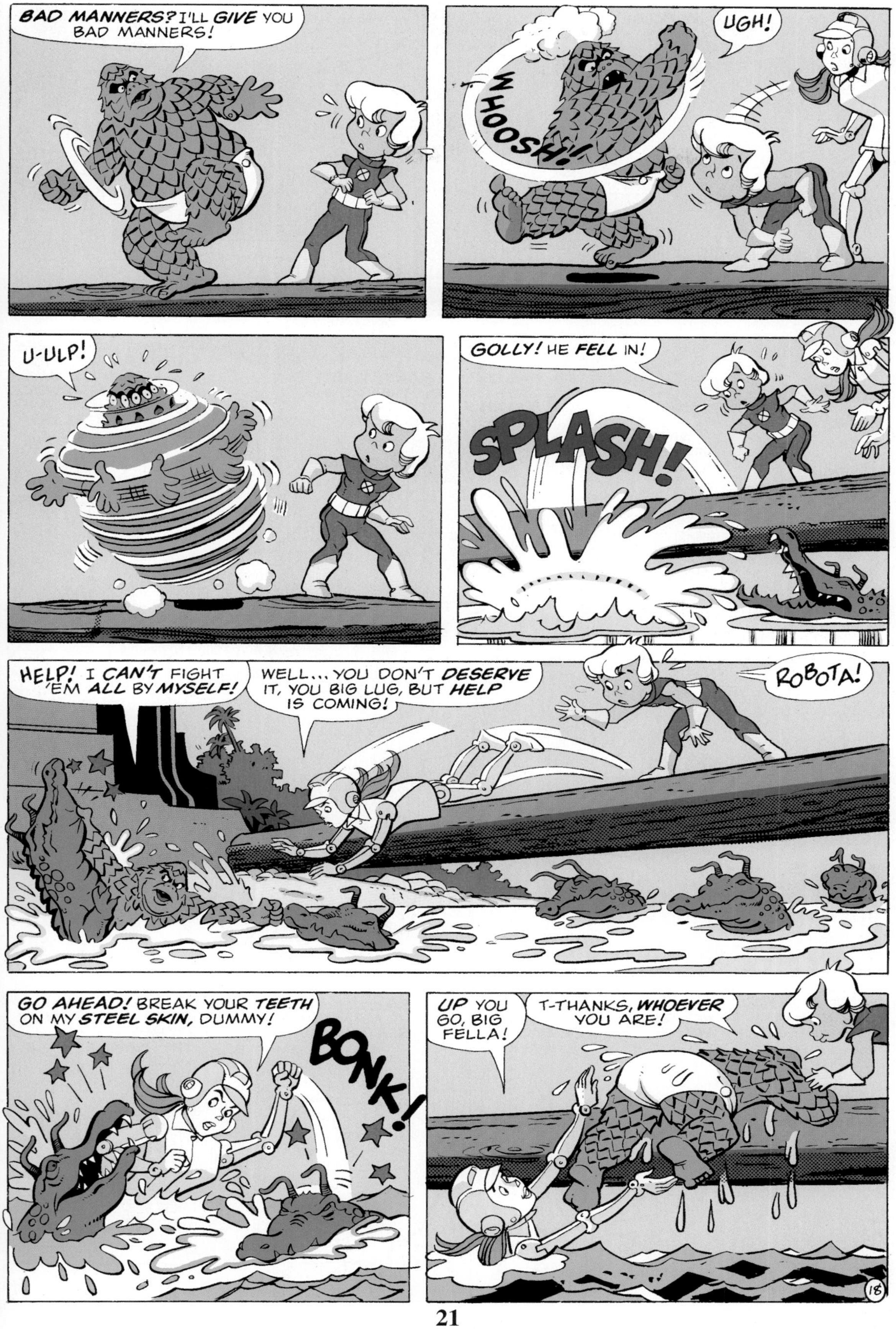
BAD MANNERS? I'LL GIVE YOU BAD MANNERS!
UGH!
WHOOSH!!
U-ULP!
GOLLY! HE FELL IN!
SPLASH!
HELP! I CAN'T FIGHT 'EM ALL BY MYSELF!
WELL... YOU DON'T DESERVE IT, YOU BIG LUG, BUT HELP IS COMING!
ROBOTA!
GO AHEAD! BREAK YOUR TEETH ON MY STEEL SKIN, DUMMY!
BONK!
UP YOU GO, BIG FELLA!
T-THANKS, WHOEVER YOU ARE!
18

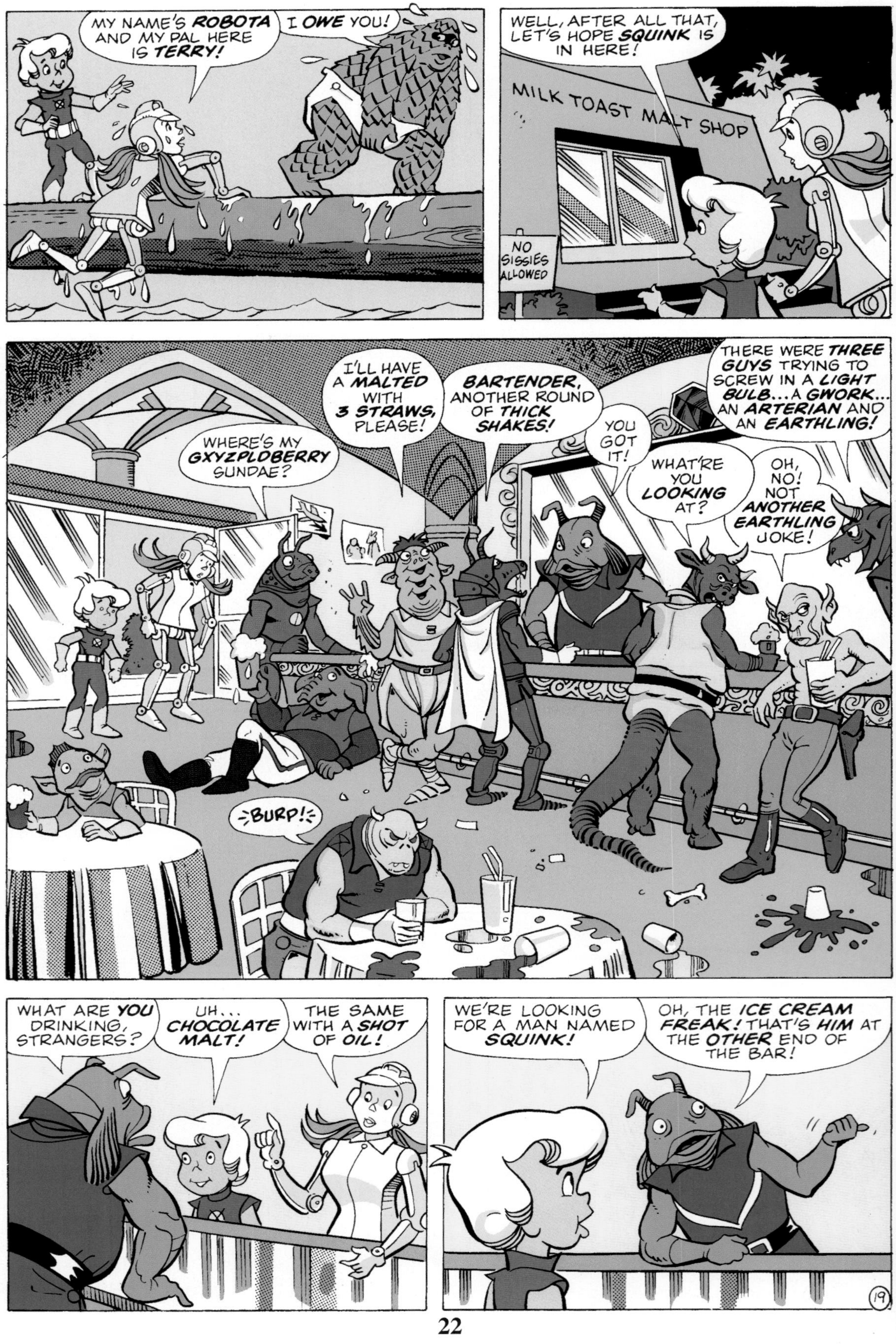

MY NAME'S ROBOTA AND MY PAL HERE IS TERRY!
I OWE YOU!
WELL, AFTER ALL THAT, LET'S HOPE SQUINK IS IN HERE!
MILK TOAST MALT SHOP
NO SISSIES ALLOWED
WHERE'S MY GXYZPLDBERRY SUNDAE?
I'LL HAVE A MALTED WITH 3 STRAWS, PLEASE!
BARTENDER, ANOTHER ROUND OF THICK SHAKES!
YOU GOT IT!
WHAT'RE YOU LOOKING AT?
OH, NO! NOT ANOTHER EARTHLING JOKE!
THERE WERE THREE GUYS TRYING TO SCREW IN A LIGHT BULB... A GWORK... AN ARTERIAN AND AN EARTHLING!
BURP!
WHAT ARE YOU DRINKING, STRANGERS?
UH... CHOCOLATE MALT!
THE SAME WITH A SHOT OF OIL!
WE'RE LOOKING FOR A MAN NAMED SQUINK!
OH, THE ICE CREAM FREAK! THAT'S HIM AT THE OTHER END OF THE BAR!
19

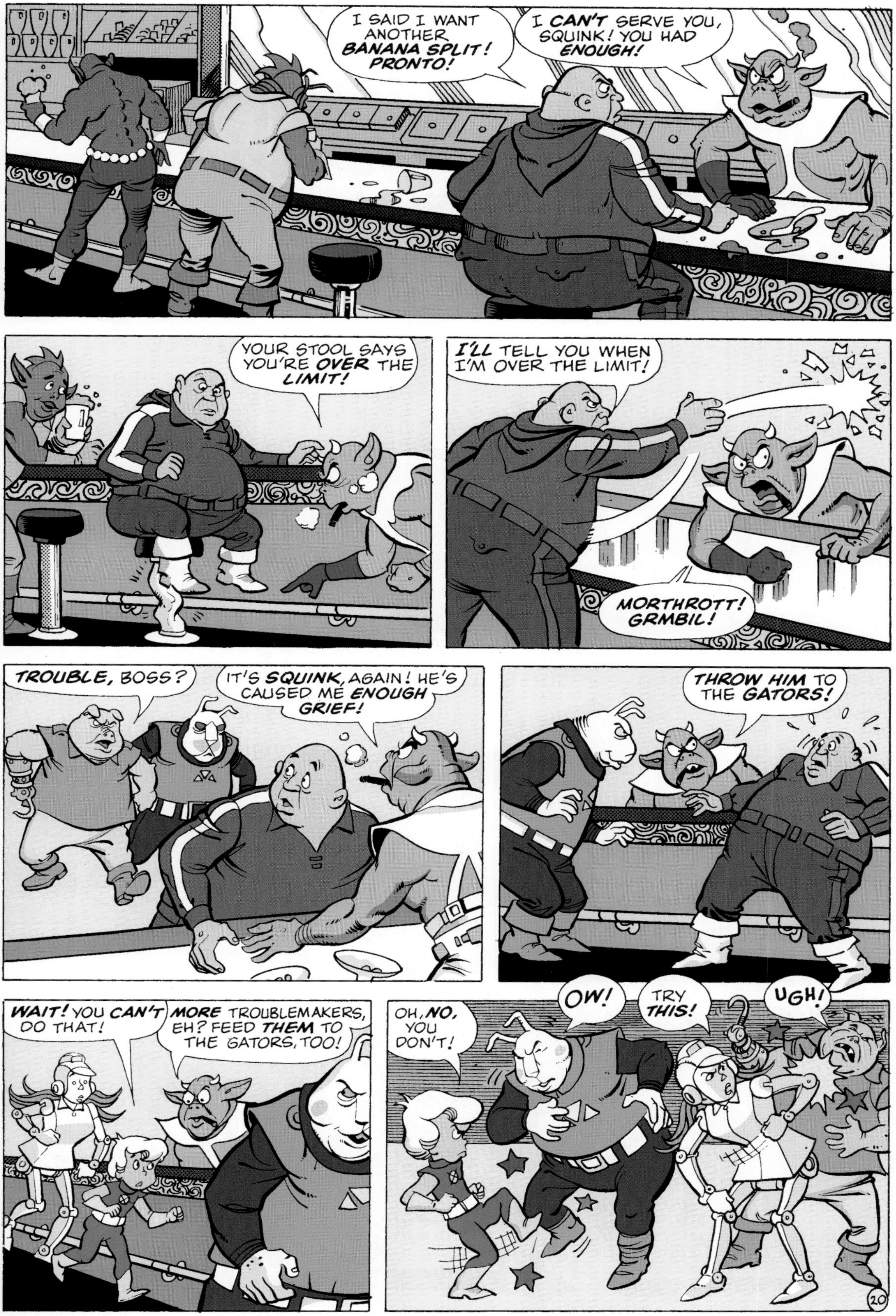

I SAID I WANT ANOTHER BANANA SPLIT! PRONTO!
I CAN'T SERVE YOU, SQUINK! YOU HAD ENOUGH!
YOUR STOOL SAYS YOU'RE OVER THE LIMIT!
I'LL TELL YOU WHEN I'M OVER THE LIMIT!
MORTHROTT! GRMBIL!
TROUBLE, BOSS?
IT'S SQUINK, AGAIN! HE'S CAUSED ME ENOUGH GRIEF!
THROW HIM TO THE GATORS!
WAIT! YOU CAN'T DO THAT!
MORE TROUBLEMAKERS, EH? FEED THEM TO THE GATORS, TOO!
OH, NO, YOU DON'T!
OW!
TRY THIS!
UGH!
20

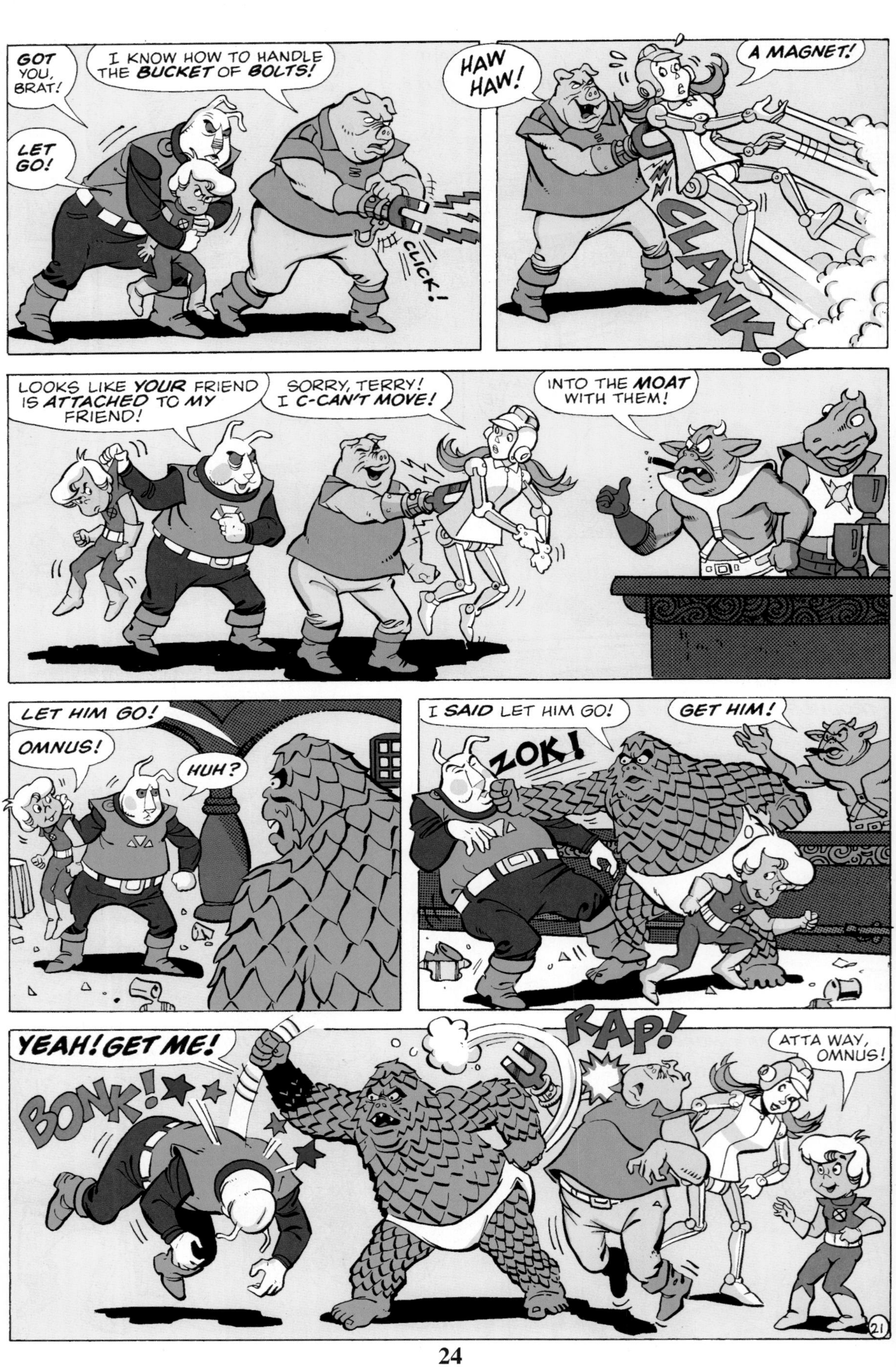

GOT YOU, BRAT!
I KNOW HOW TO HANDLE THE BUCKET OF BOLTS!
LET GO!
CLICK!
HAW HAW!
A MAGNET!
CLANK!
LOOKS LIKE YOUR FRIEND IS ATTACHED TO MY FRIEND!
SORRY, TERRY! I C-CAN'T MOVE!
INTO THE MOAT WITH THEM!
LET HIM GO!
OMNUS!
HUH?
I SAID LET HIM GO!
GET HIM!
ZOK!
YEAH! GET ME!
BONK!
RAP!
ATTA WAY, OMNUS!
21

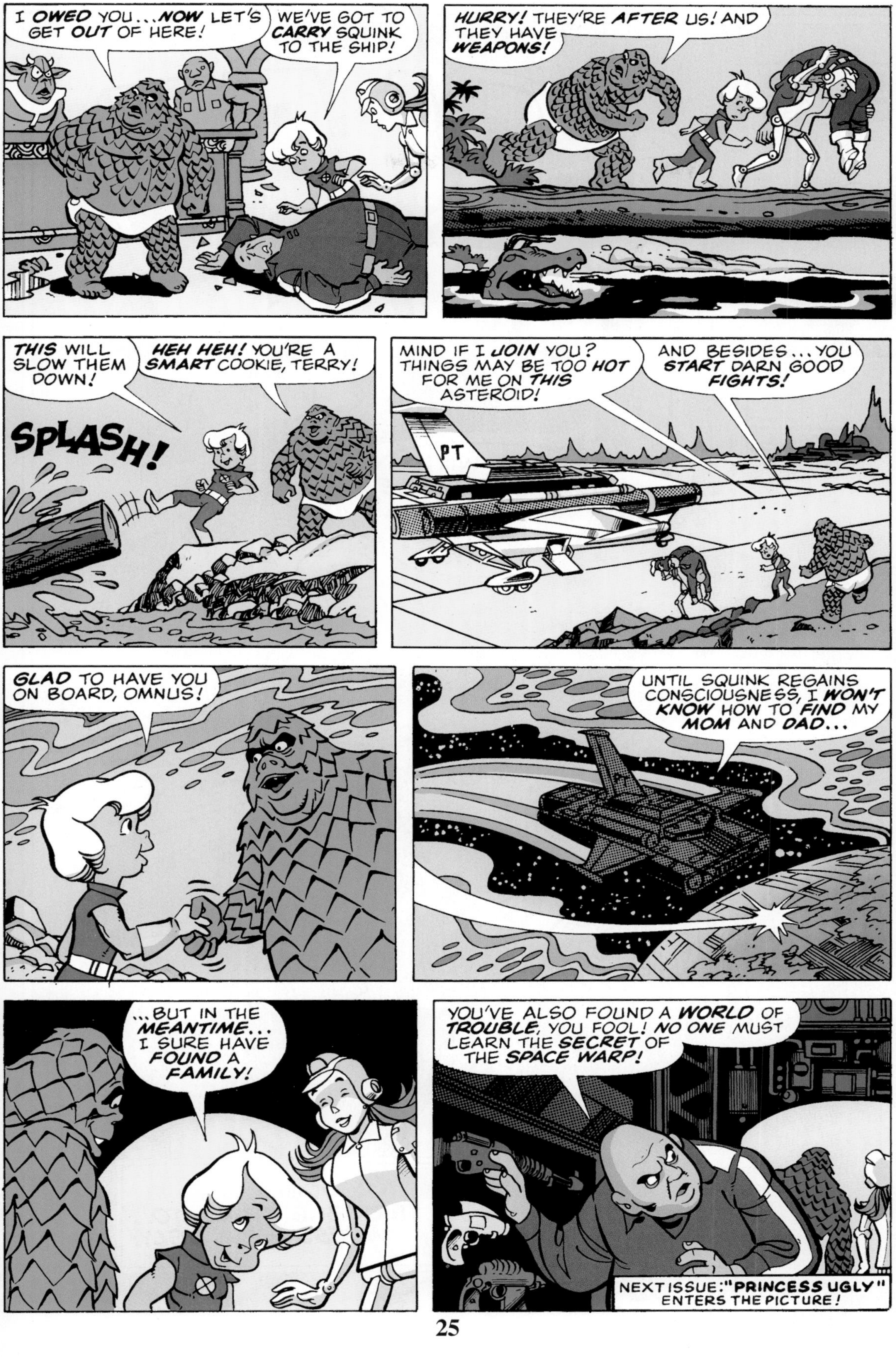

I OWED YOU...NOW LET'S GET OUT OF HERE!
WE'VE GOT TO CARRY SQUINK TO THE SHIP!
HURRY! THEY'RE AFTER US! AND THEY HAVE WEAPONS!
THIS WILL SLOW THEM DOWN!
HEH HEH! YOU'RE A SMART COOKIE, TERRY!
SPLASH!
MIND IF I JOIN YOU? THINGS MAY BE TOO HOT FOR ME ON THIS ASTEROID!
AND BESIDES... YOU START DARN GOOD FIGHTS!
PT
GLAD TO HAVE YOU ON BOARD, OMNUS!
UNTIL SQUINK REGAINS CONSCIOUSNESS, I WON'T KNOW HOW TO FIND MY MOM AND DAD...
...BUT IN THE MEANTIME... I SURE HAVE FOUND A FAMILY!
YOU'VE ALSO FOUND A WORLD OF TROUBLE, YOU FOOL! NO ONE MUST LEARN THE SECRET OF THE SPACE WARP!
NEXT ISSUE: "PRINCESS UGLY" ENTERS THE PICTURE!

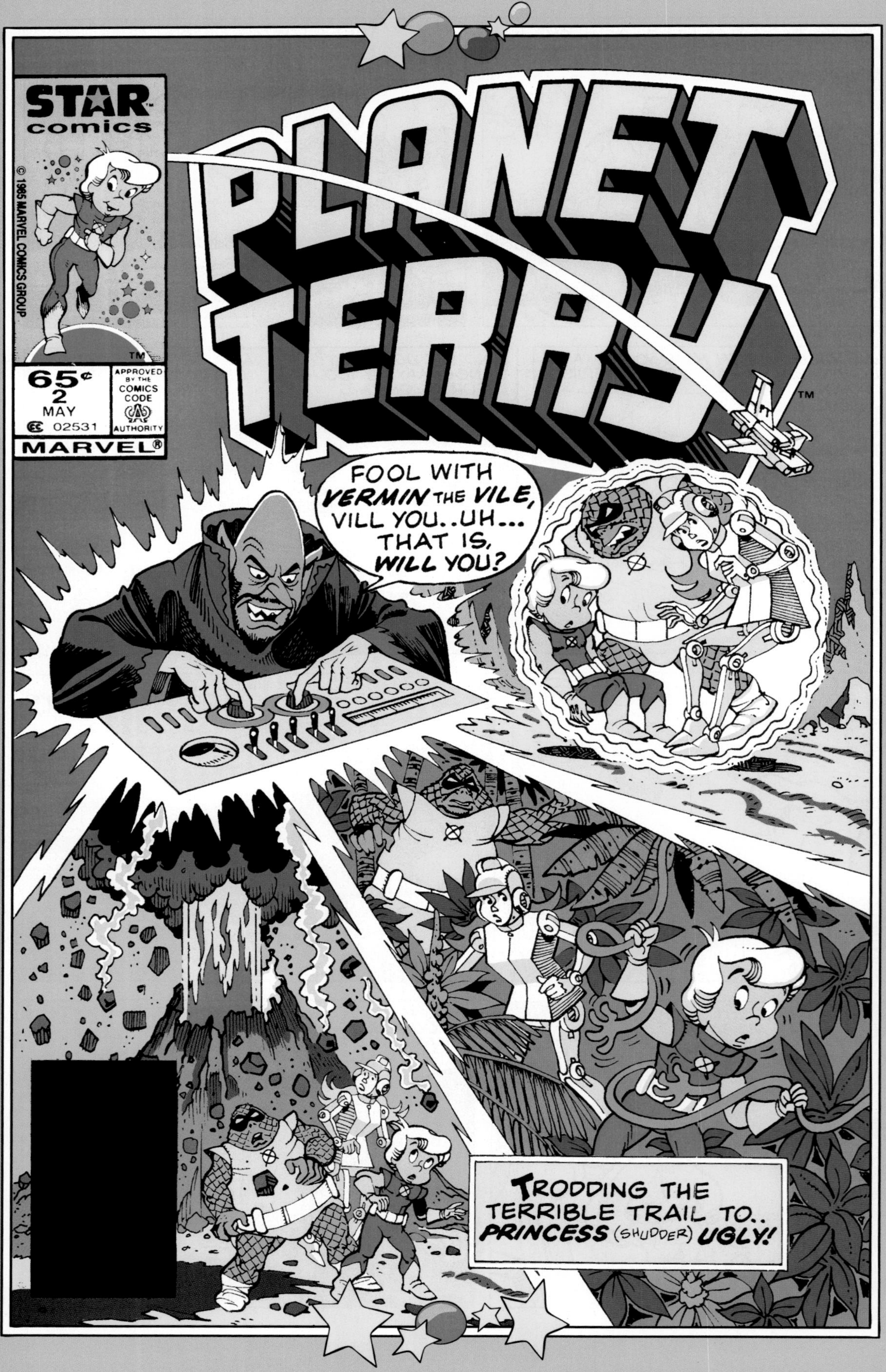

STAR comics
© 1985 MARVEL COMICS GROUP
PLANET TERRY™
65¢
2
MAY
02531
APPROVED BY THE COMICS CODE AUTHORITY
MARVEL®
FOOL WITH VERMIN THE VILE, VILL YOU..UH... THAT IS, WILL YOU?
TRODDING THE TERRIBLE TRAIL TO.. PRINCESS (SHUDDER) UGLY!

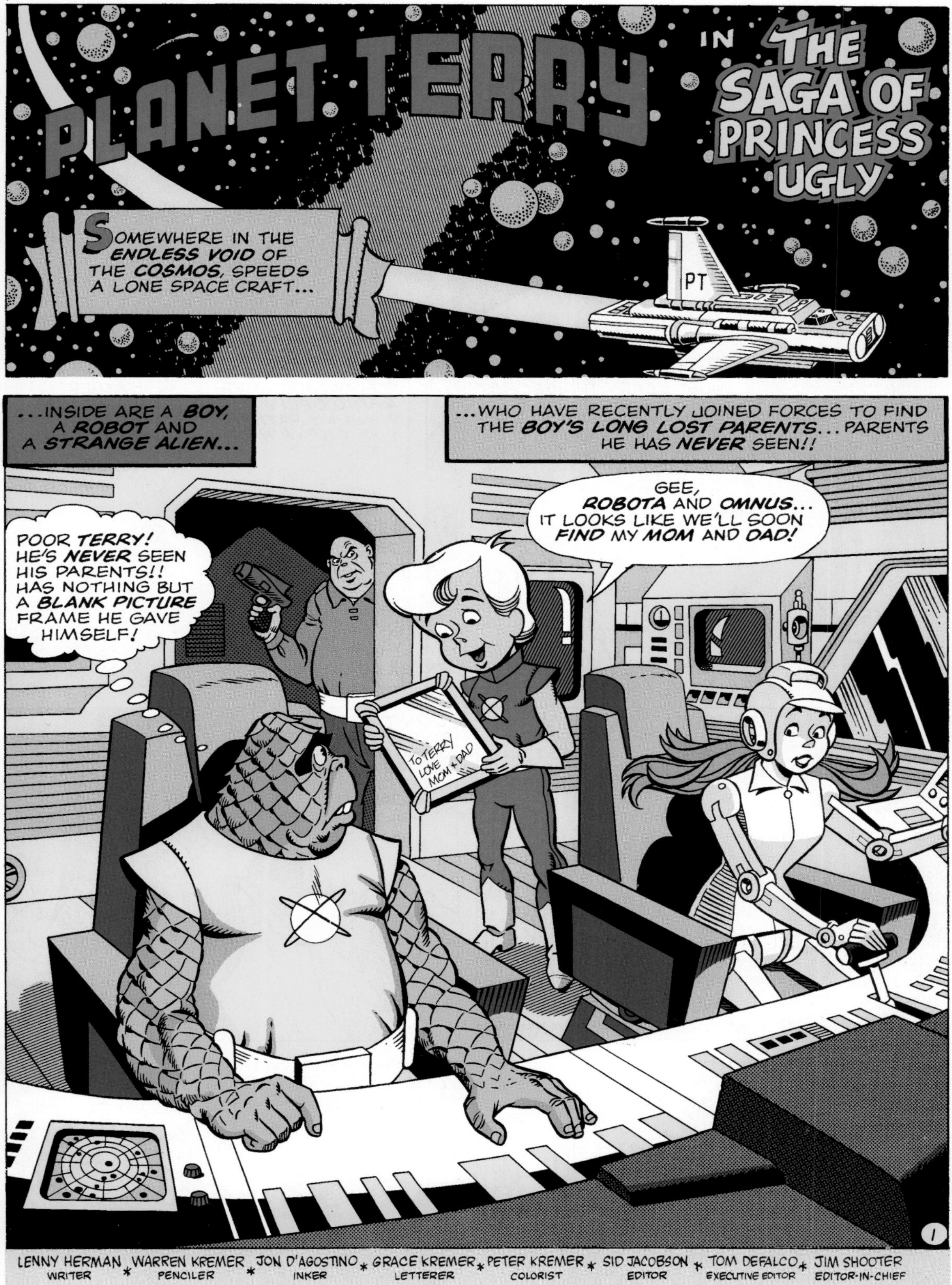
PLANET TERRY
IN
THE SAGA OF PRINCESS UGLY
SOMEWHERE IN THE ENDLESS VOID OF THE COSMOS, SPEEDS A LONE SPACE CRAFT...
PT
...INSIDE ARE A BOY, A ROBOT AND A STRANGE ALIEN...
...WHO HAVE RECENTLY JOINED FORCES TO FIND THE BOY'S LONG LOST PARENTS... PARENTS HE HAS NEVER SEEN!!
POOR TERRY! HE'S NEVER SEEN HIS PARENTS!! HAS NOTHING BUT A BLANK PICTURE FRAME HE GAVE HIMSELF!
GEE, ROBOTA AND OMNUS... IT LOOKS LIKE WE'LL SOON FIND MY MOM AND DAD!
TO TERRY LOVE MOM + DAD
1

LENNY HERMAN WRITER * WARREN KREMER PENCILER * JON D'AGOSTINO INKER * GRACE KREMER LETTERER * PETER KREMER COLORIST * SID JACOBSON EDITOR * TOM DEFALCO EXECUTIVE EDITOR * JIM SHOOTER EDITOR-IN-CHIEF

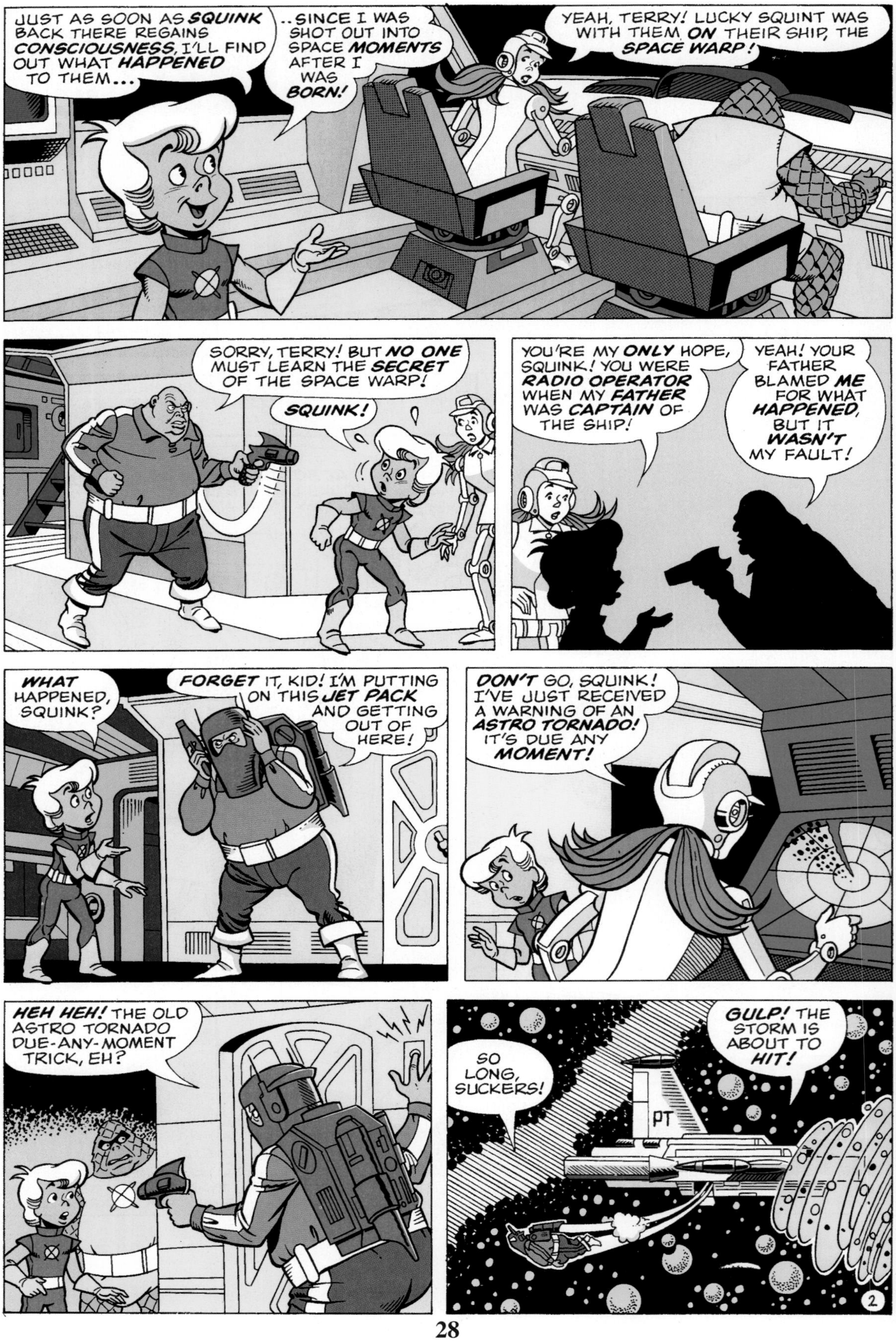
JUST AS SOON AS SQUINK BACK THERE REGAINS CONSCIOUSNESS, I'LL FIND OUT WHAT HAPPENED TO THEM...
..SINCE I WAS SHOT OUT INTO SPACE MOMENTS AFTER I WAS BORN!
YEAH, TERRY! LUCKY SQUINT WAS WITH THEM ON THEIR SHIP, THE SPACE WARP!
SORRY, TERRY! BUT NO ONE MUST LEARN THE SECRET OF THE SPACE WARP!
SQUINK!
YOU'RE MY ONLY HOPE, SQUINK! YOU WERE RADIO OPERATOR WHEN MY FATHER WAS CAPTAIN OF THE SHIP!
YEAH! YOUR FATHER BLAMED ME FOR WHAT HAPPENED, BUT IT WASN'T MY FAULT!
WHAT HAPPENED, SQUINK?
FORGET IT, KID! I'M PUTTING ON THIS JET PACK AND GETTING OUT OF HERE!
DON'T GO, SQUINK! I'VE JUST RECEIVED A WARNING OF AN ASTRO TORNADO! IT'S DUE ANY MOMENT!
HEH HEH! THE OLD ASTRO TORNADO DUE-ANY-MOMENT TRICK, EH?
SO LONG, SUCKERS!
GULP! THE STORM IS ABOUT TO HIT!
PT
2

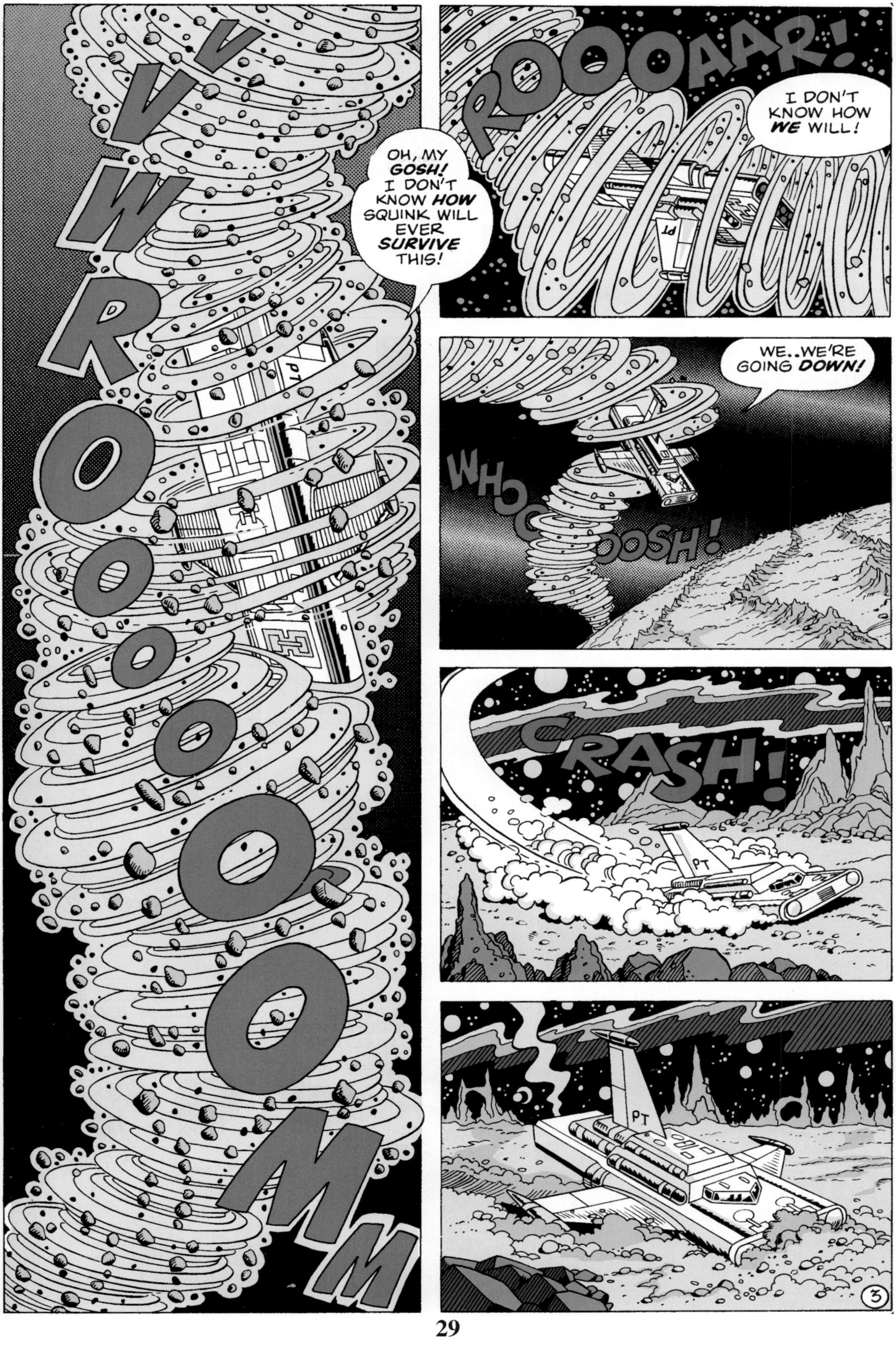

VVWROOOOOOMMM
OH, MY GOSH! I DON'T KNOW HOW SQUINK WILL EVER SURVIVE THIS!
ROOOAAR!
I DON'T KNOW HOW WE WILL!
WE..WE'RE GOING DOWN!
WHOOOOOSH!
CRASH!
3

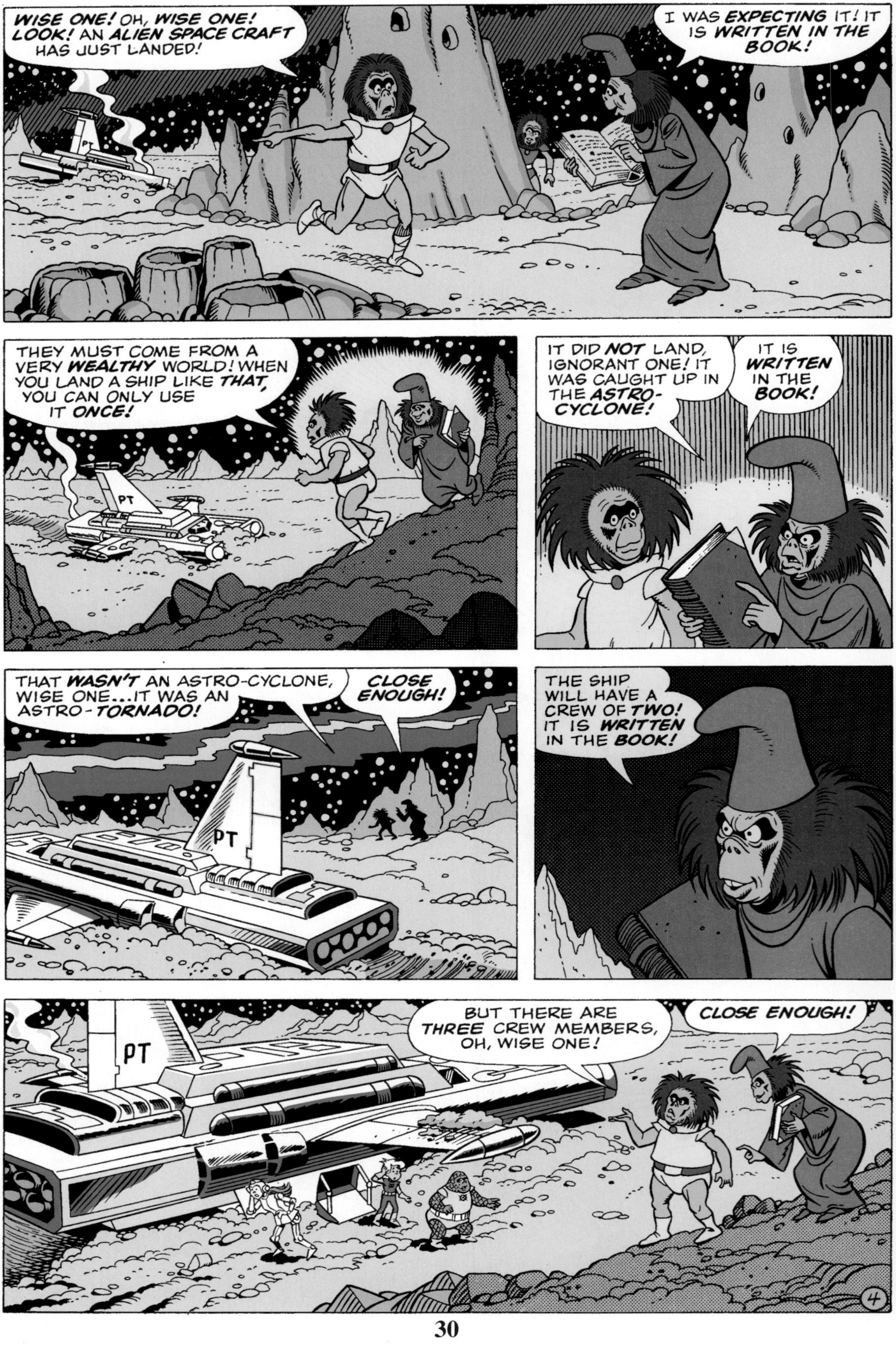
WISE ONE! OH, WISE ONE! LOOK! AN ALIEN SPACE CRAFT HAS JUST LANDED!
I WAS EXPECTING IT! IT IS WRITTEN IN THE BOOK!
THEY MUST COME FROM A VERY WEALTHY WORLD! WHEN YOU LAND A SHIP LIKE THAT, YOU CAN ONLY USE IT ONCE!
PT
IT DID NOT LAND, IGNORANT ONE! IT WAS CAUGHT UP IN THE ASTRO-CYCLONE!
IT IS WRITTEN IN THE BOOK!
THAT WASN'T AN ASTRO-CYCLONE, WISE ONE...IT WAS AN ASTRO-TORNADO!
CLOSE ENOUGH!
PT
THE SHIP WILL HAVE A CREW OF TWO! IT IS WRITTEN IN THE BOOK!
PT
BUT THERE ARE THREE CREW MEMBERS, OH, WISE ONE!
CLOSE ENOUGH!
4

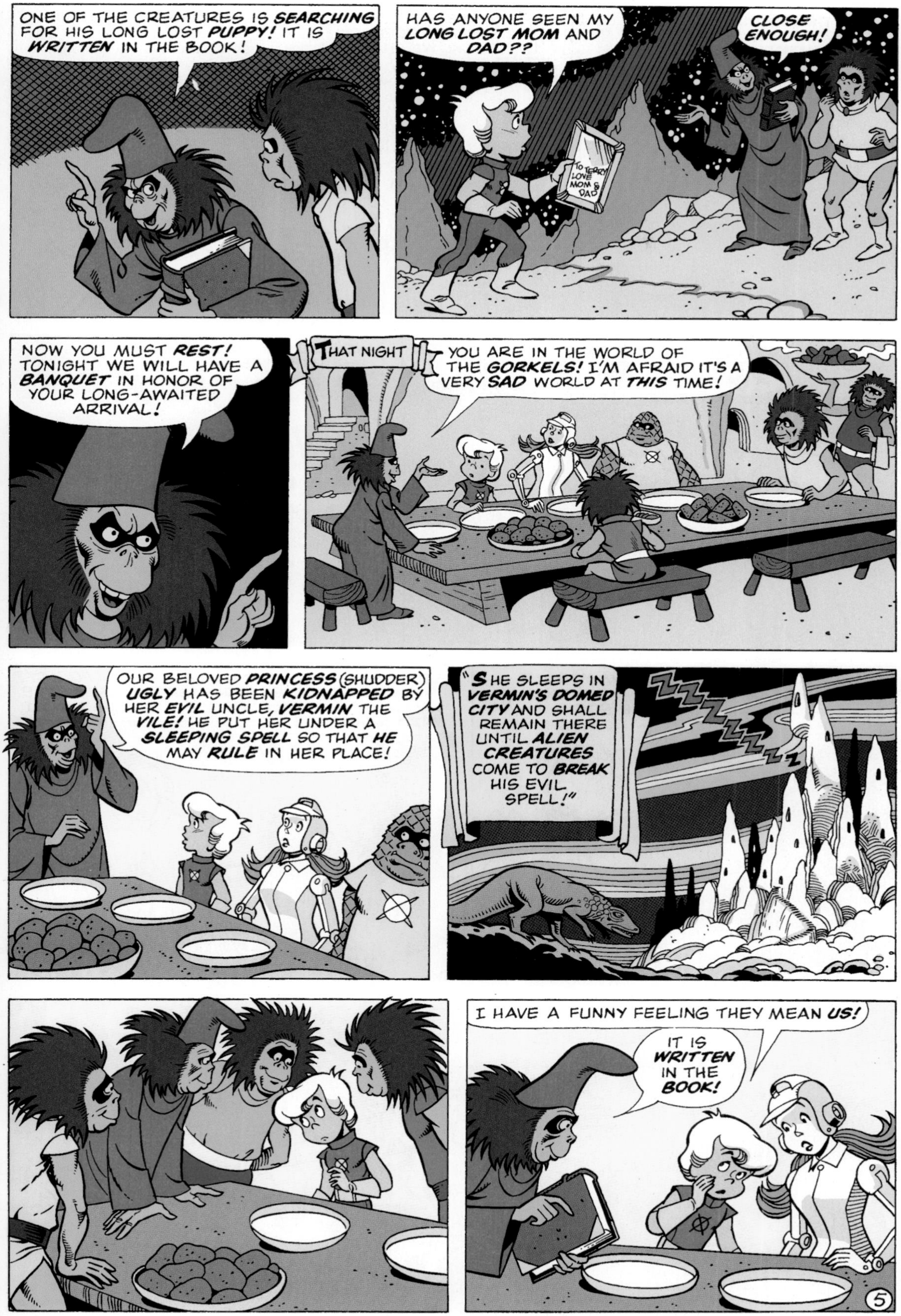
ONE OF THE CREATURES IS SEARCHING FOR HIS LONG LOST PUPPY! IT IS WRITTEN IN THE BOOK!
HAS ANYONE SEEN MY LONG LOST MOM AND DAD??
TO TERRY LOVE MOM & DAD
CLOSE ENOUGH!
NOW YOU MUST REST! TONIGHT WE WILL HAVE A BANQUET IN HONOR OF YOUR LONG-AWAITED ARRIVAL!
THAT NIGHT
YOU ARE IN THE WORLD OF THE GORKELS! I'M AFRAID IT'S A VERY SAD WORLD AT THIS TIME!
OUR BELOVED PRINCESS (SHUDDER) UGLY HAS BEEN KIDNAPPED BY HER EVIL UNCLE, VERMIN THE VILE! HE PUT HER UNDER A SLEEPING SPELL SO THAT HE MAY RULE IN HER PLACE!
"SHE SLEEPS IN VERMIN'S DOMED CITY AND SHALL REMAIN THERE UNTIL ALIEN CREATURES COME TO BREAK HIS EVIL SPELL!"
ZZZZZZ
I HAVE A FUNNY FEELING THEY MEAN US!
IT IS WRITTEN IN THE BOOK!
5

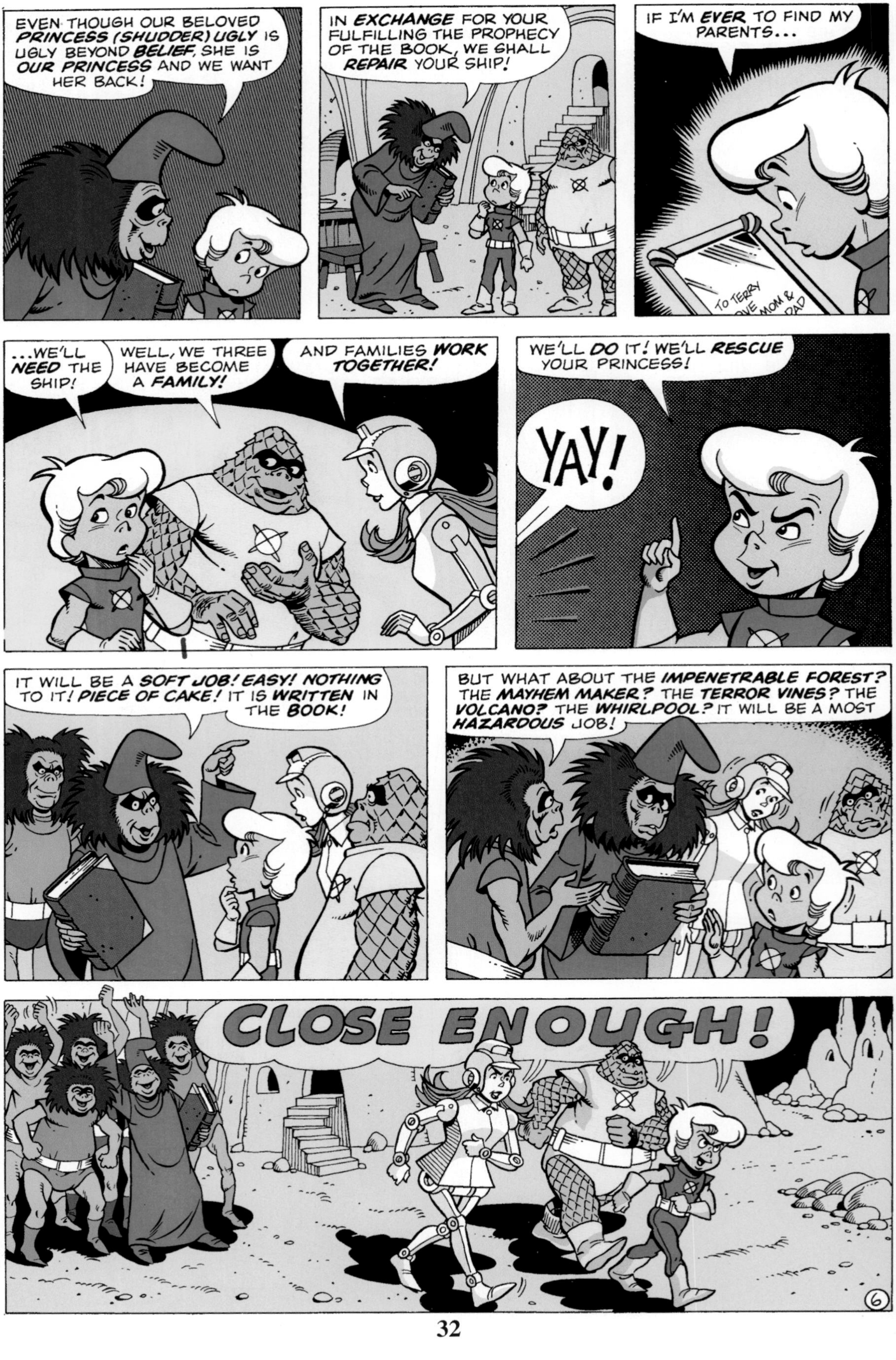
EVEN THOUGH OUR BELOVED PRINCESS (SHUDDER) UGLY IS UGLY BEYOND BELIEF, SHE IS OUR PRINCESS AND WE WANT HER BACK!
IN EXCHANGE FOR YOUR FULFILLING THE PROPHECY OF THE BOOK, WE SHALL REPAIR YOUR SHIP!
IF I'M EVER TO FIND MY PARENTS...
TO TERRY
...WE'LL NEED THE SHIP!
WELL, WE THREE HAVE BECOME A FAMILY!
AND FAMILIES WORK TOGETHER!
WE'LL DO IT! WE'LL RESCUE YOUR PRINCESS!
YAY!
IT WILL BE A SOFT JOB! EASY! NOTHING TO IT! PIECE OF CAKE! IT IS WRITTEN IN THE BOOK!
BUT WHAT ABOUT THE IMPENETRABLE FOREST? THE MAYHEM MAKER? THE TERROR VINES? THE VOLCANO? THE WHIRLPOOL? IT WILL BE A MOST HAZARDOUS JOB!
CLOSE ENOUGH!
6

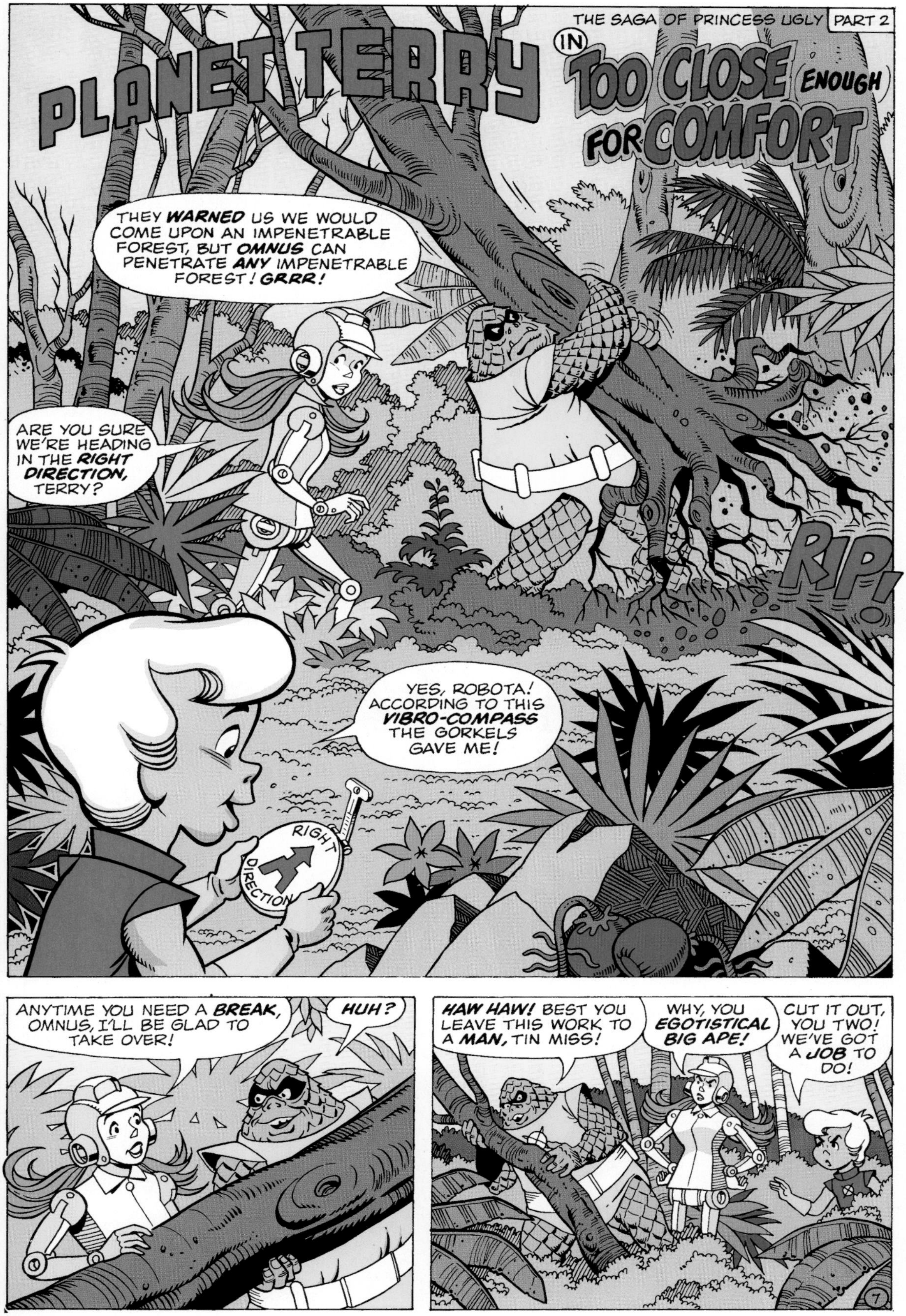
THE SAGA OF PRINCESS UGLY PART 2
PLANET TERRY IN TOO CLOSE (ENOUGH) FOR COMFORT
THEY WARNED US WE WOULD COME UPON AN IMPENETRABLE FOREST, BUT OMNUS CAN PENETRATE ANY IMPENETRABLE FOREST! GRRR!
ARE YOU SURE WE'RE HEADING IN THE RIGHT DIRECTION, TERRY?
RIP!
YES, ROBOTA! ACCORDING TO THIS VIBRO-COMPASS THE GORKELS GAVE ME!
RIGHT DIRECTION
ANYTIME YOU NEED A BREAK, OMNUS, I'LL BE GLAD TO TAKE OVER!
HUH?
HAW HAW! BEST YOU LEAVE THIS WORK TO A MAN, TIN MISS!
WHY, YOU EGOTISTICAL BIG APE!
CUT IT OUT, YOU TWO! WE'VE GOT A JOB TO DO!
7

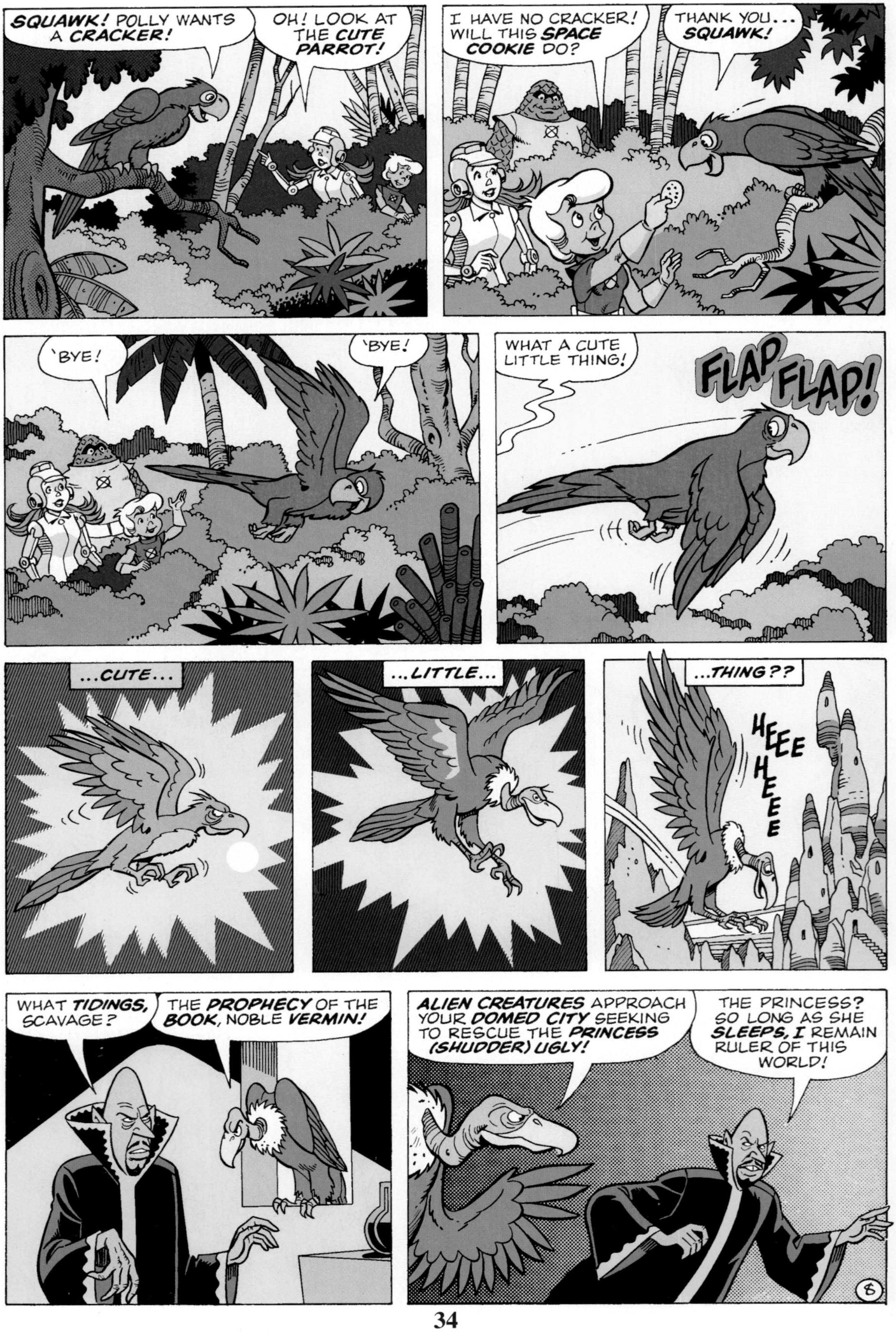
SQUAWK! POLLY WANTS A CRACKER!
OH! LOOK AT THE CUTE PARROT!
I HAVE NO CRACKER! WILL THIS SPACE COOKIE DO?
THANK YOU... SQUAWK!
`BYE!
`BYE!
WHAT A CUTE LITTLE THING!
FLAP FLAP!
...CUTE...
...LITTLE...
...THING??
HEEEE HEEEE
WHAT TIDINGS, SCAVAGE?
THE PROPHECY OF THE BOOK, NOBLE VERMIN!
ALIEN CREATURES APPROACH YOUR DOMED CITY SEEKING TO RESCUE THE PRINCESS (SHUDDER) UGLY!
THE PRINCESS? SO LONG AS SHE SLEEPS, I REMAIN RULER OF THIS WORLD!
8

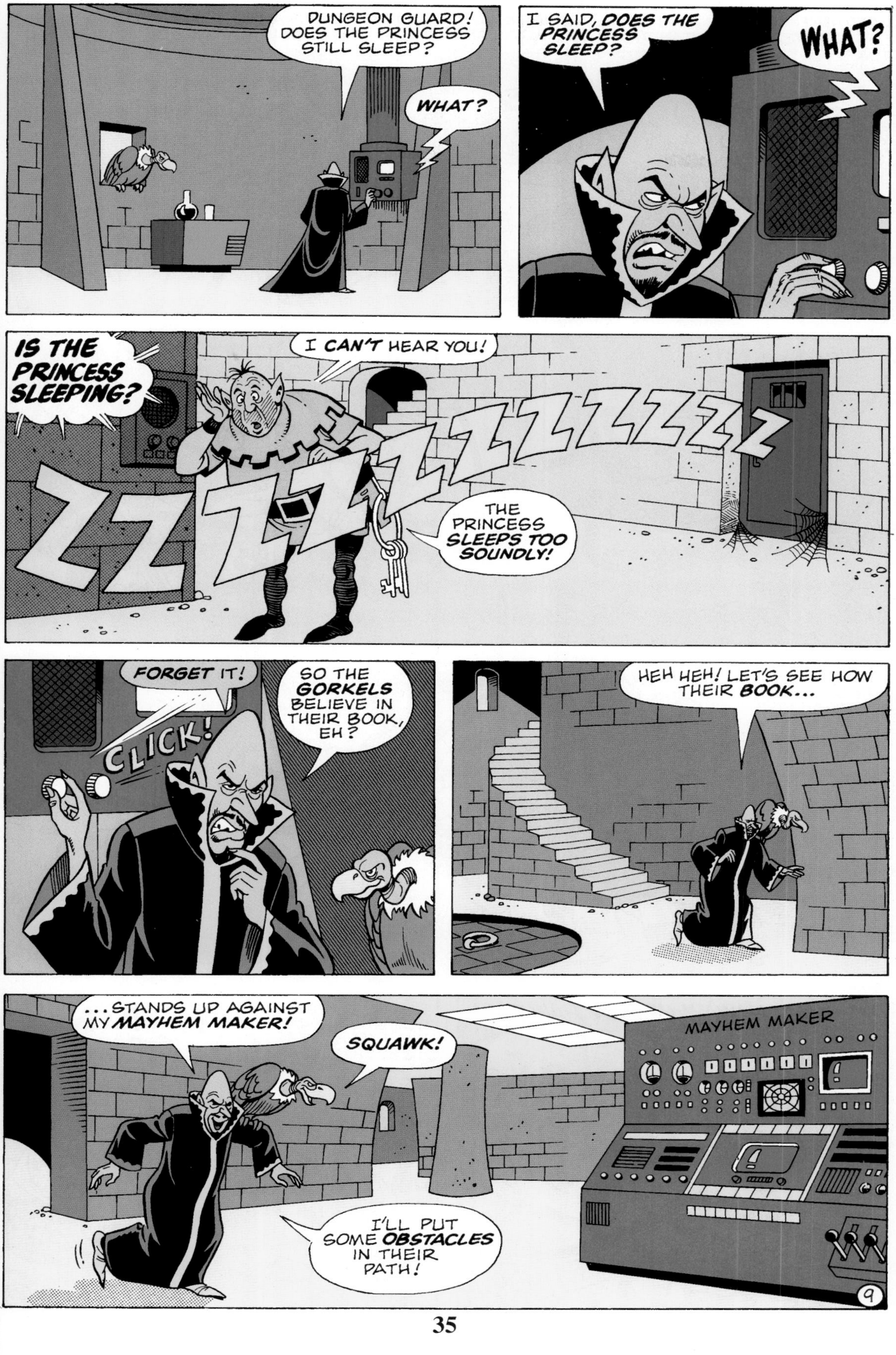
DUNGEON GUARD! DOES THE PRINCESS STILL SLEEP?
WHAT?
I SAID, DOES THE PRINCESS SLEEP?
WHAT?
IS THE PRINCESS SLEEPING?
I CAN'T HEAR YOU!
ZZZZZZZZZZZZZZ
THE PRINCESS SLEEPS TOO SOUNDLY!
FORGET IT!
CLICK!
SO THE GORKELS BELIEVE IN THEIR BOOK, EH?
HEH HEH! LET'S SEE HOW THEIR BOOK...
...STANDS UP AGAINST MY MAYHEM MAKER!
SQUAWK!
MAYHEM MAKER
I'LL PUT SOME OBSTACLES IN THEIR PATH!
9

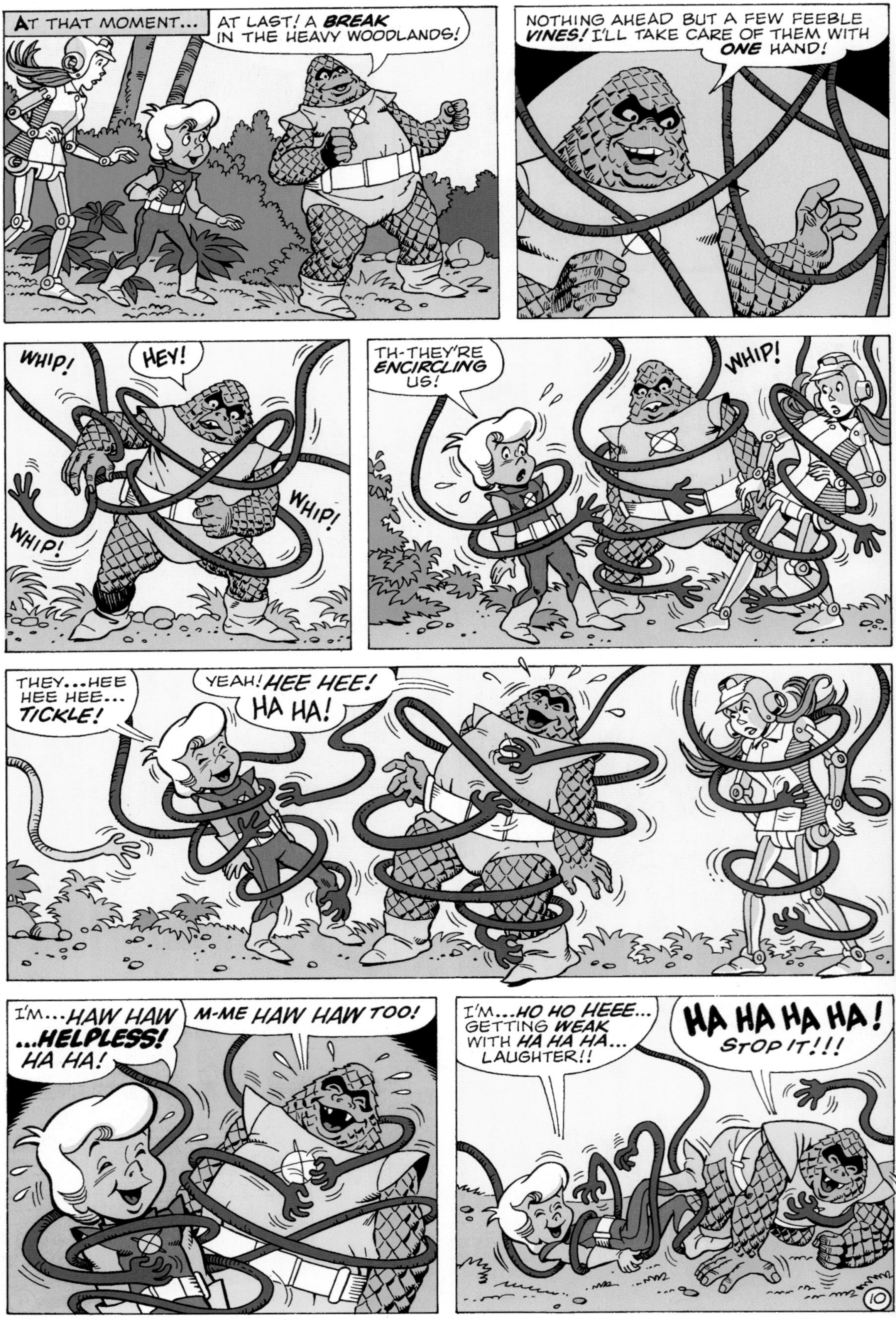
AT THAT MOMENT...
AT LAST! A BREAK IN THE HEAVY WOODLANDS!
NOTHING AHEAD BUT A FEW FEEBLE VINES! I'LL TAKE CARE OF THEM WITH ONE HAND!
WHIP!
HEY!
WHIP!
WHIP!
TH-THEY'RE ENCIRCLING US!
WHIP!
THEY...HEE HEE HEE... TICKLE!
YEAH! HEE HEE! HA HA!
I'M...HAW HAW ...HELPLESS! HA HA!
M-ME HAW HAW TOO!
I'M...HO HO HEEE... GETTING WEAK WITH HA HA HA... LAUGHTER!!
HA HA HA HA HA! STOP IT!!!
10

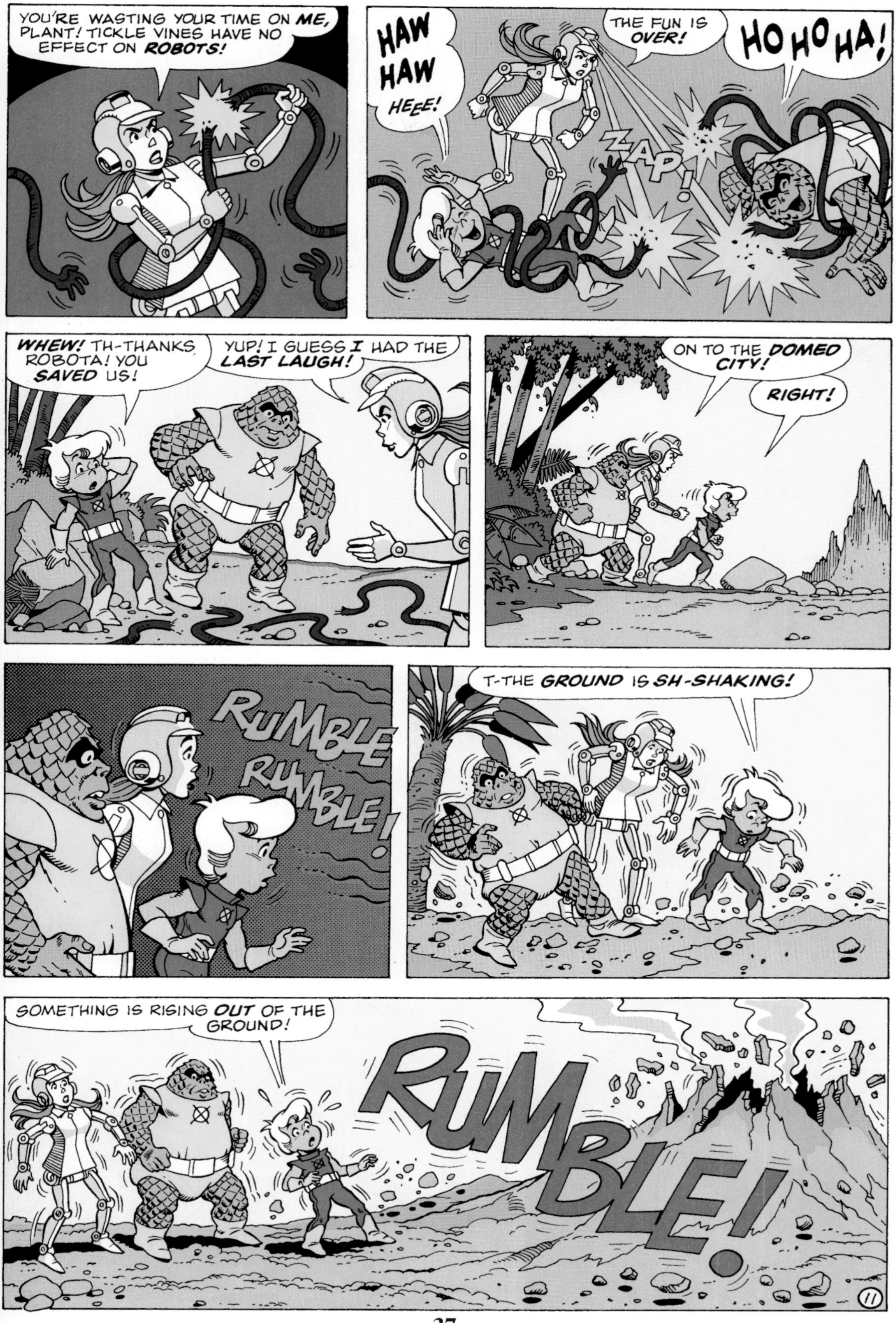
YOU'RE WASTING YOUR TIME ON ME, PLANT! TICKLE VINES HAVE NO EFFECT ON ROBOTS!
HAW HAW HEEE!
THE FUN IS OVER!
HO HO HA!
ZAP!
WHEW! TH-THANKS, ROBOTA! YOU SAVED US!
YUP! I GUESS I HAD THE LAST LAUGH!
ON TO THE DOMED CITY!
RIGHT!
RUMBLE RUMBLE!
T-THE GROUND IS SH-SHAKING!
SOMETHING IS RISING OUT OF THE GROUND!
RUMBLE!
11

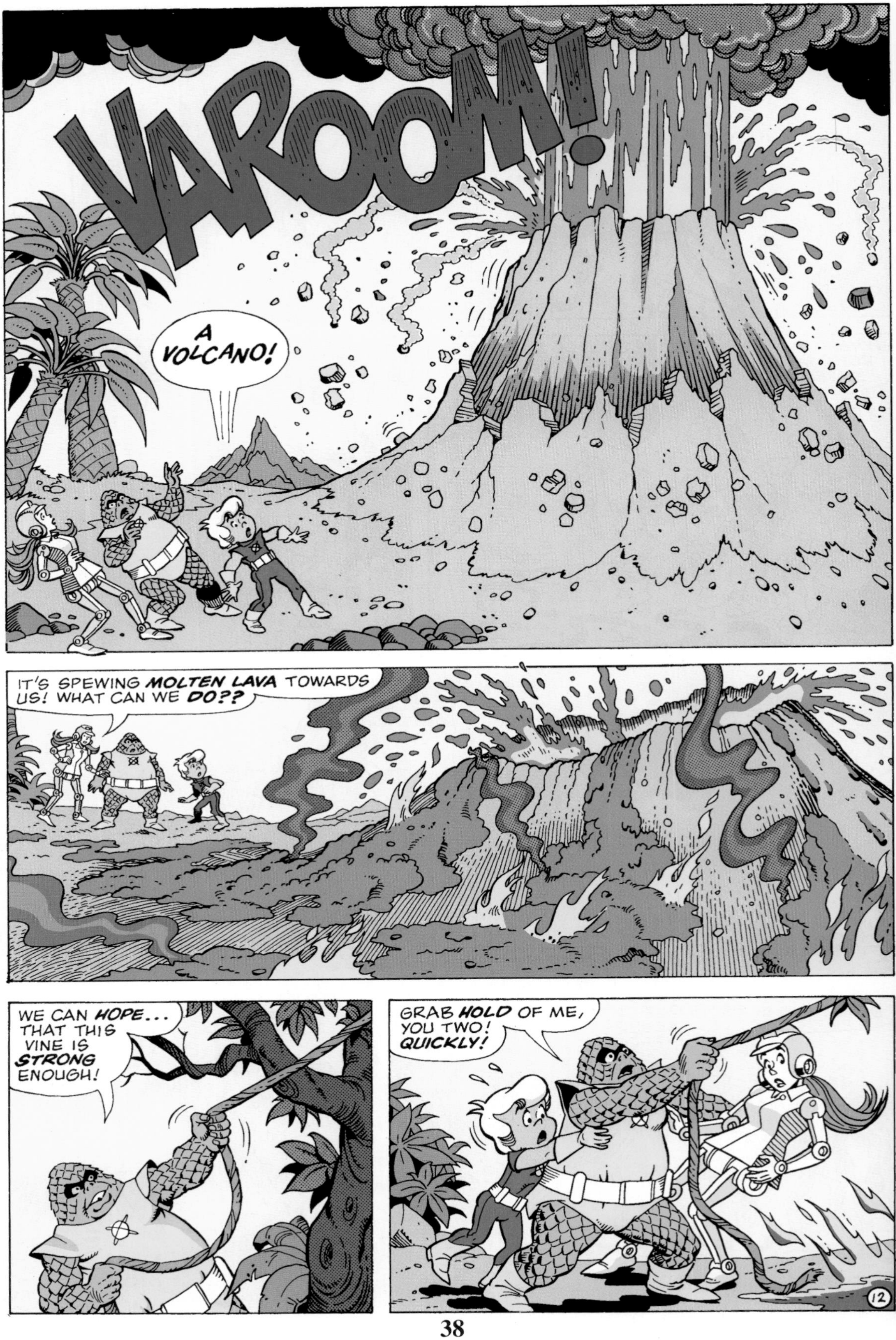
VAROOM!
A VOLCANO!
IT'S SPEWING MOLTEN LAVA TOWARDS US! WHAT CAN WE DO??
WE CAN HOPE... THAT THIS VINE IS STRONG ENOUGH!
GRAB HOLD OF ME, YOU TWO! QUICKLY!
12

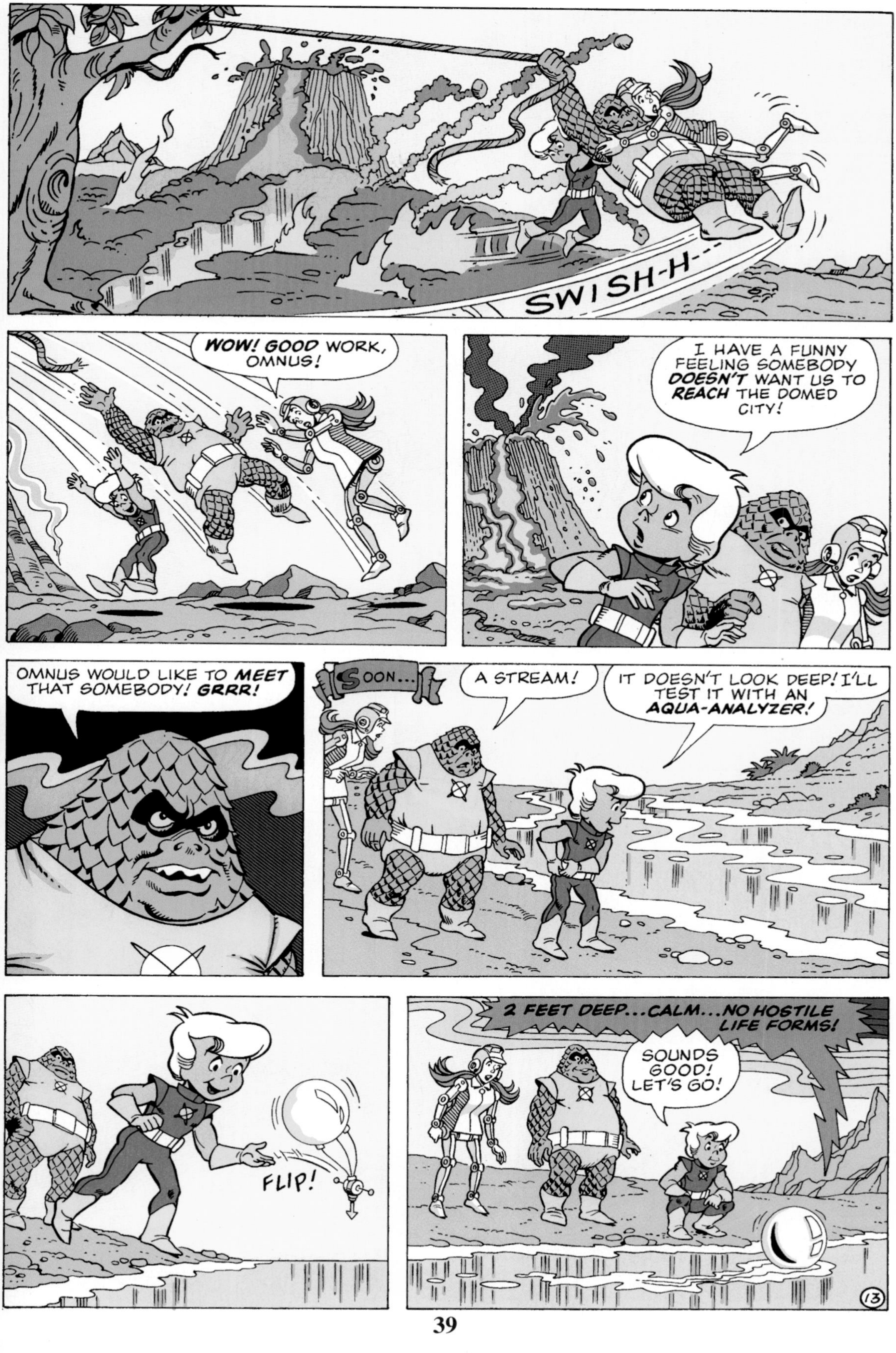
SWISH-H
WOW! GOOD WORK, OMNUS!
I HAVE A FUNNY FEELING SOMEBODY DOESN'T WANT US TO REACH THE DOMED CITY!
OMNUS WOULD LIKE TO MEET THAT SOMEBODY! GRRR!
SOON...
A STREAM!
IT DOESN'T LOOK DEEP! I'LL TEST IT WITH AN AQUA-ANALYZER!
FLIP!
2 FEET DEEP...CALM...NO HOSTILE LIFE FORMS!
SOUNDS GOOD! LET'S GO!
13

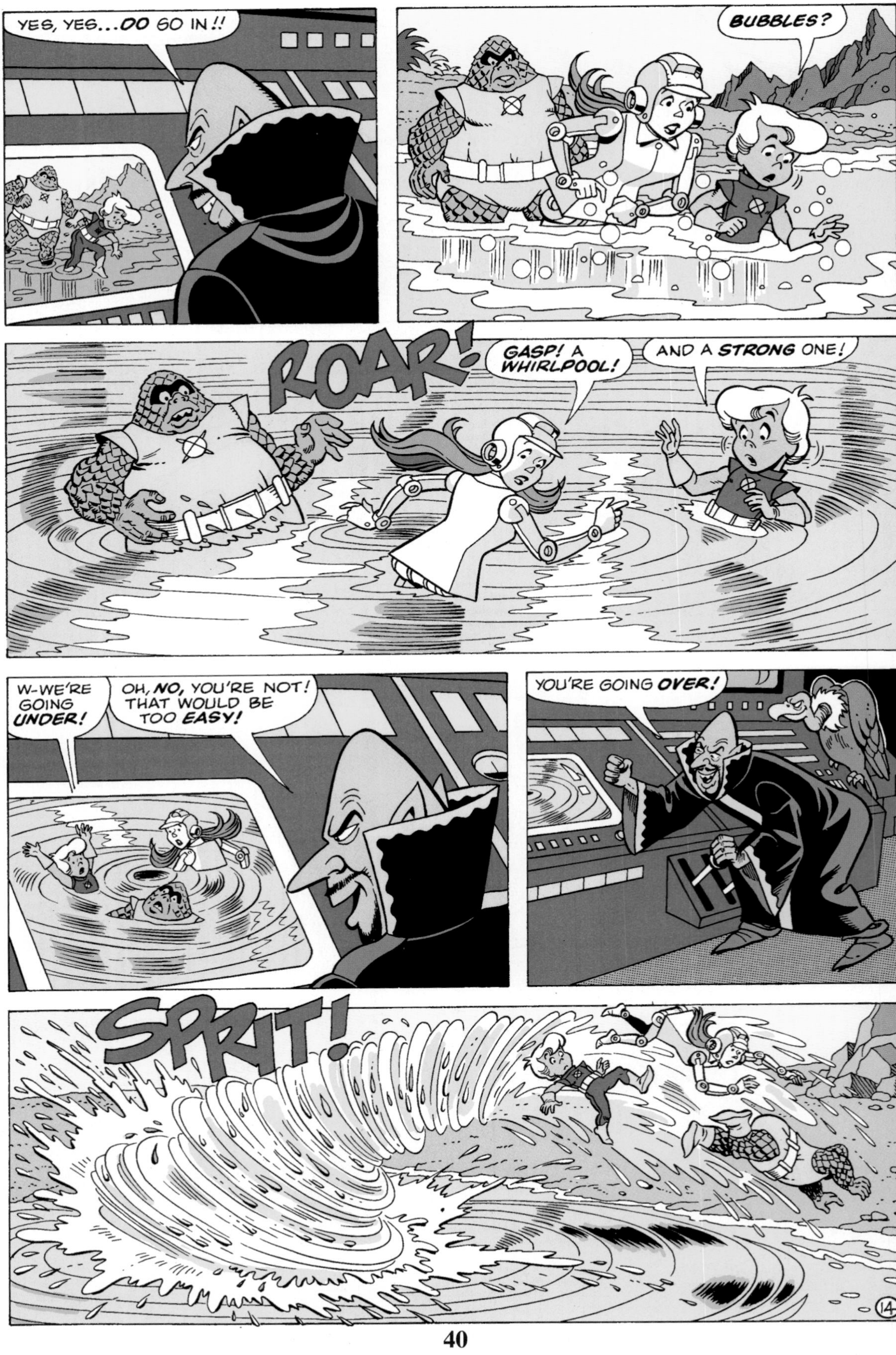

YES, YES...DO GO IN!!
BUBBLES?
ROAR!
GASP! A WHIRLPOOL!
AND A STRONG ONE!
W-WE'RE GOING UNDER!
OH, NO, YOU'RE NOT! THAT WOULD BE TOO EASY!
YOU'RE GOING OVER!
SPRIT!
14

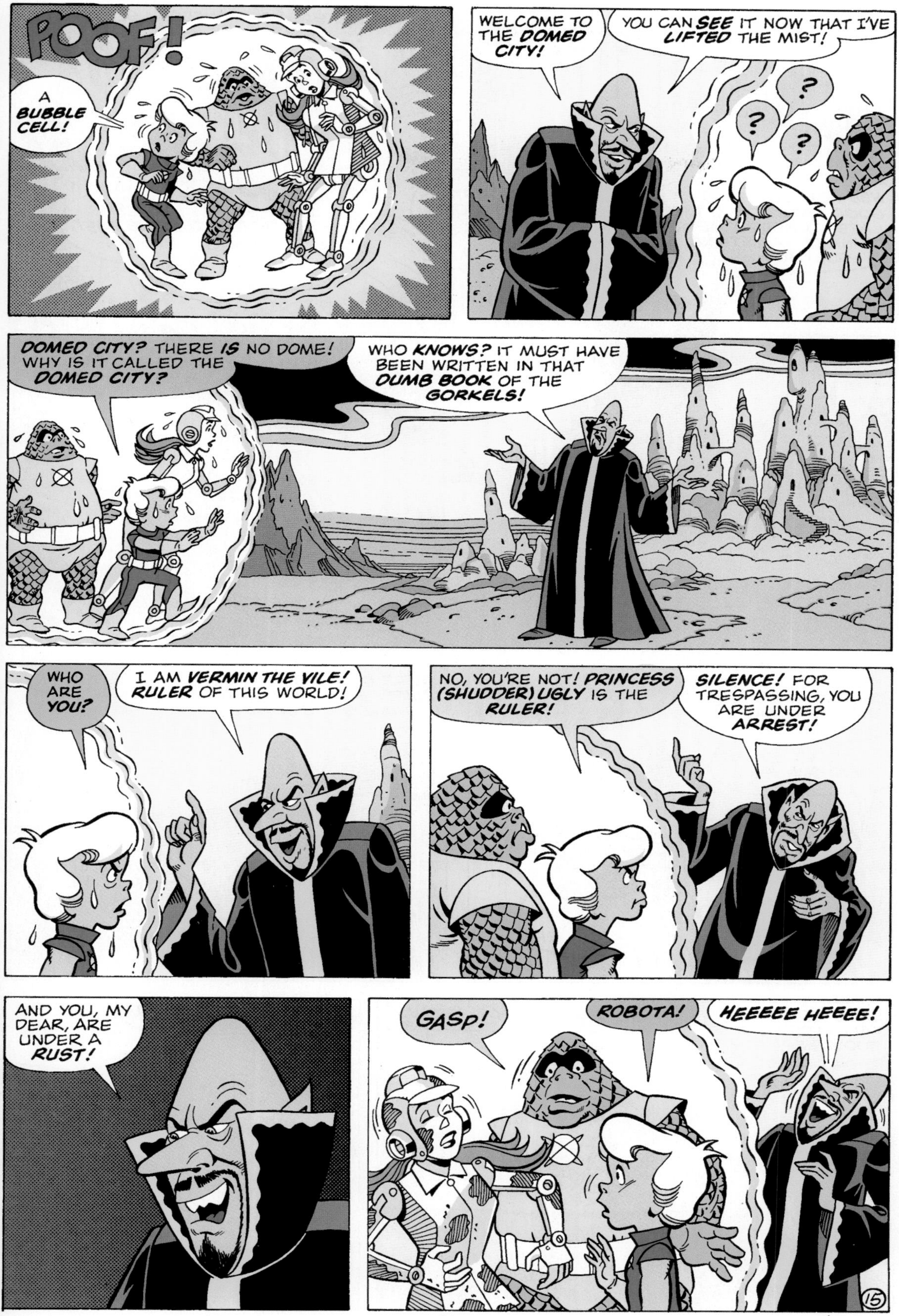
POOF!
A BUBBLE CELL!
WELCOME TO THE DOMED CITY!
YOU CAN SEE IT NOW THAT I'VE LIFTED THE MIST!
?
?
?
DOMED CITY? THERE IS NO DOME! WHY IS IT CALLED THE DOMED CITY?
WHO KNOWS? IT MUST HAVE BEEN WRITTEN IN THAT DUMB BOOK OF THE GORKELS!
WHO ARE YOU?
I AM VERMIN THE VILE! RULER OF THIS WORLD!
NO, YOU'RE NOT! PRINCESS (SHUDDER) UGLY IS THE RULER!
SILENCE! FOR TRESPASSING, YOU ARE UNDER ARREST!
AND YOU, MY DEAR, ARE UNDER A RUST!
GASp!
ROBOTA!
HEEEEE HEEEE!
15

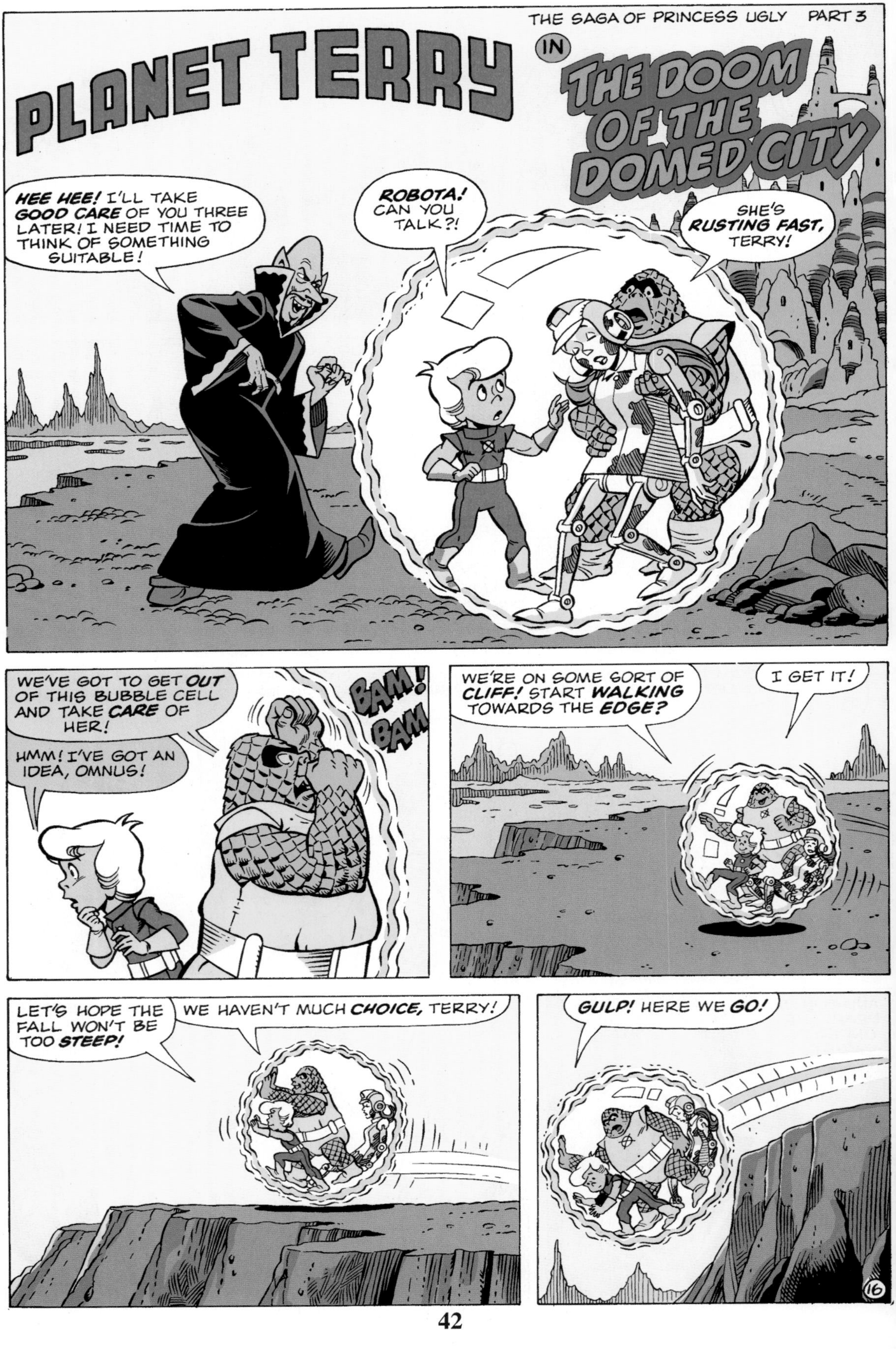
THE SAGA OF PRINCESS UGLY PART 3
PLANET TERRY
IN
THE DOOM OF THE DOMED CITY
HEE HEE! I'LL TAKE GOOD CARE OF YOU THREE LATER! I NEED TIME TO THINK OF SOMETHING SUITABLE!
ROBOTA! CAN YOU TALK?!
SHE'S RUSTING FAST, TERRY!
WE'VE GOT TO GET OUT OF THIS BUBBLE CELL AND TAKE CARE OF HER!
HMM! I'VE GOT AN IDEA, OMNUS!
BAM! BAM
WE'RE ON SOME SORT OF CLIFF! START WALKING TOWARDS THE EDGE?
I GET IT!
LET'S HOPE THE FALL WON'T BE TOO STEEP!
WE HAVEN'T MUCH CHOICE, TERRY!
GULP! HERE WE GO!
16

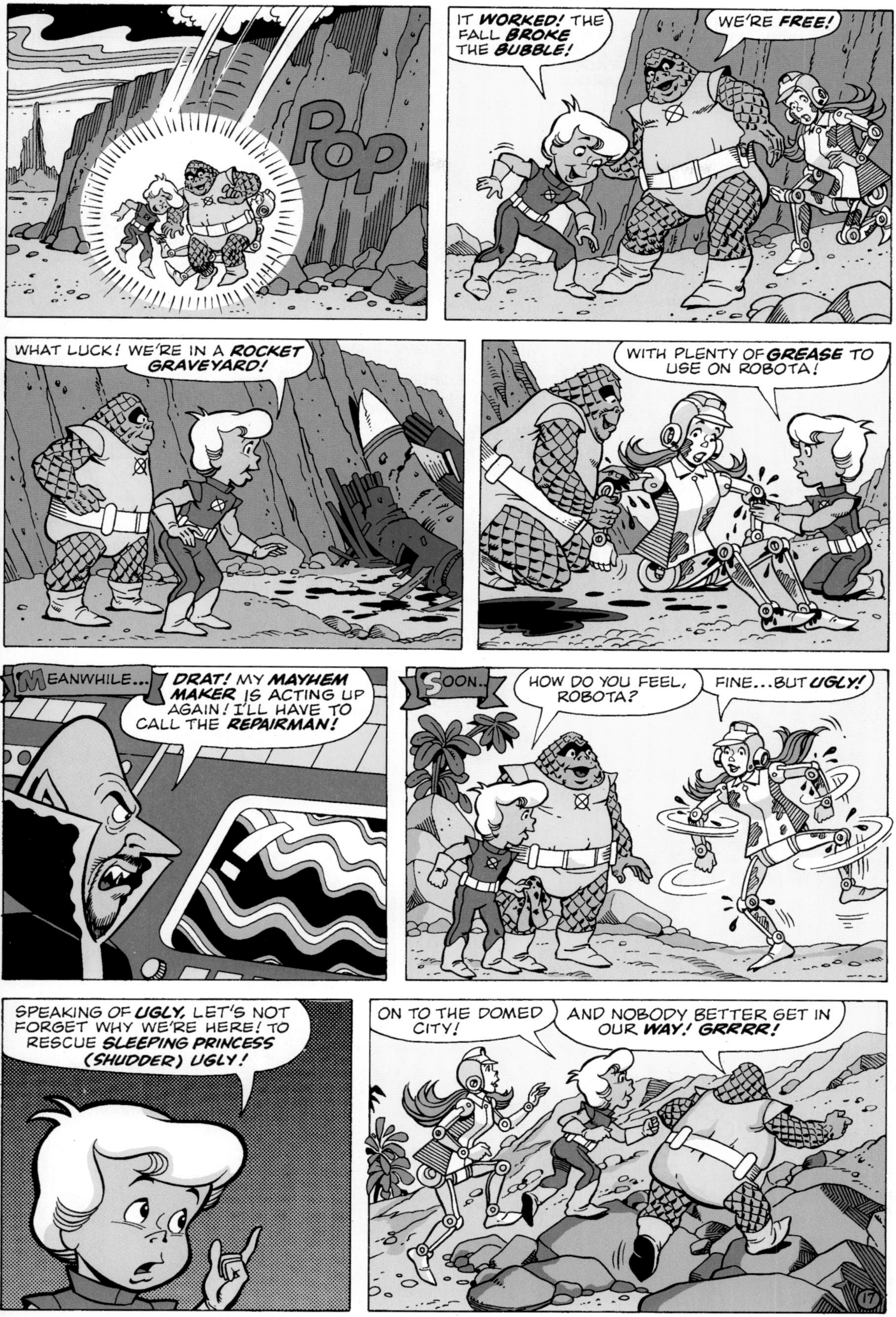
POP
IT WORKED! THE FALL BROKE THE BUBBLE!
WE'RE FREE!
WHAT LUCK! WE'RE IN A ROCKET GRAVEYARD!
WITH PLENTY OF GREASE TO USE ON ROBOTA!
MEANWHILE...
DRAT! MY MAYHEM MAKER IS ACTING UP AGAIN! I'LL HAVE TO CALL THE REPAIRMAN!
SOON...
HOW DO YOU FEEL, ROBOTA?
FINE...BUT UGLY!
SPEAKING OF UGLY, LET'S NOT FORGET WHY WE'RE HERE! TO RESCUE SLEEPING PRINCESS (SHUDDER) UGLY!
ON TO THE DOMED CITY!
AND NOBODY BETTER GET IN OUR WAY! GRRRR!
17

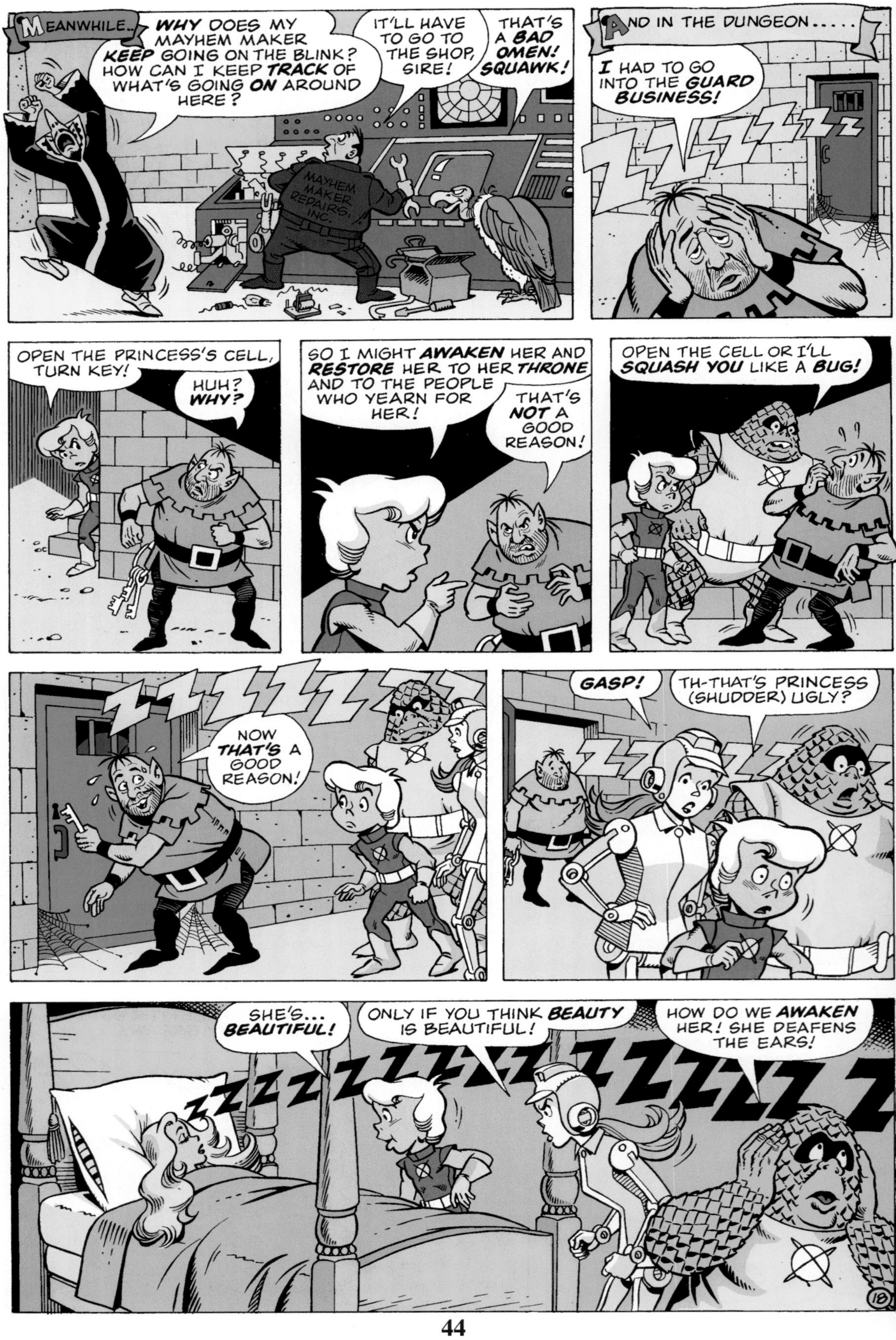
MEANWHILE..
WHY DOES MY MAYHEM MAKER KEEP GOING ON THE BLINK? HOW CAN I KEEP TRACK OF WHAT'S GOING ON AROUND HERE?
IT'LL HAVE TO GO TO THE SHOP, SIRE!
THAT'S A BAD OMEN! SQUAWK!
MAYHEM MAKER REPAIRS, INC.
AND IN THE DUNGEON.....
I HAD TO GO INTO THE GUARD BUSINESS!
ZZZZZZZZZ
OPEN THE PRINCESS'S CELL, TURN KEY!
HUH? WHY?
SO I MIGHT AWAKEN HER AND RESTORE HER TO HER THRONE AND TO THE PEOPLE WHO YEARN FOR HER!
THAT'S NOT A GOOD REASON!
OPEN THE CELL OR I'LL SQUASH YOU LIKE A BUG!
??
NOW THAT'S A GOOD REASON!
GASP!
TH-THAT'S PRINCESS (SHUDDER) UGLY?
SHE'S... BEAUTIFUL!
ONLY IF YOU THINK BEAUTY IS BEAUTIFUL!
HOW DO WE AWAKEN HER! SHE DEAFENS THE EARS!
18

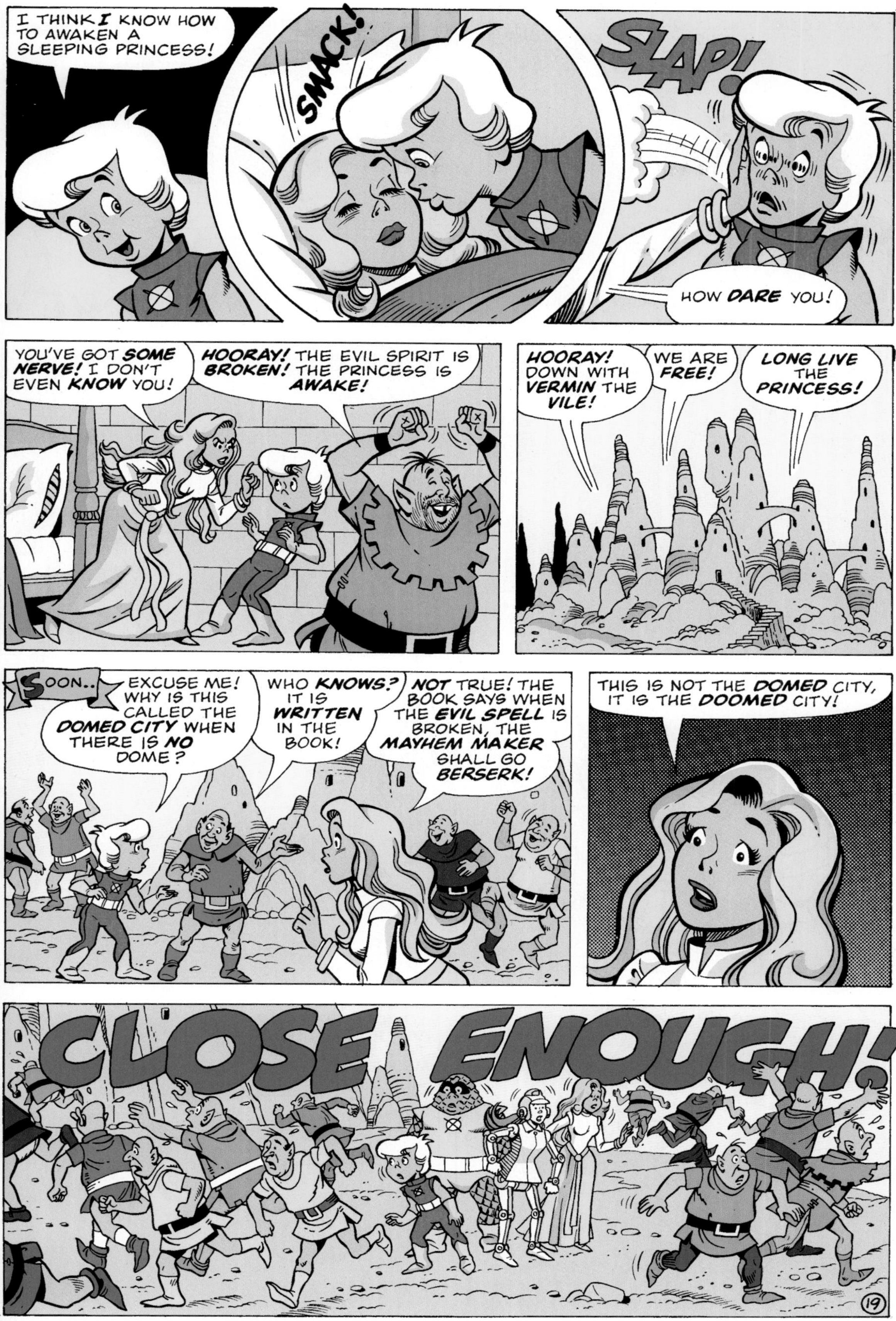
I THINK I KNOW HOW TO AWAKEN A SLEEPING PRINCESS!
SMACK!
SLAP!
HOW DARE YOU!
YOU'VE GOT SOME NERVE! I DON'T EVEN KNOW YOU!
HOORAY! THE EVIL SPIRIT IS BROKEN! THE PRINCESS IS AWAKE!
HOORAY! DOWN WITH VERMIN THE VILE!
WE ARE FREE!
LONG LIVE THE PRINCESS!
SOON..
EXCUSE ME! WHY IS THIS CALLED THE DOMED CITY WHEN THERE IS NO DOME?
WHO KNOWS? IT IS WRITTEN IN THE BOOK!
NOT TRUE! THE BOOK SAYS WHEN THE EVIL SPELL IS BROKEN, THE MAYHEM MAKER SHALL GO BERSERK!
THIS IS NOT THE DOMED CITY, IT IS THE DOOMED CITY!
CLOSE ENOUGH!
19

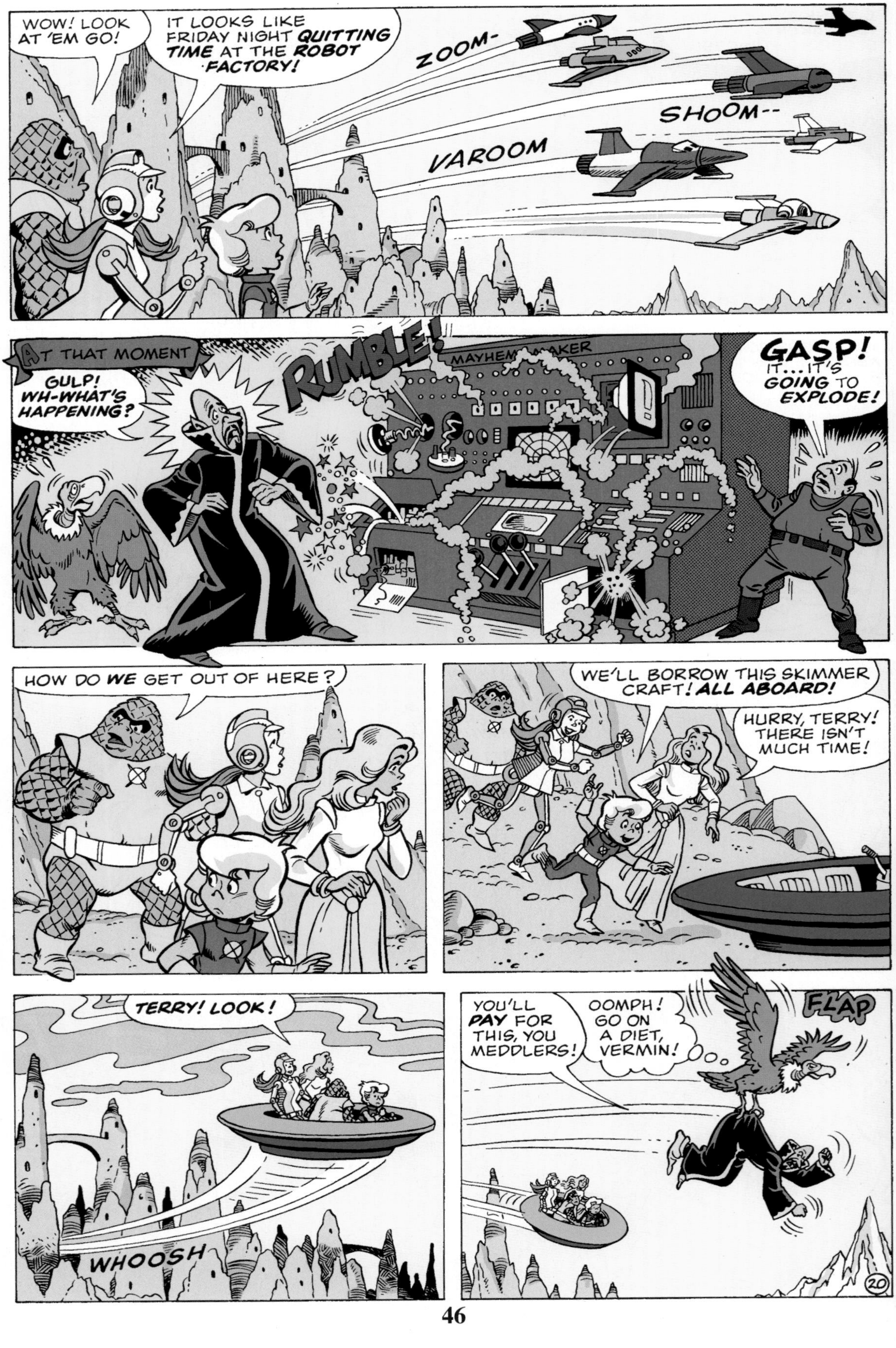

WOW! LOOK AT 'EM GO!
IT LOOKS LIKE FRIDAY NIGHT QUITTING TIME AT THE ROBOT FACTORY!
ZOOM-
SHOOM--
VAROOM
AT THAT MOMENT
GULP! WH-WHAT'S HAPPENING?
RUMBLE!
MAYHEM MAKER
GASP! IT...IT'S GOING TO EXPLODE!
HOW DO WE GET OUT OF HERE?
WE'LL BORROW THIS SKIMMER CRAFT! ALL ABOARD!
HURRY, TERRY! THERE ISN'T MUCH TIME!
TERRY! LOOK!
WHOOSH
YOU'LL PAY FOR THIS, YOU MEDDLERS!
OOMPH! GO ON A DIET, VERMIN!
FLAP
20

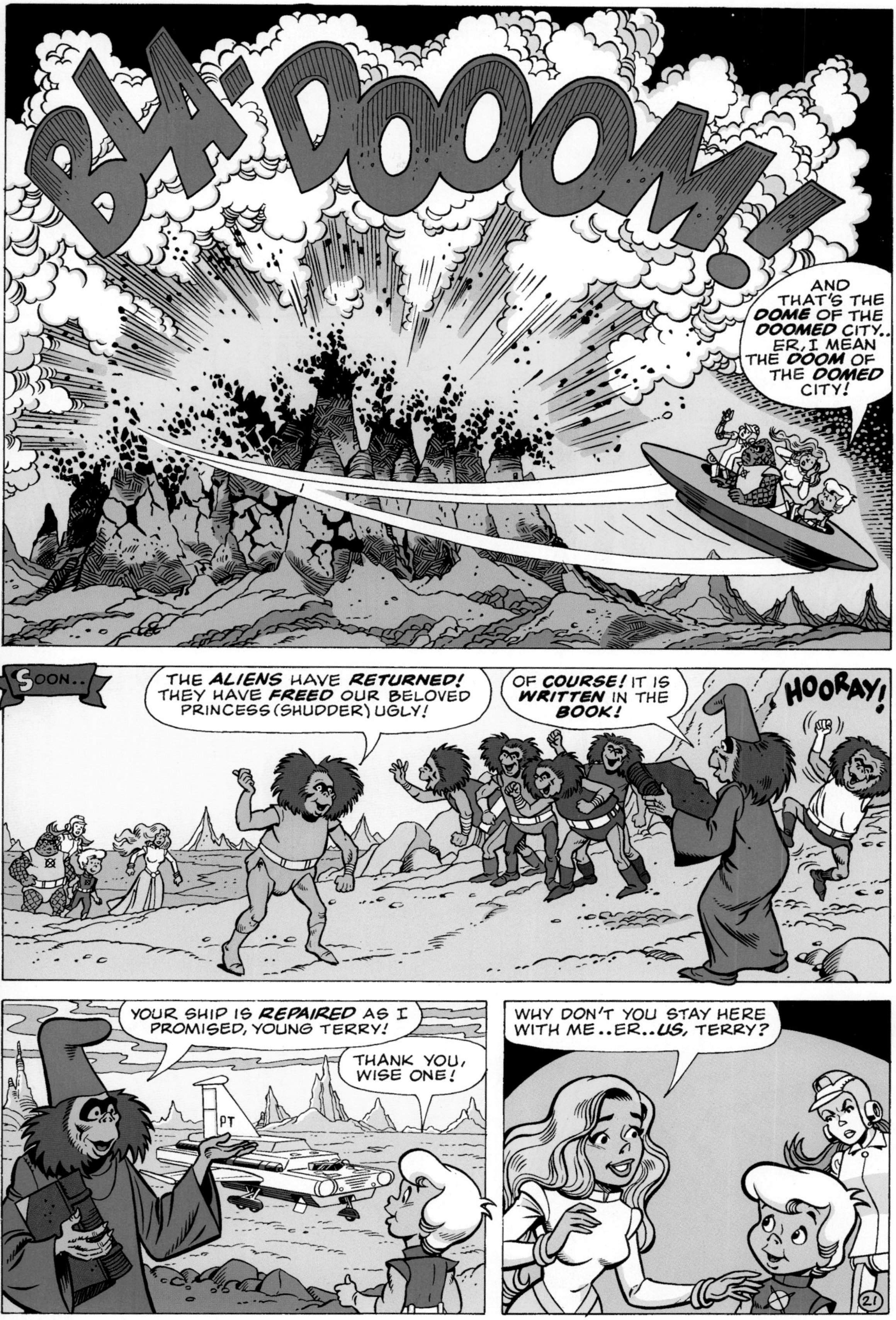
BLA-DOOOM!
AND THAT'S THE DOME OF THE DOOMED CITY.. ER, I MEAN THE DOOM OF THE DOMED CITY!
SOON..
THE ALIENS HAVE RETURNED! THEY HAVE FREED OUR BELOVED PRINCESS (SHUDDER) UGLY!
OF COURSE! IT IS WRITTEN IN THE BOOK!
HOORAY!
YOUR SHIP IS REPAIRED AS I PROMISED, YOUNG TERRY!
THANK YOU, WISE ONE!
PT
WHY DON'T YOU STAY HERE WITH ME..ER..US, TERRY?
21

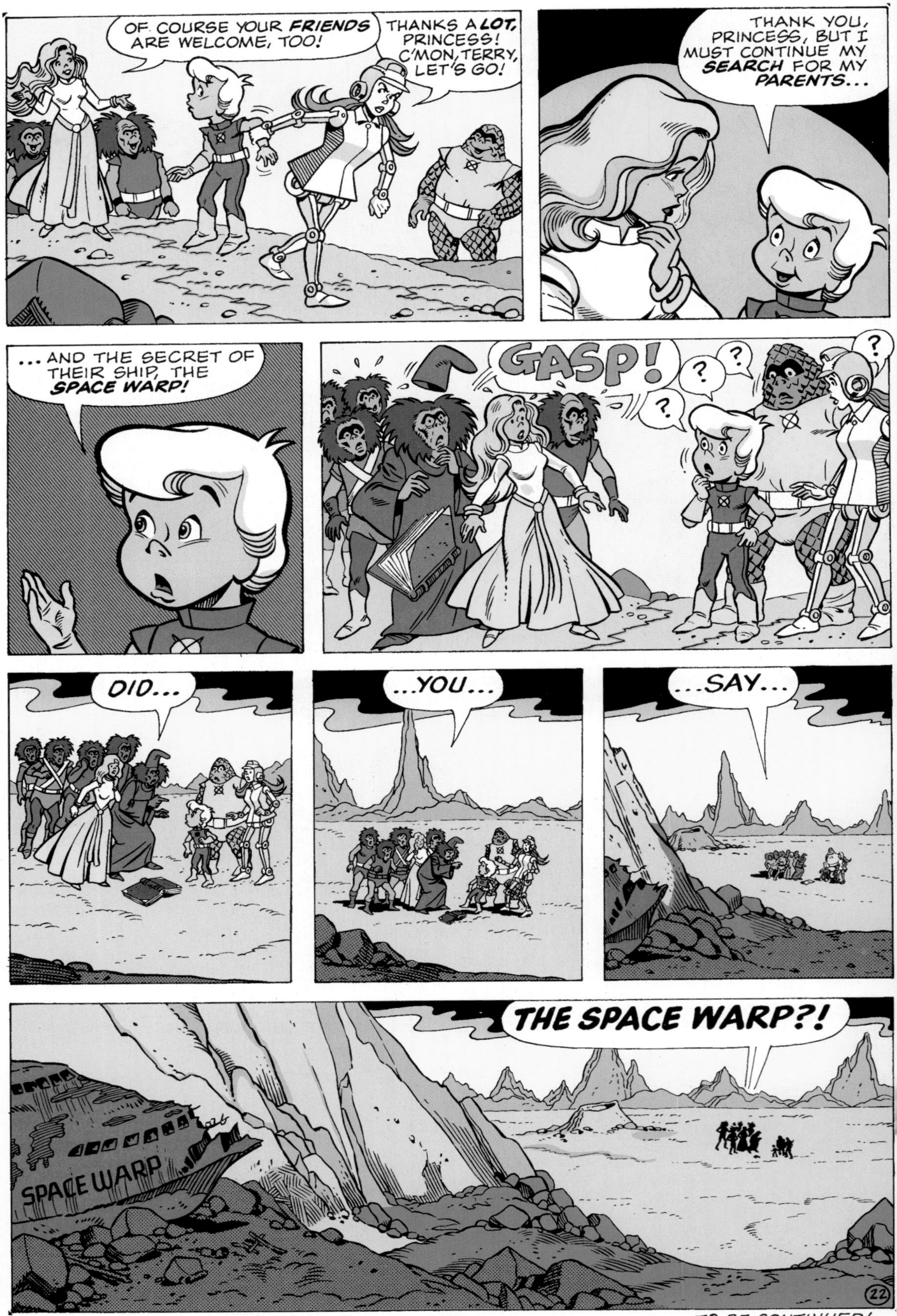
OF COURSE YOUR FRIENDS ARE WELCOME, TOO!
THANKS A LOT, PRINCESS! C'MON, TERRY, LET'S GO!
THANK YOU, PRINCESS, BUT I MUST CONTINUE MY SEARCH FOR MY PARENTS...
...AND THE SECRET OF THEIR SHIP, THE SPACE WARP!
GASP!
?
?
?
?
DID...
...YOU...
...SAY...
THE SPACE WARP?!
SPACE WARP
22

TO BE CONTINUED!

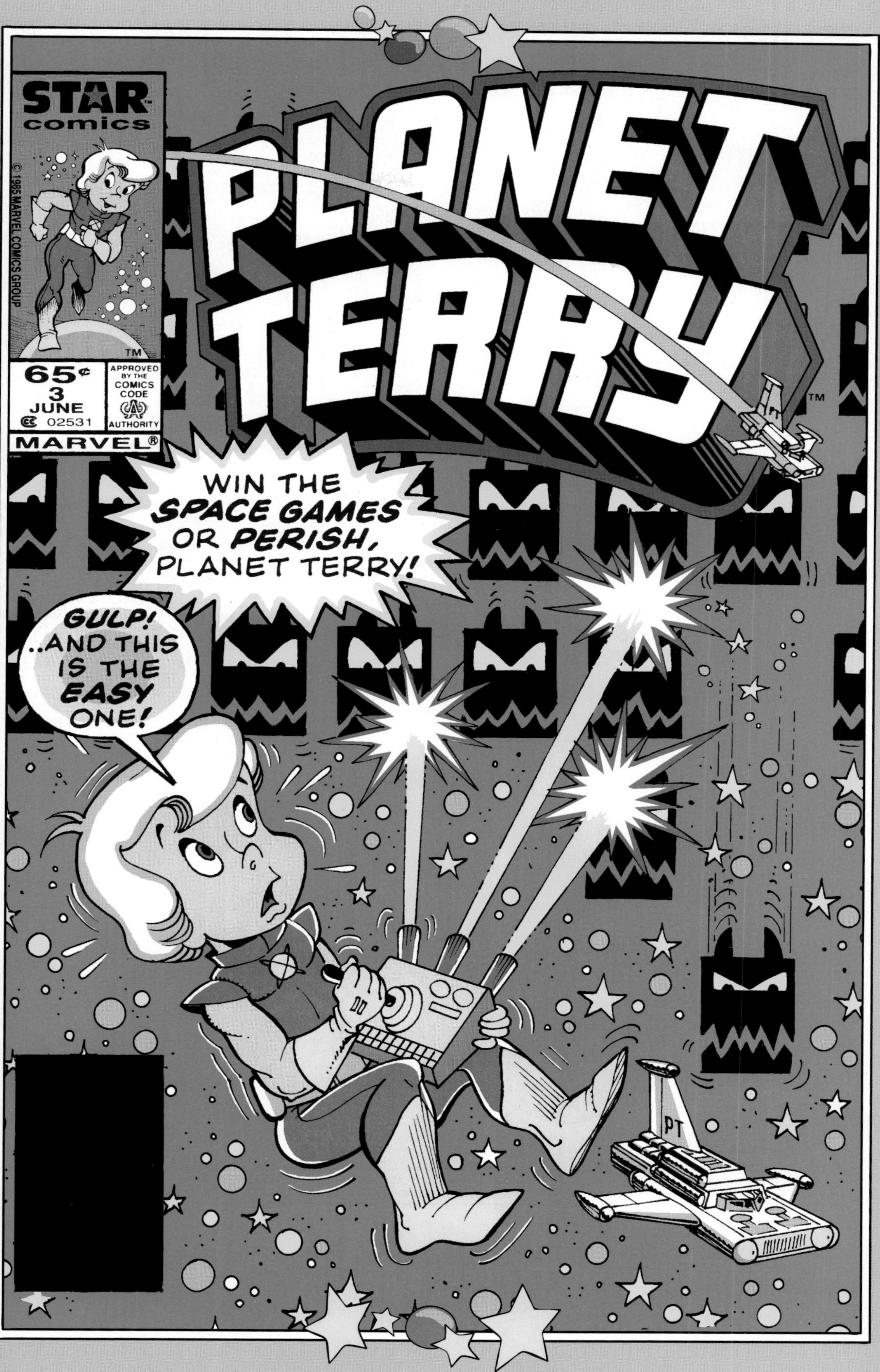
STAR comics
© 1985 MARVEL COMICS GROUP
PLANET TERRY™
65¢
3
JUNE
02531
APPROVED BY THE COMICS CODE AUTHORITY
MARVEL®
WIN THE SPACE GAMES OR PERISH, PLANET TERRY!
GULP! ..AND THIS IS THE EASY ONE!
PT

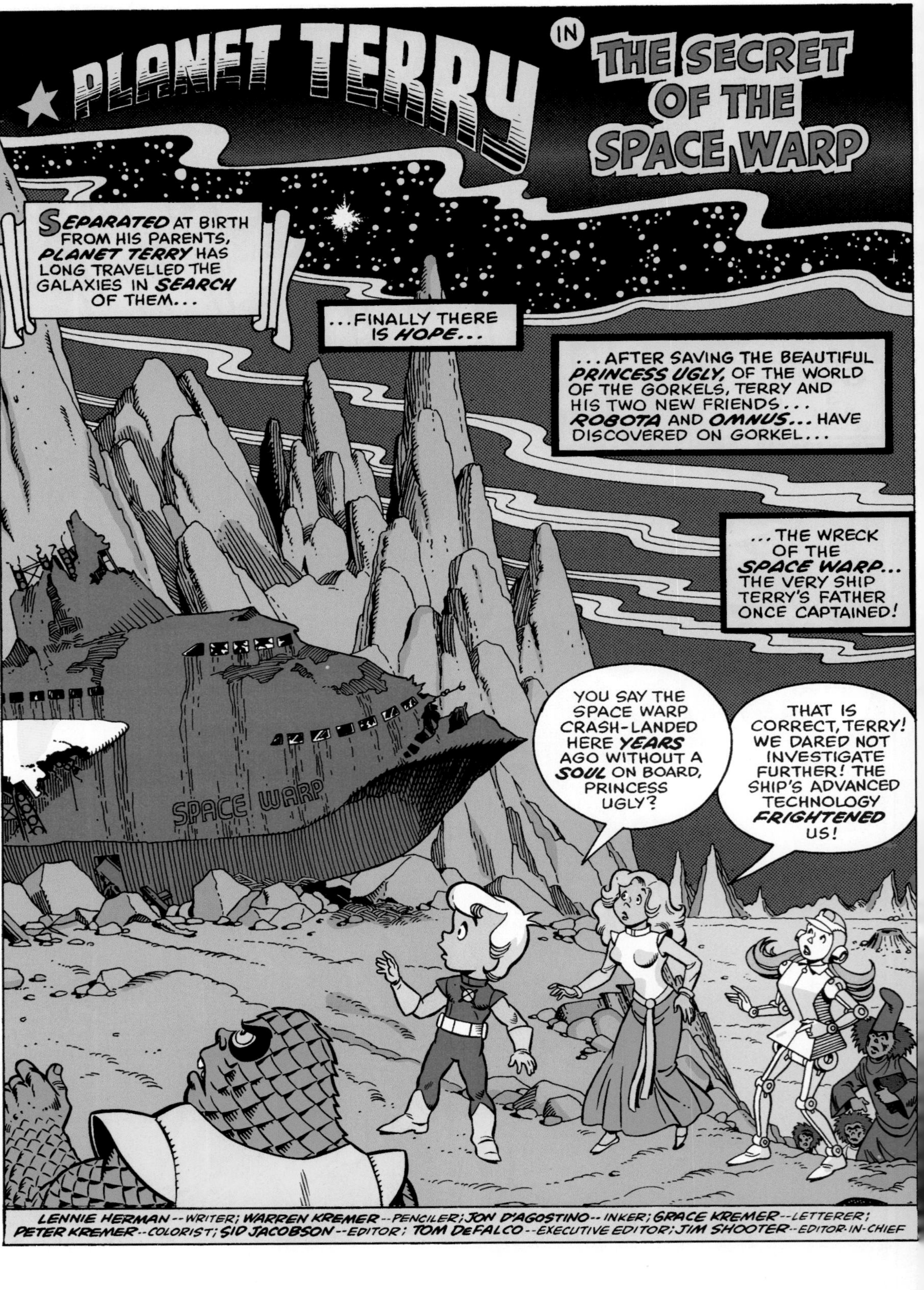
PLANET TERRY IN THE SECRET OF THE SPACE WARP
SEPARATED AT BIRTH FROM HIS PARENTS, PLANET TERRY HAS LONG TRAVELLED THE GALAXIES IN SEARCH OF THEM...
...FINALLY THERE IS HOPE...
...AFTER SAVING THE BEAUTIFUL PRINCESS UGLY, OF THE WORLD OF THE GORKELS, TERRY AND HIS TWO NEW FRIENDS... ROBOTA AND OMNUS... HAVE DISCOVERED ON GORKEL...
...THE WRECK OF THE SPACE WARP... THE VERY SHIP TERRY'S FATHER ONCE CAPTAINED!
SPACE WARP
YOU SAY THE SPACE WARP CRASH-LANDED HERE YEARS AGO WITHOUT A SOUL ON BOARD, PRINCESS UGLY?
THAT IS CORRECT, TERRY! WE DARED NOT INVESTIGATE FURTHER! THE SHIP'S ADVANCED TECHNOLOGY FRIGHTENED US!
LENNIE HERMAN--WRITER; WARREN KREMER--PENCILER; JON D'AGOSTINO--INKER; GRACE KREMER--LETTERER; PETER KREMER--COLORIST; SID JACOBSON--EDITOR; TOM DeFALCO--EXECUTIVE EDITOR; JIM SHOOTER--EDITOR-IN-CHIEF

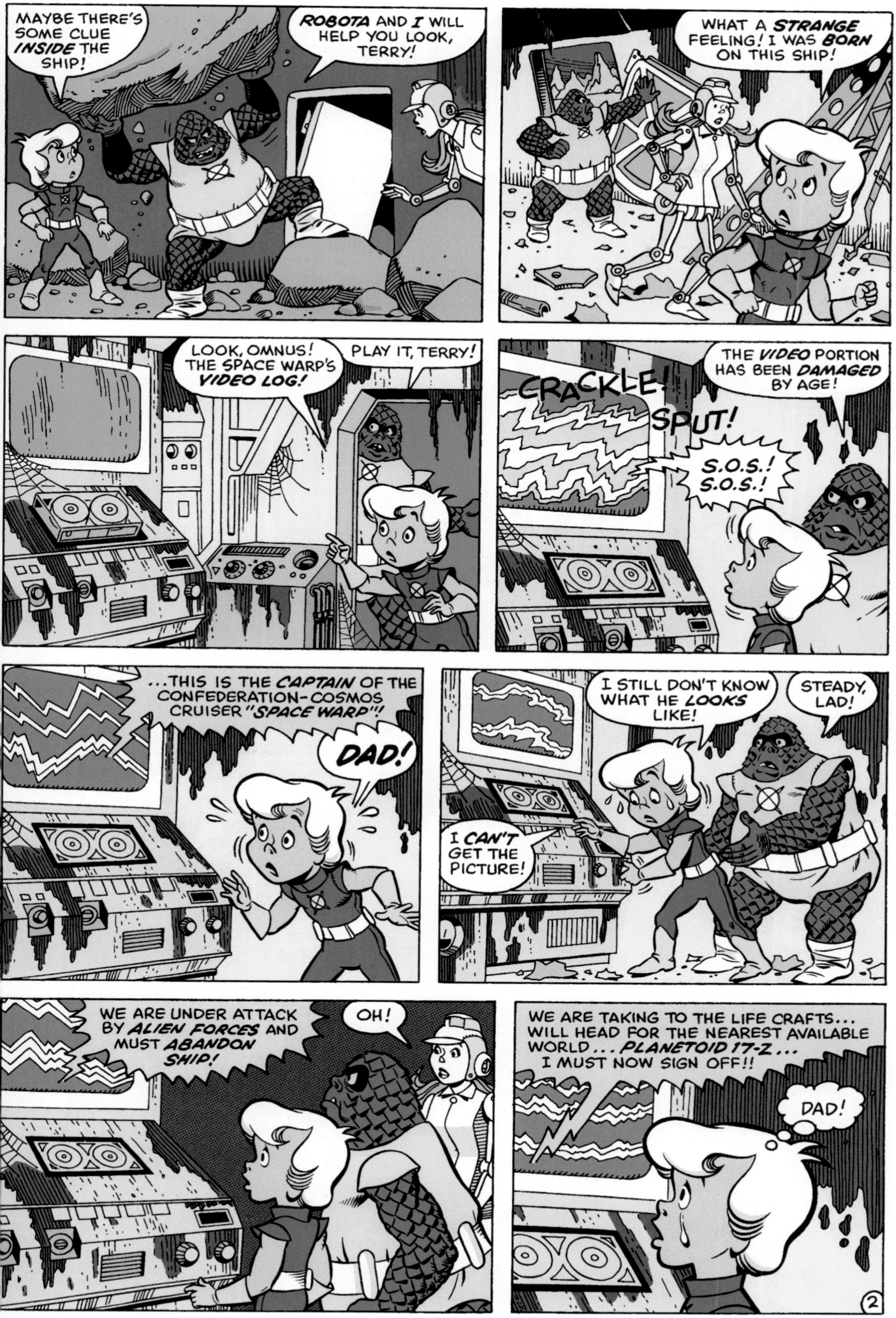
MAYBE THERE'S SOME CLUE INSIDE THE SHIP!
ROBOTA AND I WILL HELP YOU LOOK, TERRY!
WHAT A STRANGE FEELING! I WAS BORN ON THIS SHIP!
LOOK, OMNUS! THE SPACE WARP'S VIDEO LOG!
PLAY IT, TERRY!
CRACKLE!
SPUT!
THE VIDEO PORTION HAS BEEN DAMAGED BY AGE!
S.O.S.! S.O.S.!
...THIS IS THE CAPTAIN OF THE CONFEDERATION-COSMOS CRUISER "SPACE WARP"!
DAD!
I STILL DON'T KNOW WHAT HE LOOKS LIKE!
STEADY, LAD!
I CAN'T GET THE PICTURE!
WE ARE UNDER ATTACK BY ALIEN FORCES AND MUST ABANDON SHIP!
OH!
WE ARE TAKING TO THE LIFE CRAFTS... WILL HEAD FOR THE NEAREST AVAILABLE WORLD... PLANETOID 17-Z... I MUST NOW SIGN OFF!!
DAD!
2

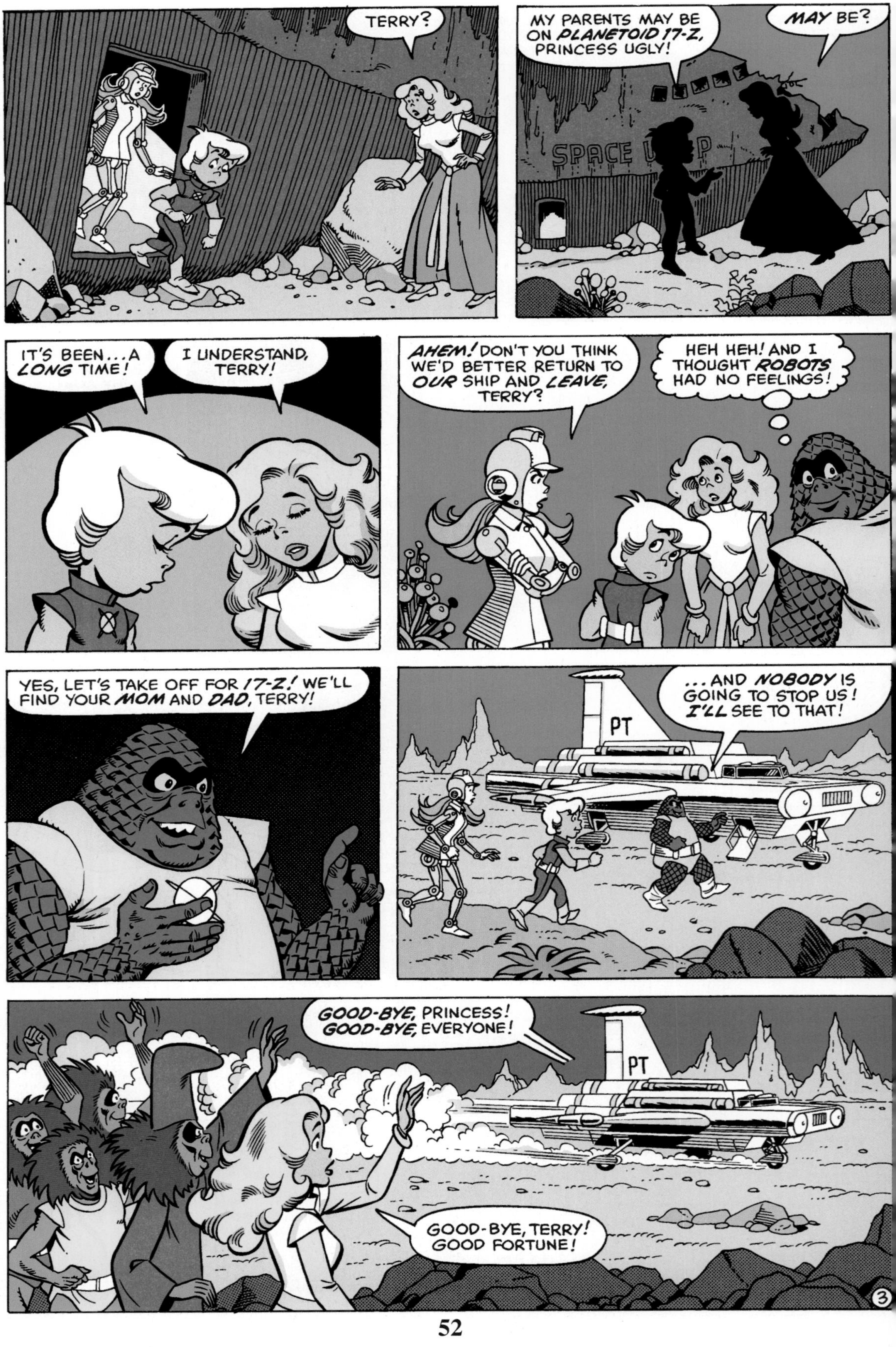
TERRY?
MY PARENTS MAY BE ON PLANETOID 17-Z, PRINCESS UGLY!
MAY BE?
SPACE U P
IT'S BEEN... A LONG TIME!
I UNDERSTAND, TERRY!
AHEM! DON'T YOU THINK WE'D BETTER RETURN TO OUR SHIP AND LEAVE, TERRY?
HEH HEH! AND I THOUGHT ROBOTS HAD NO FEELINGS!
YES, LET'S TAKE OFF FOR 17-Z! WE'LL FIND YOUR MOM AND DAD, TERRY!
PT
...AND NOBODY IS GOING TO STOP US! I'LL SEE TO THAT!
GOOD-BYE, PRINCESS! GOOD-BYE, EVERYONE!
PT
GOOD-BYE, TERRY! GOOD FORTUNE!
3

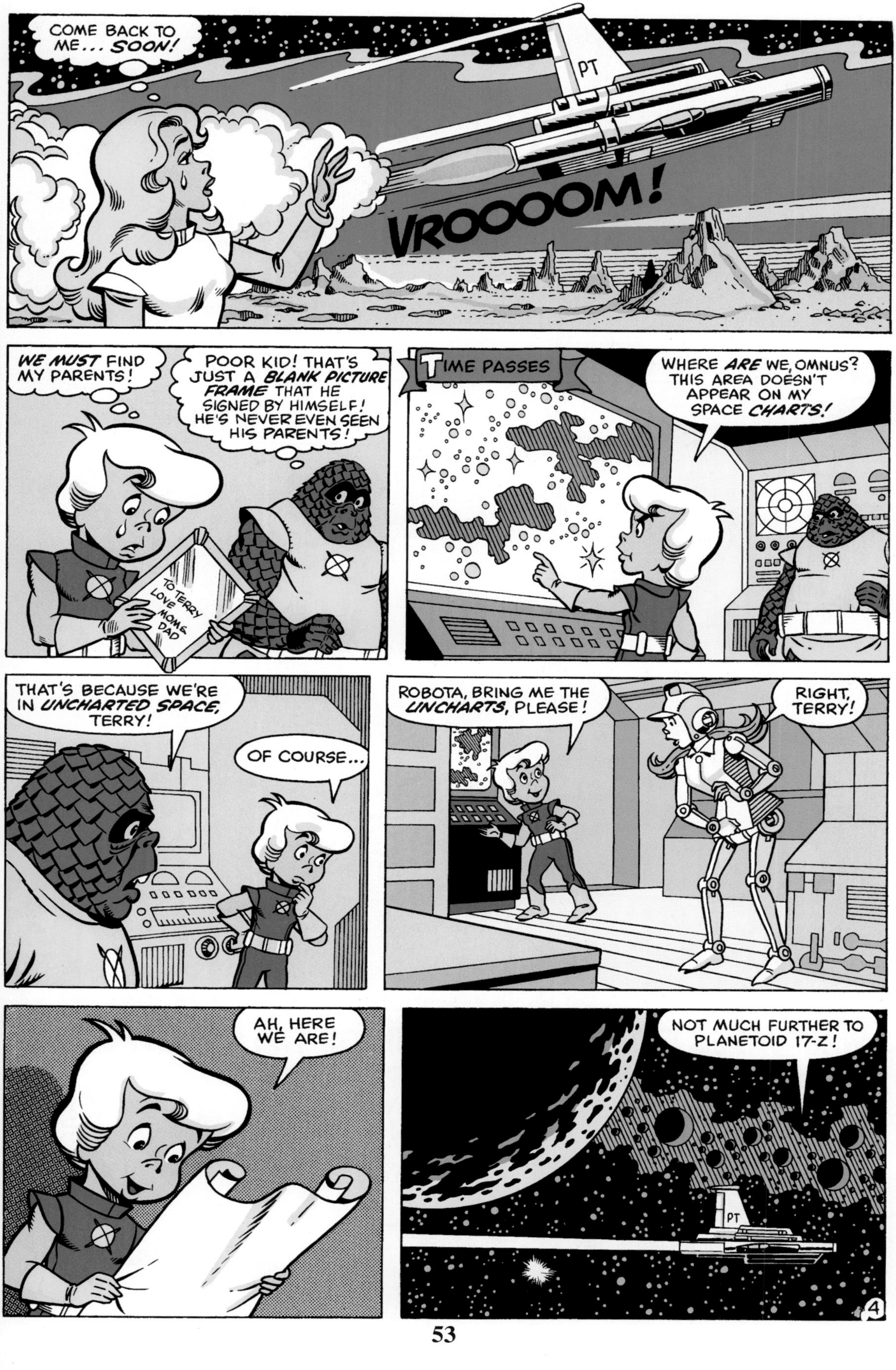
COME BACK TO ME... SOON!
PT
VROOOOM!
WE MUST FIND MY PARENTS!
POOR KID! THAT'S JUST A BLANK PICTURE FRAME THAT HE SIGNED BY HIMSELF! HE'S NEVER EVEN SEEN HIS PARENTS!
TO TERRY LOVE MOM & DAD
TIME PASSES
WHERE ARE WE, OMNUS? THIS AREA DOESN'T APPEAR ON MY SPACE CHARTS!
THAT'S BECAUSE WE'RE IN UNCHARTED SPACE, TERRY!
OF COURSE...
ROBOTA, BRING ME THE UNCHARTS, PLEASE!
RIGHT, TERRY!
AH, HERE WE ARE!
NOT MUCH FURTHER TO PLANETOID 17-Z!
PT
4

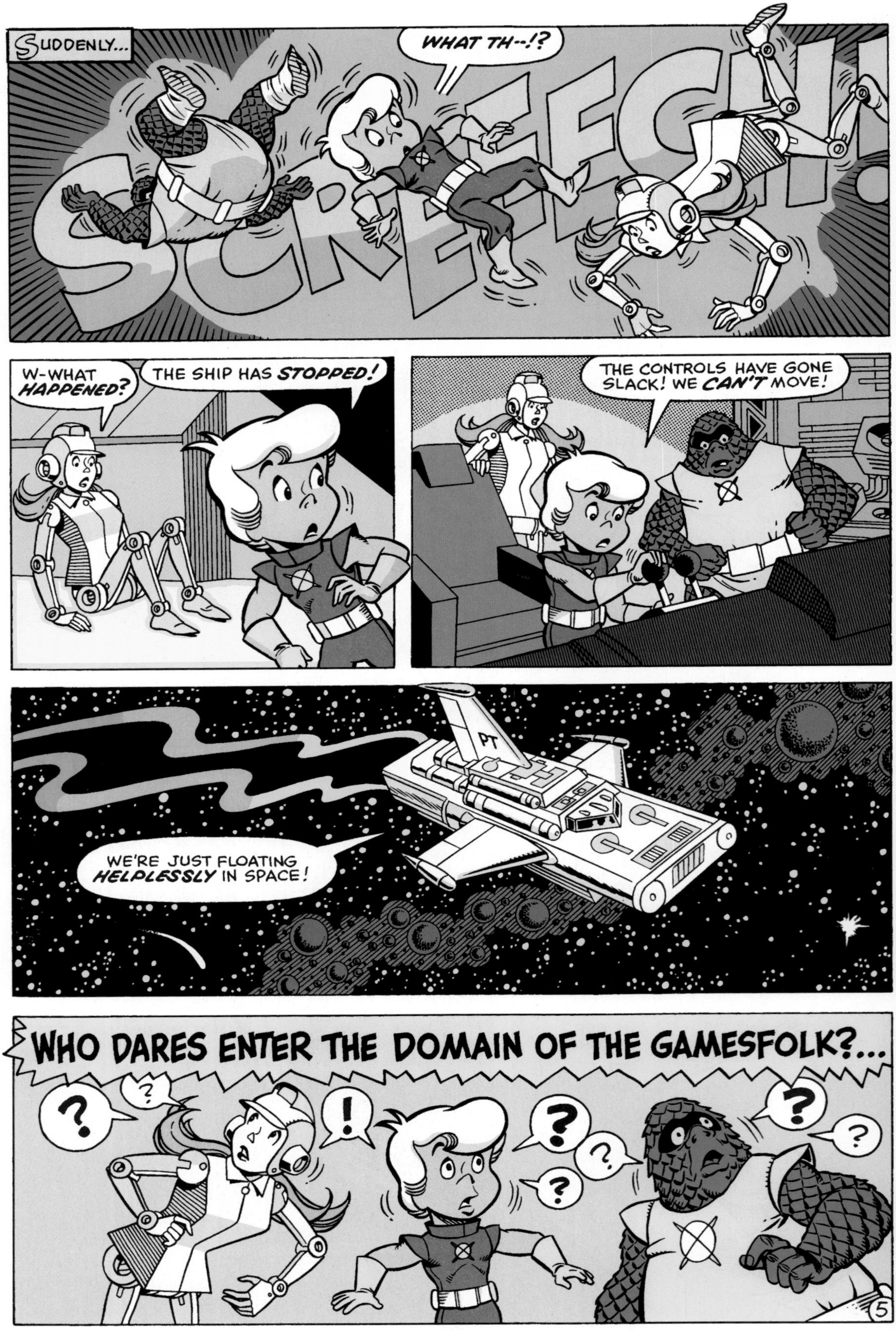
SUDDENLY...
WHAT TH--!?
SCREECH!
W-WHAT HAPPENED?
THE SHIP HAS STOPPED!
THE CONTROLS HAVE GONE SLACK! WE CAN'T MOVE!
PT
WE'RE JUST FLOATING HELPLESSLY IN SPACE!
WHO DARES ENTER THE DOMAIN OF THE GAMESFOLK?...
?
?
!
?
?
?
?
?
5

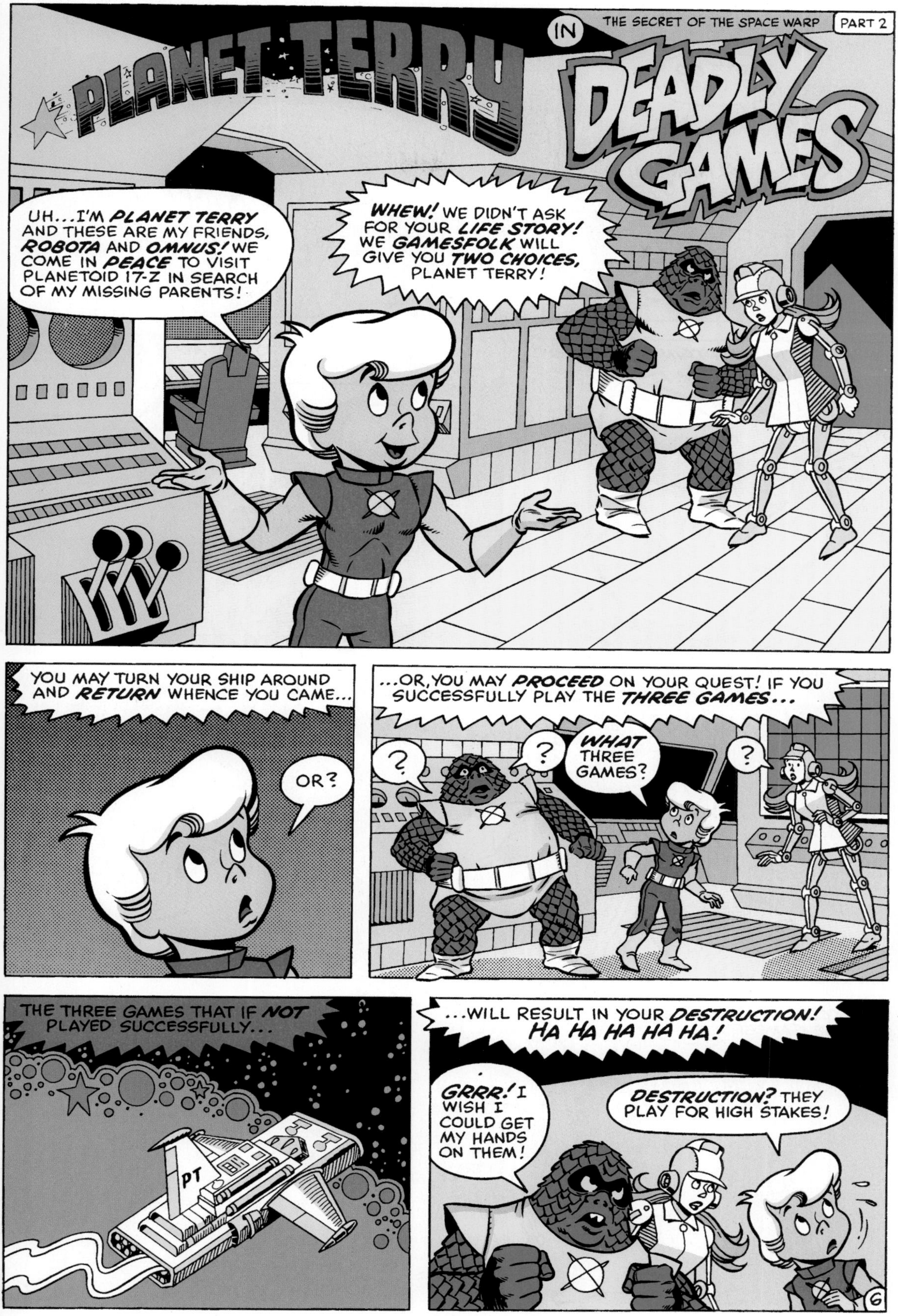
PLANET TERRY
IN
THE SECRET OF THE SPACE WARP
PART 2
DEADLY GAMES
UH...I'M PLANET TERRY AND THESE ARE MY FRIENDS, ROBOTA AND OMNUS! WE COME IN PEACE TO VISIT PLANETOID 17-Z IN SEARCH OF MY MISSING PARENTS!
WHEW! WE DIDN'T ASK FOR YOUR LIFE STORY! WE GAMESFOLK WILL GIVE YOU TWO CHOICES, PLANET TERRY!
YOU MAY TURN YOUR SHIP AROUND AND RETURN WHENCE YOU CAME...
OR?
...OR, YOU MAY PROCEED ON YOUR QUEST! IF YOU SUCCESSFULLY PLAY THE THREE GAMES...
?
?
WHAT THREE GAMES?
?
THE THREE GAMES THAT IF NOT PLAYED SUCCESSFULLY...
PT
...WILL RESULT IN YOUR DESTRUCTION! HA HA HA HA HA!
GRRR! I WISH I COULD GET MY HANDS ON THEM!
DESTRUCTION? THEY PLAY FOR HIGH STAKES!
6

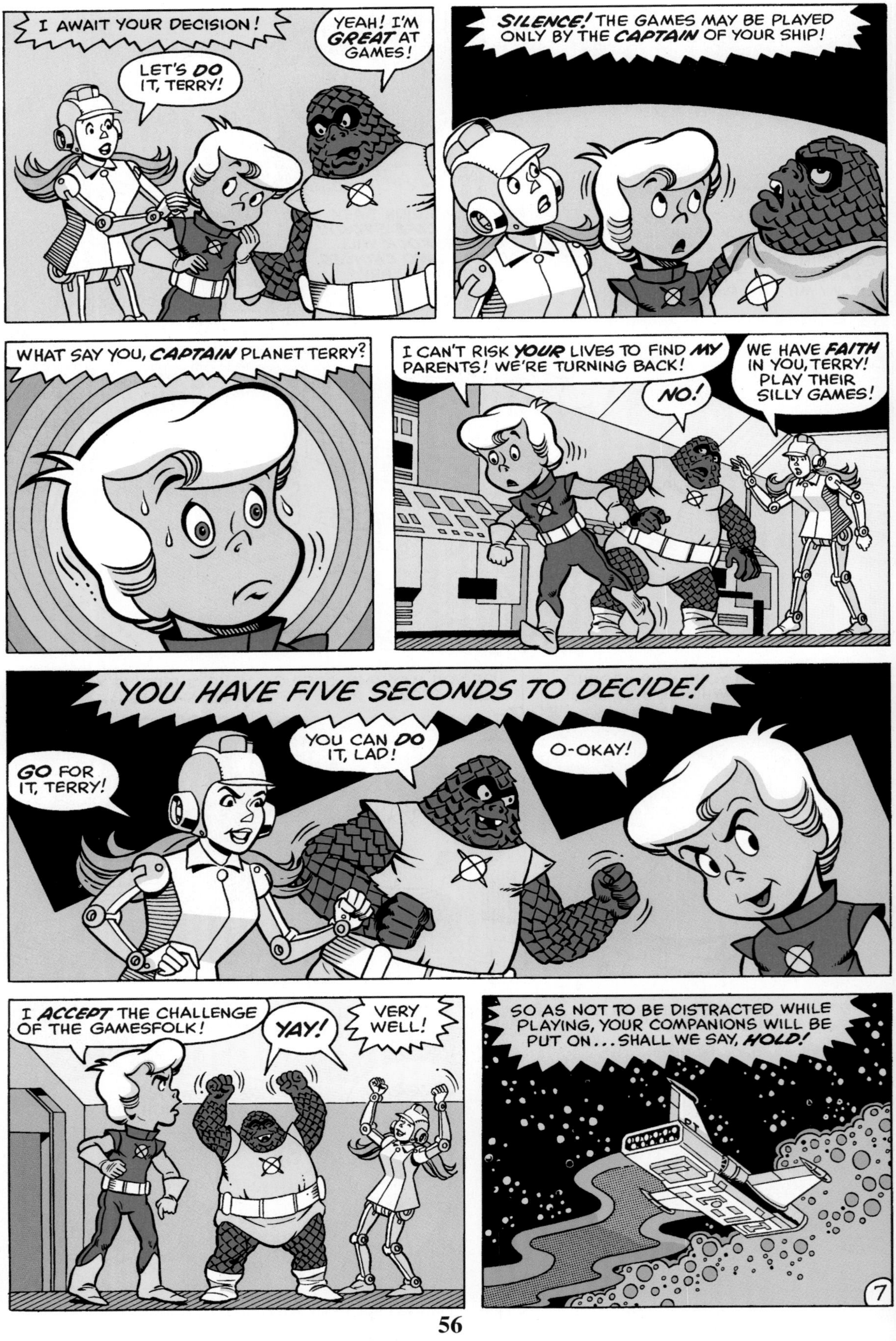
I AWAIT YOUR DECISION!
LET'S DO IT, TERRY!
YEAH! I'M GREAT AT GAMES!
SILENCE! THE GAMES MAY BE PLAYED ONLY BY THE CAPTAIN OF YOUR SHIP!
WHAT SAY YOU, CAPTAIN PLANET TERRY?
I CAN'T RISK YOUR LIVES TO FIND MY PARENTS! WE'RE TURNING BACK!
NO!
WE HAVE FAITH IN YOU, TERRY! PLAY THEIR SILLY GAMES!
YOU HAVE FIVE SECONDS TO DECIDE!
GO FOR IT, TERRY!
YOU CAN DO IT, LAD!
O-OKAY!
I ACCEPT THE CHALLENGE OF THE GAMESFOLK!
YAY!
VERY WELL!
SO AS NOT TO BE DISTRACTED WHILE PLAYING, YOUR COMPANIONS WILL BE PUT ON... SHALL WE SAY, HOLD!
7

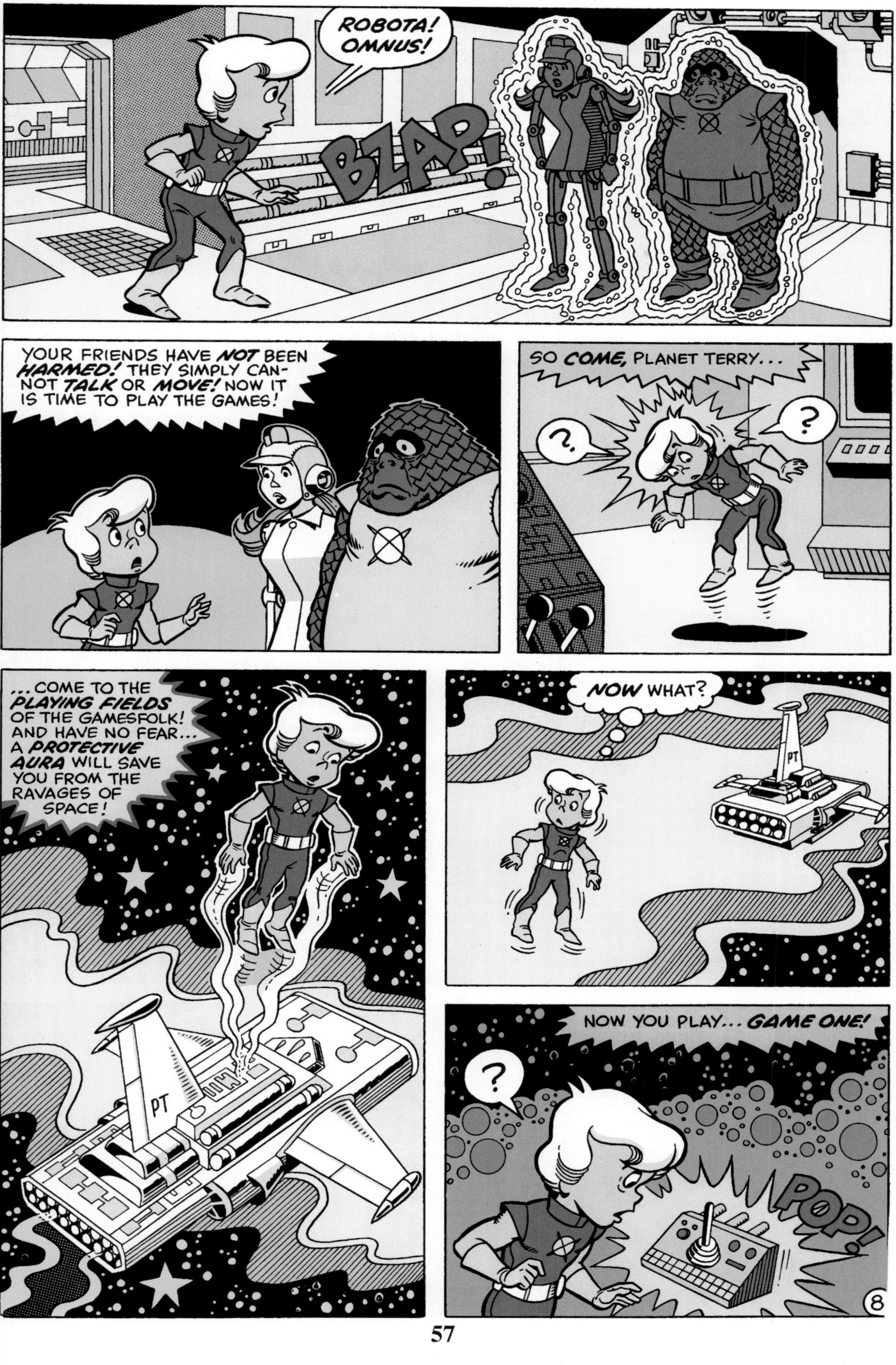
ROBOTA! OMNUS!
BZAP!
YOUR FRIENDS HAVE NOT BEEN HARMED! THEY SIMPLY CAN-NOT TALK OR MOVE! NOW IT IS TIME TO PLAY THE GAMES!
SO COME, PLANET TERRY...
?
?
...COME TO THE PLAYING FIELDS OF THE GAMESFOLK! AND HAVE NO FEAR... A PROTECTIVE AURA WILL SAVE YOU FROM THE RAVAGES OF SPACE!
PT
NOW WHAT?
PT
NOW YOU PLAY... GAME ONE!
?
POP!
8

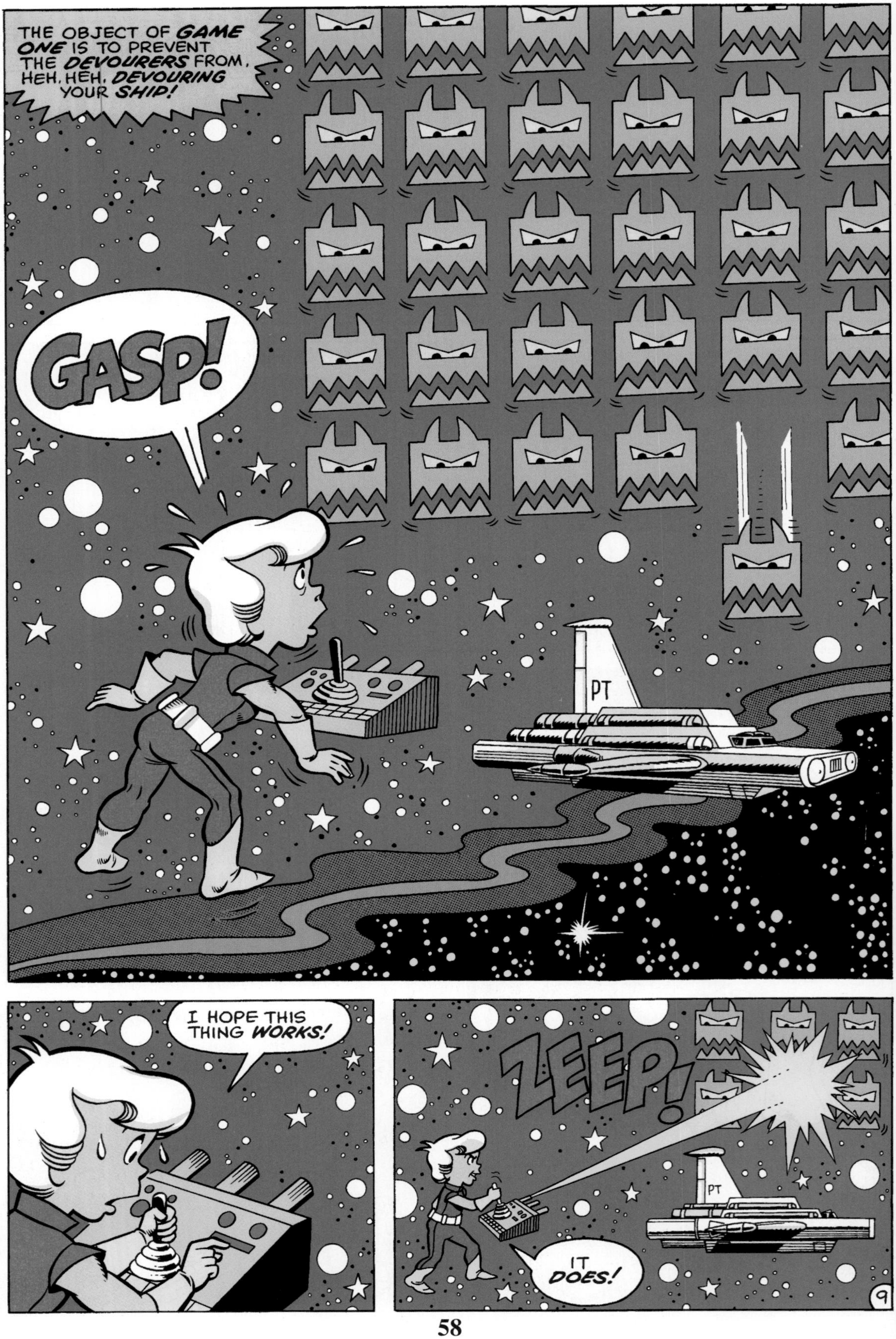
THE OBJECT OF GAME ONE IS TO PREVENT THE DEVOURERS FROM, HEH, HEH, DEVOURING YOUR SHIP!
GASP!
PT
I HOPE THIS THING WORKS!
ZEEP!
PT
IT DOES!
9

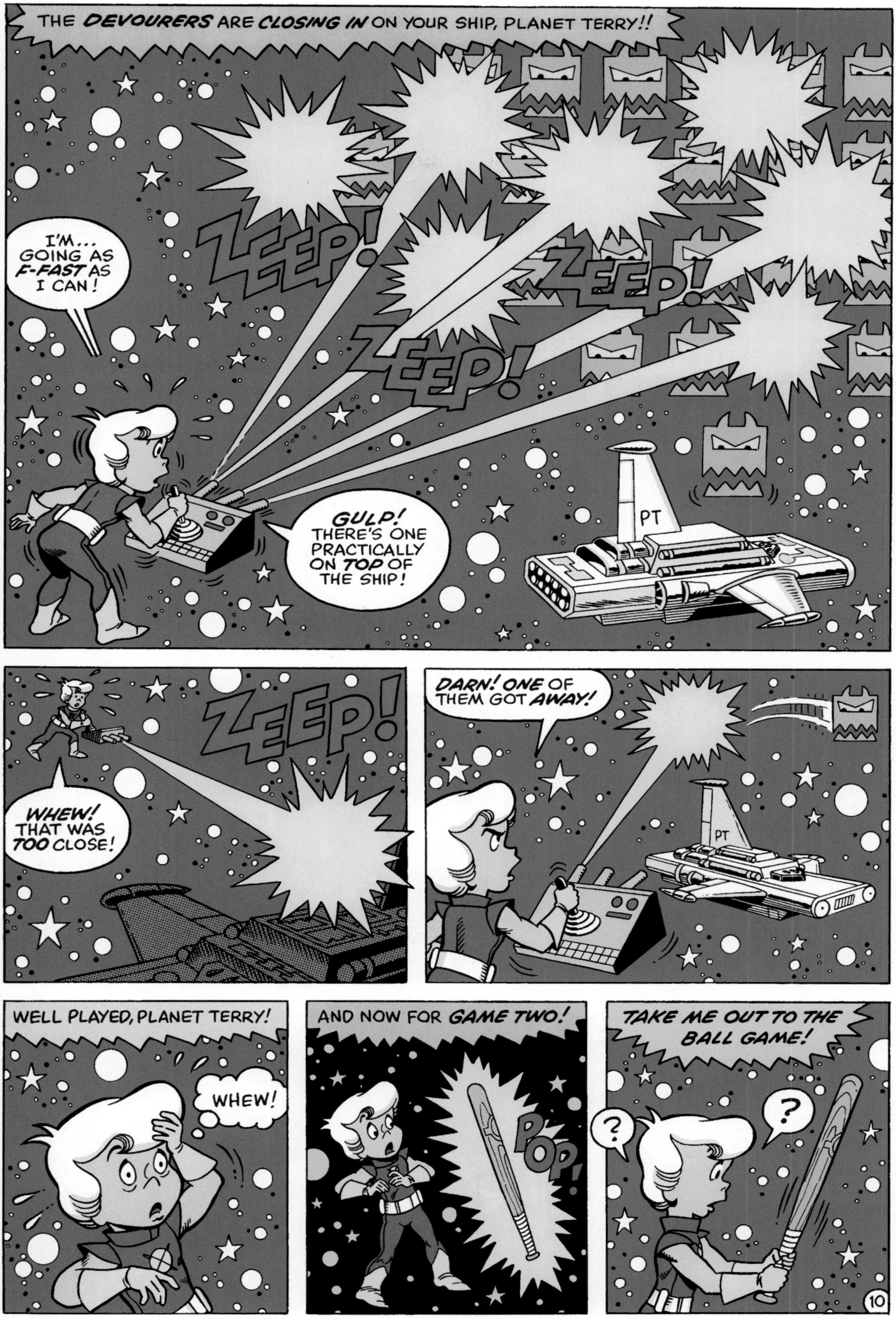

THE DEVOURERS ARE CLOSING IN ON YOUR SHIP, PLANET TERRY!!
I'M... GOING AS F-FAST AS I CAN!
ZEEP!
ZEEP!
ZEEP!
GULP! THERE'S ONE PRACTICALLY ON TOP OF THE SHIP!
PT
ZEEP!
WHEW! THAT WAS TOO CLOSE!
DARN! ONE OF THEM GOT AWAY!
PT
WELL PLAYED, PLANET TERRY!
WHEW!
AND NOW FOR GAME TWO!
POP!
TAKE ME OUT TO THE BALL GAME!
?
?
10

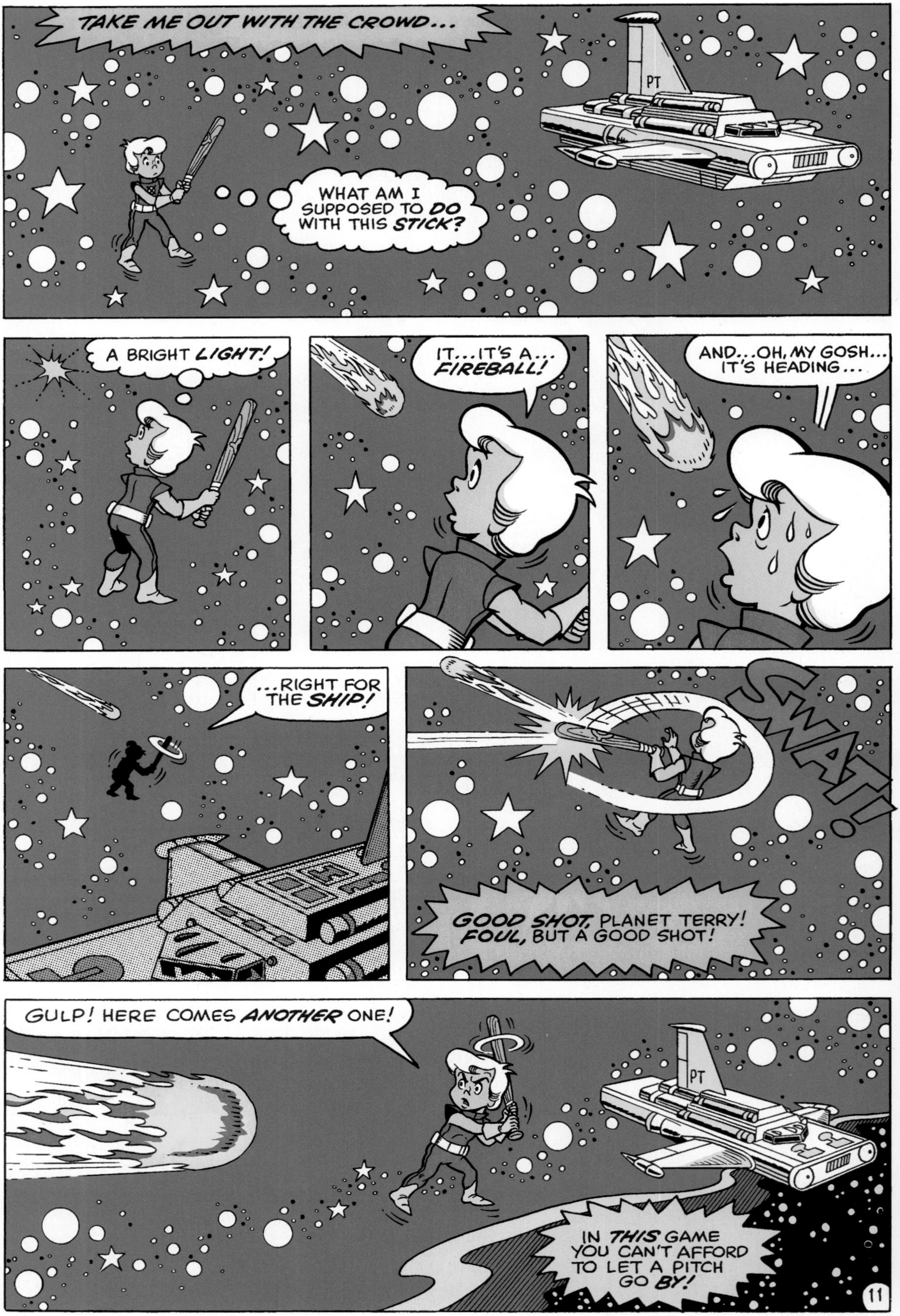
TAKE ME OUT WITH THE CROWD...
PT
WHAT AM I SUPPOSED TO DO WITH THIS STICK?
A BRIGHT LIGHT!
IT...IT'S A... FIREBALL!
AND...OH, MY GOSH... IT'S HEADING...
...RIGHT FOR THE SHIP!
SWAT!
GOOD SHOT, PLANET TERRY! FOUL, BUT A GOOD SHOT!
GULP! HERE COMES ANOTHER ONE!
PT
IN THIS GAME YOU CAN'T AFFORD TO LET A PITCH GO BY!
11

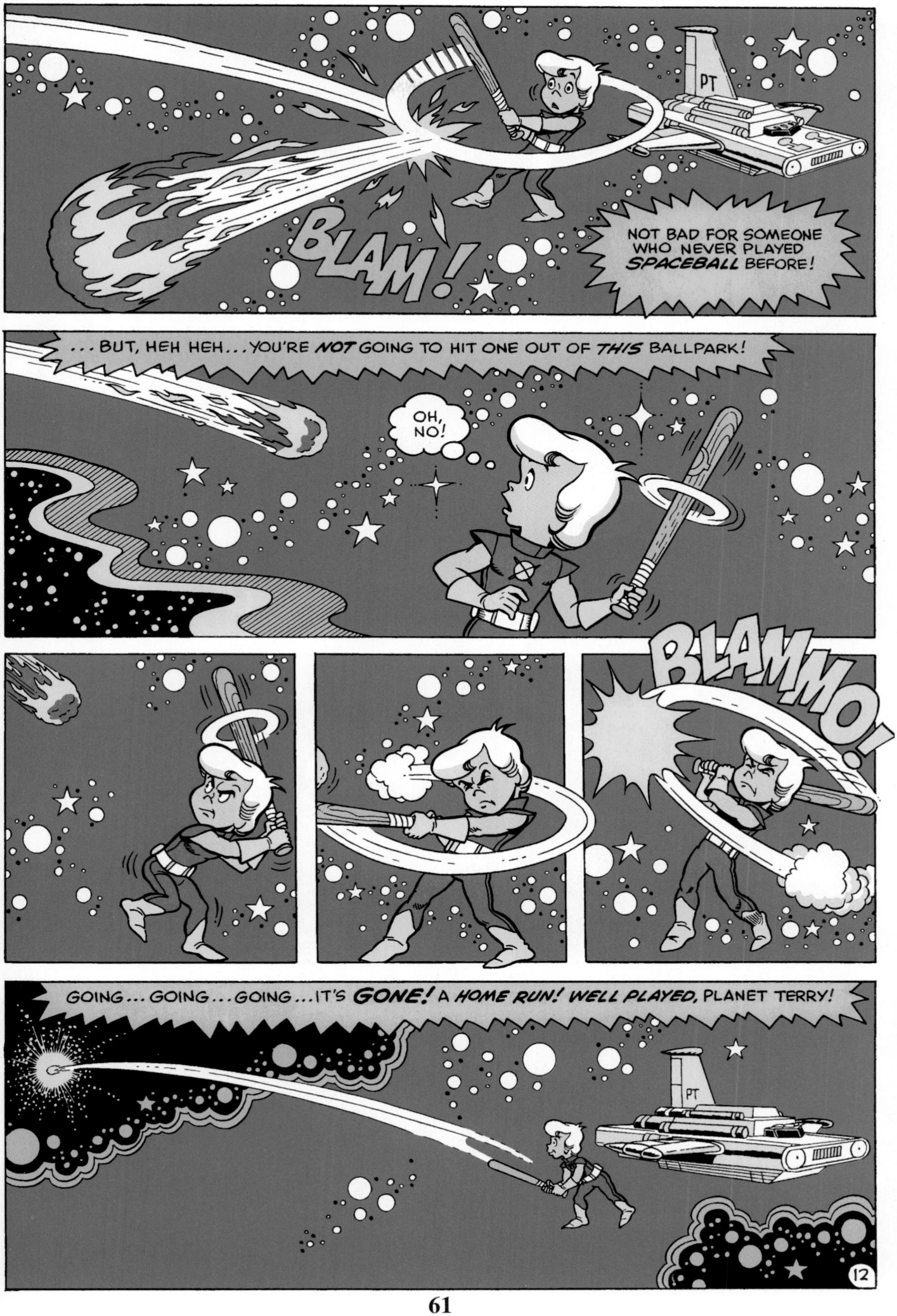
BLAM!
NOT BAD FOR SOMEONE WHO NEVER PLAYED SPACEBALL BEFORE!
...BUT, HEH HEH... YOU'RE NOT GOING TO HIT ONE OUT OF THIS BALLPARK!
OH, NO!
BLAMMO!
GOING... GOING... GOING... IT'S GONE! A HOME RUN! WELL PLAYED, PLANET TERRY!
12

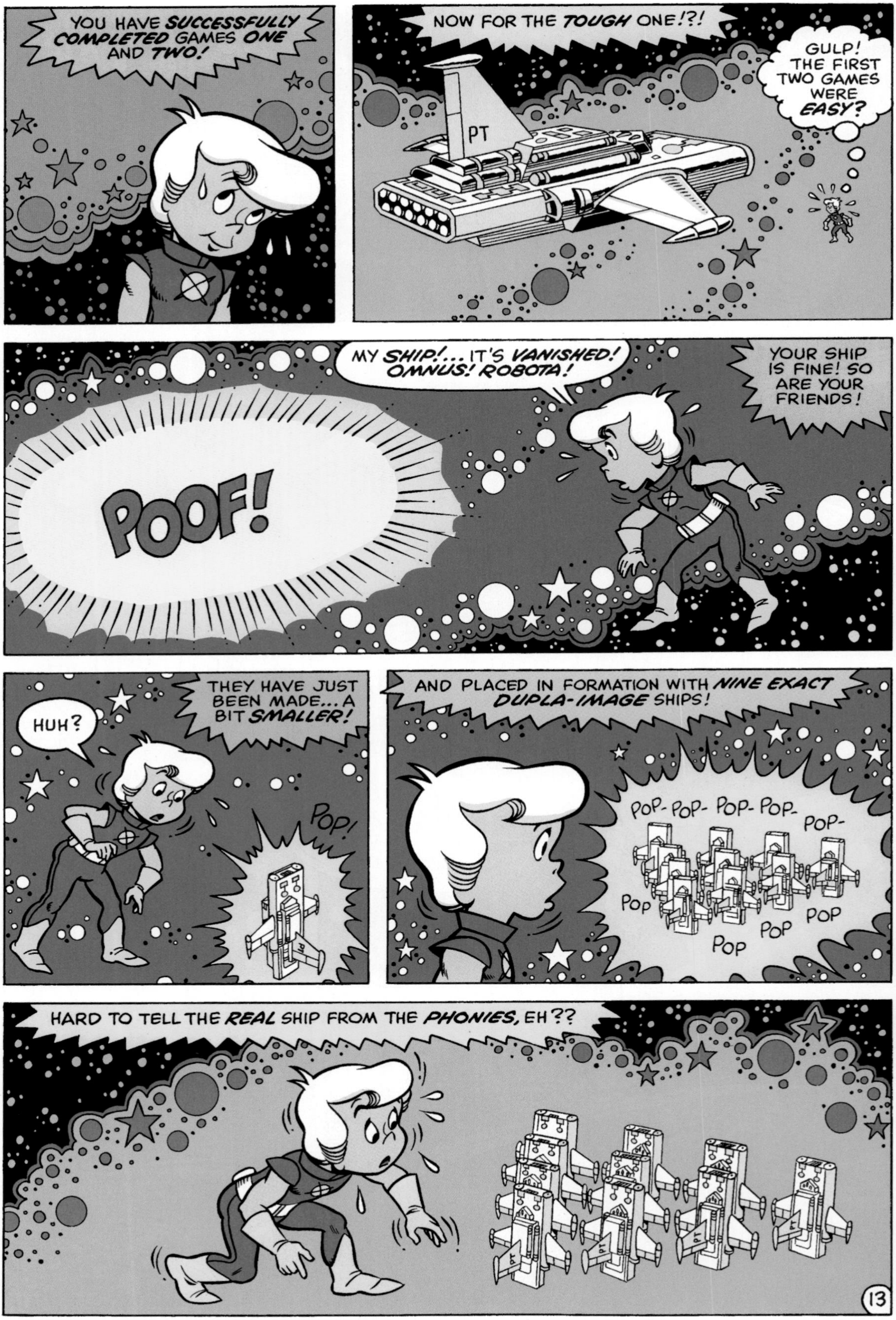
YOU HAVE SUCCESSFULLY COMPLETED GAMES ONE AND TWO!
NOW FOR THE TOUGH ONE!?!
GULP! THE FIRST TWO GAMES WERE EASY?
PT
POOF!
MY SHIP!... IT'S VANISHED! OMNUS! ROBOTA!
YOUR SHIP IS FINE! SO ARE YOUR FRIENDS!
HUH?
THEY HAVE JUST BEEN MADE... A BIT SMALLER!
POP!
AND PLACED IN FORMATION WITH NINE EXACT DUPLA-IMAGE SHIPS!
POP- POP- POP- POP- POP-
POP
POP
POP
POP
HARD TO TELL THE REAL SHIP FROM THE PHONIES, EH??
13

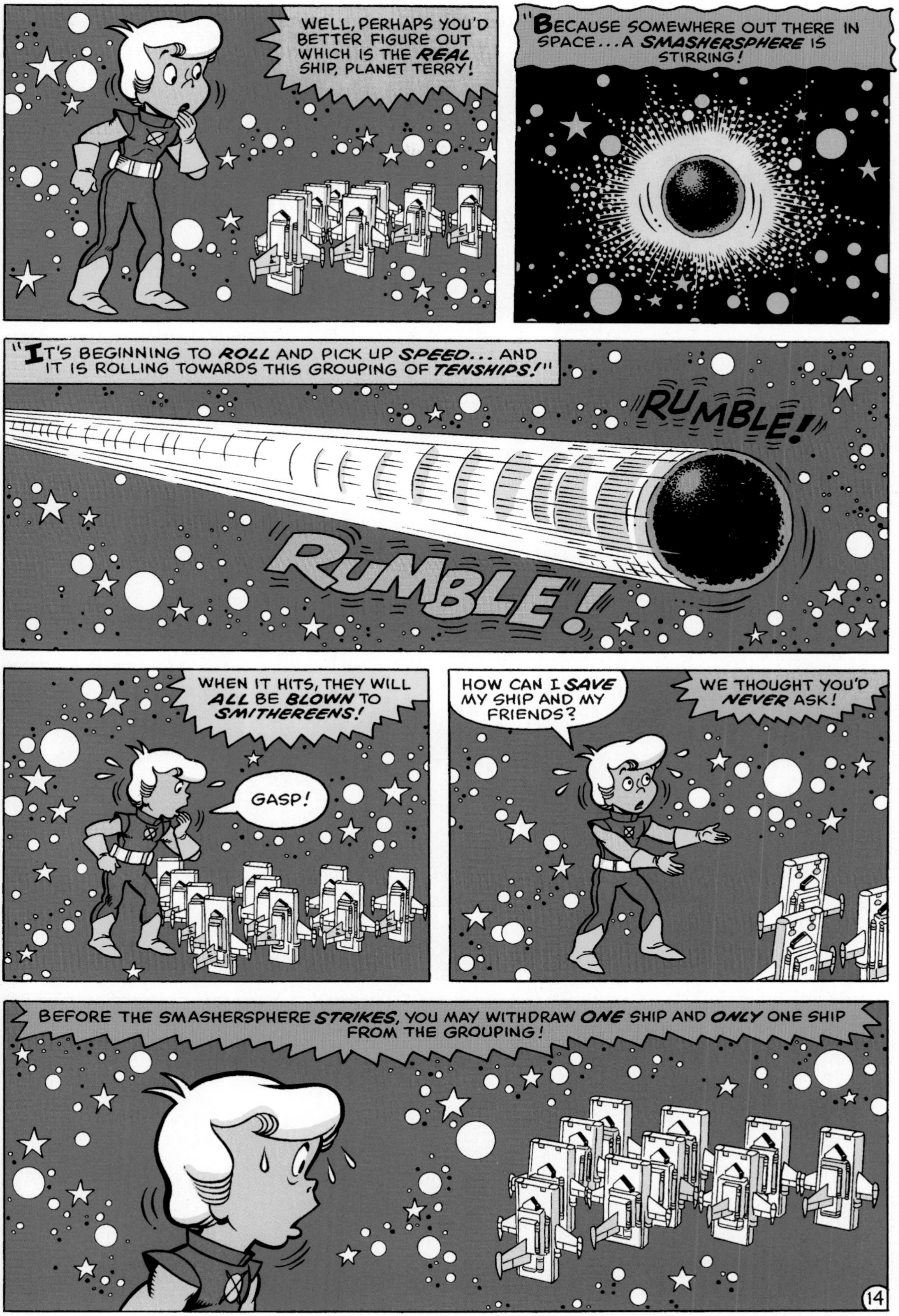
WELL, PERHAPS YOU'D BETTER FIGURE OUT WHICH IS THE REAL SHIP, PLANET TERRY!
"BECAUSE SOMEWHERE OUT THERE IN SPACE... A SMASHERSPHERE IS STIRRING!
"IT'S BEGINNING TO ROLL AND PICK UP SPEED... AND IT IS ROLLING TOWARDS THIS GROUPING OF TENSHIPS!"
RUMBLE!
RUMBLE!
WHEN IT HITS, THEY WILL ALL BE BLOWN TO SMITHEREENS!
GASP!
HOW CAN I SAVE MY SHIP AND MY FRIENDS?
WE THOUGHT YOU'D NEVER ASK!
BEFORE THE SMASHERSPHERE STRIKES, YOU MAY WITHDRAW ONE SHIP AND ONLY ONE SHIP FROM THE GROUPING!
14

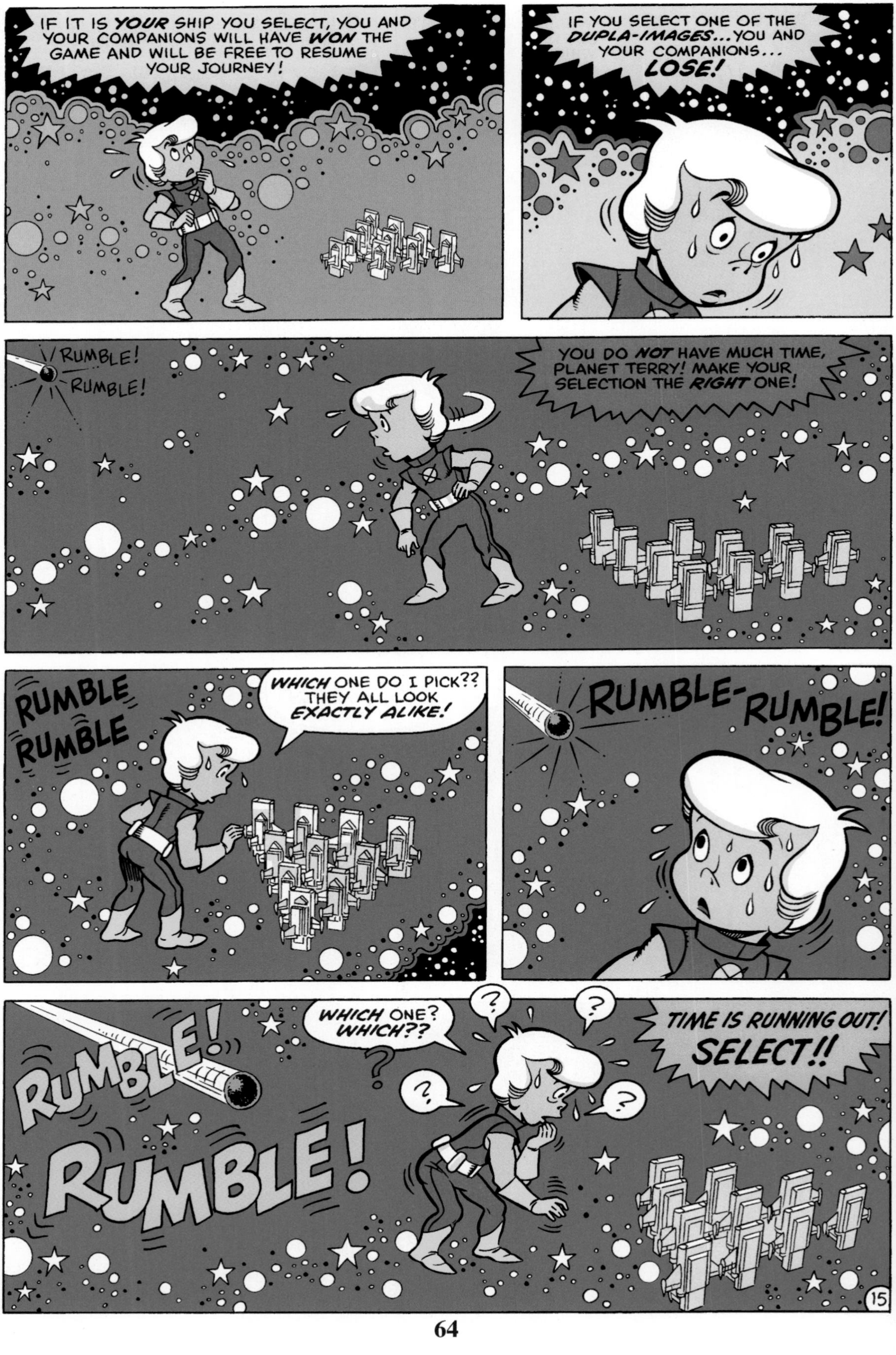
IF IT IS *YOUR* SHIP YOU SELECT, YOU AND YOUR COMPANIONS WILL HAVE *WON* THE GAME AND WILL BE FREE TO RESUME YOUR JOURNEY!
IF YOU SELECT ONE OF THE *DUPLA-IMAGES*... YOU AND YOUR COMPANIONS... *LOSE!*
RUMBLE! RUMBLE!
YOU DO *NOT* HAVE MUCH TIME, PLANET TERRY! MAKE YOUR SELECTION THE *RIGHT* ONE!
RUMBLE RUMBLE
WHICH ONE DO I PICK?? THEY ALL LOOK *EXACTLY ALIKE!*
RUMBLE-RUMBLE!
RUMBLE!
RUMBLE!
WHICH ONE? *WHICH??*
?
?
?
?
TIME IS RUNNING OUT! SELECT!!
15

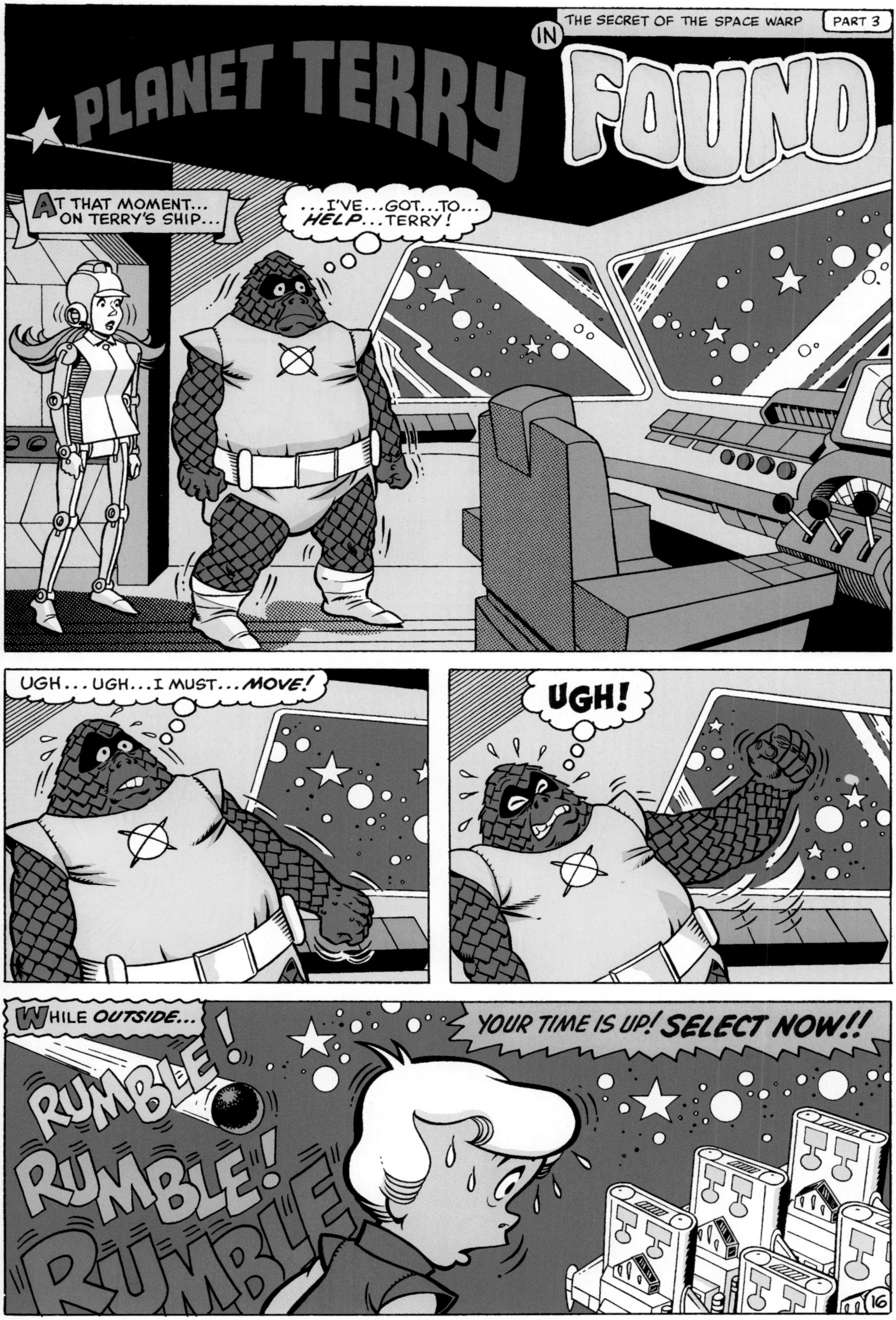
THE SECRET OF THE SPACE WARP
PART 3
PLANET TERRY
IN
FOUND
AT THAT MOMENT... ON TERRY'S SHIP...
...I'VE...GOT...TO... HELP...TERRY!
UGH...UGH...I MUST...MOVE!
UGH!
WHILE OUTSIDE...
YOUR TIME IS UP! SELECT NOW!!
RUMBLE!
RUMBLE!
RUMBLE
16

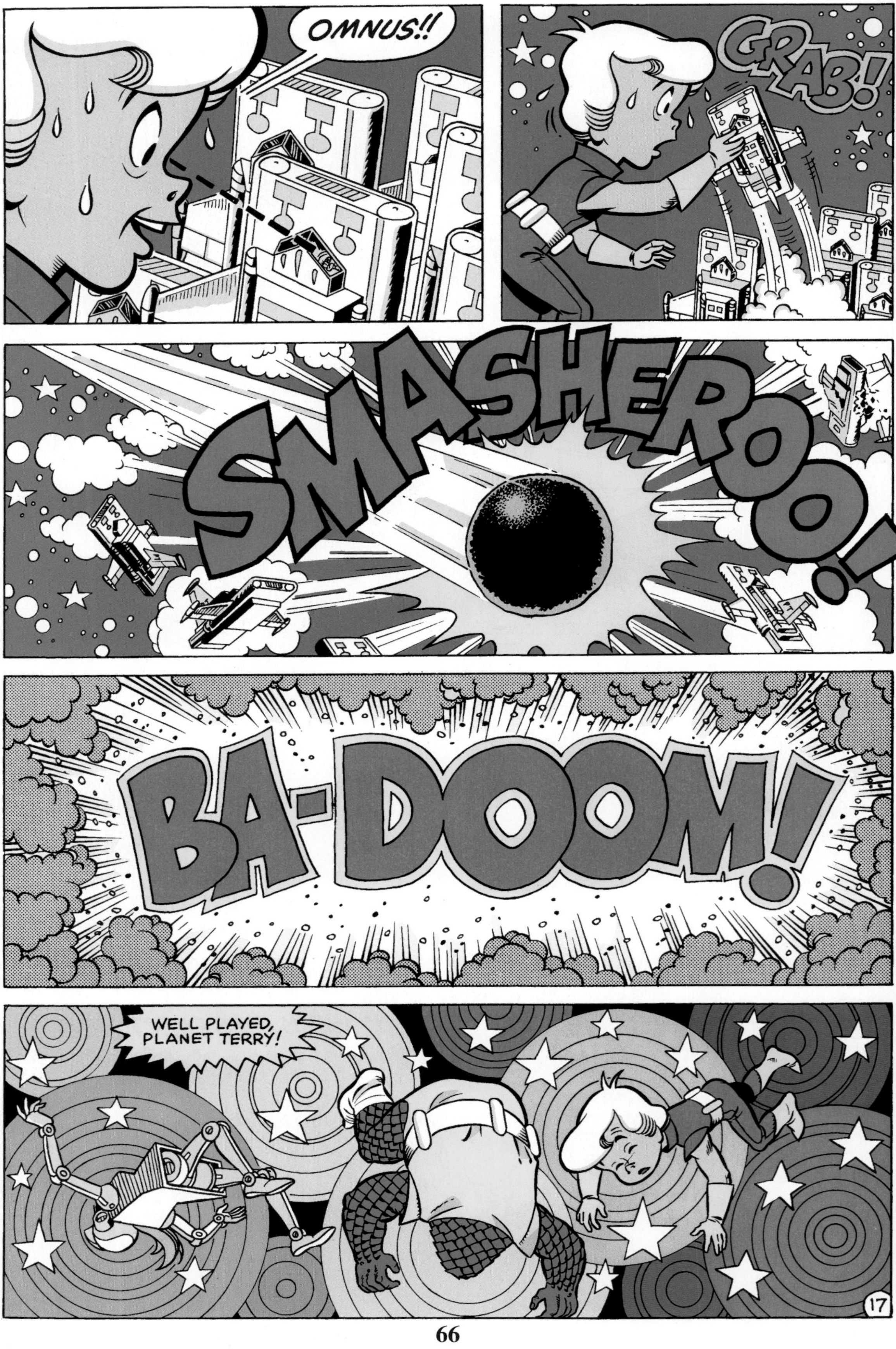
OMNUS!!
GRAB!
SMASHEROO!!
BA-DOOM!
WELL PLAYED, PLANET TERRY!
17

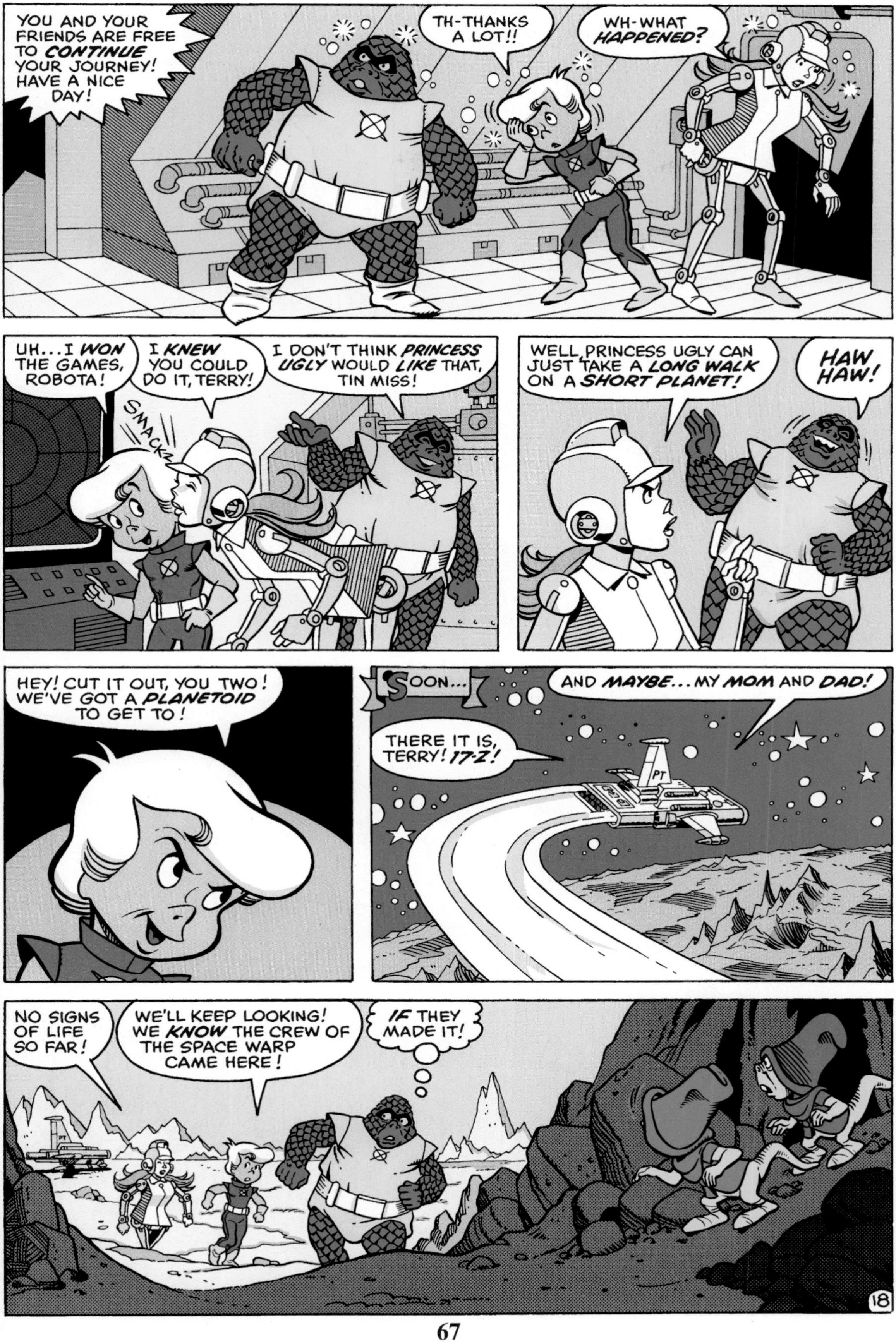
YOU AND YOUR FRIENDS ARE FREE TO CONTINUE YOUR JOURNEY! HAVE A NICE DAY!
TH-THANKS A LOT!!
WH-WHAT HAPPENED?
UH...I WON THE GAMES, ROBOTA!
I KNEW YOU COULD DO IT, TERRY!
SMACKZ
I DON'T THINK PRINCESS UGLY WOULD LIKE THAT, TIN MISS!
WELL, PRINCESS UGLY CAN JUST TAKE A LONG WALK ON A SHORT PLANET!
HAW HAW!
HEY! CUT IT OUT, YOU TWO! WE'VE GOT A PLANETOID TO GET TO!
SOON...
AND MAYBE... MY MOM AND DAD!
THERE IT IS, TERRY! 17-Z!
PT
NO SIGNS OF LIFE SO FAR!
WE'LL KEEP LOOKING! WE KNOW THE CREW OF THE SPACE WARP CAME HERE!
IF THEY MADE IT!
18

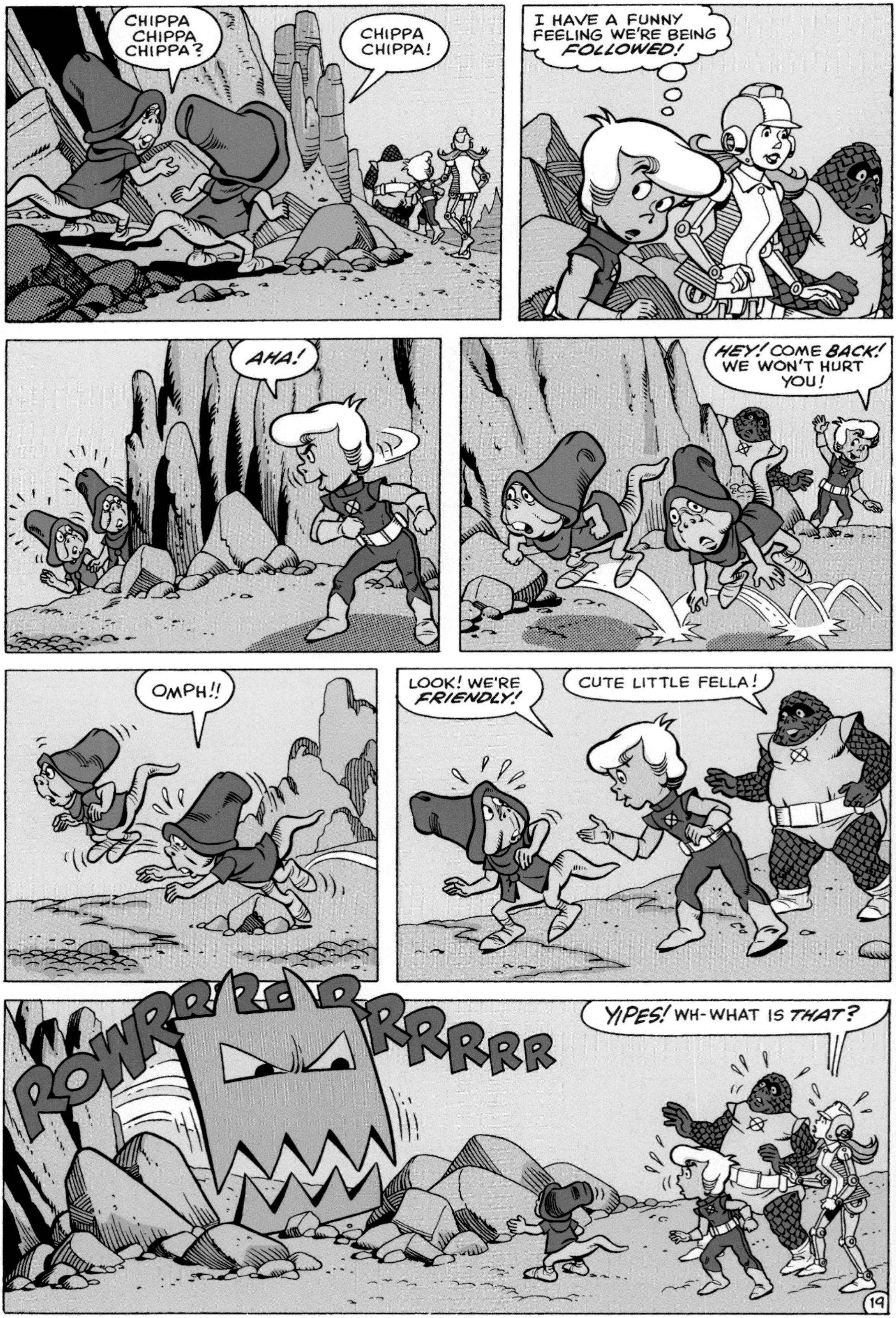
CHIPPA CHIPPA CHIPPA?
CHIPPA CHIPPA!
I HAVE A FUNNY FEELING WE'RE BEING FOLLOWED!
AHA!
HEY! COME BACK! WE WON'T HURT YOU!
OMPH!!
LOOK! WE'RE FRIENDLY!
CUTE LITTLE FELLA!
ROWRRRRRRRRRRRR
YIPES! WH-WHAT IS THAT?
19

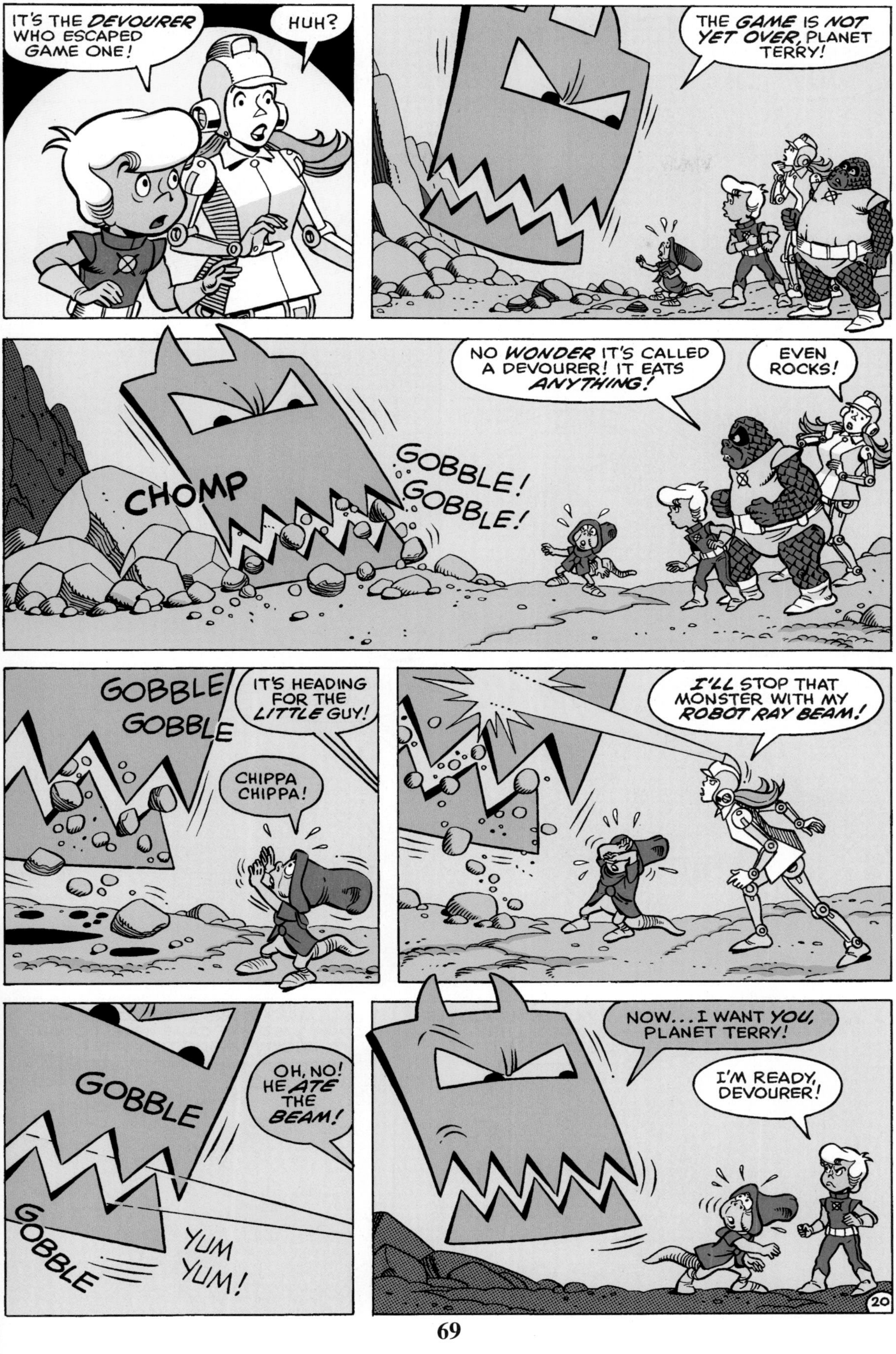

IT'S THE DEVOURER WHO ESCAPED GAME ONE!
HUH?
THE GAME IS NOT YET OVER, PLANET TERRY!
NO WONDER IT'S CALLED A DEVOURER! IT EATS ANYTHING!
EVEN ROCKS!
CHOMP
GOBBLE! GOBBLE!
GOBBLE GOBBLE
IT'S HEADING FOR THE LITTLE GUY!
CHIPPA CHIPPA!
I'LL STOP THAT MONSTER WITH MY ROBOT RAY BEAM!
GOBBLE
OH, NO! HE ATE THE BEAM!
GOBBLE
YUM YUM!
NOW... I WANT YOU, PLANET TERRY!
I'M READY, DEVOURER!
20

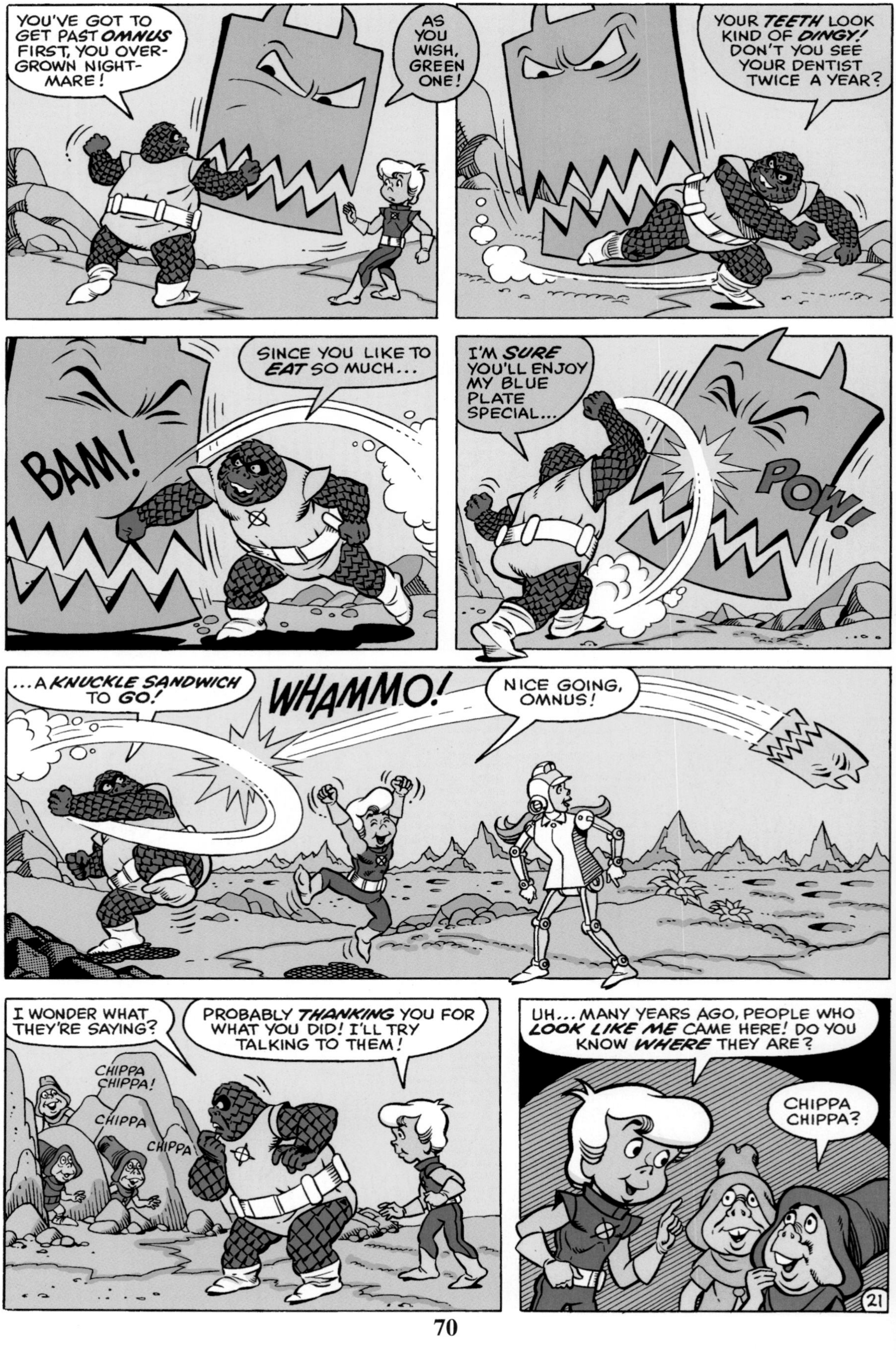
YOU'VE GOT TO GET PAST OMNUS FIRST, YOU OVER-GROWN NIGHT-MARE!
AS YOU WISH, GREEN ONE!
YOUR TEETH LOOK KIND OF DINGY! DON'T YOU SEE YOUR DENTIST TWICE A YEAR?
SINCE YOU LIKE TO EAT SO MUCH...
BAM!
I'M SURE YOU'LL ENJOY MY BLUE PLATE SPECIAL...
POW!
...A KNUCKLE SANDWICH TO GO!
WHAMMO!
NICE GOING, OMNUS!
I WONDER WHAT THEY'RE SAYING?
PROBABLY THANKING YOU FOR WHAT YOU DID! I'LL TRY TALKING TO THEM!
CHIPPA CHIPPA!
CHIPPA
CHIPPA
UH... MANY YEARS AGO, PEOPLE WHO LOOK LIKE ME CAME HERE! DO YOU KNOW WHERE THEY ARE?
CHIPPA CHIPPA?
21

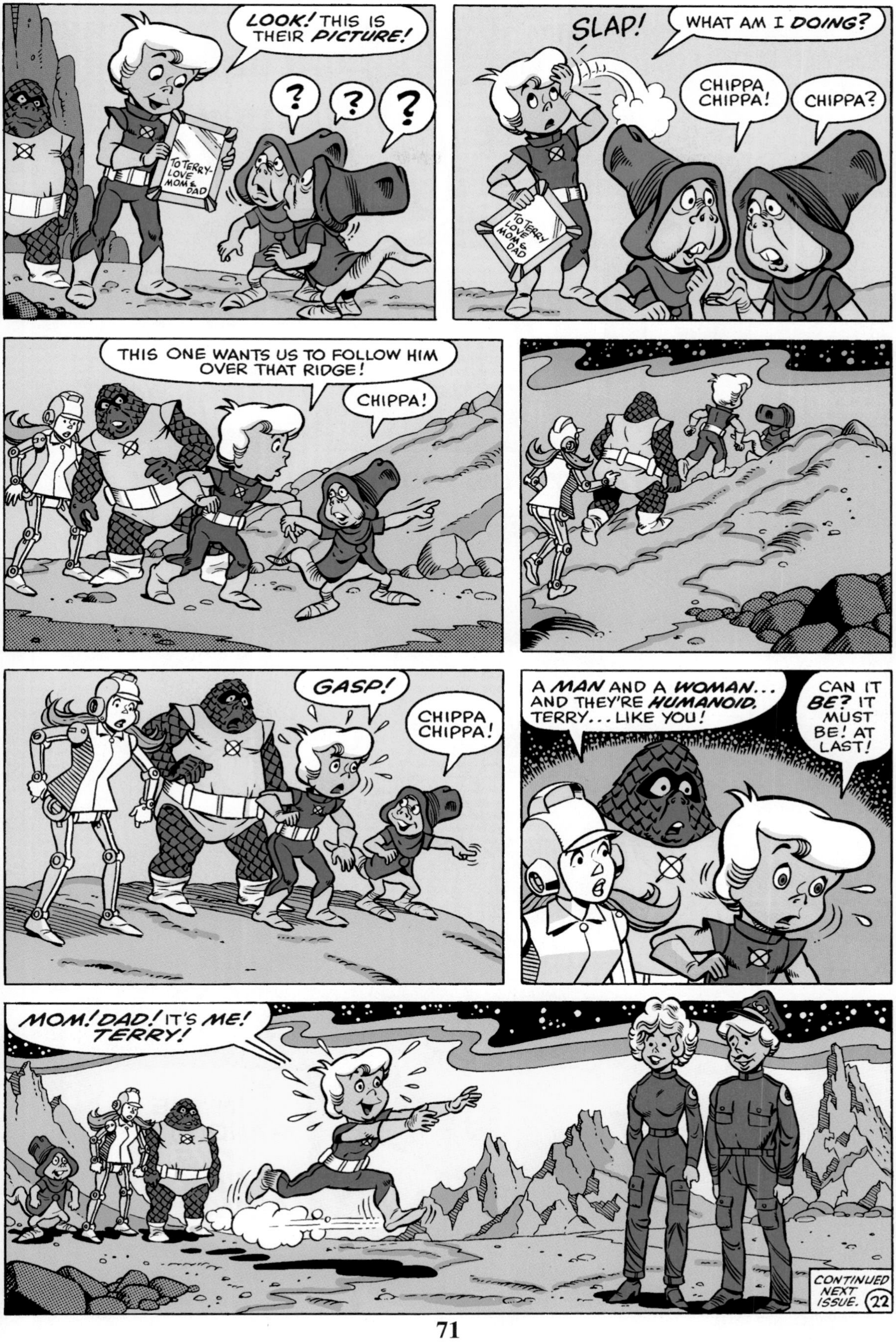
LOOK! THIS IS THEIR PICTURE!
TO TERRY-LOVE MOM & DAD
?
?
?
SLAP!
WHAT AM I DOING?
TO TERRY LOVE MOM & DAD
CHIPPA CHIPPA!
CHIPPA?
THIS ONE WANTS US TO FOLLOW HIM OVER THAT RIDGE!
CHIPPA!
GASP!
CHIPPA CHIPPA!
A MAN AND A WOMAN... AND THEY'RE HUMANOID, TERRY... LIKE YOU!
CAN IT BE? IT MUST BE! AT LAST!
MOM! DAD! IT'S ME! TERRY!
CONTINUED NEXT ISSUE.
22

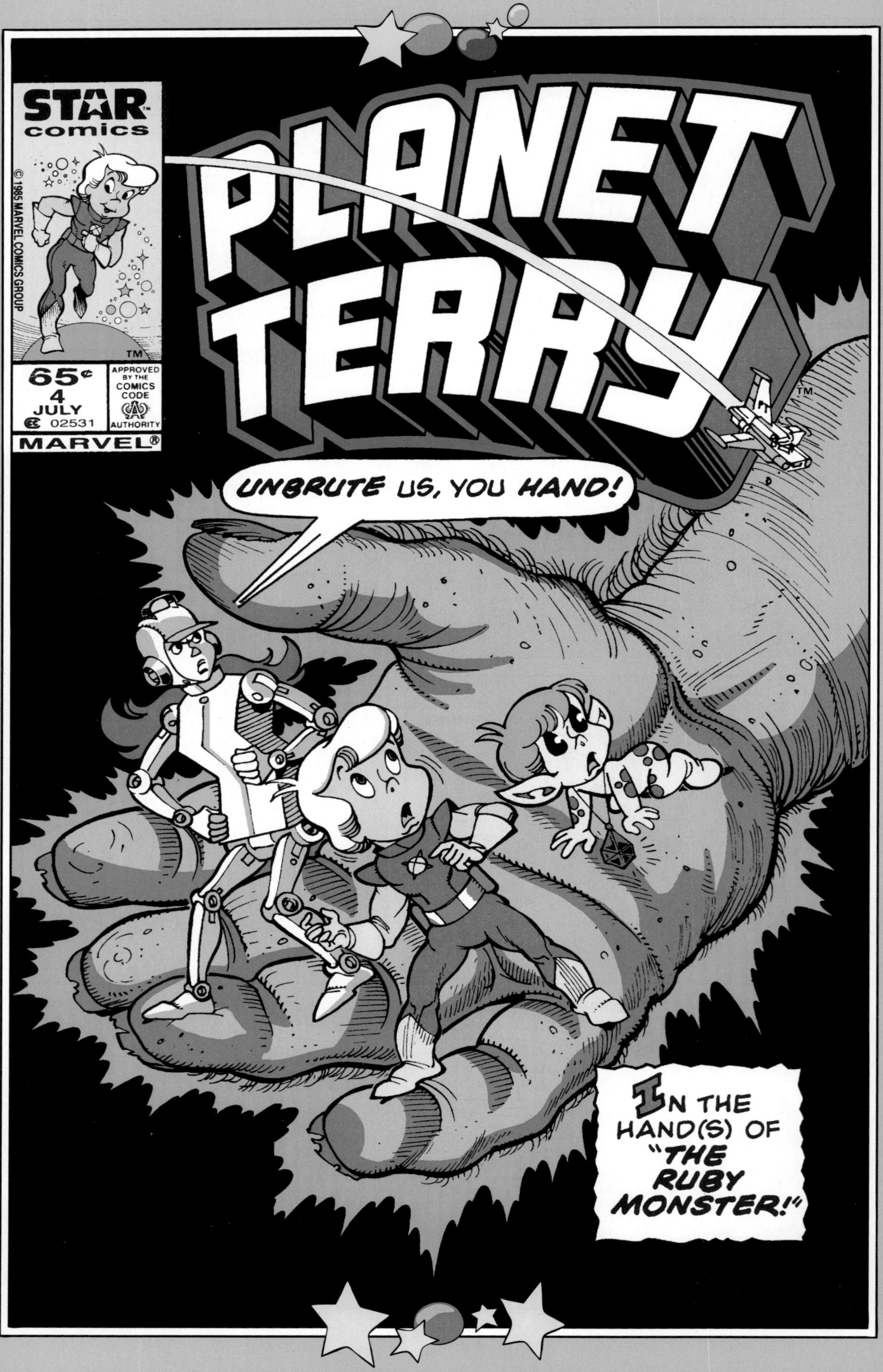
STAR comics
© 1985 MARVEL COMICS GROUP
PLANET TERRY
65¢
4
JULY
02531
APPROVED BY THE COMICS CODE AUTHORITY
MARVEL
UNBRUTE US, YOU HAND!
IN THE HAND(S) OF "THE RUBY MONSTER!"

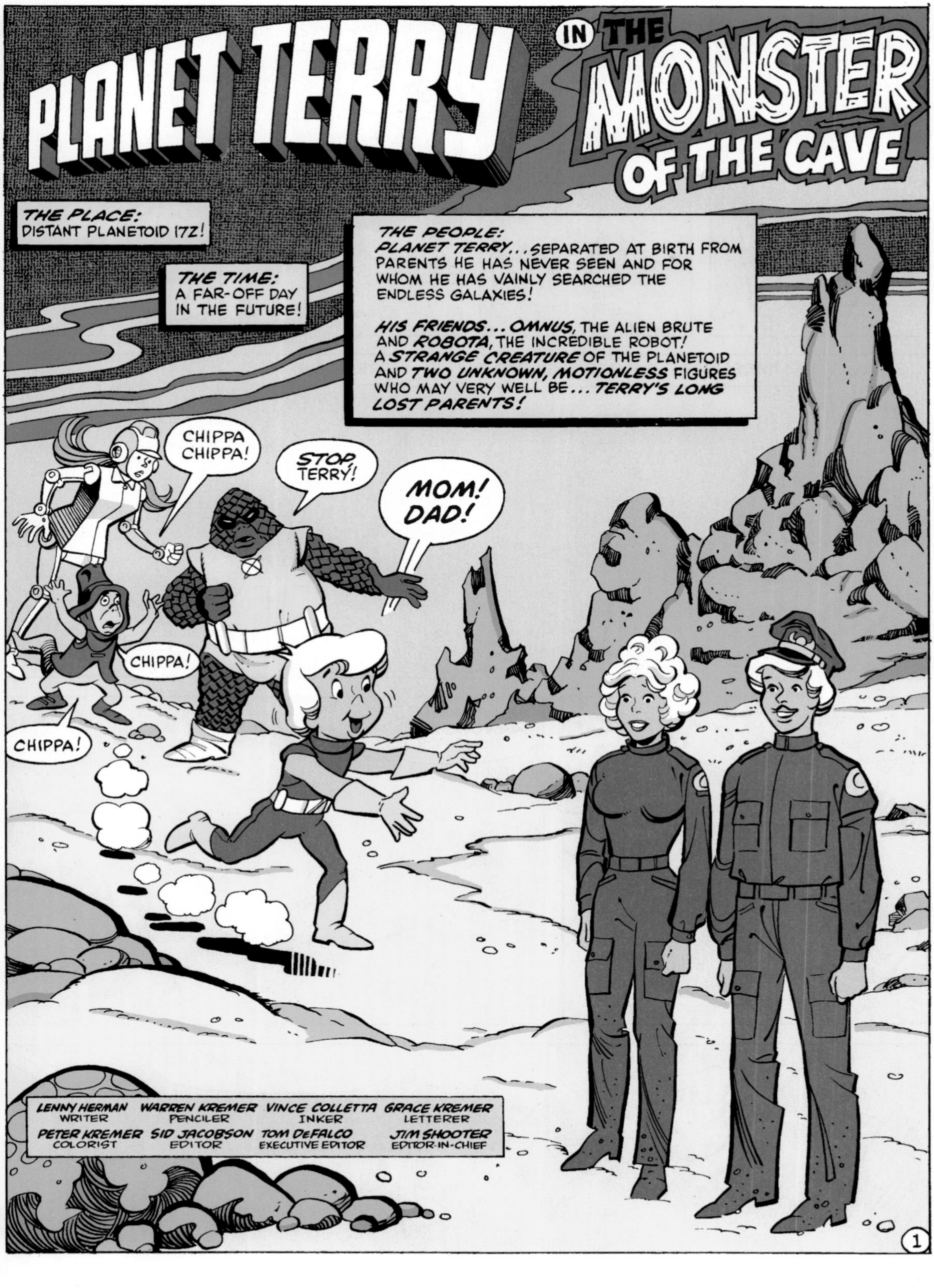
PLANET TERRY
IN THE MONSTER OF THE CAVE
THE PLACE: DISTANT PLANETOID 17Z!
THE TIME: A FAR-OFF DAY IN THE FUTURE!
THE PEOPLE: PLANET TERRY... SEPARATED AT BIRTH FROM PARENTS HE HAS NEVER SEEN AND FOR WHOM HE HAS VAINLY SEARCHED THE ENDLESS GALAXIES!
HIS FRIENDS... OMNUS, THE ALIEN BRUTE AND ROBOTA, THE INCREDIBLE ROBOT! A STRANGE CREATURE OF THE PLANETOID AND TWO UNKNOWN, MOTIONLESS FIGURES WHO MAY VERY WELL BE... TERRY'S LONG LOST PARENTS!
CHIPPA CHIPPA!
STOP, TERRY!
MOM! DAD!
CHIPPA!
CHIPPA!
LENNY HERMAN WRITER
WARREN KREMER PENCILER
VINCE COLLETTA INKER
GRACE KREMER LETTERER
PETER KREMER COLORIST
SID JACOBSON EDITOR
TOM DeFALCO EXECUTIVE EDITOR
JIM SHOOTER EDITOR-IN-CHIEF
1

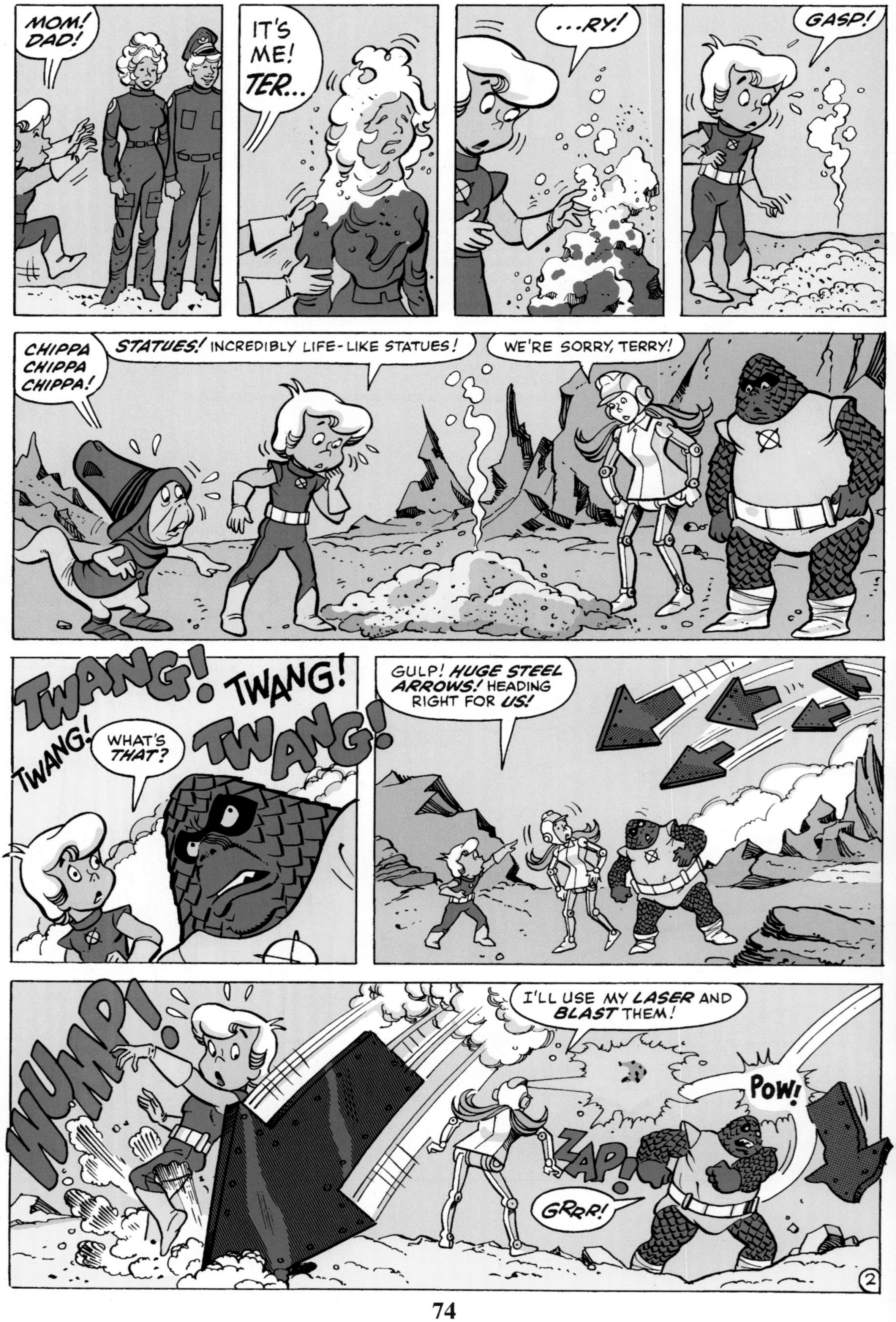
MOM! DAD!
IT'S ME! TER...
...RY!
GASP!
CHIPPA CHIPPA CHIPPA!
STATUES! INCREDIBLY LIFE-LIKE STATUES!
WE'RE SORRY, TERRY!
TWANG!
TWANG!
TWANG!
TWANG!
WHAT'S THAT?
GULP! HUGE STEEL ARROWS! HEADING RIGHT FOR US!
WUMP!
I'LL USE MY LASER AND BLAST THEM!
POW!
ZAP!
GRRR!
2

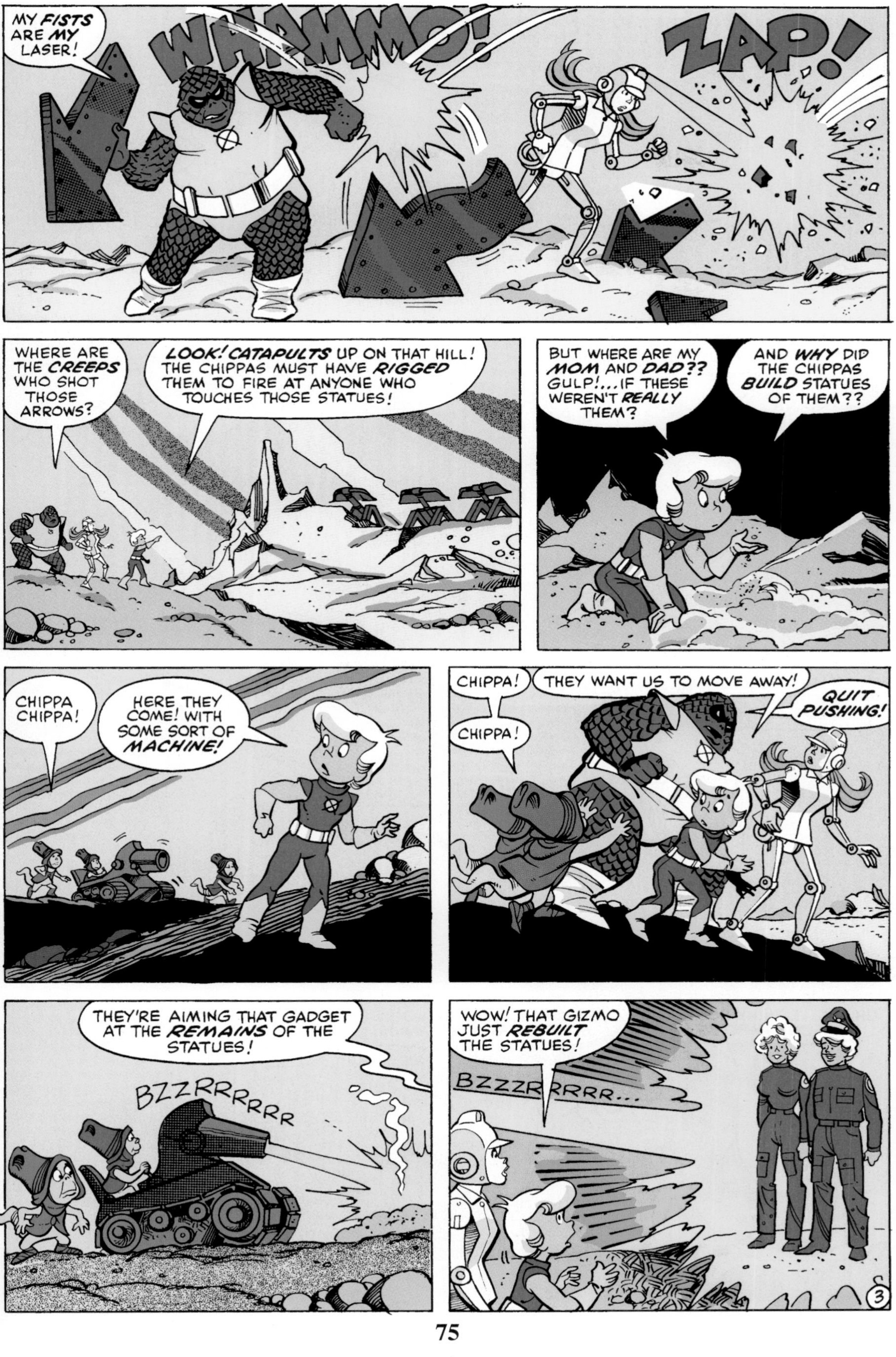
MY FISTS ARE MY LASER!
WHAMMO!
ZAP!
WHERE ARE THE CREEPS WHO SHOT THOSE ARROWS?
LOOK! CATAPULTS UP ON THAT HILL! THE CHIPPAS MUST HAVE RIGGED THEM TO FIRE AT ANYONE WHO TOUCHES THOSE STATUES!
BUT WHERE ARE MY MOM AND DAD?? GULP!...IF THESE WEREN'T REALLY THEM?
AND WHY DID THE CHIPPAS BUILD STATUES OF THEM??
CHIPPA CHIPPA!
HERE THEY COME! WITH SOME SORT OF MACHINE!
CHIPPA!
CHIPPA!
THEY WANT US TO MOVE AWAY!
QUIT PUSHING!
THEY'RE AIMING THAT GADGET AT THE REMAINS OF THE STATUES!
BZZRRRRRR
WOW! THAT GIZMO JUST REBUILT THE STATUES!
BZZZRRRRR...
3

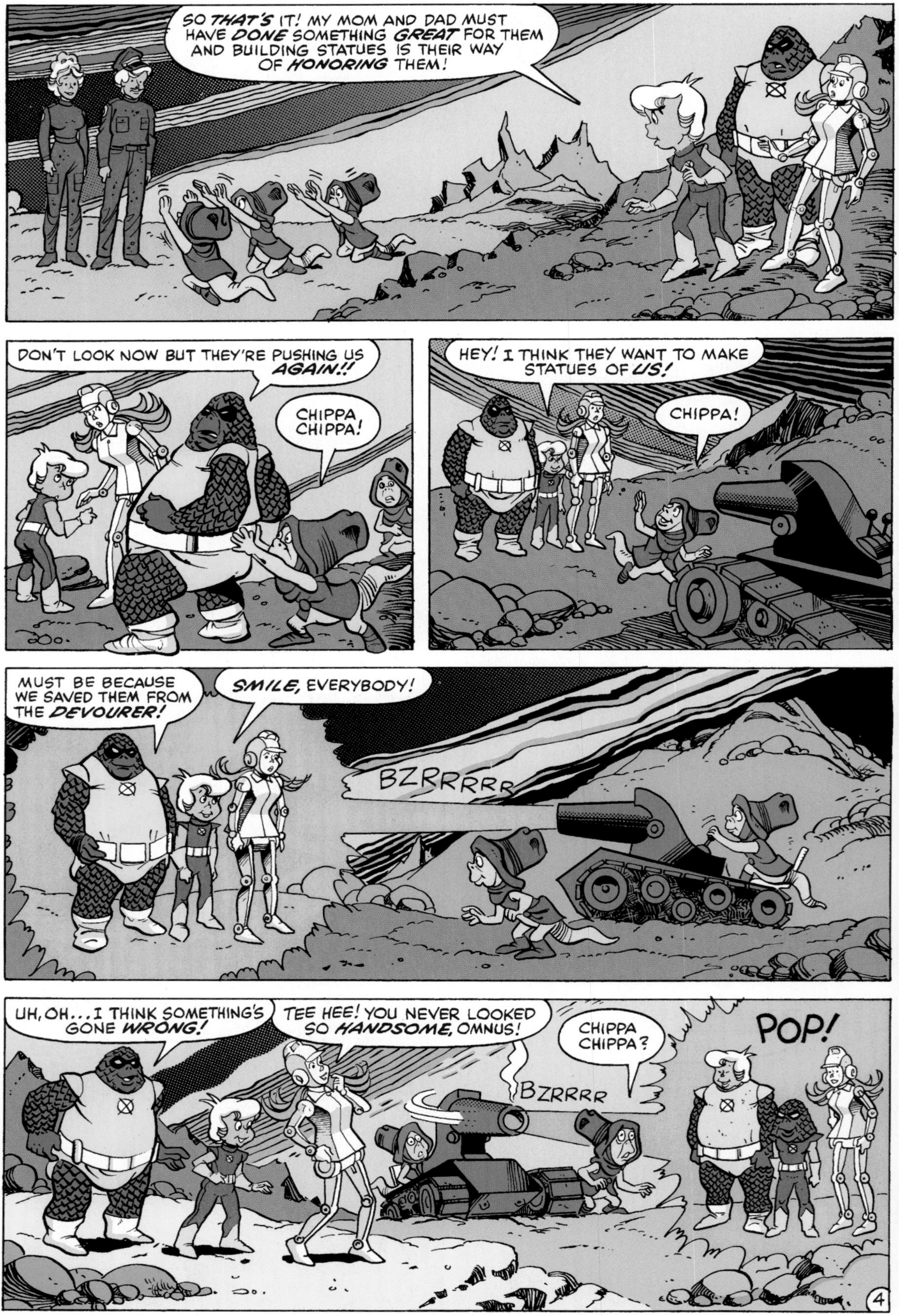
SO THAT'S IT! MY MOM AND DAD MUST HAVE DONE SOMETHING GREAT FOR THEM AND BUILDING STATUES IS THEIR WAY OF HONORING THEM!
DON'T LOOK NOW BUT THEY'RE PUSHING US AGAIN!!
CHIPPA CHIPPA!
HEY! I THINK THEY WANT TO MAKE STATUES OF US!
CHIPPA!
MUST BE BECAUSE WE SAVED THEM FROM THE DEVOURER!
SMILE, EVERYBODY!
BZRRRRRR
UH, OH... I THINK SOMETHING'S GONE WRONG!
TEE HEE! YOU NEVER LOOKED SO HANDSOME, OMNUS!
CHIPPA CHIPPA?
BZRRRR
POP!
4

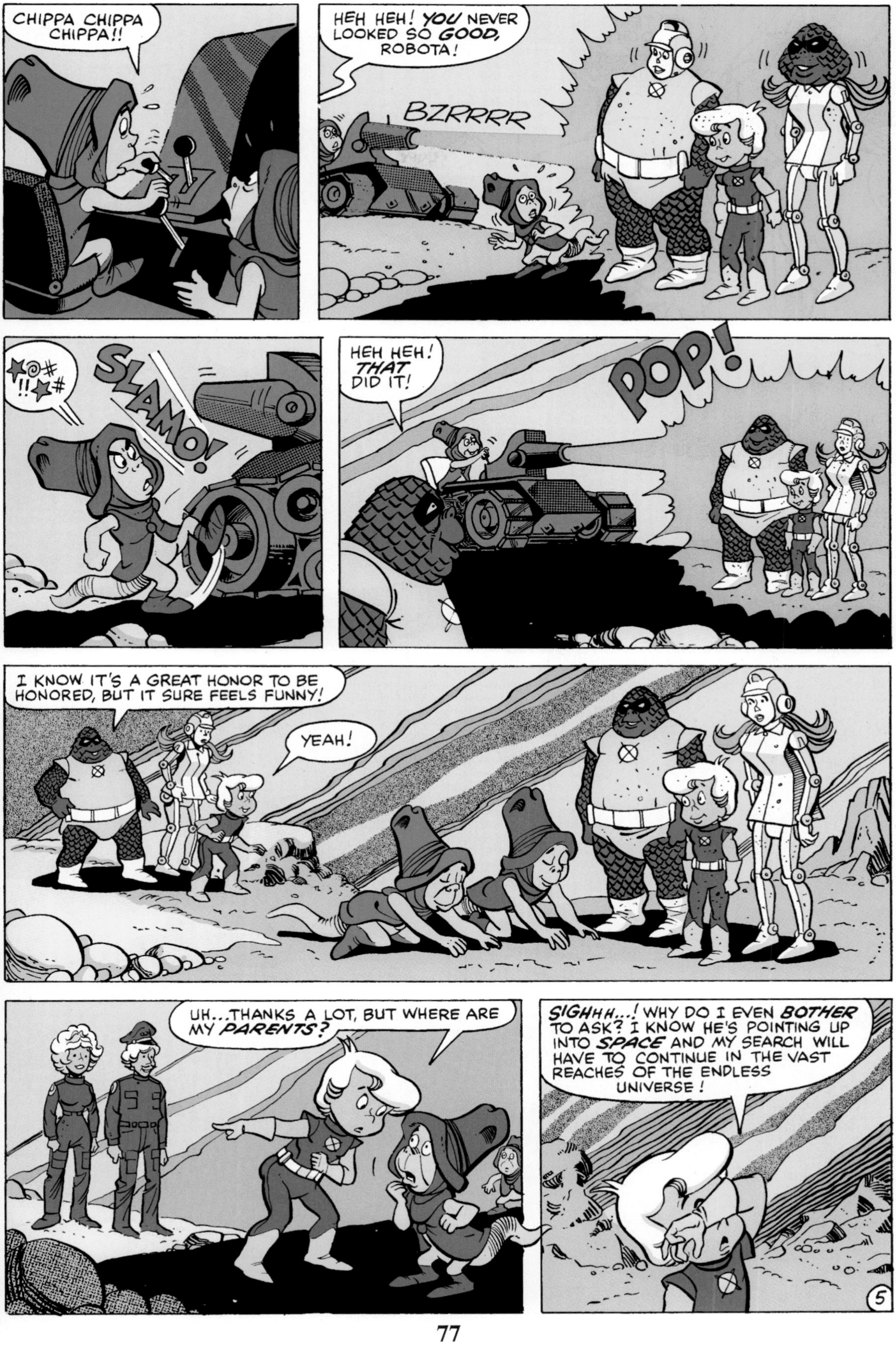
CHIPPA CHIPPA CHIPPA!!
HEH HEH! YOU NEVER LOOKED SO GOOD, ROBOTA!
BZRRRRR
SLAMO!
HEH HEH! THAT DID IT!
POP!
I KNOW IT'S A GREAT HONOR TO BE HONORED, BUT IT SURE FEELS FUNNY!
YEAH!
UH...THANKS A LOT, BUT WHERE ARE MY PARENTS?
SIGHHH...! WHY DO I EVEN BOTHER TO ASK? I KNOW HE'S POINTING UP INTO SPACE AND MY SEARCH WILL HAVE TO CONTINUE IN THE VAST REACHES OF THE ENDLESS UNIVERSE!
5

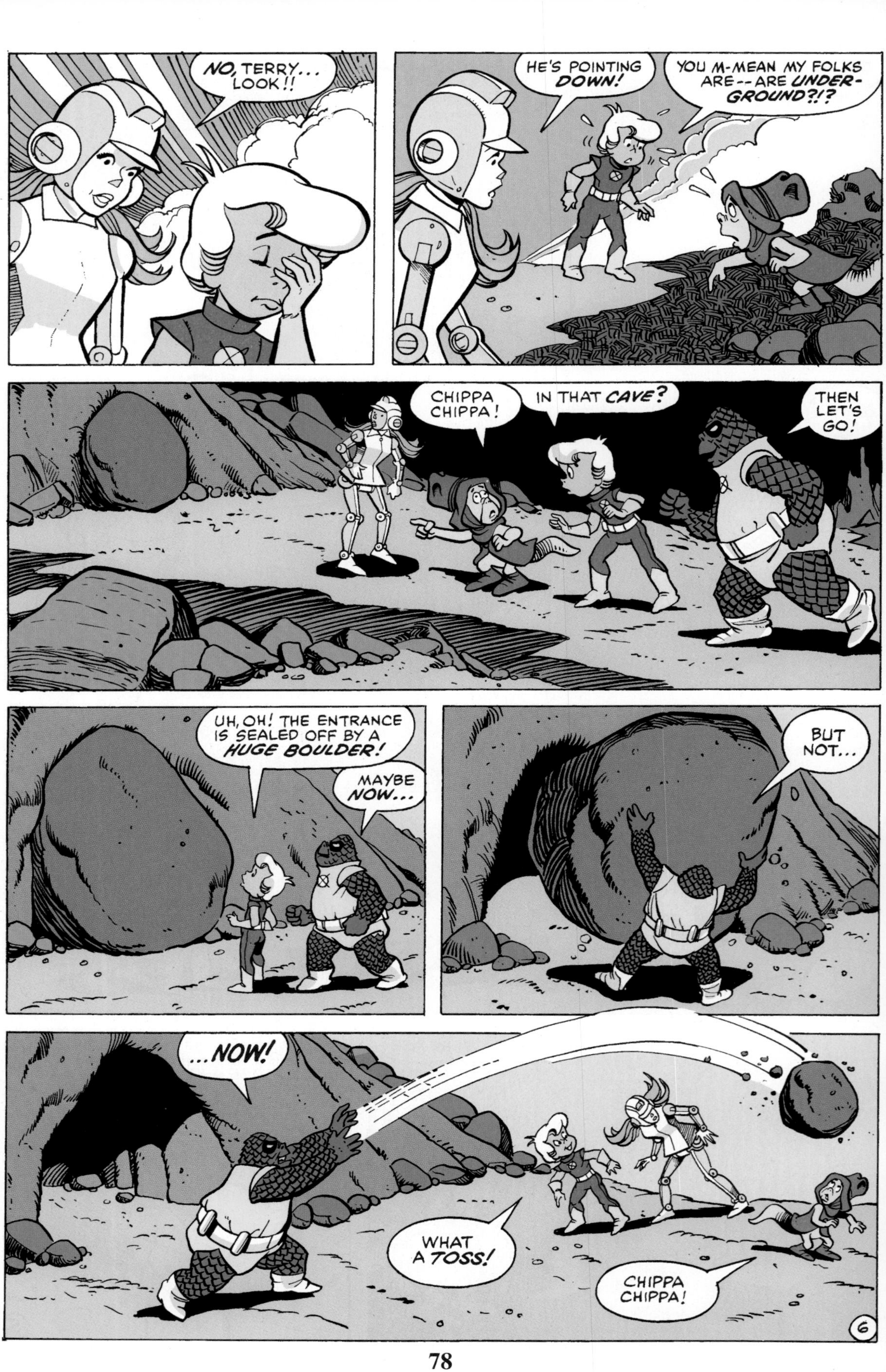
NO, TERRY... LOOK!!
HE'S POINTING DOWN!
YOU M-MEAN MY FOLKS ARE--ARE UNDERGROUND?!?
CHIPPA CHIPPA!
IN THAT CAVE?
THEN LET'S GO!
UH, OH! THE ENTRANCE IS SEALED OFF BY A HUGE BOULDER!
MAYBE NOW...
BUT NOT...
...NOW!
WHAT A TOSS!
CHIPPA CHIPPA!
6

THE CHIPPAS ARE RUNNING AWAY... AS IF THEY'RE *AFRAID* OF SOMETHING IN THIS CAVE!

WELL, IF MY *FOLKS* ARE IN THERE, THEY MAY *NEED* ME!

LET'S GO!

LIGHT! WHAT KIND OF CAVE IS *LIT UP?*

ONE THAT'S BEING *USED,* I'D SAY!

STEPS! TO *WHERE??*

WE'LL SOON FIND OUT! STAY ALERT, OMNUS AND ROBOTA! WE DON'T KNOW *WHAT* TO EXPECT!

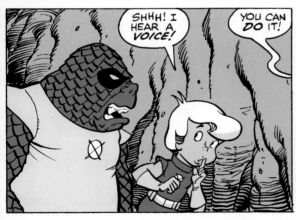

SHHH! I HEAR A *VOICE!*

YOU CAN *DO IT!*

IT'S COMING FROM *BEHIND* THAT *DOOR!*

YOU CAN *DO IT!* YOU CAN *DO IT!*

READY?

READY!

HI! ARE *YOU* HERE TO TAKE THE *TEST,* TOO?

7

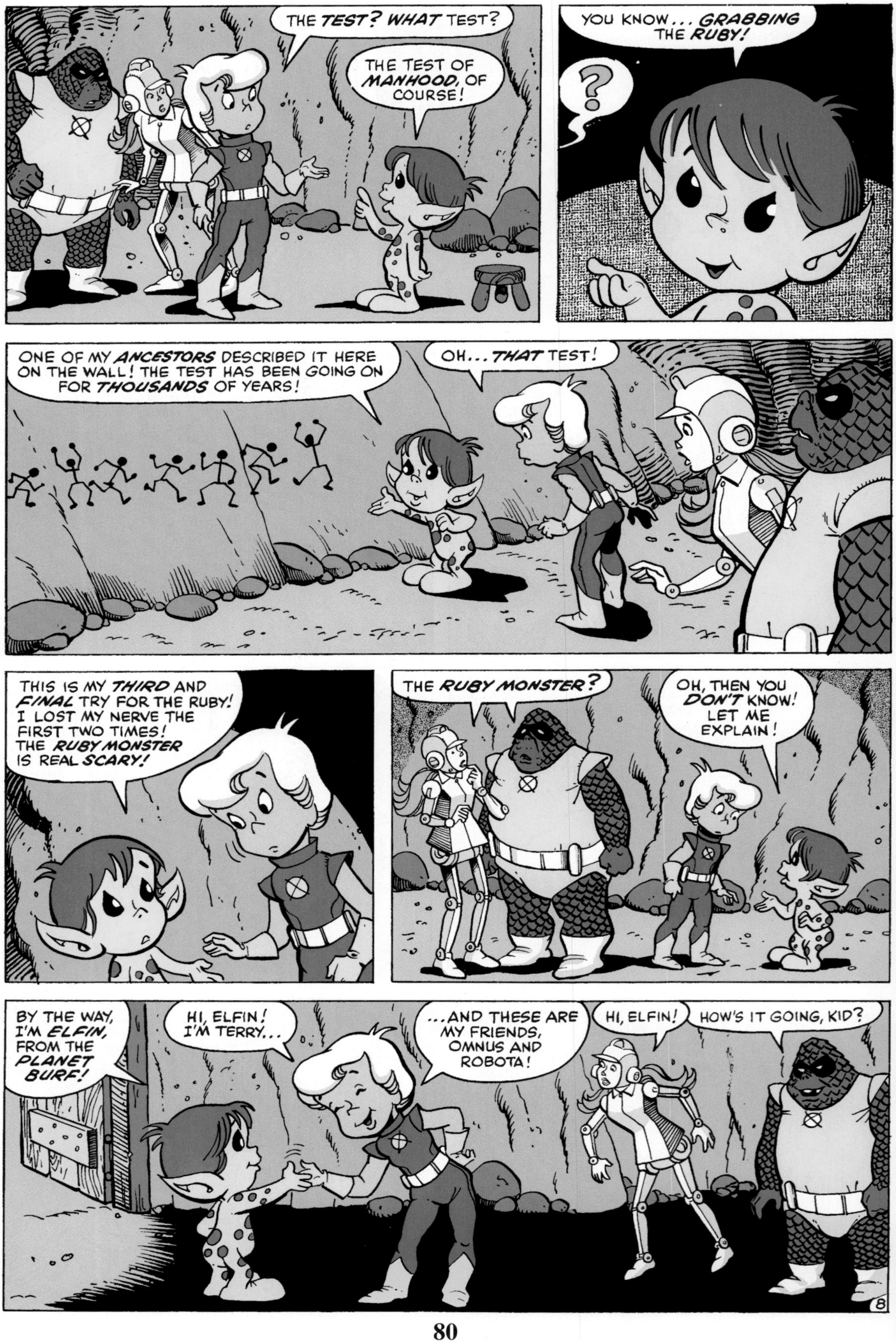
THE TEST? WHAT TEST?
THE TEST OF MANHOOD, OF COURSE!
YOU KNOW... GRABBING THE RUBY!
?
ONE OF MY ANCESTORS DESCRIBED IT HERE ON THE WALL! THE TEST HAS BEEN GOING ON FOR THOUSANDS OF YEARS!
OH... THAT TEST!
THIS IS MY THIRD AND FINAL TRY FOR THE RUBY! I LOST MY NERVE THE FIRST TWO TIMES! THE RUBY MONSTER IS REAL SCARY!
THE RUBY MONSTER?
OH, THEN YOU DON'T KNOW! LET ME EXPLAIN!
BY THE WAY, I'M ELFIN, FROM THE PLANET BURF!
HI, ELFIN! I'M TERRY...
...AND THESE ARE MY FRIENDS, OMNUS AND ROBOTA!
HI, ELFIN!
HOW'S IT GOING, KID?
8

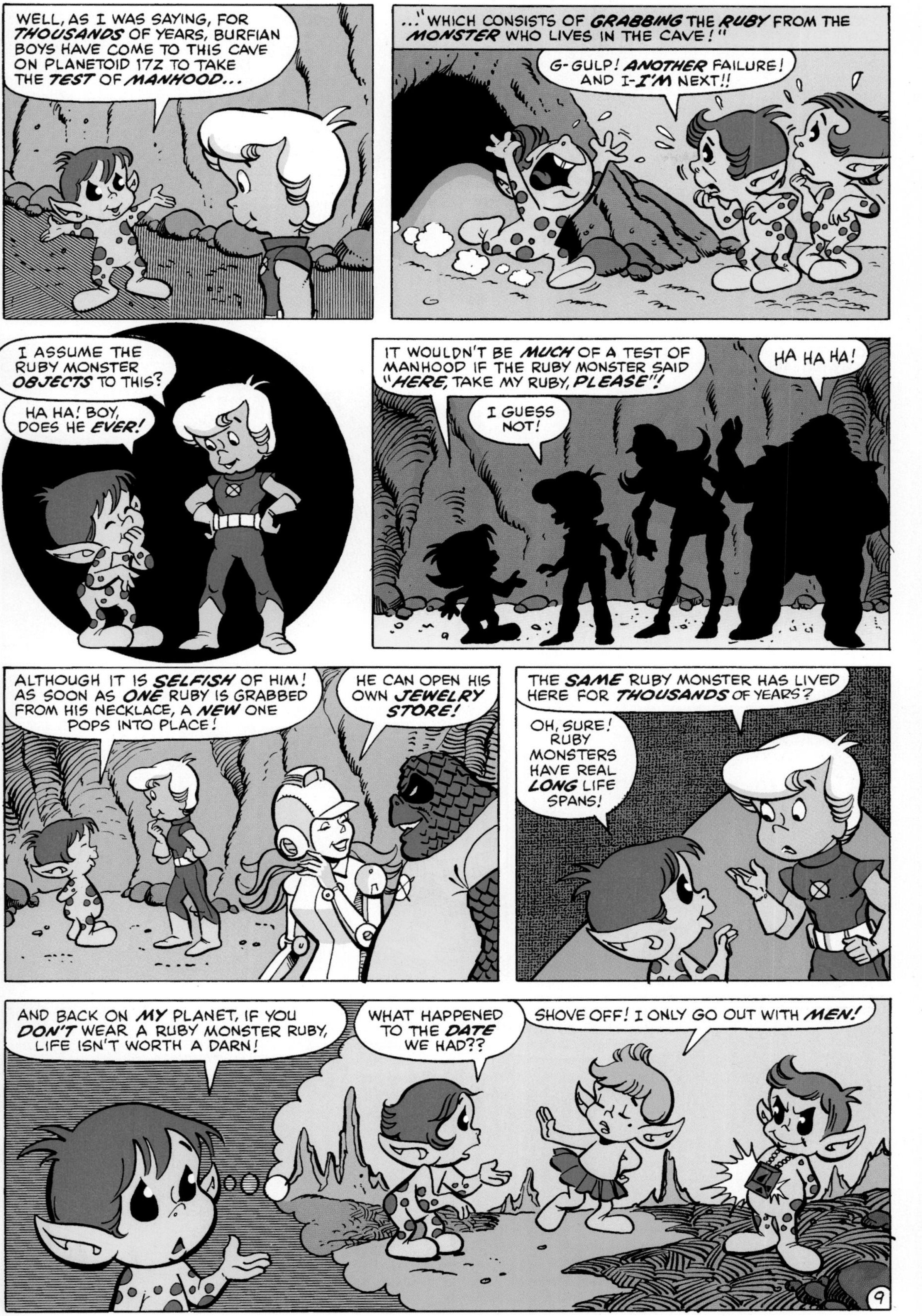
WELL, AS I WAS SAYING, FOR THOUSANDS OF YEARS, BURFIAN BOYS HAVE COME TO THIS CAVE ON PLANETOID 17Z TO TAKE THE TEST OF MANHOOD...
..."WHICH CONSISTS OF GRABBING THE RUBY FROM THE MONSTER WHO LIVES IN THE CAVE!"
G-GULP! ANOTHER FAILURE! AND I-I'M NEXT!!
I ASSUME THE RUBY MONSTER OBJECTS TO THIS?
HA HA! BOY, DOES HE EVER!
IT WOULDN'T BE MUCH OF A TEST OF MANHOOD IF THE RUBY MONSTER SAID "HERE, TAKE MY RUBY, PLEASE"!
HA HA HA!
I GUESS NOT!
ALTHOUGH IT IS SELFISH OF HIM! AS SOON AS ONE RUBY IS GRABBED FROM HIS NECKLACE, A NEW ONE POPS INTO PLACE!
HE CAN OPEN HIS OWN JEWELRY STORE!
THE SAME RUBY MONSTER HAS LIVED HERE FOR THOUSANDS OF YEARS?
OH, SURE! RUBY MONSTERS HAVE REAL LONG LIFE SPANS!
AND BACK ON MY PLANET, IF YOU DON'T WEAR A RUBY MONSTER RUBY, LIFE ISN'T WORTH A DARN!
WHAT HAPPENED TO THE DATE WE HAD??
SHOVE OFF! I ONLY GO OUT WITH MEN!
9

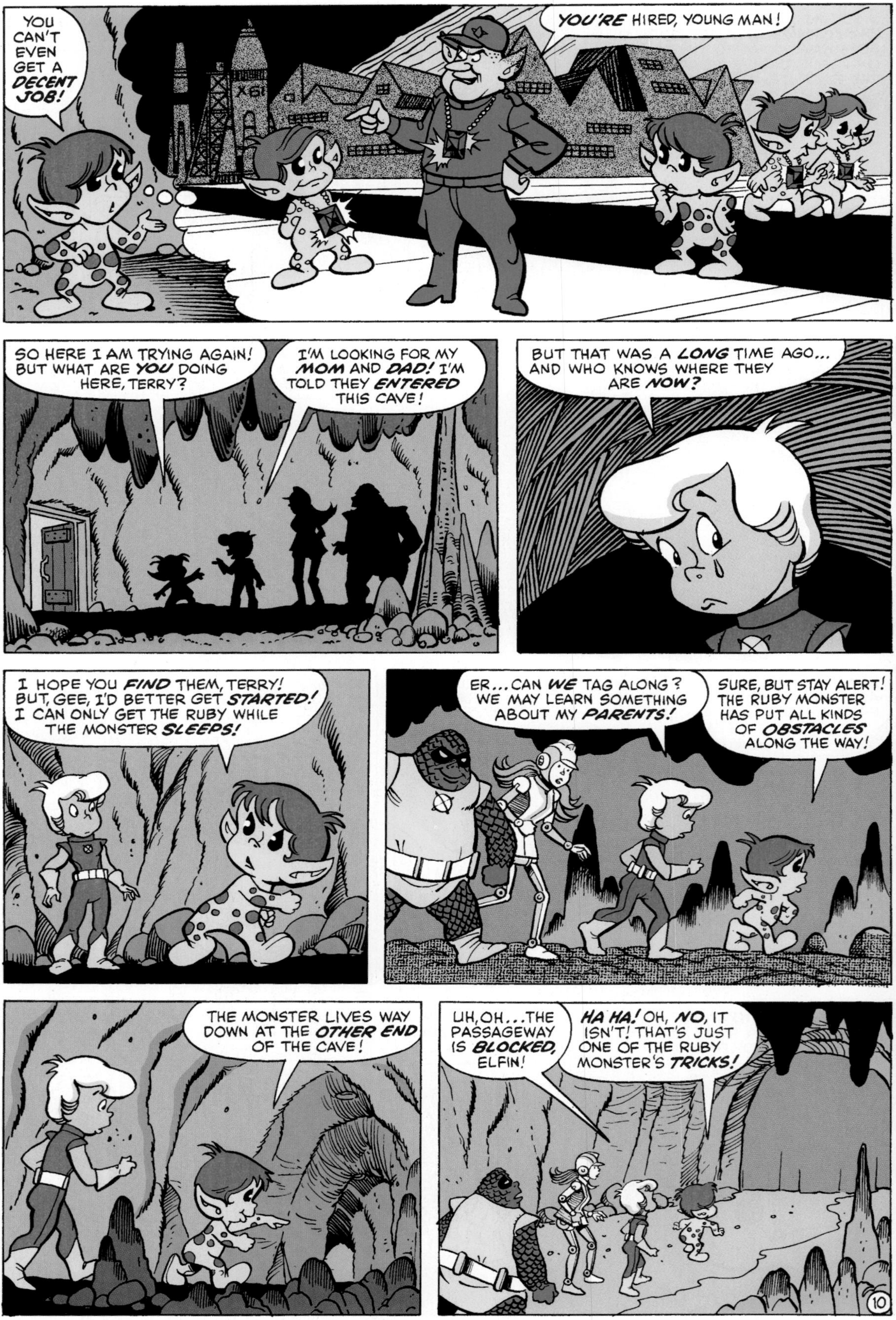
YOU CAN'T EVEN GET A DECENT JOB!
YOU'RE HIRED, YOUNG MAN!
SO HERE I AM TRYING AGAIN! BUT WHAT ARE YOU DOING HERE, TERRY?
I'M LOOKING FOR MY MOM AND DAD! I'M TOLD THEY ENTERED THIS CAVE!
BUT THAT WAS A LONG TIME AGO... AND WHO KNOWS WHERE THEY ARE NOW?
I HOPE YOU FIND THEM, TERRY! BUT, GEE, I'D BETTER GET STARTED! I CAN ONLY GET THE RUBY WHILE THE MONSTER SLEEPS!
ER... CAN WE TAG ALONG? WE MAY LEARN SOMETHING ABOUT MY PARENTS!
SURE, BUT STAY ALERT! THE RUBY MONSTER HAS PUT ALL KINDS OF OBSTACLES ALONG THE WAY!
THE MONSTER LIVES WAY DOWN AT THE OTHER END OF THE CAVE!
UH, OH... THE PASSAGEWAY IS BLOCKED, ELFIN!
HA HA! OH, NO, IT ISN'T! THAT'S JUST ONE OF THE RUBY MONSTER'S TRICKS!
10

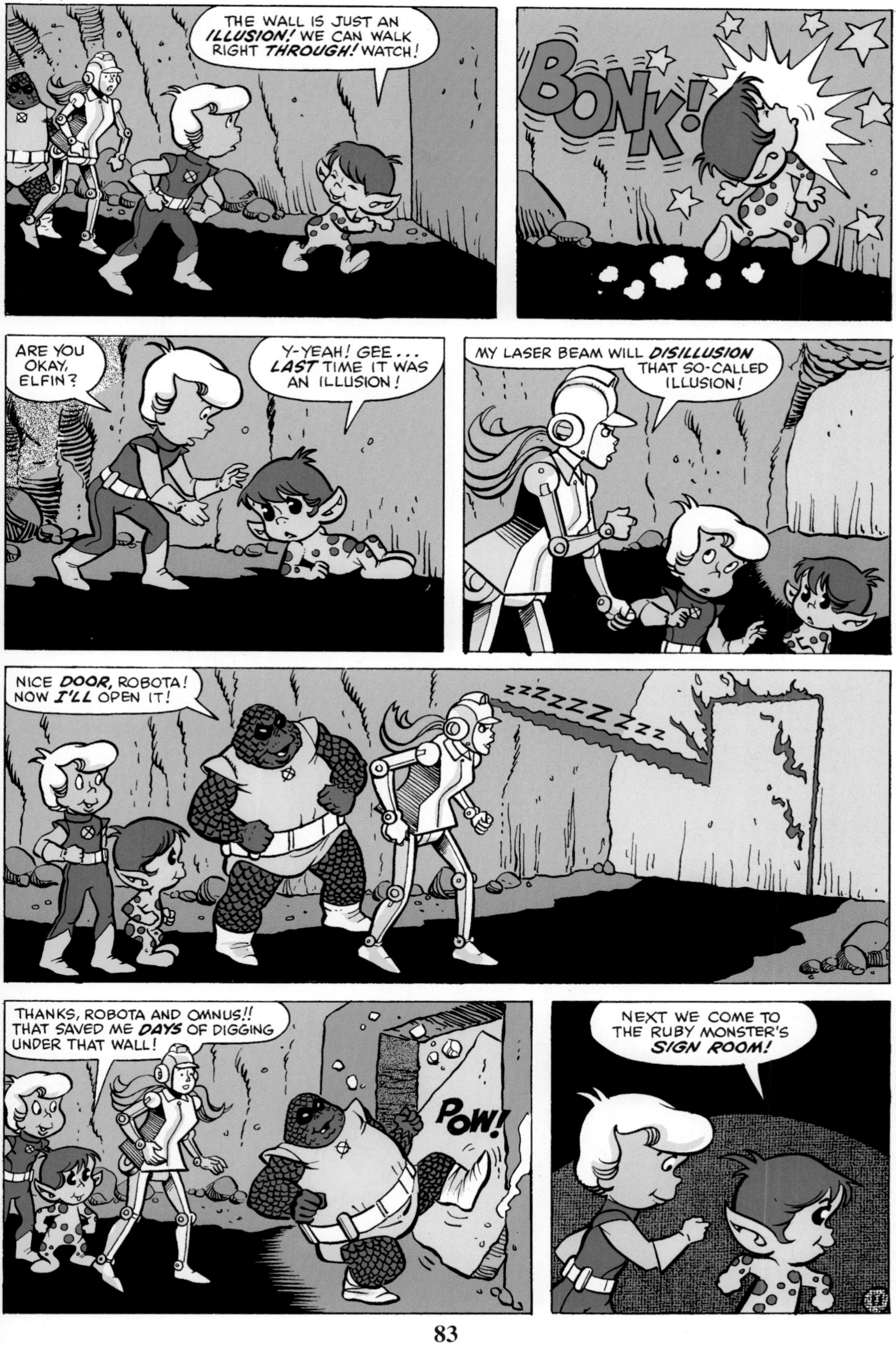
THE WALL IS JUST AN ILLUSION! WE CAN WALK RIGHT THROUGH! WATCH!
BONK!
ARE YOU OKAY, ELFIN?
Y-YEAH! GEE... LAST TIME IT WAS AN ILLUSION!
MY LASER BEAM WILL DISILLUSION THAT SO-CALLED ILLUSION!
NICE DOOR, ROBOTA! NOW I'LL OPEN IT!
zzzZZZZZzzz
THANKS, ROBOTA AND OMNUS!! THAT SAVED ME DAYS OF DIGGING UNDER THAT WALL!
POW!
NEXT WE COME TO THE RUBY MONSTER'S SIGN ROOM!
11

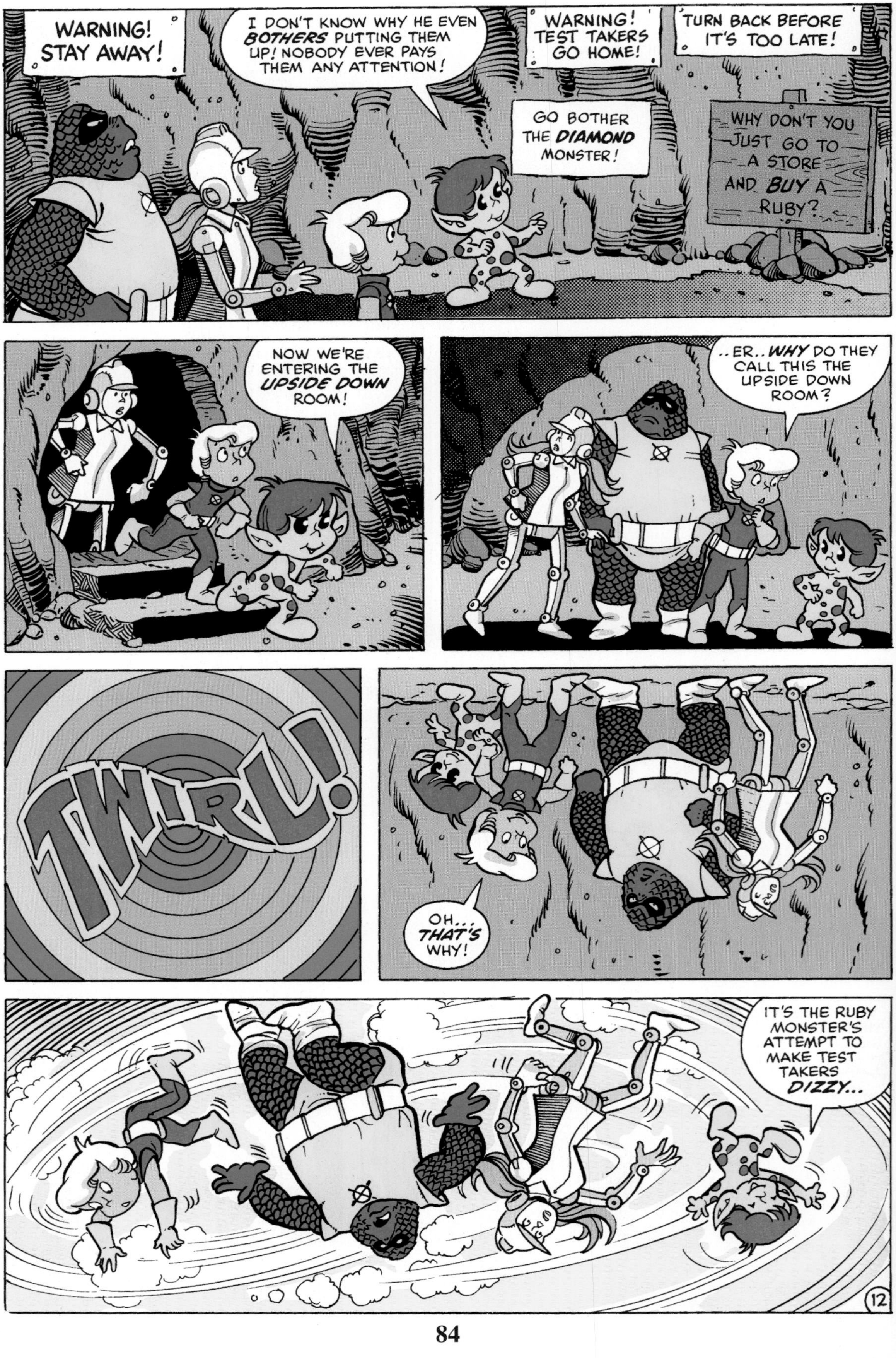

WARNING! STAY AWAY!
I DON'T KNOW WHY HE EVEN BOTHERS PUTTING THEM UP! NOBODY EVER PAYS THEM ANY ATTENTION!
WARNING! TEST TAKERS GO HOME!
TURN BACK BEFORE IT'S TOO LATE!
GO BOTHER THE DIAMOND MONSTER!
WHY DON'T YOU JUST GO TO A STORE AND BUY A RUBY?
NOW WE'RE ENTERING THE UPSIDE DOWN ROOM!
..ER..WHY DO THEY CALL THIS THE UPSIDE DOWN ROOM?
TWIRL!
OH... THAT'S WHY!
IT'S THE RUBY MONSTER'S ATTEMPT TO MAKE TEST TAKERS DIZZY...
12

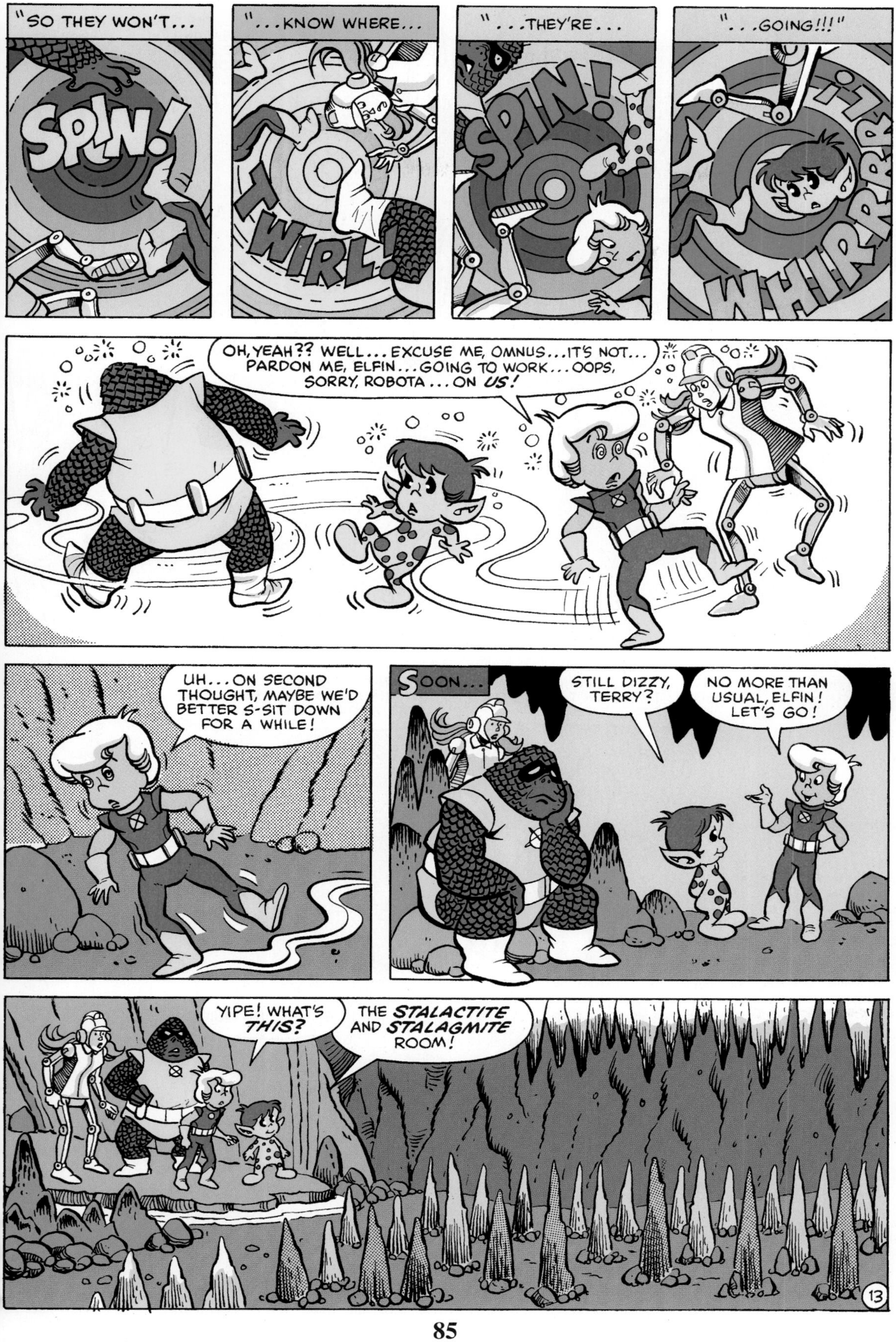
"SO THEY WON'T...
SPIN!
"...KNOW WHERE...
TWIRL!
"...THEY'RE...
SPIN!
"...GOING!!!"
WHIRRRRL-!
OH, YEAH?? WELL... EXCUSE ME, OMNUS... IT'S NOT... PARDON ME, ELFIN... GOING TO WORK... OOPS, SORRY, ROBOTA... ON US!
UH... ON SECOND THOUGHT, MAYBE WE'D BETTER S-SIT DOWN FOR A WHILE!
SOON...
STILL DIZZY, TERRY?
NO MORE THAN USUAL, ELFIN! LET'S GO!
YIPE! WHAT'S THIS?
THE STALACTITE AND STALAGMITE ROOM!
13

STALACTITES AND STALAGMITES? WHAT'S THE DIFFERENCE?

WELL, THE STALACTITES ARE *SHARP* AND THE STALAGMITES ARE *SHARPER!* AND IN THIS ROOM THEY *MOVE!* C'MON, LET'S MAKE A RUN FOR IT!

ZAP!

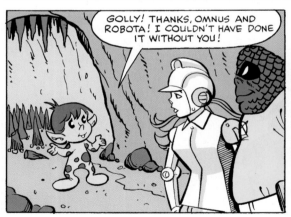

GOLLY! THANKS, OMNUS AND ROBOTA! I COULDN'T HAVE DONE IT WITHOUT YOU!

AND NOW...*GULP*...THE *LAIR* OF THE *RUBY MONSTER* IS JUST AROUND THE CORNER!

DON'T WORRY, ELFIN! WE'LL *HELP* YOU GET YOUR RUBY!

NO! I'VE GOT TO GET IT *MYSELF!* THAT'S THE TEST!

SHHHH! BE QUIET!

14

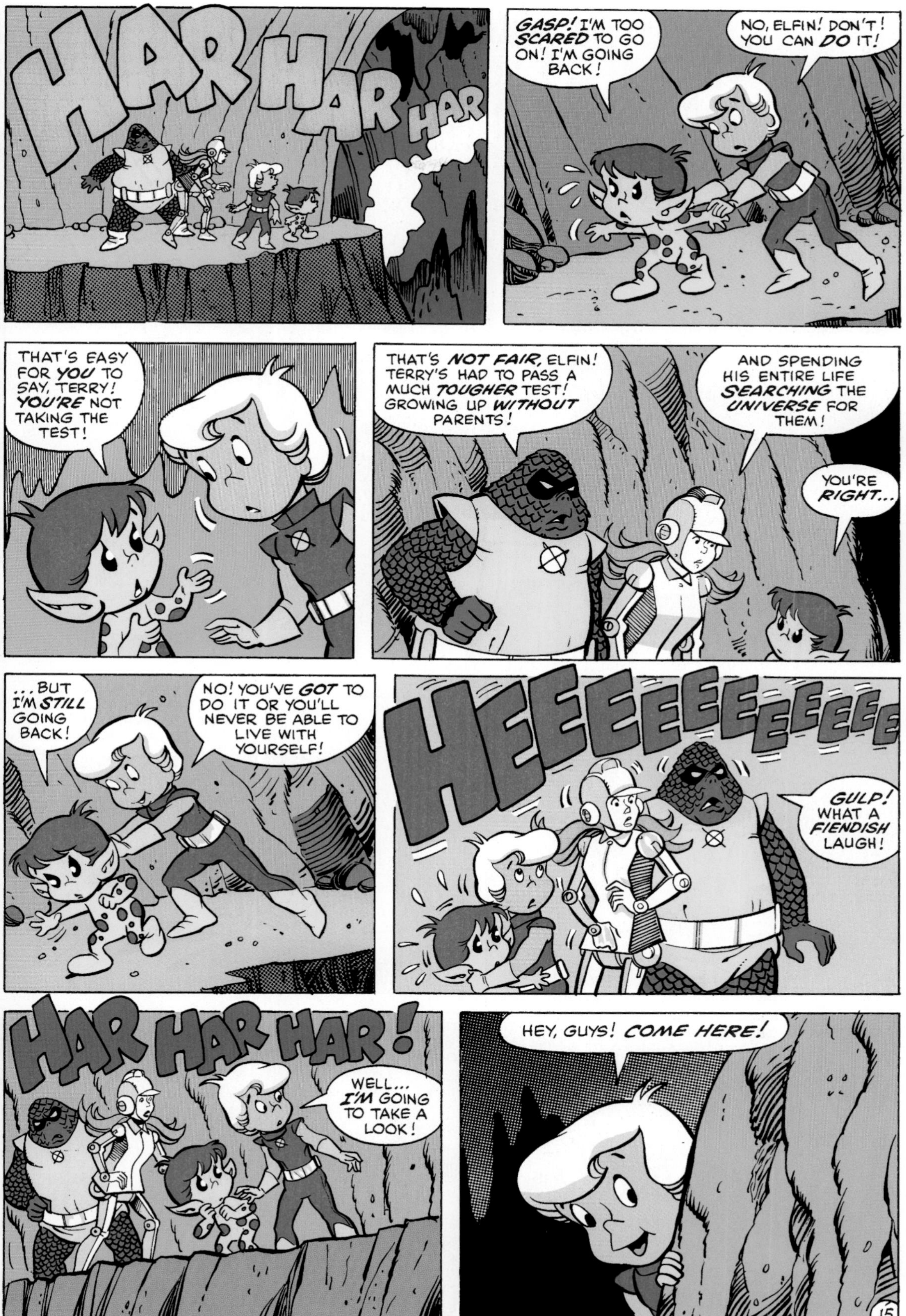
HAR HAR HAR
GASP! I'M TOO SCARED TO GO ON! I'M GOING BACK!
NO, ELFIN! DON'T! YOU CAN DO IT!
THAT'S EASY FOR YOU TO SAY, TERRY! YOU'RE NOT TAKING THE TEST!
THAT'S NOT FAIR, ELFIN! TERRY'S HAD TO PASS A MUCH TOUGHER TEST! GROWING UP WITHOUT PARENTS!
AND SPENDING HIS ENTIRE LIFE SEARCHING THE UNIVERSE FOR THEM!
YOU'RE RIGHT...
...BUT I'M STILL GOING BACK!
NO! YOU'VE GOT TO DO IT OR YOU'LL NEVER BE ABLE TO LIVE WITH YOURSELF!
HEEEEEEEEEE
GULP! WHAT A FIENDISH LAUGH!
HAR HAR HAR!
WELL... I'M GOING TO TAKE A LOOK!
HEY, GUYS! COME HERE!
15

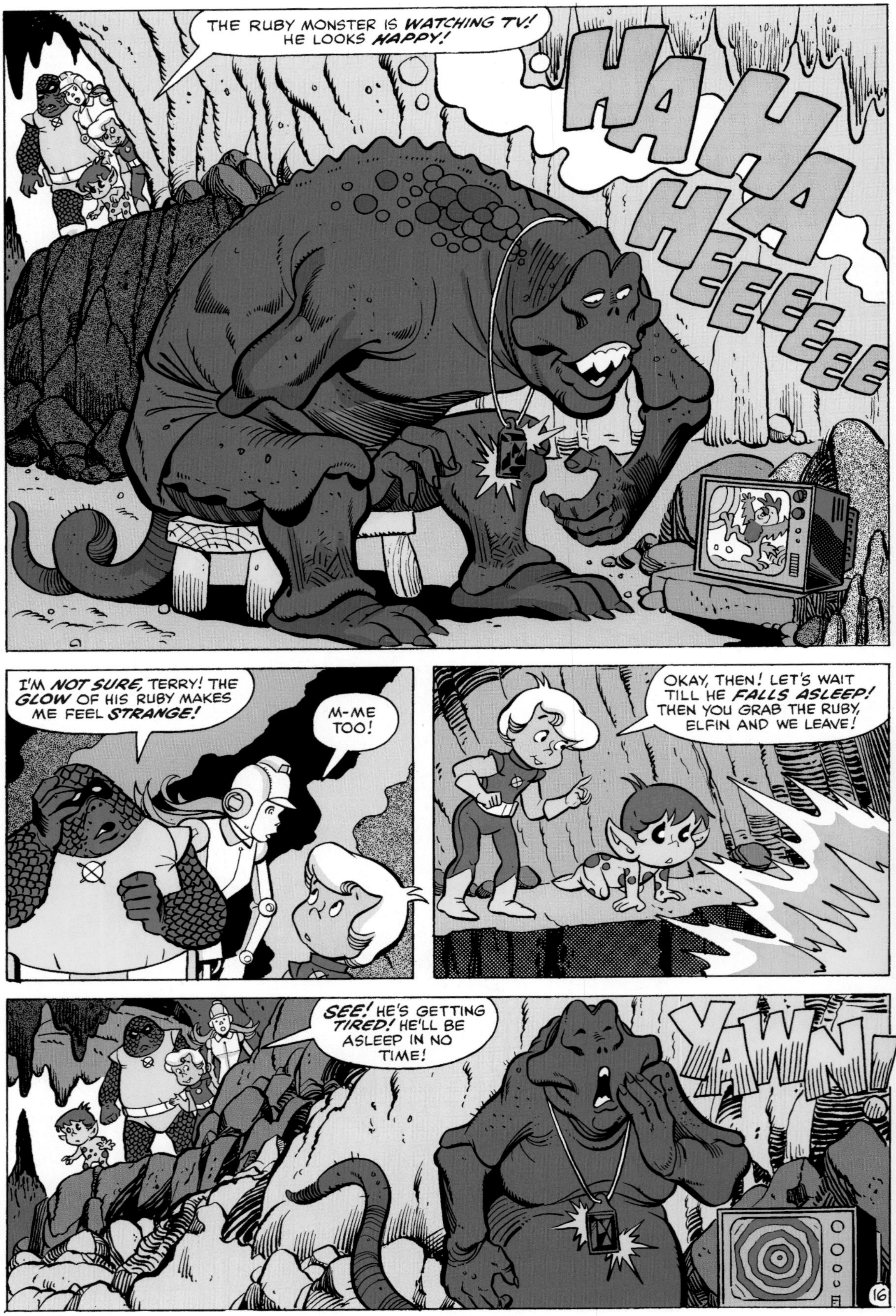
THE RUBY MONSTER IS WATCHING TV! HE LOOKS HAPPY!
HA HA HA HEEEEEEEE
I'M NOT SURE, TERRY! THE GLOW OF HIS RUBY MAKES ME FEEL STRANGE!
M-ME TOO!
OKAY, THEN! LET'S WAIT TILL HE FALLS ASLEEP! THEN YOU GRAB THE RUBY, ELFIN AND WE LEAVE!
SEE! HE'S GETTING TIRED! HE'LL BE ASLEEP IN NO TIME!
YAWN!
16

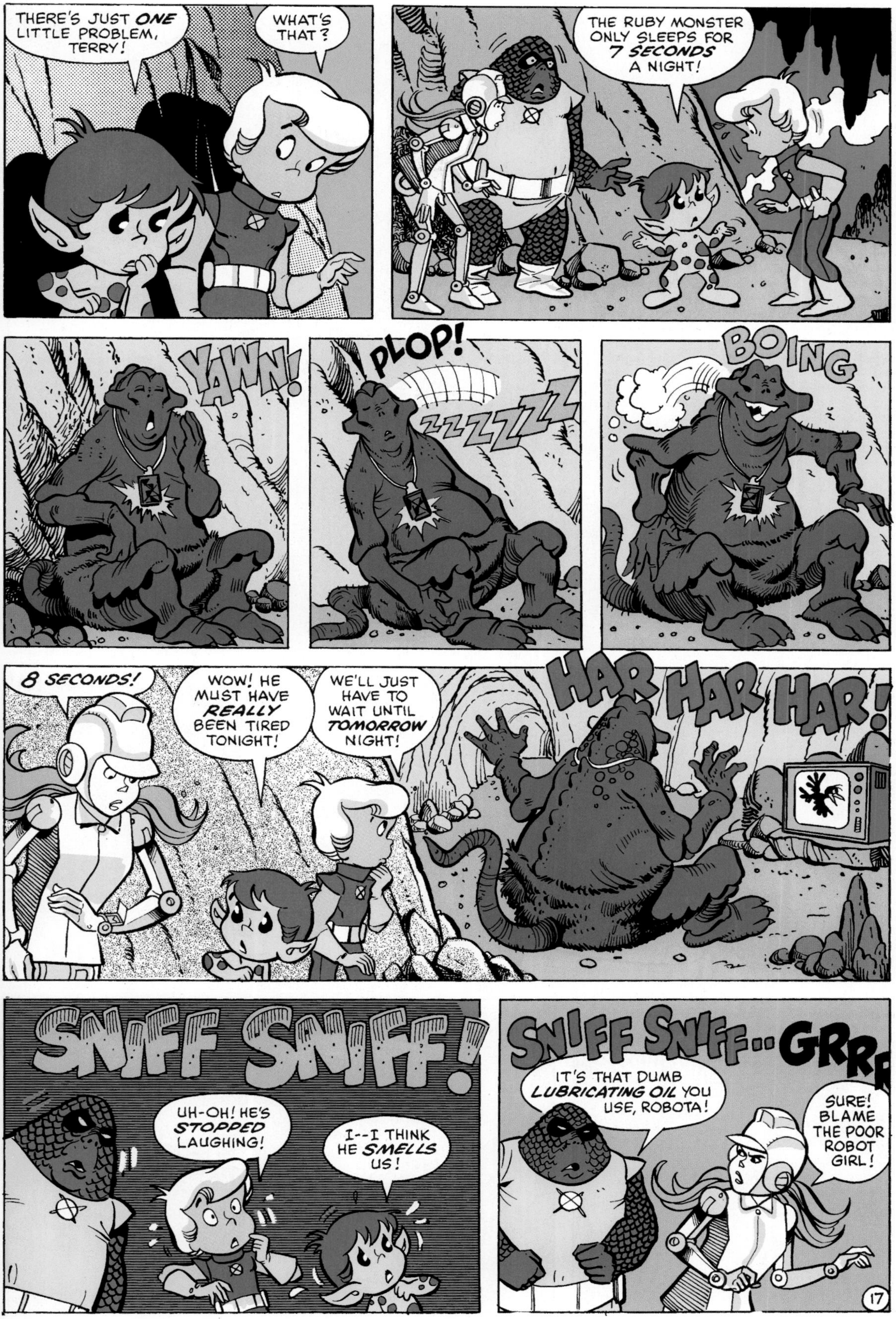
THERE'S JUST ONE LITTLE PROBLEM, TERRY!
WHAT'S THAT?
THE RUBY MONSTER ONLY SLEEPS FOR 7 SECONDS A NIGHT!
YAWN!
PLOP!
ZZZZZZZ
BOING
8 SECONDS!
WOW! HE MUST HAVE REALLY BEEN TIRED TONIGHT!
WE'LL JUST HAVE TO WAIT UNTIL TOMORROW NIGHT!
HAR HAR HAR!
SNIFF SNIFF!
UH-OH! HE'S STOPPED LAUGHING!
I--I THINK HE SMELLS US!
SNIFF SNIFF..GRRR
IT'S THAT DUMB LUBRICATING OIL YOU USE, ROBOTA!
SURE! BLAME THE POOR ROBOT GIRL!
17

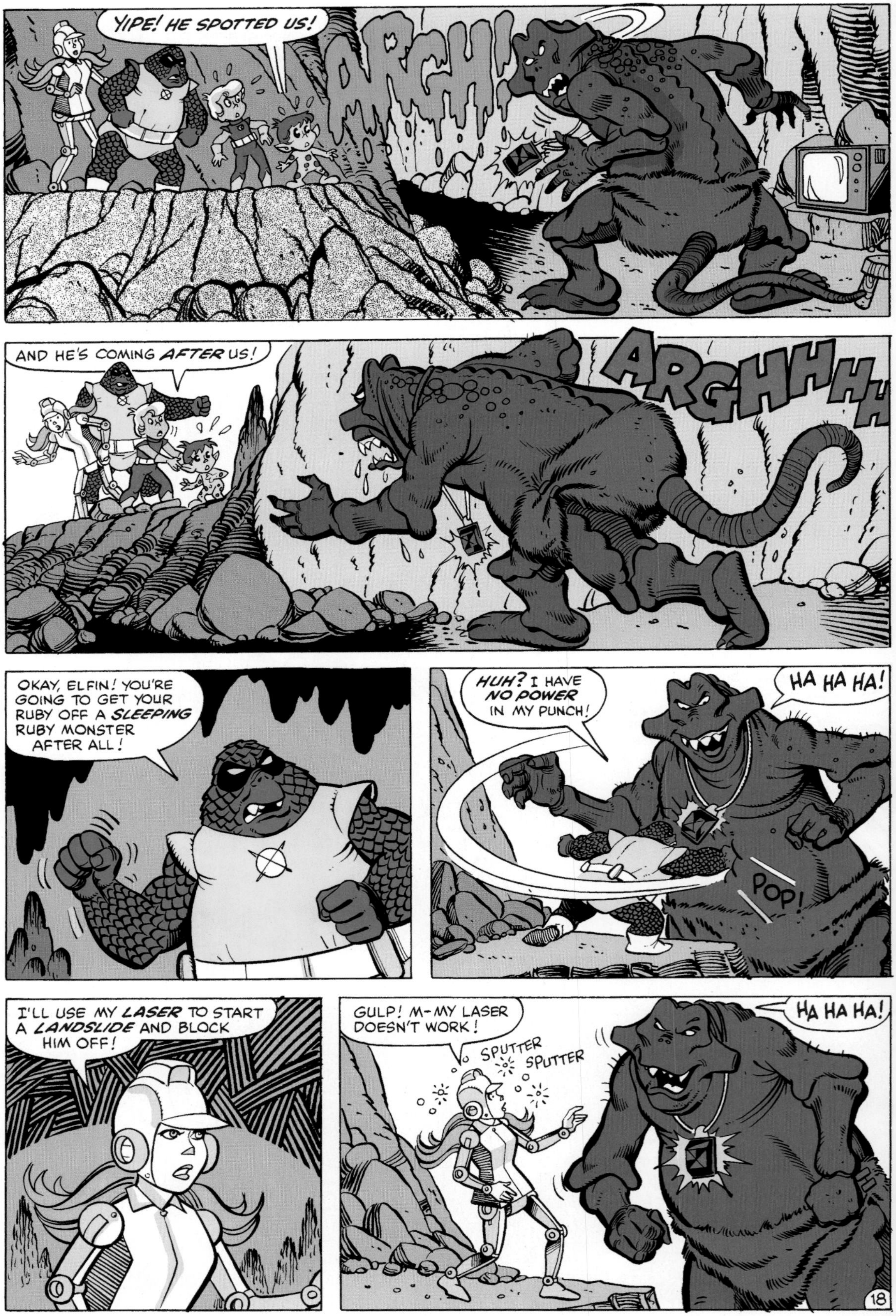
YIPE! HE SPOTTED US!
ARGH!
AND HE'S COMING AFTER US!
ARGHHHHH
OKAY, ELFIN! YOU'RE GOING TO GET YOUR RUBY OFF A SLEEPING RUBY MONSTER AFTER ALL!
HUH? I HAVE NO POWER IN MY PUNCH!
HA HA HA!
POP!
I'LL USE MY LASER TO START A LANDSLIDE AND BLOCK HIM OFF!
GULP! M-MY LASER DOESN'T WORK!
SPUTTER SPUTTER
HA HA HA!
18

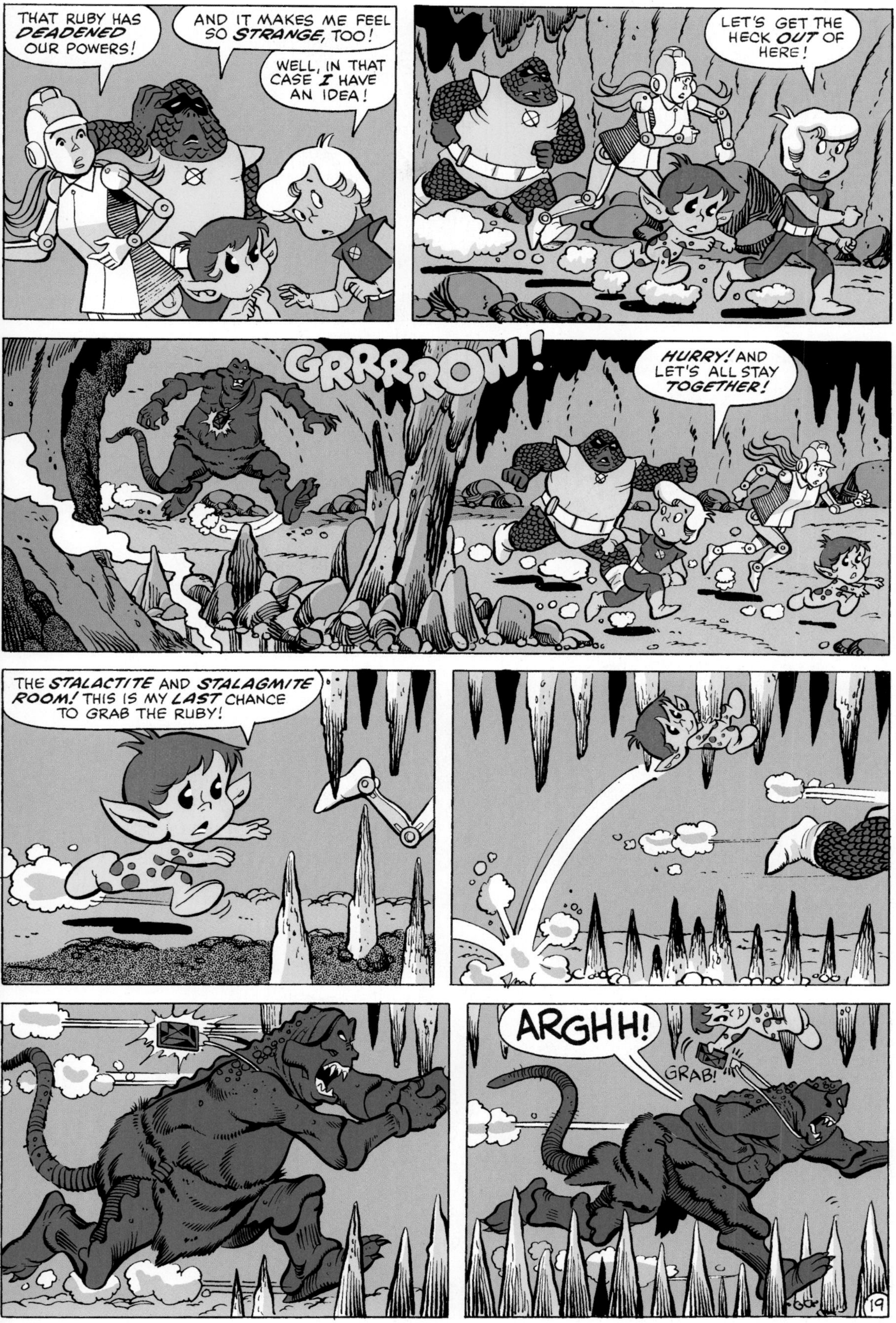
THAT RUBY HAS *DEADENED* OUR POWERS!
AND IT MAKES ME FEEL SO *STRANGE*, TOO!
WELL, IN THAT CASE *I* HAVE AN IDEA!
LET'S GET THE HECK *OUT* OF HERE!
GRRRROW!
HURRY! AND LET'S ALL STAY *TOGETHER!*
THE *STALACTITE* AND *STALAGMITE ROOM!* THIS IS MY *LAST* CHANCE TO GRAB THE RUBY!
ARGHH!
GRAB!
19

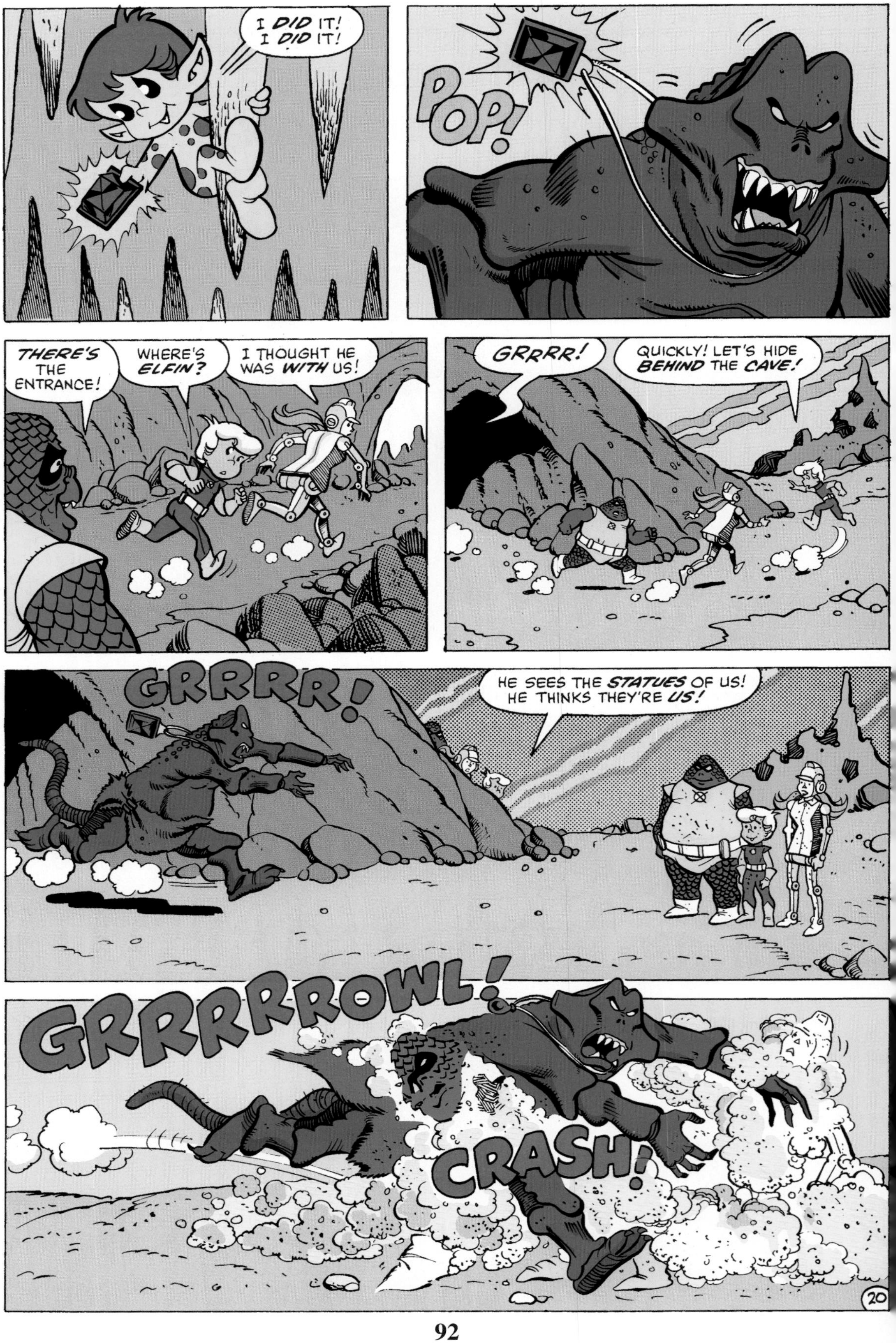
I DID IT! I DID IT!
POP!
THERE'S THE ENTRANCE!
WHERE'S ELFIN?
I THOUGHT HE WAS WITH US!
GRRRR!
QUICKLY! LET'S HIDE BEHIND THE CAVE!
GRRRRR!
HE SEES THE STATUES OF US! HE THINKS THEY'RE US!
GRRRRROWL!
CRASH!
20

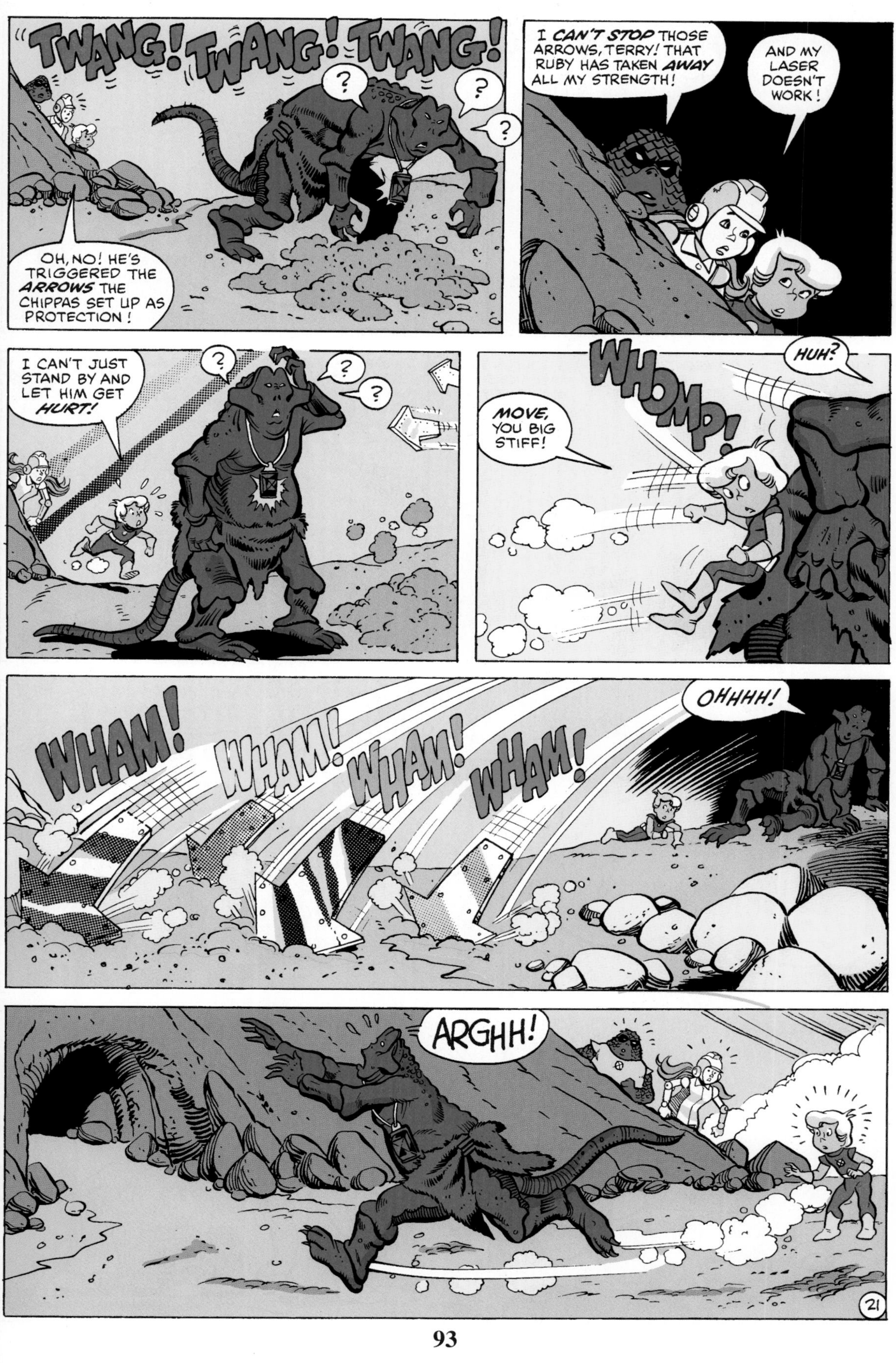

TWANG! TWANG! TWANG!
?
?
?
OH, NO! HE'S TRIGGERED THE ARROWS THE CHIPPAS SET UP AS PROTECTION!
I CAN'T STOP THOSE ARROWS, TERRY! THAT RUBY HAS TAKEN AWAY ALL MY STRENGTH!
AND MY LASER DOESN'T WORK!
I CAN'T JUST STAND BY AND LET HIM GET HURT!
?
?
?
WHOMP!
HUH?
MOVE, YOU BIG STIFF!
WHAM! WHAM! WHAM! WHAM!
OHHHH!
ARGHH!
21

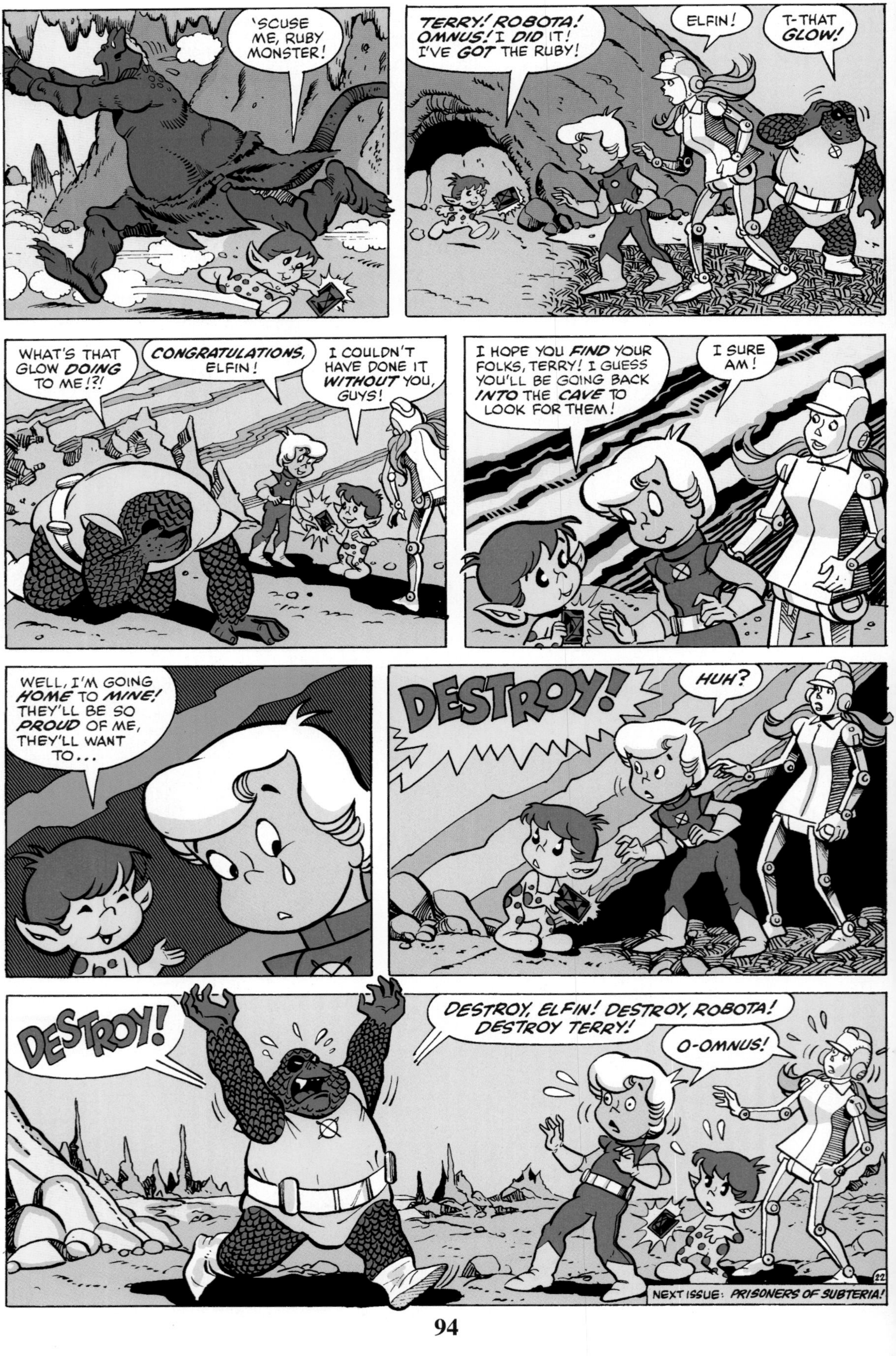
'SCUSE ME, RUBY MONSTER!
TERRY! ROBOTA! OMNUS! I DID IT! I'VE GOT THE RUBY!
ELFIN!
T-THAT GLOW!
WHAT'S THAT GLOW DOING TO ME!?!
CONGRATULATIONS, ELFIN!
I COULDN'T HAVE DONE IT WITHOUT YOU, GUYS!
I HOPE YOU FIND YOUR FOLKS, TERRY! I GUESS YOU'LL BE GOING BACK INTO THE CAVE TO LOOK FOR THEM!
I SURE AM!
WELL, I'M GOING HOME TO MINE! THEY'LL BE SO PROUD OF ME, THEY'LL WANT TO...
DESTROY!
HUH?
DESTROY!
DESTROY, ELFIN! DESTROY, ROBOTA! DESTROY TERRY!
O-OMNUS!
22
NEXT ISSUE: PRISONERS OF SUBTERIA!

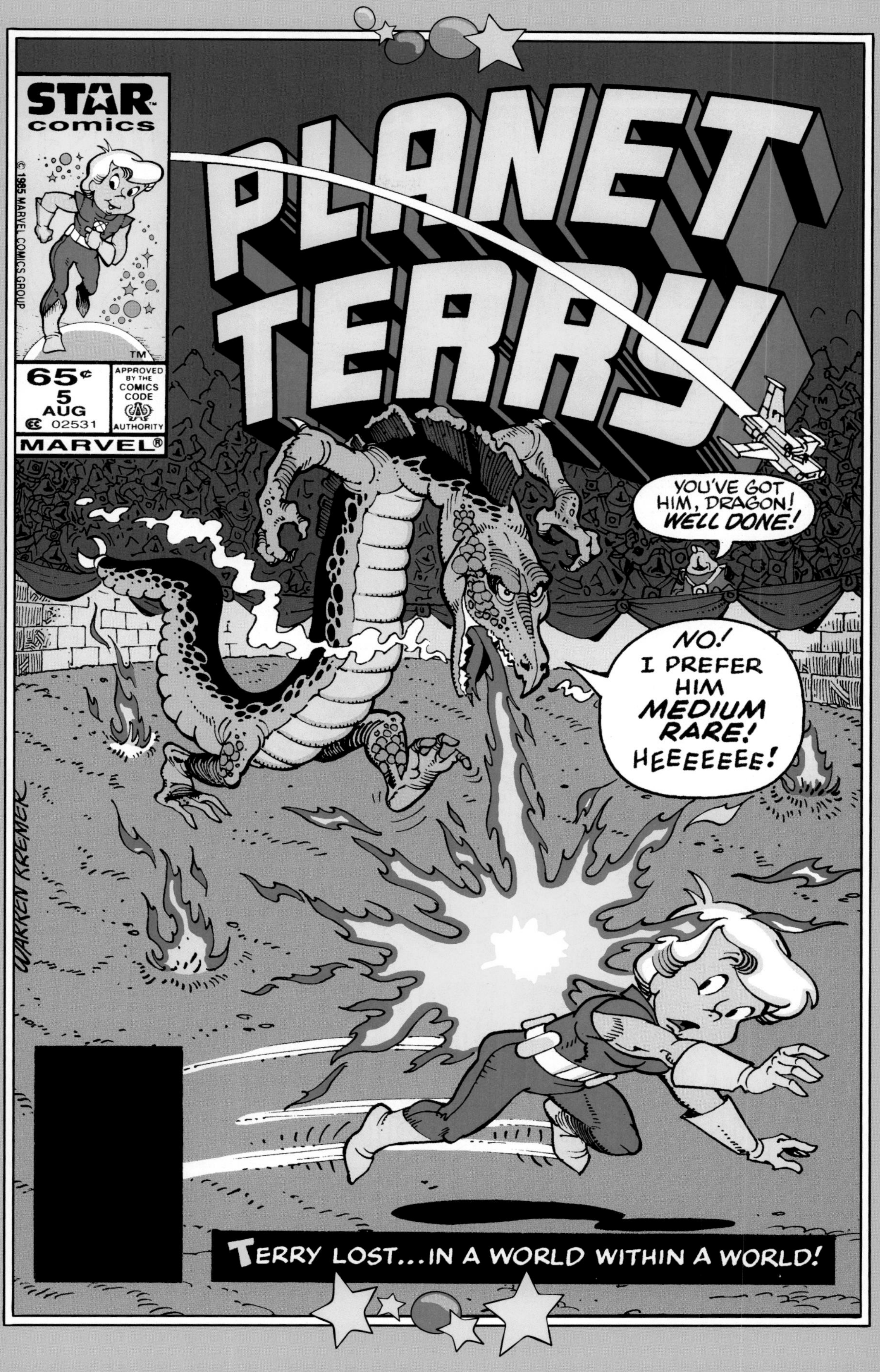
STAR comics
© 1985 MARVEL COMICS GROUP
65¢
5
AUG
02531
APPROVED BY THE COMICS CODE AUTHORITY
MARVEL
PLANET TERRY
YOU'VE GOT HIM, DRAGON! WELL DONE!
NO! I PREFER HIM MEDIUM RARE! HEEEEEEE!
WARREN KREMER
TERRY LOST...IN A WORLD WITHIN A WORLD!

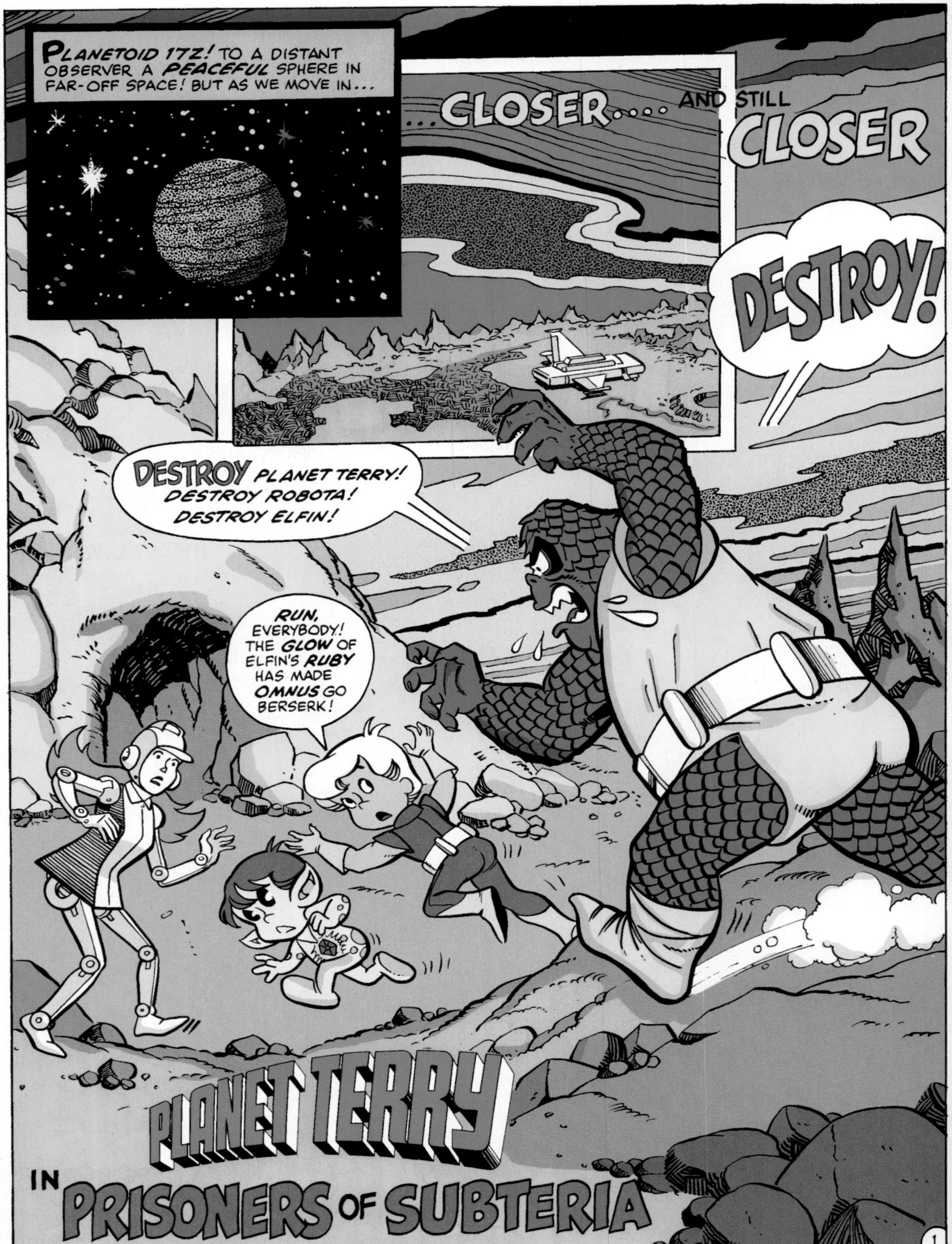

PLANETOID 17Z! TO A DISTANT OBSERVER A PEACEFUL SPHERE IN FAR-OFF SPACE! BUT AS WE MOVE IN...
...CLOSER.... AND STILL CLOSER
DESTROY!
DESTROY PLANET TERRY! DESTROY ROBOTA! DESTROY ELFIN!
RUN, EVERYBODY! THE GLOW OF ELFIN'S RUBY HAS MADE OMNUS GO BERSERK!
PLANET TERRY
IN PRISONERS OF SUBTERIA
1

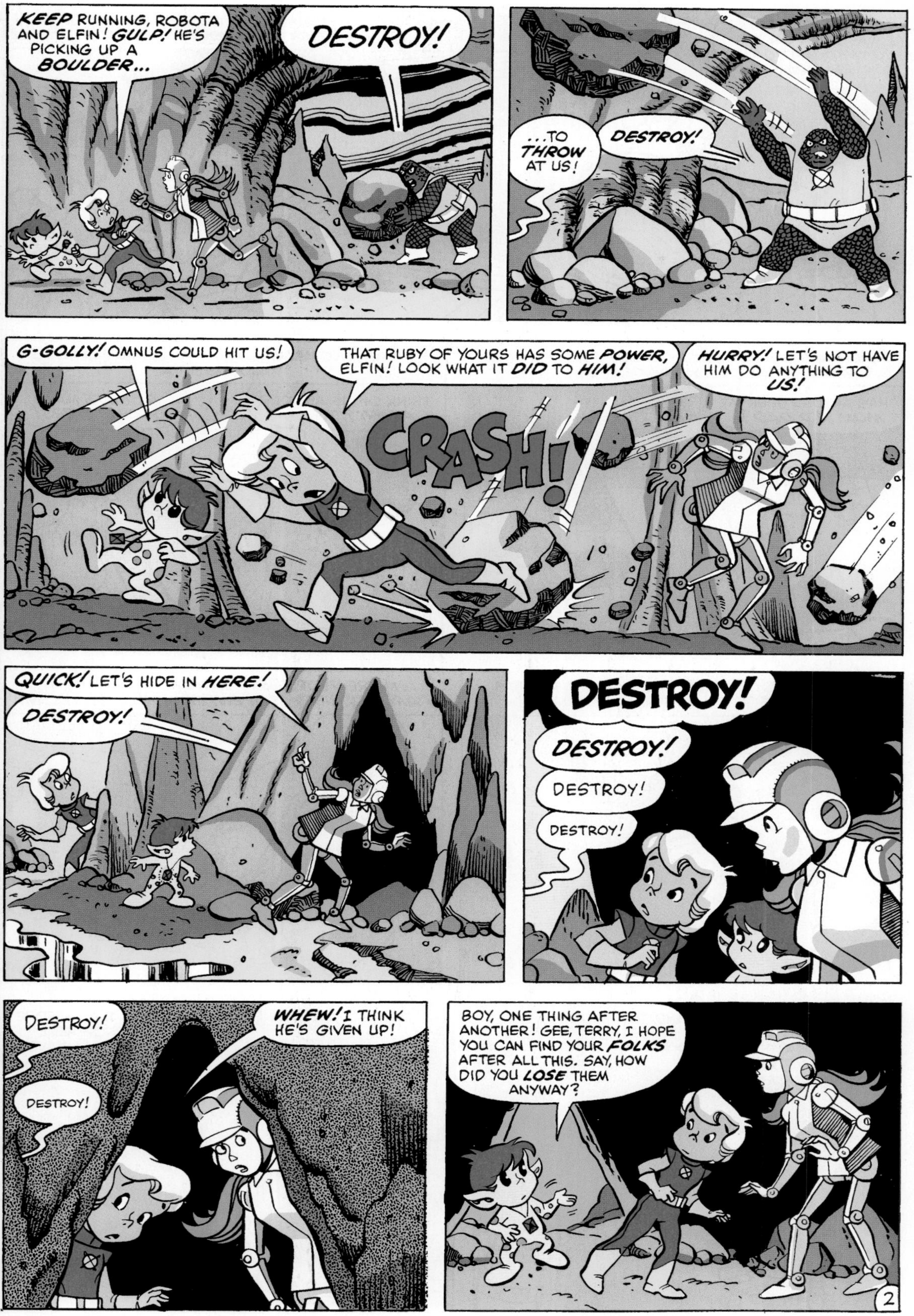
KEEP RUNNING, ROBOTA AND ELFIN! GULP! HE'S PICKING UP A BOULDER...
DESTROY!
...TO THROW AT US!
DESTROY!
G-GOLLY! OMNUS COULD HIT US!
THAT RUBY OF YOURS HAS SOME POWER, ELFIN! LOOK WHAT IT DID TO HIM!
HURRY! LET'S NOT HAVE HIM DO ANYTHING TO US!
CRASH!
QUICK! LET'S HIDE IN HERE!
DESTROY!
DESTROY!
DESTROY!
DESTROY!
DESTROY!
DESTROY!
WHEW! I THINK HE'S GIVEN UP!
DESTROY!
BOY, ONE THING AFTER ANOTHER! GEE, TERRY, I HOPE YOU CAN FIND YOUR FOLKS AFTER ALL THIS. SAY, HOW DID YOU LOSE THEM ANYWAY?
2

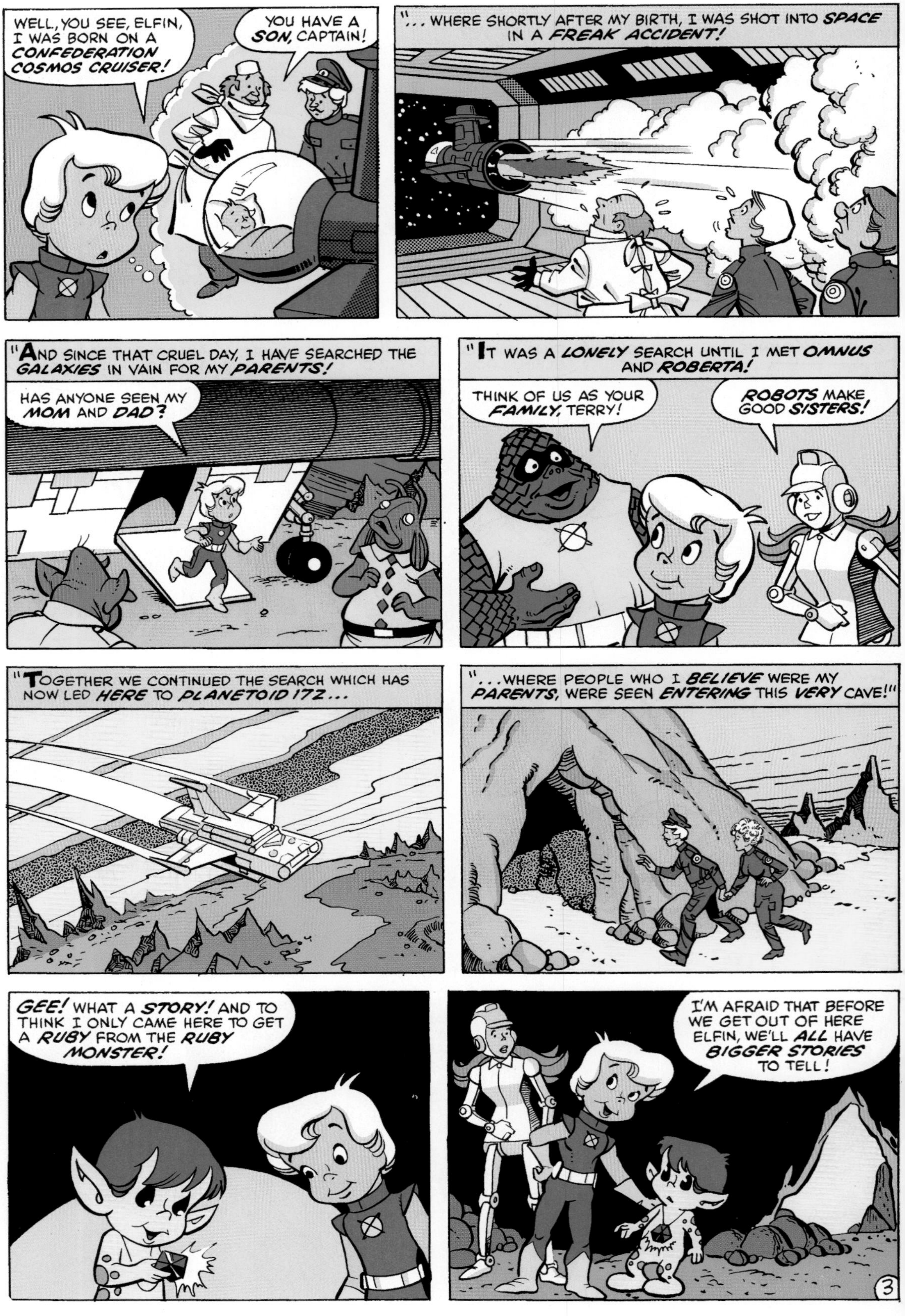
WELL, YOU SEE, ELFIN, I WAS BORN ON A CONFEDERATION COSMOS CRUISER!
YOU HAVE A SON, CAPTAIN!
"...WHERE SHORTLY AFTER MY BIRTH, I WAS SHOT INTO SPACE IN A FREAK ACCIDENT!
"AND SINCE THAT CRUEL DAY, I HAVE SEARCHED THE GALAXIES IN VAIN FOR MY PARENTS!
HAS ANYONE SEEN MY MOM AND DAD?
"IT WAS A LONELY SEARCH UNTIL I MET OMNUS AND ROBERTA!
THINK OF US AS YOUR FAMILY, TERRY!
ROBOTS MAKE GOOD SISTERS!
"TOGETHER WE CONTINUED THE SEARCH WHICH HAS NOW LED HERE TO PLANETOID 172...
"...WHERE PEOPLE WHO I BELIEVE WERE MY PARENTS, WERE SEEN ENTERING THIS VERY CAVE!"
GEE! WHAT A STORY! AND TO THINK I ONLY CAME HERE TO GET A RUBY FROM THE RUBY MONSTER!
I'M AFRAID THAT BEFORE WE GET OUT OF HERE ELFIN, WE'LL ALL HAVE BIGGER STORIES TO TELL!
3

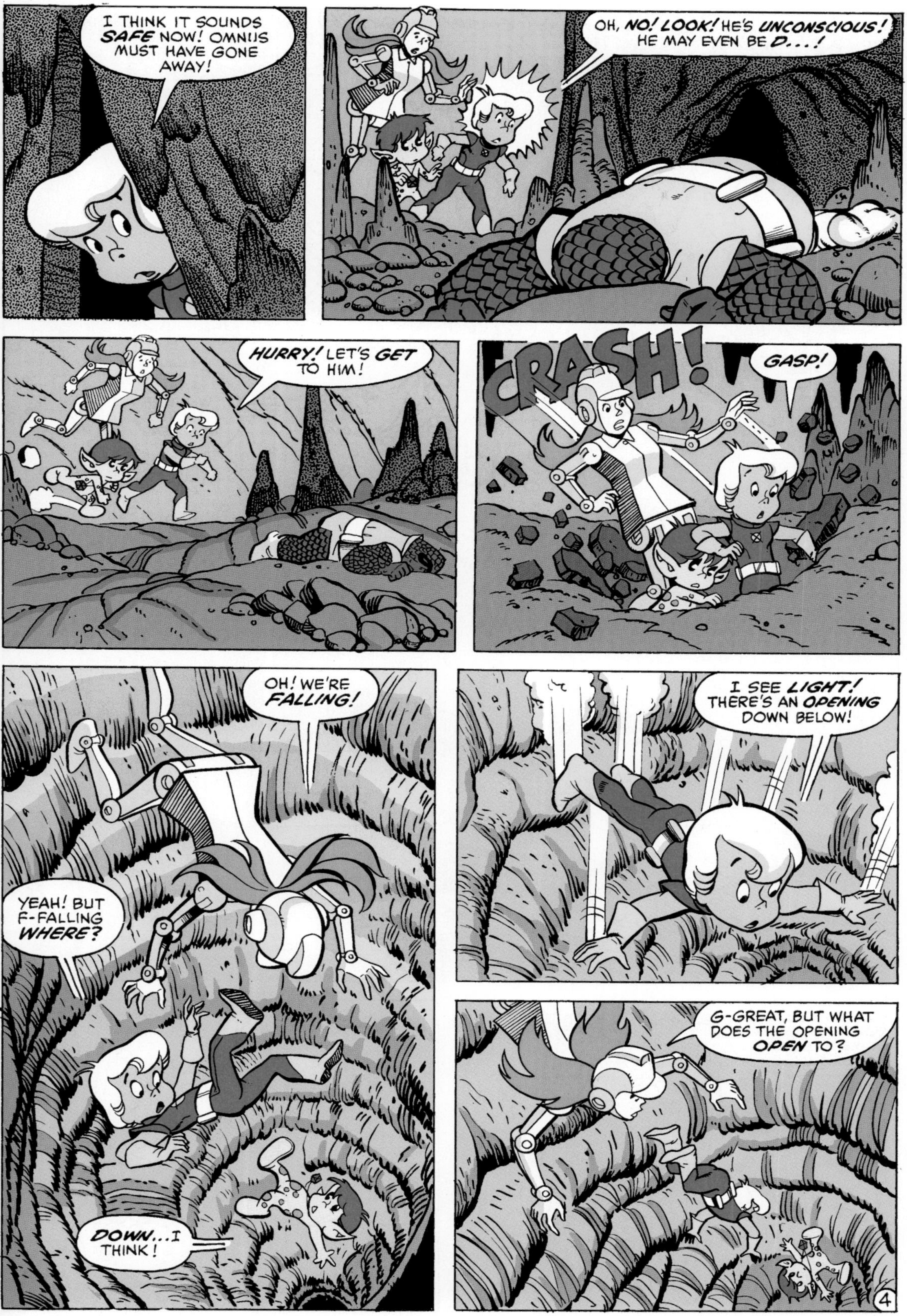
I THINK IT SOUNDS SAFE NOW! OMNIUS MUST HAVE GONE AWAY!
OH, NO! LOOK! HE'S UNCONSCIOUS! HE MAY EVEN BE D...!
HURRY! LET'S GET TO HIM!
CRASH!
GASP!
OH! WE'RE FALLING!
YEAH! BUT F-FALLING WHERE?
DOWN... I THINK!
I SEE LIGHT! THERE'S AN OPENING DOWN BELOW!
G-GREAT, BUT WHAT DOES THE OPENING OPEN TO?
4

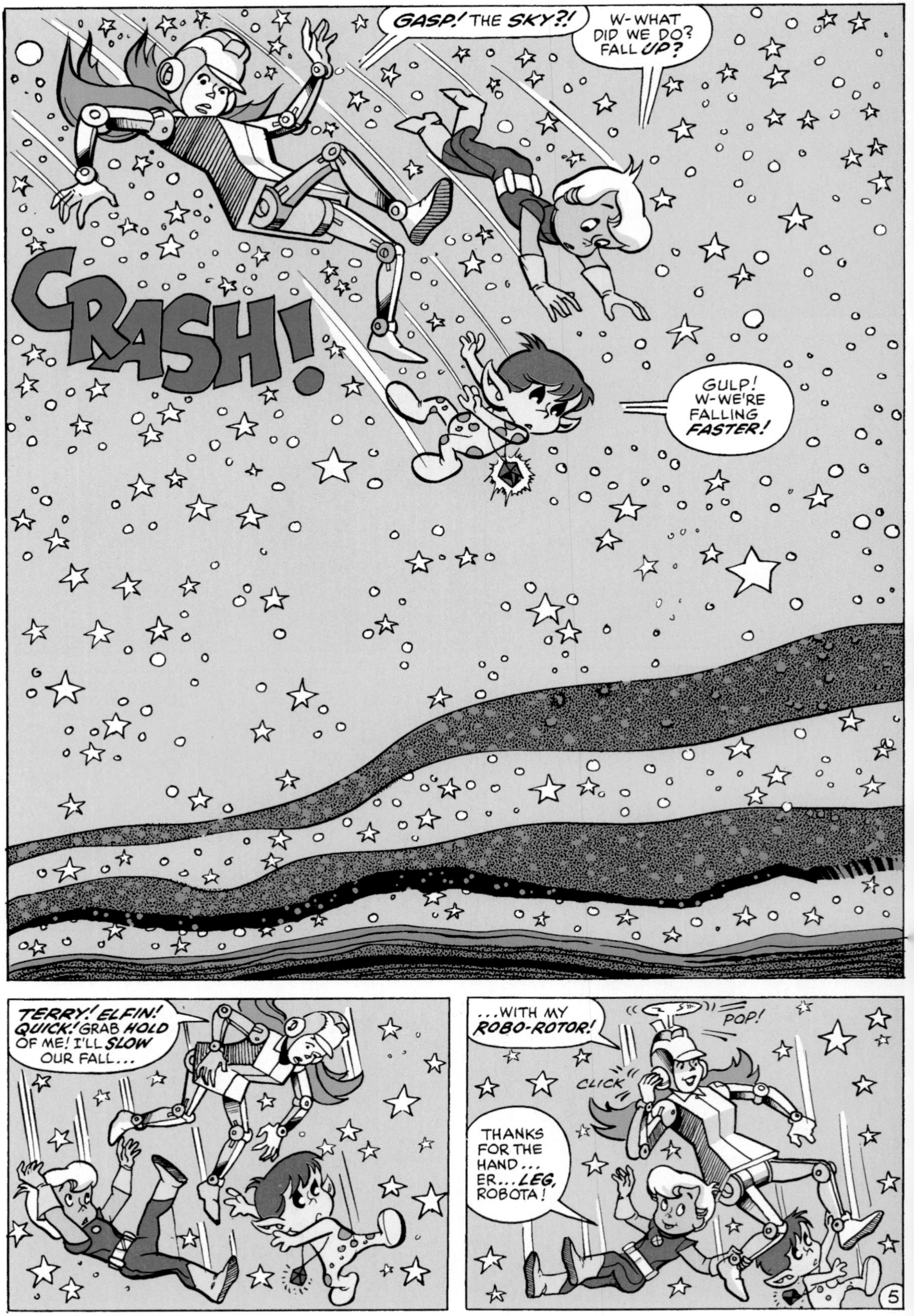
GASP! THE SKY?!
W-WHAT DID WE DO? FALL UP?
CRASH!
GULP! W-WE'RE FALLING FASTER!
TERRY! ELFIN! QUICK! GRAB HOLD OF ME! I'LL SLOW OUR FALL...
...WITH MY ROBO-ROTOR!
POP!
CLICK
THANKS FOR THE HAND... ER...LEG, ROBOTA!
5

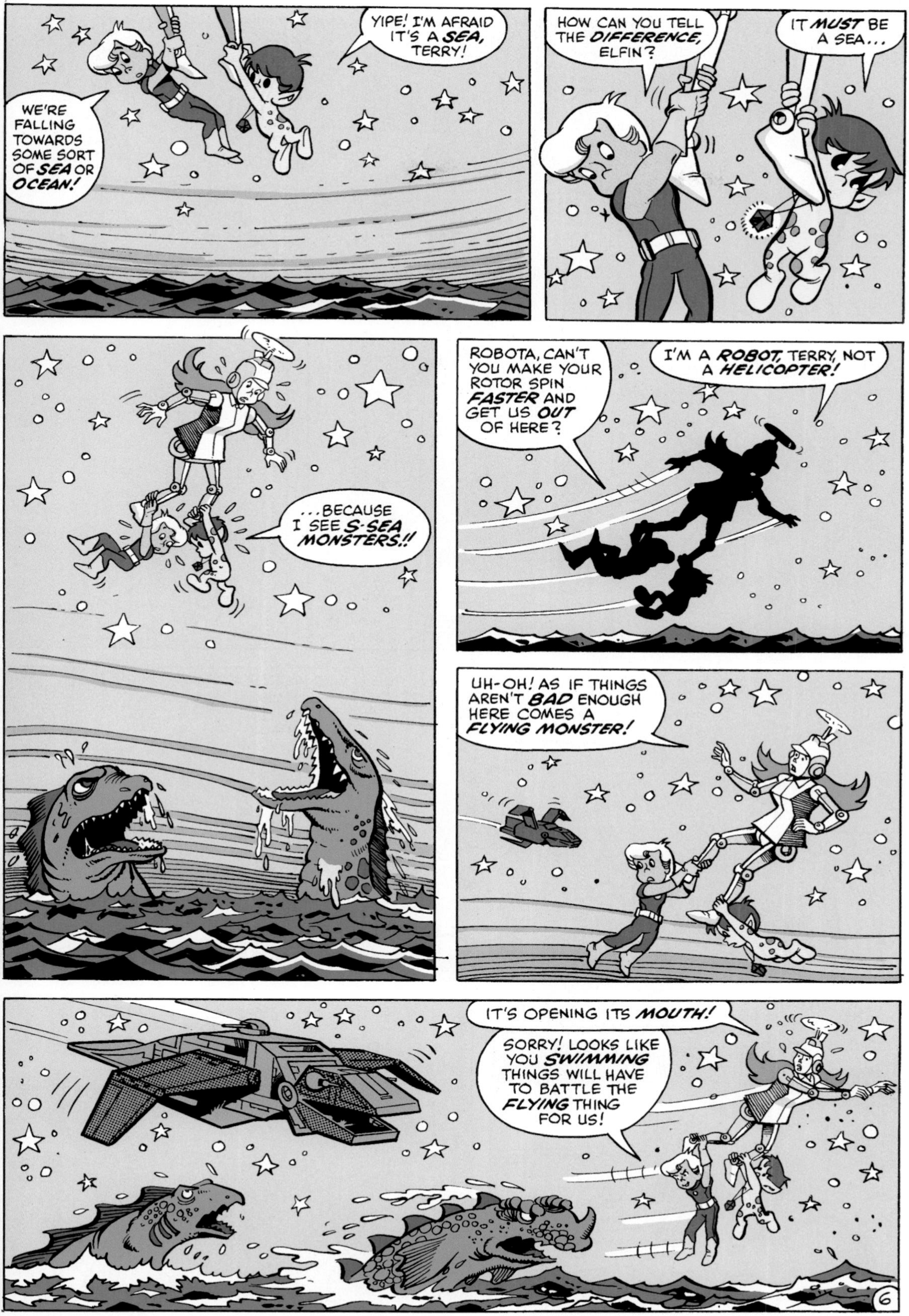
WE'RE FALLING TOWARDS SOME SORT OF SEA OR OCEAN!
YIPE! I'M AFRAID IT'S A SEA, TERRY!
HOW CAN YOU TELL THE DIFFERENCE, ELFIN?
IT MUST BE A SEA...
...BECAUSE I SEE S-SEA MONSTERS!!
ROBOTA, CAN'T YOU MAKE YOUR ROTOR SPIN FASTER AND GET US OUT OF HERE?
I'M A ROBOT, TERRY, NOT A HELICOPTER!
UH-OH! AS IF THINGS AREN'T BAD ENOUGH HERE COMES A FLYING MONSTER!
IT'S OPENING ITS MOUTH!
SORRY! LOOKS LIKE YOU SWIMMING THINGS WILL HAVE TO BATTLE THE FLYING THING FOR US!
6

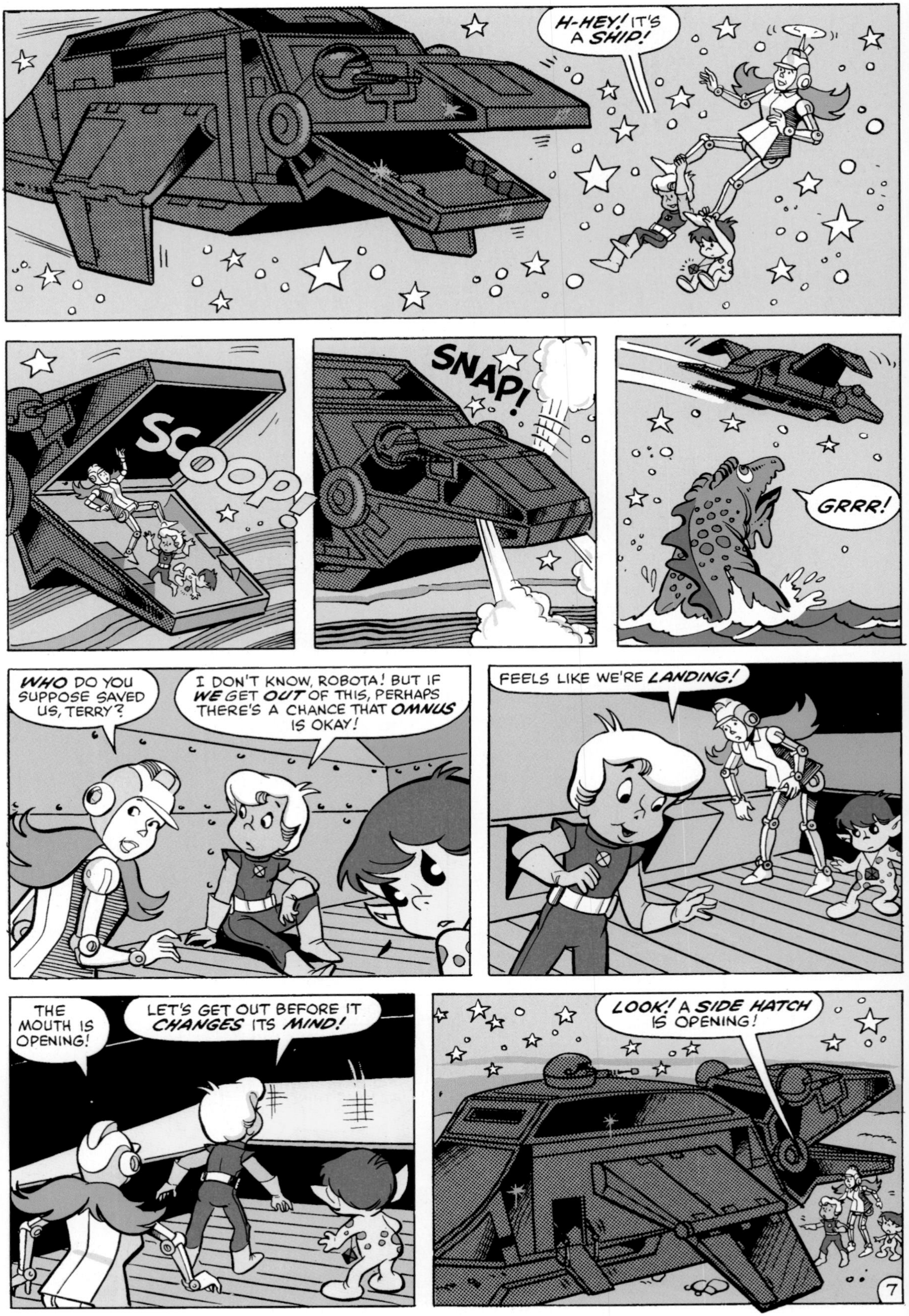
H-HEY! IT'S A SHIP!
SCOOP!
SNAP!
GRRR!
WHO DO YOU SUPPOSE SAVED US, TERRY?
I DON'T KNOW, ROBOTA! BUT IF WE GET OUT OF THIS, PERHAPS THERE'S A CHANCE THAT OMNUS IS OKAY!
FEELS LIKE WE'RE LANDING!
THE MOUTH IS OPENING!
LET'S GET OUT BEFORE IT CHANGES ITS MIND!
LOOK! A SIDE HATCH IS OPENING!
7

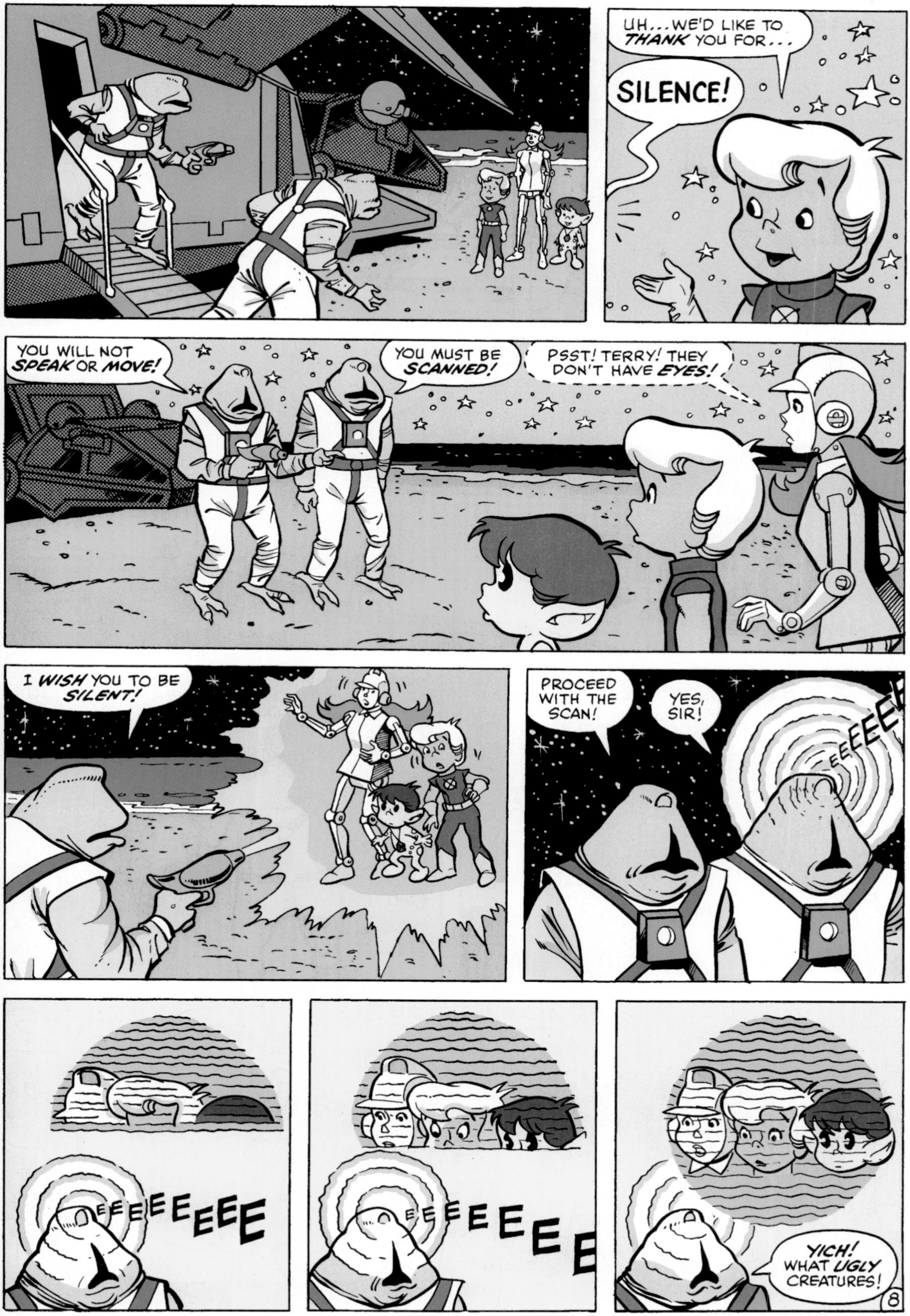
UH...WE'D LIKE TO THANK YOU FOR...
SILENCE!
YOU WILL NOT SPEAK OR MOVE!
YOU MUST BE SCANNED!
PSST! TERRY! THEY DON'T HAVE EYES!
I WISH YOU TO BE SILENT!
PROCEED WITH THE SCAN!
YES, SIR!
EEEEEEEE
EEEEEEEEEE
EEEEEEEEEE
YICH! WHAT UGLY CREATURES!
8

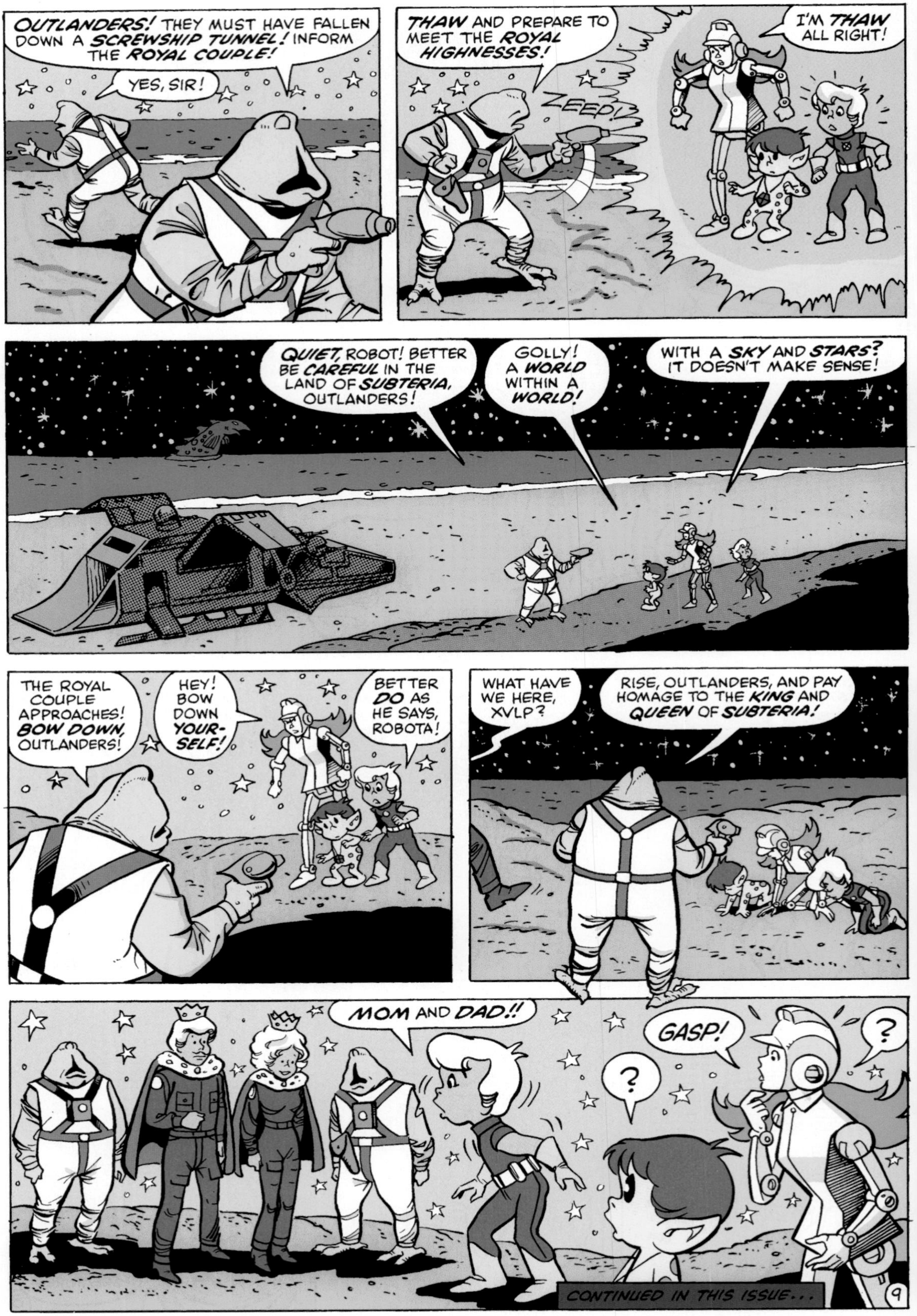
OUTLANDERS! THEY MUST HAVE FALLEN DOWN A SCREWSHIP TUNNEL! INFORM THE ROYAL COUPLE!
YES, SIR!
THAW AND PREPARE TO MEET THE ROYAL HIGHNESSES!
ZEEP!
I'M THAW ALL RIGHT!
QUIET, ROBOT! BETTER BE CAREFUL IN THE LAND OF SUBTERIA, OUTLANDERS!
GOLLY! A WORLD WITHIN A WORLD!
WITH A SKY AND STARS? IT DOESN'T MAKE SENSE!
THE ROYAL COUPLE APPROACHES! BOW DOWN, OUTLANDERS!
HEY! BOW DOWN YOURSELF!
BETTER DO AS HE SAYS, ROBOTA!
WHAT HAVE WE HERE, XVLP?
RISE, OUTLANDERS, AND PAY HOMAGE TO THE KING AND QUEEN OF SUBTERIA!
MOM AND DAD!!
GASP!
?
?
CONTINUED IN THIS ISSUE...
9

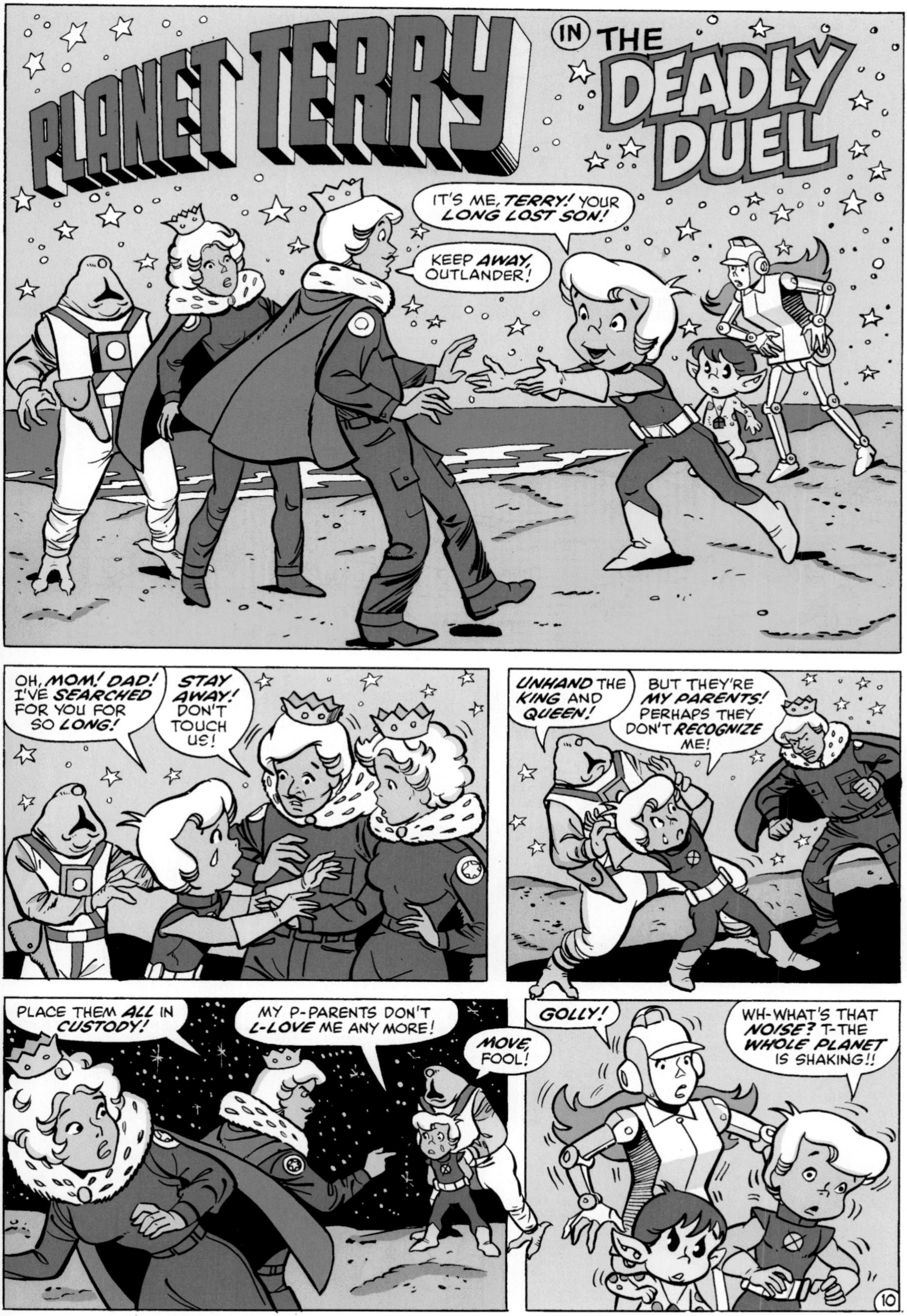
PLANET TERRY
IN THE DEADLY DUEL
IT'S ME, TERRY! YOUR LONG LOST SON!
KEEP AWAY, OUTLANDER!
OH, MOM! DAD! I'VE SEARCHED FOR YOU FOR SO LONG!
STAY AWAY! DON'T TOUCH US!
UNHAND THE KING AND QUEEN!
BUT THEY'RE MY PARENTS! PERHAPS THEY DON'T RECOGNIZE ME!
PLACE THEM ALL IN CUSTODY!
MY P-PARENTS DON'T L-LOVE ME ANY MORE!
MOVE, FOOL!
GOLLY!
WH-WHAT'S THAT NOISE? T-THE WHOLE PLANET IS SHAKING!!
10

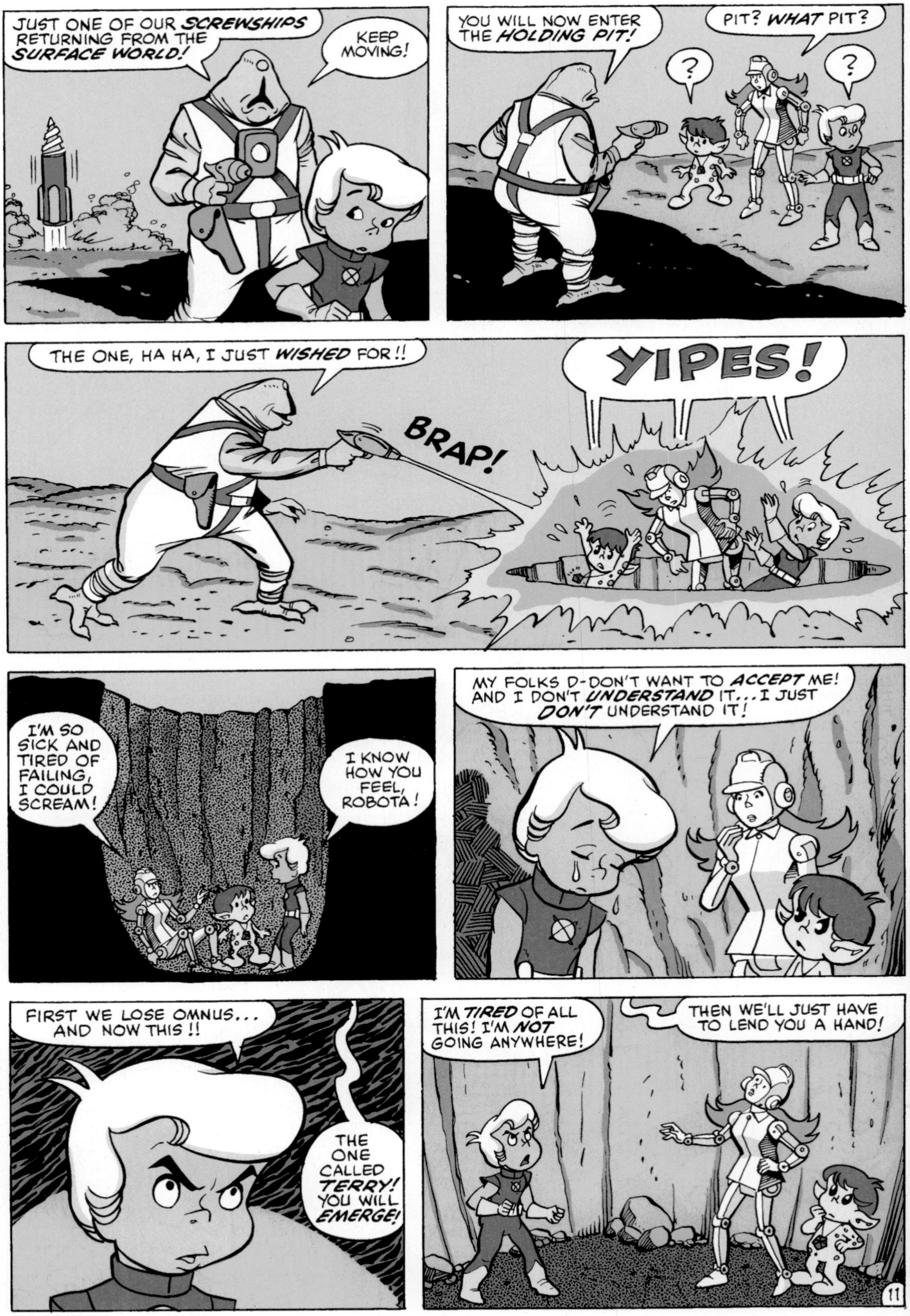
JUST ONE OF OUR SCREWSHIPS RETURNING FROM THE SURFACE WORLD!
KEEP MOVING!
YOU WILL NOW ENTER THE HOLDING PIT!
PIT? WHAT PIT?
?
?
THE ONE, HA HA, I JUST WISHED FOR!!
BRAP!
YIPES!
I'M SO SICK AND TIRED OF FAILING, I COULD SCREAM!
I KNOW HOW YOU FEEL, ROBOTA!
MY FOLKS D-DON'T WANT TO ACCEPT ME! AND I DON'T UNDERSTAND IT... I JUST DON'T UNDERSTAND IT!
FIRST WE LOSE OMNUS... AND NOW THIS!!
THE ONE CALLED TERRY! YOU WILL EMERGE!
I'M TIRED OF ALL THIS! I'M NOT GOING ANYWHERE!
THEN WE'LL JUST HAVE TO LEND YOU A HAND!
11

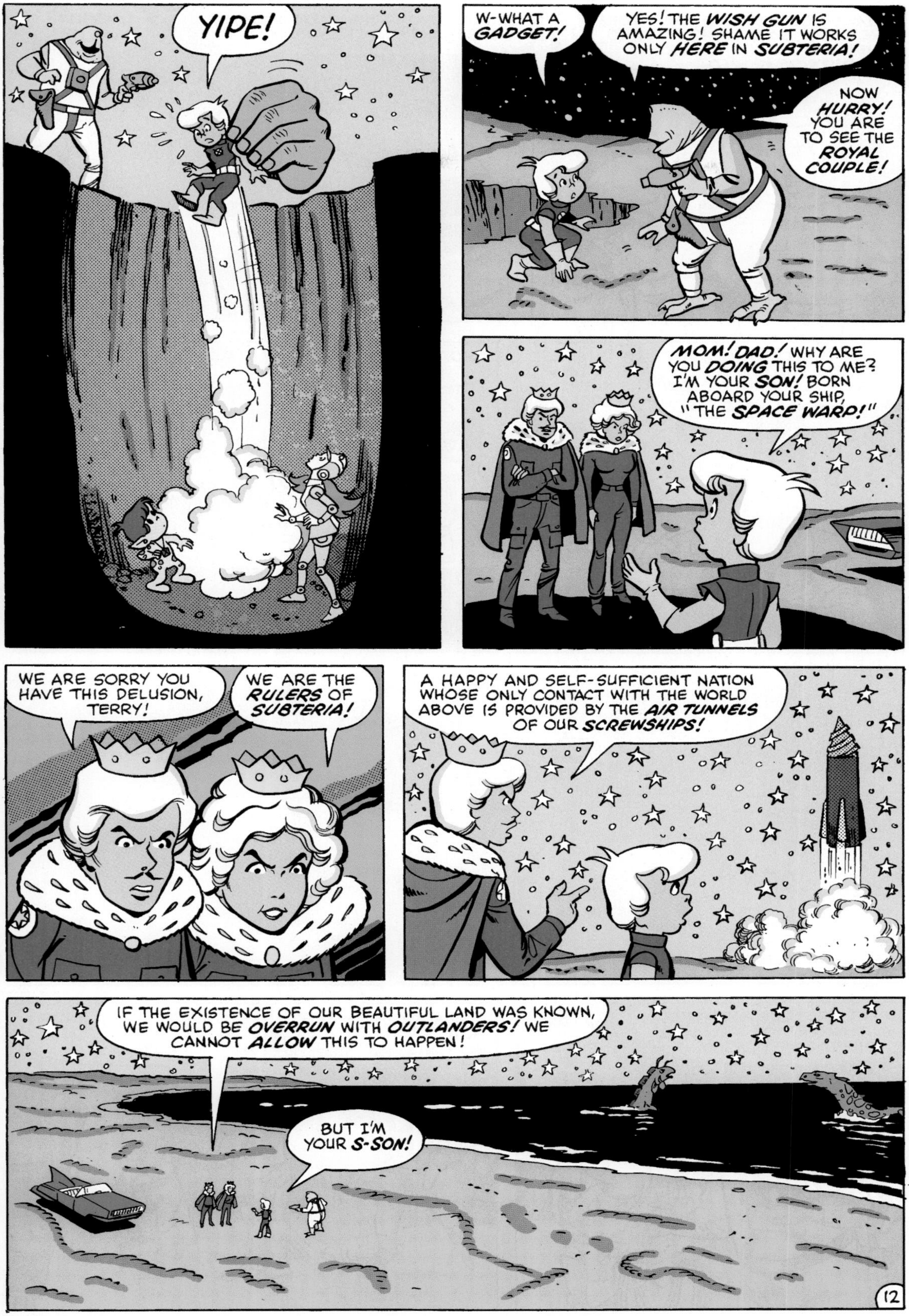
YIPE!
W-WHAT A GADGET!
YES! THE WISH GUN IS AMAZING! SHAME IT WORKS ONLY HERE IN SUBTERIA!
NOW HURRY! YOU ARE TO SEE THE ROYAL COUPLE!
MOM! DAD! WHY ARE YOU DOING THIS TO ME? I'M YOUR SON! BORN ABOARD YOUR SHIP, "THE SPACE WARP!"
WE ARE SORRY YOU HAVE THIS DELUSION, TERRY!
WE ARE THE RULERS OF SUBTERIA!
A HAPPY AND SELF-SUFFICIENT NATION WHOSE ONLY CONTACT WITH THE WORLD ABOVE IS PROVIDED BY THE AIR TUNNELS OF OUR SCREWSHIPS!
IF THE EXISTENCE OF OUR BEAUTIFUL LAND WAS KNOWN, WE WOULD BE OVERRUN WITH OUTLANDERS! WE CANNOT ALLOW THIS TO HAPPEN!
BUT I'M YOUR S-SON!
12

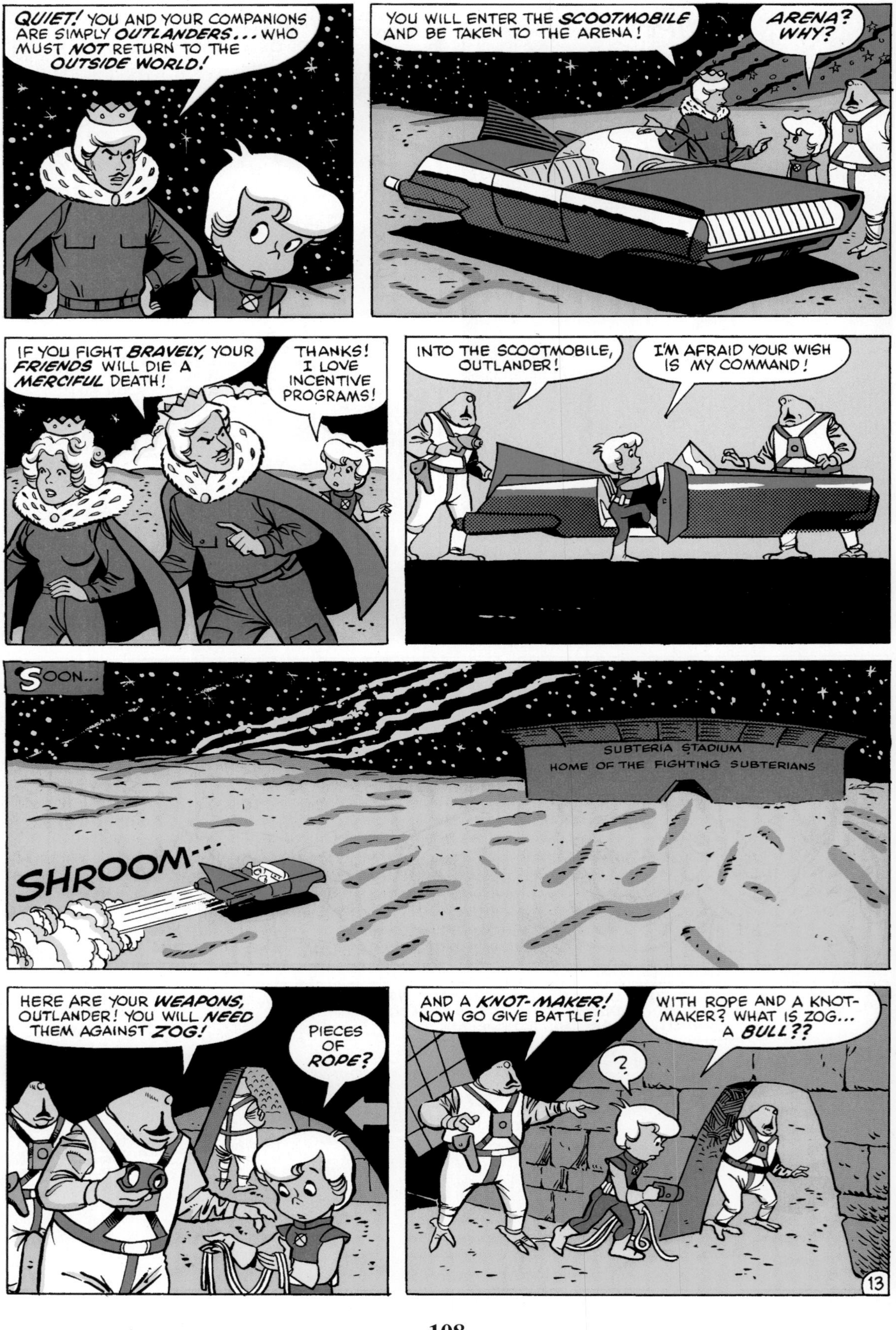
QUIET! YOU AND YOUR COMPANIONS ARE SIMPLY OUTLANDERS... WHO MUST NOT RETURN TO THE OUTSIDE WORLD!
YOU WILL ENTER THE SCOOTMOBILE AND BE TAKEN TO THE ARENA!
ARENA? WHY?
IF YOU FIGHT BRAVELY, YOUR FRIENDS WILL DIE A MERCIFUL DEATH!
THANKS! I LOVE INCENTIVE PROGRAMS!
INTO THE SCOOTMOBILE, OUTLANDER!
I'M AFRAID YOUR WISH IS MY COMMAND!
SOON...
SUBTERIA STADIUM
HOME OF THE FIGHTING SUBTERIANS
SHROOM---
HERE ARE YOUR WEAPONS, OUTLANDER! YOU WILL NEED THEM AGAINST ZOG!
PIECES OF ROPE?
AND A KNOT-MAKER! NOW GO GIVE BATTLE!
WITH ROPE AND A KNOT-MAKER? WHAT IS ZOG... A BULL??
?
13

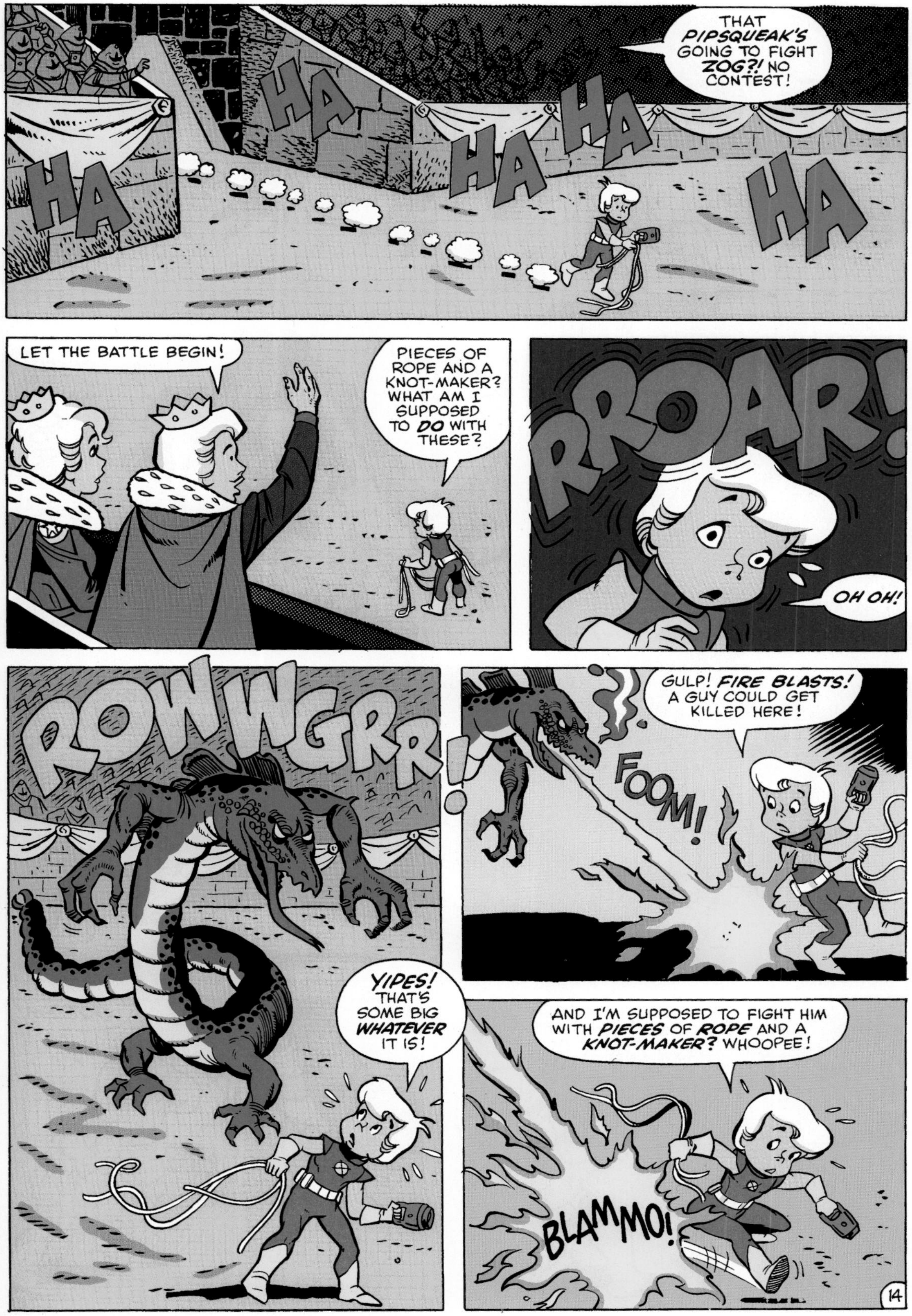
HA
HA
HA
HA
THAT PIPSQUEAK'S GOING TO FIGHT ZOG?! NO CONTEST!
HA
HA
LET THE BATTLE BEGIN!
PIECES OF ROPE AND A KNOT-MAKER? WHAT AM I SUPPOSED TO DO WITH THESE?
RROAR!
OH OH!
ROWWGRR!
YIPES! THAT'S SOME BIG WHATEVER IT IS!
GULP! FIRE BLASTS! A GUY COULD GET KILLED HERE!
FOOM!
AND I'M SUPPOSED TO FIGHT HIM WITH PIECES OF ROPE AND A KNOT-MAKER? WHOOPEE!
BLAMMO!
14

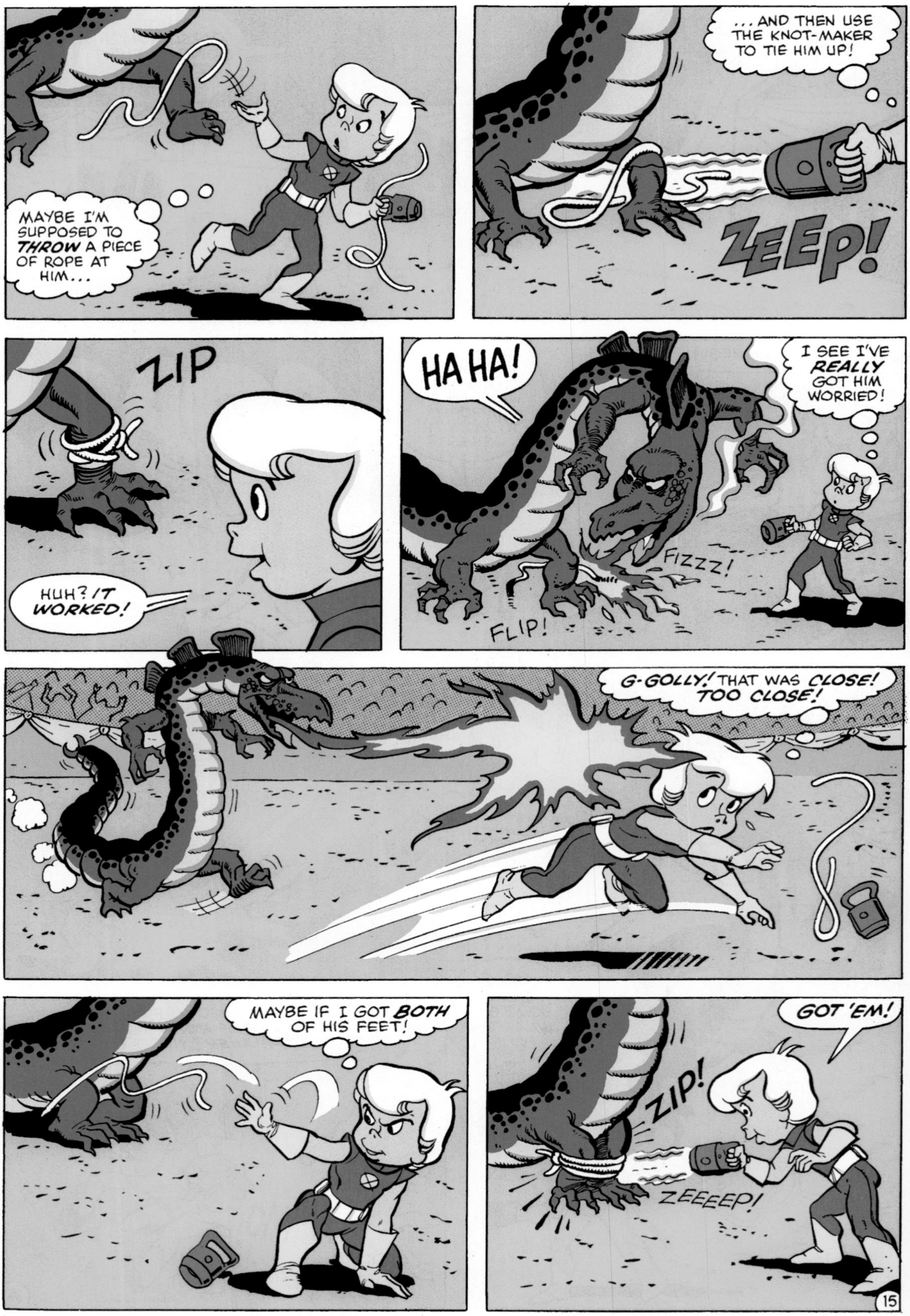
MAYBE I'M SUPPOSED TO THROW A PIECE OF ROPE AT HIM...
...AND THEN USE THE KNOT-MAKER TO TIE HIM UP!
ZEEP!
ZIP
HUH? IT WORKED!
HA HA!
I SEE I'VE REALLY GOT HIM WORRIED!
FIZZZ!
FLIP!
G-GOLLY! THAT WAS CLOSE! TOO CLOSE!
MAYBE IF I GOT BOTH OF HIS FEET!
GOT 'EM!
ZIP!
ZEEEEP!
15

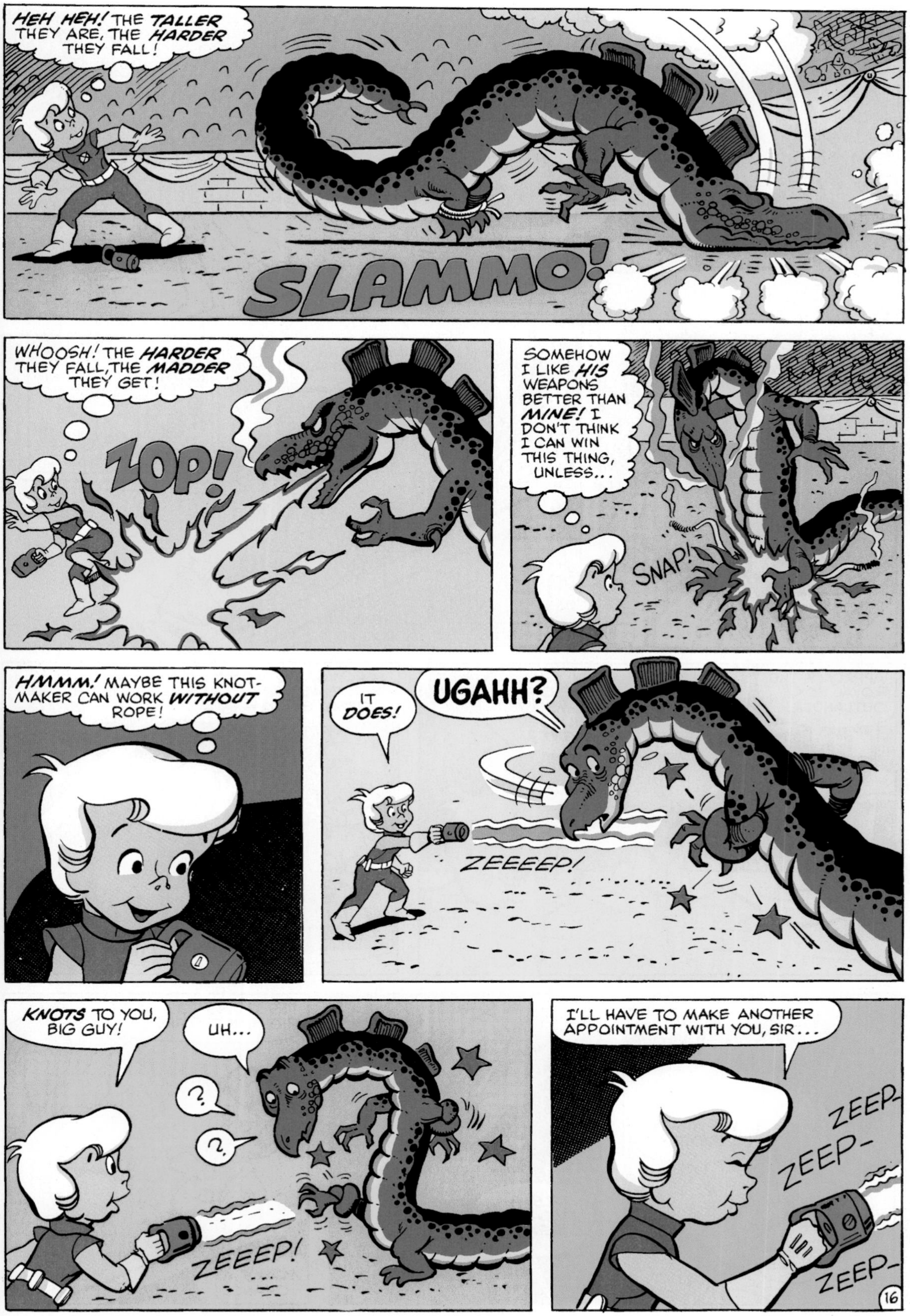
HEH HEH! THE TALLER THEY ARE, THE HARDER THEY FALL!
SLAMMO!
WHOOSH! THE HARDER THEY FALL, THE MADDER THEY GET!
ZOP!
SOMEHOW I LIKE HIS WEAPONS BETTER THAN MINE! I DON'T THINK I CAN WIN THIS THING, UNLESS...
SNAP!
HMMM! MAYBE THIS KNOT-MAKER CAN WORK WITHOUT ROPE!
IT DOES!
UGAHH?
ZEEEEP!
KNOTS TO YOU, BIG GUY!
UH...
?
?
ZEEEP!
I'LL HAVE TO MAKE ANOTHER APPOINTMENT WITH YOU, SIR...
ZEEP-
ZEEP-
ZEEP-
16

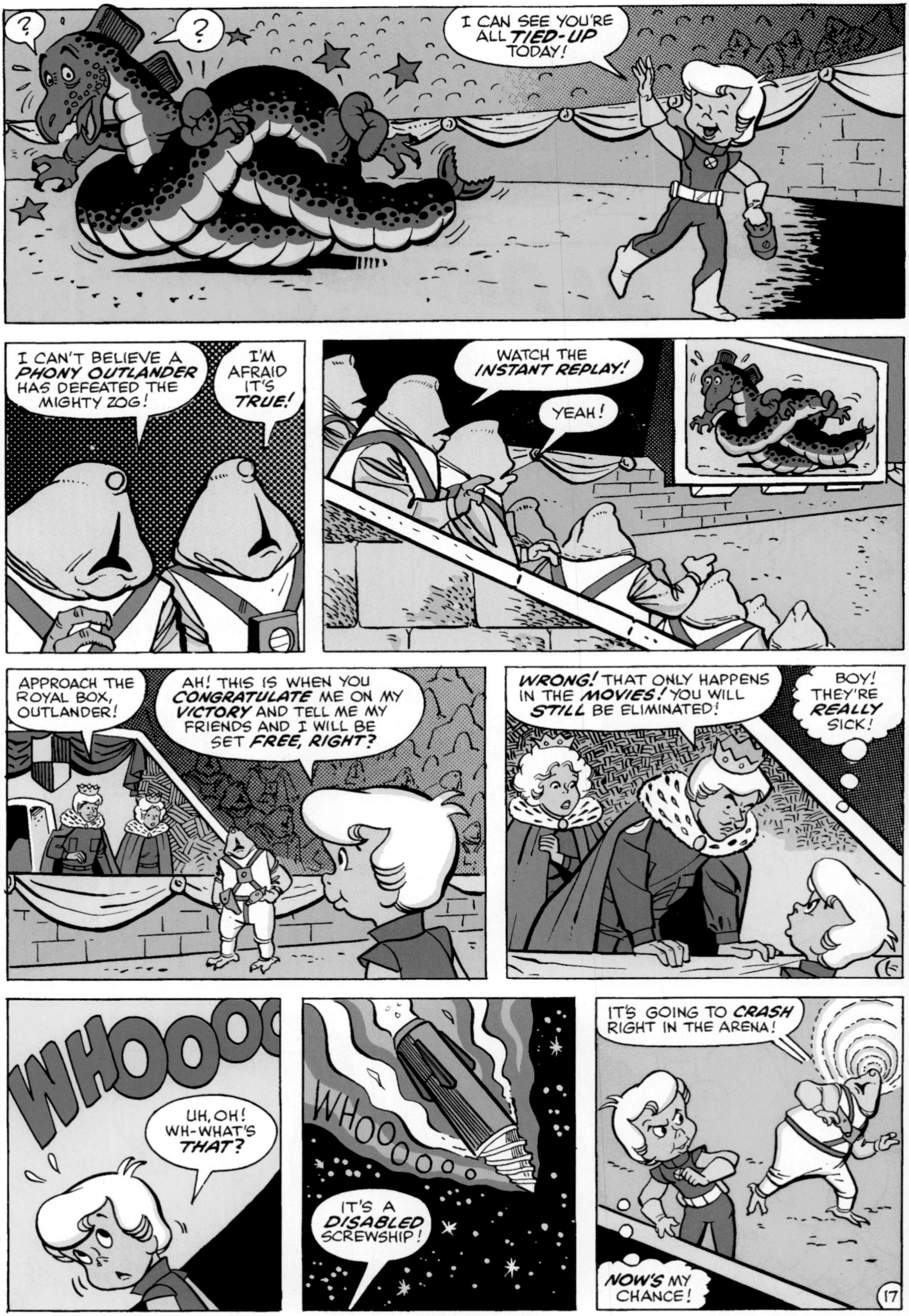
?
?
I CAN SEE YOU'RE ALL TIED-UP TODAY!
I CAN'T BELIEVE A PHONY OUTLANDER HAS DEFEATED THE MIGHTY ZOG!
I'M AFRAID IT'S TRUE!
WATCH THE INSTANT REPLAY!
YEAH!
APPROACH THE ROYAL BOX, OUTLANDER!
AH! THIS IS WHEN YOU CONGRATULATE ME ON MY VICTORY AND TELL ME MY FRIENDS AND I WILL BE SET FREE, RIGHT?
WRONG! THAT ONLY HAPPENS IN THE MOVIES! YOU WILL STILL BE ELIMINATED!
BOY! THEY'RE REALLY SICK!
WHOOOO
UH, OH! WH-WHAT'S THAT?
WHOOooooo
IT'S A DISABLED SCREWSHIP!
IT'S GOING TO CRASH RIGHT IN THE ARENA!
NOW'S MY CHANCE!
17

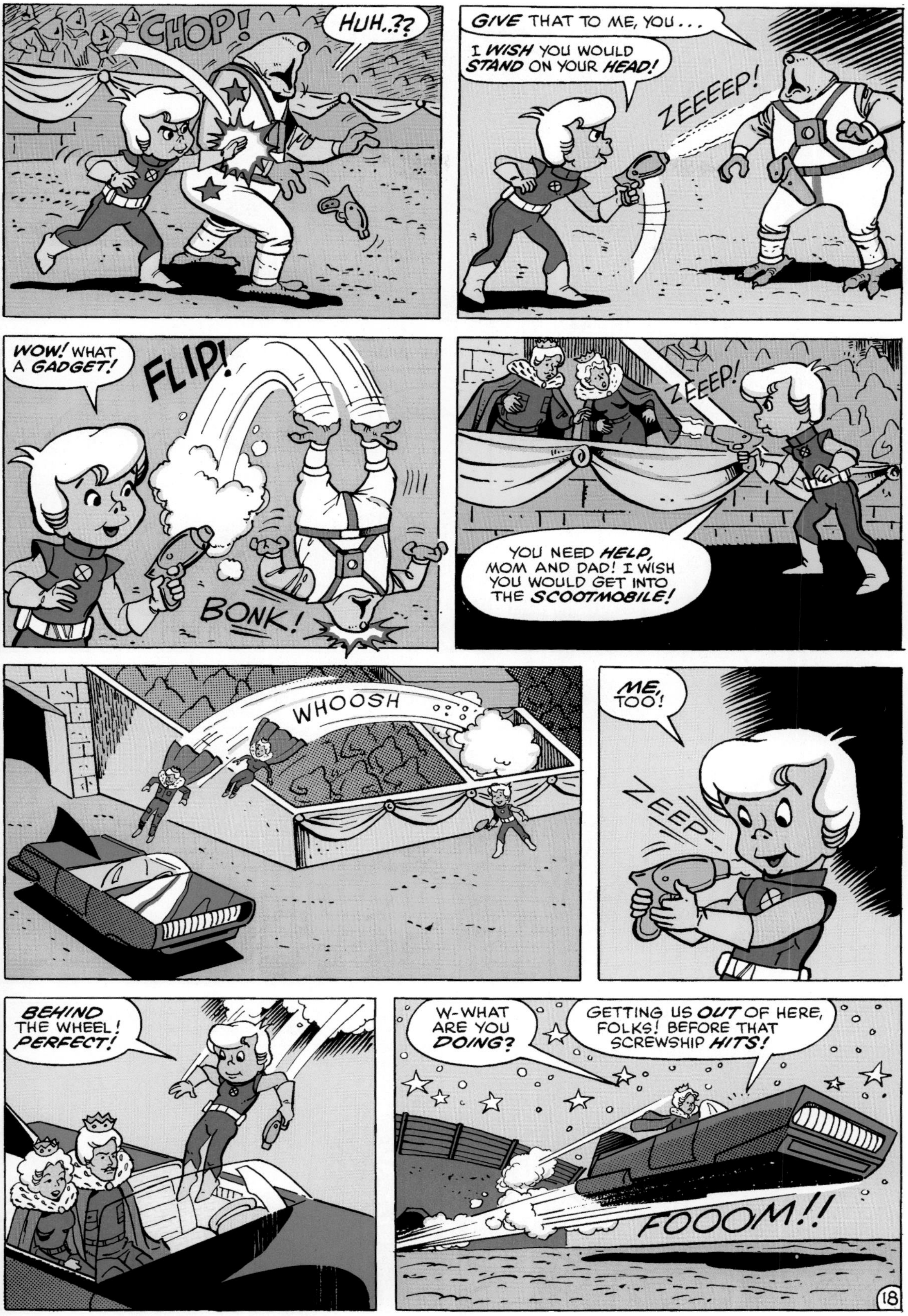
CHOP!
HUH..??
GIVE THAT TO ME, YOU...
I WISH YOU WOULD STAND ON YOUR HEAD!
ZEEEEP!
WOW! WHAT A GADGET!
FLIP!
BONK!
ZEEEP!
YOU NEED HELP, MOM AND DAD! I WISH YOU WOULD GET INTO THE SCOOTMOBILE!
WHOOSH
ME, TOO!
ZEEP--
BEHIND THE WHEEL! PERFECT!
W-WHAT ARE YOU DOING?
GETTING US OUT OF HERE, FOLKS! BEFORE THAT SCREWSHIP HITS!
FOOOM!!
18

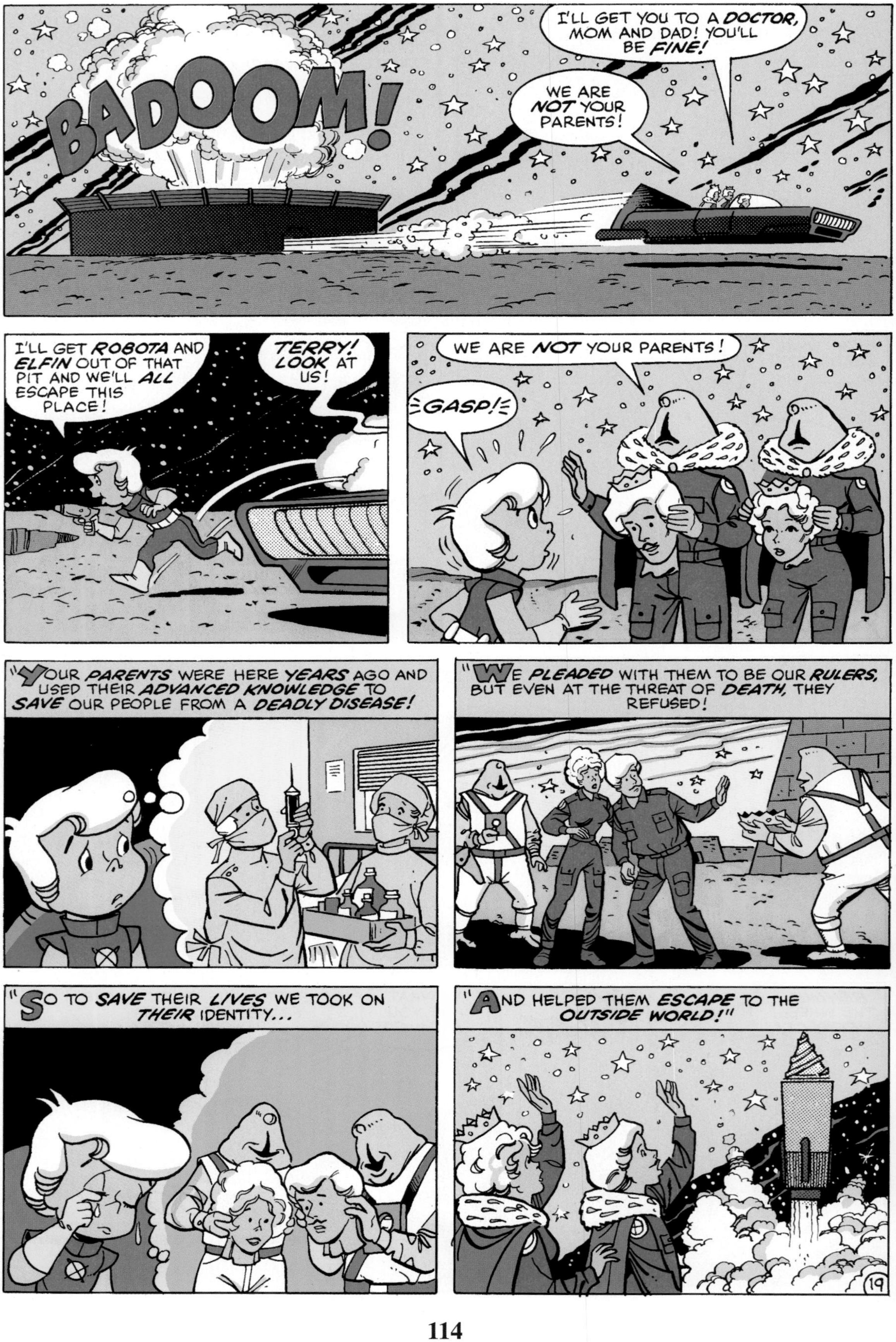
BADOOOM!
I'LL GET YOU TO A DOCTOR, MOM AND DAD! YOU'LL BE FINE!
WE ARE NOT YOUR PARENTS!
I'LL GET ROBOTA AND ELFIN OUT OF THAT PIT AND WE'LL ALL ESCAPE THIS PLACE!
TERRY! LOOK AT US!
WE ARE NOT YOUR PARENTS!
GASP!
"YOUR PARENTS WERE HERE YEARS AGO AND USED THEIR ADVANCED KNOWLEDGE TO SAVE OUR PEOPLE FROM A DEADLY DISEASE!
"WE PLEADED WITH THEM TO BE OUR RULERS, BUT EVEN AT THE THREAT OF DEATH, THEY REFUSED!
"SO TO SAVE THEIR LIVES WE TOOK ON THEIR IDENTITY...
"AND HELPED THEM ESCAPE TO THE OUTSIDE WORLD!"
19

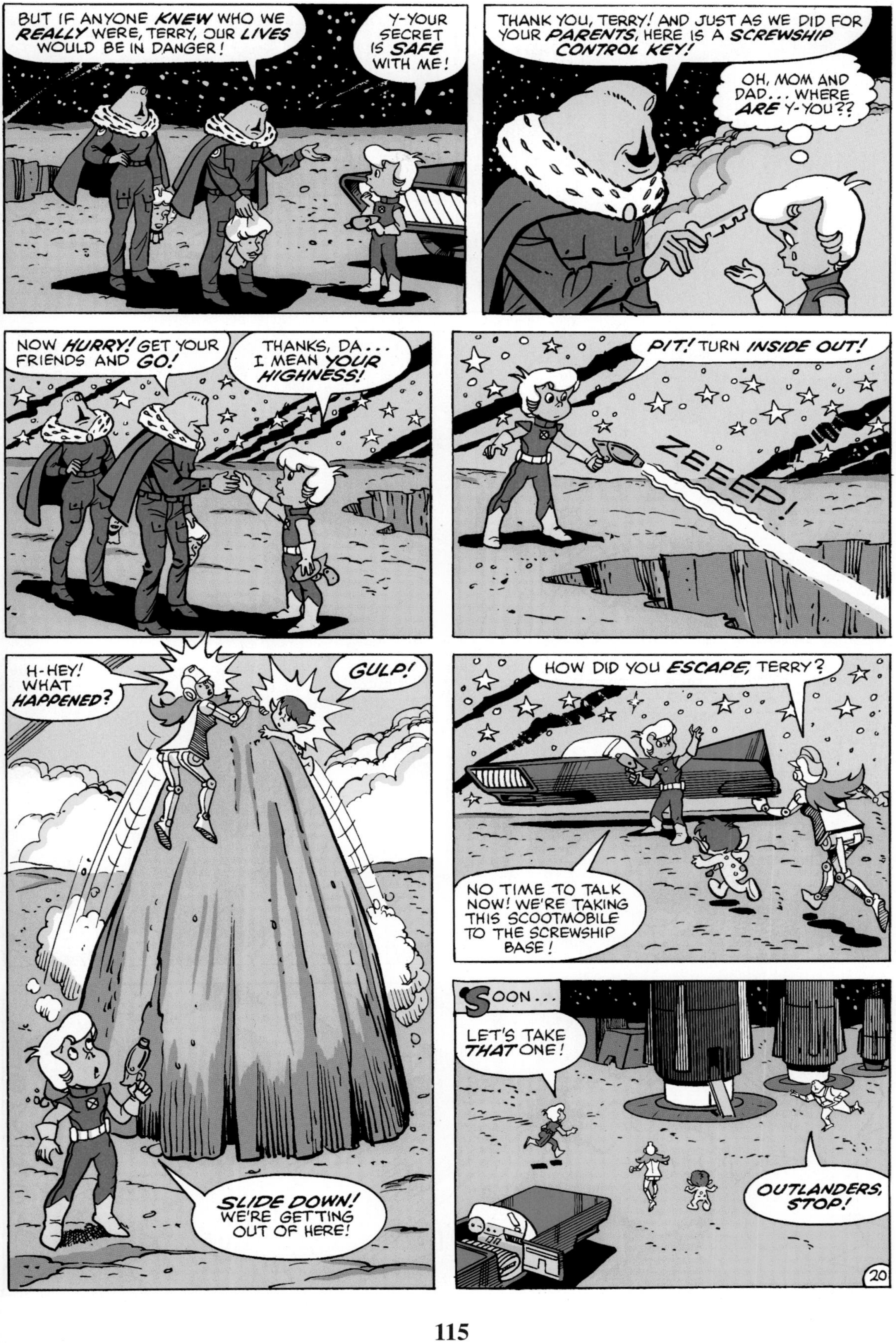
BUT IF ANYONE KNEW WHO WE REALLY WERE, TERRY, OUR LIVES WOULD BE IN DANGER!
Y-YOUR SECRET IS SAFE WITH ME!
THANK YOU, TERRY! AND JUST AS WE DID FOR YOUR PARENTS, HERE IS A SCREWSHIP CONTROL KEY!
OH, MOM AND DAD... WHERE ARE Y-YOU??
NOW HURRY! GET YOUR FRIENDS AND GO!
THANKS, DA... I MEAN YOUR HIGHNESS!
PIT! TURN INSIDE OUT!
ZEEEP!
H-HEY! WHAT HAPPENED?
GULP!
SLIDE DOWN! WE'RE GETTING OUT OF HERE!
HOW DID YOU ESCAPE, TERRY?
NO TIME TO TALK NOW! WE'RE TAKING THIS SCOOTMOBILE TO THE SCREWSHIP BASE!
SOON...
LET'S TAKE THAT ONE!
OUTLANDERS, STOP!
20

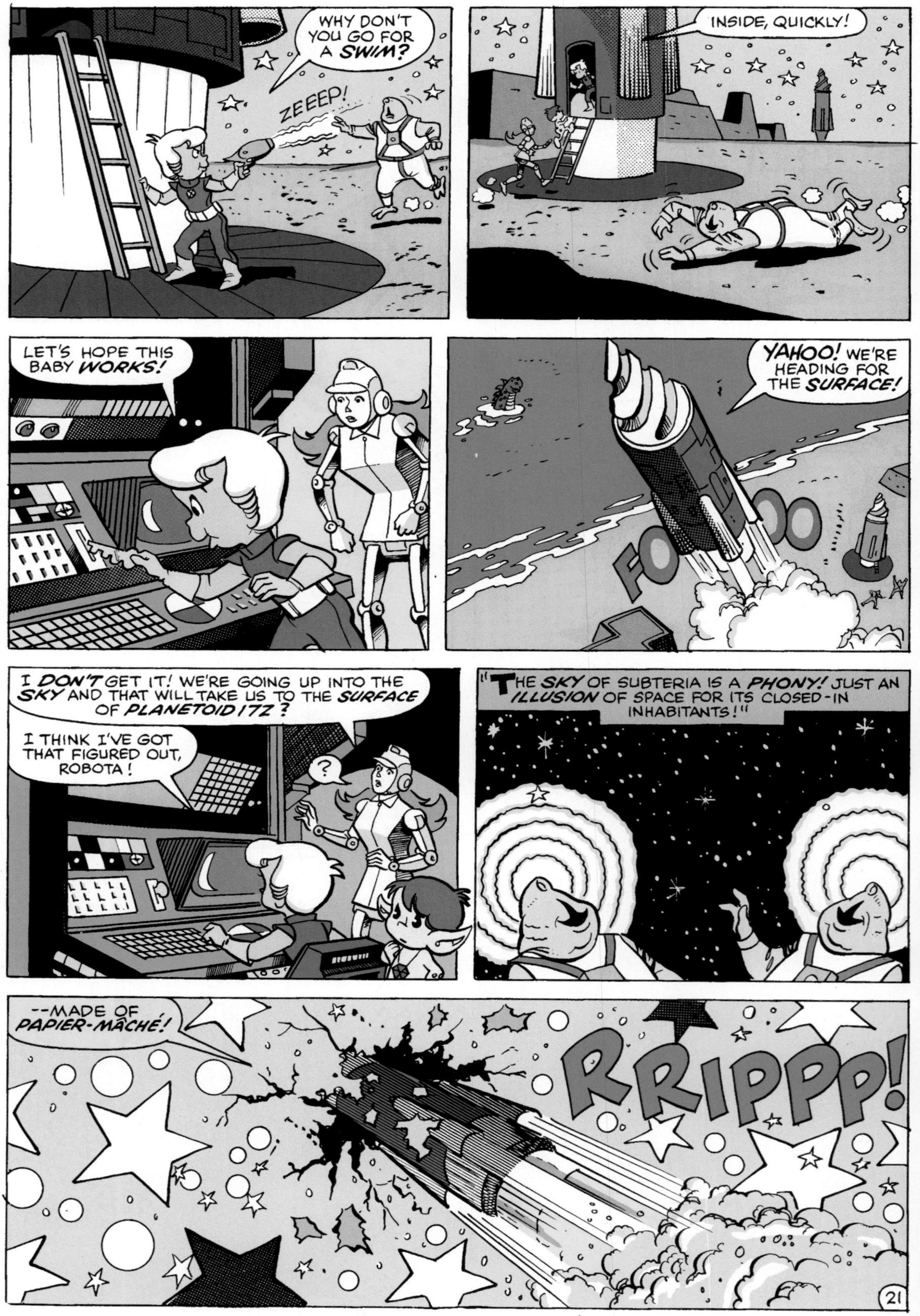
WHY DON'T YOU GO FOR A SWIM?
ZEEEP!
INSIDE, QUICKLY!
LET'S HOPE THIS BABY WORKS!
YAHOO! WE'RE HEADING FOR THE SURFACE!
FOOOO
I DON'T GET IT! WE'RE GOING UP INTO THE SKY AND THAT WILL TAKE US TO THE SURFACE OF PLANETOID 17Z?
I THINK I'VE GOT THAT FIGURED OUT, ROBOTA!
?
"THE SKY OF SUBTERIA IS A PHONY! JUST AN ILLUSION OF SPACE FOR ITS CLOSED-IN INHABITANTS!"
--MADE OF PAPIER-MÂCHÉ!
RRIPPP!
21

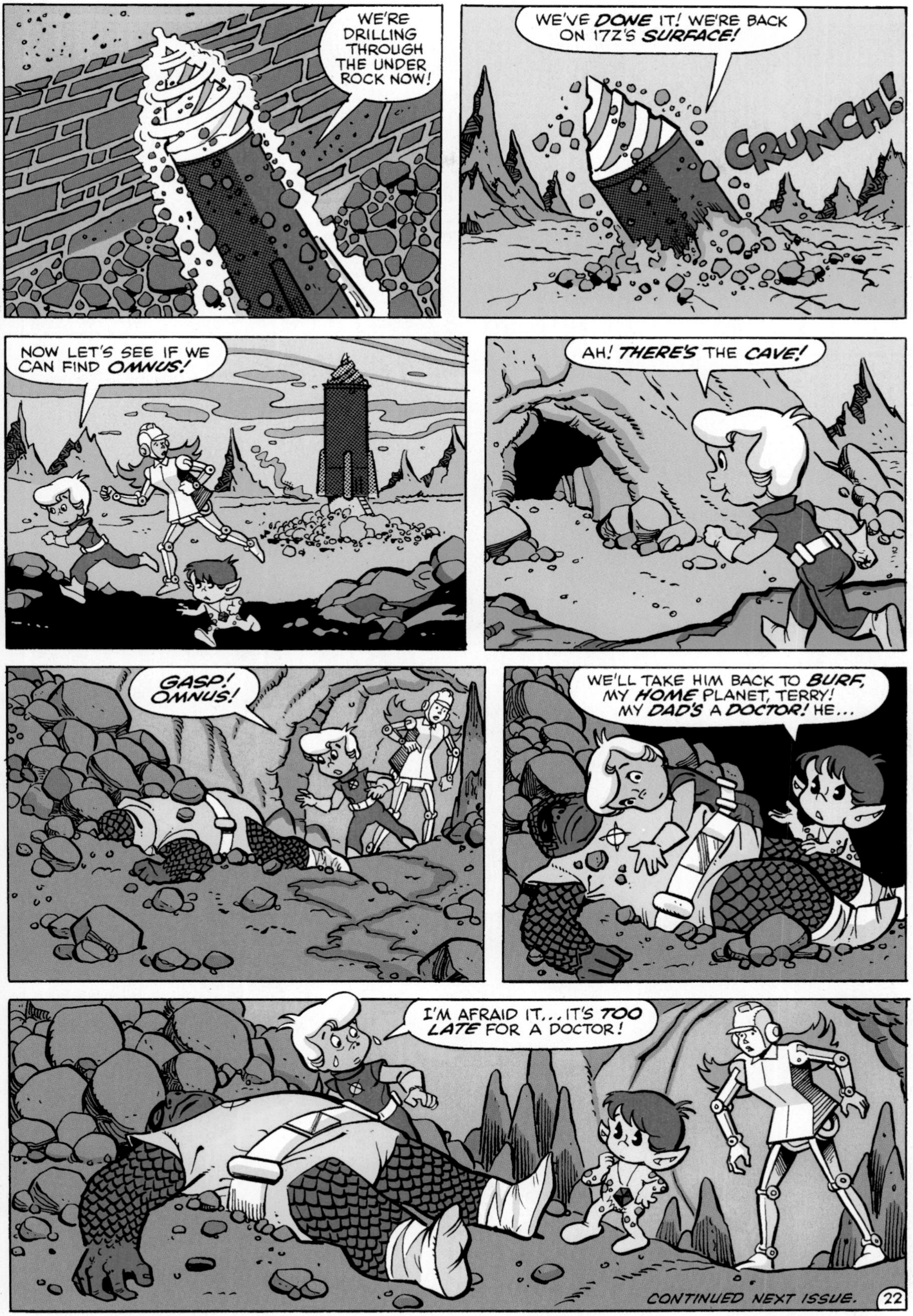
WE'RE DRILLING THROUGH THE UNDER ROCK NOW!
WE'VE DONE IT! WE'RE BACK ON 17Z'S SURFACE!
CRUNCH!
NOW LET'S SEE IF WE CAN FIND OMNUS!
AH! THERE'S THE CAVE!
GASP! OMNUS!
WE'LL TAKE HIM BACK TO BURF, MY HOME PLANET, TERRY! MY DAD'S A DOCTOR! HE...
I'M AFRAID IT... IT'S TOO LATE FOR A DOCTOR!
CONTINUED NEXT ISSUE.
22

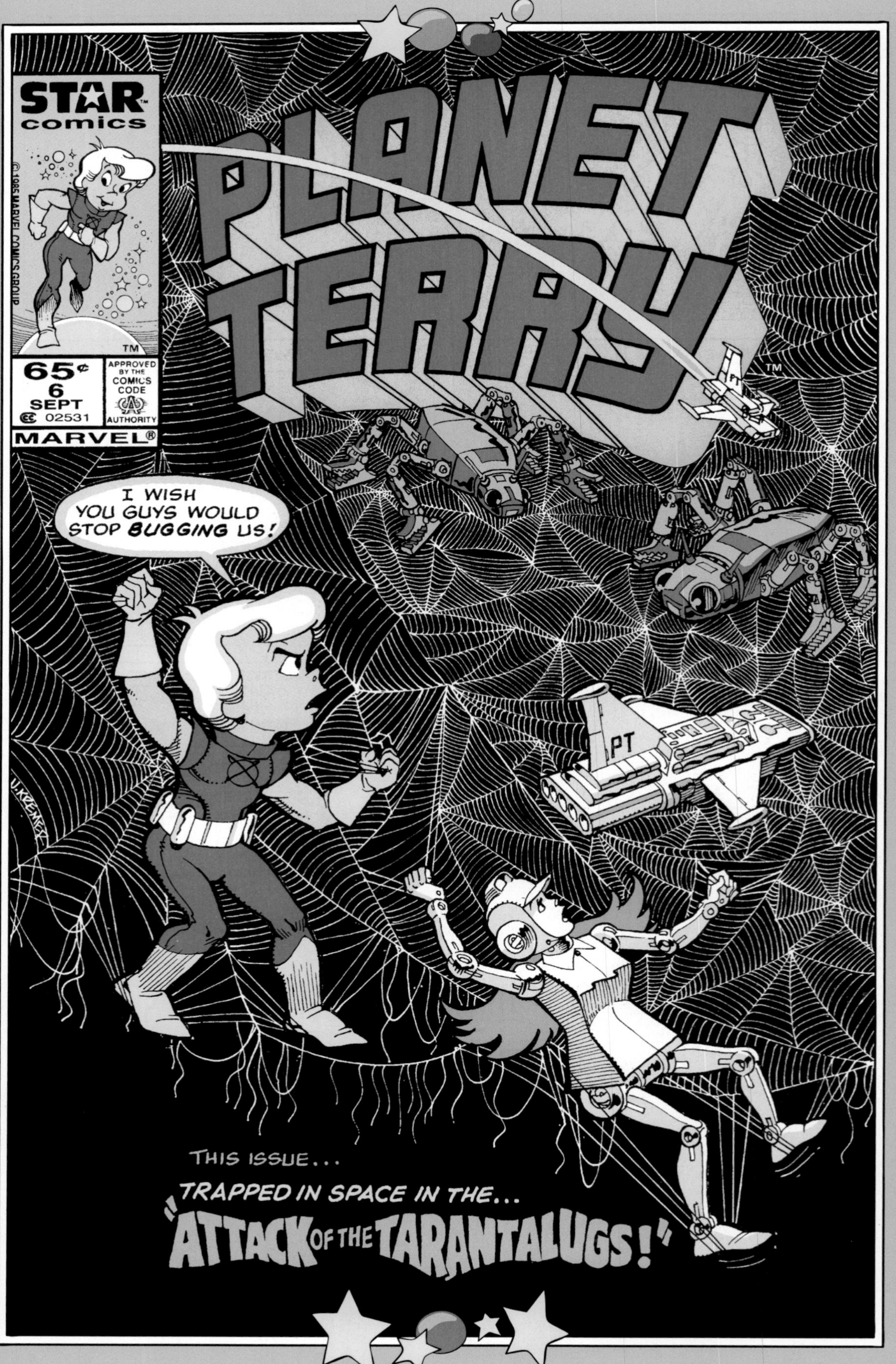
STAR comics
© 1985 MARVEL COMICS GROUP
65¢
6
SEPT
02531
APPROVED BY THE COMICS CODE AUTHORITY
MARVEL®
PLANET TERRY™
I WISH YOU GUYS WOULD STOP BUGGING US!
THIS ISSUE...
TRAPPED IN SPACE IN THE...
"ATTACK OF THE TARANTALUGS!"

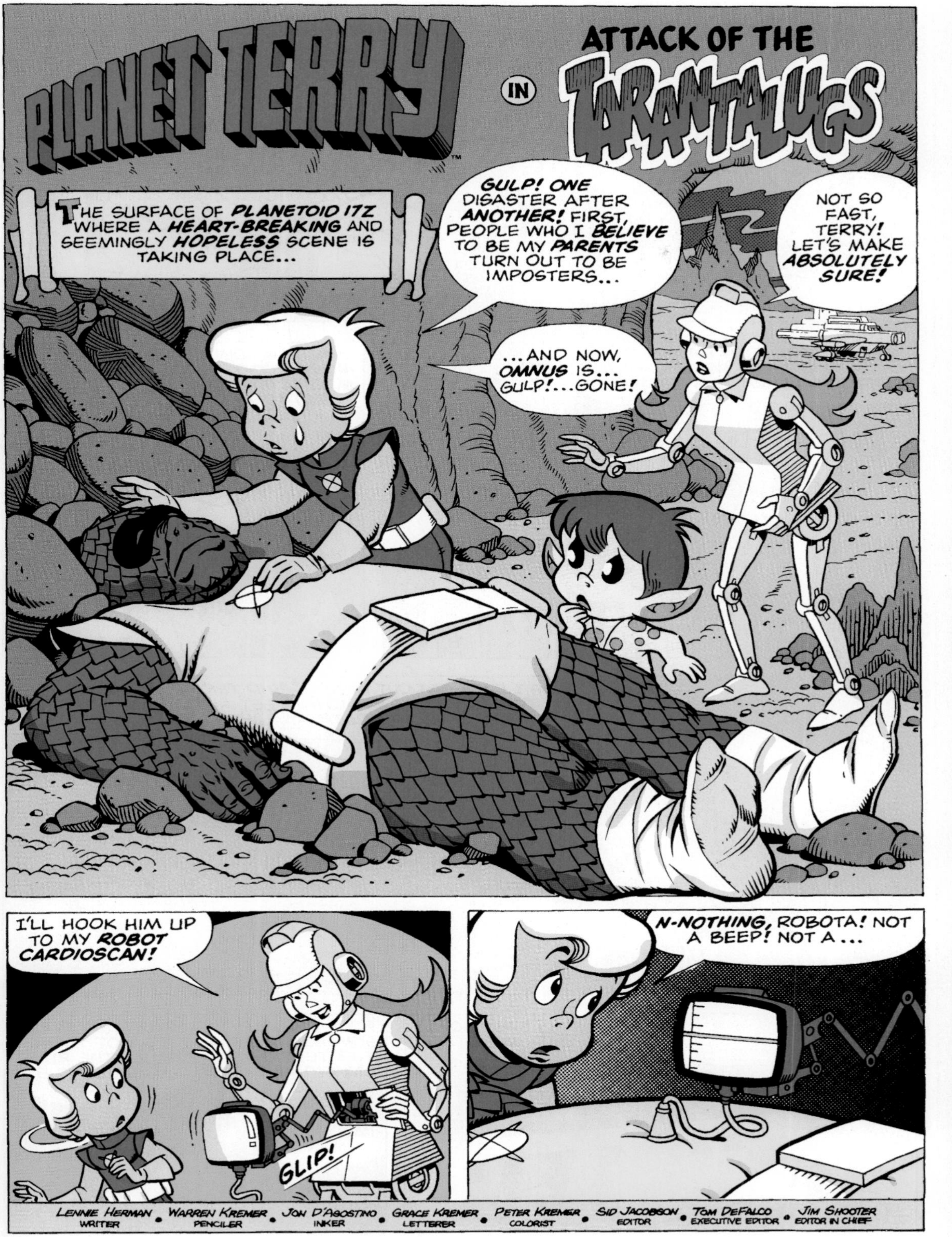

PLANET TERRY
IN
ATTACK OF THE
TARANTALUGS
THE SURFACE OF PLANETOID 17Z WHERE A HEART-BREAKING AND SEEMINGLY HOPELESS SCENE IS TAKING PLACE...
GULP! ONE DISASTER AFTER ANOTHER! FIRST, PEOPLE WHO I BELIEVE TO BE MY PARENTS TURN OUT TO BE IMPOSTERS...
...AND NOW, OMNUS IS... GULP!...GONE!
NOT SO FAST, TERRY! LET'S MAKE ABSOLUTELY SURE!
I'LL HOOK HIM UP TO MY ROBOT CARDIOSCAN!
GLIP!
N-NOTHING, ROBOTA! NOT A BEEP! NOT A...
LENNIE HERMAN WRITER • WARREN KREMER PENCILER • JON D'AGOSTINO INKER • GRACE KREMER LETTERER • PETER KREMER COLORIST • SID JACOBSON EDITOR • TOM DEFALCO EXECUTIVE EDITOR • JIM SHOOTER EDITOR IN CHIEF

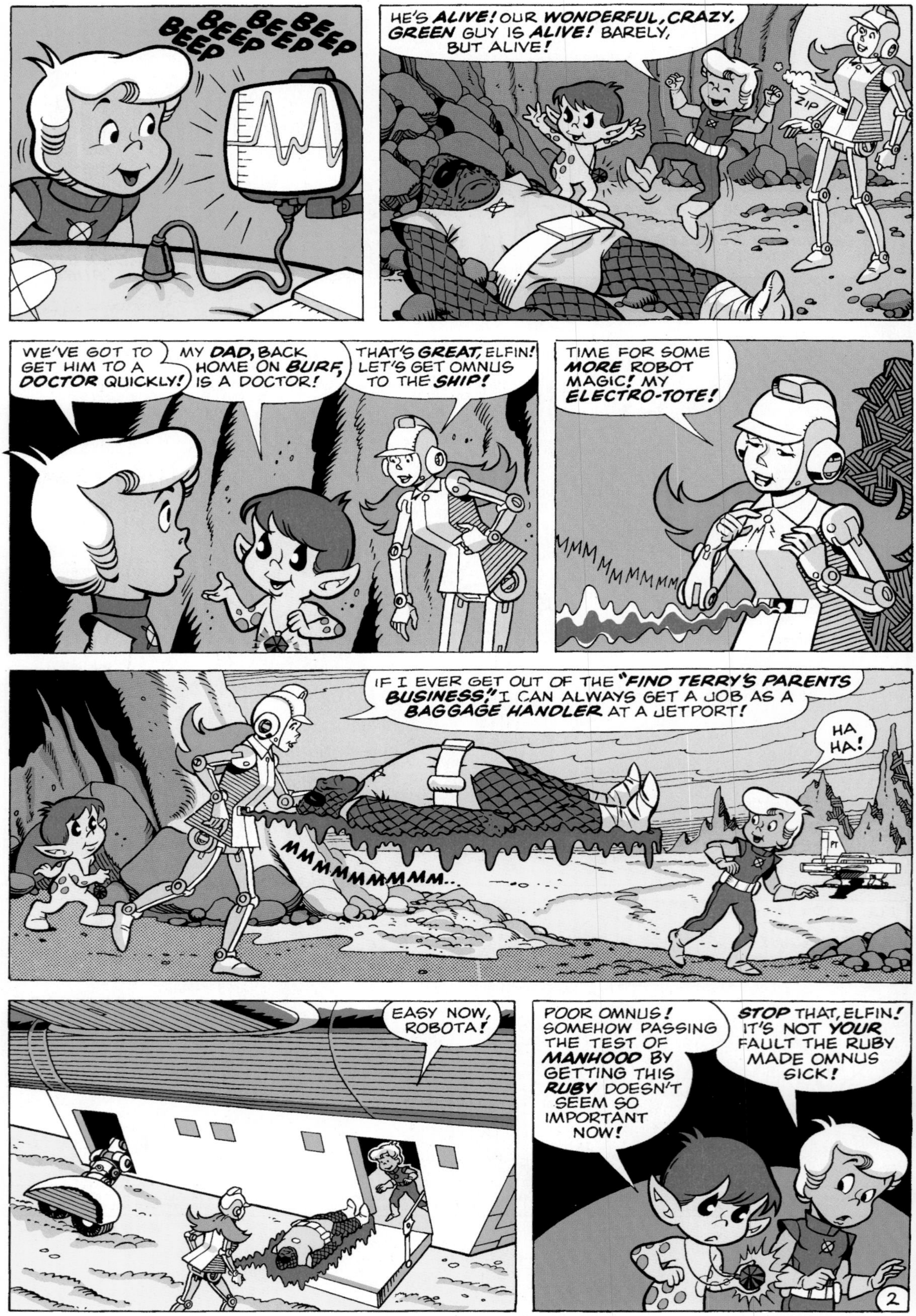
BEEP BEEP BEEP BEEP
HE'S ALIVE! OUR WONDERFUL, CRAZY, GREEN GUY IS ALIVE! BARELY, BUT ALIVE!
ZIP
WE'VE GOT TO GET HIM TO A DOCTOR QUICKLY!
MY DAD, BACK HOME ON BURF, IS A DOCTOR!
THAT'S GREAT, ELFIN! LET'S GET OMNUS TO THE SHIP!
TIME FOR SOME MORE ROBOT MAGIC! MY ELECTRO-TOTE!
MMMMMMMMMMM
IF I EVER GET OUT OF THE "FIND TERRY'S PARENTS BUSINESS," I CAN ALWAYS GET A JOB AS A BAGGAGE HANDLER AT A JETPORT!
HA HA!
MMMMMMMMMMM...
EASY NOW, ROBOTA!
POOR OMNUS! SOMEHOW PASSING THE TEST OF MANHOOD BY GETTING THIS RUBY DOESN'T SEEM SO IMPORTANT NOW!
STOP THAT, ELFIN! IT'S NOT YOUR FAULT THE RUBY MADE OMNUS SICK!
2

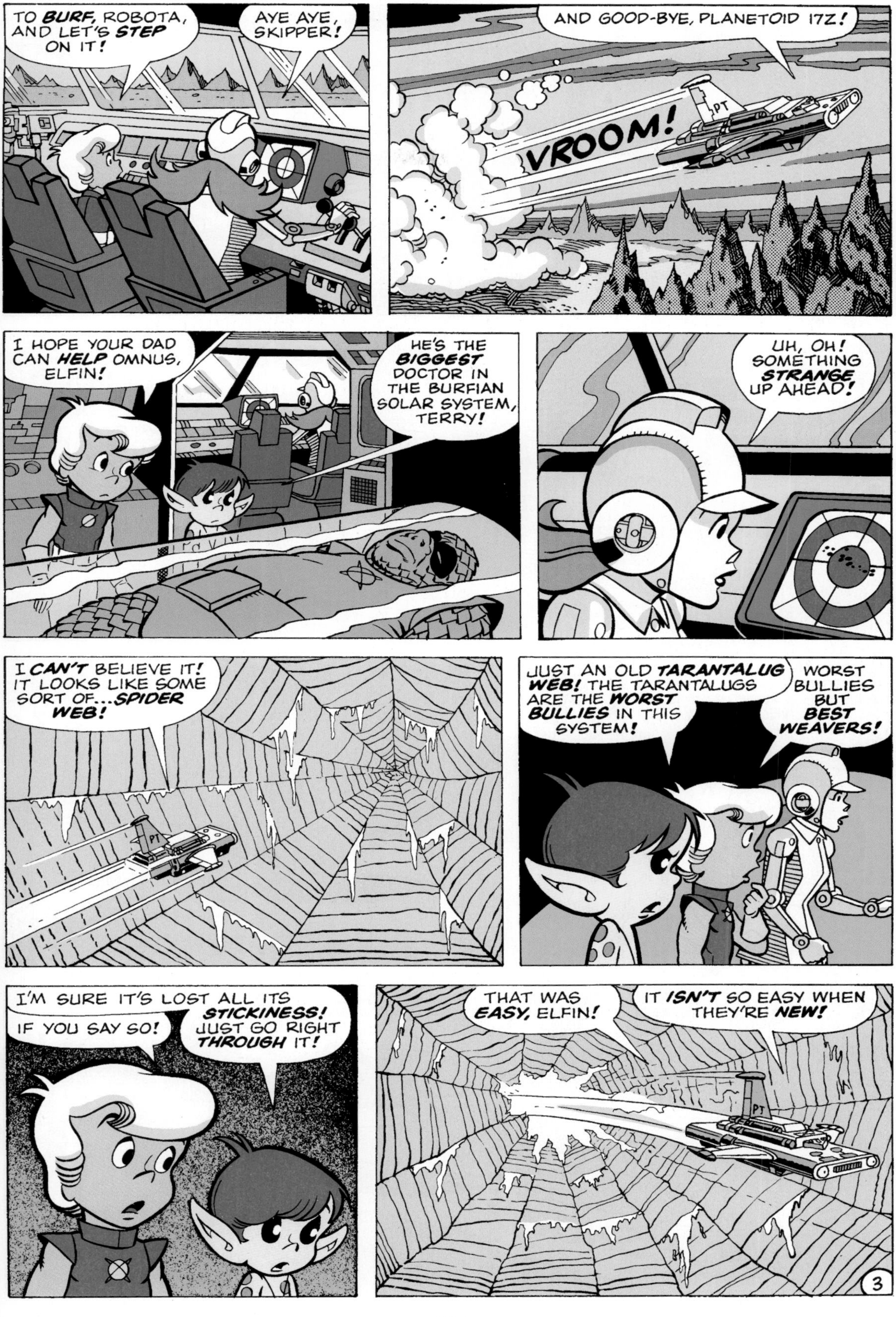

TO BURF, ROBOTA, AND LET'S STEP ON IT!
AYE AYE, SKIPPER!
AND GOOD-BYE, PLANETOID 17Z!
VROOM!
PT
I HOPE YOUR DAD CAN HELP OMNUS, ELFIN!
HE'S THE BIGGEST DOCTOR IN THE BURFIAN SOLAR SYSTEM, TERRY!
UH, OH! SOMETHING STRANGE UP AHEAD!
I CAN'T BELIEVE IT! IT LOOKS LIKE SOME SORT OF...SPIDER WEB!
PT
JUST AN OLD TARANTALUG WEB! THE TARANTALUGS ARE THE WORST BULLIES IN THIS SYSTEM!
WORST BULLIES BUT BEST WEAVERS!
I'M SURE IT'S LOST ALL ITS STICKINESS! JUST GO RIGHT THROUGH IT!
IF YOU SAY SO!
THAT WAS EASY, ELFIN!
IT ISN'T SO EASY WHEN THEY'RE NEW!
PT
3

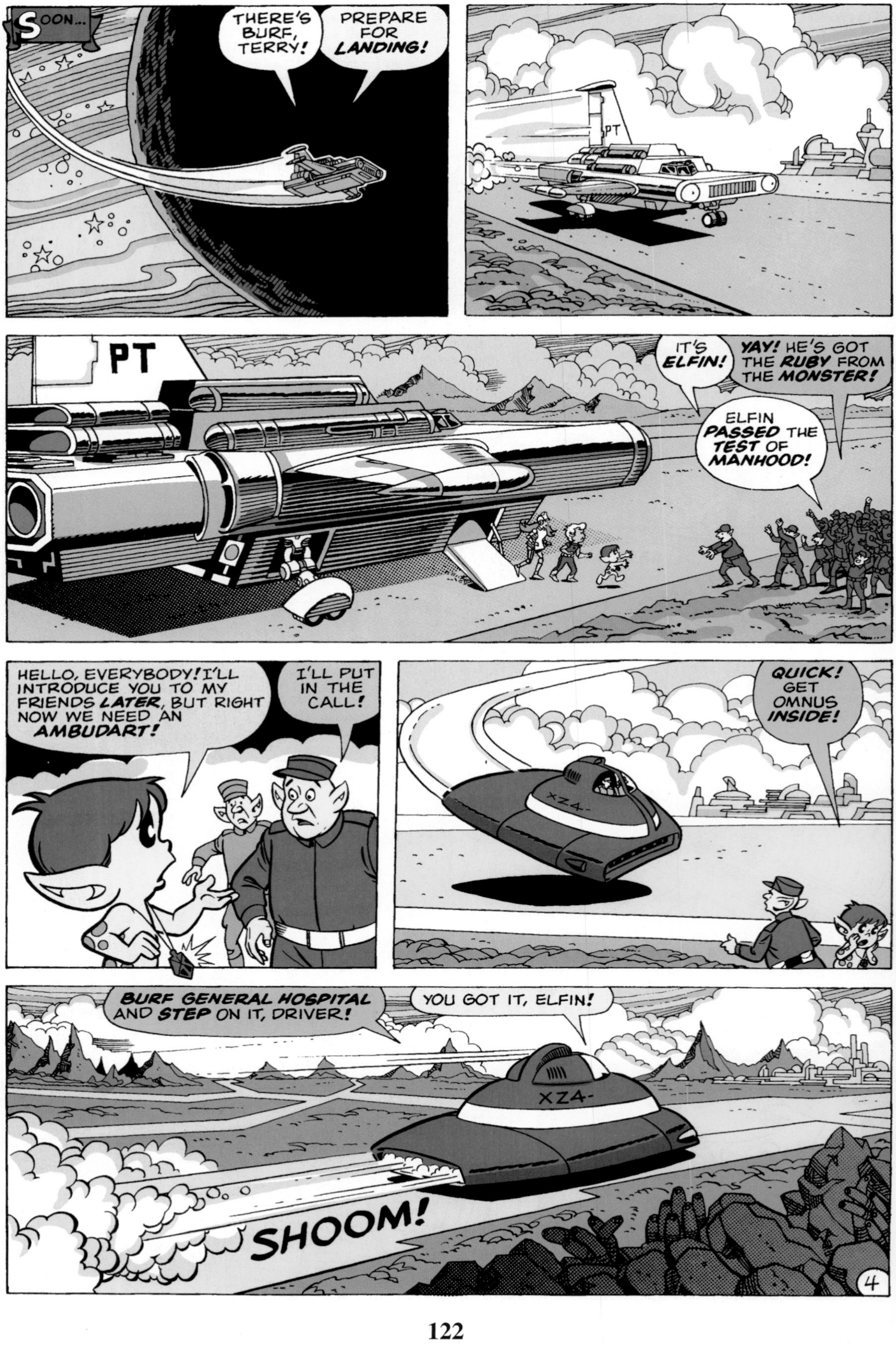
SOON...
THERE'S BURF, TERRY!
PREPARE FOR LANDING!
PT
PT
IT'S ELFIN!
YAY! HE'S GOT THE RUBY FROM THE MONSTER!
ELFIN PASSED THE TEST OF MANHOOD!
HELLO, EVERYBODY! I'LL INTRODUCE YOU TO MY FRIENDS LATER, BUT RIGHT NOW WE NEED AN AMBUDART!
I'LL PUT IN THE CALL!
QUICK! GET OMNUS INSIDE!
XZ4-
BURF GENERAL HOSPITAL AND STEP ON IT, DRIVER!
YOU GOT IT, ELFIN!
XZ4-
SHOOM!
4

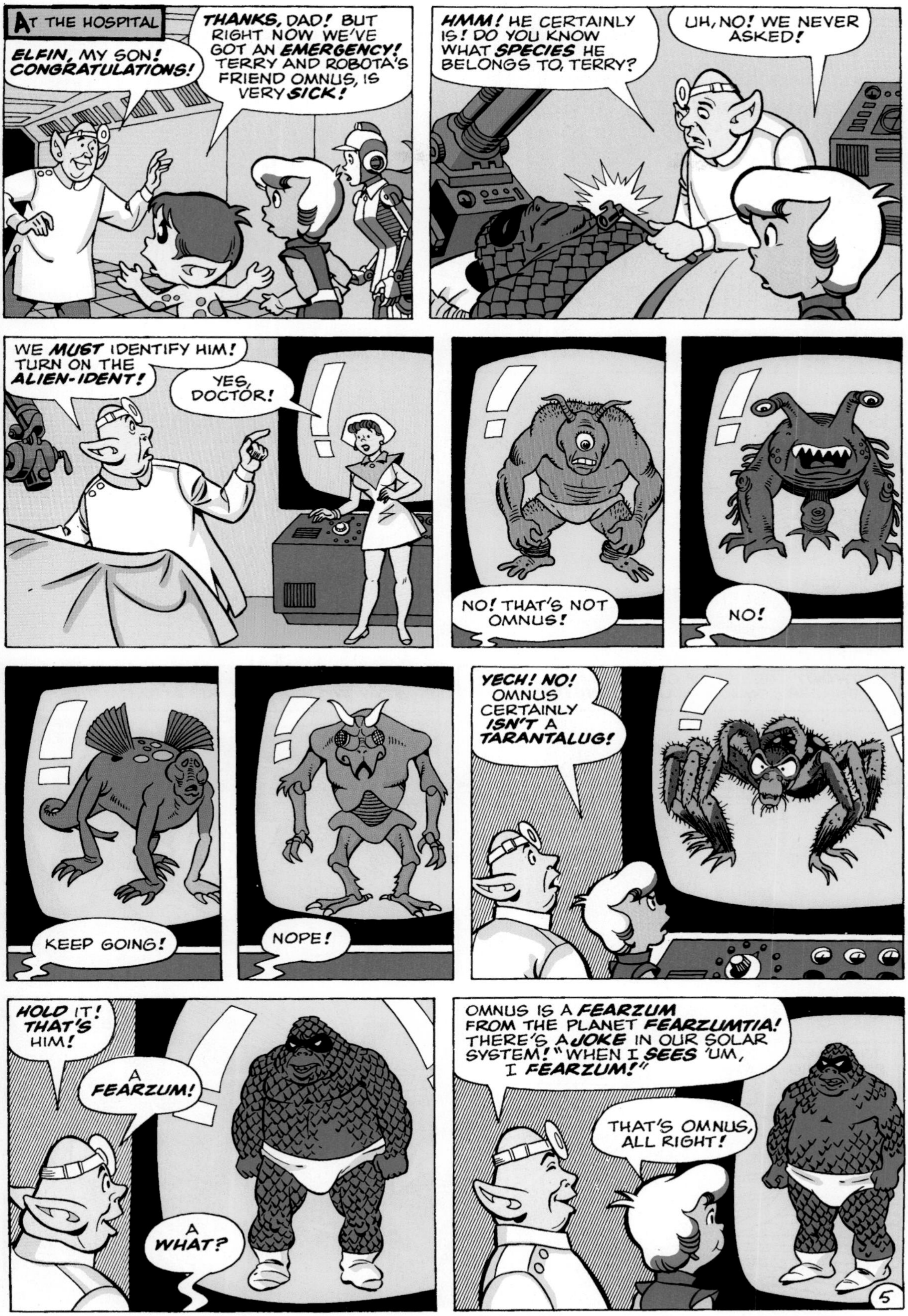
AT THE HOSPITAL
ELFIN, MY SON! CONGRATULATIONS!
THANKS, DAD! BUT RIGHT NOW WE'VE GOT AN EMERGENCY! TERRY AND ROBOTA'S FRIEND OMNUS, IS VERY SICK!
HMM! HE CERTAINLY IS! DO YOU KNOW WHAT SPECIES HE BELONGS TO, TERRY?
UH, NO! WE NEVER ASKED!
WE MUST IDENTIFY HIM! TURN ON THE ALIEN-IDENT!
YES, DOCTOR!
NO! THAT'S NOT OMNUS!
NO!
KEEP GOING!
NOPE!
YECH! NO! OMNUS CERTAINLY ISN'T A TARANTALUG!
HOLD IT! THAT'S HIM!
A FEARZUM!
A WHAT?
OMNUS IS A FEARZUM FROM THE PLANET FEARZUMTIA! THERE'S A JOKE IN OUR SOLAR SYSTEM! "WHEN I SEES 'UM, I FEARZUM!"
THAT'S OMNUS, ALL RIGHT!
5

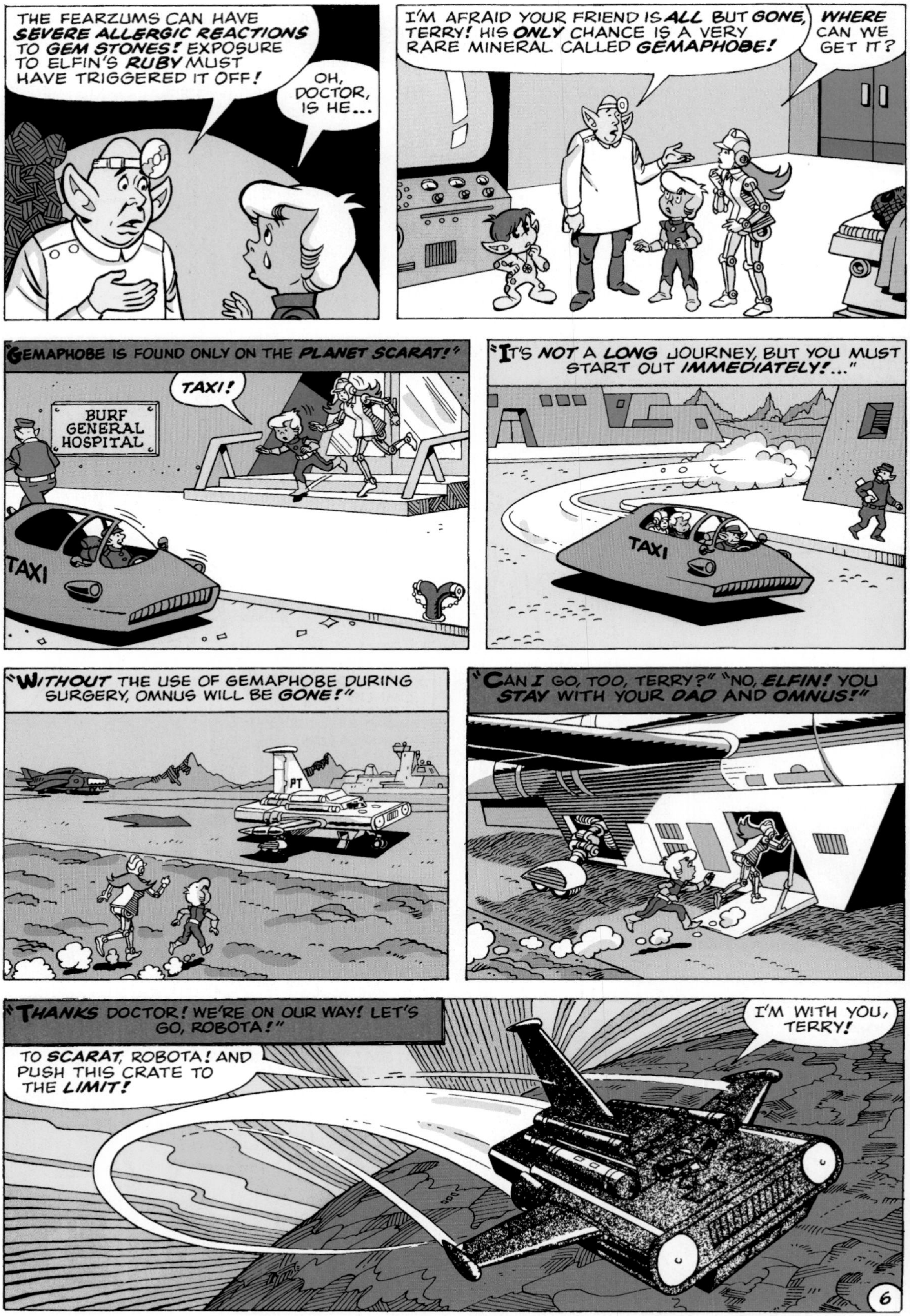
THE FEARZUMS CAN HAVE SEVERE ALLERGIC REACTIONS TO GEM STONES! EXPOSURE TO ELFIN'S RUBY MUST HAVE TRIGGERED IT OFF!
OH, DOCTOR, IS HE...
I'M AFRAID YOUR FRIEND IS ALL BUT GONE, TERRY! HIS ONLY CHANCE IS A VERY RARE MINERAL CALLED GEMAPHOBE!
WHERE CAN WE GET IT?
"GEMAPHOBE IS FOUND ONLY ON THE PLANET SCARAT!"
TAXI!
BURF GENERAL HOSPITAL
TAXI
"IT'S NOT A LONG JOURNEY, BUT YOU MUST START OUT IMMEDIATELY!..."
TAXI
"WITHOUT THE USE OF GEMAPHOBE DURING SURGERY, OMNUS WILL BE GONE!"
PT
"CAN I GO, TOO, TERRY?" "NO, ELFIN! YOU STAY WITH YOUR DAD AND OMNUS!"
"THANKS DOCTOR! WE'RE ON OUR WAY! LET'S GO, ROBOTA!"
I'M WITH YOU, TERRY!
TO SCARAT, ROBOTA! AND PUSH THIS CRATE TO THE LIMIT!
6

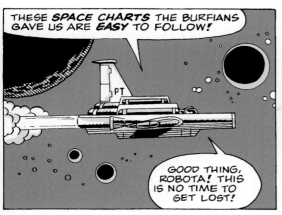

THESE *SPACE CHARTS* THE BURFIANS GAVE US ARE *EASY* TO FOLLOW!

GOOD THING, ROBOTA! THIS IS NO TIME TO GET LOST!

THAT'S IT, TERRY! SCARAT! STRAIGHT AHEAD?

THERE'S SOMETHING...*STRANGE* AROUND THE PLANET! IT LOOKS...*FAMILIAR!*

GASP! IT'S A *WEB*, ROBOTA! LIKE THE ONE WE SAW ON THE WAY TO BURF!

BUT MUCH *LARGER!* IT'S *SURROUNDING* THE PLANET!

ATTENTION! THIS IS *CAPTAIN STING* OF THE TARANTALUG SIEGE FORCE!

THE PLANET SCARAT IS UNDER *TARANTALUG BLOCKADE!* ANY ATTEMPT TO *BREAK* THIS BLOCKADE WILL RESULT IN YOUR *DESTRUCTION!* TURN BACK!

WE *CAN'T* TURN BACK, ROBOTA! WE *MUST* GET THE GEMAPHOBE FOR OMNUS!

I K-KNOW, TERRY!

FULL SPEED AHEAD! WE'LL BREAK *THROUGH* THAT WEB!

7

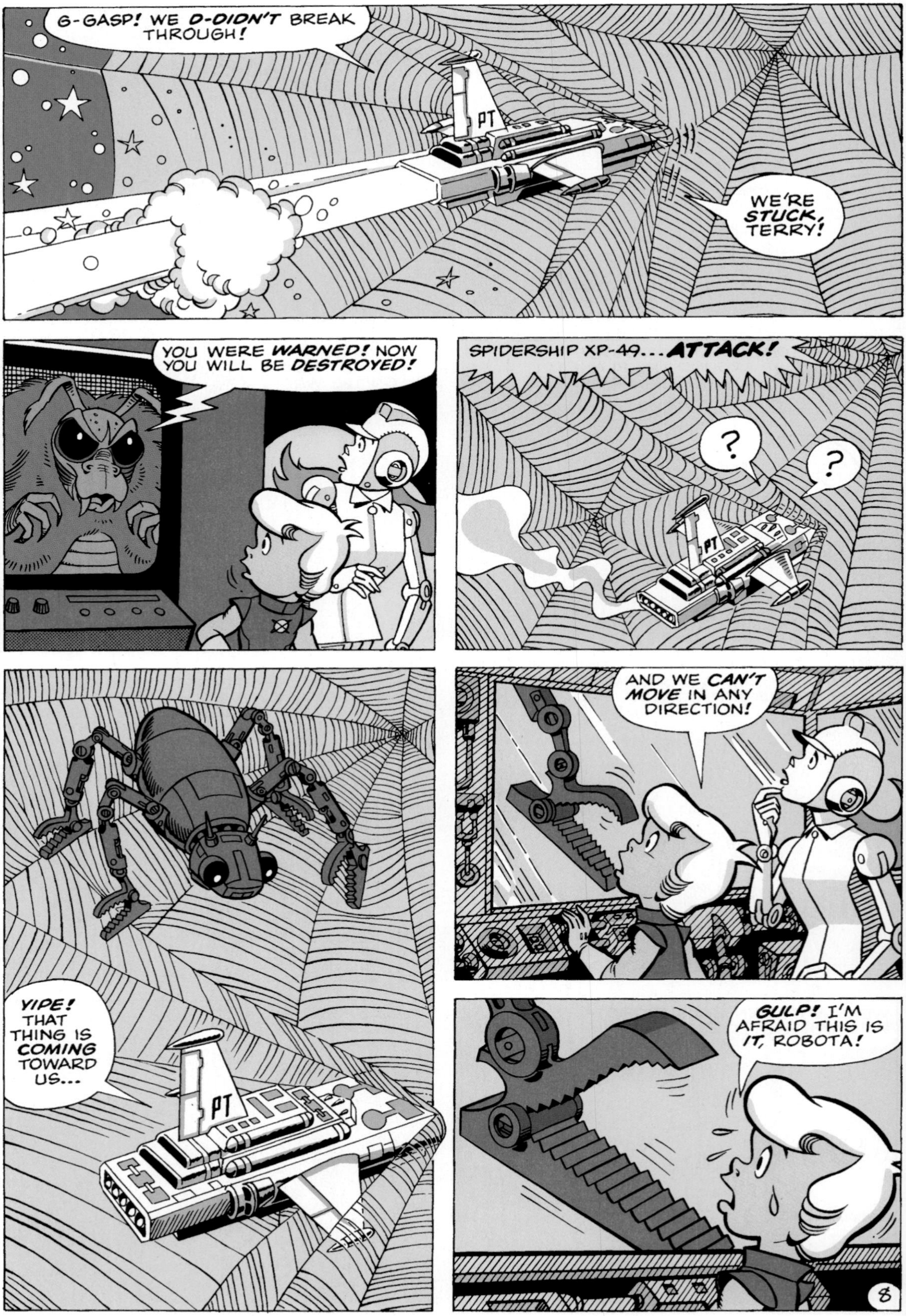
G-GASP! WE D-DIDN'T BREAK THROUGH!
WE'RE STUCK, TERRY!
YOU WERE WARNED! NOW YOU WILL BE DESTROYED!
SPIDERSHIP XP-49... ATTACK!
?
?
AND WE CAN'T MOVE IN ANY DIRECTION!
YIPE! THAT THING IS COMING TOWARD US...
GULP! I'M AFRAID THIS IS IT, ROBOTA!
8

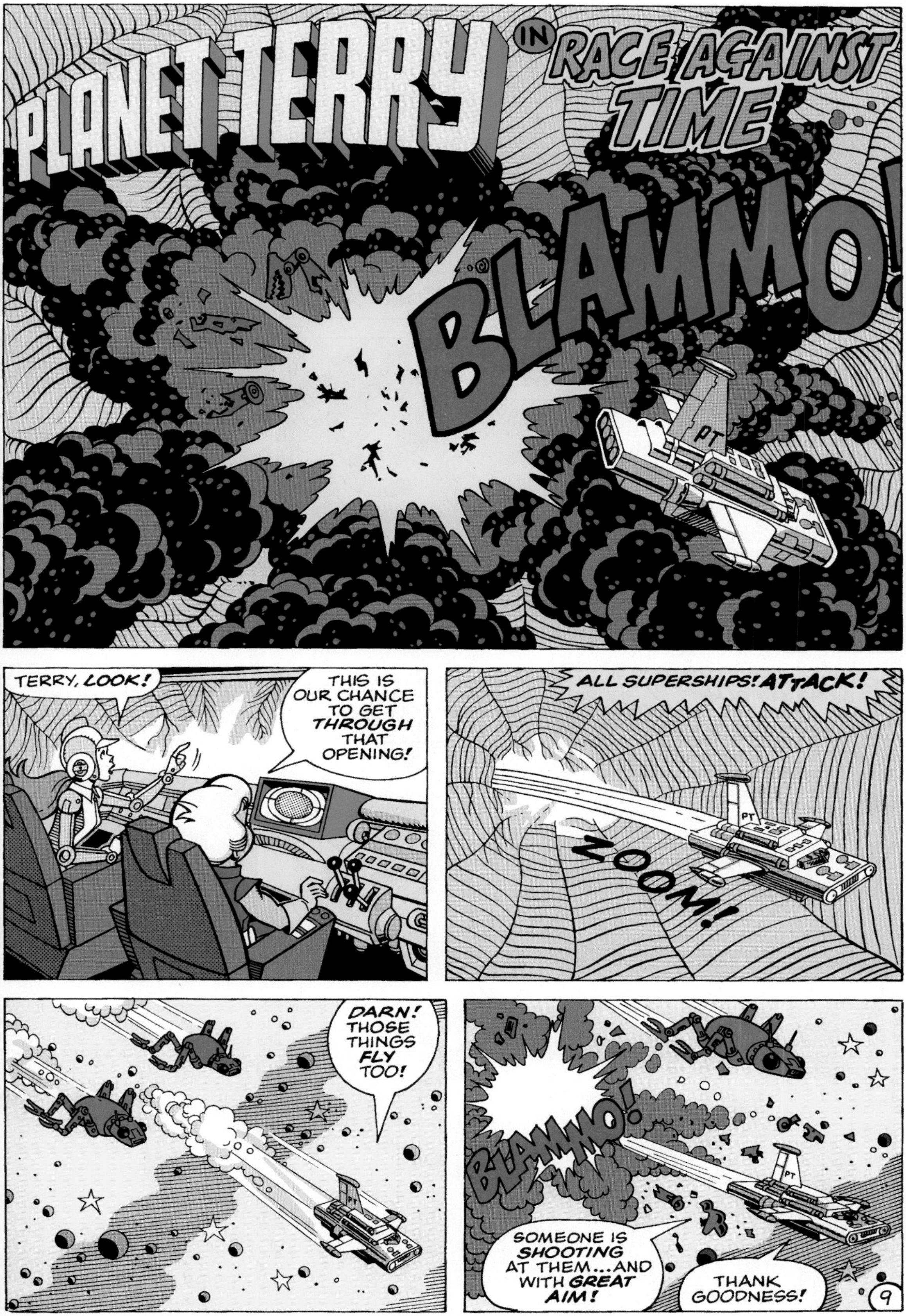
PLANET TERRY
IN
RACE AGAINST TIME
BLAMMO!
PT
TERRY, LOOK!
THIS IS OUR CHANCE TO GET THROUGH THAT OPENING!
ALL SUPERSHIPS! ATTACK!
ZOOM!
DARN! THOSE THINGS FLY TOO!
BLAMMO!
SOMEONE IS SHOOTING AT THEM...AND WITH GREAT AIM!
THANK GOODNESS!
9

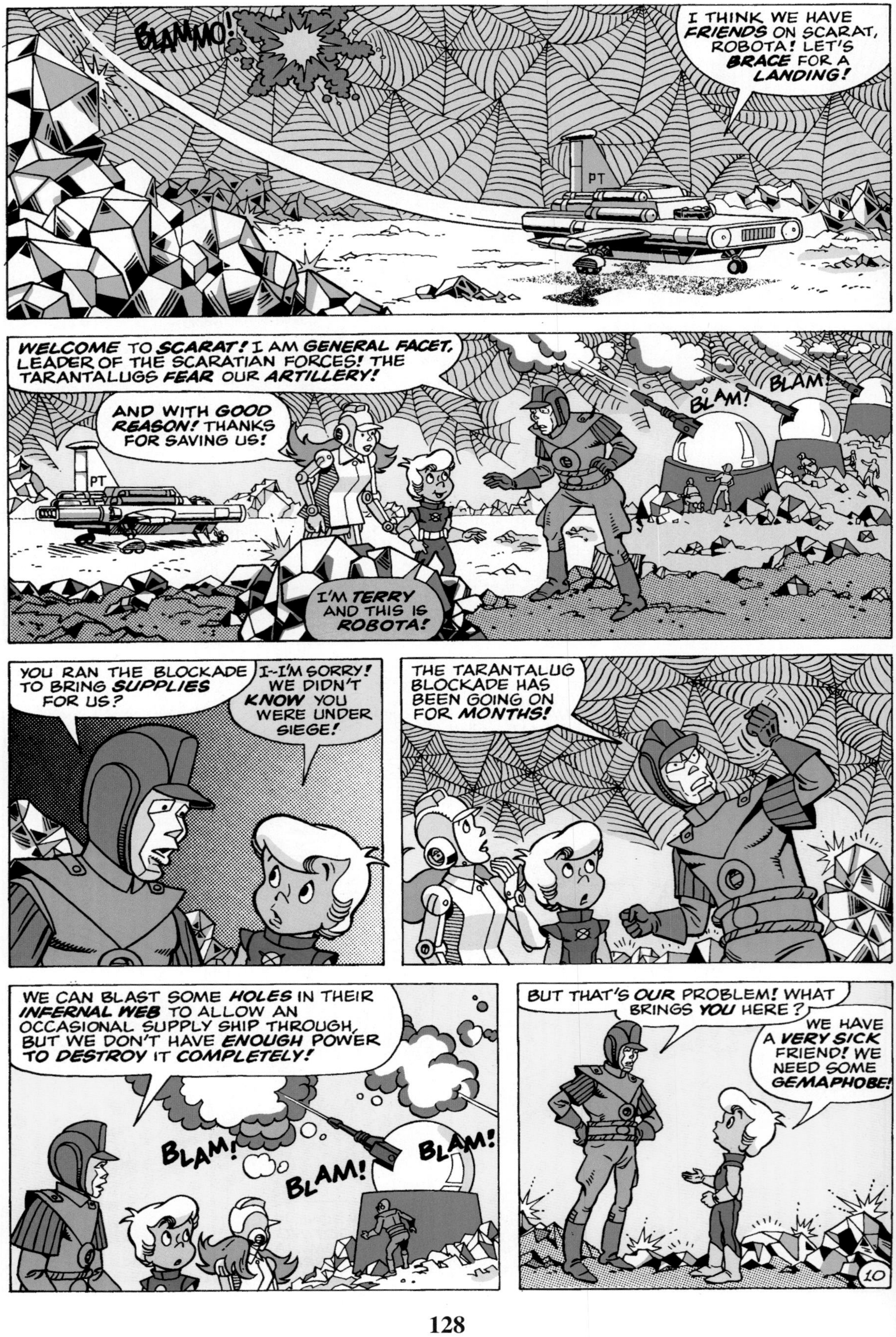

BLAMMO!
I THINK WE HAVE FRIENDS ON SCARAT, ROBOTA! LET'S BRACE FOR A LANDING!
PT
WELCOME TO SCARAT! I AM GENERAL FACET, LEADER OF THE SCARATIAN FORCES! THE TARANTALUGS FEAR OUR ARTILLERY!
AND WITH GOOD REASON! THANKS FOR SAVING US!
BLAM!
BLAM!
PT
I'M TERRY AND THIS IS ROBOTA!
YOU RAN THE BLOCKADE TO BRING SUPPLIES FOR US?
I--I'M SORRY! WE DIDN'T KNOW YOU WERE UNDER SIEGE!
THE TARANTALUG BLOCKADE HAS BEEN GOING ON FOR MONTHS!
WE CAN BLAST SOME HOLES IN THEIR INFERNAL WEB TO ALLOW AN OCCASIONAL SUPPLY SHIP THROUGH, BUT WE DON'T HAVE ENOUGH POWER TO DESTROY IT COMPLETELY!
BLAM!
BLAM!
BLAM!
BUT THAT'S OUR PROBLEM! WHAT BRINGS YOU HERE?
WE HAVE A VERY SICK FRIEND! WE NEED SOME GEMAPHOBE!
10

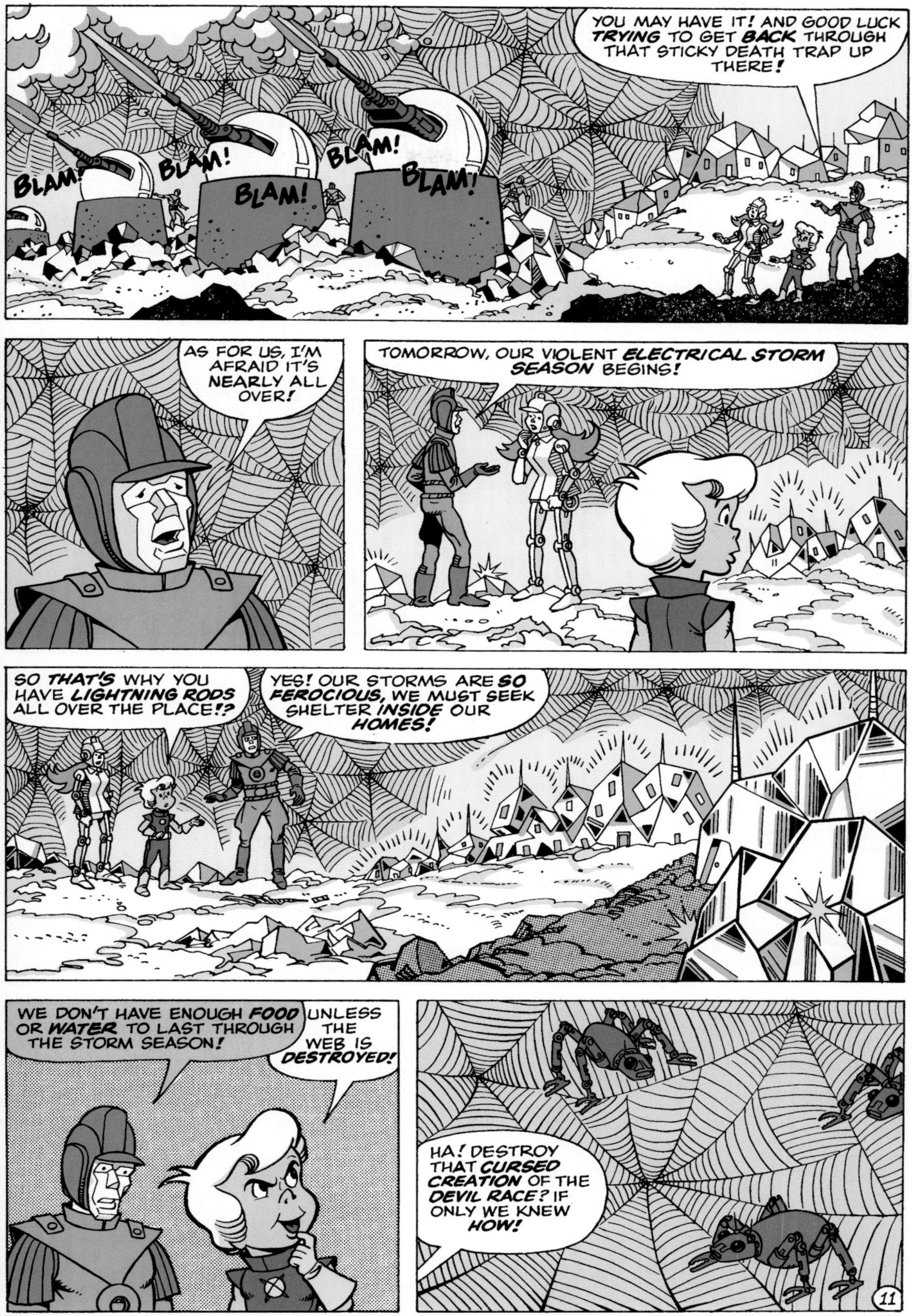
YOU MAY HAVE IT! AND GOOD LUCK TRYING TO GET BACK THROUGH THAT STICKY DEATH TRAP UP THERE!
BLAM!
BLAM!
BLAM!
BLAM!
BLAM!
AS FOR US, I'M AFRAID IT'S NEARLY ALL OVER!
TOMORROW, OUR VIOLENT ELECTRICAL STORM SEASON BEGINS!
SO THAT'S WHY YOU HAVE LIGHTNING RODS ALL OVER THE PLACE!?
YES! OUR STORMS ARE SO FEROCIOUS, WE MUST SEEK SHELTER INSIDE OUR HOMES!
WE DON'T HAVE ENOUGH FOOD OR WATER TO LAST THROUGH THE STORM SEASON!
UNLESS THE WEB IS DESTROYED!
HA! DESTROY THAT CURSED CREATION OF THE DEVIL RACE? IF ONLY WE KNEW HOW!
11

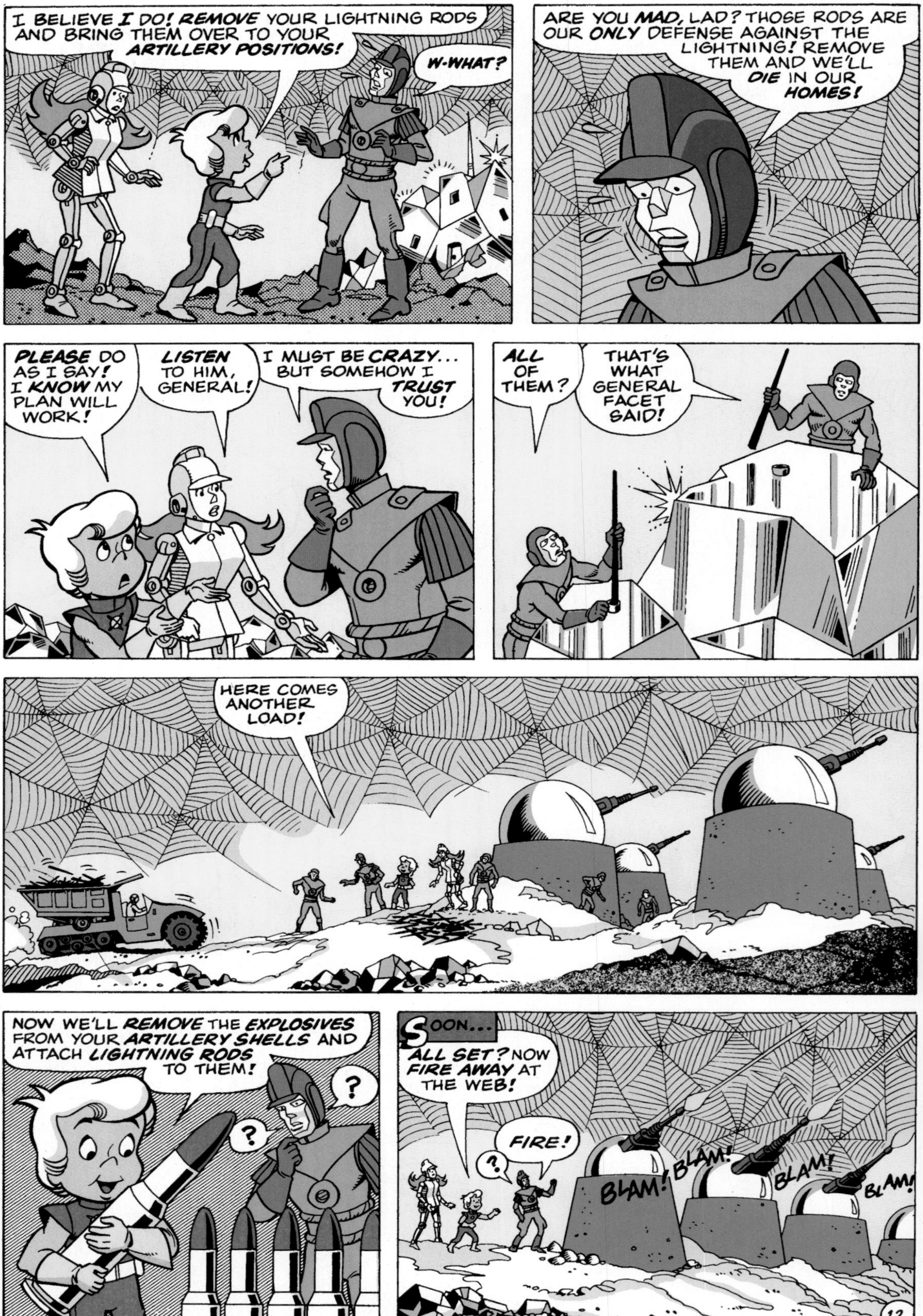
I BELIEVE I DO! REMOVE YOUR LIGHTNING RODS AND BRING THEM OVER TO YOUR ARTILLERY POSITIONS!
W-WHAT?
ARE YOU MAD, LAD? THOSE RODS ARE OUR ONLY DEFENSE AGAINST THE LIGHTNING! REMOVE THEM AND WE'LL DIE IN OUR HOMES!
PLEASE DO AS I SAY! I KNOW MY PLAN WILL WORK!
LISTEN TO HIM, GENERAL!
I MUST BE CRAZY... BUT SOMEHOW I TRUST YOU!
ALL OF THEM?
THAT'S WHAT GENERAL FACET SAID!
HERE COMES ANOTHER LOAD!
NOW WE'LL REMOVE THE EXPLOSIVES FROM YOUR ARTILLERY SHELLS AND ATTACH LIGHTNING RODS TO THEM!
?
?
SOON...
ALL SET? NOW FIRE AWAY AT THE WEB!
?
FIRE!
BLAM! BLAM! BLAM! BLAM!
12

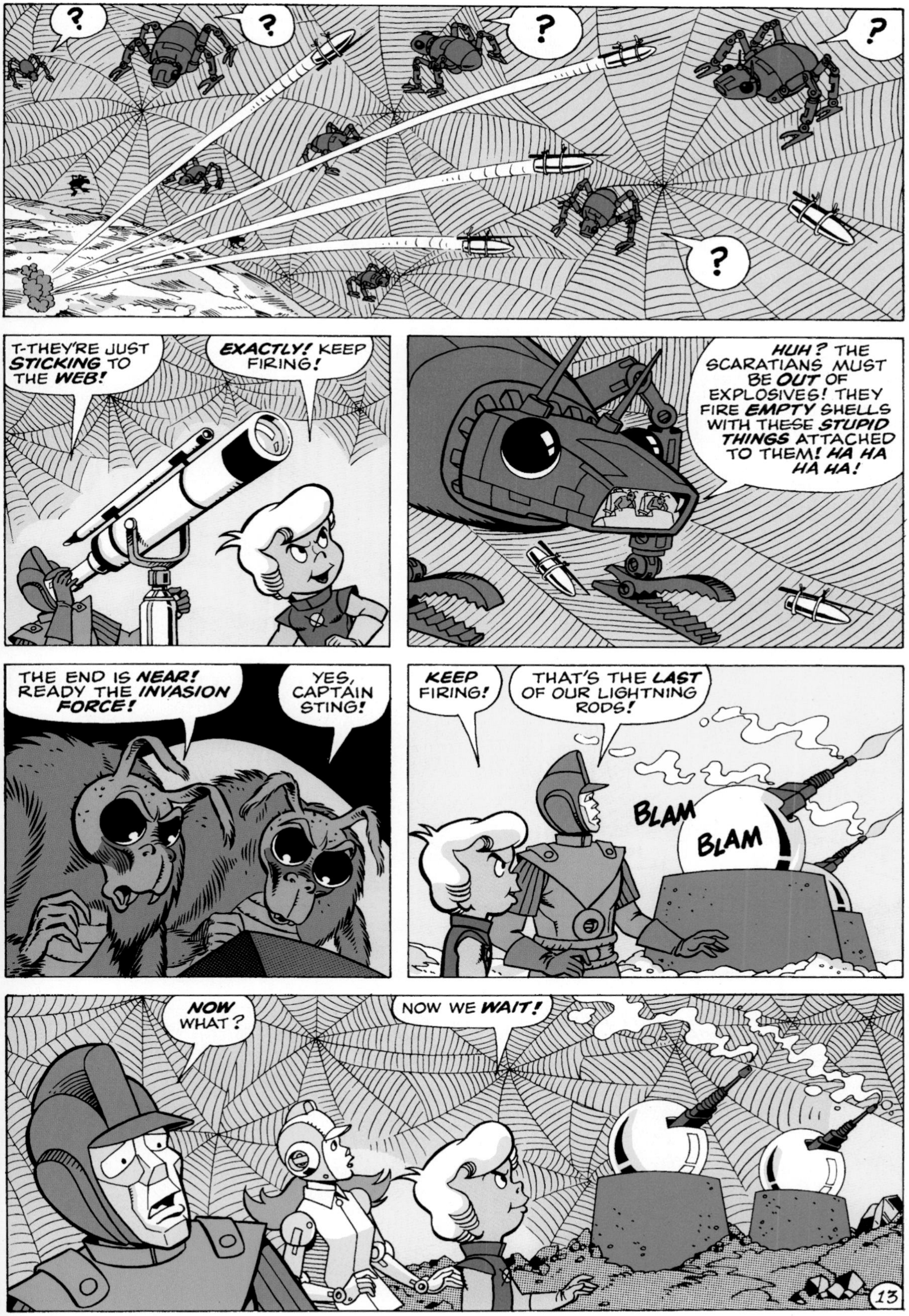
?
?
?
?
?
T-THEY'RE JUST STICKING TO THE WEB!
EXACTLY! KEEP FIRING!
HUH? THE SCARATIANS MUST BE OUT OF EXPLOSIVES! THEY FIRE EMPTY SHELLS WITH THESE STUPID THINGS ATTACHED TO THEM! HA HA HA HA!
THE END IS NEAR! READY THE INVASION FORCE!
YES, CAPTAIN STING!
KEEP FIRING!
THAT'S THE LAST OF OUR LIGHTNING RODS!
BLAM
BLAM
NOW WHAT?
NOW WE WAIT!
13

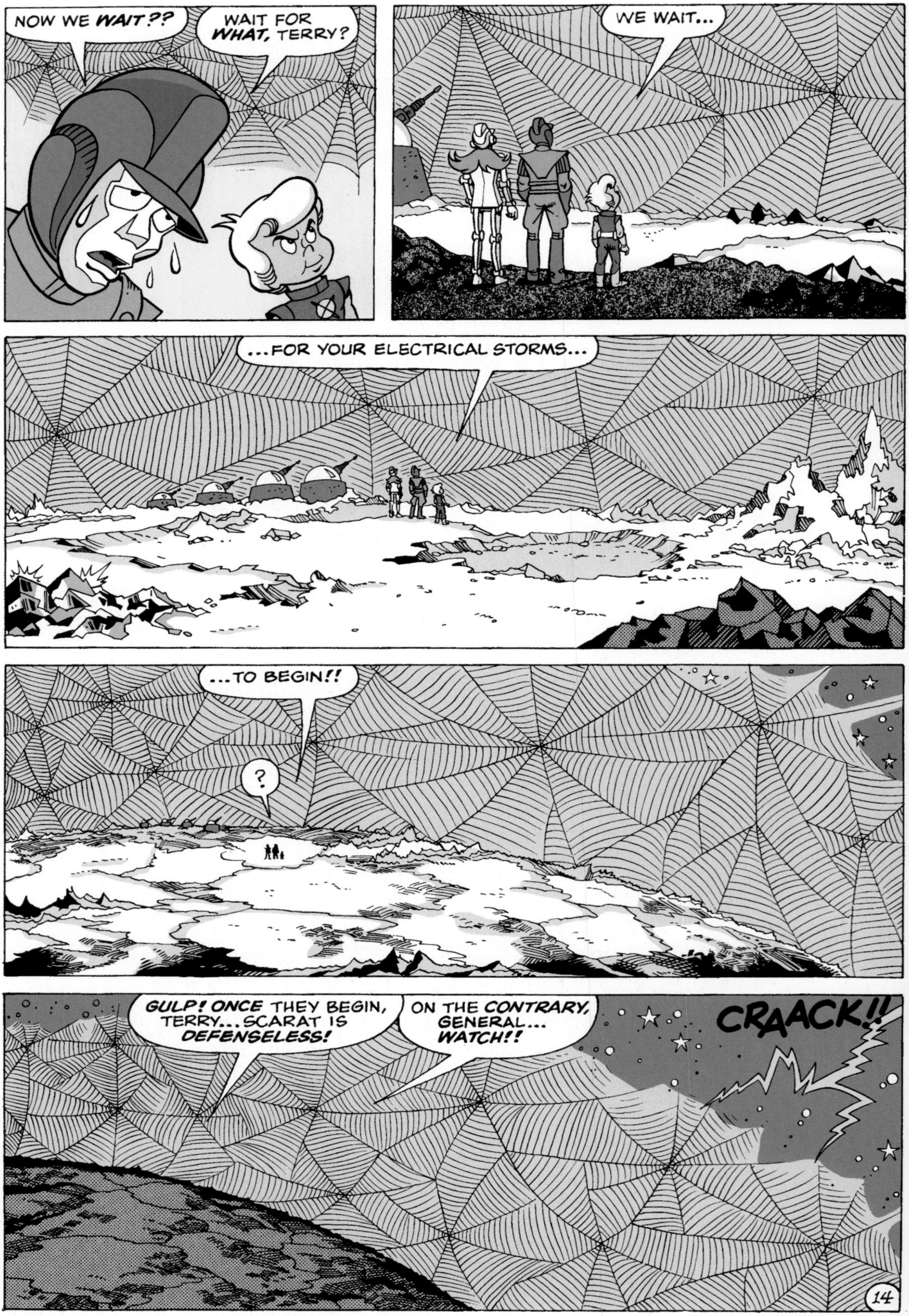
NOW WE WAIT??
WAIT FOR WHAT, TERRY?
WE WAIT...
...FOR YOUR ELECTRICAL STORMS...
...TO BEGIN!!
?
GULP! ONCE THEY BEGIN, TERRY...SCARAT IS DEFENSELESS!
ON THE CONTRARY, GENERAL... WATCH!!
CRAACK!!
14

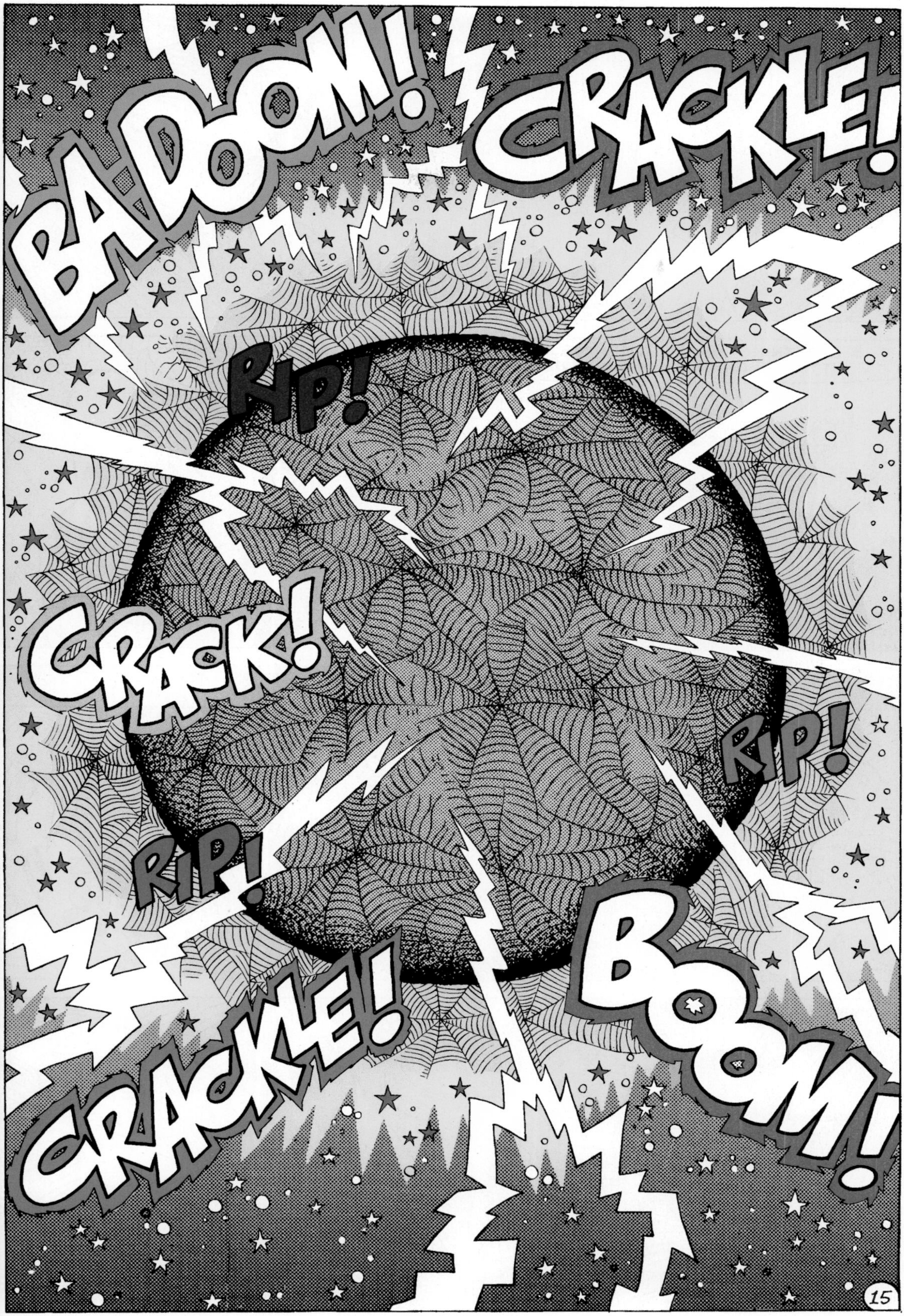
BA-DOOM!
CRACKLE!
RIP!
CRACK!
RIP!
RIP!
CRACKLE!
BOOM!
15

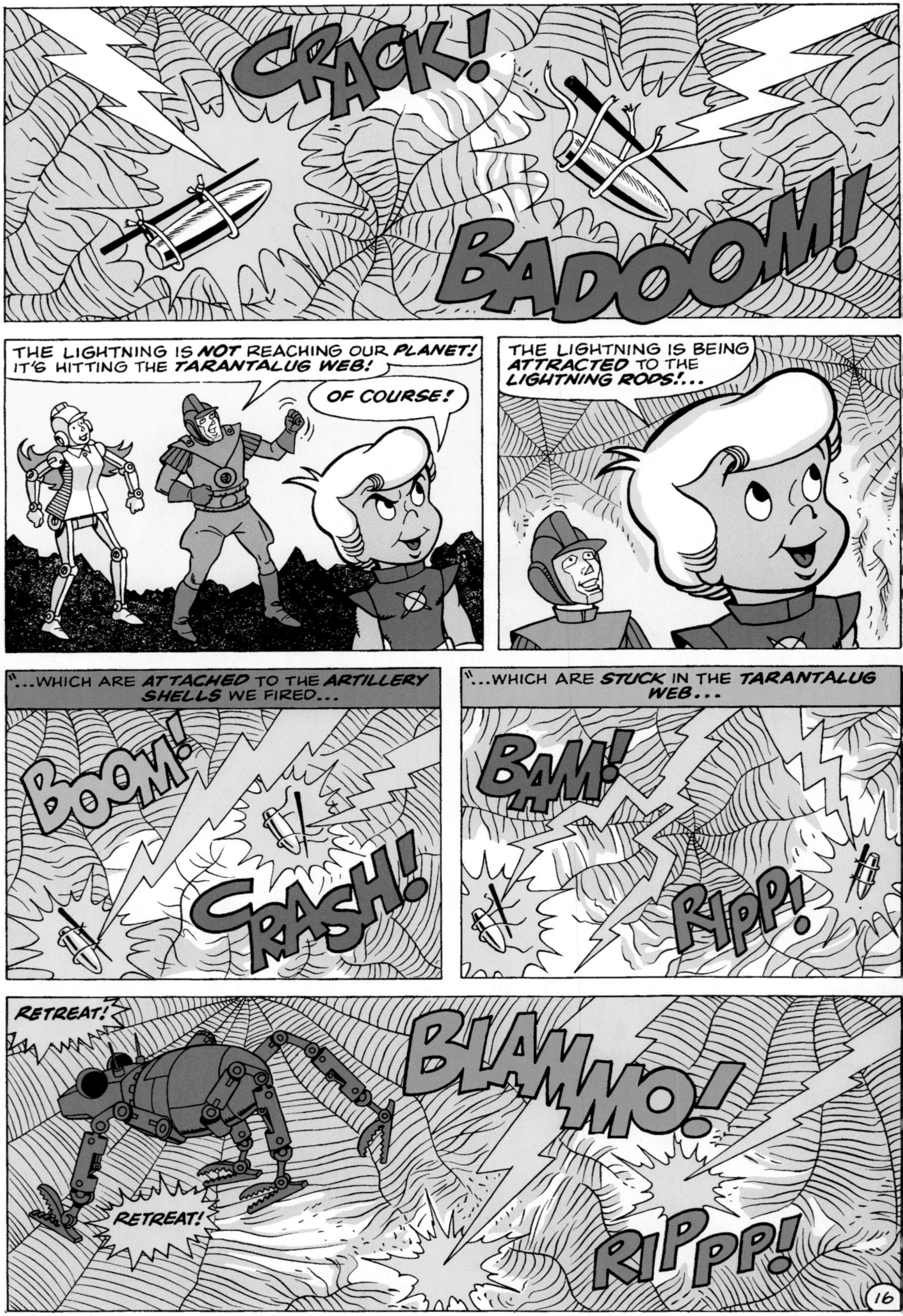
CRACK!
BADOOOM!
THE LIGHTNING IS NOT REACHING OUR PLANET! IT'S HITTING THE TARANTALUG WEB!
OF COURSE!
THE LIGHTNING IS BEING ATTRACTED TO THE LIGHTNING RODS!...
"...WHICH ARE ATTACHED TO THE ARTILLERY SHELLS WE FIRED...
BOOM!
CRASH!
"...WHICH ARE STUCK IN THE TARANTALUG WEB...
BAM!
RIPP!
RETREAT!
RETREAT!
BLAMMO!
RIPPPP!
16

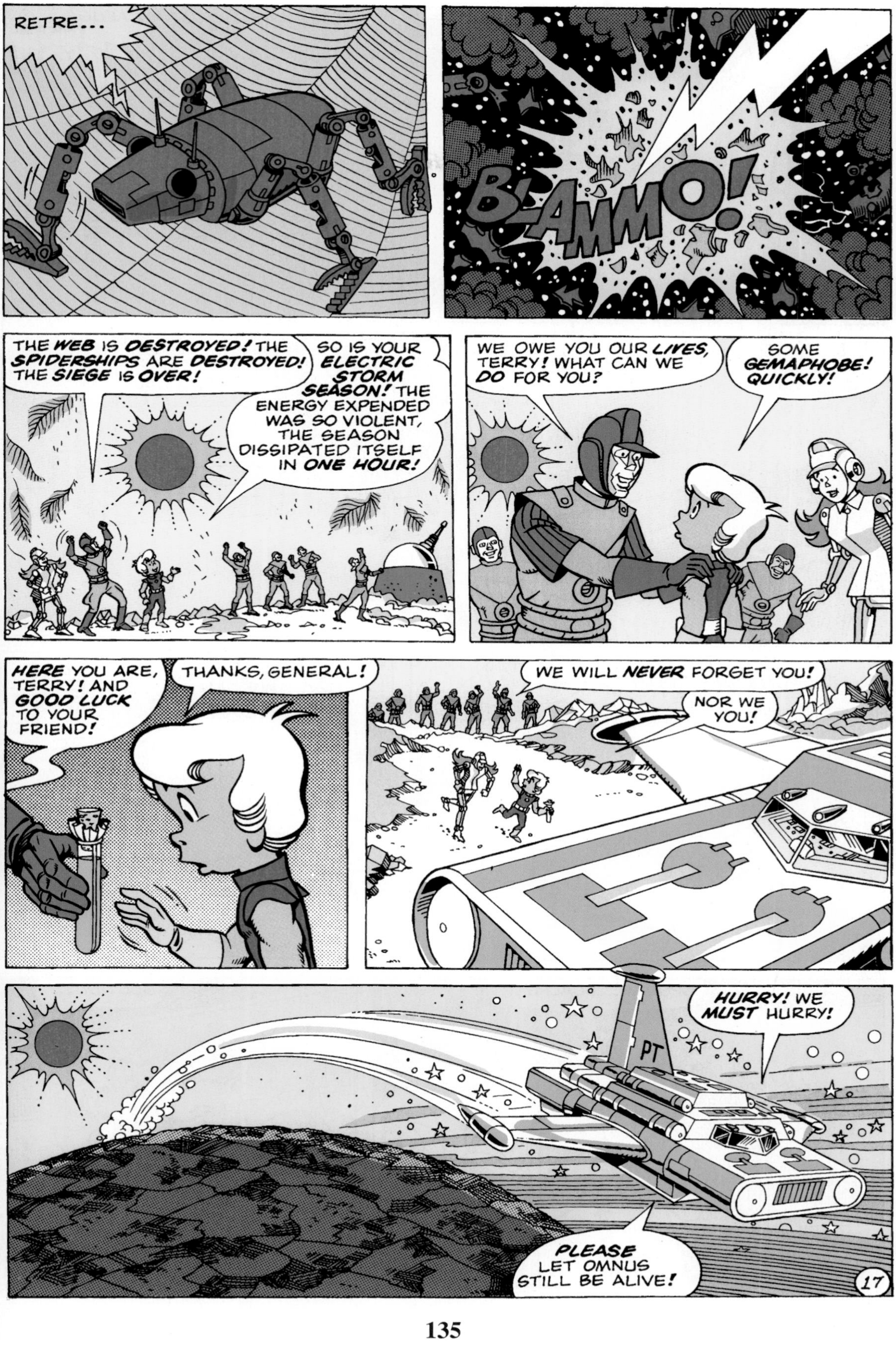
RETRE...
BLAMMO!
THE WEB IS DESTROYED! THE SPIDERSHIPS ARE DESTROYED! THE SIEGE IS OVER!
SO IS YOUR ELECTRIC STORM SEASON! THE ENERGY EXPENDED WAS SO VIOLENT, THE SEASON DISSIPATED ITSELF IN ONE HOUR!
WE OWE YOU OUR LIVES, TERRY! WHAT CAN WE DO FOR YOU?
SOME GEMAPHOBE! QUICKLY!
HERE YOU ARE, TERRY! AND GOOD LUCK TO YOUR FRIEND!
THANKS, GENERAL!
WE WILL NEVER FORGET YOU!
NOR WE YOU!
PT
HURRY! WE MUST HURRY!
PLEASE LET OMNUS STILL BE ALIVE!
17

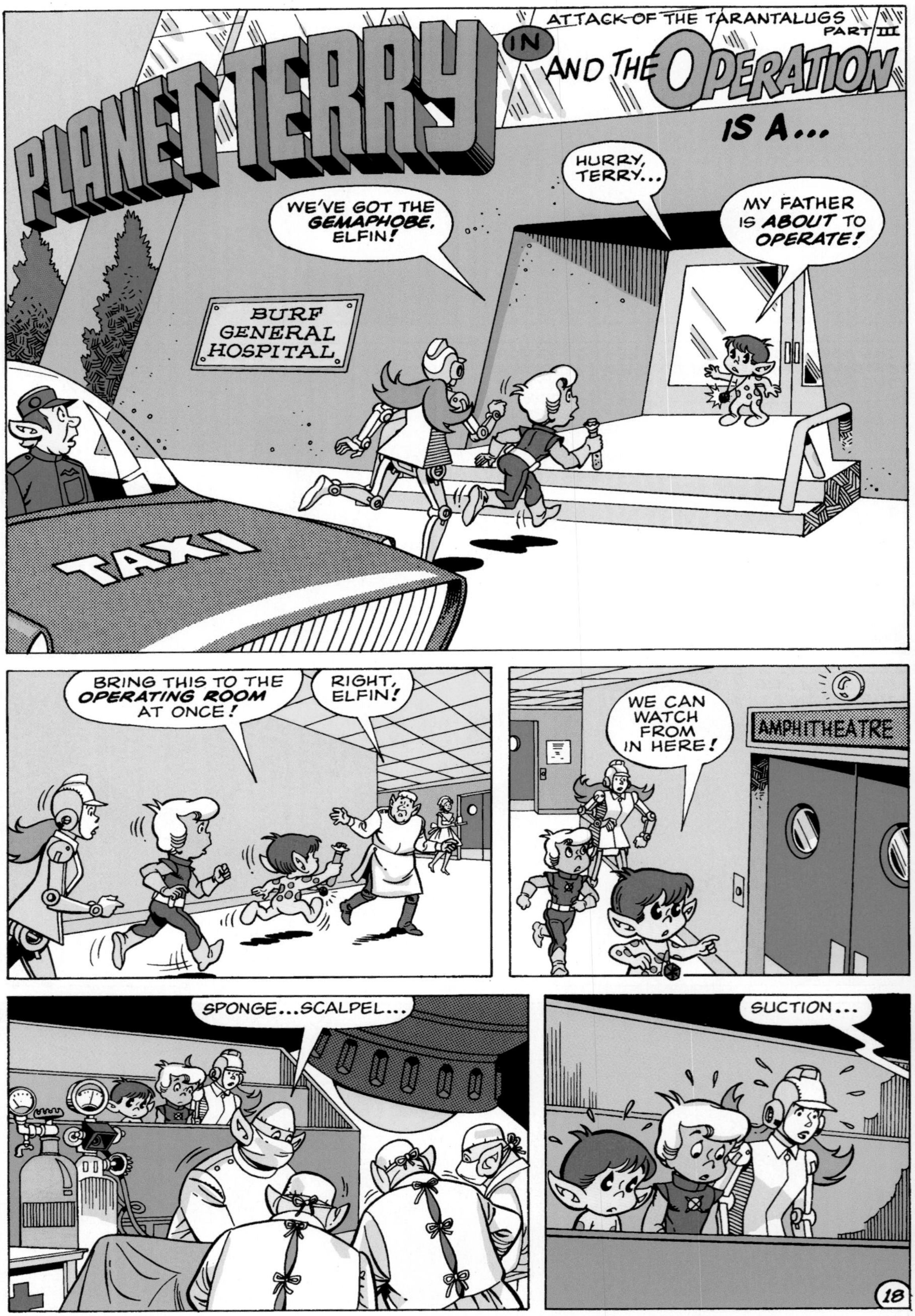
PLANET TERRY
IN
ATTACK OF THE TARANTALUGS
PART III
AND THE OPERATION
IS A...
WE'VE GOT THE GEMAPHOBE, ELFIN!
HURRY, TERRY...
MY FATHER IS ABOUT TO OPERATE!
BURF GENERAL HOSPITAL
TAXI
BRING THIS TO THE OPERATING ROOM AT ONCE!
RIGHT, ELFIN!
WE CAN WATCH FROM IN HERE!
AMPHITHEATRE
SPONGE...SCALPEL...
SUCTION...
18

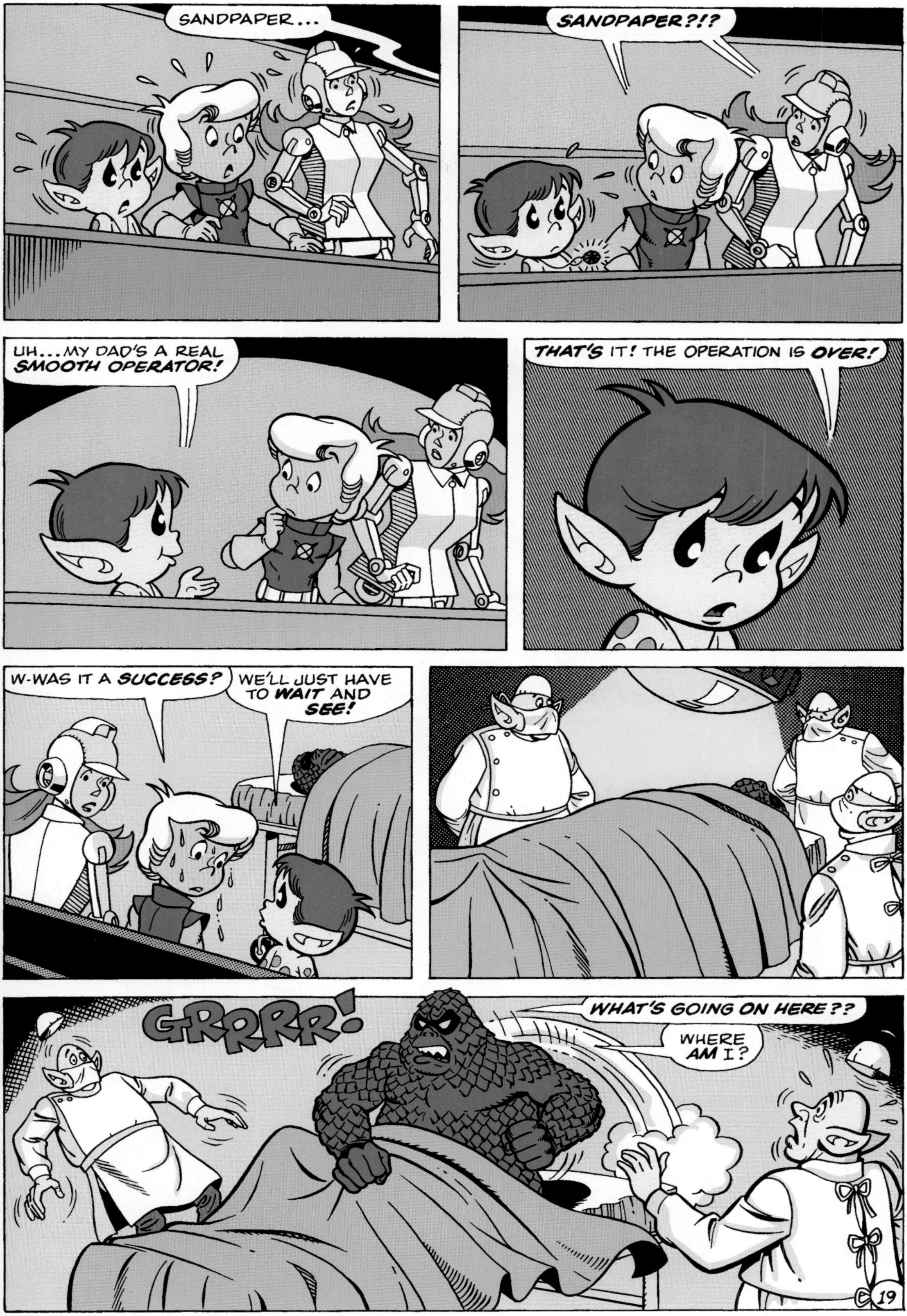
SANDPAPER...
SANDPAPER?!?
UH...MY DAD'S A REAL SMOOTH OPERATOR!
THAT'S IT! THE OPERATION IS OVER!
W-WAS IT A SUCCESS?
WE'LL JUST HAVE TO WAIT AND SEE!
GRRRR!
WHAT'S GOING ON HERE??
WHERE AM I?
19

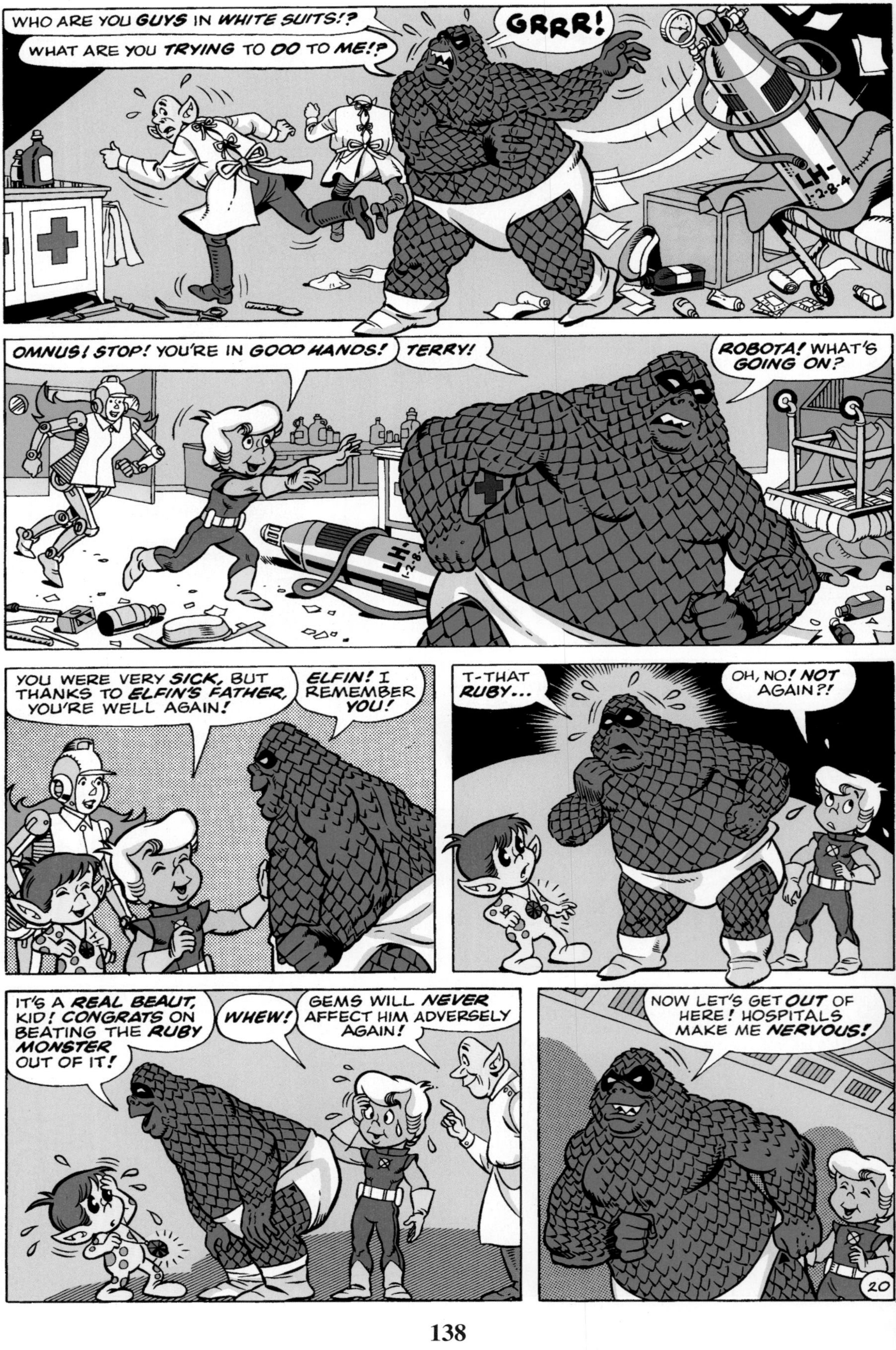
WHO ARE YOU GUYS IN WHITE SUITS!?
WHAT ARE YOU TRYING TO DO TO ME!?
GRRR!
LH-
1-2-8-4
OMNUS! STOP! YOU'RE IN GOOD HANDS!
TERRY!
ROBOTA! WHAT'S GOING ON?
YOU WERE VERY SICK, BUT THANKS TO ELFIN'S FATHER, YOU'RE WELL AGAIN!
ELFIN! I REMEMBER YOU!
T-THAT RUBY...
OH, NO! NOT AGAIN?!
IT'S A REAL BEAUT, KID! CONGRATS ON BEATING THE RUBY MONSTER OUT OF IT!
WHEW!
GEMS WILL NEVER AFFECT HIM ADVERSELY AGAIN!
NOW LET'S GET OUT OF HERE! HOSPITALS MAKE ME NERVOUS!
20

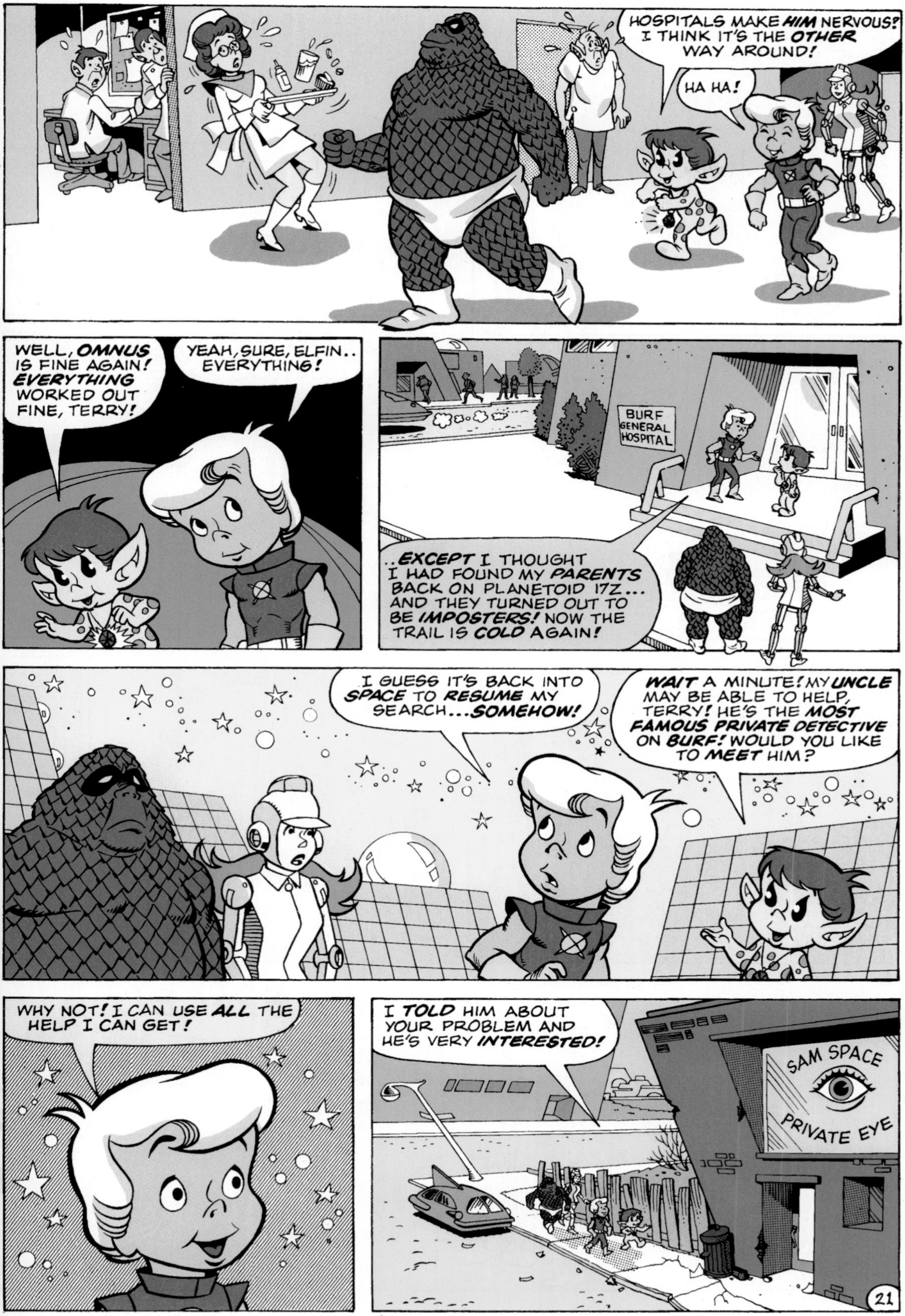
HOSPITALS MAKE HIM NERVOUS? I THINK IT'S THE OTHER WAY AROUND!
HA HA!
WELL, OMNUS IS FINE AGAIN! EVERYTHING WORKED OUT FINE, TERRY!
YEAH, SURE, ELFIN.. EVERYTHING!
BURF GENERAL HOSPITAL
..EXCEPT I THOUGHT I HAD FOUND MY PARENTS BACK ON PLANETOID 17Z... AND THEY TURNED OUT TO BE IMPOSTERS! NOW THE TRAIL IS COLD AGAIN!
I GUESS IT'S BACK INTO SPACE TO RESUME MY SEARCH...SOMEHOW!
WAIT A MINUTE! MY UNCLE MAY BE ABLE TO HELP, TERRY! HE'S THE MOST FAMOUS PRIVATE DETECTIVE ON BURF! WOULD YOU LIKE TO MEET HIM?
WHY NOT! I CAN USE ALL THE HELP I CAN GET!
I TOLD HIM ABOUT YOUR PROBLEM AND HE'S VERY INTERESTED!
SAM SPACE PRIVATE EYE
21

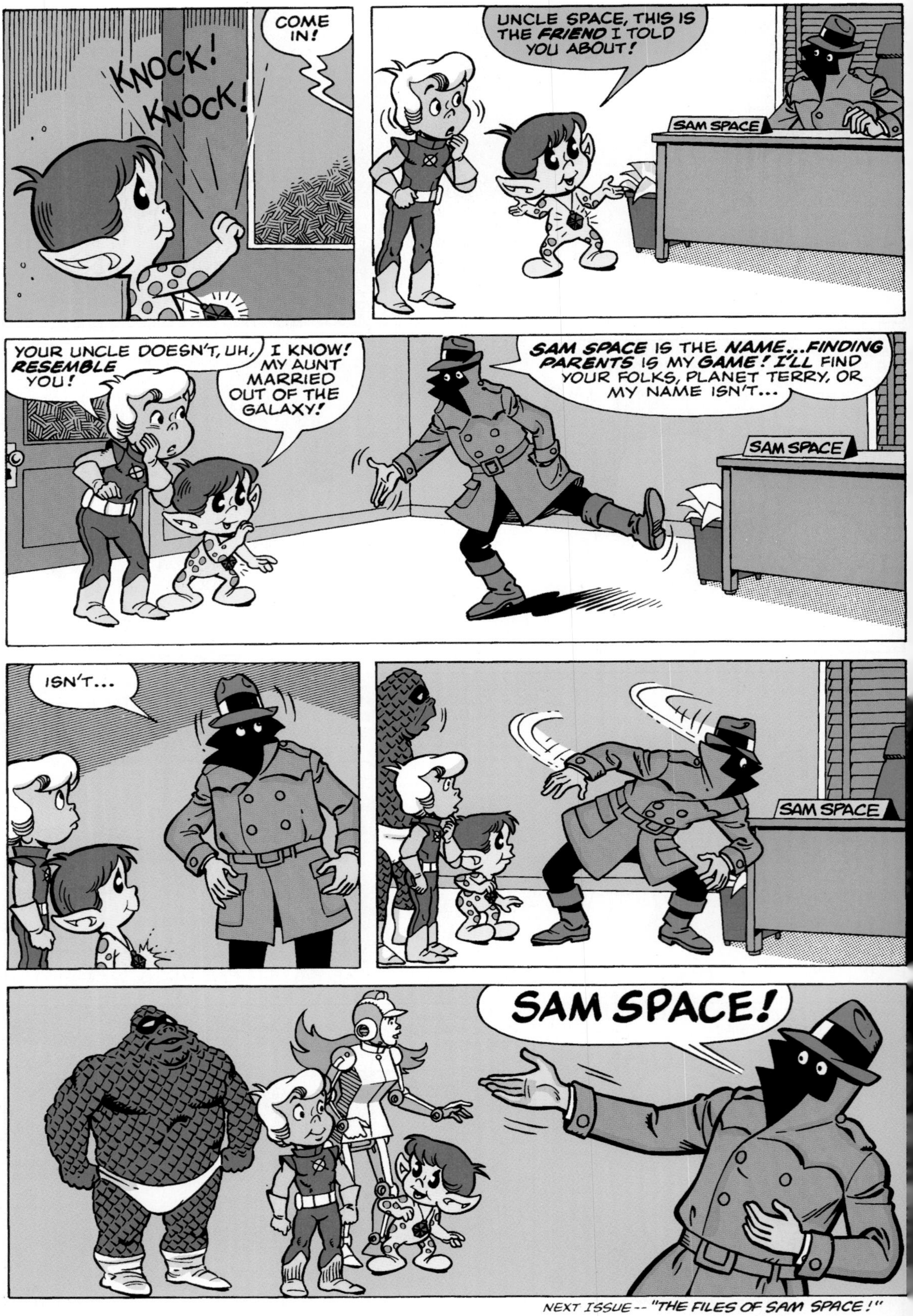
KNOCK! KNOCK!
COME IN!
UNCLE SPACE, THIS IS THE FRIEND I TOLD YOU ABOUT!
SAM SPACE
YOUR UNCLE DOESN'T, UH, RESEMBLE YOU!
I KNOW! MY AUNT MARRIED OUT OF THE GALAXY!
SAM SPACE IS THE NAME...FINDING PARENTS IS MY GAME! I'LL FIND YOUR FOLKS, PLANET TERRY, OR MY NAME ISN'T...
SAM SPACE
ISN'T...
SAM SPACE
SAM SPACE!
NEXT ISSUE -- "THE FILES OF SAM SPACE!"

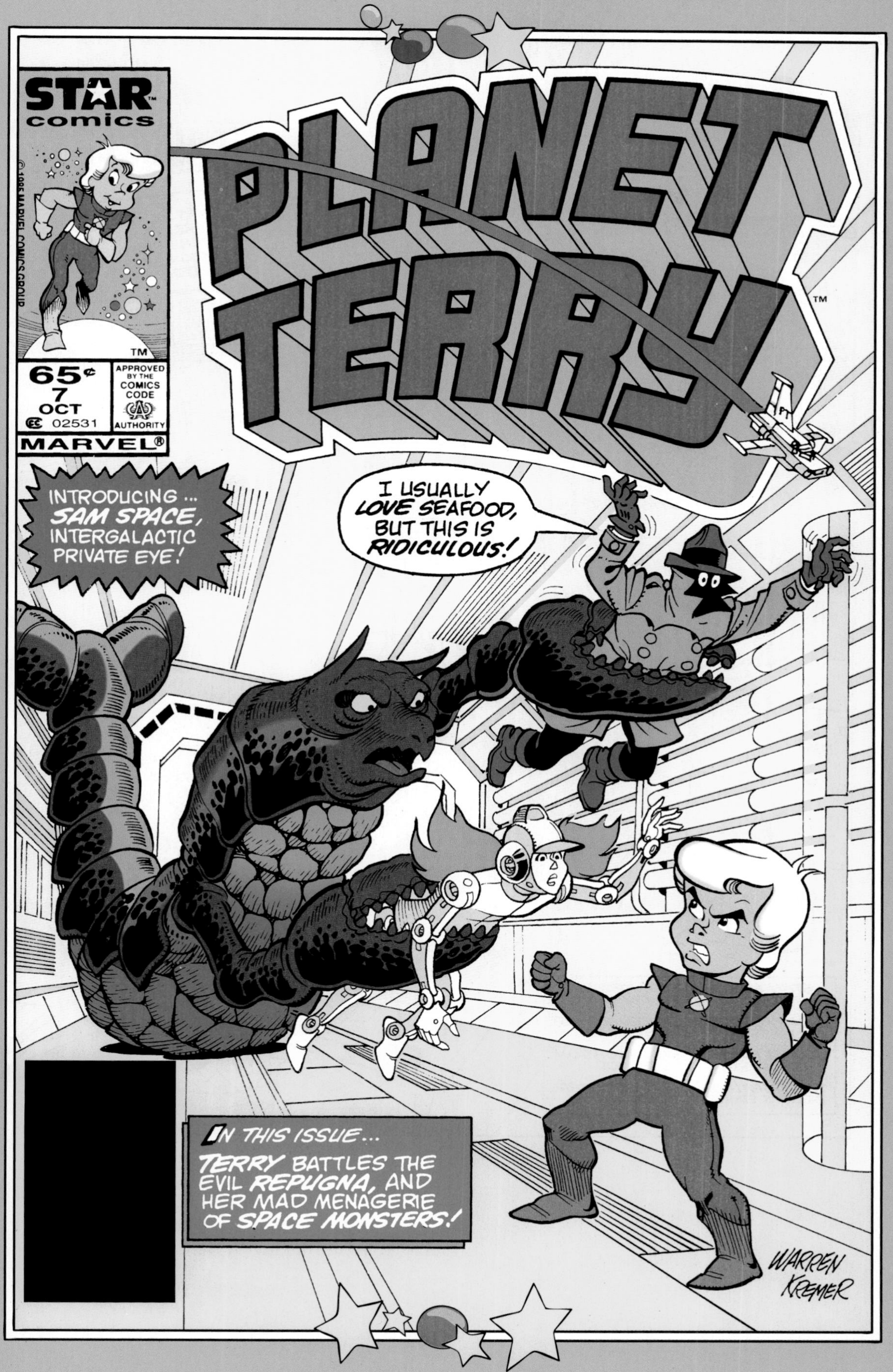
STAR comics
© 1985 MARVEL COMICS GROUP
PLANET TERRY
65¢
7
OCT
02531
APPROVED BY THE COMICS CODE AUTHORITY
MARVEL
INTRODUCING ... SAM SPACE, INTERGALACTIC PRIVATE EYE!
I USUALLY LOVE SEAFOOD, BUT THIS IS RIDICULOUS!
IN THIS ISSUE...
TERRY BATTLES THE EVIL REPUGNA, AND HER MAD MENAGERIE OF SPACE MONSTERS!
WARREN KREMER

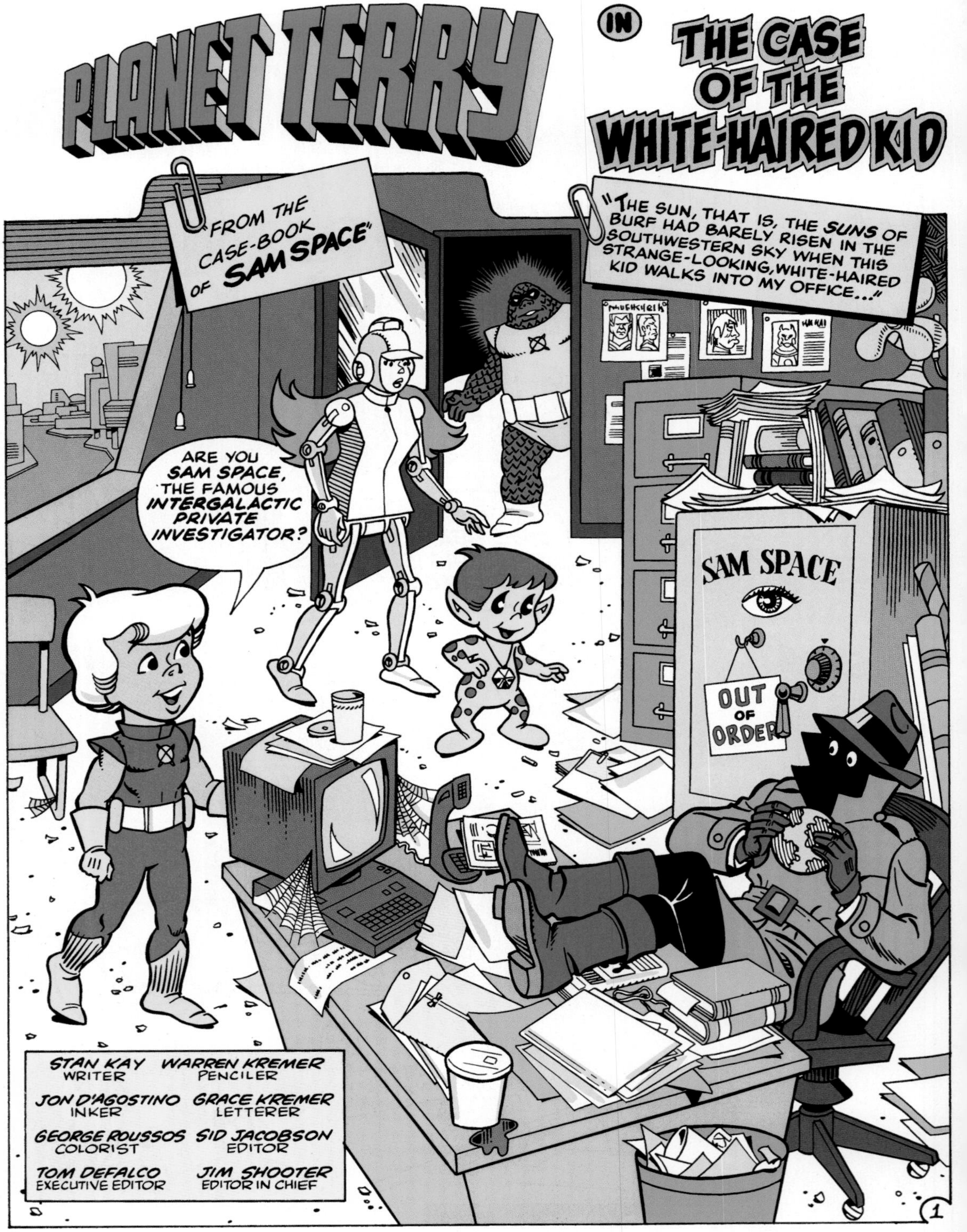
PLANET TERRY
IN
THE CASE OF THE WHITE-HAIRED KID
"FROM THE CASE-BOOK OF SAM SPACE"
"THE SUN, THAT IS, THE SUNS OF BURF HAD BARELY RISEN IN THE SOUTHWESTERN SKY WHEN THIS STRANGE-LOOKING, WHITE-HAIRED KID WALKS INTO MY OFFICE..."
ARE YOU SAM SPACE, THE FAMOUS INTERGALACTIC PRIVATE INVESTIGATOR?
SAM SPACE
OUT OF ORDER
STAN KAY WRITER
WARREN KREMER PENCILER
JON D'AGOSTINO INKER
GRACE KREMER LETTERER
GEORGE ROUSSOS COLORIST
SID JACOBSON EDITOR
TOM DEFALCO EXECUTIVE EDITOR
JIM SHOOTER EDITOR IN CHIEF
1

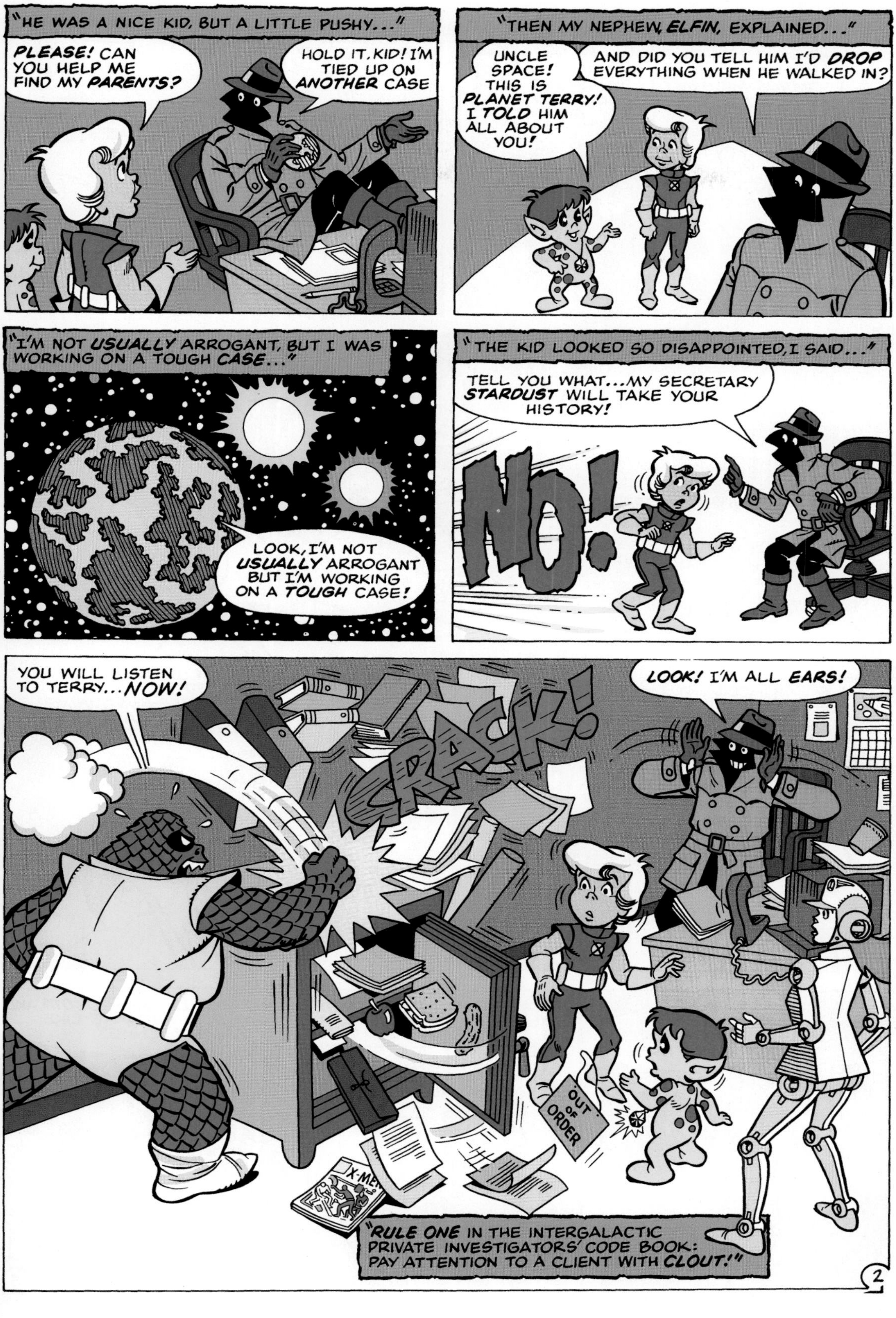
"HE WAS A NICE KID, BUT A LITTLE PUSHY..."
PLEASE! CAN YOU HELP ME FIND MY PARENTS?
HOLD IT, KID! I'M TIED UP ON ANOTHER CASE
"THEN MY NEPHEW, ELFIN, EXPLAINED..."
UNCLE SPACE! THIS IS PLANET TERRY! I TOLD HIM ALL ABOUT YOU!
AND DID YOU TELL HIM I'D DROP EVERYTHING WHEN HE WALKED IN?
"I'M NOT USUALLY ARROGANT, BUT I WAS WORKING ON A TOUGH CASE..."
LOOK, I'M NOT USUALLY ARROGANT BUT I'M WORKING ON A TOUGH CASE!
"THE KID LOOKED SO DISAPPOINTED, I SAID..."
TELL YOU WHAT...MY SECRETARY STARDUST WILL TAKE YOUR HISTORY!
NO!
YOU WILL LISTEN TO TERRY...NOW!
LOOK! I'M ALL EARS!
CRACK!
OUT OF ORDER
X-MEN
"RULE ONE IN THE INTERGALACTIC PRIVATE INVESTIGATORS' CODE BOOK: PAY ATTENTION TO A CLIENT WITH CLOUT!"
2

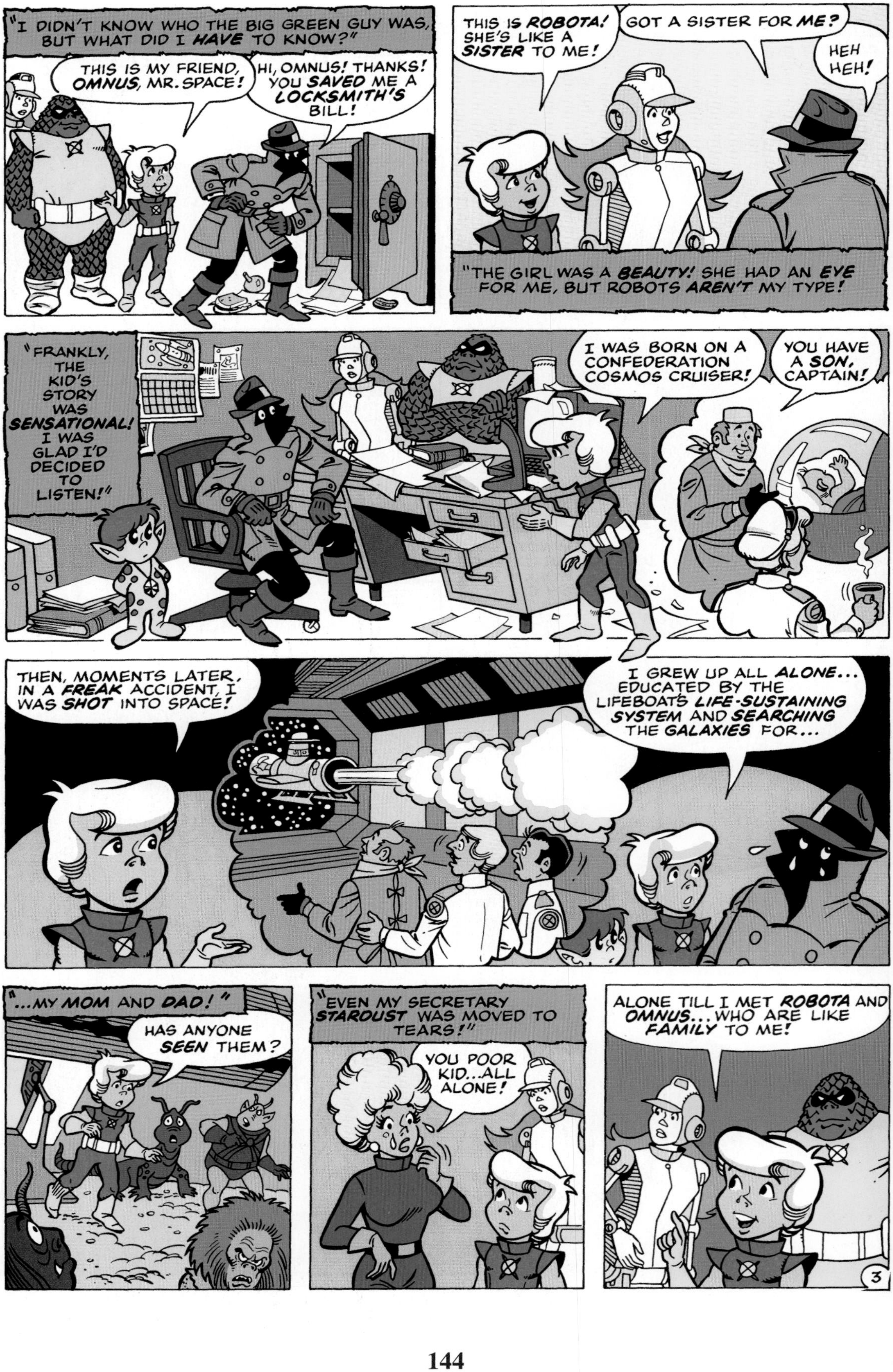
"I DIDN'T KNOW WHO THE BIG GREEN GUY WAS, BUT WHAT DID I HAVE TO KNOW?"
THIS IS MY FRIEND, OMNUS, MR. SPACE!
HI, OMNUS! THANKS! YOU SAVED ME A LOCKSMITH'S BILL!
THIS IS ROBOTA! SHE'S LIKE A SISTER TO ME!
GOT A SISTER FOR ME?
HEH HEH!
"THE GIRL WAS A BEAUTY! SHE HAD AN EYE FOR ME, BUT ROBOTS AREN'T MY TYPE!
"FRANKLY, THE KID'S STORY WAS SENSATIONAL! I WAS GLAD I'D DECIDED TO LISTEN!"
I WAS BORN ON A CONFEDERATION COSMOS CRUISER!
YOU HAVE A SON, CAPTAIN!
THEN, MOMENTS LATER, IN A FREAK ACCIDENT, I WAS SHOT INTO SPACE!
I GREW UP ALL ALONE... EDUCATED BY THE LIFEBOAT'S LIFE-SUSTAINING SYSTEM AND SEARCHING THE GALAXIES FOR...
"...MY MOM AND DAD!"
HAS ANYONE SEEN THEM?
"EVEN MY SECRETARY STARDUST WAS MOVED TO TEARS!"
YOU POOR KID...ALL ALONE!
ALONE TILL I MET ROBOTA AND OMNUS... WHO ARE LIKE FAMILY TO ME!
3

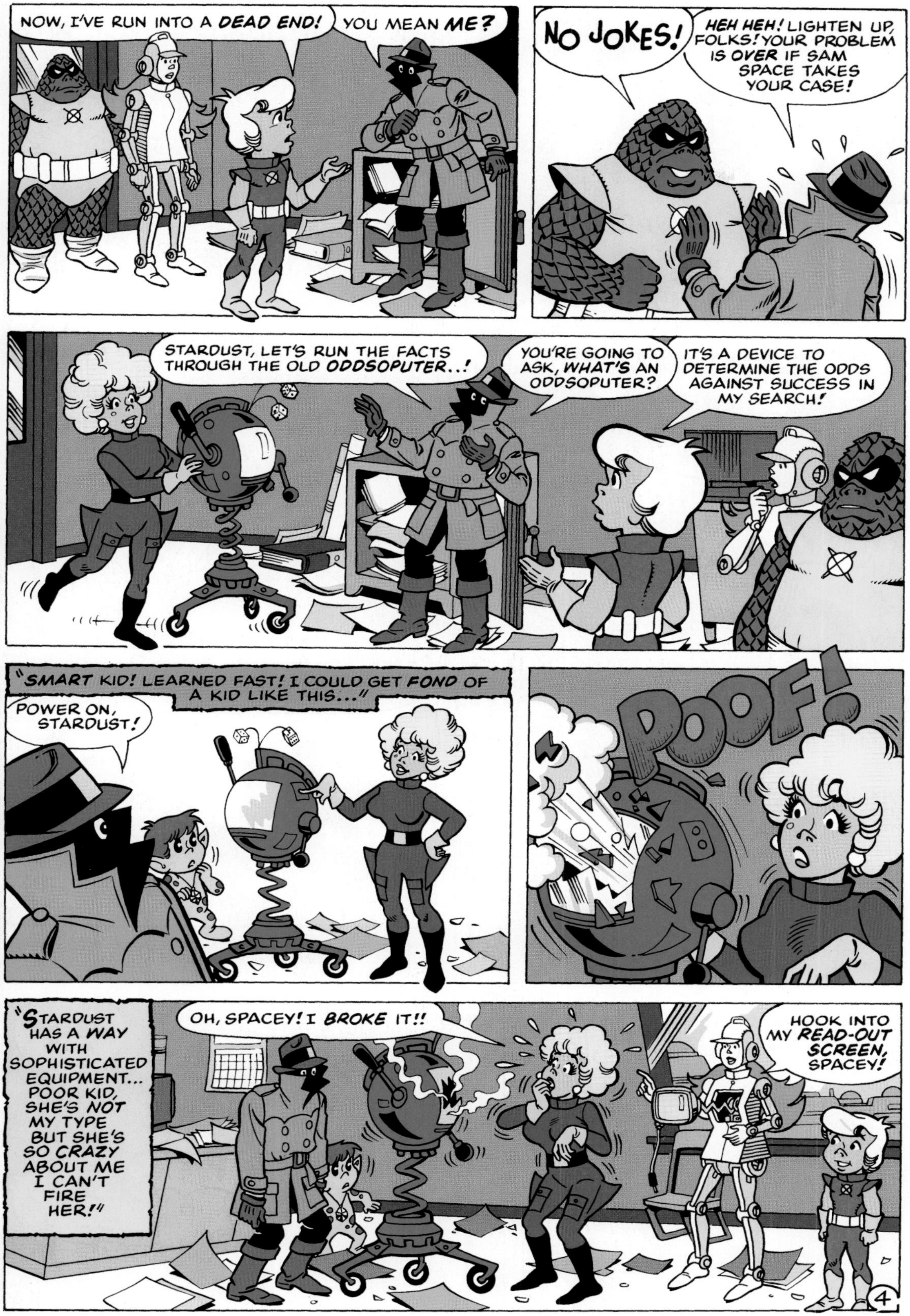
NOW, I'VE RUN INTO A DEAD END!
YOU MEAN ME?
NO JOKES!
HEH HEH! LIGHTEN UP, FOLKS! YOUR PROBLEM IS OVER IF SAM SPACE TAKES YOUR CASE!
STARDUST, LET'S RUN THE FACTS THROUGH THE OLD ODDSOPUTER...!
YOU'RE GOING TO ASK, WHAT'S AN ODDSOPUTER?
IT'S A DEVICE TO DETERMINE THE ODDS AGAINST SUCCESS IN MY SEARCH!
"SMART KID! LEARNED FAST! I COULD GET FOND OF A KID LIKE THIS..."
POWER ON, STARDUST!
POOF!
"STARDUST HAS A WAY WITH SOPHISTICATED EQUIPMENT... POOR KID, SHE'S NOT MY TYPE BUT SHE'S SO CRAZY ABOUT ME I CAN'T FIRE HER!"
OH, SPACEY! I BROKE IT!!
HOOK INTO MY READ-OUT SCREEN, SPACEY!
4

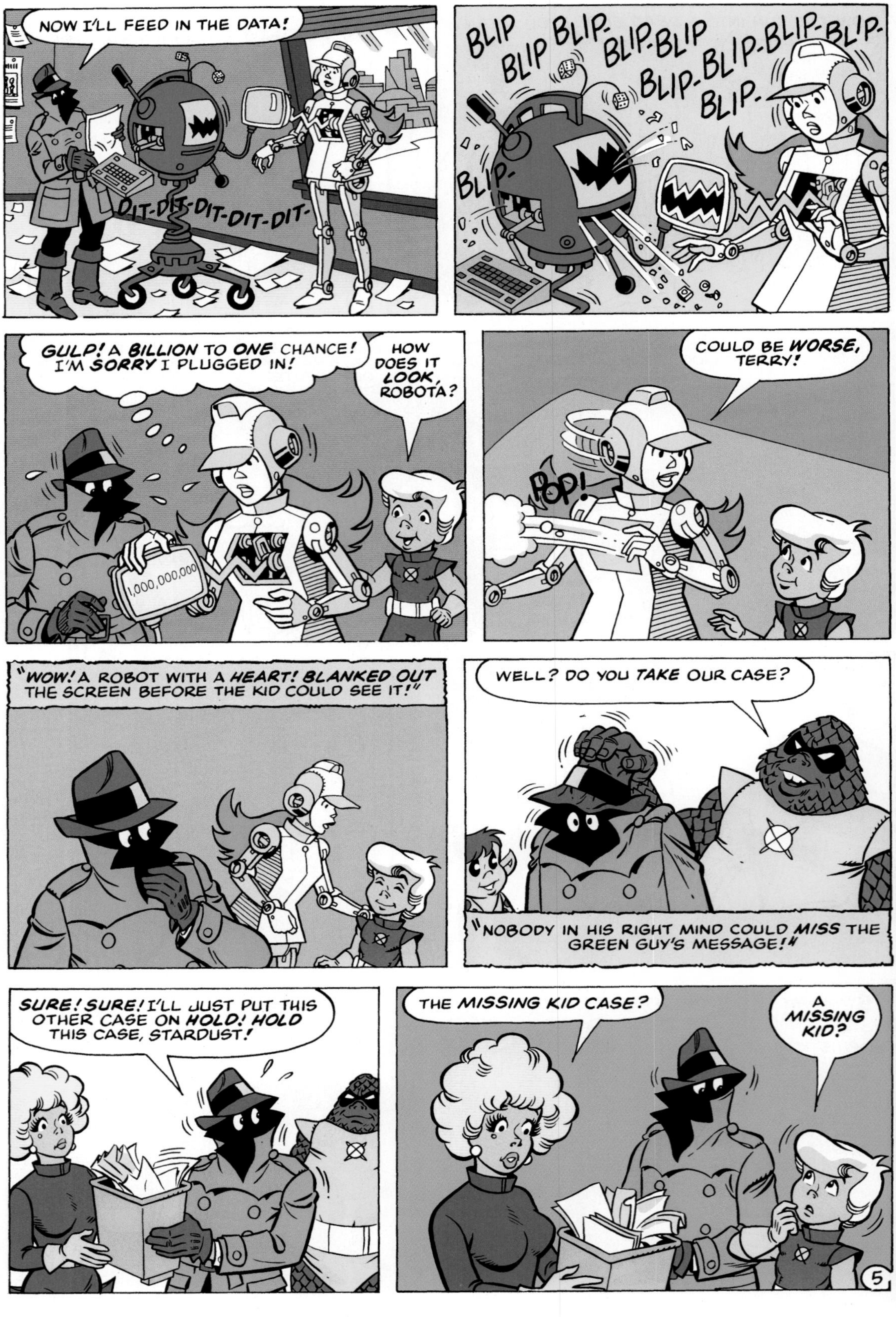
NOW I'LL FEED IN THE DATA!
DIT-DIT-DIT-DIT-DIT-
BLIP BLIP BLIP-BLIP-BLIP BLIP-BLIP-BLIP-BLIP-BLIP- BLIP- BLIP-
GULP! A BILLION TO ONE CHANCE! I'M SORRY I PLUGGED IN!
1,000,000,000
HOW DOES IT LOOK, ROBOTA?
COULD BE WORSE, TERRY!
POP!
"WOW! A ROBOT WITH A HEART! BLANKED OUT THE SCREEN BEFORE THE KID COULD SEE IT!"
WELL? DO YOU TAKE OUR CASE?
"NOBODY IN HIS RIGHT MIND COULD MISS THE GREEN GUY'S MESSAGE!"
SURE! SURE! I'LL JUST PUT THIS OTHER CASE ON HOLD! HOLD THIS CASE, STARDUST!
THE MISSING KID CASE?
A MISSING KID?
5

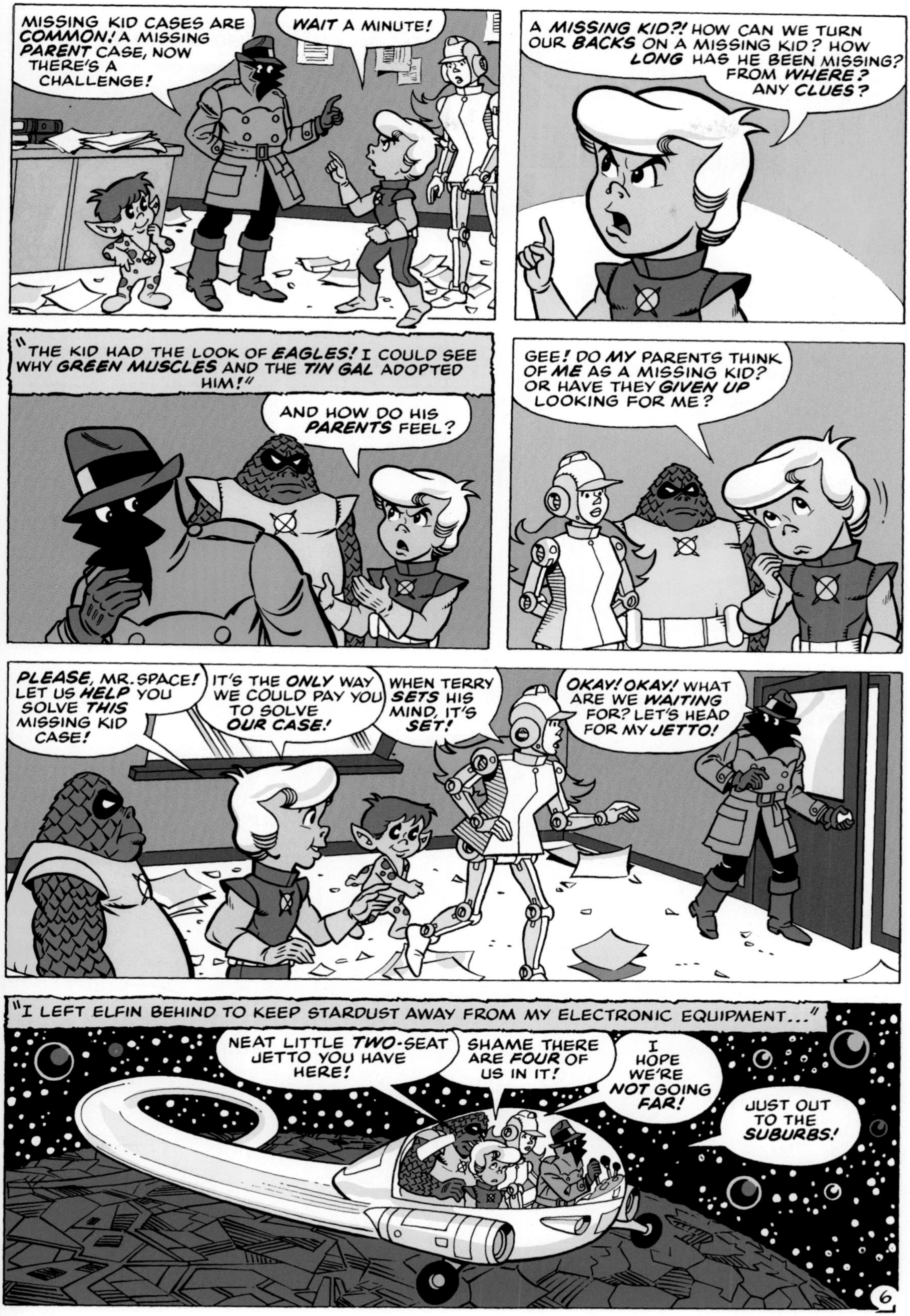
MISSING KID CASES ARE COMMON! A MISSING PARENT CASE, NOW THERE'S A CHALLENGE!
WAIT A MINUTE!
A MISSING KID?! HOW CAN WE TURN OUR BACKS ON A MISSING KID? HOW LONG HAS HE BEEN MISSING? FROM WHERE? ANY CLUES?
"THE KID HAD THE LOOK OF EAGLES! I COULD SEE WHY GREEN MUSCLES AND THE TIN GAL ADOPTED HIM!"
AND HOW DO HIS PARENTS FEEL?
GEE! DO MY PARENTS THINK OF ME AS A MISSING KID? OR HAVE THEY GIVEN UP LOOKING FOR ME?
PLEASE, MR. SPACE! LET US HELP YOU SOLVE THIS MISSING KID CASE!
IT'S THE ONLY WAY WE COULD PAY YOU TO SOLVE OUR CASE!
WHEN TERRY SETS HIS MIND, IT'S SET!
OKAY! OKAY! WHAT ARE WE WAITING FOR? LET'S HEAD FOR MY JETTO!
"I LEFT ELFIN BEHIND TO KEEP STARDUST AWAY FROM MY ELECTRONIC EQUIPMENT..."
NEAT LITTLE TWO-SEAT JETTO YOU HAVE HERE!
SHAME THERE ARE FOUR OF US IN IT!
I HOPE WE'RE NOT GOING FAR!
JUST OUT TO THE SUBURBS!
6

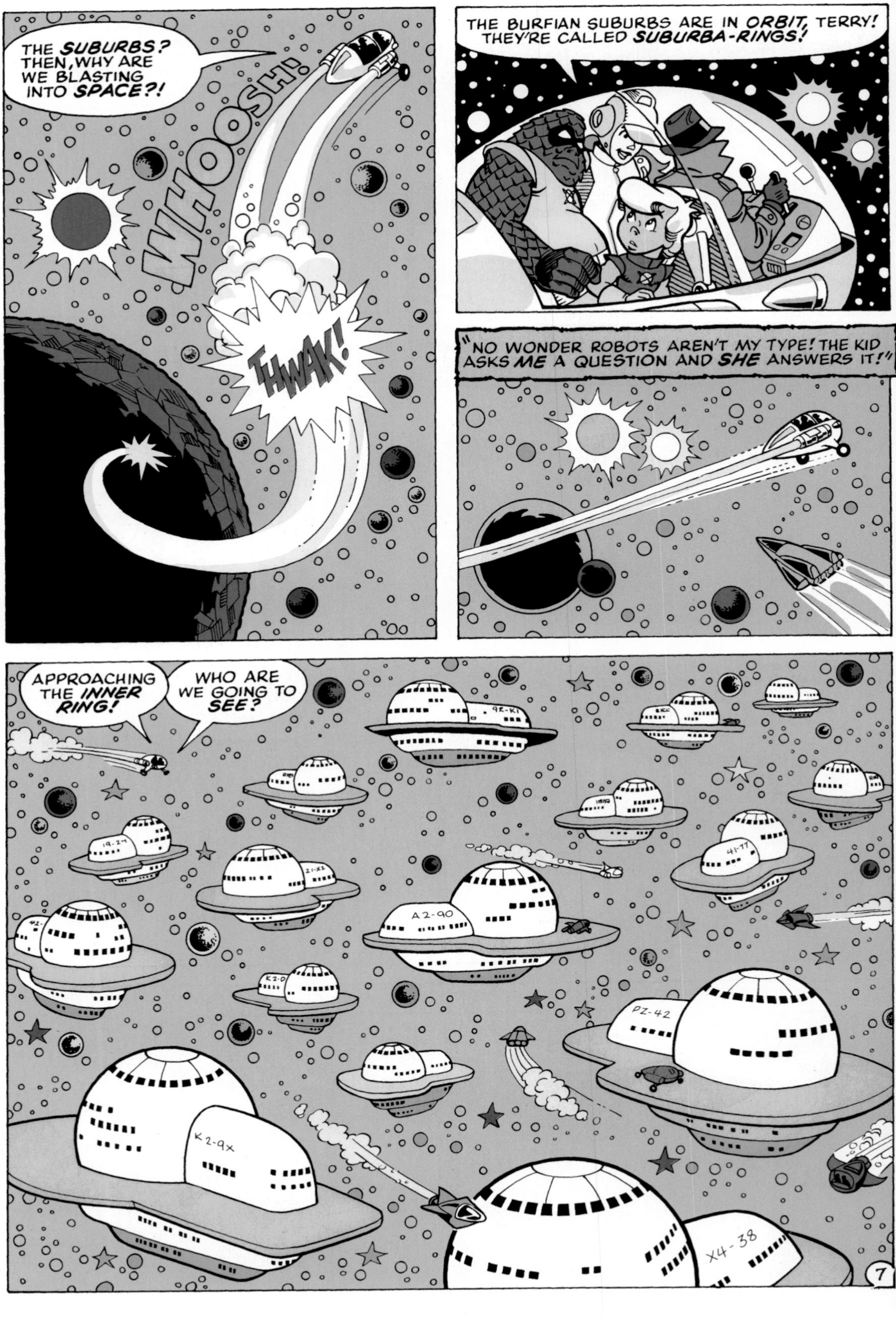
THE SUBURBS? THEN, WHY ARE WE BLASTING INTO SPACE?!
WHOOSH!
THWAK!
THE BURFIAN SUBURBS ARE IN ORBIT, TERRY! THEY'RE CALLED SUBURBA-RINGS!
"NO WONDER ROBOTS AREN'T MY TYPE! THE KID ASKS ME A QUESTION AND SHE ANSWERS IT!"
APPROACHING THE INNER RING!
WHO ARE WE GOING TO SEE?
A2-90
PZ-42
K2-9X
X4-38
7

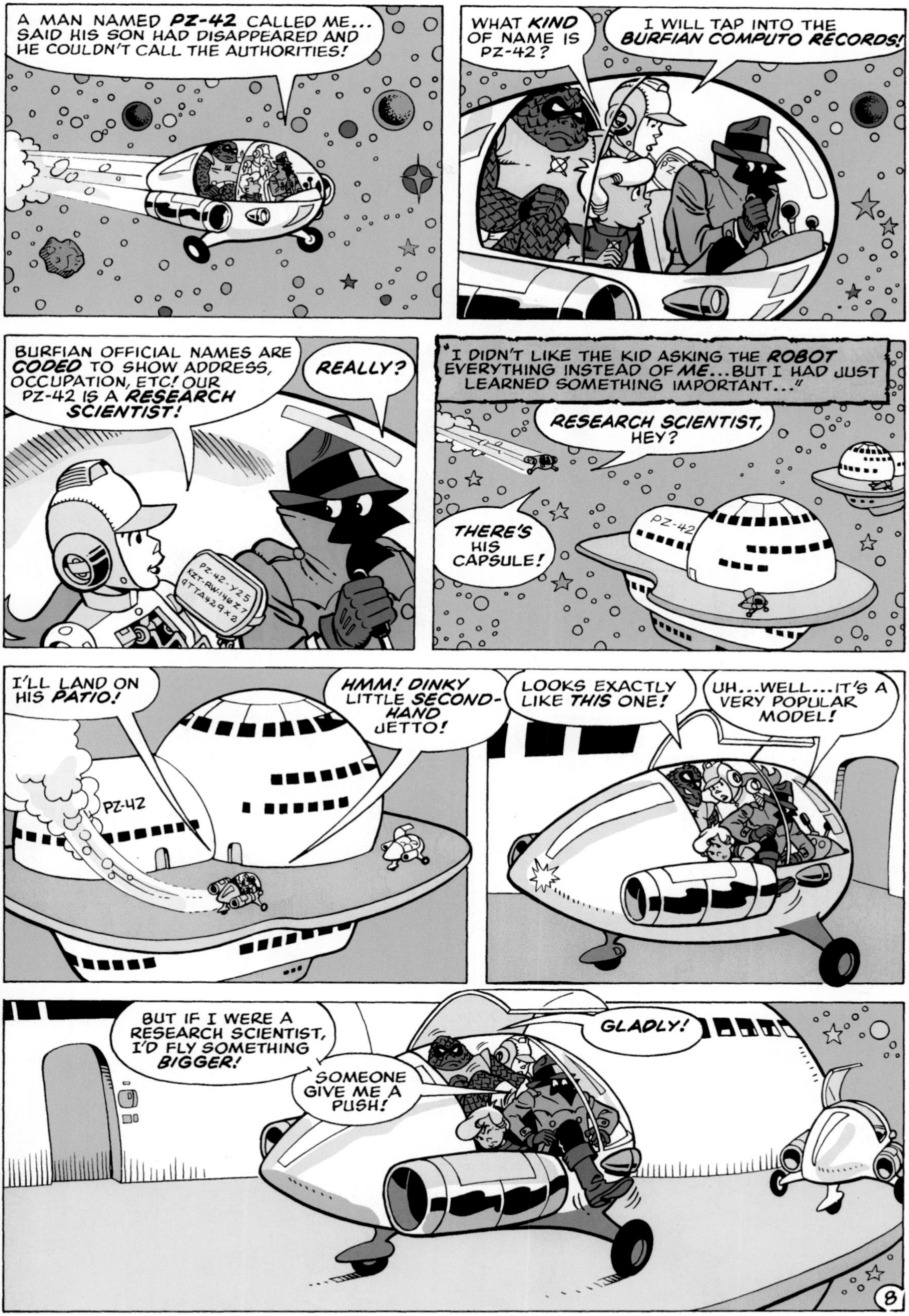

A MAN NAMED PZ-42 CALLED ME... SAID HIS SON HAD DISAPPEARED AND HE COULDN'T CALL THE AUTHORITIES!
WHAT KIND OF NAME IS PZ-42?
I WILL TAP INTO THE BURFIAN COMPUTO RECORDS!
BURFIAN OFFICIAL NAMES ARE CODED TO SHOW ADDRESS, OCCUPATION, ETC! OUR PZ-42 IS A RESEARCH SCIENTIST!
REALLY?
PZ-42-Y25 KZT-RW-146Z7 9TTA429x2
"I DIDN'T LIKE THE KID ASKING THE ROBOT EVERYTHING INSTEAD OF ME...BUT I HAD JUST LEARNED SOMETHING IMPORTANT..."
RESEARCH SCIENTIST, HEY?
THERE'S HIS CAPSULE!
PZ-42
I'LL LAND ON HIS PATIO!
HMM! DINKY LITTLE SECOND-HAND JETTO!
PZ-42
LOOKS EXACTLY LIKE THIS ONE!
UH...WELL...IT'S A VERY POPULAR MODEL!
BUT IF I WERE A RESEARCH SCIENTIST, I'D FLY SOMETHING BIGGER!
SOMEONE GIVE ME A PUSH!
GLADLY!
8

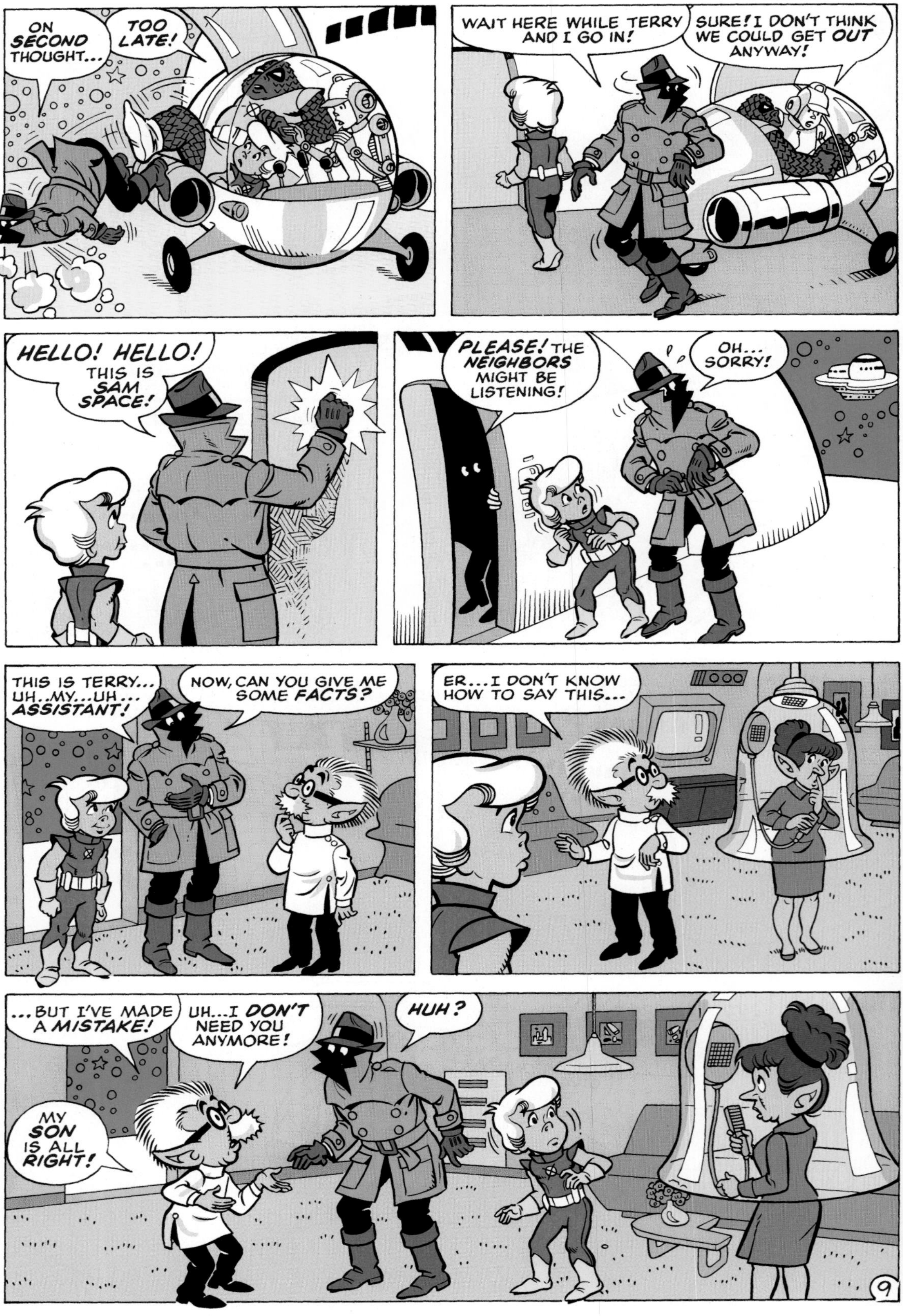
ON SECOND THOUGHT...
TOO LATE!
WAIT HERE WHILE TERRY AND I GO IN!
SURE! I DON'T THINK WE COULD GET OUT ANYWAY!
HELLO! HELLO! THIS IS SAM SPACE!
PLEASE! THE NEIGHBORS MIGHT BE LISTENING!
OH... SORRY!
THIS IS TERRY... UH..MY...UH... ASSISTANT!
NOW, CAN YOU GIVE ME SOME FACTS?
ER...I DON'T KNOW HOW TO SAY THIS...
...BUT I'VE MADE A MISTAKE!
MY SON IS ALL RIGHT!
UH...I DON'T NEED YOU ANYMORE!
HUH?
9

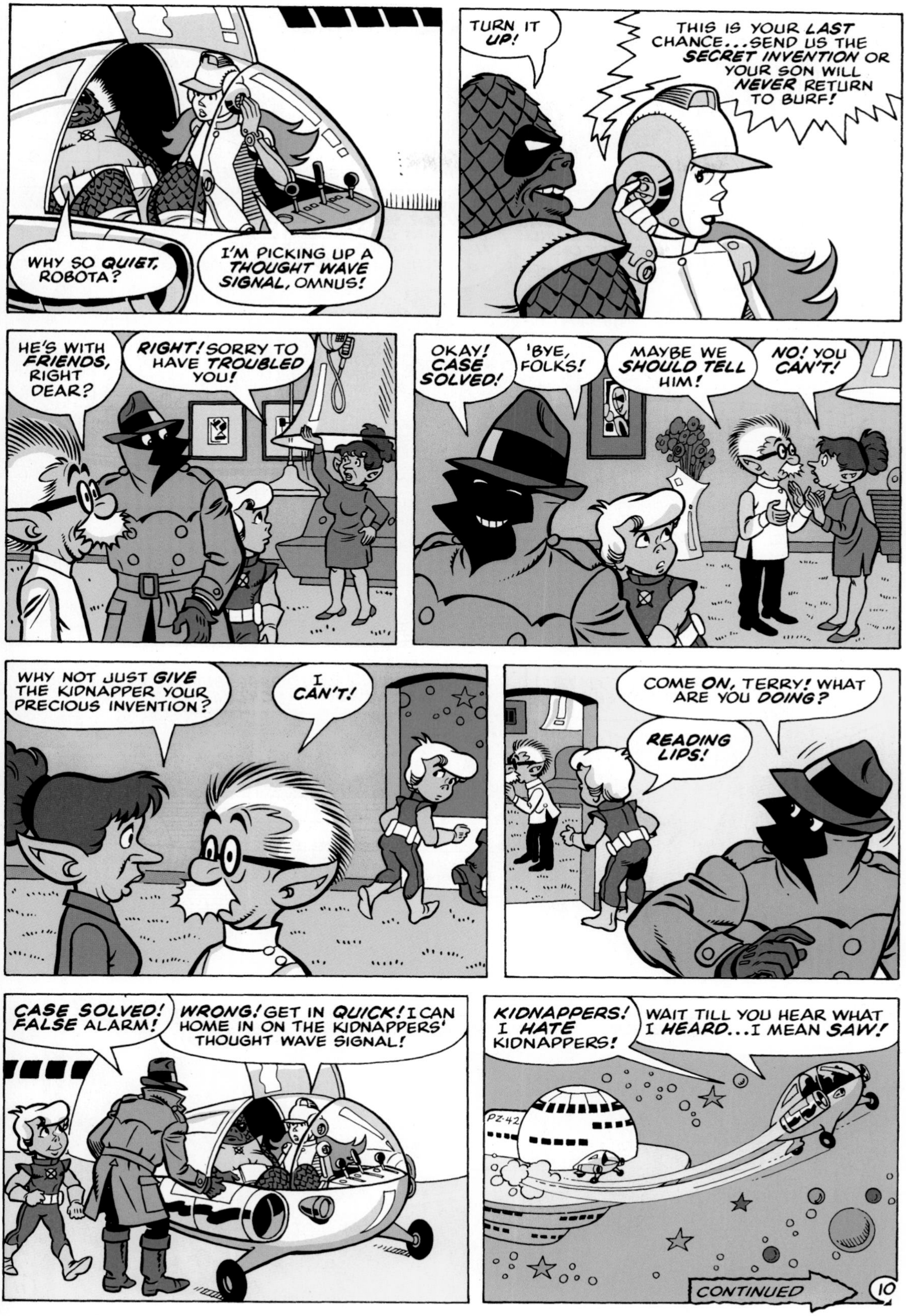
WHY SO QUIET, ROBOTA?
I'M PICKING UP A THOUGHT WAVE SIGNAL, OMNUS!
TURN IT UP!
THIS IS YOUR LAST CHANCE...SEND US THE SECRET INVENTION OR YOUR SON WILL NEVER RETURN TO BURF!
HE'S WITH FRIENDS, RIGHT DEAR?
RIGHT! SORRY TO HAVE TROUBLED YOU!
OKAY! CASE SOLVED!
'BYE, FOLKS!
MAYBE WE SHOULD TELL HIM!
NO! YOU CAN'T!
WHY NOT JUST GIVE THE KIDNAPPER YOUR PRECIOUS INVENTION?
I CAN'T!
COME ON, TERRY! WHAT ARE YOU DOING?
READING LIPS!
CASE SOLVED! FALSE ALARM!
WRONG! GET IN QUICK! I CAN HOME IN ON THE KIDNAPPERS' THOUGHT WAVE SIGNAL!
KIDNAPPERS! I HATE KIDNAPPERS!
WAIT TILL YOU HEAR WHAT I HEARD...I MEAN SAW!
PZ-42
CONTINUED
10

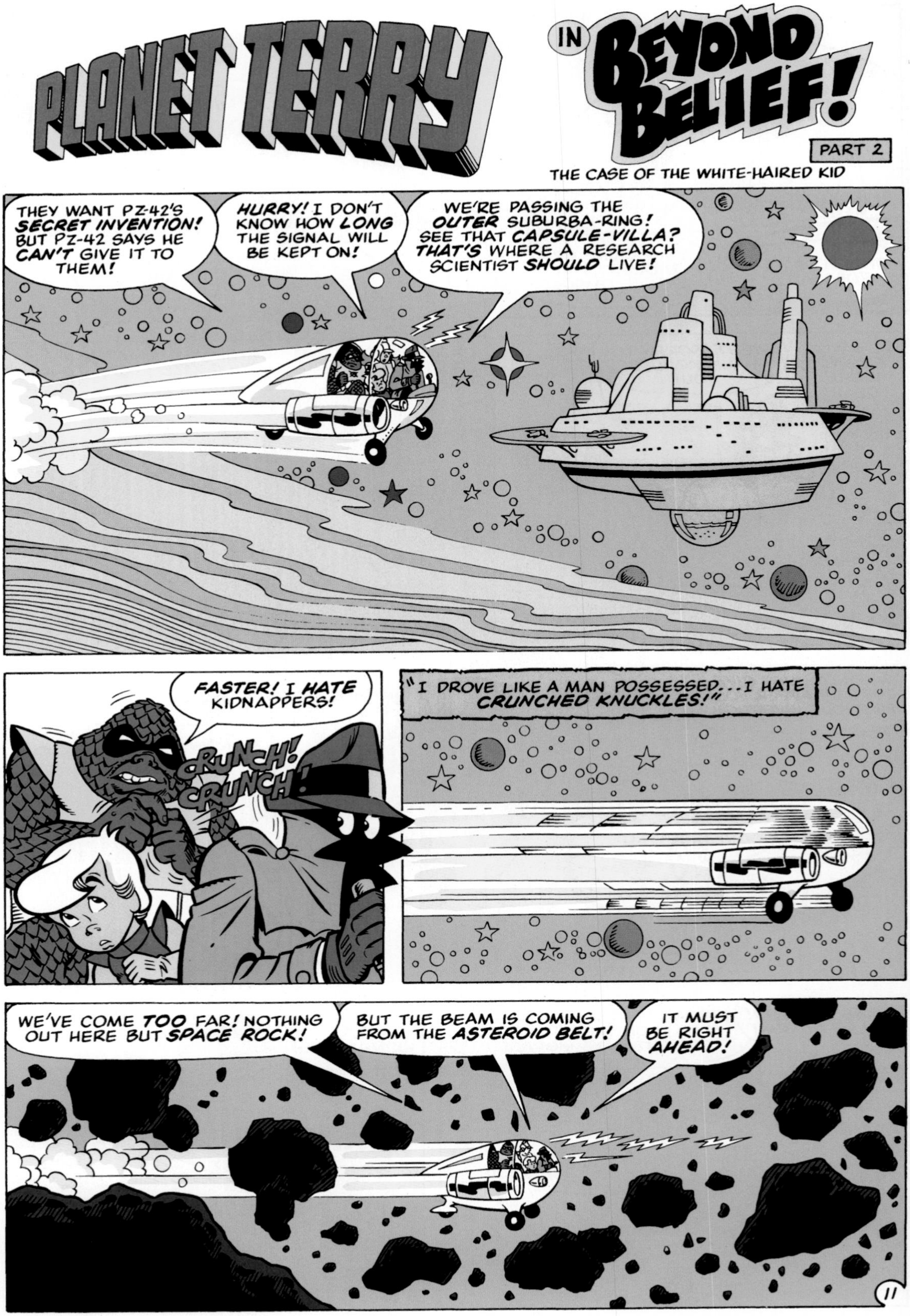

PLANET TERRY
IN
BEYOND BELIEF!
PART 2
THE CASE OF THE WHITE-HAIRED KID
THEY WANT PZ-42'S SECRET INVENTION! BUT PZ-42 SAYS HE CAN'T GIVE IT TO THEM!
HURRY! I DON'T KNOW HOW LONG THE SIGNAL WILL BE KEPT ON!
WE'RE PASSING THE OUTER SUBURBA-RING! SEE THAT CAPSULE-VILLA? THAT'S WHERE A RESEARCH SCIENTIST SHOULD LIVE!
FASTER! I HATE KIDNAPPERS!
CRUNCH! CRUNCH!
"I DROVE LIKE A MAN POSSESSED...I HATE CRUNCHED KNUCKLES!"
WE'VE COME TOO FAR! NOTHING OUT HERE BUT SPACE ROCK!
BUT THE BEAM IS COMING FROM THE ASTEROID BELT!
IT MUST BE RIGHT AHEAD!
11

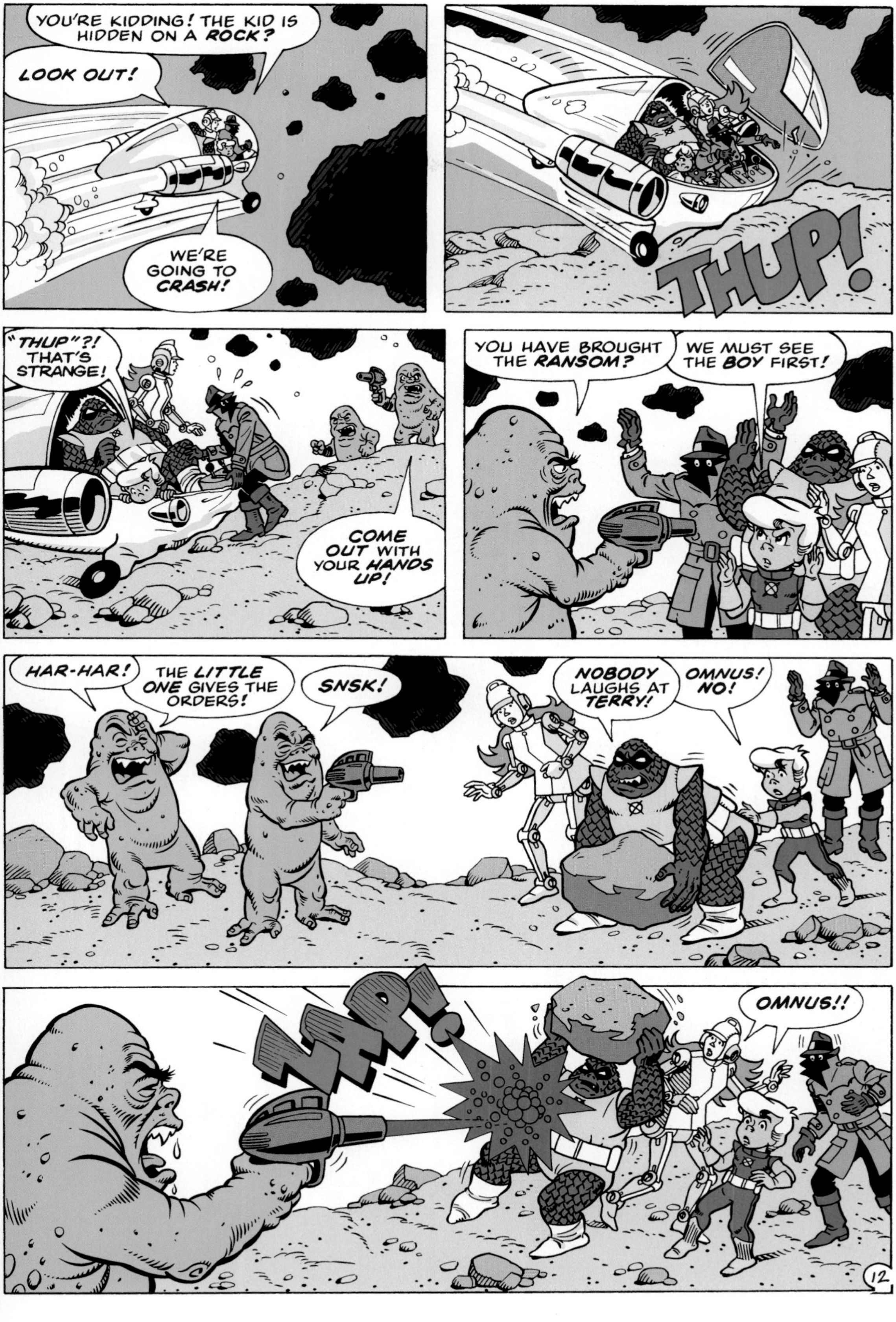
YOU'RE KIDDING! THE KID IS HIDDEN ON A ROCK?
LOOK OUT!
WE'RE GOING TO CRASH!
THUP!
"THUP"?! THAT'S STRANGE!
COME OUT WITH YOUR HANDS UP!
YOU HAVE BROUGHT THE RANSOM?
WE MUST SEE THE BOY FIRST!
HAR-HAR!
THE LITTLE ONE GIVES THE ORDERS!
SNSK!
NOBODY LAUGHS AT TERRY!
OMNUS! NO!
ZAP!
OMNUS!!
12

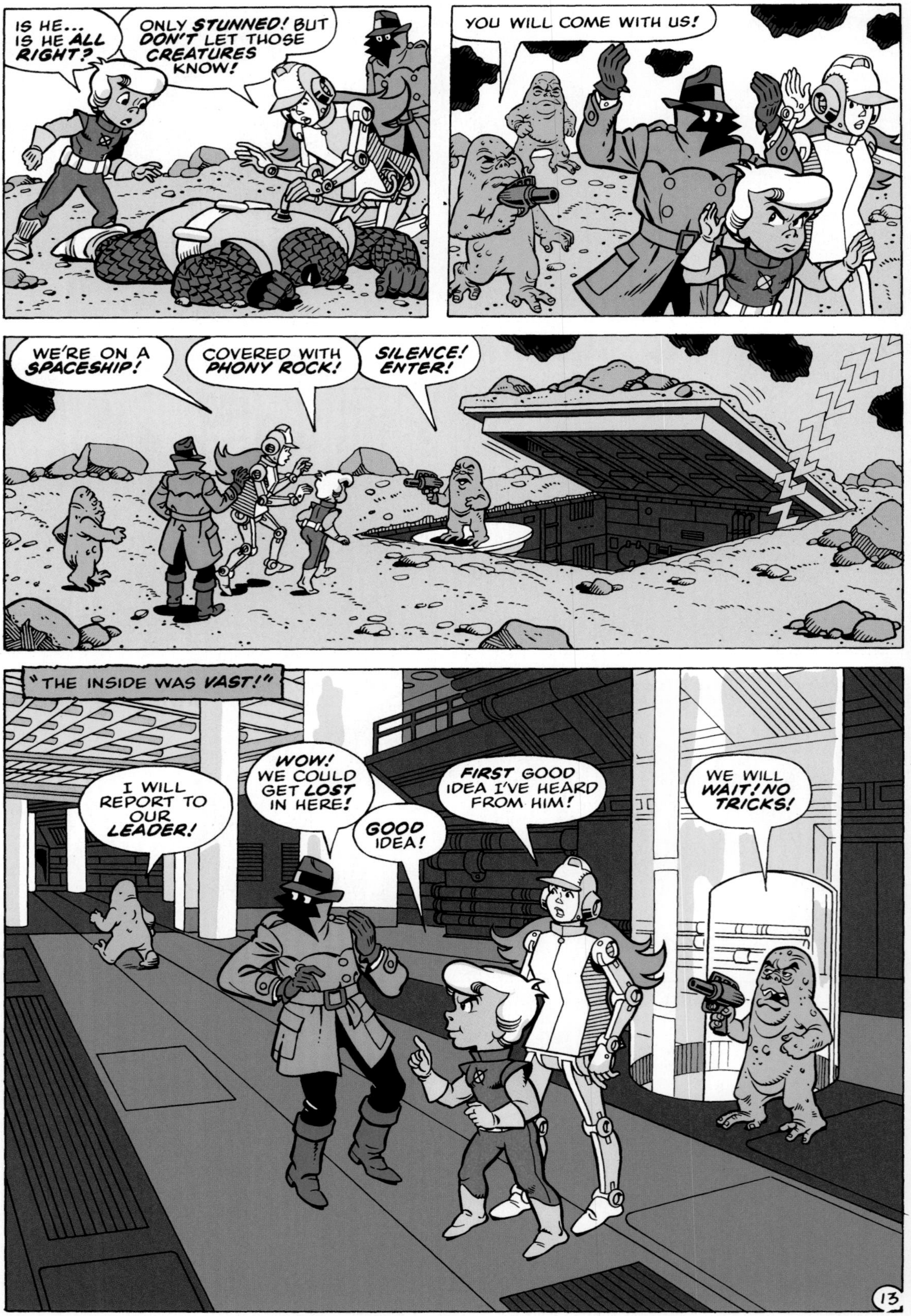
IS HE... IS HE ALL RIGHT?
ONLY STUNNED! BUT DON'T LET THOSE CREATURES KNOW!
YOU WILL COME WITH US!
WE'RE ON A SPACESHIP!
COVERED WITH PHONY ROCK!
SILENCE! ENTER!
"THE INSIDE WAS VAST!"
I WILL REPORT TO OUR LEADER!
WOW! WE COULD GET LOST IN HERE!
GOOD IDEA!
FIRST GOOD IDEA I'VE HEARD FROM HIM!
WE WILL WAIT! NO TRICKS!
13

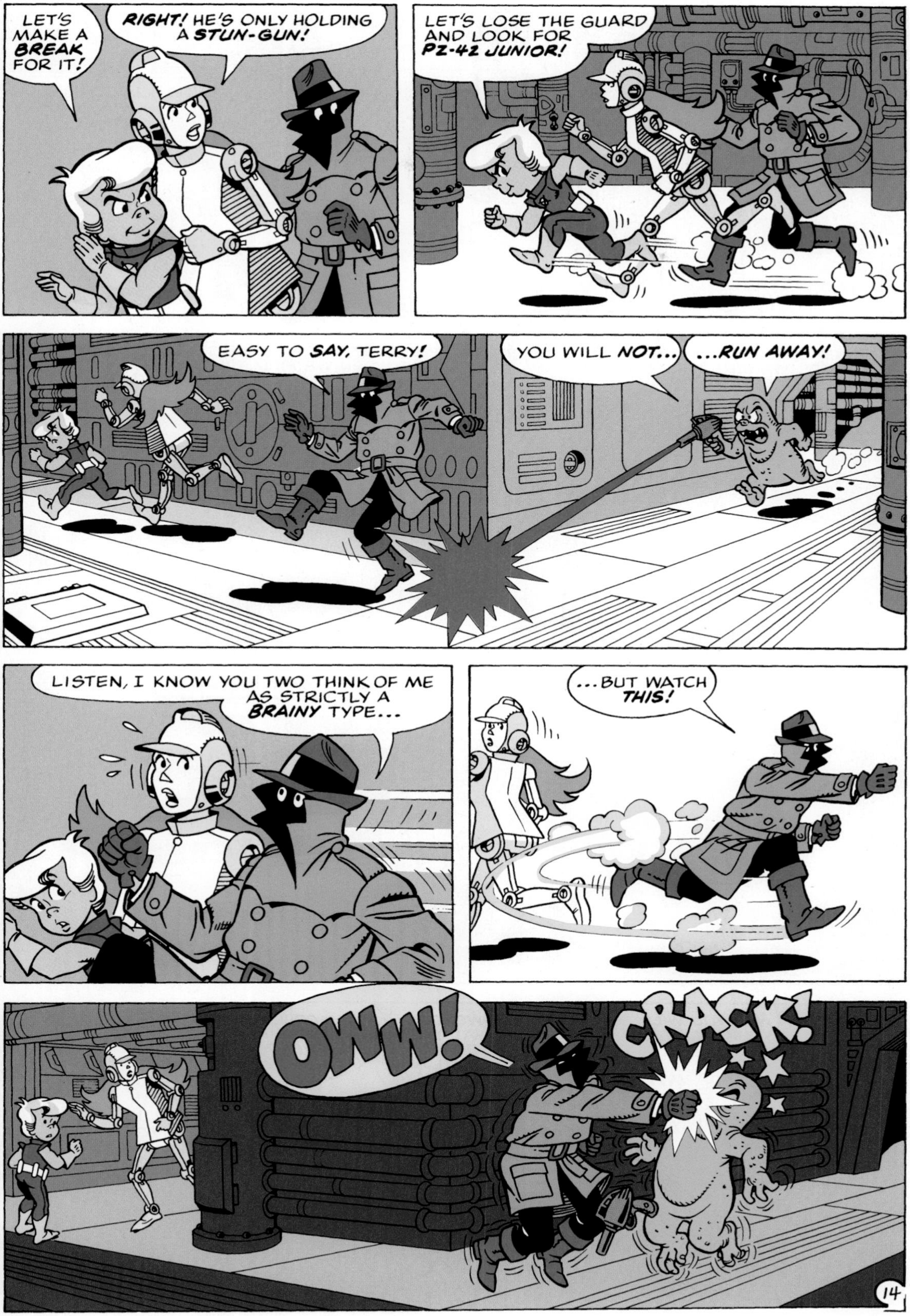
LET'S MAKE A BREAK FOR IT!
RIGHT! HE'S ONLY HOLDING A STUN-GUN!
LET'S LOSE THE GUARD AND LOOK FOR PZ-42 JUNIOR!
EASY TO SAY, TERRY!
YOU WILL NOT...
...RUN AWAY!
LISTEN, I KNOW YOU TWO THINK OF ME AS STRICTLY A BRAINY TYPE...
...BUT WATCH THIS!
OWW!
CRACK!
14

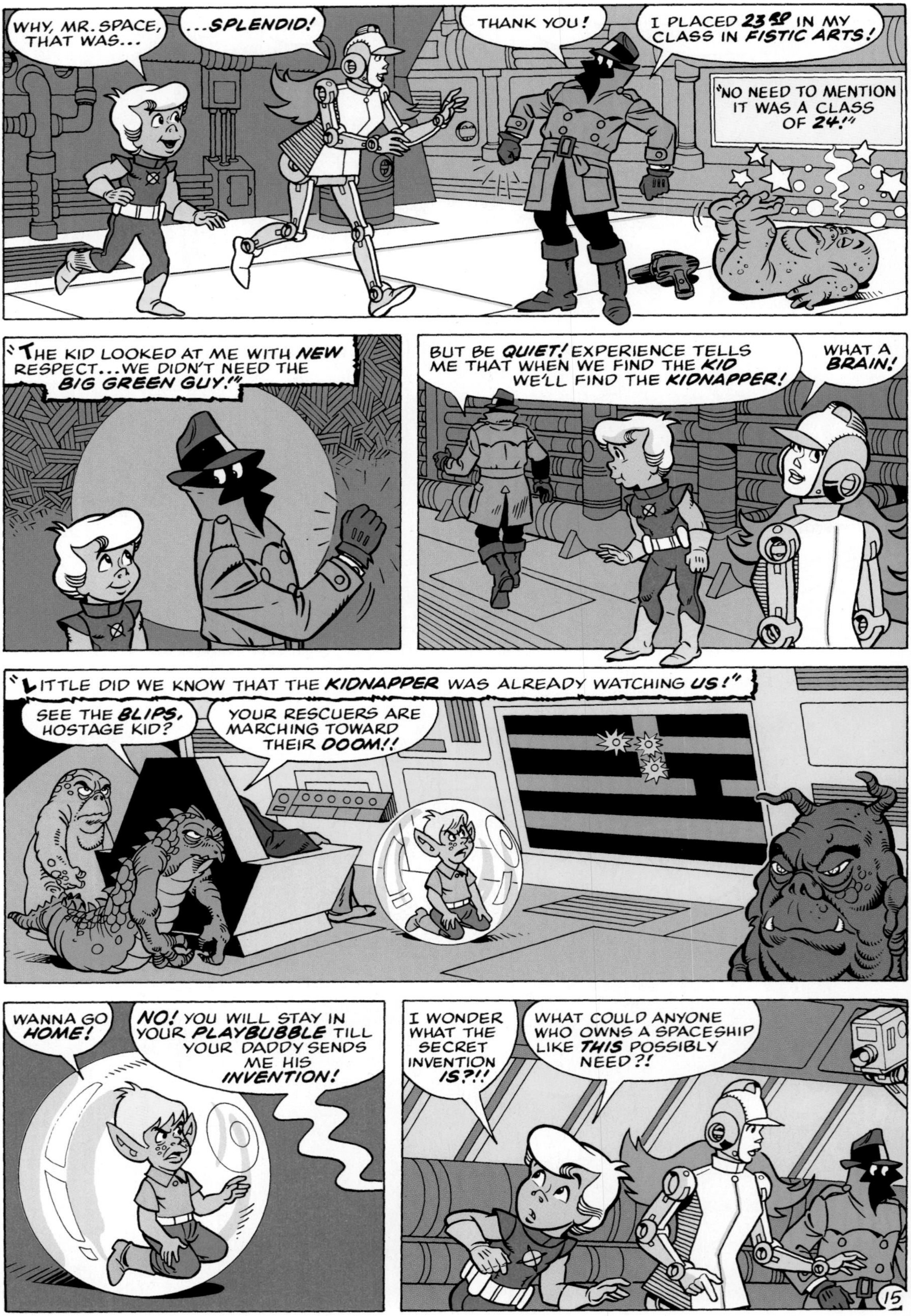
WHY, MR. SPACE, THAT WAS...
...SPLENDID!
THANK YOU!
I PLACED 23RD IN MY CLASS IN FISTIC ARTS!
"NO NEED TO MENTION IT WAS A CLASS OF 24!"
"THE KID LOOKED AT ME WITH NEW RESPECT...WE DIDN'T NEED THE BIG GREEN GUY!"
BUT BE QUIET! EXPERIENCE TELLS ME THAT WHEN WE FIND THE KID WE'LL FIND THE KIDNAPPER!
WHAT A BRAIN!
"LITTLE DID WE KNOW THAT THE KIDNAPPER WAS ALREADY WATCHING US!"
SEE THE BLIPS, HOSTAGE KID?
YOUR RESCUERS ARE MARCHING TOWARD THEIR DOOM!!
WANNA GO HOME!
NO! YOU WILL STAY IN YOUR PLAYBUBBLE TILL YOUR DADDY SENDS ME HIS INVENTION!
I WONDER WHAT THE SECRET INVENTION IS?!!
WHAT COULD ANYONE WHO OWNS A SPACESHIP LIKE THIS POSSIBLY NEED?!
15

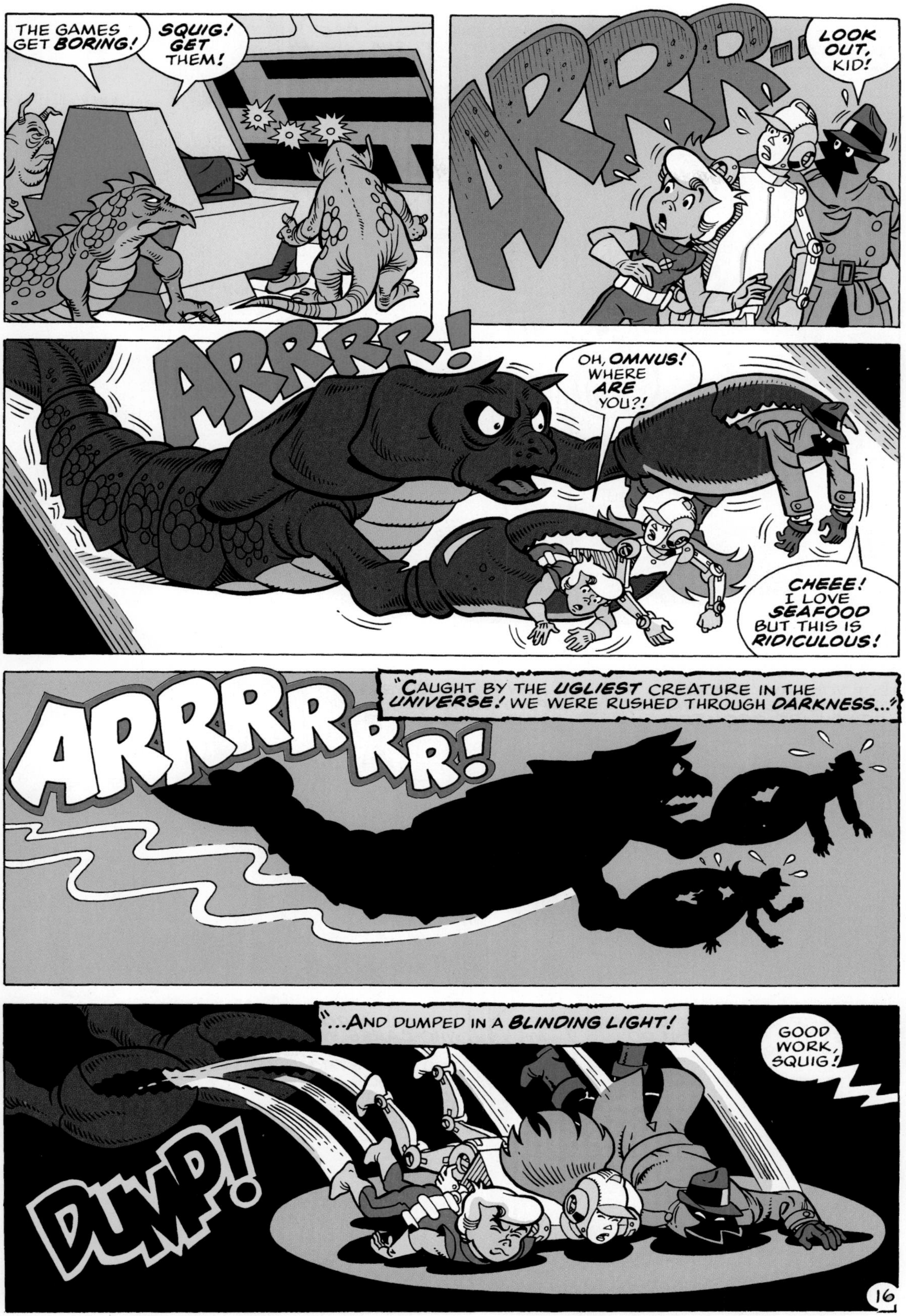
THE GAMES GET BORING!
SQUIG! GET THEM!
ARRR-
LOOK OUT, KID!
ARRRRR!
OH, OMNUS! WHERE ARE YOU?!
CHEEE! I LOVE SEAFOOD BUT THIS IS RIDICULOUS!
"CAUGHT BY THE UGLIEST CREATURE IN THE UNIVERSE! WE WERE RUSHED THROUGH DARKNESS..."
ARRRRRRR!
"...AND DUMPED IN A BLINDING LIGHT!
GOOD WORK, SQUIG!
DUMP!
16

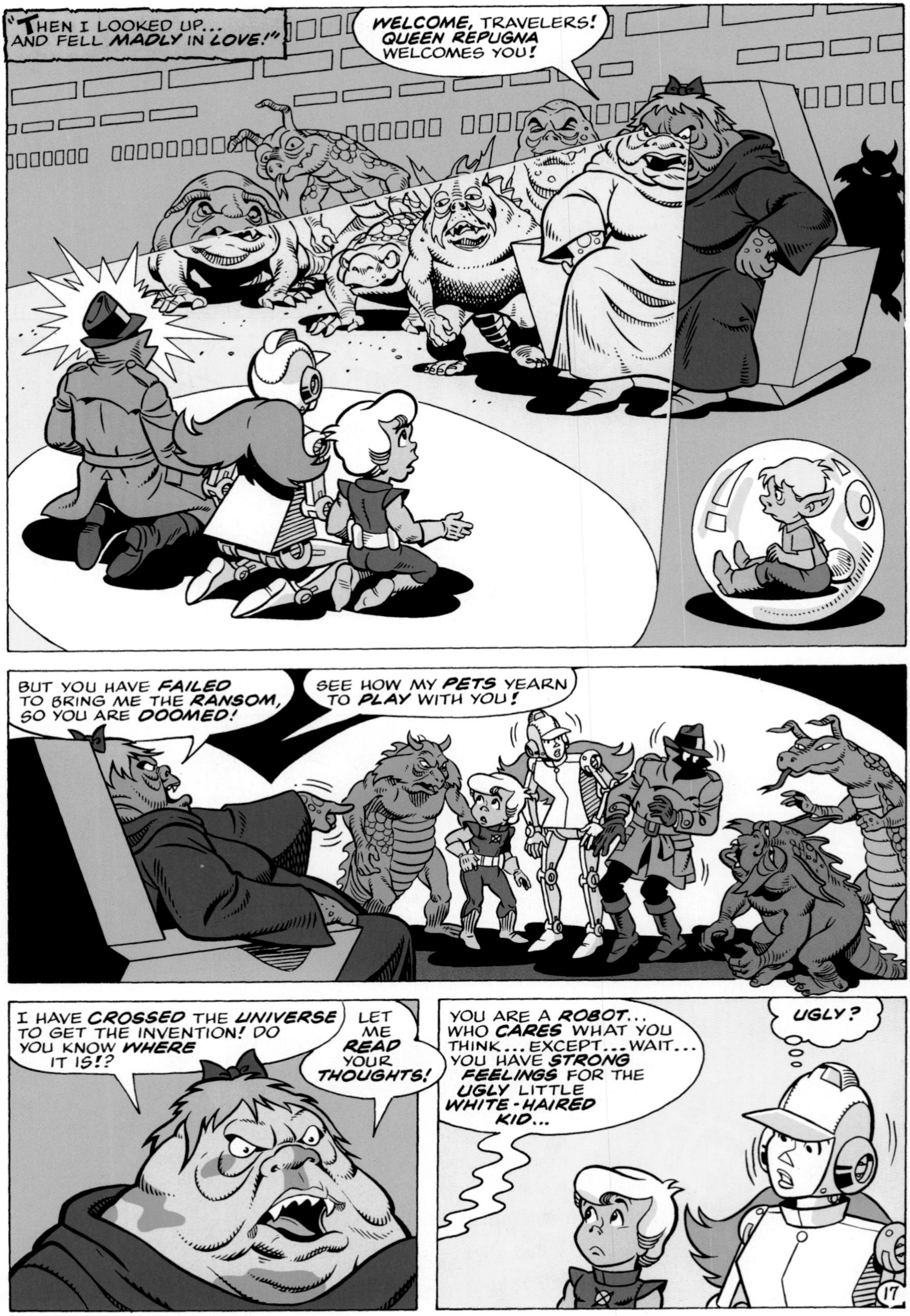
"THEN I LOOKED UP... AND FELL MADLY IN LOVE!"
WELCOME, TRAVELERS! QUEEN REPUGNA WELCOMES YOU!
BUT YOU HAVE FAILED TO BRING ME THE RANSOM, SO YOU ARE DOOMED!
SEE HOW MY PETS YEARN TO PLAY WITH YOU!
I HAVE CROSSED THE UNIVERSE TO GET THE INVENTION! DO YOU KNOW WHERE IT IS!?
LET ME READ YOUR THOUGHTS!
YOU ARE A ROBOT... WHO CARES WHAT YOU THINK... EXCEPT... WAIT... YOU HAVE STRONG FEELINGS FOR THE UGLY LITTLE WHITE-HAIRED KID...
UGLY?
17

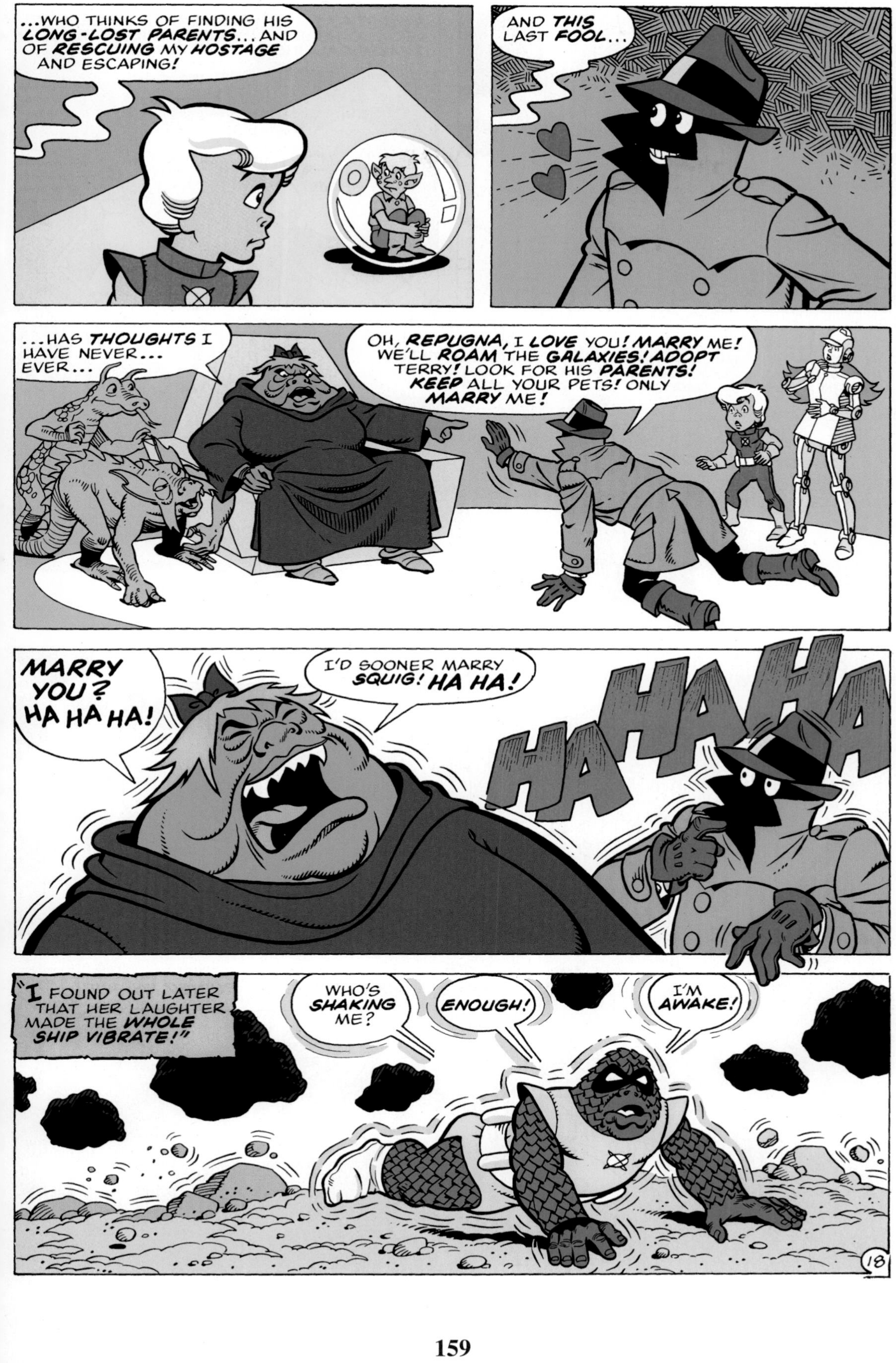
...WHO THINKS OF FINDING HIS LONG-LOST PARENTS... AND OF RESCUING MY HOSTAGE AND ESCAPING!
AND THIS LAST FOOL...
...HAS THOUGHTS I HAVE NEVER... EVER...
OH, REPUGNA, I LOVE YOU! MARRY ME! WE'LL ROAM THE GALAXIES! ADOPT TERRY! LOOK FOR HIS PARENTS! KEEP ALL YOUR PETS! ONLY MARRY ME!
MARRY YOU? HA HA HA HA!
I'D SOONER MARRY SQUIG! HA HA!
HA HA HA HA HA
"I FOUND OUT LATER THAT HER LAUGHTER MADE THE WHOLE SHIP VIBRATE!"
WHO'S SHAKING ME?
ENOUGH!
I'M AWAKE!
18

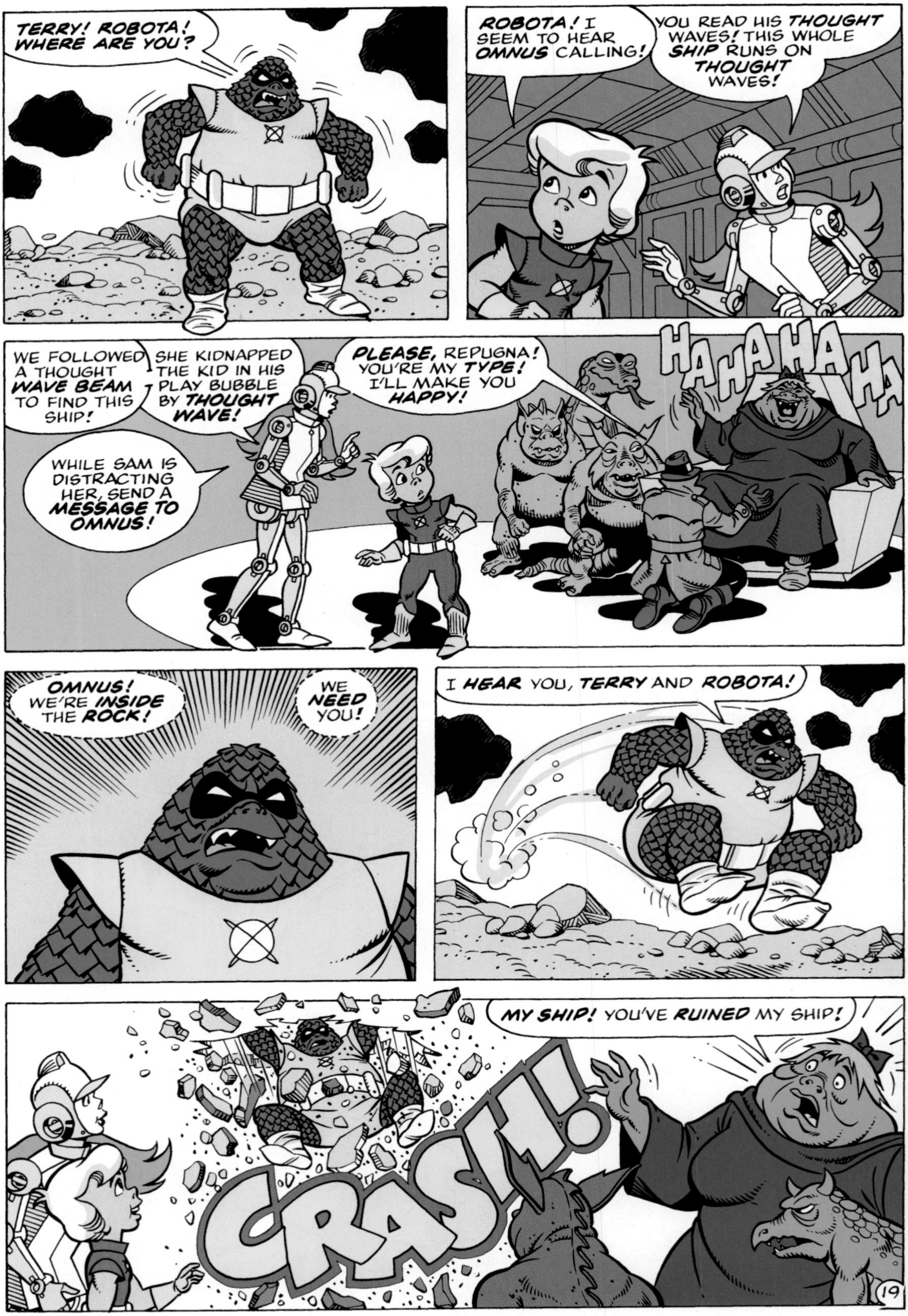
TERRY! ROBOTA! WHERE ARE YOU?
ROBOTA! I SEEM TO HEAR OMNUS CALLING!
YOU READ HIS THOUGHT WAVES! THIS WHOLE SHIP RUNS ON THOUGHT WAVES!
WE FOLLOWED A THOUGHT WAVE BEAM TO FIND THIS SHIP!
SHE KIDNAPPED THE KID IN HIS PLAY BUBBLE BY THOUGHT WAVE!
PLEASE, REPUGNA! YOU'RE MY TYPE! I'LL MAKE YOU HAPPY!
HAHAHAHA
WHILE SAM IS DISTRACTING HER, SEND A MESSAGE TO OMNUS!
OMNUS! WE'RE INSIDE THE ROCK!
WE NEED YOU!
I HEAR YOU, TERRY AND ROBOTA!
MY SHIP! YOU'VE RUINED MY SHIP!
CRASH!!
19

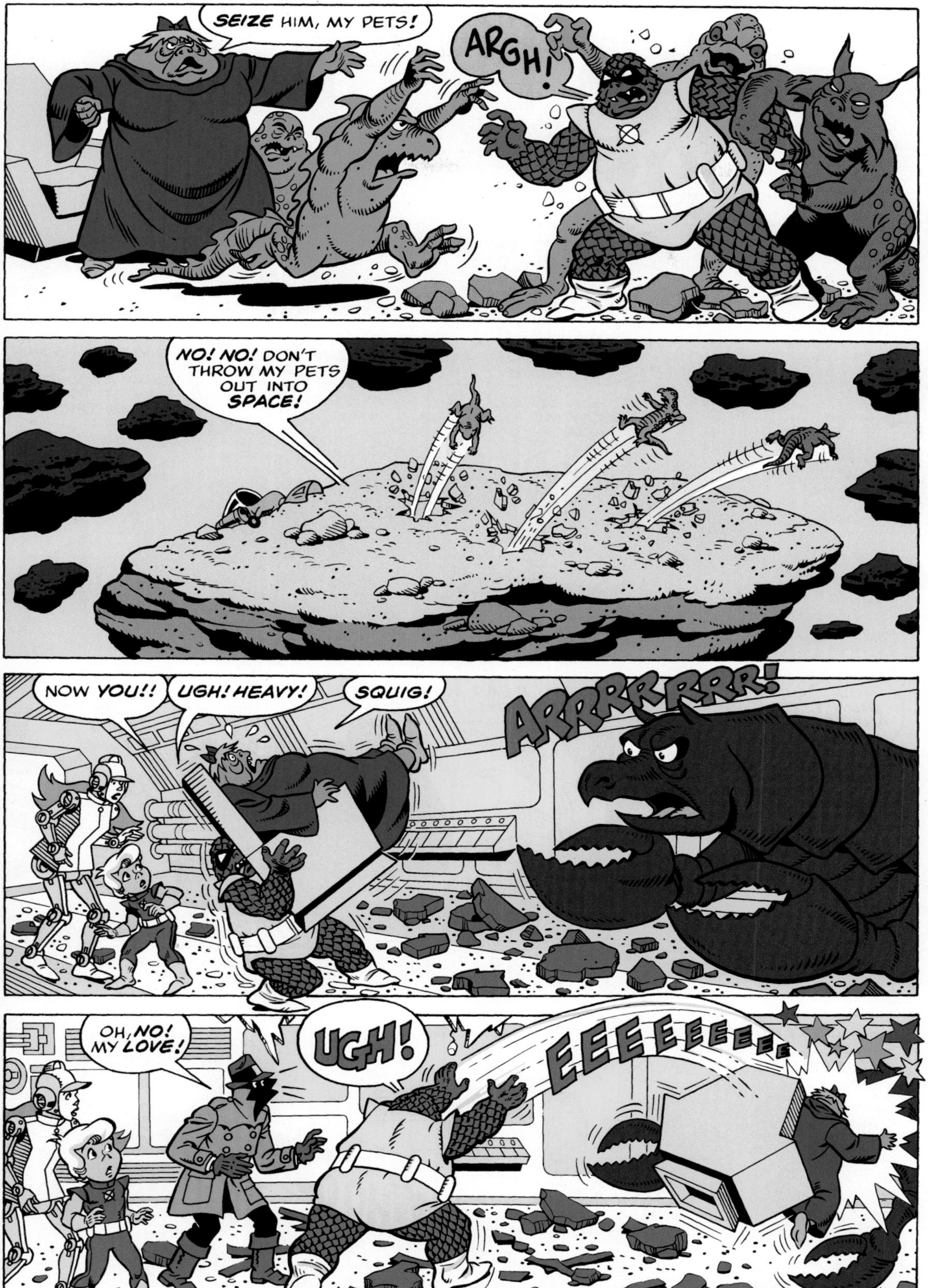
SEIZE HIM, MY PETS!
ARGH!
NO! NO! DON'T THROW MY PETS OUT INTO SPACE!
NOW YOU!!
UGH! HEAVY!
SQUIG!
ARRRRRRR!
OH, NO! MY LOVE!
UGH!
EEEEEEEEE
20

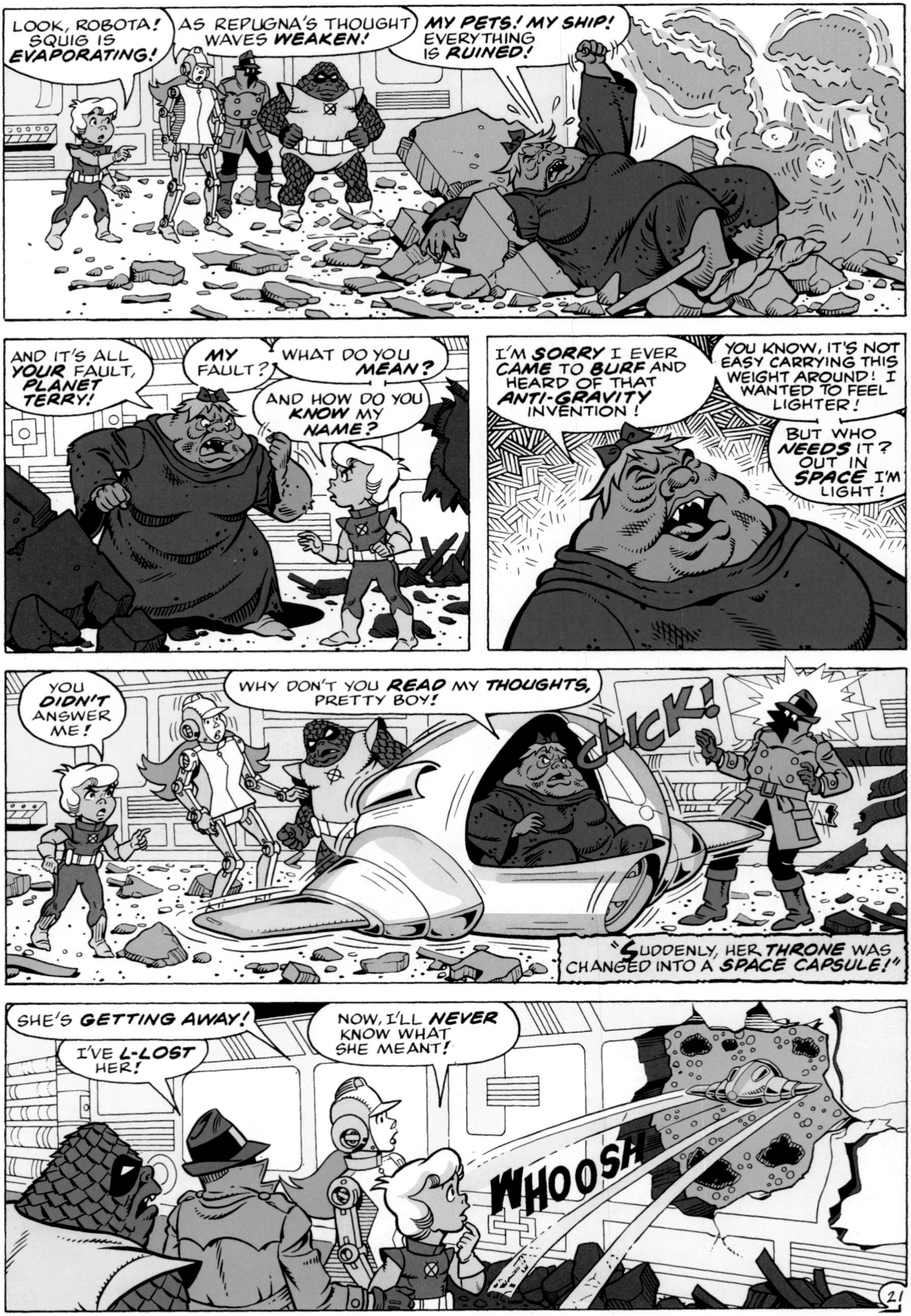
LOOK, ROBOTA! SQUIG IS EVAPORATING!
AS REPUGNA'S THOUGHT WAVES WEAKEN!
MY PETS! MY SHIP! EVERYTHING IS RUINED!
AND IT'S ALL YOUR FAULT, PLANET TERRY!
MY FAULT?
WHAT DO YOU MEAN?
AND HOW DO YOU KNOW MY NAME?
I'M SORRY I EVER CAME TO BURF AND HEARD OF THAT ANTI-GRAVITY INVENTION!
YOU KNOW, IT'S NOT EASY CARRYING THIS WEIGHT AROUND! I WANTED TO FEEL LIGHTER!
BUT WHO NEEDS IT? OUT IN SPACE I'M LIGHT!
YOU DIDN'T ANSWER ME!
WHY DON'T YOU READ MY THOUGHTS, PRETTY BOY!
CLICK!
"SUDDENLY, HER THRONE WAS CHANGED INTO A SPACE CAPSULE!"
SHE'S GETTING AWAY!
I'VE L-LOST HER!
NOW, I'LL NEVER KNOW WHAT SHE MEANT!
WHOOSH
21

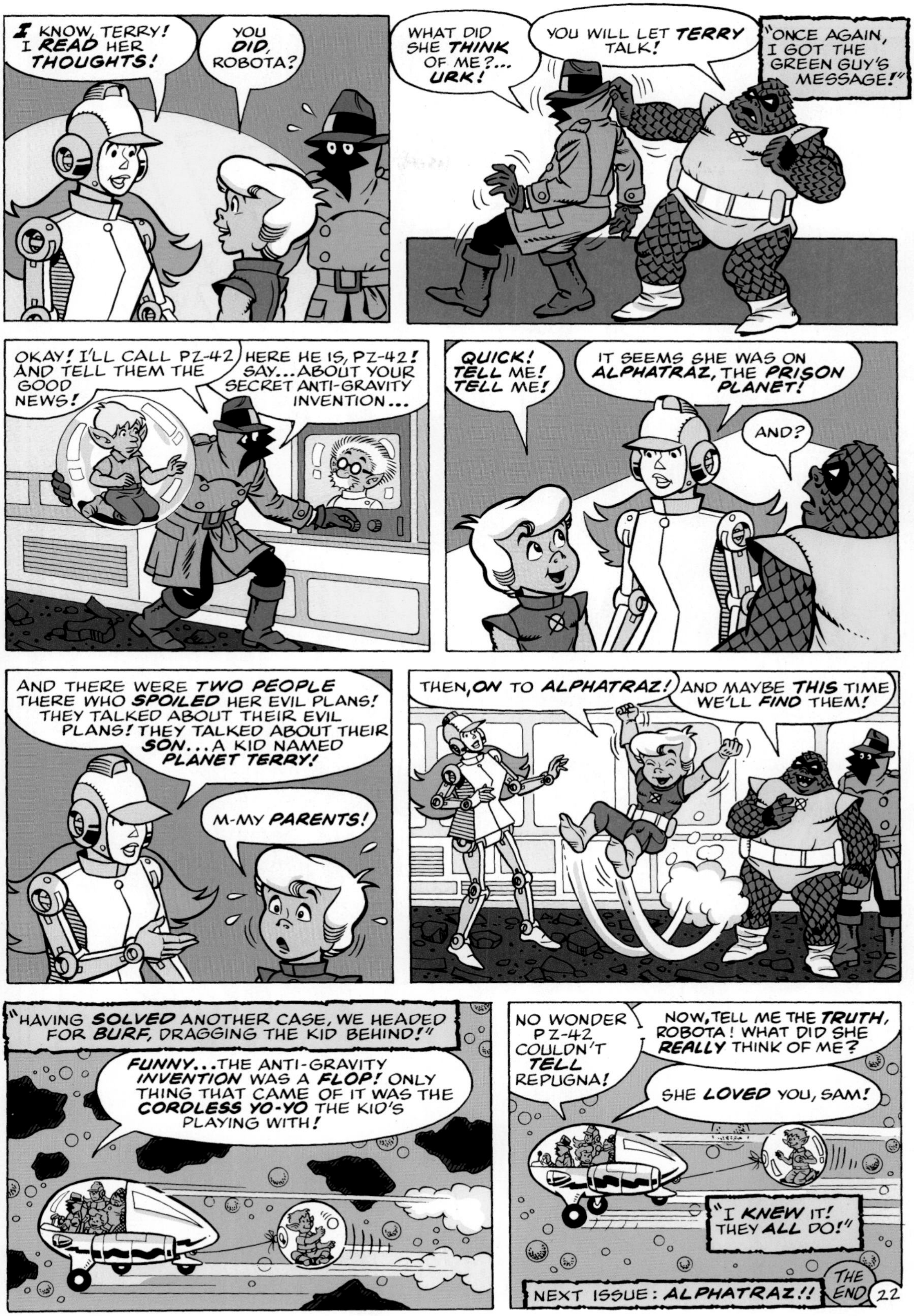
I KNOW, TERRY! I READ HER THOUGHTS!
YOU DID, ROBOTA?
WHAT DID SHE THINK OF ME?... URK!
YOU WILL LET TERRY TALK!
"ONCE AGAIN, I GOT THE GREEN GUY'S MESSAGE!"
OKAY! I'LL CALL PZ-42 AND TELL THEM THE GOOD NEWS!
HERE HE IS, PZ-42! SAY...ABOUT YOUR SECRET ANTI-GRAVITY INVENTION...
QUICK! TELL ME! TELL ME!
IT SEEMS SHE WAS ON ALPHATRAZ, THE PRISON PLANET!
AND?
AND THERE WERE TWO PEOPLE THERE WHO SPOILED HER EVIL PLANS! THEY TALKED ABOUT THEIR EVIL PLANS! THEY TALKED ABOUT THEIR SON...A KID NAMED PLANET TERRY!
M-MY PARENTS!
THEN, ON TO ALPHATRAZ!
AND MAYBE THIS TIME WE'LL FIND THEM!
"HAVING SOLVED ANOTHER CASE, WE HEADED FOR BURF, DRAGGING THE KID BEHIND!"
FUNNY...THE ANTI-GRAVITY INVENTION WAS A FLOP! ONLY THING THAT CAME OF IT WAS THE CORDLESS YO-YO THE KID'S PLAYING WITH!
NO WONDER PZ-42 COULDN'T TELL REPUGNA!
NOW, TELL ME THE TRUTH, ROBOTA! WHAT DID SHE REALLY THINK OF ME?
SHE LOVED YOU, SAM!
"I KNEW IT! THEY ALL DO!"
NEXT ISSUE: ALPHATRAZ!!
THE END
22

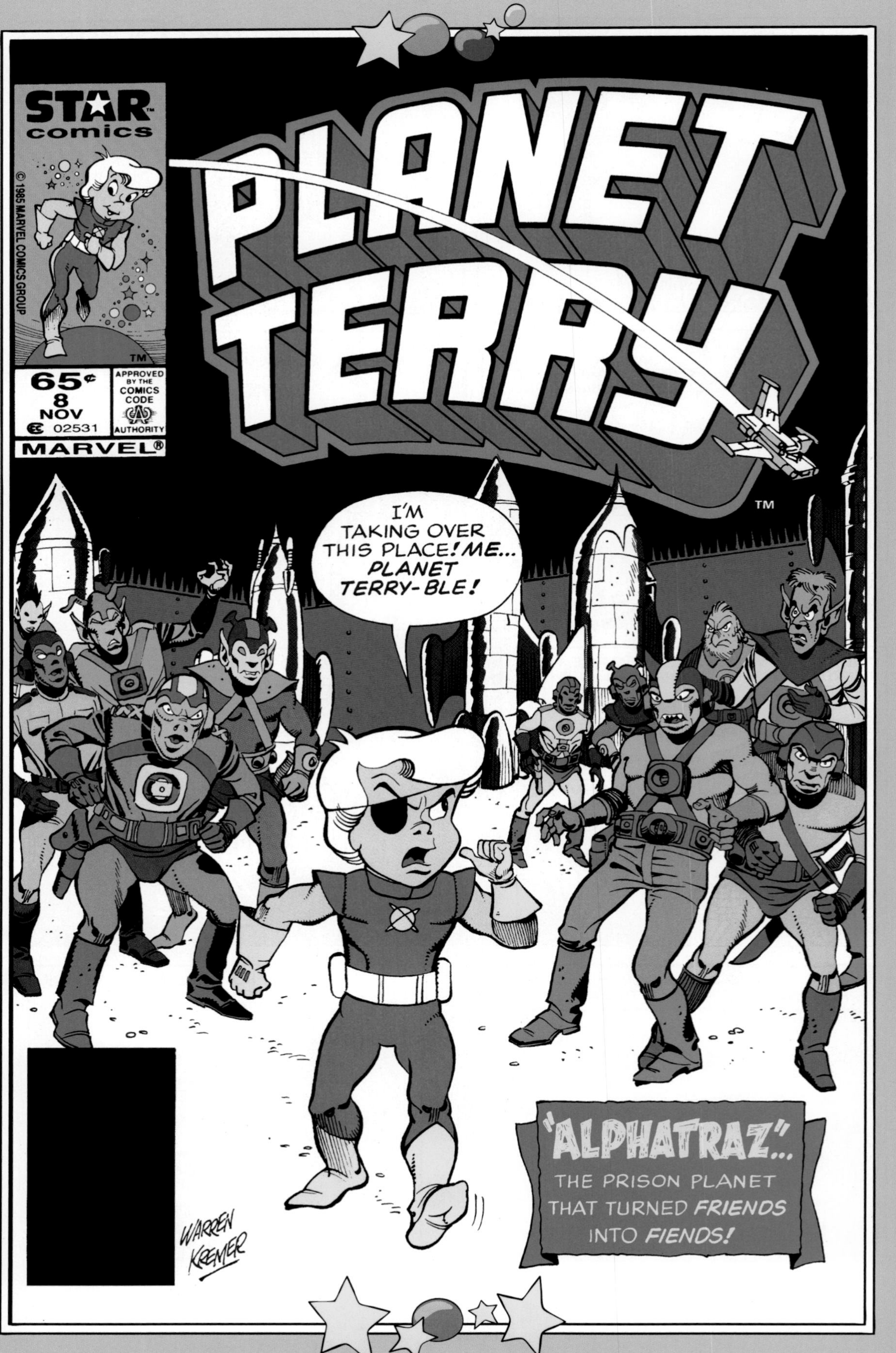
STAR™ comics
© 1985 MARVEL COMICS GROUP
65¢
8
NOV
02531
APPROVED BY THE COMICS CODE AUTHORITY
MARVEL®
PLANET TERRY™
I'M TAKING OVER THIS PLACE! ME... PLANET TERRY-BLE!
"ALPHATRAZ"... THE PRISON PLANET THAT TURNED FRIENDS INTO FIENDS!
WARREN KREMER

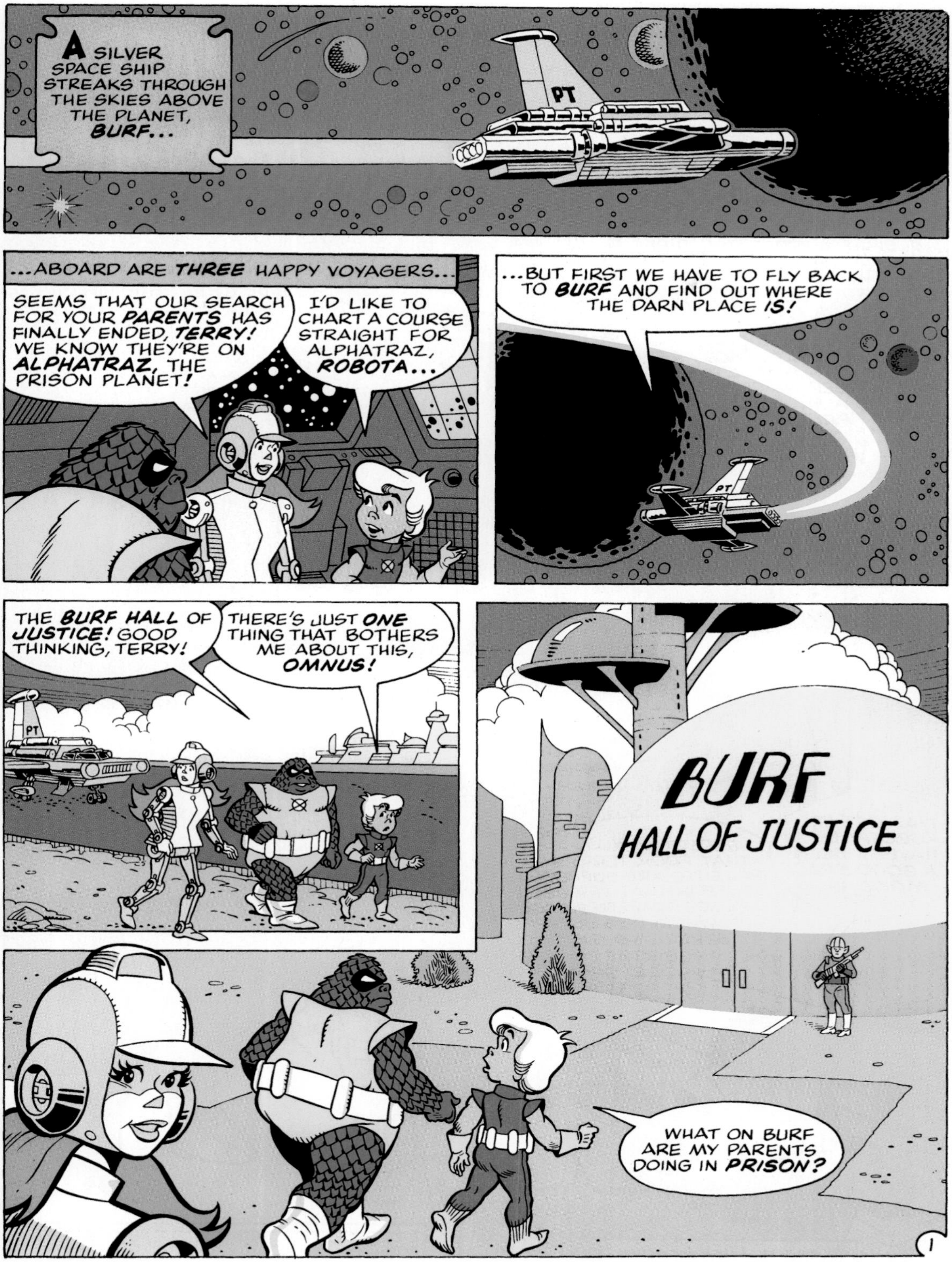
A SILVER SPACE SHIP STREAKS THROUGH THE SKIES ABOVE THE PLANET, BURF...
PT
...ABOARD ARE THREE HAPPY VOYAGERS...
SEEMS THAT OUR SEARCH FOR YOUR PARENTS HAS FINALLY ENDED, TERRY! WE KNOW THEY'RE ON ALPHATRAZ, THE PRISON PLANET!
I'D LIKE TO CHART A COURSE STRAIGHT FOR ALPHATRAZ, ROBOTA...
...BUT FIRST WE HAVE TO FLY BACK TO BURF AND FIND OUT WHERE THE DARN PLACE IS!
THE BURF HALL OF JUSTICE! GOOD THINKING, TERRY!
THERE'S JUST ONE THING THAT BOTHERS ME ABOUT THIS, OMNUS!
BURF
HALL OF JUSTICE
WHAT ON BURF ARE MY PARENTS DOING IN PRISON?
1

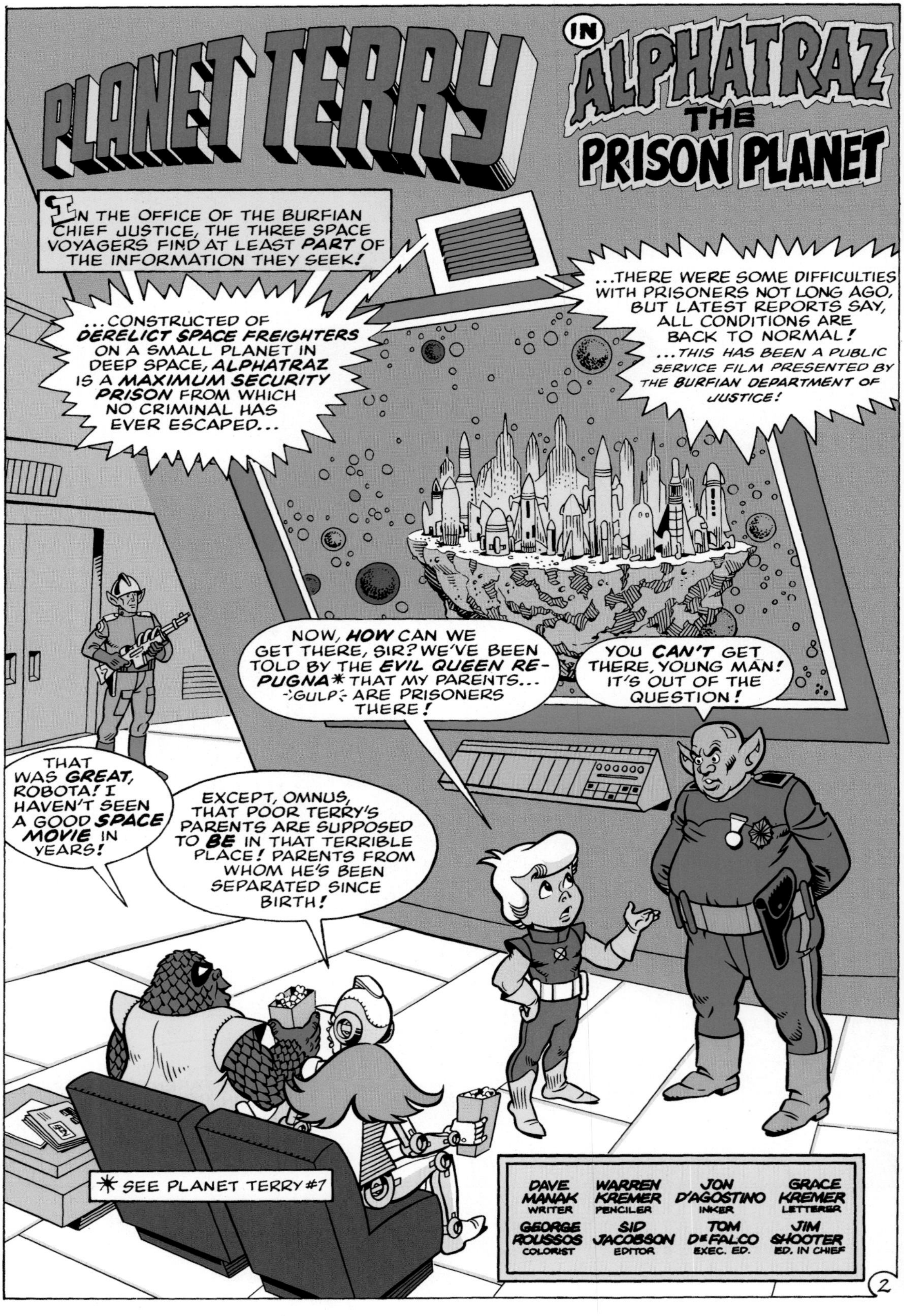
PLANET TERRY
IN
ALPHATRAZ THE PRISON PLANET
IN THE OFFICE OF THE BURFIAN CHIEF JUSTICE, THE THREE SPACE VOYAGERS FIND AT LEAST PART OF THE INFORMATION THEY SEEK!
...CONSTRUCTED OF DERELICT SPACE FREIGHTERS ON A SMALL PLANET IN DEEP SPACE, ALPHATRAZ IS A MAXIMUM SECURITY PRISON FROM WHICH NO CRIMINAL HAS EVER ESCAPED...
...THERE WERE SOME DIFFICULTIES WITH PRISONERS NOT LONG AGO, BUT LATEST REPORTS SAY, ALL CONDITIONS ARE BACK TO NORMAL! ...THIS HAS BEEN A PUBLIC SERVICE FILM PRESENTED BY THE BURFIAN DEPARTMENT OF JUSTICE!
NOW, HOW CAN WE GET THERE, SIR? WE'VE BEEN TOLD BY THE EVIL QUEEN REPUGNA* THAT MY PARENTS... GULP ARE PRISONERS THERE!
YOU CAN'T GET THERE, YOUNG MAN! IT'S OUT OF THE QUESTION!
THAT WAS GREAT, ROBOTA! I HAVEN'T SEEN A GOOD SPACE MOVIE IN YEARS!
EXCEPT, OMNUS, THAT POOR TERRY'S PARENTS ARE SUPPOSED TO BE IN THAT TERRIBLE PLACE! PARENTS FROM WHOM HE'S BEEN SEPARATED SINCE BIRTH!
* SEE PLANET TERRY #7
DAVE MANAK WRITER
WARREN KREMER PENCILER
JON D'AGOSTINO INKER
GRACE KREMER LETTERER
GEORGE ROUSSOS COLORIST
SID JACOBSON EDITOR
TOM DEFALCO EXEC. ED.
JIM SHOOTER ED. IN CHIEF
2

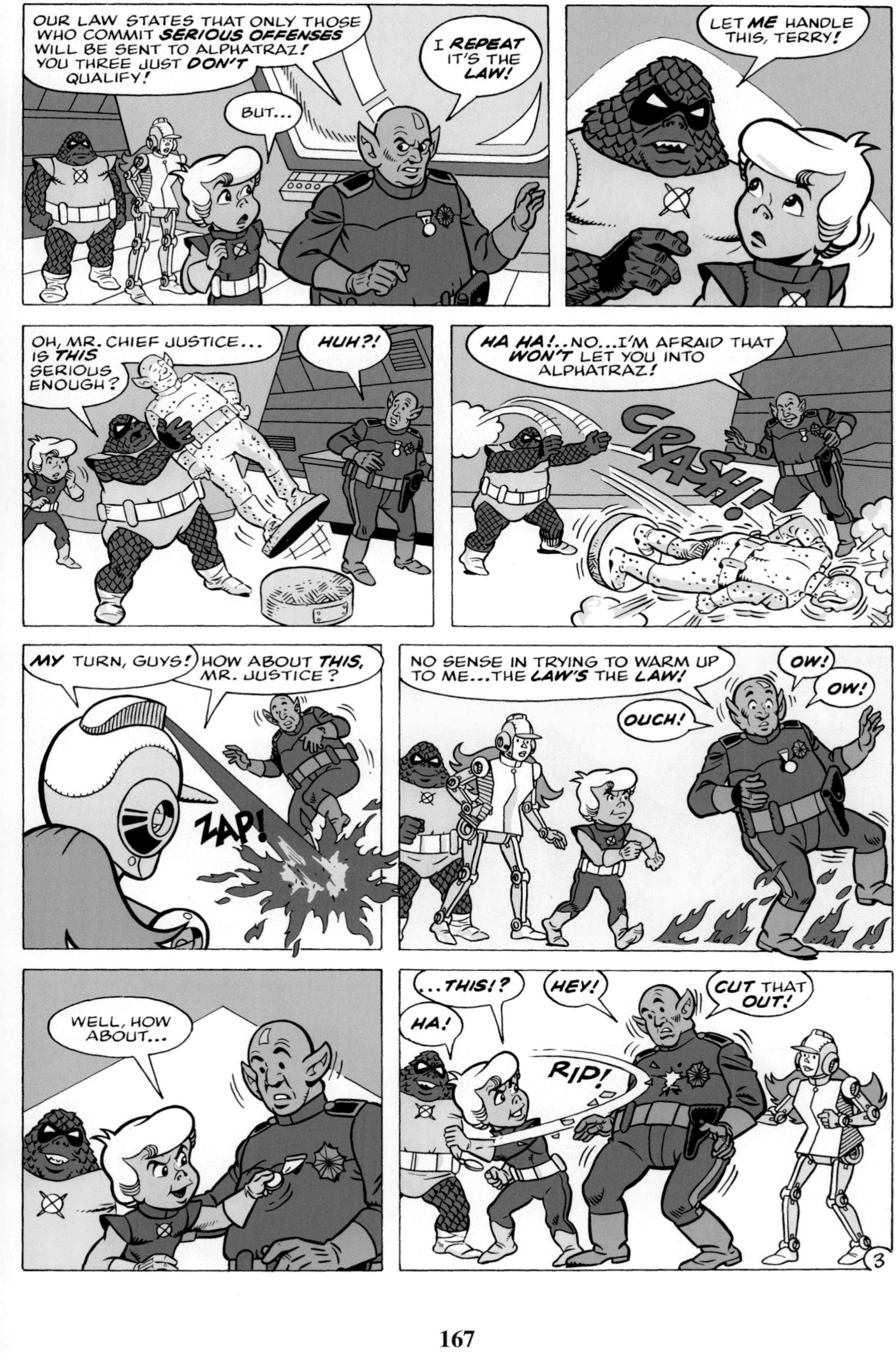
OUR LAW STATES THAT ONLY THOSE WHO COMMIT SERIOUS OFFENSES WILL BE SENT TO ALPHATRAZ! YOU THREE JUST DON'T QUALIFY!
BUT...
I REPEAT IT'S THE LAW!
LET ME HANDLE THIS, TERRY!
OH, MR. CHIEF JUSTICE... IS THIS SERIOUS ENOUGH?
HUH?!
HA HA!..NO...I'M AFRAID THAT WON'T LET YOU INTO ALPHATRAZ!
CRASH!
MY TURN, GUYS!
HOW ABOUT THIS, MR. JUSTICE?
ZAP!
NO SENSE IN TRYING TO WARM UP TO ME...THE LAW'S THE LAW!
OUCH!
OW!
OW!
WELL, HOW ABOUT...
HA!
...THIS!?
HEY!
CUT THAT OUT!
RIP!
3

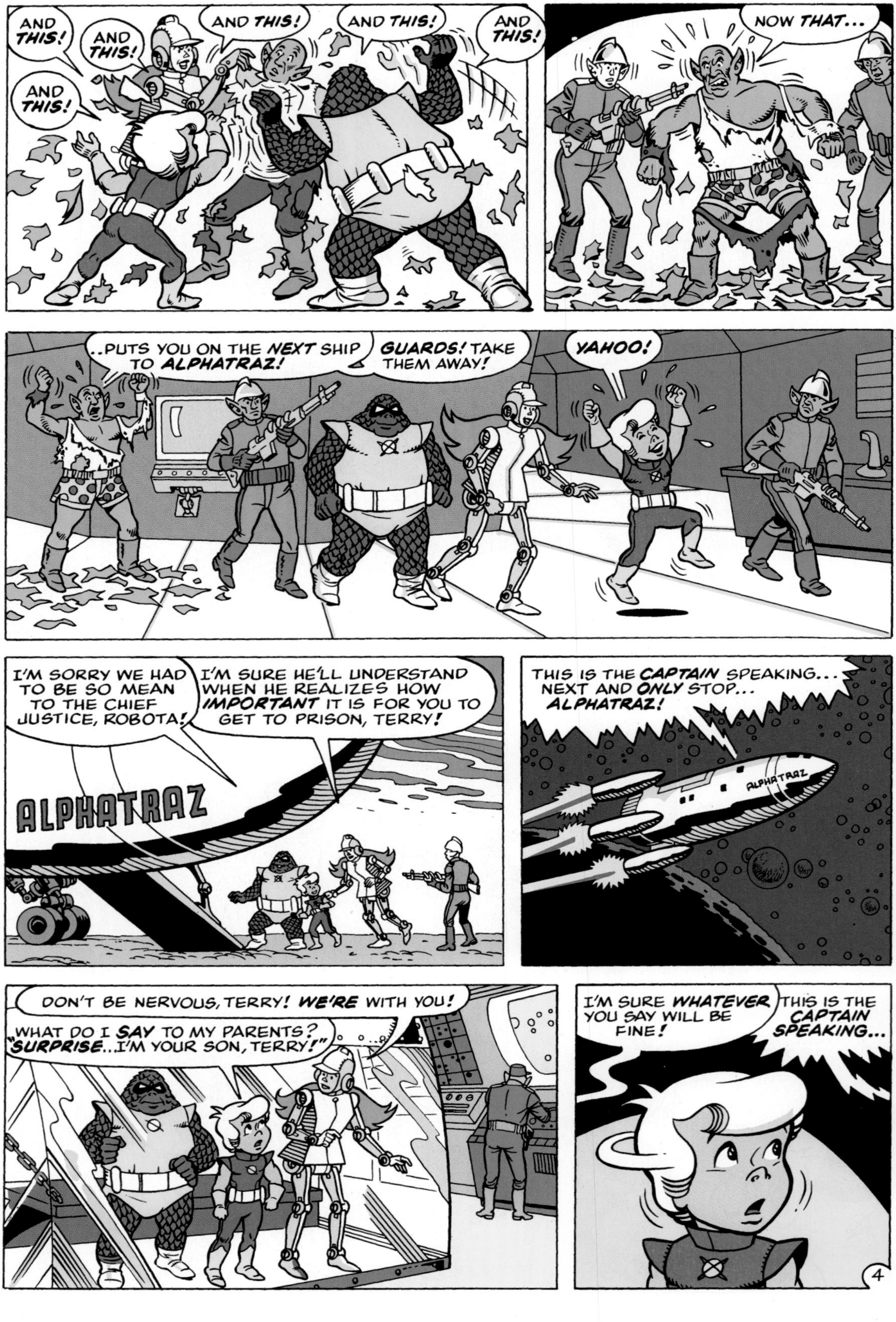

AND THIS!
AND THIS!
AND THIS!
AND THIS!
AND THIS!
AND THIS!
NOW THAT...
..PUTS YOU ON THE NEXT SHIP TO ALPHATRAZ!
GUARDS! TAKE THEM AWAY!
YAHOO!
I'M SORRY WE HAD TO BE SO MEAN TO THE CHIEF JUSTICE, ROBOTA!
I'M SURE HE'LL UNDERSTAND WHEN HE REALIZES HOW IMPORTANT IT IS FOR YOU TO GET TO PRISON, TERRY!
ALPHATRAZ
THIS IS THE CAPTAIN SPEAKING... NEXT AND ONLY STOP... ALPHATRAZ!
ALPHATRAZ
DON'T BE NERVOUS, TERRY! WE'RE WITH YOU!
WHAT DO I SAY TO MY PARENTS? "SURPRISE...I'M YOUR SON, TERRY!"
I'M SURE WHATEVER YOU SAY WILL BE FINE!
THIS IS THE CAPTAIN SPEAKING...
4

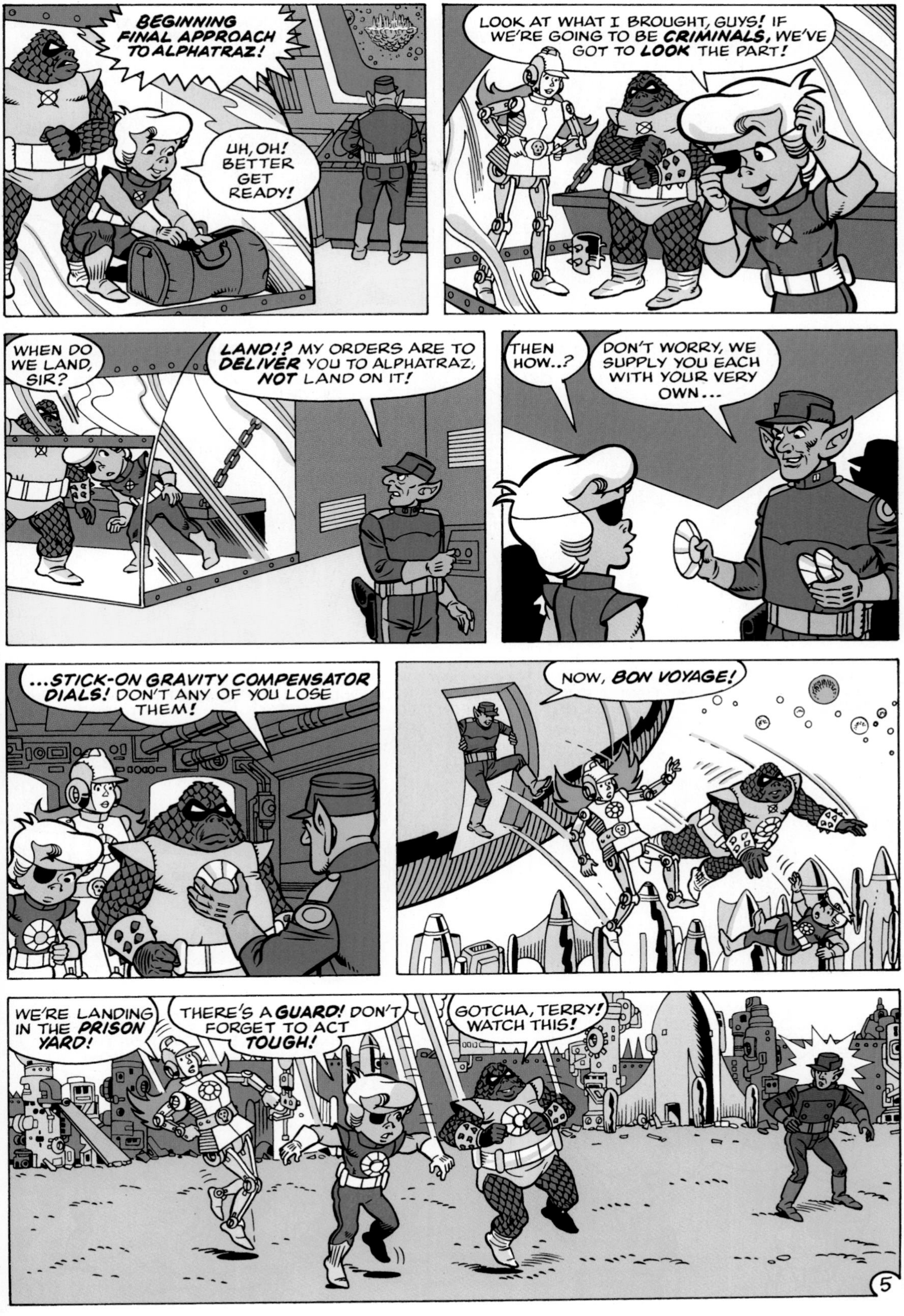
BEGINNING FINAL APPROACH TO ALPHATRAZ!
UH, OH! BETTER GET READY!
LOOK AT WHAT I BROUGHT, GUYS! IF WE'RE GOING TO BE CRIMINALS, WE'VE GOT TO LOOK THE PART!
WHEN DO WE LAND, SIR?
LAND!? MY ORDERS ARE TO DELIVER YOU TO ALPHATRAZ, NOT LAND ON IT!
THEN HOW..?
DON'T WORRY, WE SUPPLY YOU EACH WITH YOUR VERY OWN...
...STICK-ON GRAVITY COMPENSATOR DIALS! DON'T ANY OF YOU LOSE THEM!
NOW, BON VOYAGE!
WE'RE LANDING IN THE PRISON YARD!
THERE'S A GUARD! DON'T FORGET TO ACT TOUGH!
GOTCHA, TERRY! WATCH THIS!
5

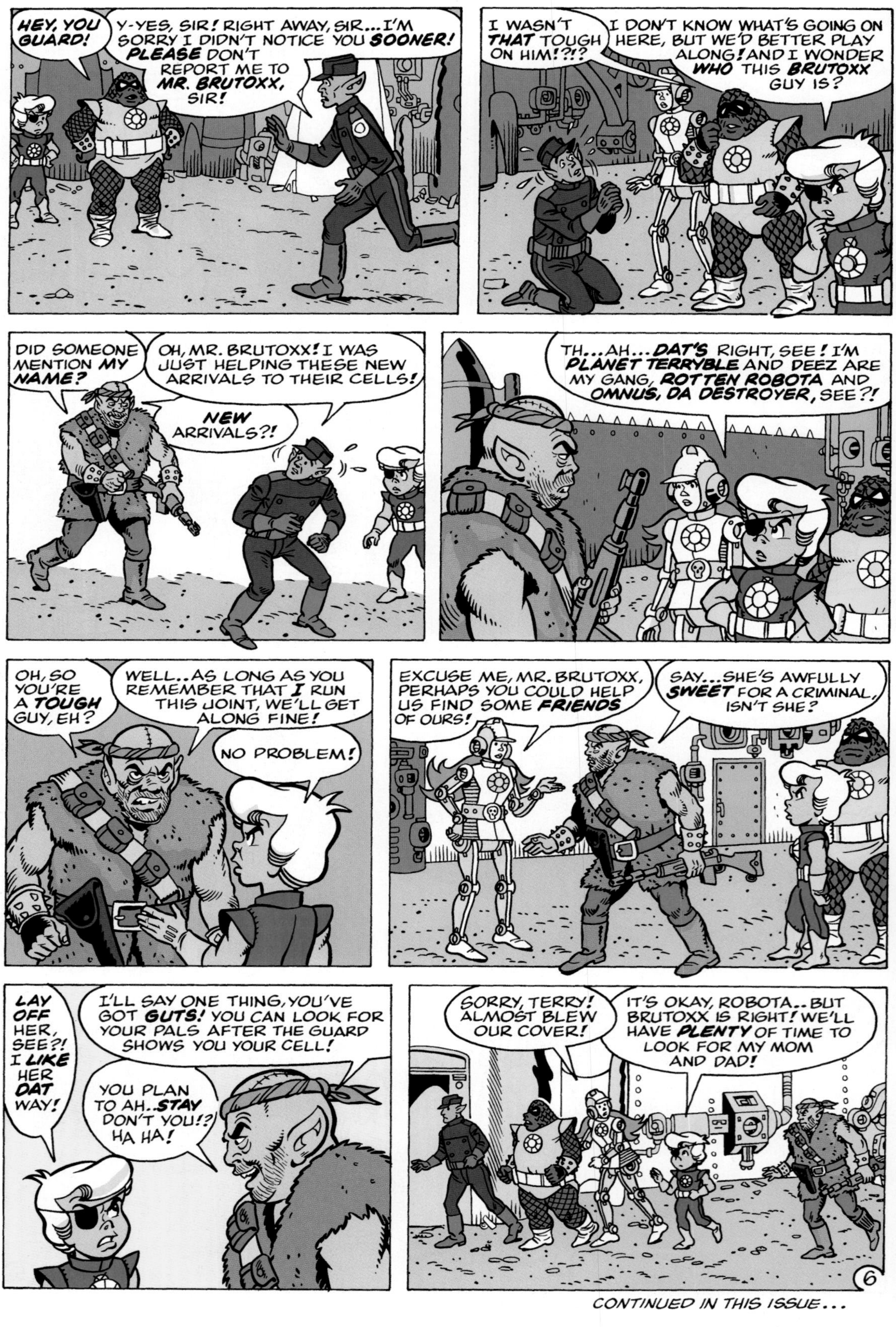
HEY, YOU GUARD!
Y-YES, SIR! RIGHT AWAY, SIR... I'M SORRY I DIDN'T NOTICE YOU SOONER! PLEASE DON'T REPORT ME TO MR. BRUTOXX, SIR!
I WASN'T THAT TOUGH ON HIM!?!?
I DON'T KNOW WHAT'S GOING ON HERE, BUT WE'D BETTER PLAY ALONG! AND I WONDER WHO THIS BRUTOXX GUY IS?
DID SOMEONE MENTION MY NAME?
OH, MR. BRUTOXX! I WAS JUST HELPING THESE NEW ARRIVALS TO THEIR CELLS!
NEW ARRIVALS?!
TH...AH...DAT'S RIGHT, SEE! I'M PLANET TERRYBLE AND DEEZ ARE MY GANG, ROTTEN ROBOTA AND OMNUS, DA DESTROYER, SEE?!
OH, SO YOU'RE A TOUGH GUY, EH?
WELL..AS LONG AS YOU REMEMBER THAT I RUN THIS JOINT, WE'LL GET ALONG FINE!
NO PROBLEM!
EXCUSE ME, MR. BRUTOXX, PERHAPS YOU COULD HELP US FIND SOME FRIENDS OF OURS!
SAY...SHE'S AWFULLY SWEET FOR A CRIMINAL, ISN'T SHE?
LAY OFF HER, SEE?! I LIKE HER DAT WAY!
I'LL SAY ONE THING, YOU'VE GOT GUTS! YOU CAN LOOK FOR YOUR PALS AFTER THE GUARD SHOWS YOU YOUR CELL!
YOU PLAN TO AH..STAY DON'T YOU!? HA HA!
SORRY, TERRY! ALMOST BLEW OUR COVER!
IT'S OKAY, ROBOTA.. BUT BRUTOXX IS RIGHT! WE'LL HAVE PLENTY OF TIME TO LOOK FOR MY MOM AND DAD!
6

CONTINUED IN THIS ISSUE...

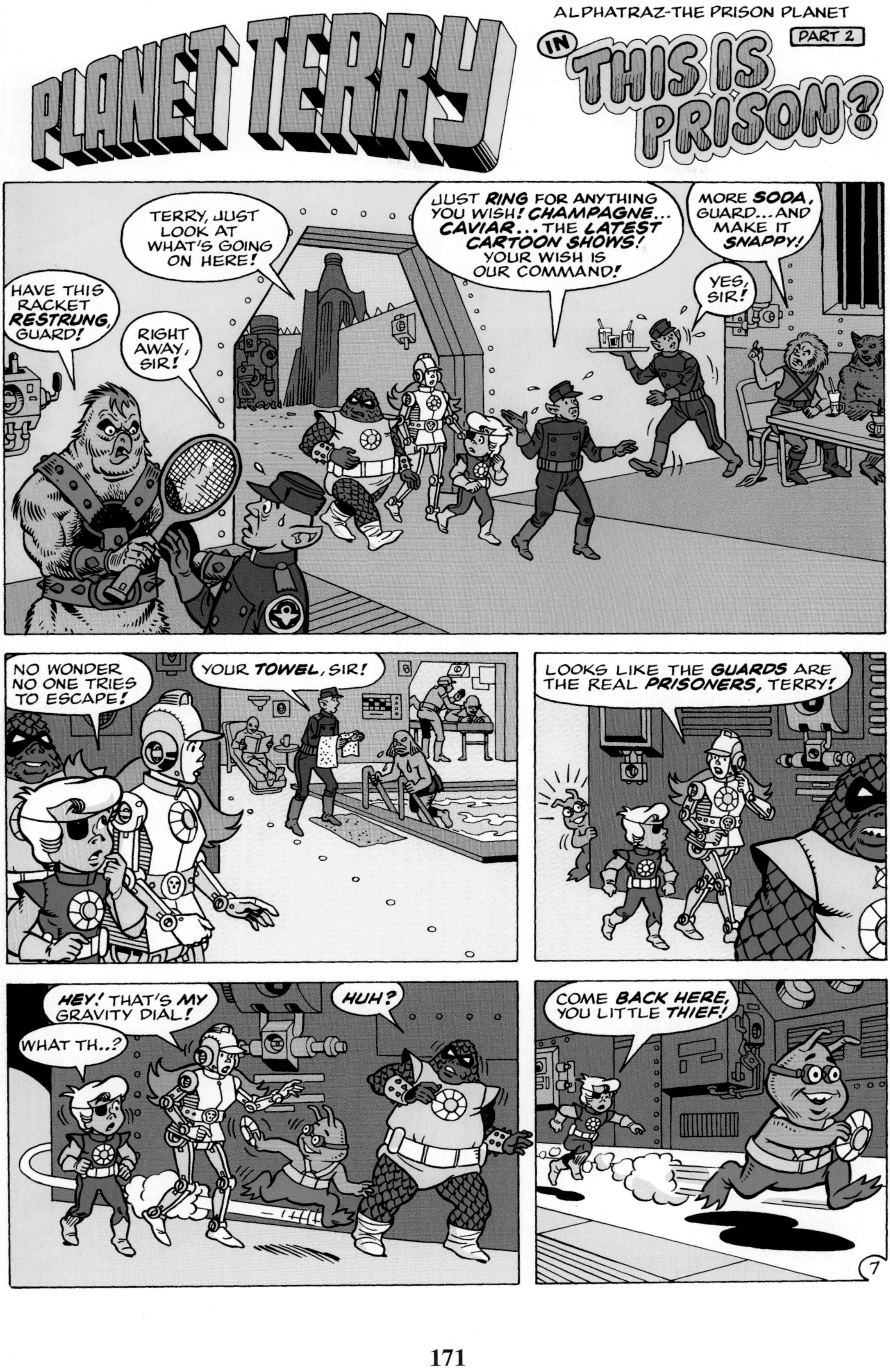
PLANET TERRY
ALPHATRAZ-THE PRISON PLANET
PART 2
IN
THIS IS PRISON?
HAVE THIS RACKET RESTRUNG, GUARD!
RIGHT AWAY, SIR!
TERRY, JUST LOOK AT WHAT'S GOING ON HERE!
JUST RING FOR ANYTHING YOU WISH! CHAMPAGNE... CAVIAR... THE LATEST CARTOON SHOWS! YOUR WISH IS OUR COMMAND!
MORE SODA, GUARD... AND MAKE IT SNAPPY!
YES, SIR!
NO WONDER NO ONE TRIES TO ESCAPE!
YOUR TOWEL, SIR!
LOOKS LIKE THE GUARDS ARE THE REAL PRISONERS, TERRY!
HEY! THAT'S MY GRAVITY DIAL!
HUH?
WHAT TH..?
COME BACK HERE, YOU LITTLE THIEF!
7

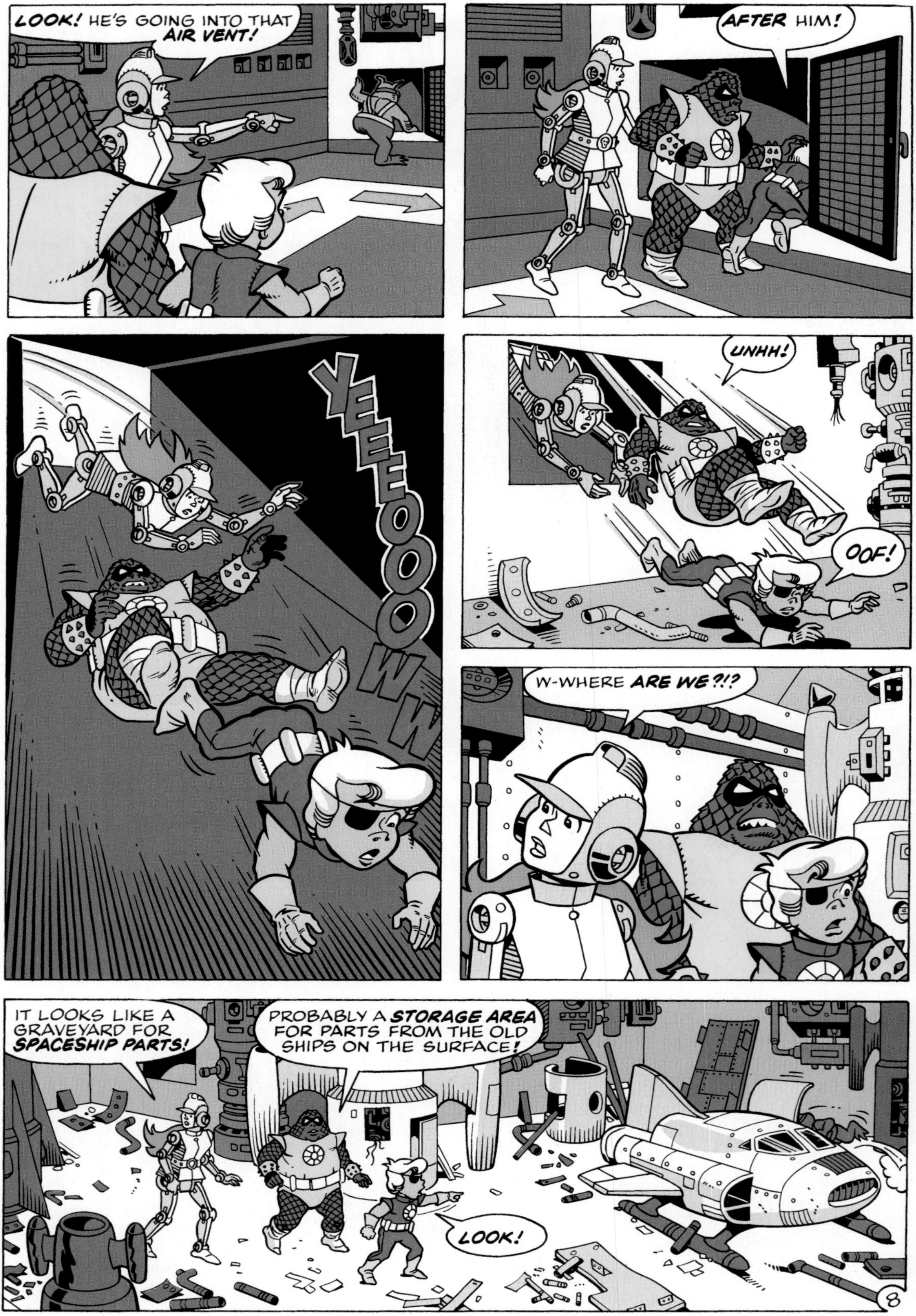
LOOK! HE'S GOING INTO THAT AIR VENT!
AFTER HIM!
YEEEOOOWW
UNHH!
OOF!
W-WHERE ARE WE?!?
IT LOOKS LIKE A GRAVEYARD FOR SPACESHIP PARTS!
PROBABLY A STORAGE AREA FOR PARTS FROM THE OLD SHIPS ON THE SURFACE!
LOOK!
8

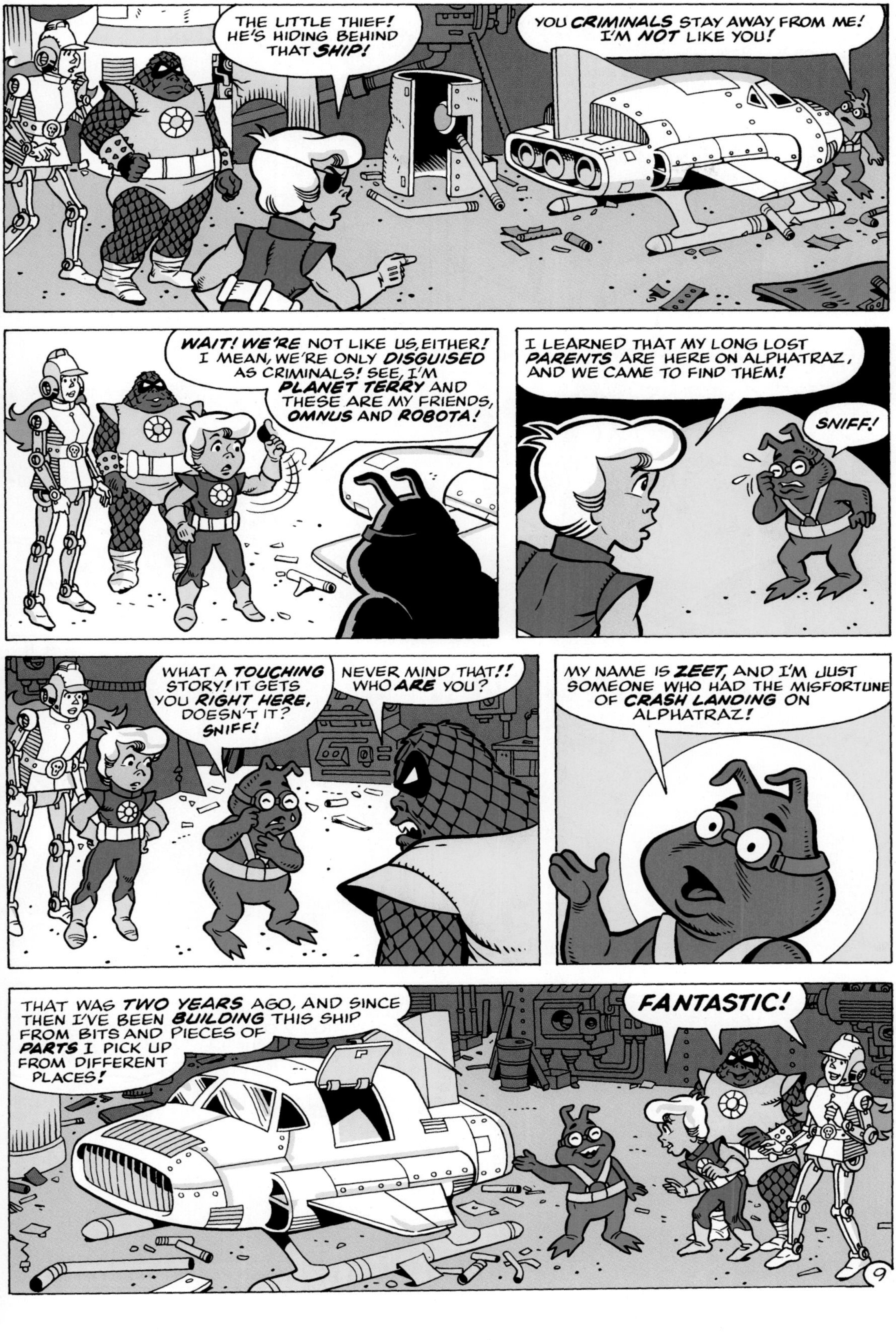
THE LITTLE THIEF! HE'S HIDING BEHIND THAT SHIP!
YOU CRIMINALS STAY AWAY FROM ME! I'M NOT LIKE YOU!
WAIT! WE'RE NOT LIKE US, EITHER! I MEAN, WE'RE ONLY DISGUISED AS CRIMINALS! SEE, I'M PLANET TERRY AND THESE ARE MY FRIENDS, OMNUS AND ROBOTA!
I LEARNED THAT MY LONG LOST PARENTS ARE HERE ON ALPHATRAZ, AND WE CAME TO FIND THEM!
SNIFF!
WHAT A TOUCHING STORY! IT GETS YOU RIGHT HERE, DOESN'T IT? SNIFF!
NEVER MIND THAT!! WHO ARE YOU?
MY NAME IS ZEET, AND I'M JUST SOMEONE WHO HAD THE MISFORTUNE OF CRASH LANDING ON ALPHATRAZ!
THAT WAS TWO YEARS AGO, AND SINCE THEN I'VE BEEN BUILDING THIS SHIP FROM BITS AND PIECES OF PARTS I PICK UP FROM DIFFERENT PLACES!
FANTASTIC!
9

SO, YOU NEEDED MY GRAVITY DIAL FOR YOUR *SHIP?*

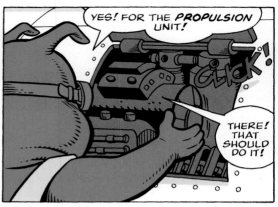

YES! FOR THE *PROPULSION* UNIT!

CLICK!

THERE! THAT SHOULD DO IT!

NOW I JUST HAVE TO DIG A TUNNEL BIG ENOUGH TO FLY OUT OF HERE!

THAT COULD TAKE *TWENTY YEARS!*

UNLESS *WE* LEND A HAND, ROBOTA!

A *HAND* AND A *LASER,* HUNK OF GREEN!

ONE *SHIP-SIZED TUNNEL* COMING UP!

BLEEEZAM!

ZZZZSSAAMMM!

FASTER, ROBOTA! I'M *GAINING* ON YOU!

YOUR FRIENDS CERTAINLY ARE NICE, TERRY!

AND THEY'RE *MORE* THAN FRIENDS, ZEET! SINCE I MET OMNUS AND ROBOTA,✳ I FEEL I'M PART OF A *REAL FAMILY!*

✳ SEE PLANET TERRY #1

10

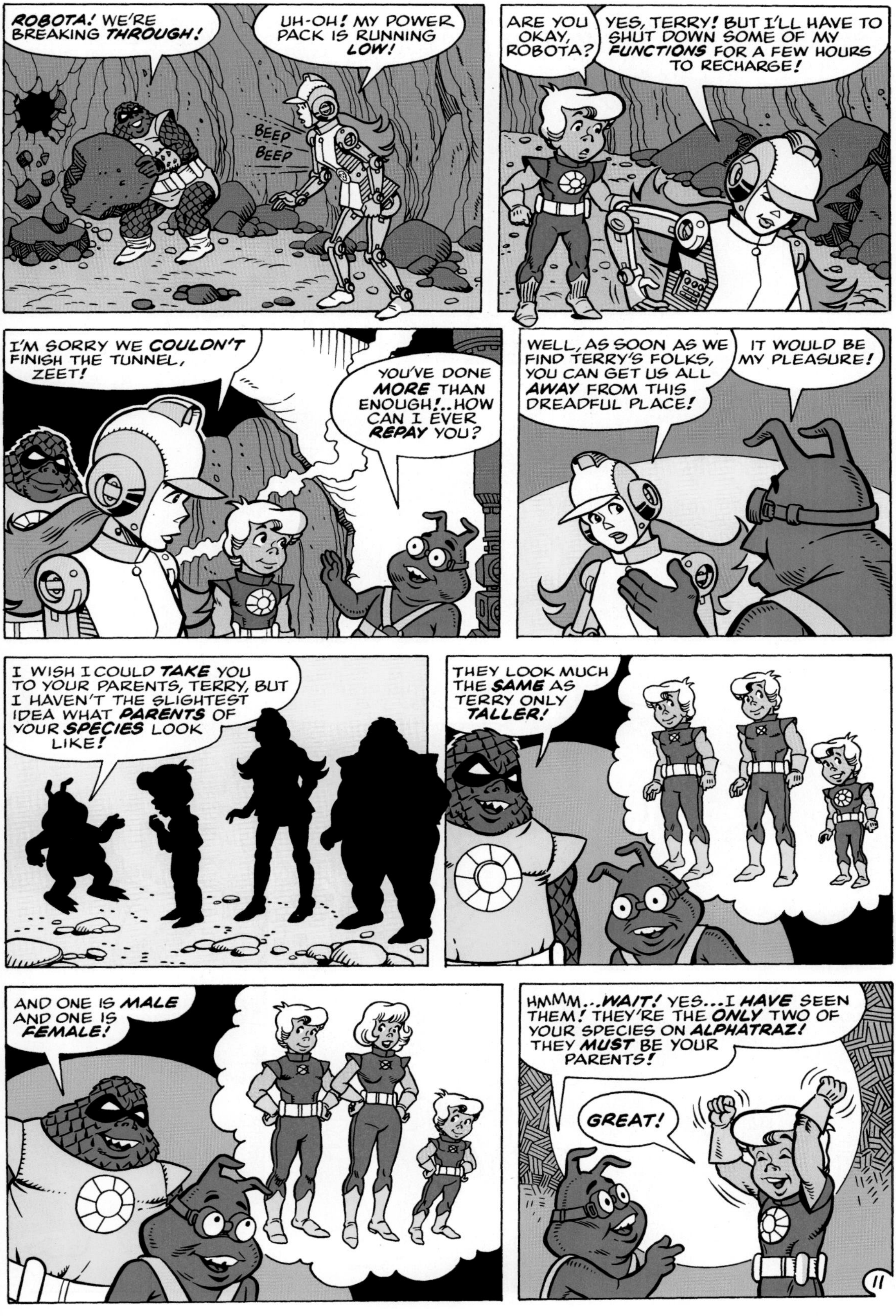
ROBOTA! WE'RE BREAKING THROUGH!
UH-OH! MY POWER PACK IS RUNNING LOW!
BEEP BEEP
ARE YOU OKAY, ROBOTA?
YES, TERRY! BUT I'LL HAVE TO SHUT DOWN SOME OF MY FUNCTIONS FOR A FEW HOURS TO RECHARGE!
I'M SORRY WE COULDN'T FINISH THE TUNNEL, ZEET!
YOU'VE DONE MORE THAN ENOUGH!..HOW CAN I EVER REPAY YOU?
WELL, AS SOON AS WE FIND TERRY'S FOLKS, YOU CAN GET US ALL AWAY FROM THIS DREADFUL PLACE!
IT WOULD BE MY PLEASURE!
I WISH I COULD TAKE YOU TO YOUR PARENTS, TERRY, BUT I HAVEN'T THE SLIGHTEST IDEA WHAT PARENTS OF YOUR SPECIES LOOK LIKE!
THEY LOOK MUCH THE SAME AS TERRY ONLY TALLER!
AND ONE IS MALE AND ONE IS FEMALE!
HMMM...WAIT! YES...I HAVE SEEN THEM! THEY'RE THE ONLY TWO OF YOUR SPECIES ON ALPHATRAZ! THEY MUST BE YOUR PARENTS!
GREAT!
11

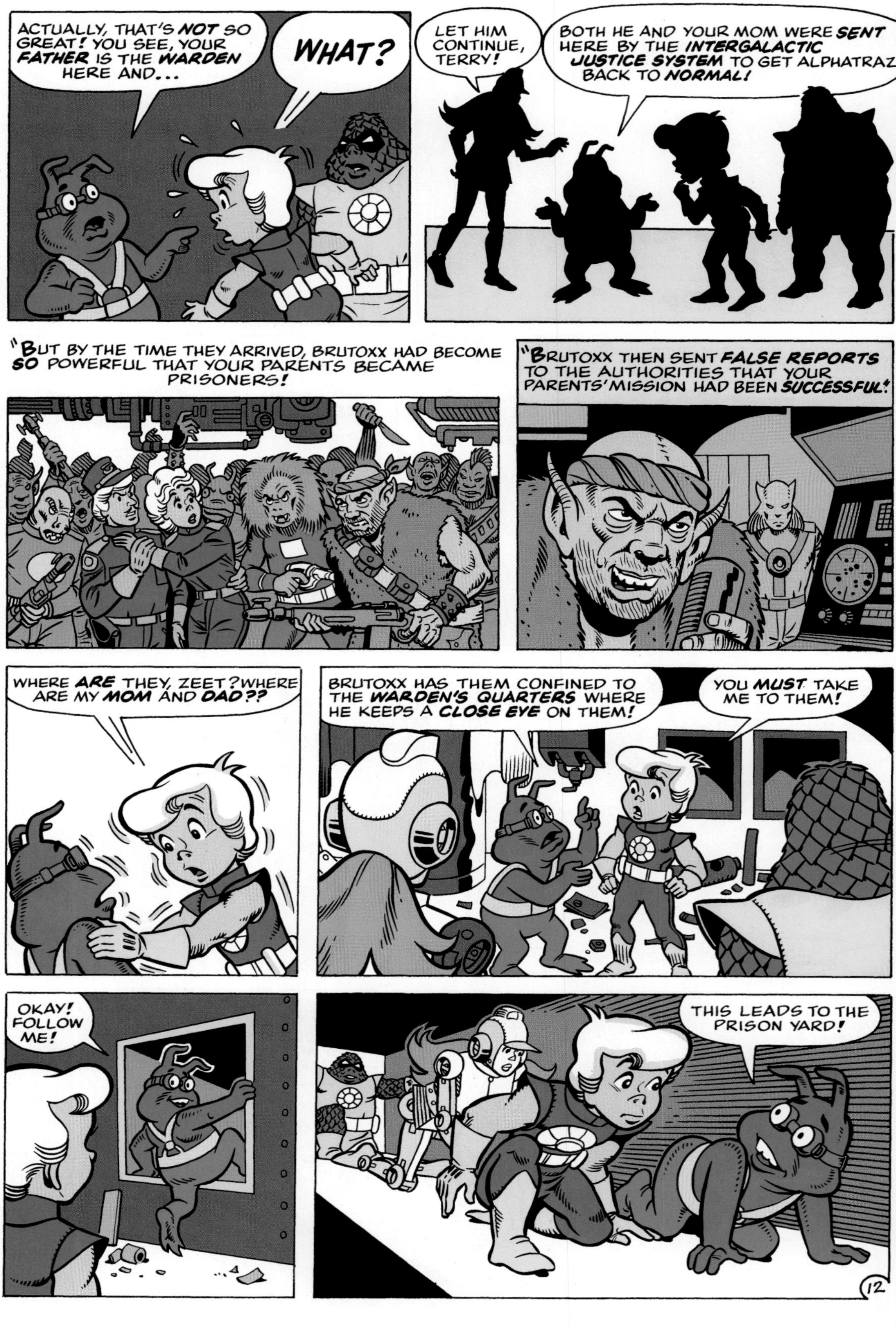
ACTUALLY, THAT'S NOT SO GREAT! YOU SEE, YOUR FATHER IS THE WARDEN HERE AND...
WHAT?
LET HIM CONTINUE, TERRY!
BOTH HE AND YOUR MOM WERE SENT HERE BY THE INTERGALACTIC JUSTICE SYSTEM TO GET ALPHATRAZ BACK TO NORMAL!
"BUT BY THE TIME THEY ARRIVED, BRUTOXX HAD BECOME SO POWERFUL THAT YOUR PARENTS BECAME PRISONERS!
"BRUTOXX THEN SENT FALSE REPORTS TO THE AUTHORITIES THAT YOUR PARENTS' MISSION HAD BEEN SUCCESSFUL!"
WHERE ARE THEY, ZEET? WHERE ARE MY MOM AND DAD??
BRUTOXX HAS THEM CONFINED TO THE WARDEN'S QUARTERS WHERE HE KEEPS A CLOSE EYE ON THEM!
YOU MUST TAKE ME TO THEM!
OKAY! FOLLOW ME!
THIS LEADS TO THE PRISON YARD!
12

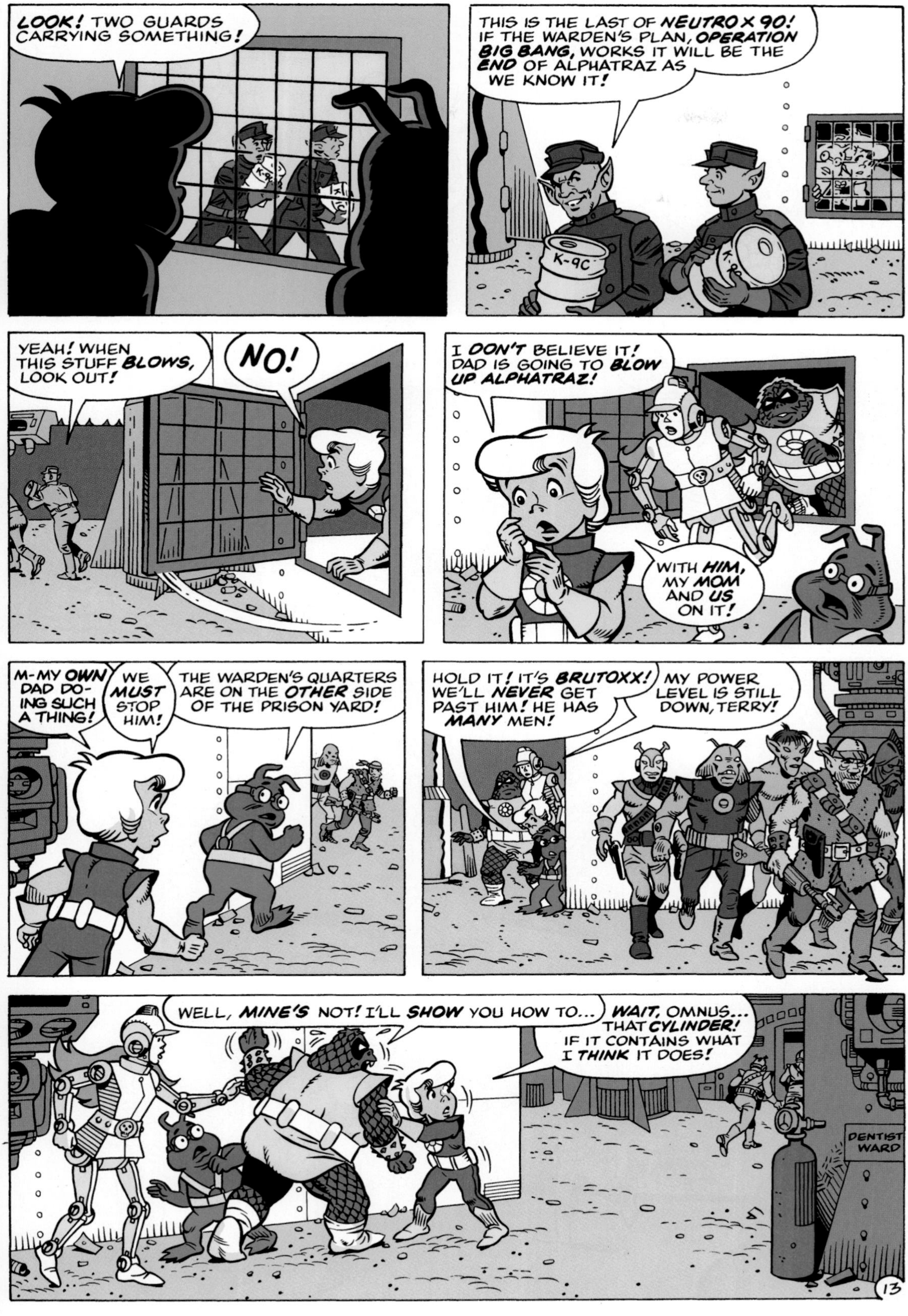
LOOK! TWO GUARDS CARRYING SOMETHING!
THIS IS THE LAST OF NEUTRO X 90! IF THE WARDEN'S PLAN, OPERATION BIG BANG, WORKS IT WILL BE THE END OF ALPHATRAZ AS WE KNOW IT!
K-9C
YEAH! WHEN THIS STUFF BLOWS, LOOK OUT!
NO!
I DON'T BELIEVE IT! DAD IS GOING TO BLOW UP ALPHATRAZ!
WITH HIM, MY MOM AND US ON IT!
M-MY OWN DAD DOING SUCH A THING!
WE MUST STOP HIM!
THE WARDEN'S QUARTERS ARE ON THE OTHER SIDE OF THE PRISON YARD!
HOLD IT! IT'S BRUTOXX! WE'LL NEVER GET PAST HIM! HE HAS MANY MEN!
MY POWER LEVEL IS STILL DOWN, TERRY!
WELL, MINE'S NOT! I'LL SHOW YOU HOW TO...
WAIT, OMNUS... THAT CYLINDER! IF IT CONTAINS WHAT I THINK IT DOES!
DENTIST WARD
13

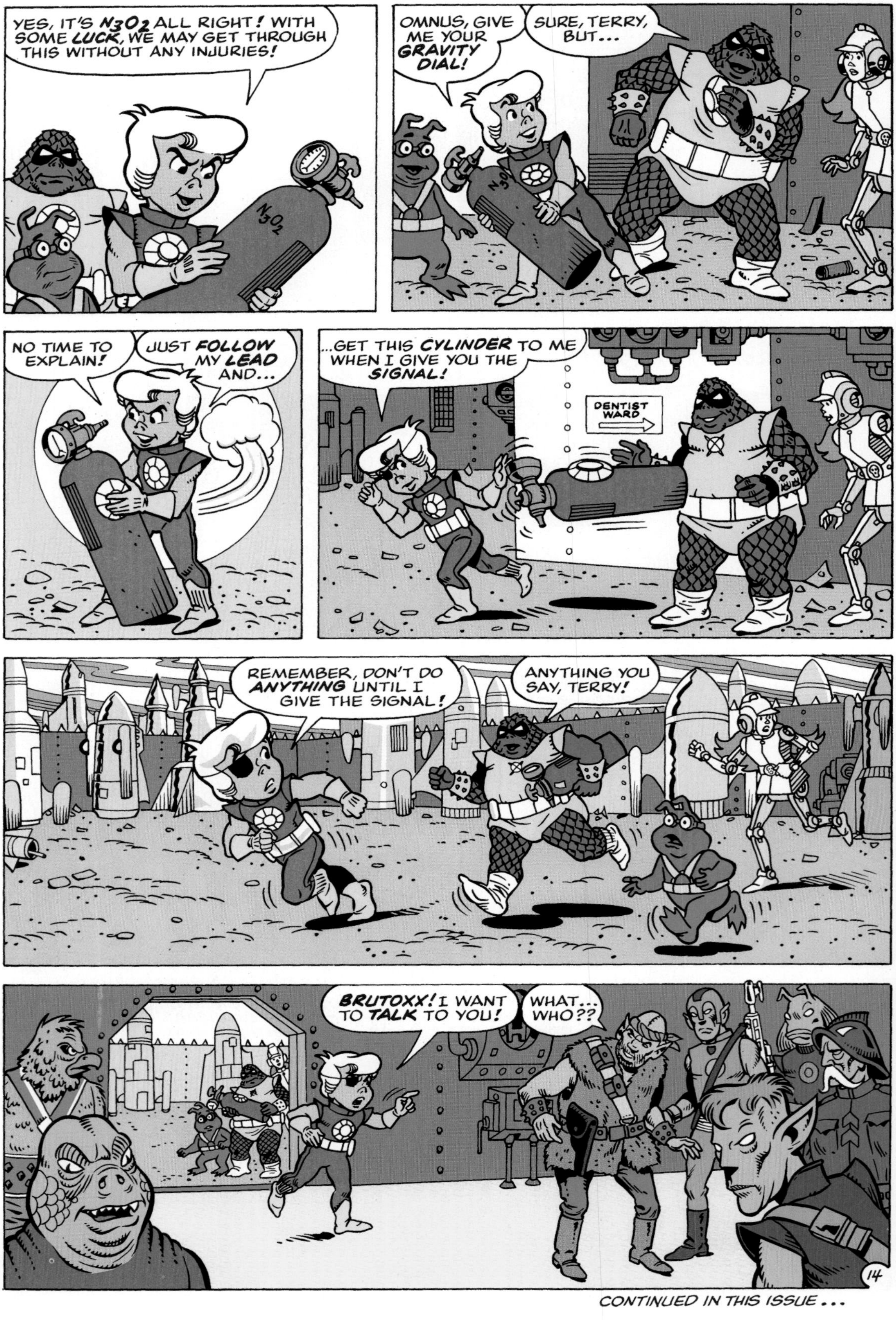
YES, IT'S N_3O_2 ALL RIGHT! WITH SOME LUCK, WE MAY GET THROUGH THIS WITHOUT ANY INJURIES!
N_3O_2
OMNUS, GIVE ME YOUR GRAVITY DIAL!
SURE, TERRY, BUT...
NO TIME TO EXPLAIN!
JUST FOLLOW MY LEAD AND...
...GET THIS CYLINDER TO ME WHEN I GIVE YOU THE SIGNAL!
DENTIST WARD
REMEMBER, DON'T DO ANYTHING UNTIL I GIVE THE SIGNAL!
ANYTHING YOU SAY, TERRY!
BRUTOXX! I WANT TO TALK TO YOU!
WHAT... WHO??
14

CONTINUED IN THIS ISSUE...

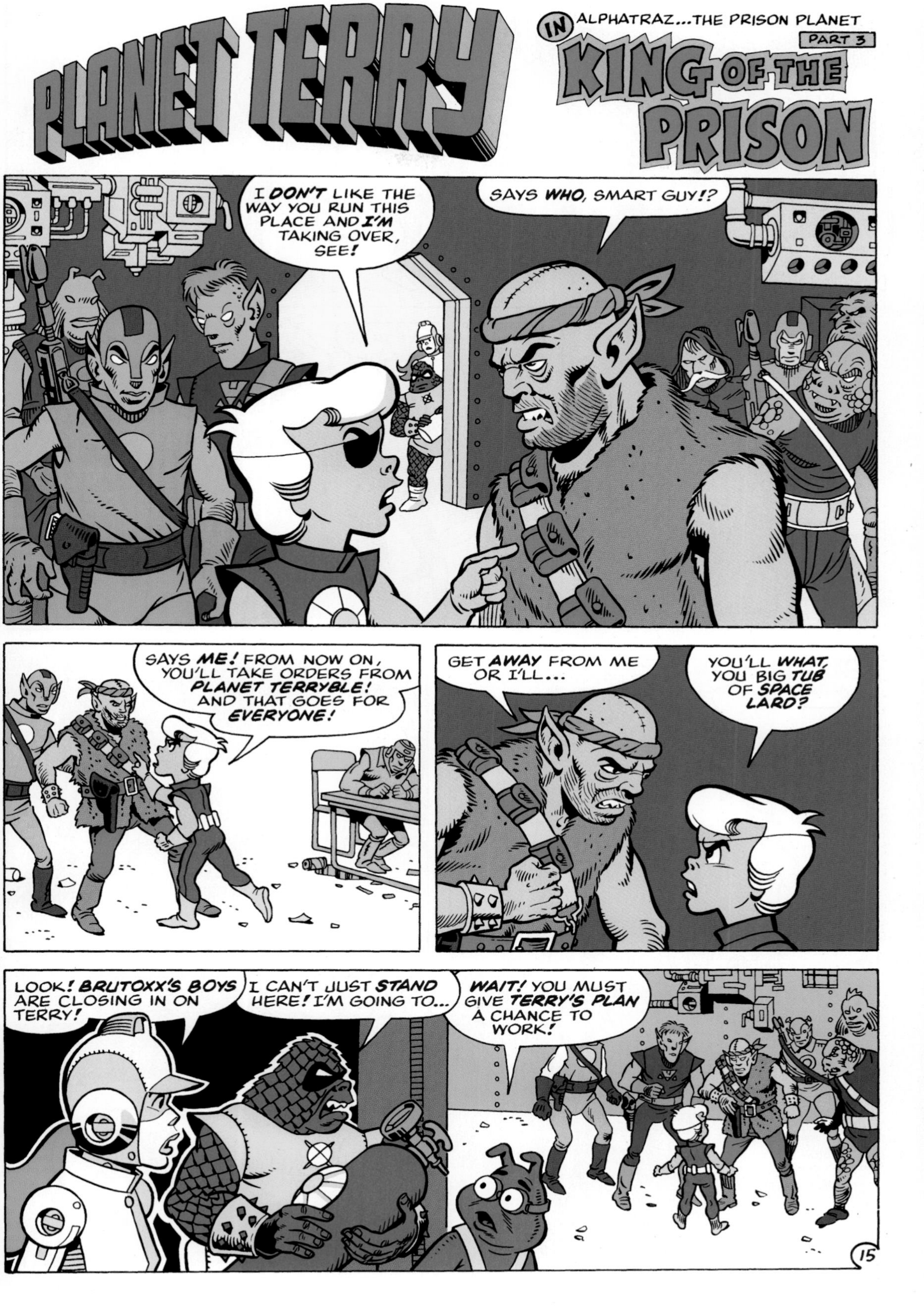
PLANET TERRY
IN ALPHATRAZ...THE PRISON PLANET
PART 3
KING OF THE PRISON
I DON'T LIKE THE WAY YOU RUN THIS PLACE AND I'M TAKING OVER, SEE!
SAYS WHO, SMART GUY!?
SAYS ME! FROM NOW ON, YOU'LL TAKE ORDERS FROM PLANET TERRYBLE! AND THAT GOES FOR EVERYONE!
GET AWAY FROM ME OR I'LL...
YOU'LL WHAT, YOU BIG TUB OF SPACE LARD?
LOOK! BRUTOXX'S BOYS ARE CLOSING IN ON TERRY!
I CAN'T JUST STAND HERE! I'M GOING TO...
WAIT! YOU MUST GIVE TERRY'S PLAN A CHANCE TO WORK!
15

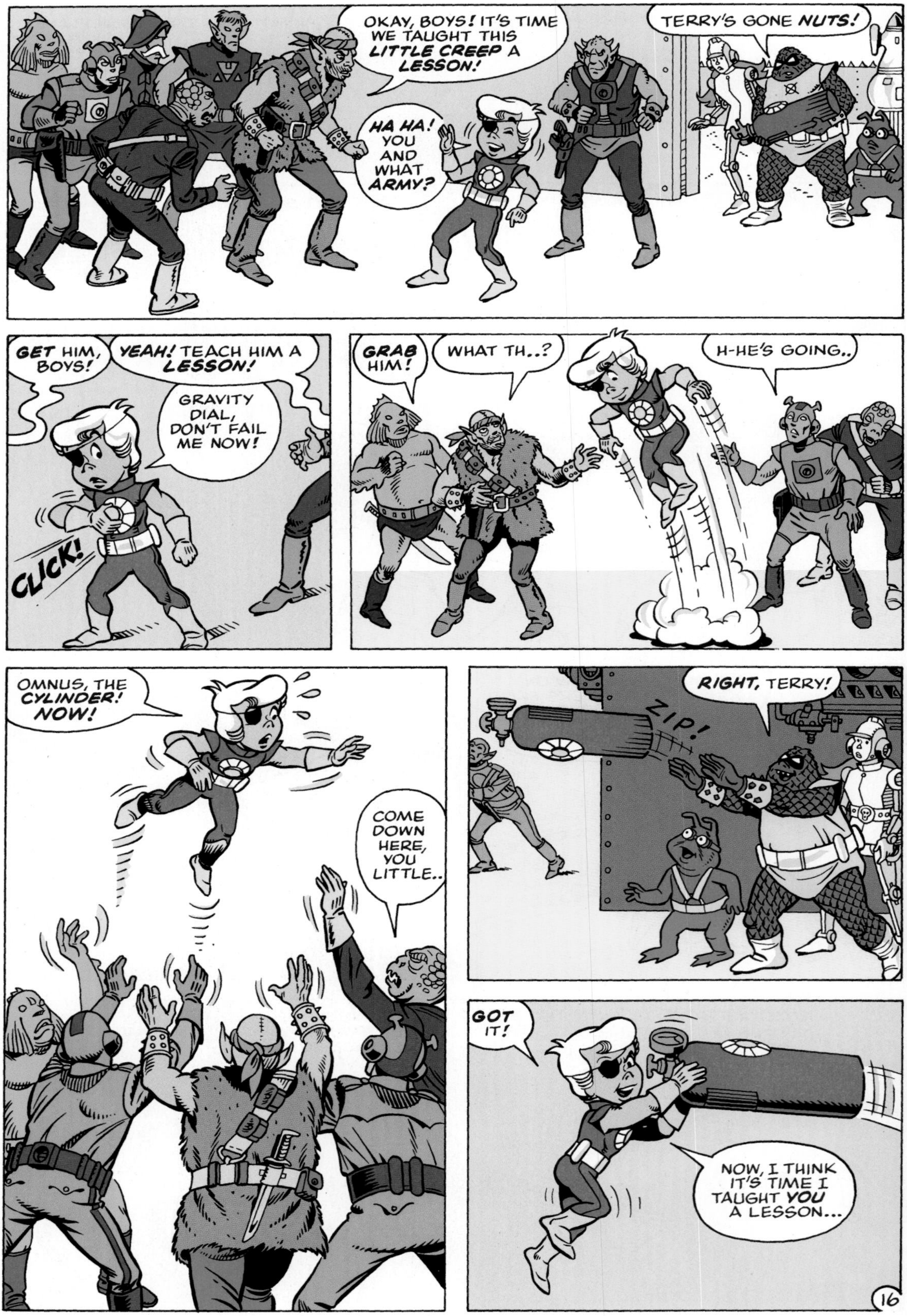
OKAY, BOYS! IT'S TIME WE TAUGHT THIS LITTLE CREEP A LESSON!
TERRY'S GONE NUTS!
HA HA! YOU AND WHAT ARMY?
GET HIM, BOYS!
YEAH! TEACH HIM A LESSON!
GRAVITY DIAL, DON'T FAIL ME NOW!
CLICK!
GRAB HIM!
WHAT TH..?
H-HE'S GOING..
OMNUS, THE CYLINDER! NOW!
COME DOWN HERE, YOU LITTLE..
RIGHT, TERRY!
ZIP!
GOT IT!
NOW, I THINK IT'S TIME I TAUGHT YOU A LESSON...
16

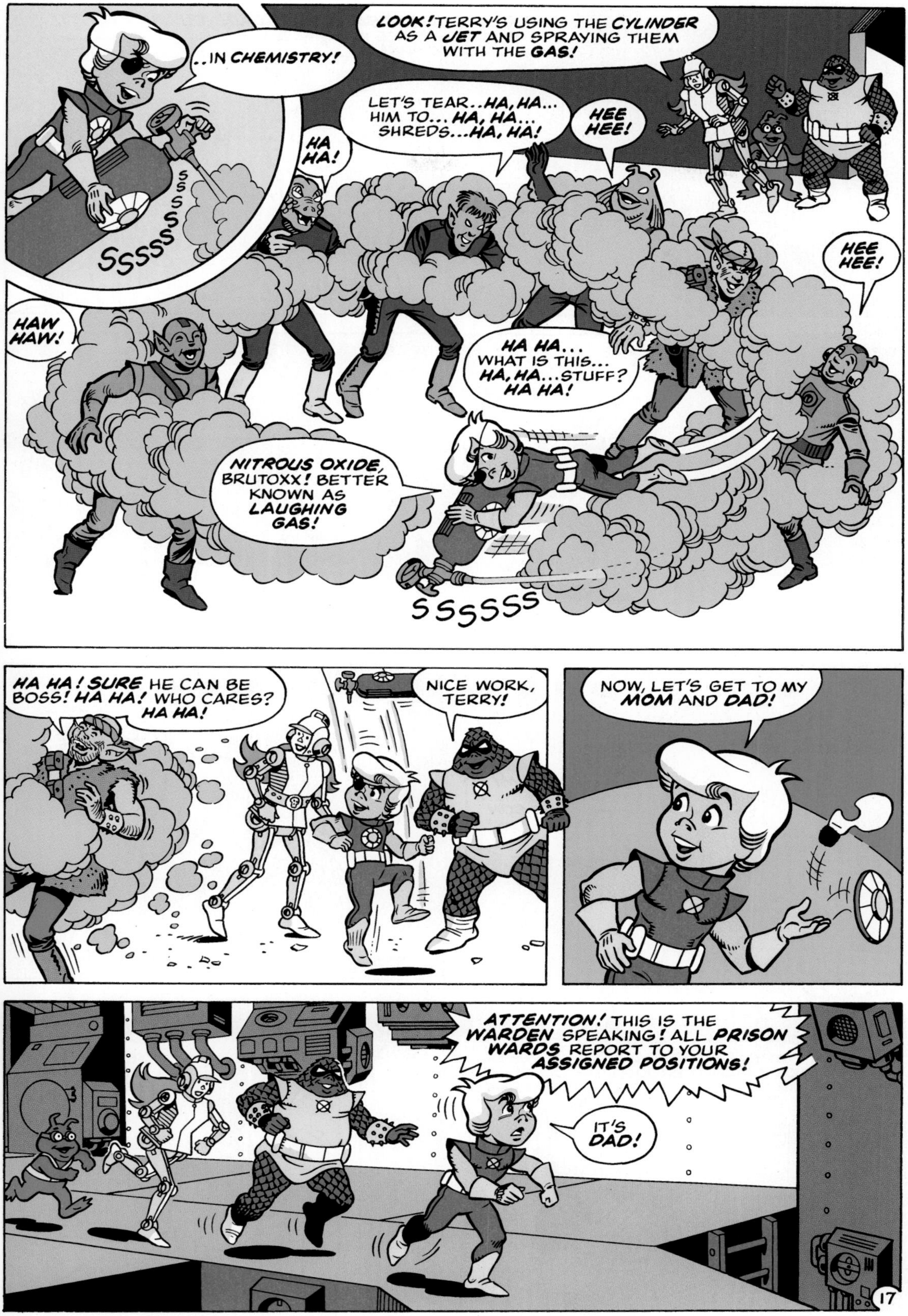

..IN CHEMISTRY!
LOOK! TERRY'S USING THE CYLINDER AS A JET AND SPRAYING THEM WITH THE GAS!
SSSSSSSS
HA HA!
LET'S TEAR..HA, HA... HIM TO... HA, HA... SHREDS...HA, HA!
HEE HEE!
HEE HEE!
HAW HAW!
HA HA... WHAT IS THIS... HA, HA...STUFF? HA HA!
NITROUS OXIDE, BRUTOXX! BETTER KNOWN AS LAUGHING GAS!
SSSSSS
HA HA! SURE HE CAN BE BOSS! HA HA! WHO CARES? HA HA!
NICE WORK, TERRY!
NOW, LET'S GET TO MY MOM AND DAD!
ATTENTION! THIS IS THE WARDEN SPEAKING! ALL PRISON WARDS REPORT TO YOUR ASSIGNED POSITIONS!
IT'S DAD!
17

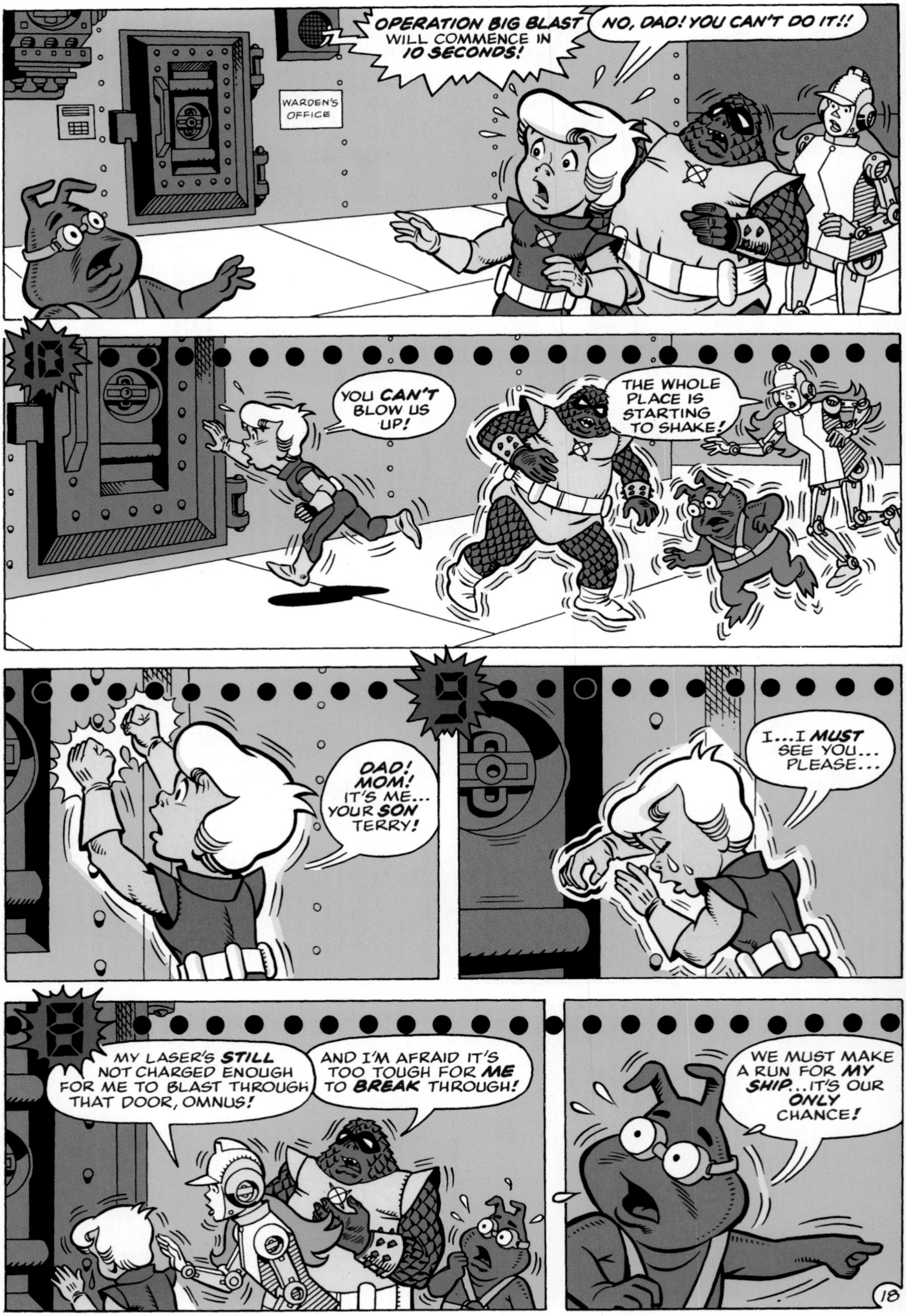
OPERATION BIG BLAST WILL COMMENCE IN 10 SECONDS!
NO, DAD! YOU CAN'T DO IT!!
WARDEN'S OFFICE
YOU CAN'T BLOW US UP!
THE WHOLE PLACE IS STARTING TO SHAKE!
DAD! MOM! IT'S ME... YOUR SON TERRY!
I...I MUST SEE YOU... PLEASE...
MY LASER'S STILL NOT CHARGED ENOUGH FOR ME TO BLAST THROUGH THAT DOOR, OMNUS!
AND I'M AFRAID IT'S TOO TOUGH FOR ME TO BREAK THROUGH!
WE MUST MAKE A RUN FOR MY SHIP...IT'S OUR ONLY CHANCE!
18

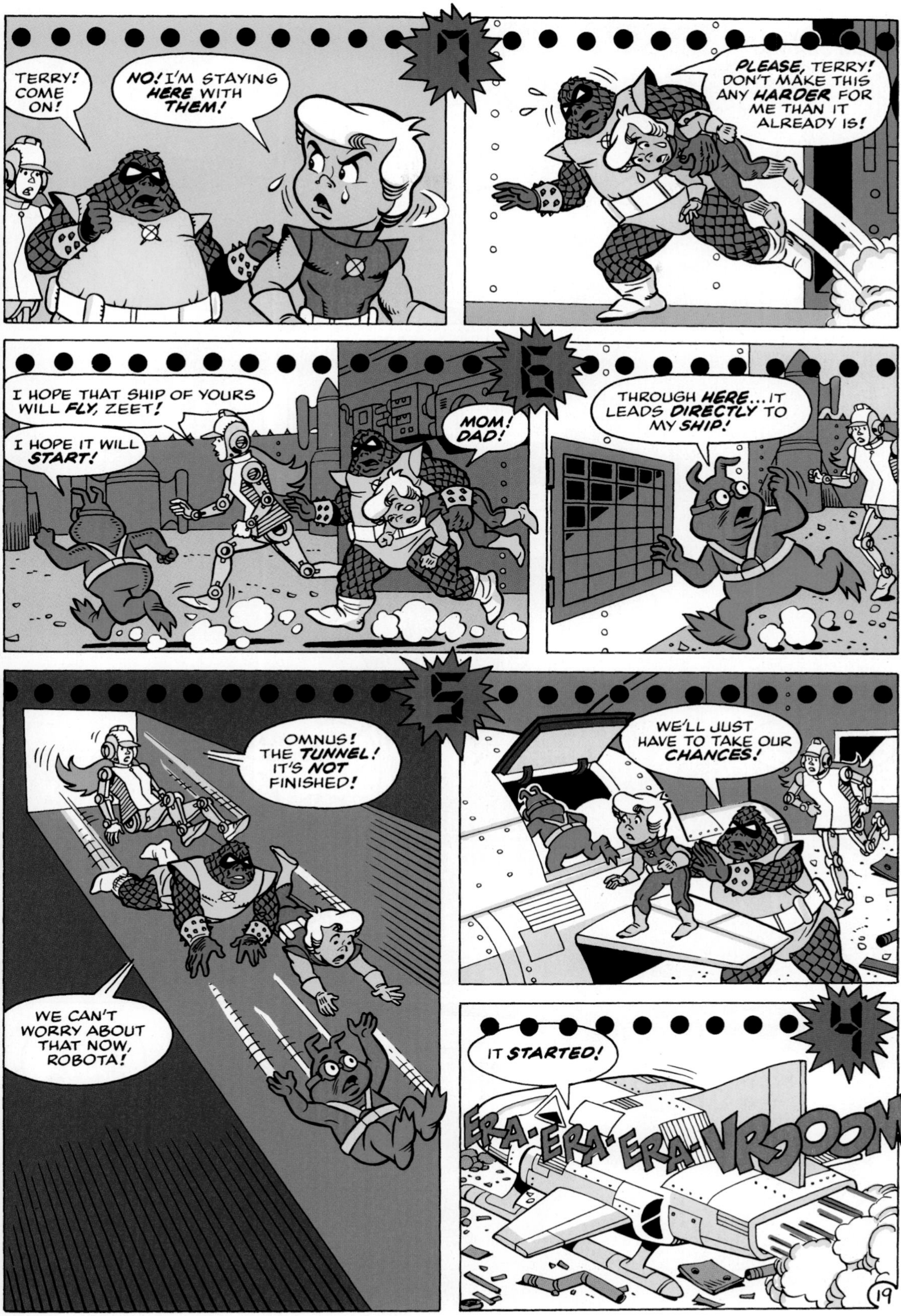
TERRY! COME ON!
NO! I'M STAYING HERE WITH THEM!
PLEASE, TERRY! DON'T MAKE THIS ANY HARDER FOR ME THAN IT ALREADY IS!
I HOPE THAT SHIP OF YOURS WILL FLY, ZEET!
I HOPE IT WILL START!
MOM! DAD!
THROUGH HERE... IT LEADS DIRECTLY TO MY SHIP!
OMNUS! THE TUNNEL! IT'S NOT FINISHED!
WE CAN'T WORRY ABOUT THAT NOW, ROBOTA!
WE'LL JUST HAVE TO TAKE OUR CHANCES!
IT STARTED!
ERA-ERA-ERA-VROOOM
19

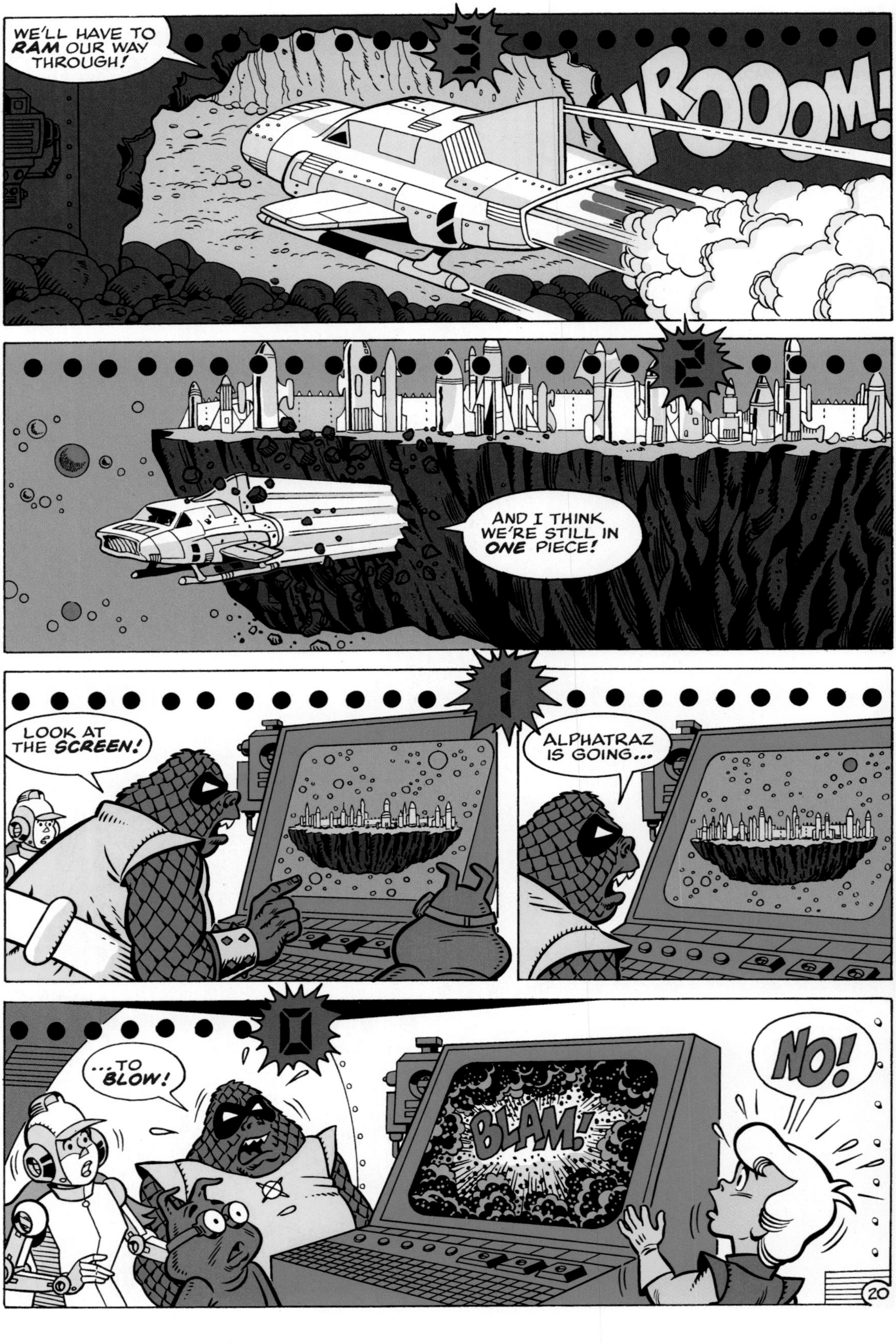
WE'LL HAVE TO RAM OUR WAY THROUGH!
VROOOM!
AND I THINK WE'RE STILL IN ONE PIECE!
LOOK AT THE SCREEN!
ALPHATRAZ IS GOING...
...TO BLOW!
BLAM!
NO!
20

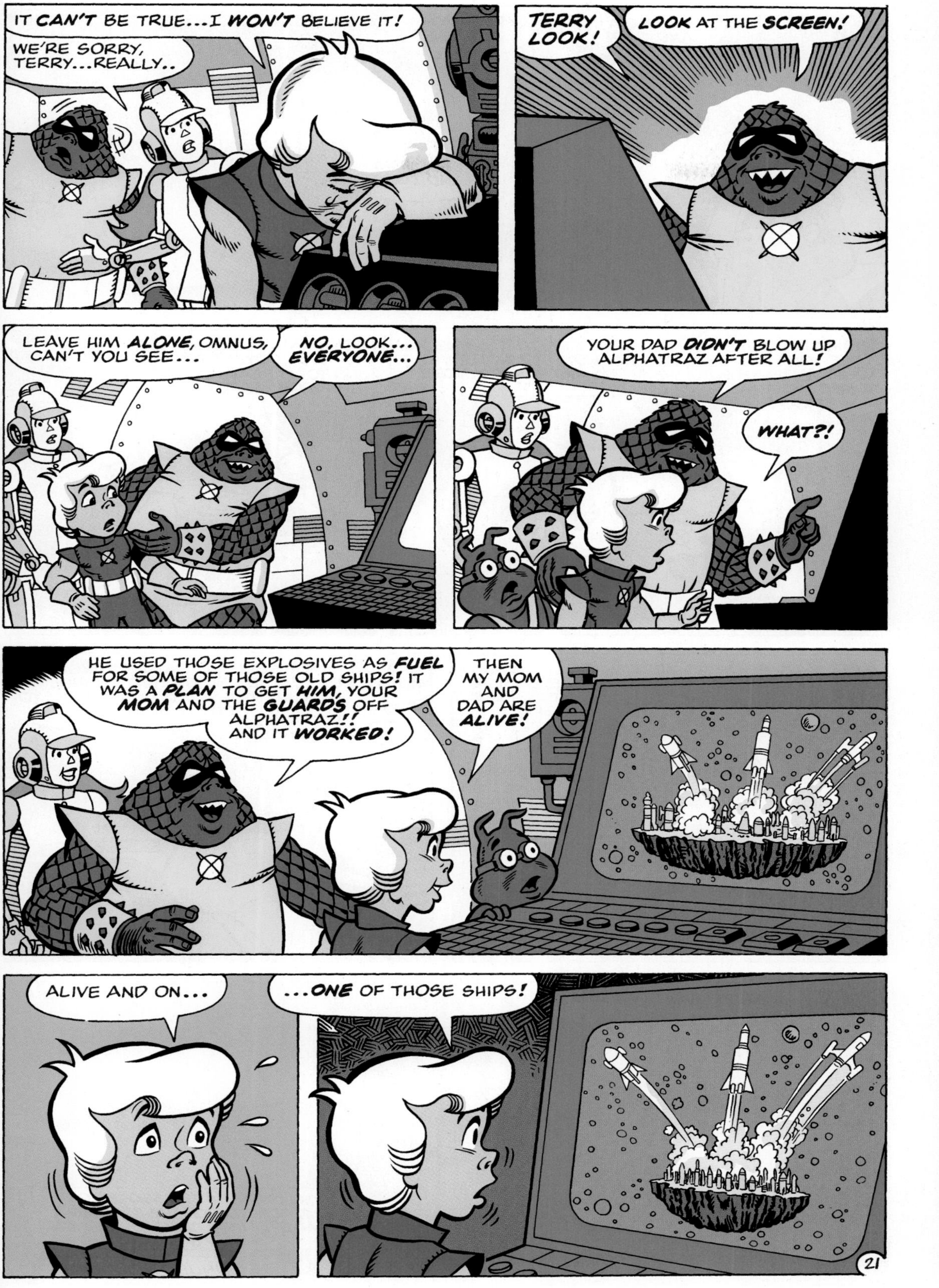
IT CAN'T BE TRUE...I WON'T BELIEVE IT!
WE'RE SORRY, TERRY...REALLY..
TERRY LOOK!
LOOK AT THE SCREEN!
LEAVE HIM ALONE, OMNUS, CAN'T YOU SEE...
NO. LOOK... EVERYONE...
YOUR DAD DIDN'T BLOW UP ALPHATRAZ AFTER ALL!
WHAT?!
HE USED THOSE EXPLOSIVES AS FUEL FOR SOME OF THOSE OLD SHIPS! IT WAS A PLAN TO GET HIM, YOUR MOM AND THE GUARDS OFF ALPHATRAZ!! AND IT WORKED!
THEN MY MOM AND DAD ARE ALIVE!
ALIVE AND ON...
...ONE OF THOSE SHIPS!
21

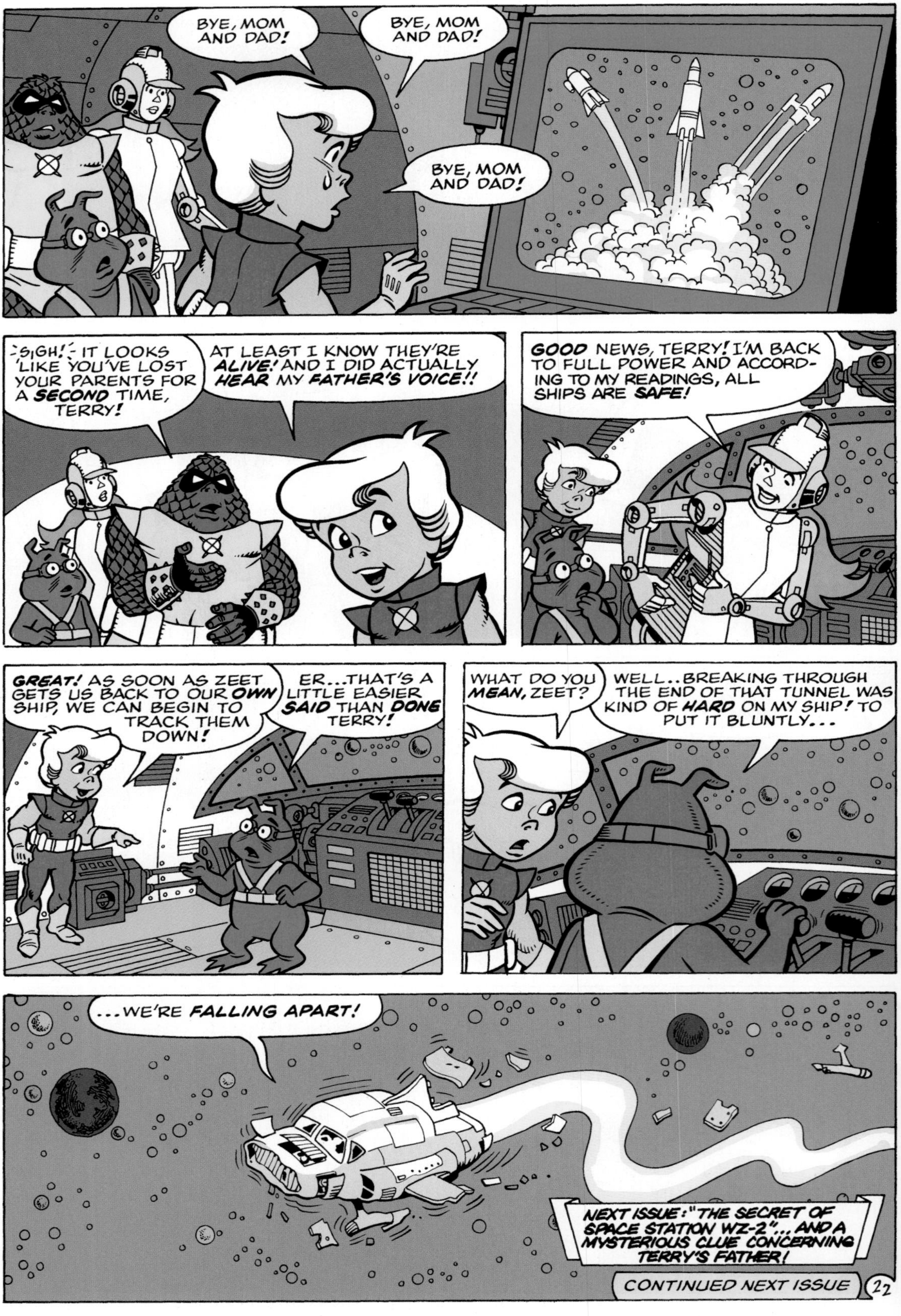
BYE, MOM AND DAD!
BYE, MOM AND DAD!
BYE, MOM AND DAD!
-SIGH!- IT LOOKS LIKE YOU'VE LOST YOUR PARENTS FOR A SECOND TIME, TERRY!
AT LEAST I KNOW THEY'RE ALIVE! AND I DID ACTUALLY HEAR MY FATHER'S VOICE!!
GOOD NEWS, TERRY! I'M BACK TO FULL POWER AND ACCORDING TO MY READINGS, ALL SHIPS ARE SAFE!
GREAT! AS SOON AS ZEET GETS US BACK TO OUR OWN SHIP, WE CAN BEGIN TO TRACK THEM DOWN!
ER...THAT'S A LITTLE EASIER SAID THAN DONE TERRY!
WHAT DO YOU MEAN, ZEET?
WELL..BREAKING THROUGH THE END OF THAT TUNNEL WAS KIND OF HARD ON MY SHIP! TO PUT IT BLUNTLY...
...WE'RE FALLING APART!
NEXT ISSUE: "THE SECRET OF SPACE STATION WZ-2"... AND A MYSTERIOUS CLUE CONCERNING TERRY'S FATHER!
CONTINUED NEXT ISSUE
22

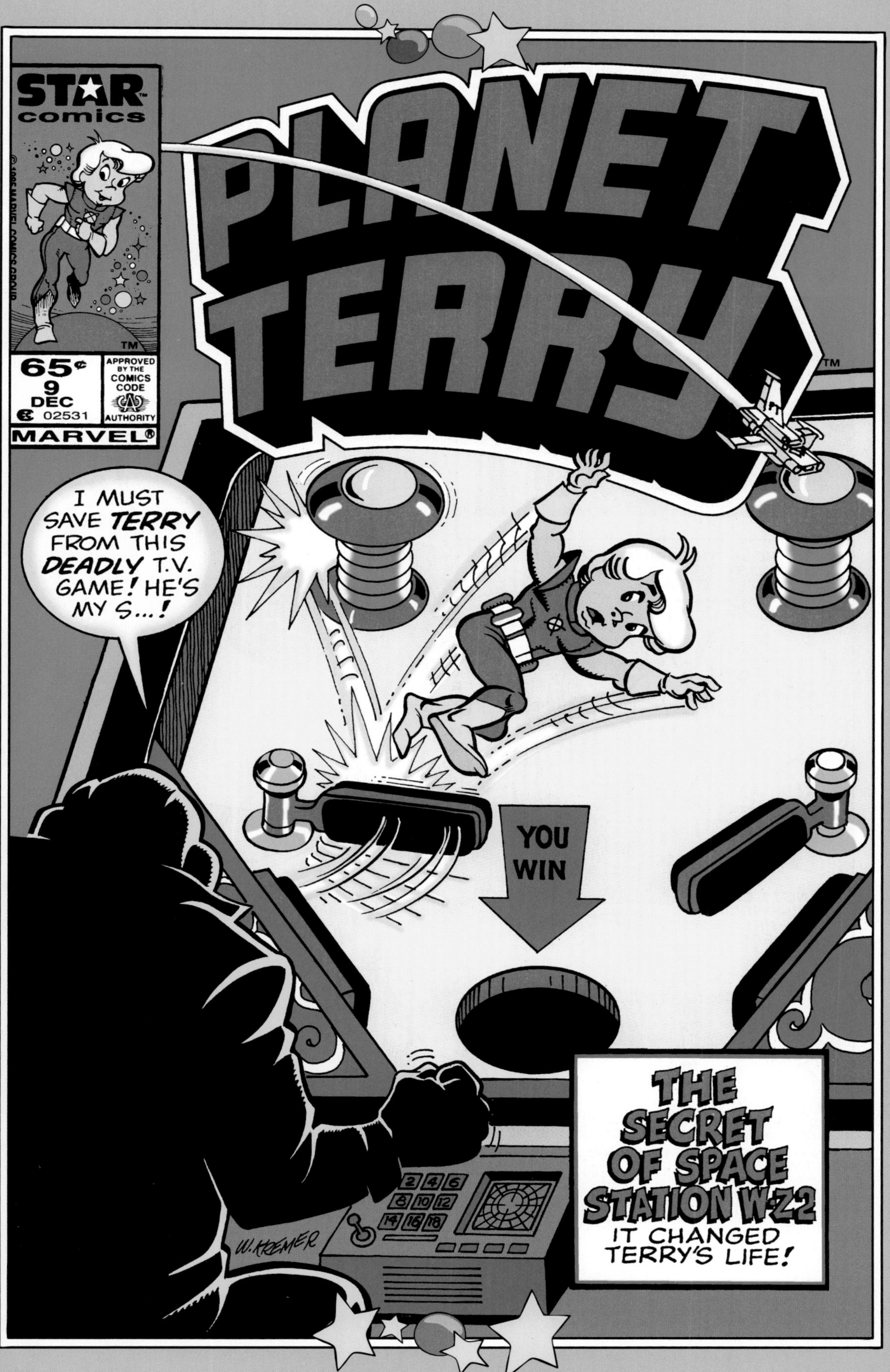
STAR comics
© 1985 MARVEL COMICS GROUP
PLANET TERRY
65¢
9
DEC
02531
APPROVED BY THE COMICS CODE AUTHORITY
MARVEL
I MUST SAVE TERRY FROM THIS DEADLY T.V. GAME! HE'S MY S...!
YOU WIN
W. KREMER
2 4 6 8 10 12 14 16 18
THE SECRET OF SPACE STATION W-Z-2
IT CHANGED TERRY'S LIFE!

SOMEWHERE IN SPACE, A CRIPPLED SPACE CRAFT...HAVING ESCAPED FROM THE PRISON PLANET, *ALPHATRAZ*...FIGHTS FOR SURVIVAL! IS THIS THE END FOR ITS PASSENGERS... *PLANET TERRY*, THE YOUTHFUL WHITE-HAIRED HERO; *ROBOTA*, THE INCREDIBLE ROBOT; *OMNUS*, THE ALIEN BRUTE; AND *ZEET*, THE STRANGER FROM ALPHATRAZ? IS THIS THE END, TOO, FOR TERRY'S LIFELONG DREAM OF FINDING HIS LONG-LOST PARENTS?

PLANET TERRY

IN THE SECRET OF SPACE STATION W-Z2

WE'VE UNDERGONE A TREMENDOUS SHOCK, TERRY! THE SHIP'S BREAKING UP!

URRG! OMNUS WILL KEEP THIS HULL IN ONE PIECE UNTIL THE UNIVERSE ITSELF BREAKS APART!

WE'LL HOLD THE SHIP TOGETHER, ZEET! JUST TRY TO KEEP HER STEADY!

RIGHT, TERRY!

OH, NO! I CAN'T LASER-WELD THESE PRESSURE LEAKS FAST ENOUGH!

BZAP!

1

DAVE MANAK WRITER • **WARREN KREMER** PENCILLER • **JON D'AGOSTINO** INKER • **GEORGE ROUSSOS** COLORIST • **SID JACOBSON** EDITOR • **TOM DEFALCO** EXEC. EDITOR • **JIM SHOOTER** EDITOR IN CHIEF

TERRY, LOOK OUT!
YEOW!
ZZZT!
NOW IT'S THE ELECTRICAL SYSTEM! WE CAN'T HOLD ON MUCH LONGER!
I KNOW, TERRY! BUT WHERE DO WE FIND A PLACE TO LAND...
...WHEN WE'RE... GULP! IN THE MIDDLE OF NOWHERE!?!
WAIT! OUR SENSORS JUST PICKED UP A LARGE NEARBY SATELLITE!
LET'S HEAD FOR IT!
BLIP-BLIP-
BLIP-
W-ZZ
NO NEED TO!
IT'S HEADING FOR US!
AND IT'S BIG ENOUGH TO LAND ON!
W-ZZ?? WHAT IN THE UNIVERSE IS THAT?
W-ZZ
I DON'T KNOW...BUT WE'LL GULP SOON FIND OUT!
W-ZZ
2

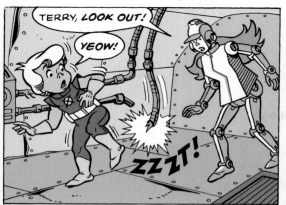

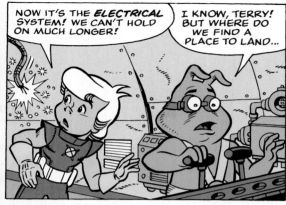

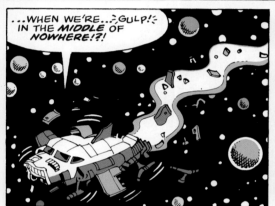

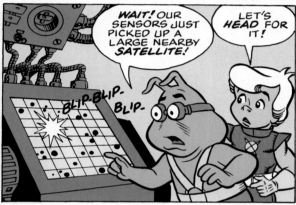

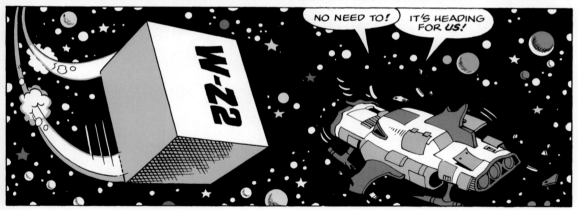

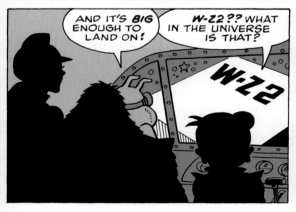

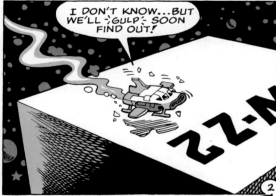

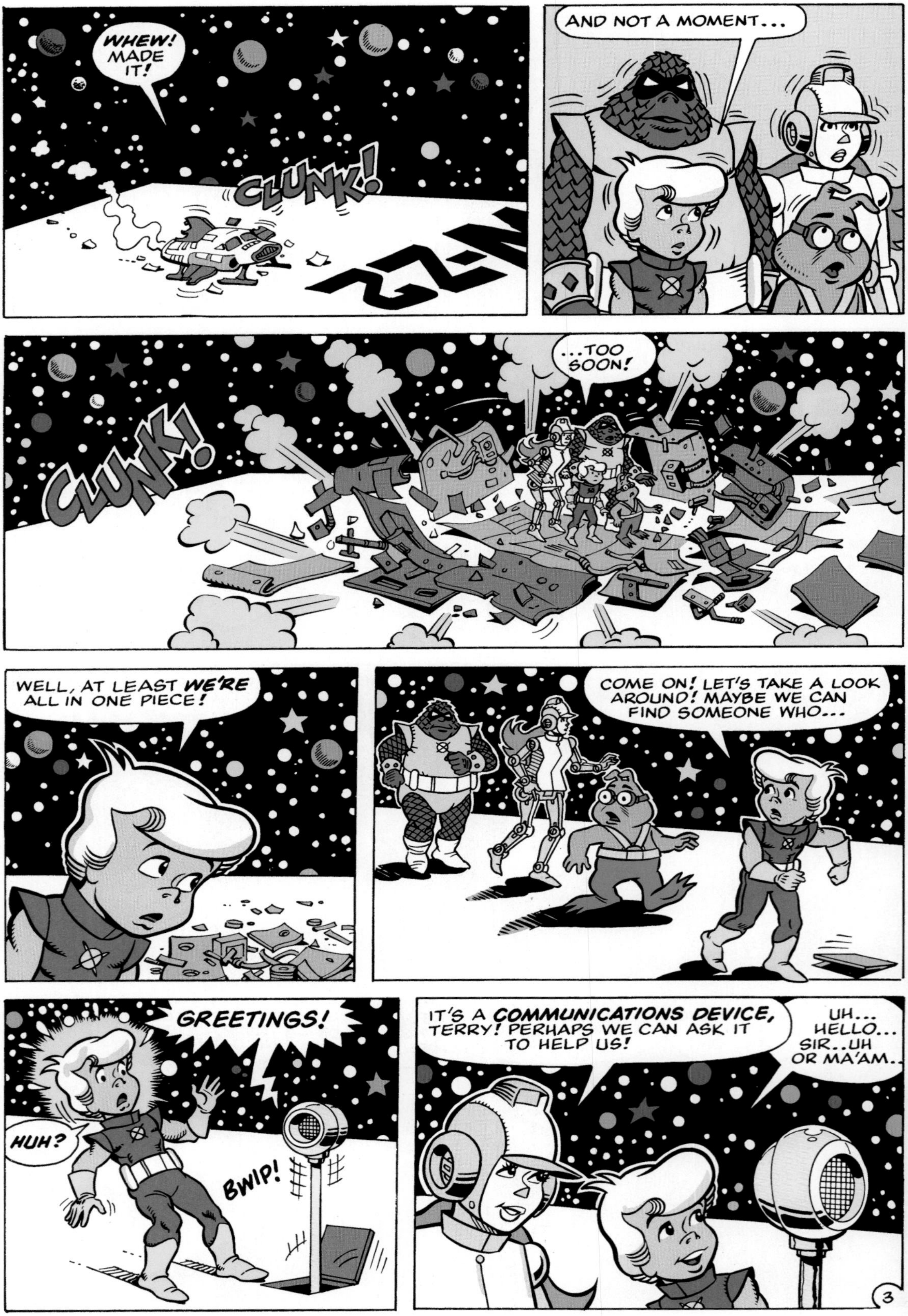
WHEW! MADE IT!
CLUNK!
ZZ-N
AND NOT A MOMENT...
...TOO SOON!
CLUNK!
WELL, AT LEAST WE'RE ALL IN ONE PIECE!
COME ON! LET'S TAKE A LOOK AROUND! MAYBE WE CAN FIND SOMEONE WHO...
GREETINGS!
HUH?
BWIP!
IT'S A COMMUNICATIONS DEVICE, TERRY! PERHAPS WE CAN ASK IT TO HELP US!
UH... HELLO... SIR..UH OR MA'AM..
3

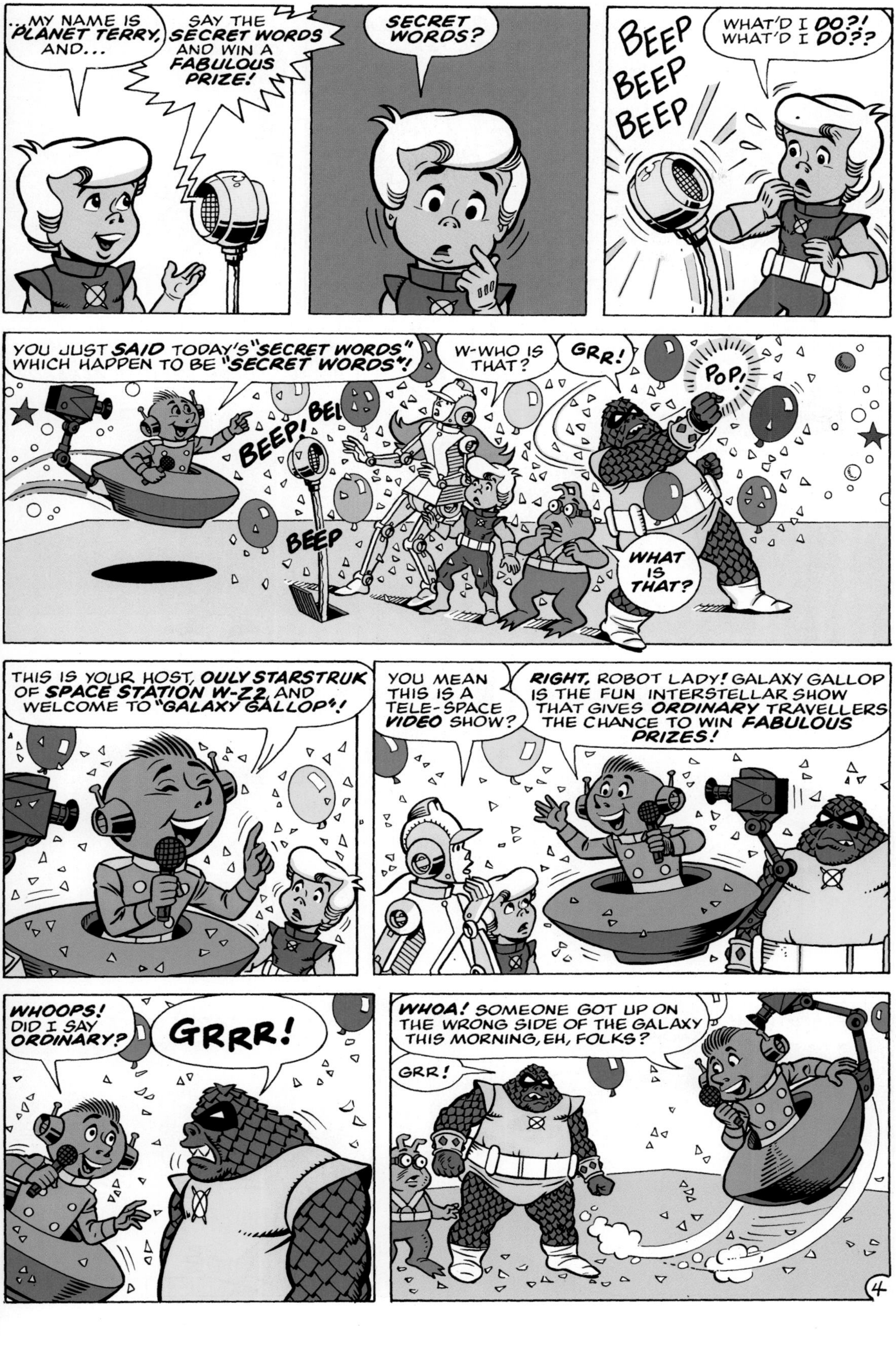
...MY NAME IS PLANET TERRY, AND...
SAY THE SECRET WORDS AND WIN A FABULOUS PRIZE!
SECRET WORDS?
BEEP BEEP BEEP
WHAT'D I DO?! WHAT'D I DO??
YOU JUST SAID TODAY'S "SECRET WORDS" WHICH HAPPEN TO BE "SECRET WORDS"!
W-WHO IS THAT?
GRR!
POP!
BEEP! BE
BEEP
WHAT IS THAT?
THIS IS YOUR HOST, OULY STARSTRUK OF SPACE STATION W-Z2, AND WELCOME TO "GALAXY GALLOP"!
YOU MEAN THIS IS A TELE-SPACE VIDEO SHOW?
RIGHT, ROBOT LADY! GALAXY GALLOP IS THE FUN INTERSTELLAR SHOW THAT GIVES ORDINARY TRAVELLERS THE CHANCE TO WIN FABULOUS PRIZES!
WHOOPS! DID I SAY ORDINARY?
GRRR!
WHOA! SOMEONE GOT UP ON THE WRONG SIDE OF THE GALAXY THIS MORNING, EH, FOLKS?
GRR!
4

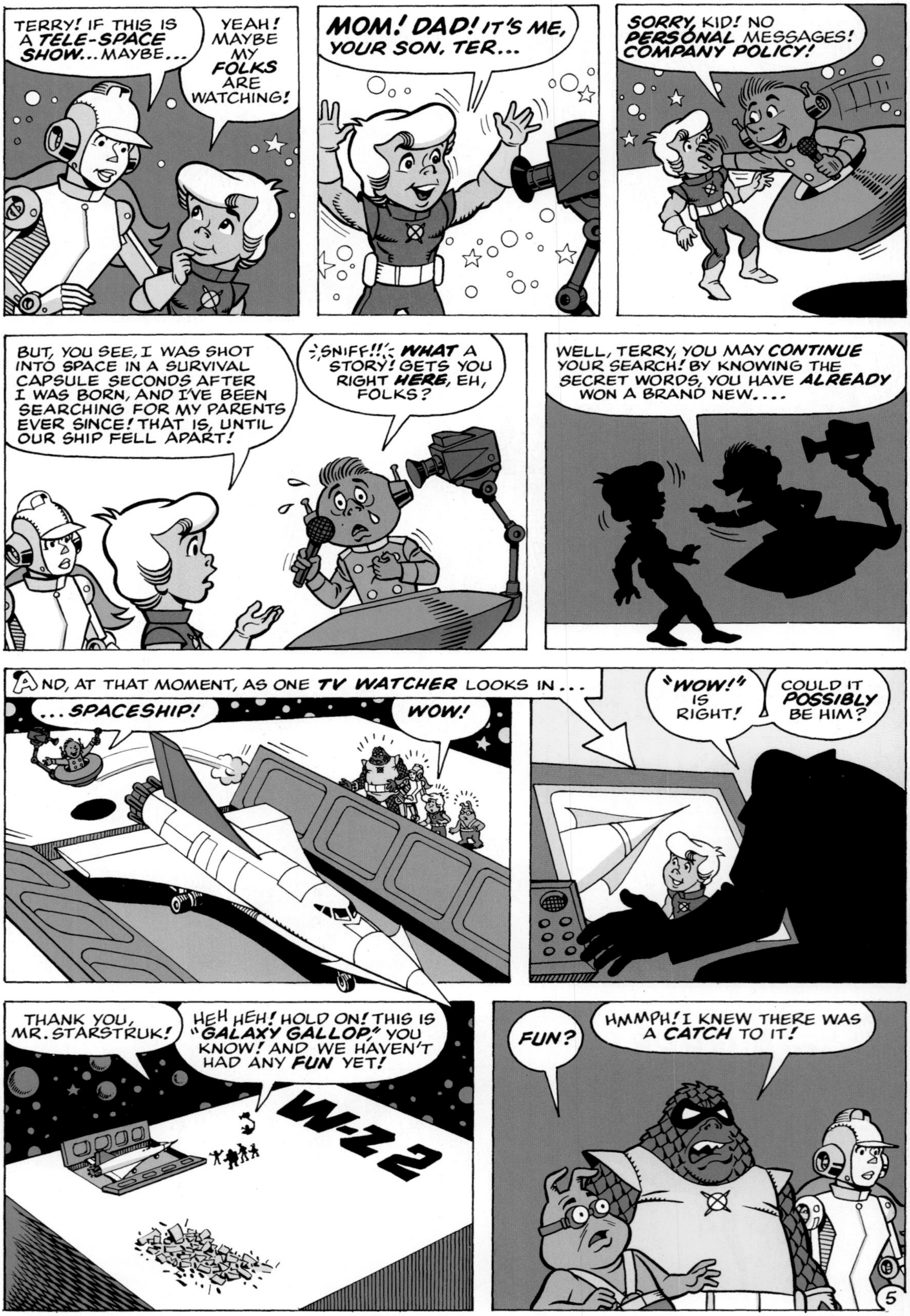
TERRY! IF THIS IS A TELE-SPACE SHOW... MAYBE...
YEAH! MAYBE MY FOLKS ARE WATCHING!
MOM! DAD! IT'S ME, YOUR SON, TER...
SORRY, KID! NO PERSONAL MESSAGES! COMPANY POLICY!
BUT, YOU SEE, I WAS SHOT INTO SPACE IN A SURVIVAL CAPSULE SECONDS AFTER I WAS BORN, AND I'VE BEEN SEARCHING FOR MY PARENTS EVER SINCE! THAT IS, UNTIL OUR SHIP FELL APART!
SNIFF!! WHAT A STORY! GETS YOU RIGHT HERE, EH, FOLKS?
WELL, TERRY, YOU MAY CONTINUE YOUR SEARCH! BY KNOWING THE SECRET WORDS, YOU HAVE ALREADY WON A BRAND NEW....
AND, AT THAT MOMENT, AS ONE TV WATCHER LOOKS IN...
...SPACESHIP!
WOW!
"WOW!" IS RIGHT!
COULD IT POSSIBLY BE HIM?
THANK YOU, MR. STARSTRUK!
HEH HEH! HOLD ON! THIS IS "GALAXY GALLOP," YOU KNOW! AND WE HAVEN'T HAD ANY FUN YET!
W-22
FUN?
HMMPH! I KNEW THERE WAS A CATCH TO IT!
5

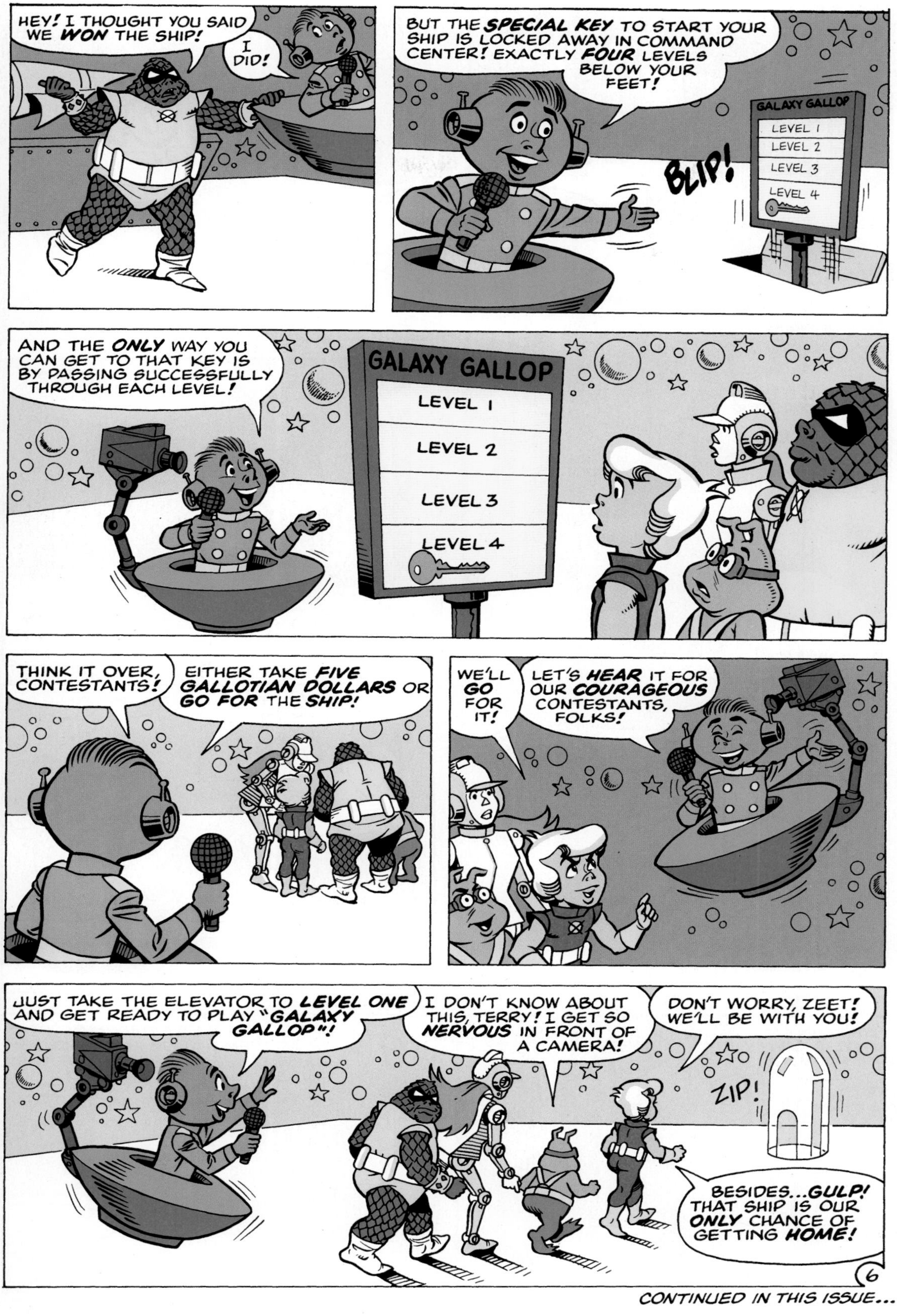

HEY! I THOUGHT YOU SAID WE WON THE SHIP!
I DID!
BUT THE SPECIAL KEY TO START YOUR SHIP IS LOCKED AWAY IN COMMAND CENTER! EXACTLY FOUR LEVELS BELOW YOUR FEET!
GALAXY GALLOP
LEVEL 1
LEVEL 2
LEVEL 3
LEVEL 4
BLIP!
AND THE ONLY WAY YOU CAN GET TO THAT KEY IS BY PASSING SUCCESSFULLY THROUGH EACH LEVEL!
GALAXY GALLOP
LEVEL 1
LEVEL 2
LEVEL 3
LEVEL 4
THINK IT OVER, CONTESTANTS!
EITHER TAKE FIVE GALLOTIAN DOLLARS OR GO FOR THE SHIP!
WE'LL GO FOR IT!
LET'S HEAR IT FOR OUR COURAGEOUS CONTESTANTS, FOLKS!
JUST TAKE THE ELEVATOR TO LEVEL ONE AND GET READY TO PLAY "GALAXY GALLOP"!
I DON'T KNOW ABOUT THIS, TERRY! I GET SO NERVOUS IN FRONT OF A CAMERA!
DON'T WORRY, ZEET! WE'LL BE WITH YOU!
ZIP!
BESIDES...GULP! THAT SHIP IS OUR ONLY CHANCE OF GETTING HOME!
6

CONTINUED IN THIS ISSUE...

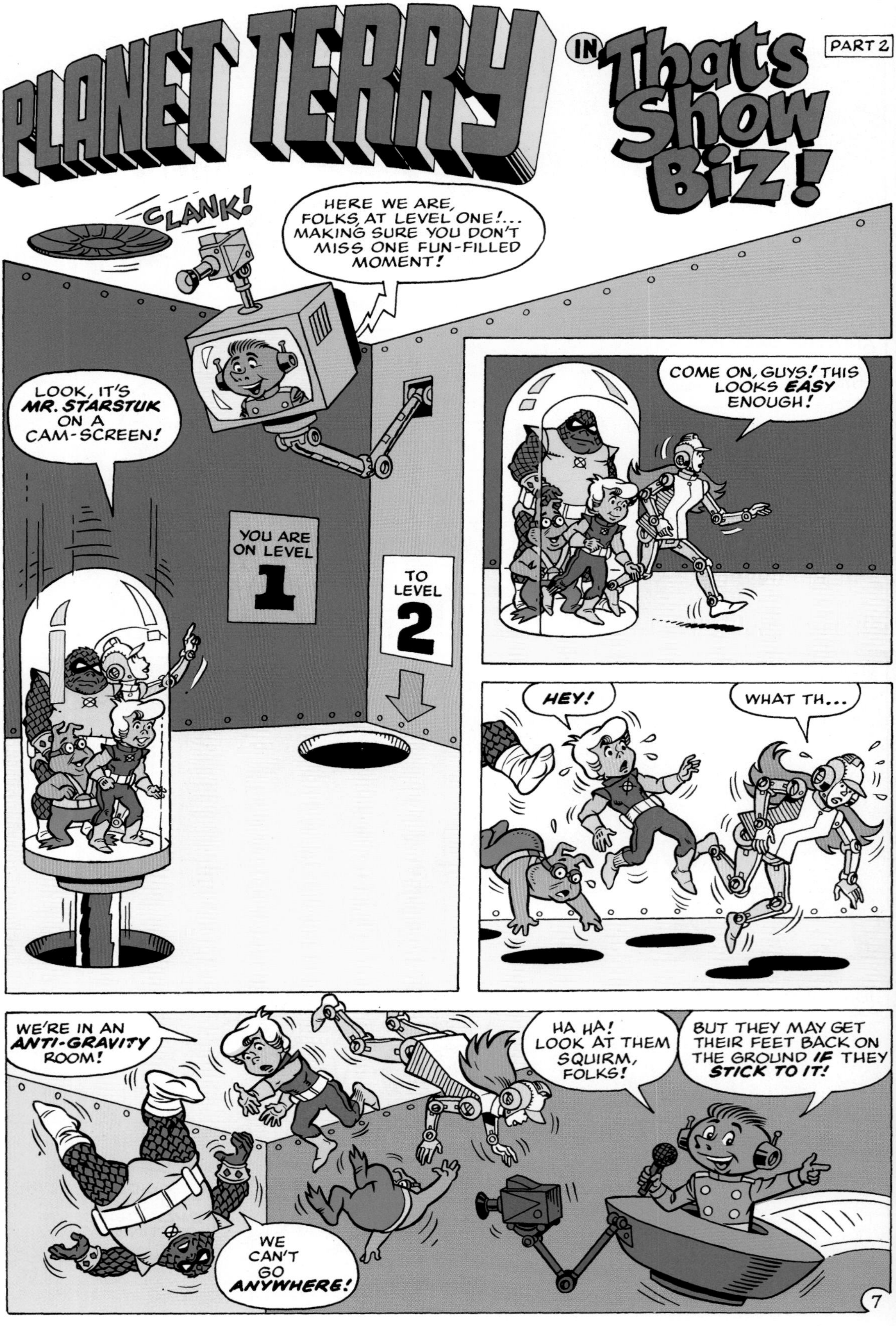
PLANET TERRY
IN
Thats Show Biz!
PART 2
CLANK!
HERE WE ARE, FOLKS, AT LEVEL ONE!... MAKING SURE YOU DON'T MISS ONE FUN-FILLED MOMENT!
LOOK, IT'S MR. STARSTUK ON A CAM-SCREEN!
YOU ARE ON LEVEL 1
TO LEVEL 2
COME ON, GUYS! THIS LOOKS EASY ENOUGH!
HEY!
WHAT TH...
WE'RE IN AN ANTI-GRAVITY ROOM!
HA HA! LOOK AT THEM SQUIRM, FOLKS!
BUT THEY MAY GET THEIR FEET BACK ON THE GROUND IF THEY STICK TO IT!
WE CAN'T GO ANYWHERE!
7

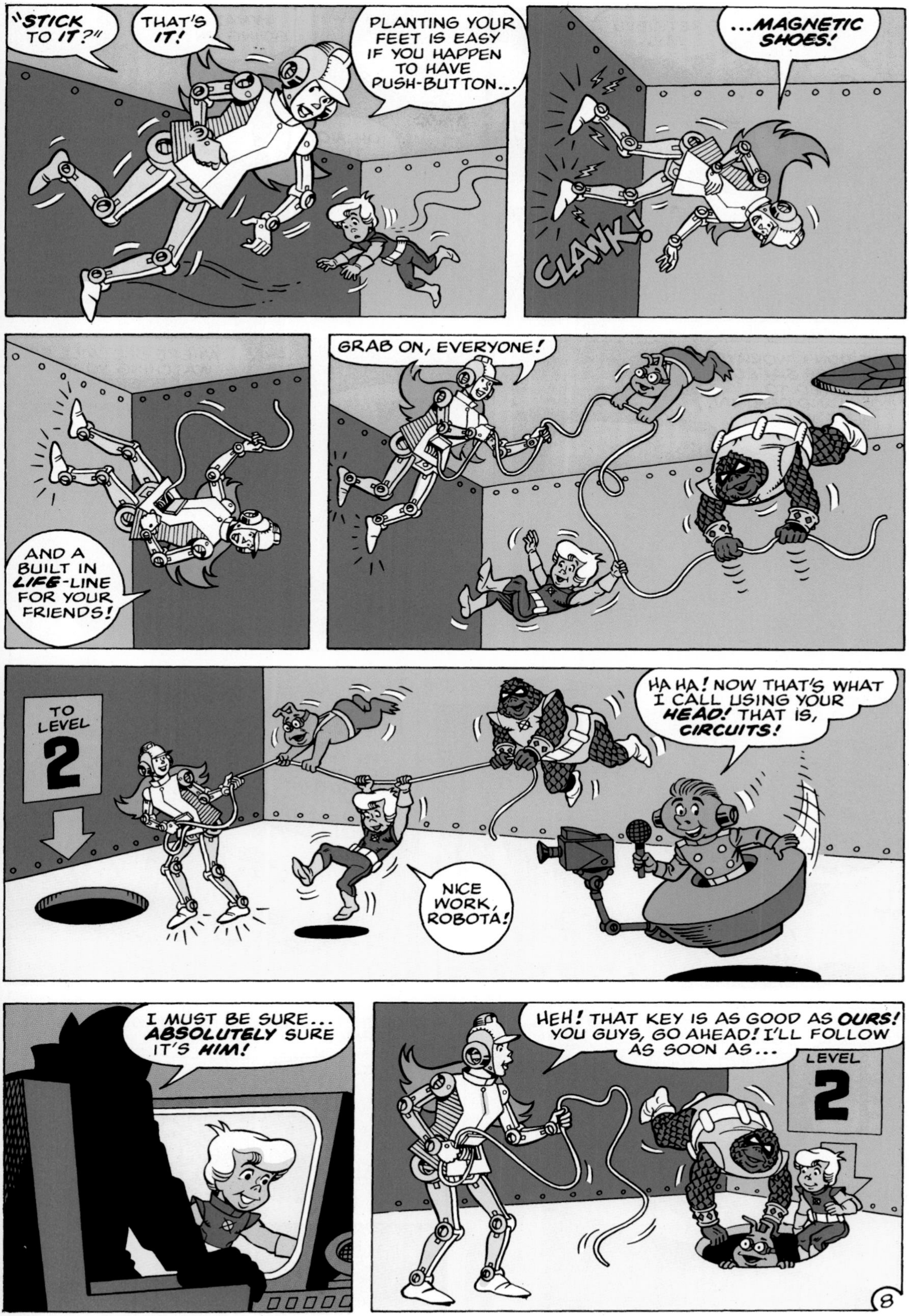

"STICK TO IT?"
THAT'S IT!
PLANTING YOUR FEET IS EASY IF YOU HAPPEN TO HAVE PUSH-BUTTON...
...MAGNETIC SHOES!
CLANK!
AND A BUILT IN LIFE-LINE FOR YOUR FRIENDS!
GRAB ON, EVERYONE!
TO LEVEL 2
HA HA! NOW THAT'S WHAT I CALL USING YOUR HEAD! THAT IS, CIRCUITS!
NICE WORK, ROBOTA!
I MUST BE SURE... ABSOLUTELY SURE IT'S HIM!
HEH! THAT KEY IS AS GOOD AS OURS! YOU GUYS, GO AHEAD! I'LL FOLLOW AS SOON AS...
LEVEL 2
8

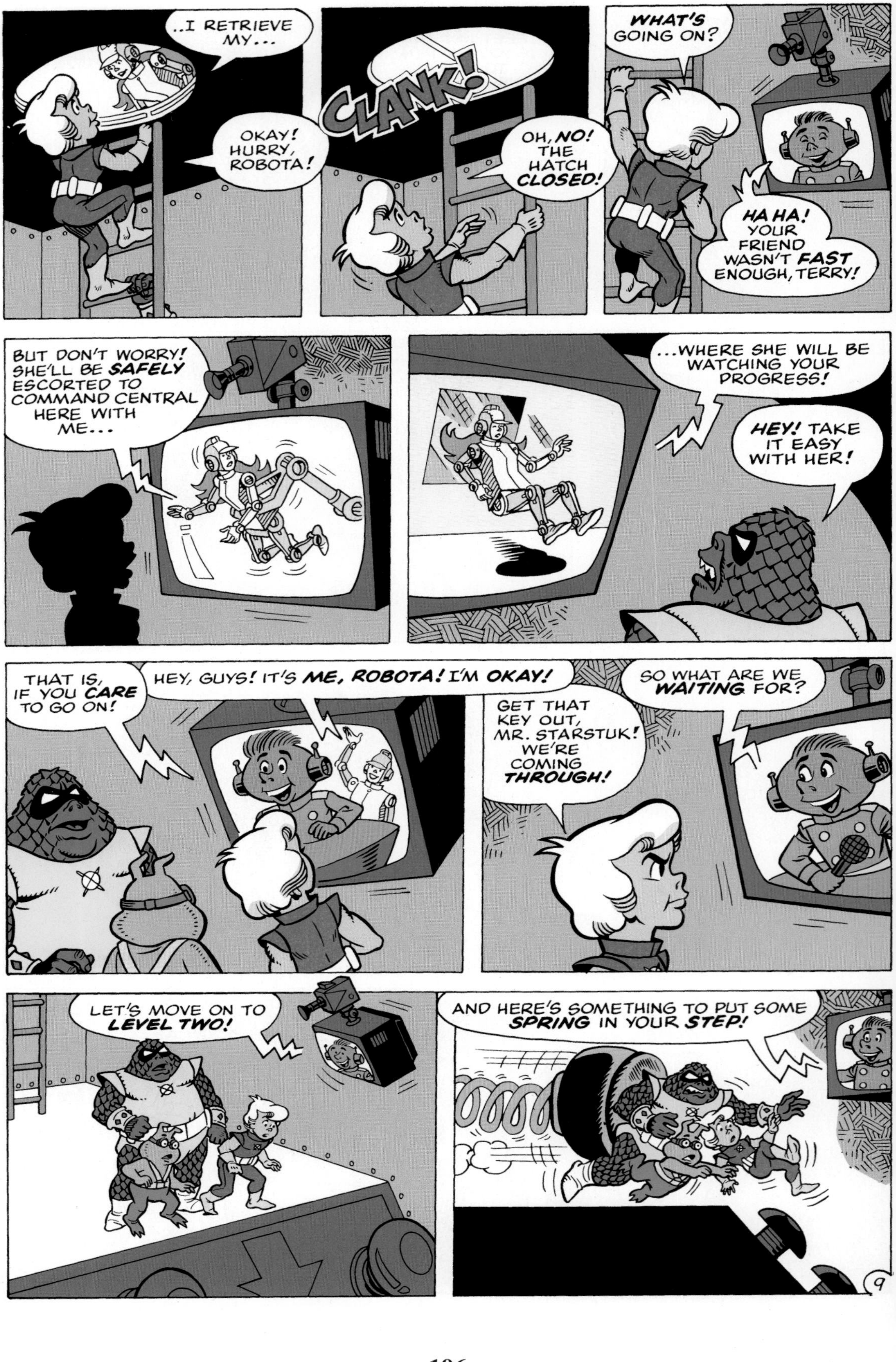
..I RETRIEVE MY...
OKAY! HURRY, ROBOTA!
CLANK!
OH, NO! THE HATCH CLOSED!
WHAT'S GOING ON?
HA HA! YOUR FRIEND WASN'T FAST ENOUGH, TERRY!
BUT DON'T WORRY! SHE'LL BE SAFELY ESCORTED TO COMMAND CENTRAL HERE WITH ME...
...WHERE SHE WILL BE WATCHING YOUR PROGRESS!
HEY! TAKE IT EASY WITH HER!
THAT IS, IF YOU CARE TO GO ON!
HEY, GUYS! IT'S ME, ROBOTA! I'M OKAY!
GET THAT KEY OUT, MR. STARSTUK! WE'RE COMING THROUGH!
SO WHAT ARE WE WAITING FOR?
LET'S MOVE ON TO LEVEL TWO!
AND HERE'S SOMETHING TO PUT SOME SPRING IN YOUR STEP!
9

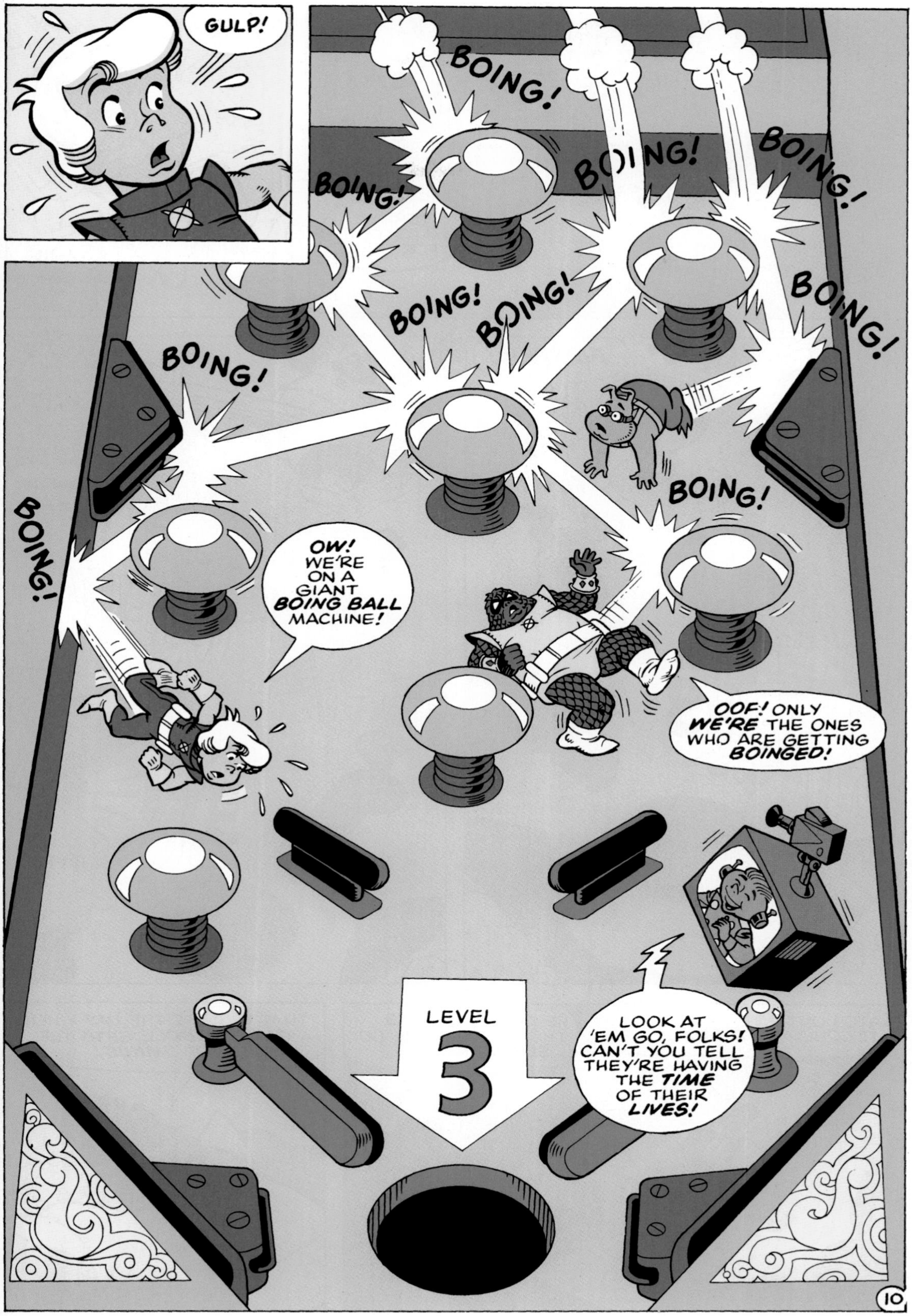

GULP!
BOING!
BOING!
BOING!
BOING!
BOING!
BOING!
BOING!
BOING!
BOING!
BOING!
OW! WE'RE ON A GIANT BOING BALL MACHINE!
OOF! ONLY WE'RE THE ONES WHO ARE GETTING BOINGED!
LEVEL 3
LOOK AT 'EM GO, FOLKS! CAN'T YOU TELL THEY'RE HAVING THE TIME OF THEIR LIVES!
10

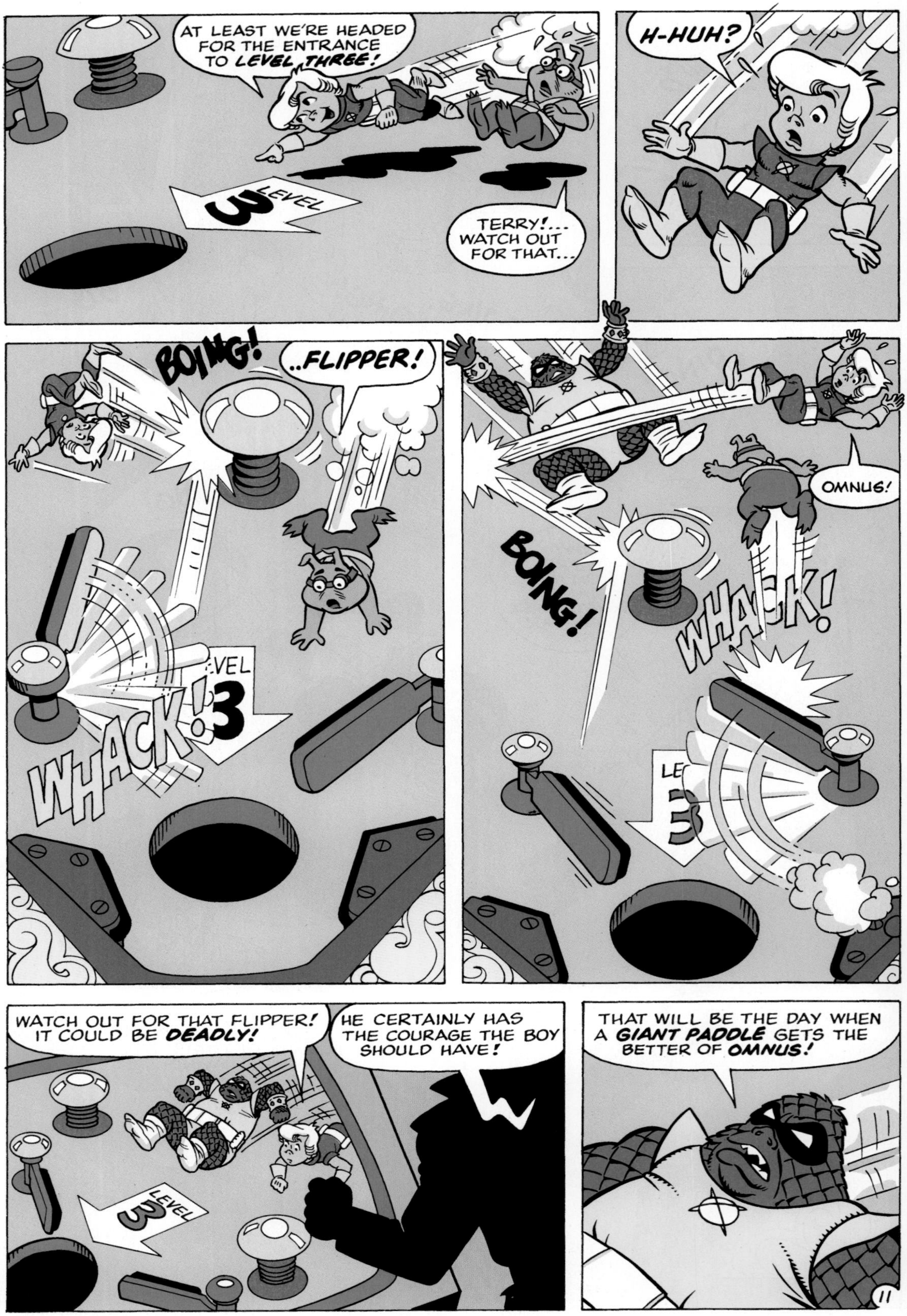

AT LEAST WE'RE HEADED FOR THE ENTRANCE TO LEVEL THREE!
LEVEL 3
TERRY!... WATCH OUT FOR THAT...
H-HUH?
BOING!
..FLIPPER!
LEVEL 3
WHACK!
OMNUS!
BOING!
WHACK!
WATCH OUT FOR THAT FLIPPER! IT COULD BE DEADLY!
HE CERTAINLY HAS THE COURAGE THE BOY SHOULD HAVE!
LEVEL 3
THAT WILL BE THE DAY WHEN A GIANT PADDLE GETS THE BETTER OF OMNUS!
11

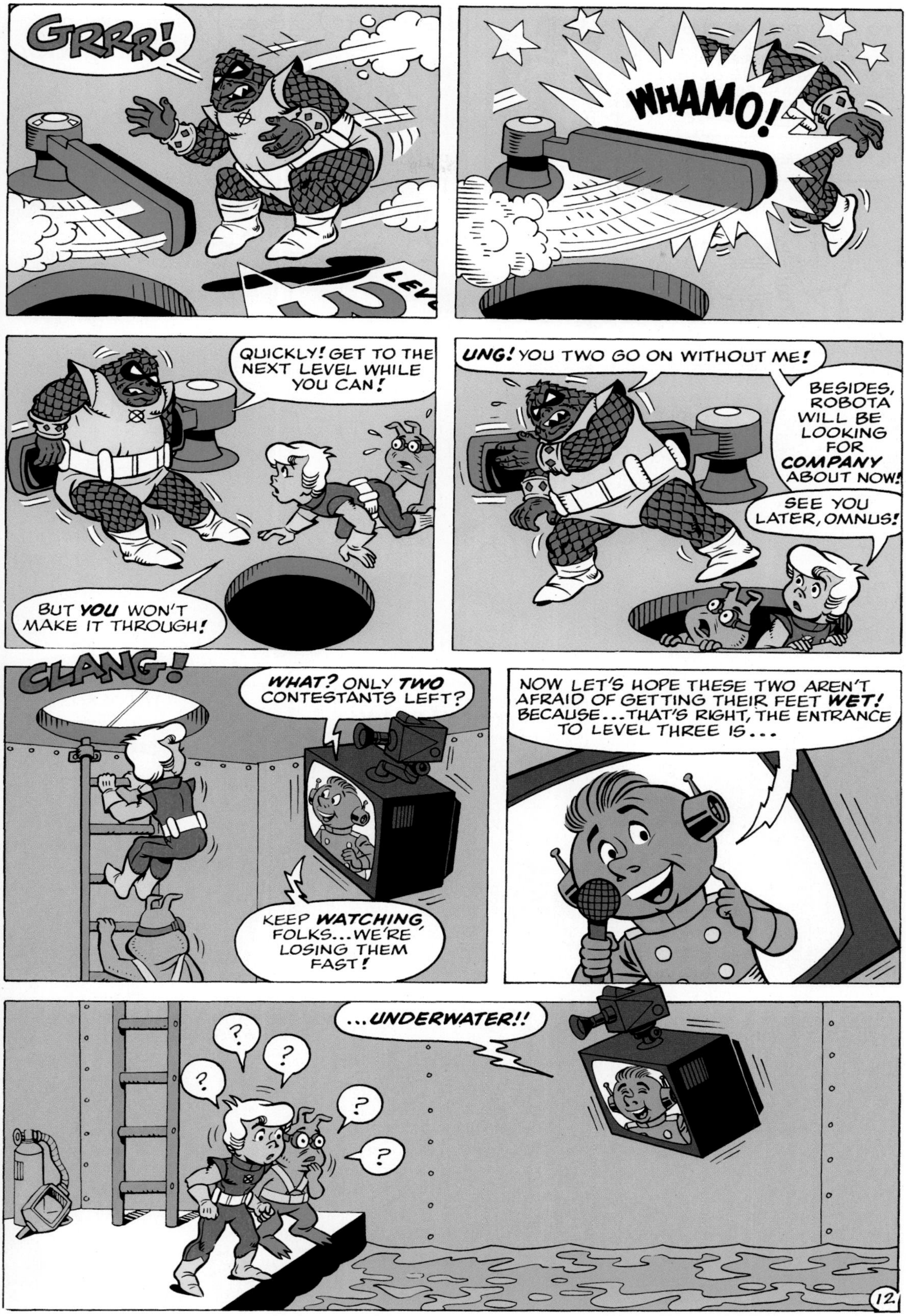
GRRR!
WHAMO!
QUICKLY! GET TO THE NEXT LEVEL WHILE YOU CAN!
BUT YOU WON'T MAKE IT THROUGH!
UNG! YOU TWO GO ON WITHOUT ME!
BESIDES, ROBOTA WILL BE LOOKING FOR COMPANY ABOUT NOW!
SEE YOU LATER, OMNUS!
CLANG!
WHAT? ONLY TWO CONTESTANTS LEFT?
KEEP WATCHING, FOLKS...WE'RE LOSING THEM FAST!
NOW LET'S HOPE THESE TWO AREN'T AFRAID OF GETTING THEIR FEET WET! BECAUSE...THAT'S RIGHT, THE ENTRANCE TO LEVEL THREE IS...
...UNDERWATER!!
?
?
?
?
?
12

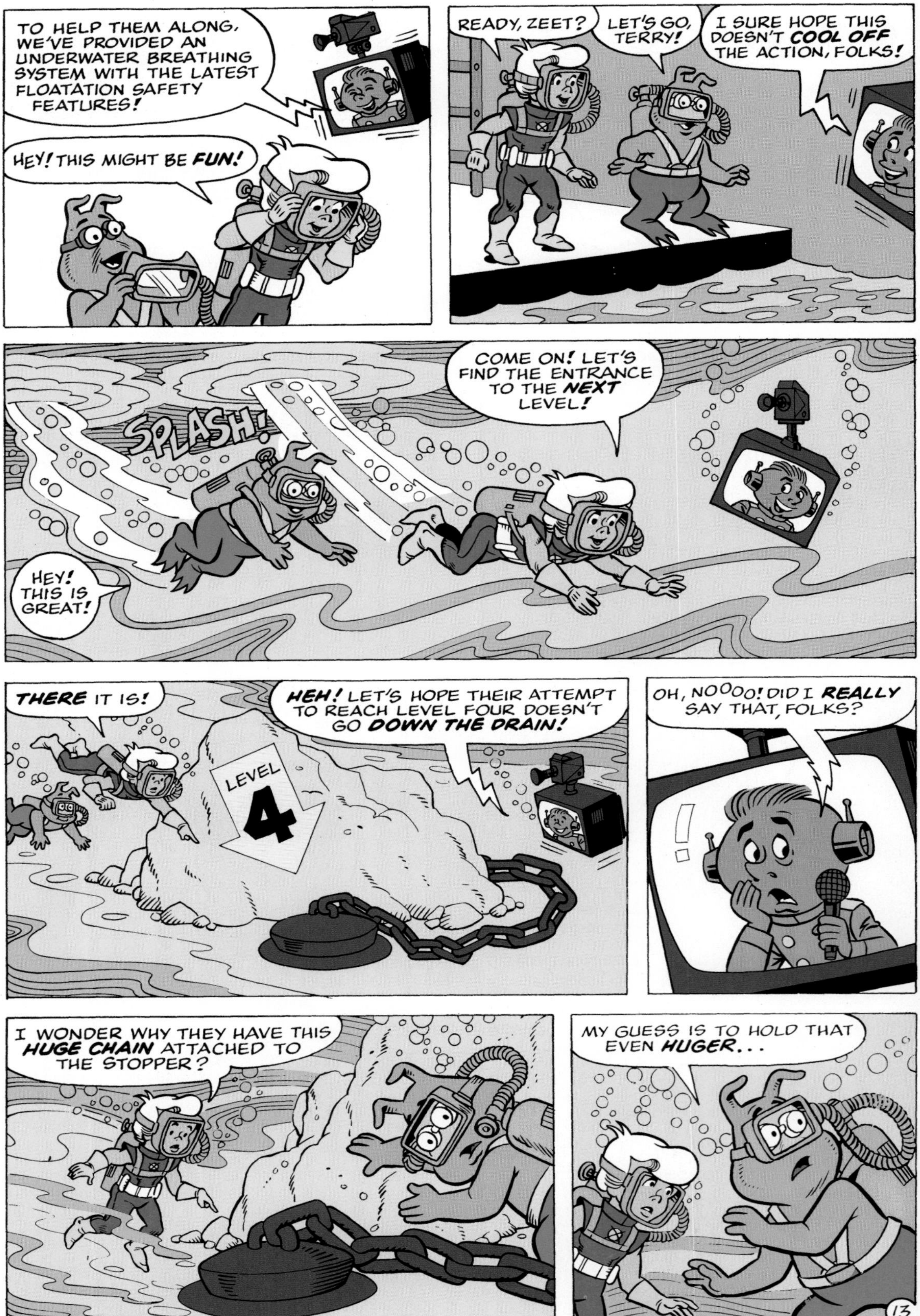
TO HELP THEM ALONG, WE'VE PROVIDED AN UNDERWATER BREATHING SYSTEM WITH THE LATEST FLOATATION SAFETY FEATURES!
HEY! THIS MIGHT BE FUN!
READY, ZEET?
LET'S GO, TERRY!
I SURE HOPE THIS DOESN'T COOL OFF THE ACTION, FOLKS!
SPLASH!
COME ON! LET'S FIND THE ENTRANCE TO THE NEXT LEVEL!
HEY! THIS IS GREAT!
THERE IT IS!
HEH! LET'S HOPE THEIR ATTEMPT TO REACH LEVEL FOUR DOESN'T GO DOWN THE DRAIN!
LEVEL 4
OH, NOOOO! DID I REALLY SAY THAT, FOLKS?
I WONDER WHY THEY HAVE THIS HUGE CHAIN ATTACHED TO THE STOPPER?
MY GUESS IS TO HOLD THAT EVEN HUGER...
13

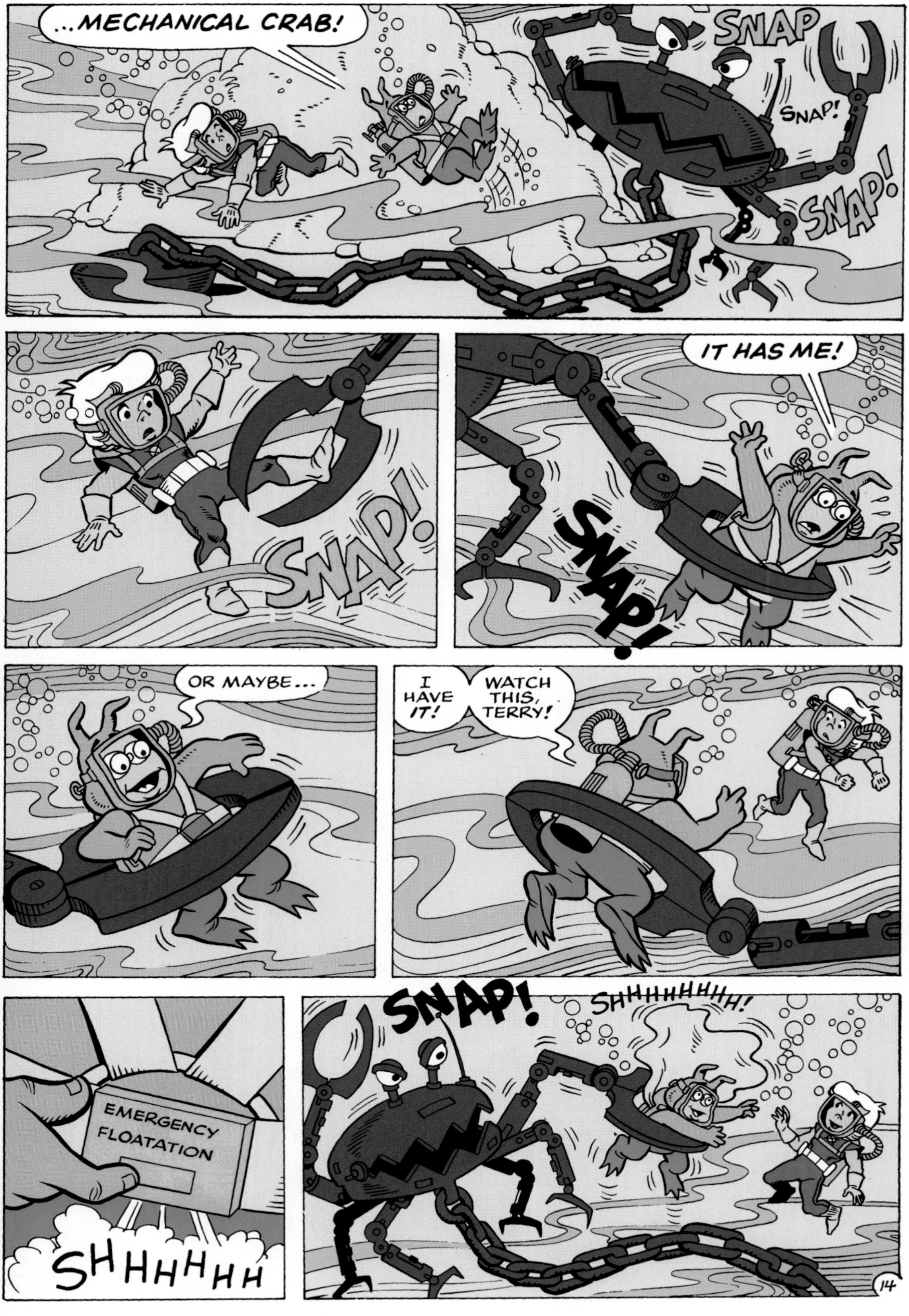
...MECHANICAL CRAB!
SNAP
SNAP!
SNAP!
SNAP!
IT HAS ME!
SNAP!
OR MAYBE...
I HAVE IT!
WATCH THIS, TERRY!
EMERGENCY FLOATATION
SHHHHHHH
SNAP!
SHHHHHHHH!
14

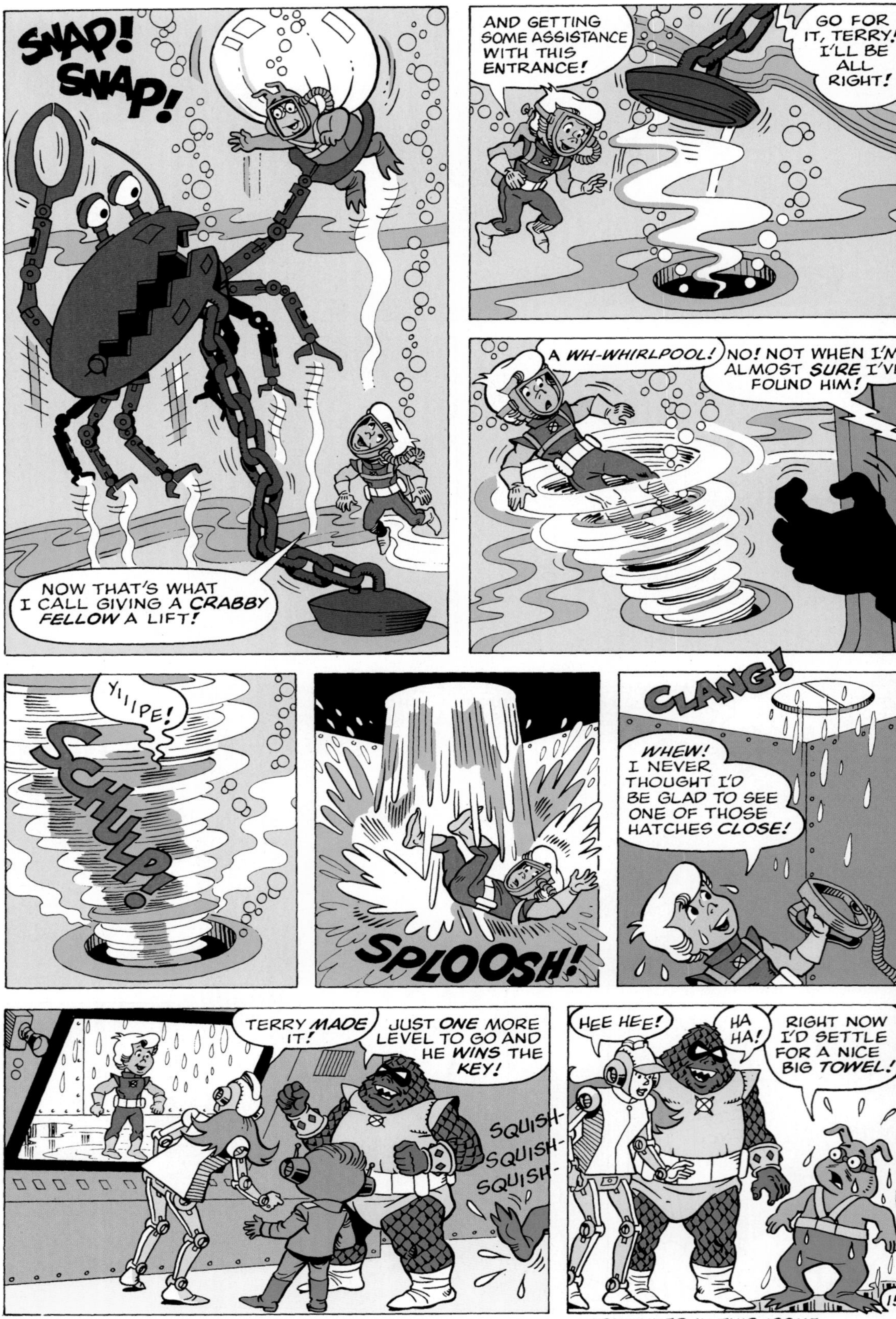
SNAP! SNAP!
NOW THAT'S WHAT I CALL GIVING A CRABBY FELLOW A LIFT!
AND GETTING SOME ASSISTANCE WITH THIS ENTRANCE!
GO FOR IT, TERRY! I'LL BE ALL RIGHT!
A WH-WHIRLPOOL!
NO! NOT WHEN I'M ALMOST SURE I'VE FOUND HIM!
YIIIPE!
SCHULP!
SPLOOSH!
CLANG!
WHEW! I NEVER THOUGHT I'D BE GLAD TO SEE ONE OF THOSE HATCHES CLOSE!
TERRY MADE IT!
JUST ONE MORE LEVEL TO GO AND HE WINS THE KEY!
SQUISH- SQUISH- SQUISH-
HEE HEE!
HA HA!
RIGHT NOW I'D SETTLE FOR A NICE BIG TOWEL!
15

CONTINUED IN THIS ISSUE...

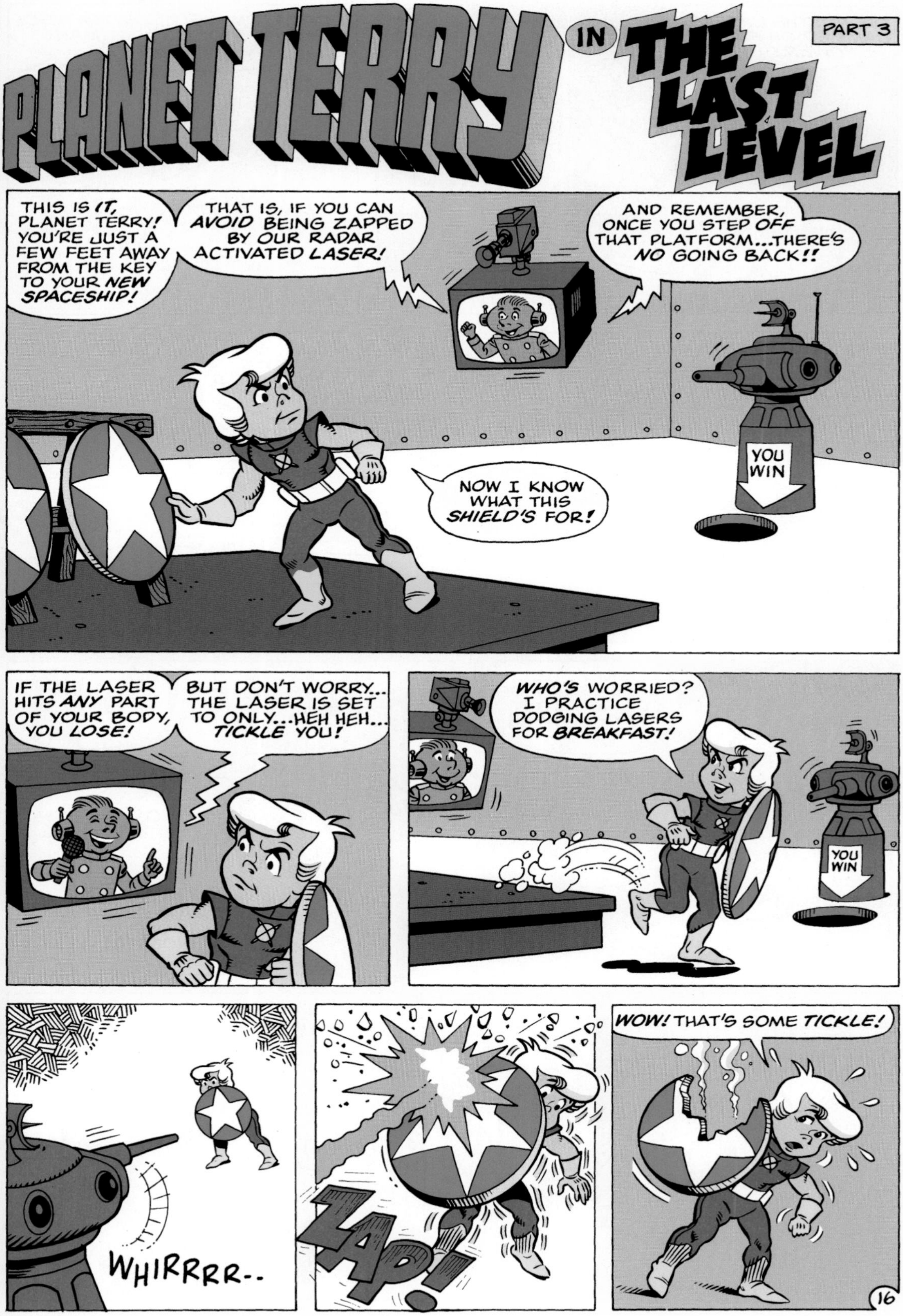

PLANET TERRY IN THE LAST LEVEL
PART 3
THIS IS IT, PLANET TERRY! YOU'RE JUST A FEW FEET AWAY FROM THE KEY TO YOUR NEW SPACESHIP!
THAT IS, IF YOU CAN AVOID BEING ZAPPED BY OUR RADAR ACTIVATED LASER!
AND REMEMBER, ONCE YOU STEP OFF THAT PLATFORM...THERE'S NO GOING BACK!!
YOU WIN
NOW I KNOW WHAT THIS SHIELD'S FOR!
IF THE LASER HITS ANY PART OF YOUR BODY, YOU LOSE!
BUT DON'T WORRY... THE LASER IS SET TO ONLY...HEH HEH... TICKLE YOU!
WHO'S WORRIED? I PRACTICE DODGING LASERS FOR BREAKFAST!
YOU WIN
WHIRRRR--
ZAP!!
WOW! THAT'S SOME TICKLE!
16

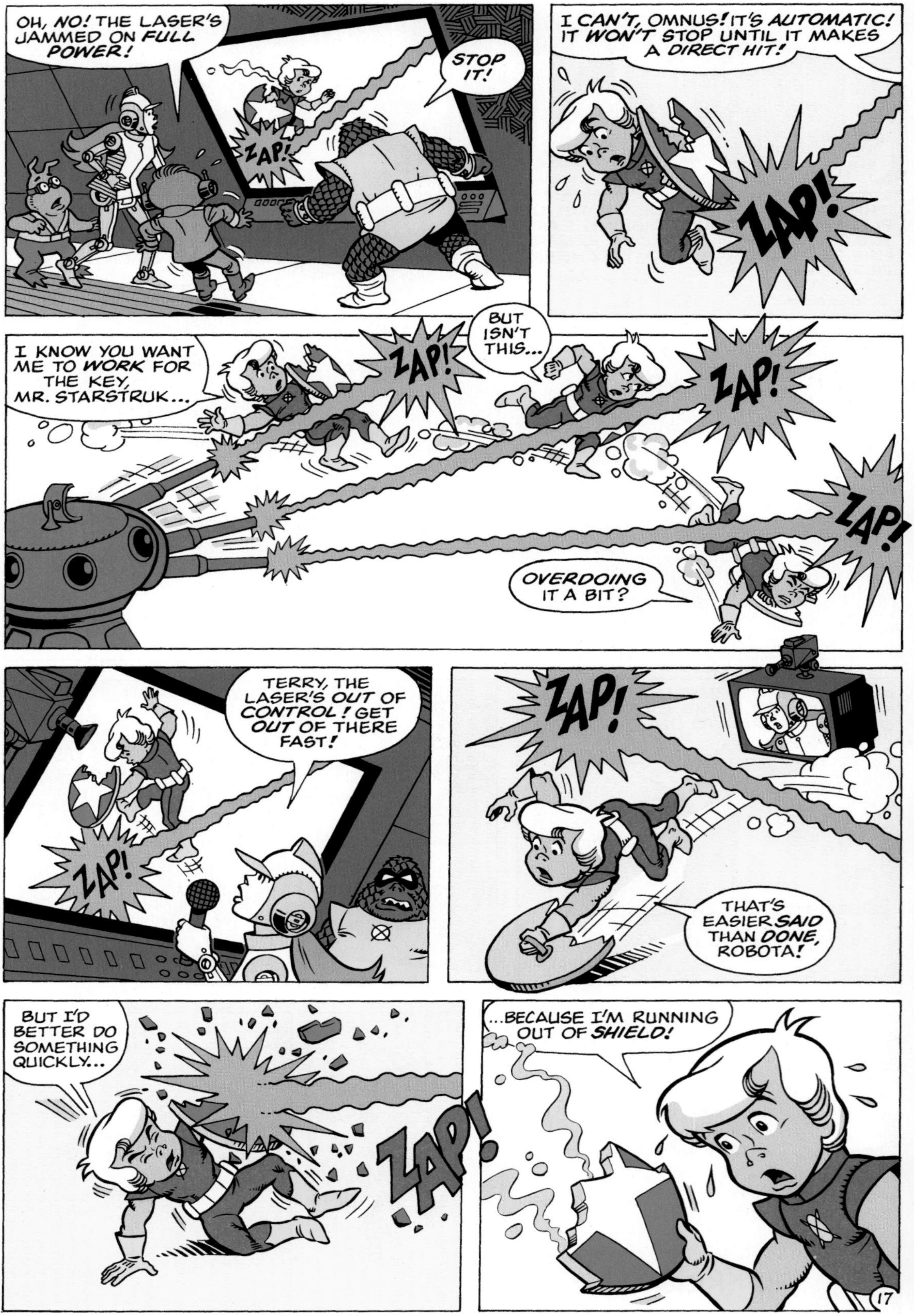

OH, NO! THE LASER'S JAMMED ON FULL POWER!
STOP IT!
ZAP!
I CAN'T, OMNUS! IT'S AUTOMATIC! IT WON'T STOP UNTIL IT MAKES A DIRECT HIT!
ZAP!
I KNOW YOU WANT ME TO WORK FOR THE KEY, MR. STARSTRUK...
ZAP!
BUT ISN'T THIS...
ZAP!
ZAP!
OVERDOING IT A BIT?
TERRY, THE LASER'S OUT OF CONTROL! GET OUT OF THERE FAST!
ZAP!
ZAP!
THAT'S EASIER SAID THAN DONE, ROBOTA!
BUT I'D BETTER DO SOMETHING QUICKLY...
ZAP!
...BECAUSE I'M RUNNING OUT OF SHIELD!
17

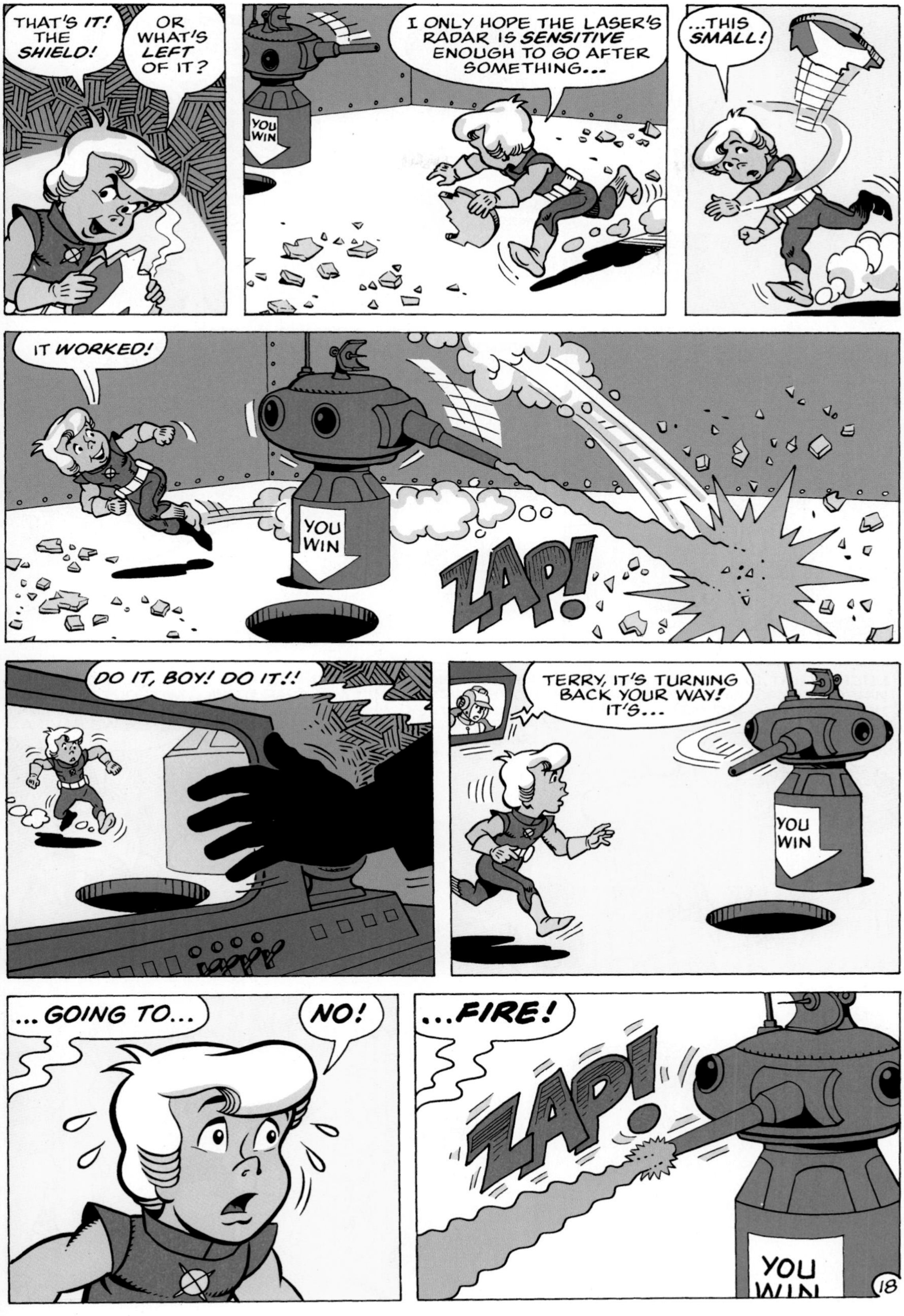
THAT'S IT! THE SHIELD!
OR WHAT'S LEFT OF IT?
I ONLY HOPE THE LASER'S RADAR IS SENSITIVE ENOUGH TO GO AFTER SOMETHING...
YOU WIN
...THIS SMALL!
IT WORKED!
YOU WIN
ZAP!
DO IT, BOY! DO IT!!
TERRY, IT'S TURNING BACK YOUR WAY! IT'S...
YOU WIN
...GOING TO...
NO!
...FIRE!
ZAP!
YOU
18

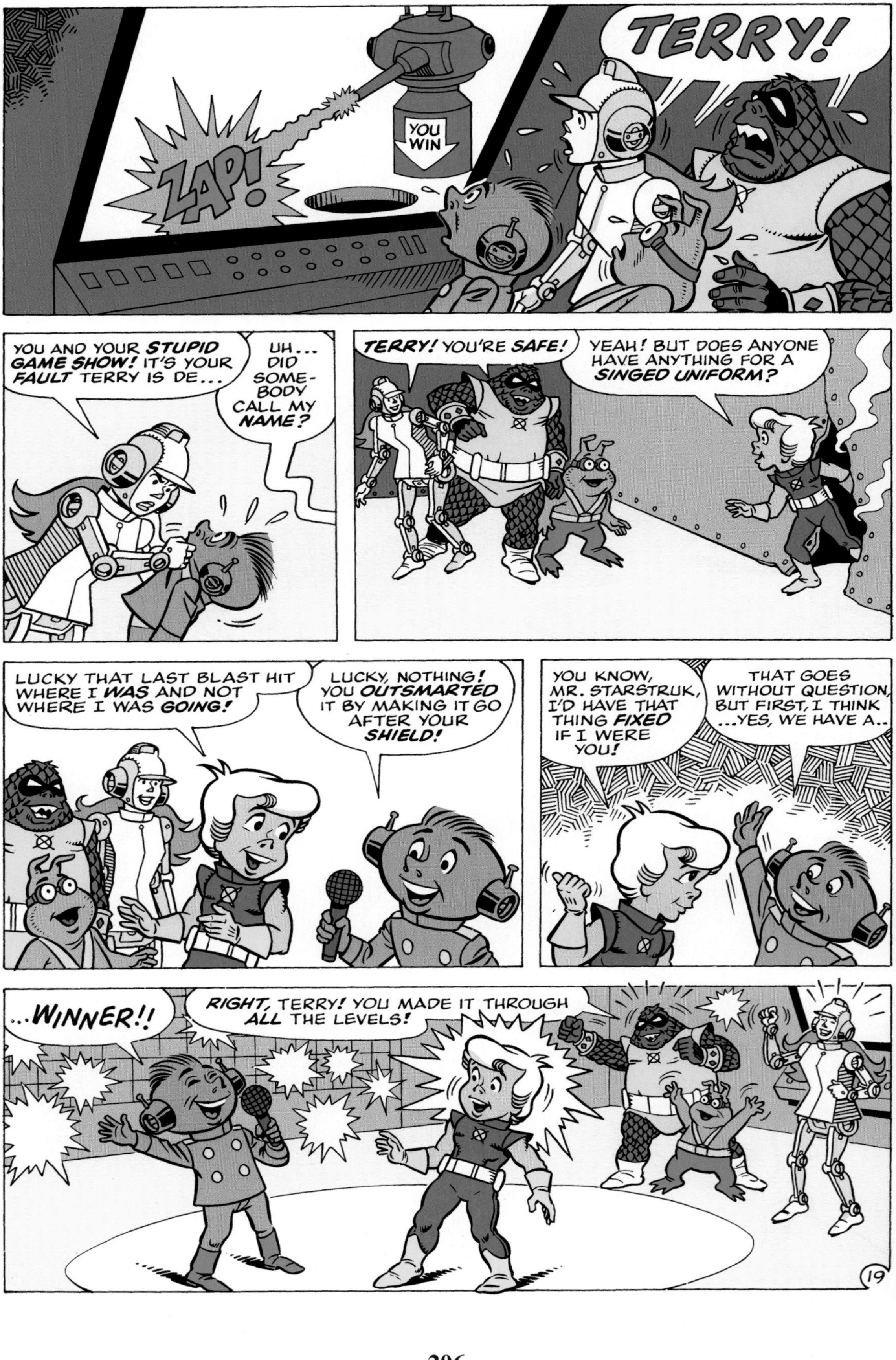
YOU WIN
ZAP!
TERRY!
YOU AND YOUR STUPID GAME SHOW! IT'S YOUR FAULT TERRY IS DE...
UH... DID SOMEBODY CALL MY NAME?
TERRY! YOU'RE SAFE!
YEAH! BUT DOES ANYONE HAVE ANYTHING FOR A SINGED UNIFORM?
LUCKY THAT LAST BLAST HIT WHERE I WAS AND NOT WHERE I WAS GOING!
LUCKY, NOTHING! YOU OUTSMARTED IT BY MAKING IT GO AFTER YOUR SHIELD!
YOU KNOW, MR. STARSTRUK, I'D HAVE THAT THING FIXED IF I WERE YOU!
THAT GOES WITHOUT QUESTION, BUT FIRST, I THINK ...YES, WE HAVE A..
...WINNER!!
RIGHT, TERRY! YOU MADE IT THROUGH ALL THE LEVELS!
19

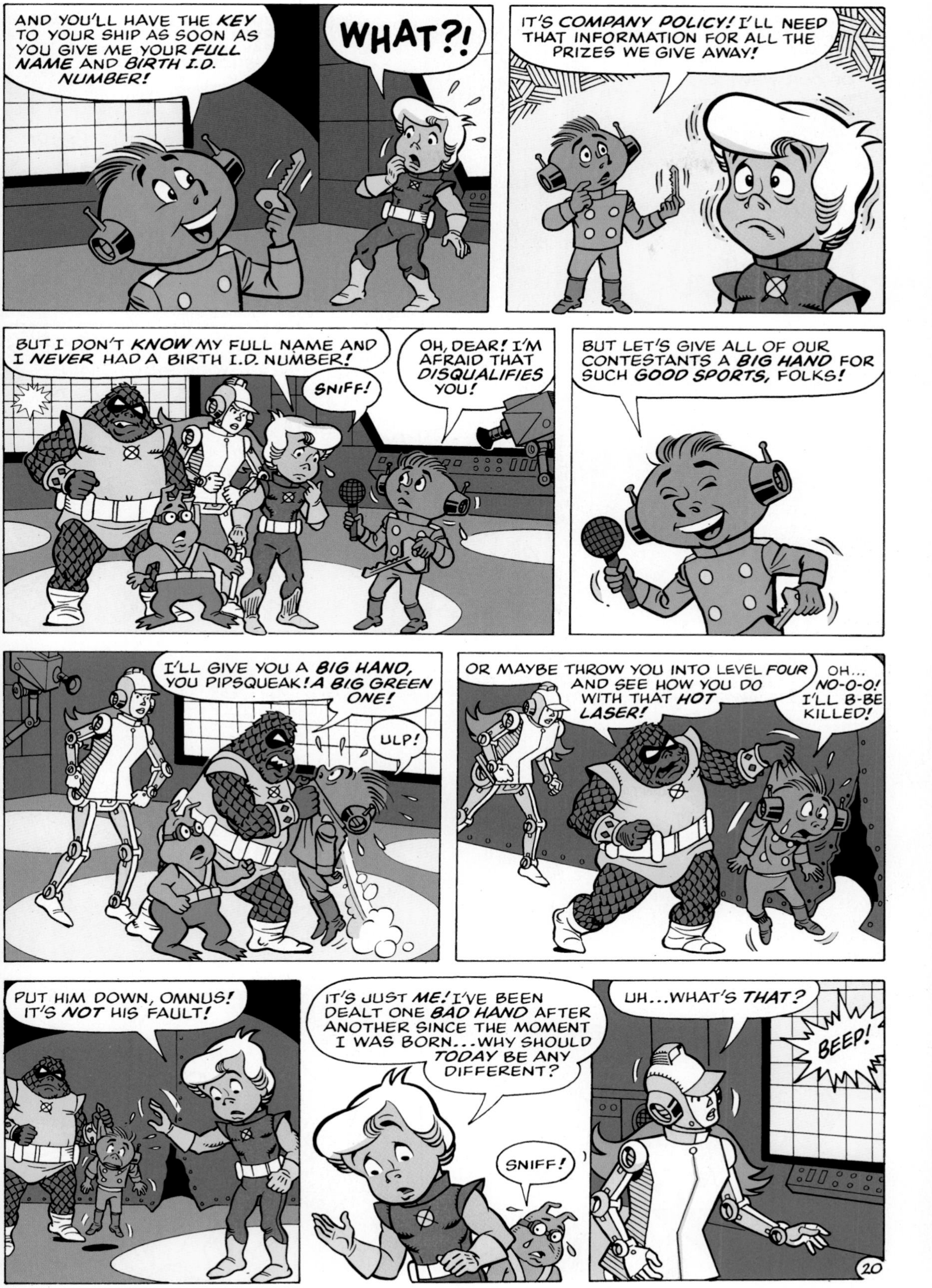
AND YOU'LL HAVE THE KEY TO YOUR SHIP AS SOON AS YOU GIVE ME YOUR FULL NAME AND BIRTH I.D. NUMBER!
WHAT?!
IT'S COMPANY POLICY! I'LL NEED THAT INFORMATION FOR ALL THE PRIZES WE GIVE AWAY!
BUT I DON'T KNOW MY FULL NAME AND I NEVER HAD A BIRTH I.D. NUMBER!
SNIFF!
OH, DEAR! I'M AFRAID THAT DISQUALIFIES YOU!
BUT LET'S GIVE ALL OF OUR CONTESTANTS A BIG HAND FOR SUCH GOOD SPORTS, FOLKS!
I'LL GIVE YOU A BIG HAND, YOU PIPSQUEAK! A BIG GREEN ONE!
ULP!
OR MAYBE THROW YOU INTO LEVEL FOUR AND SEE HOW YOU DO WITH THAT HOT LASER!
OH... NO-O-O! I'LL B-BE KILLED!
PUT HIM DOWN, OMNUS! IT'S NOT HIS FAULT!
IT'S JUST ME! I'VE BEEN DEALT ONE BAD HAND AFTER ANOTHER SINCE THE MOMENT I WAS BORN...WHY SHOULD TODAY BE ANY DIFFERENT?
SNIFF!
UH...WHAT'S THAT?
BEEP!
20

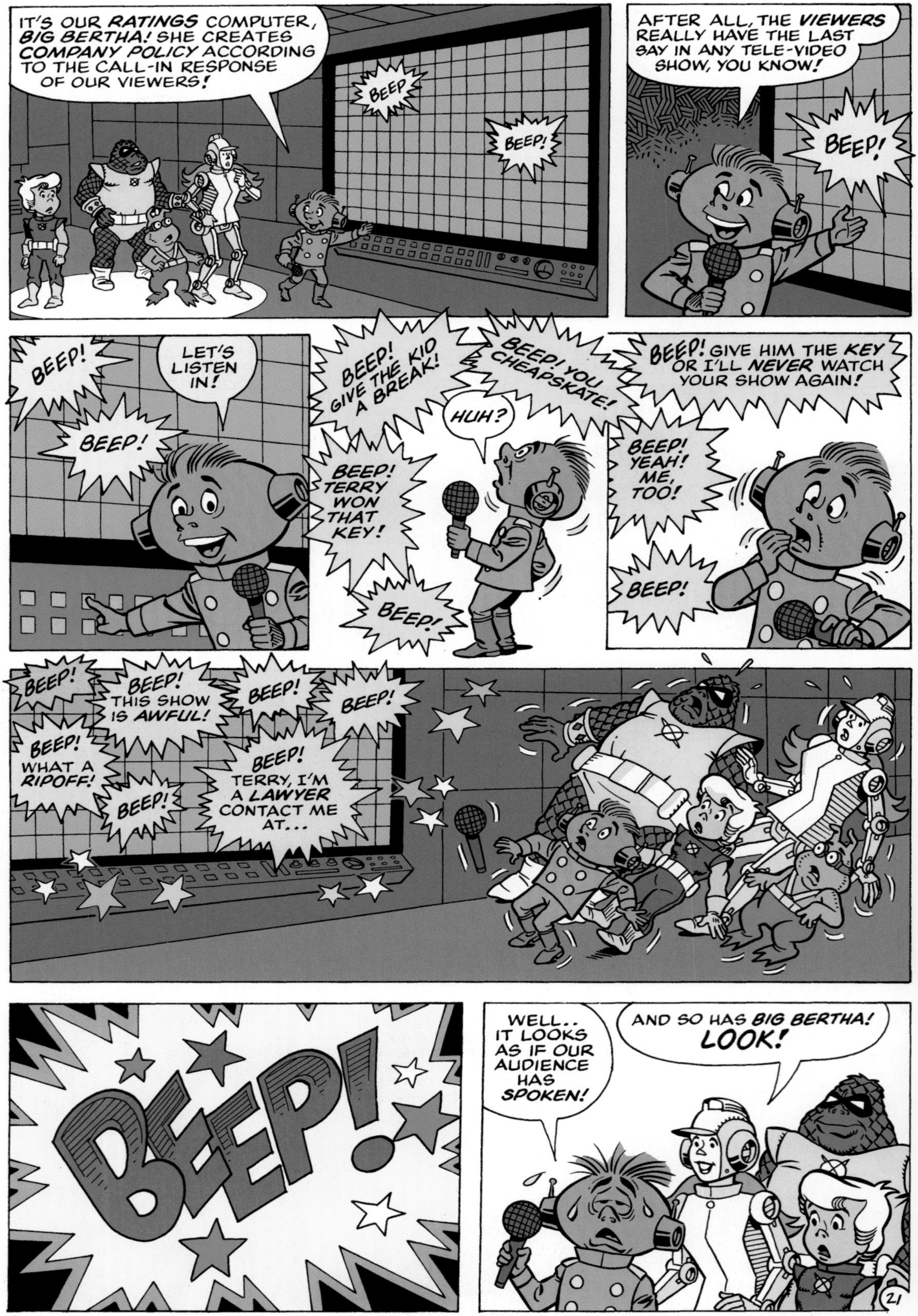
IT'S OUR RATINGS COMPUTER, BIG BERTHA! SHE CREATES COMPANY POLICY ACCORDING TO THE CALL-IN RESPONSE OF OUR VIEWERS!
BEEP
BEEP!
AFTER ALL, THE VIEWERS REALLY HAVE THE LAST SAY IN ANY TELE-VIDEO SHOW, YOU KNOW!
BEEP!
BEEP!
LET'S LISTEN IN!
BEEP!
BEEP! GIVE THE KID A BREAK!
BEEP! YOU CHEAPSKATE!
HUH?
BEEP! TERRY WON THAT KEY!
BEEP!
BEEP! GIVE HIM THE KEY OR I'LL NEVER WATCH YOUR SHOW AGAIN!
BEEP! YEAH! ME, TOO!
BEEP!
BEEP!
BEEP! THIS SHOW IS AWFUL!
BEEP!
BEEP!
BEEP! WHAT A RIPOFF!
BEEP!
BEEP! TERRY, I'M A LAWYER CONTACT ME AT...
BEEP!
WELL.. IT LOOKS AS IF OUR AUDIENCE HAS SPOKEN!
AND SO HAS BIG BERTHA! LOOK!
21

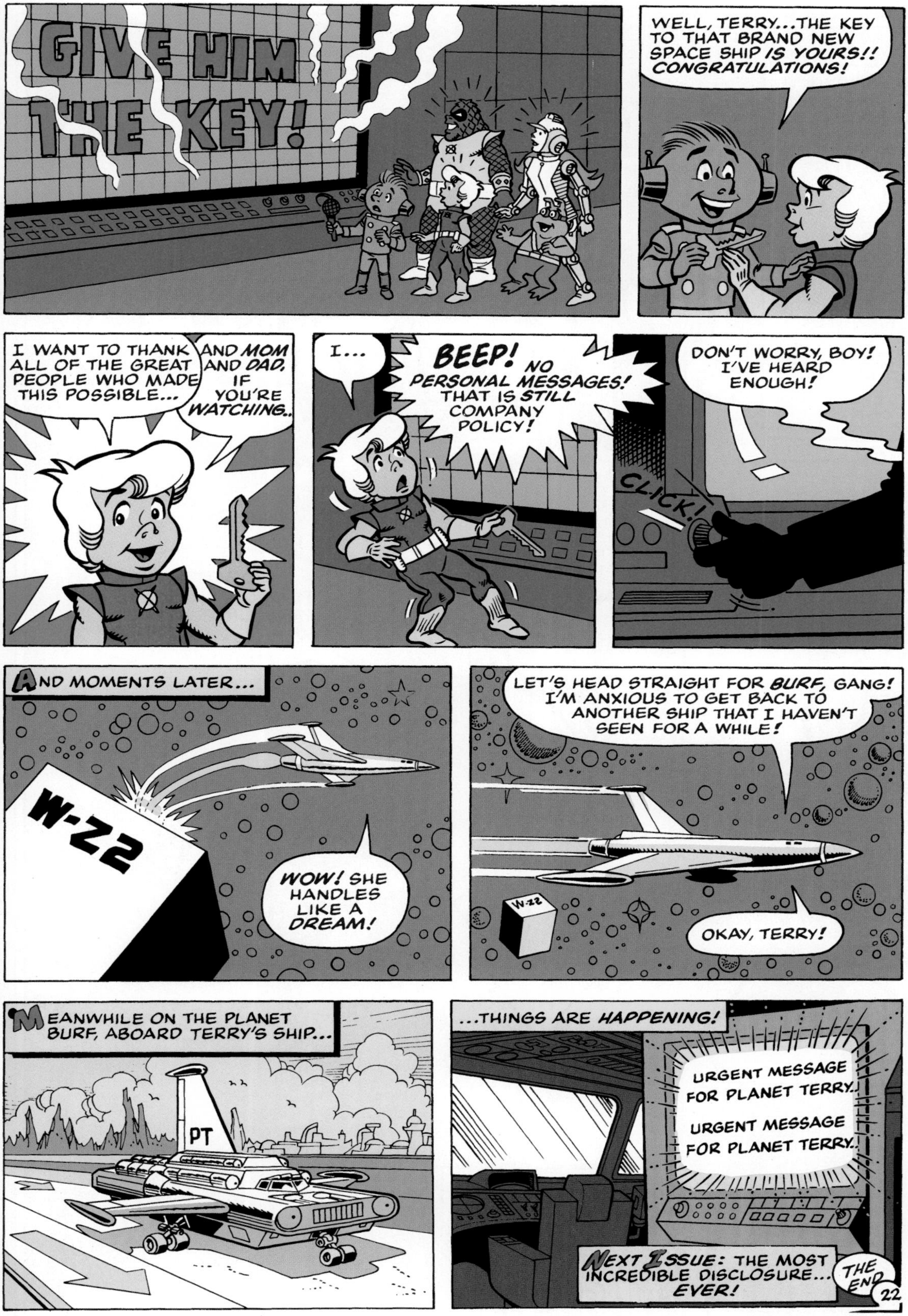
GIVE HIM THE KEY!
WELL, TERRY... THE KEY TO THAT BRAND NEW SPACE SHIP IS YOURS!! CONGRATULATIONS!
I WANT TO THANK ALL OF THE GREAT PEOPLE WHO MADE THIS POSSIBLE...
AND MOM AND DAD, IF YOU'RE WATCHING..
I...
BEEP! NO PERSONAL MESSAGES! THAT IS STILL COMPANY POLICY!
DON'T WORRY, BOY! I'VE HEARD ENOUGH!
CLICK!
AND MOMENTS LATER...
W-22
WOW! SHE HANDLES LIKE A DREAM!
LET'S HEAD STRAIGHT FOR BURF, GANG! I'M ANXIOUS TO GET BACK TO ANOTHER SHIP THAT I HAVEN'T SEEN FOR A WHILE!
W-22
OKAY, TERRY!
MEANWHILE ON THE PLANET BURF, ABOARD TERRY'S SHIP...
PT
...THINGS ARE HAPPENING!
URGENT MESSAGE FOR PLANET TERRY.
URGENT MESSAGE FOR PLANET TERRY.
NEXT ISSUE: THE MOST INCREDIBLE DISCLOSURE... EVER!
THE END
22

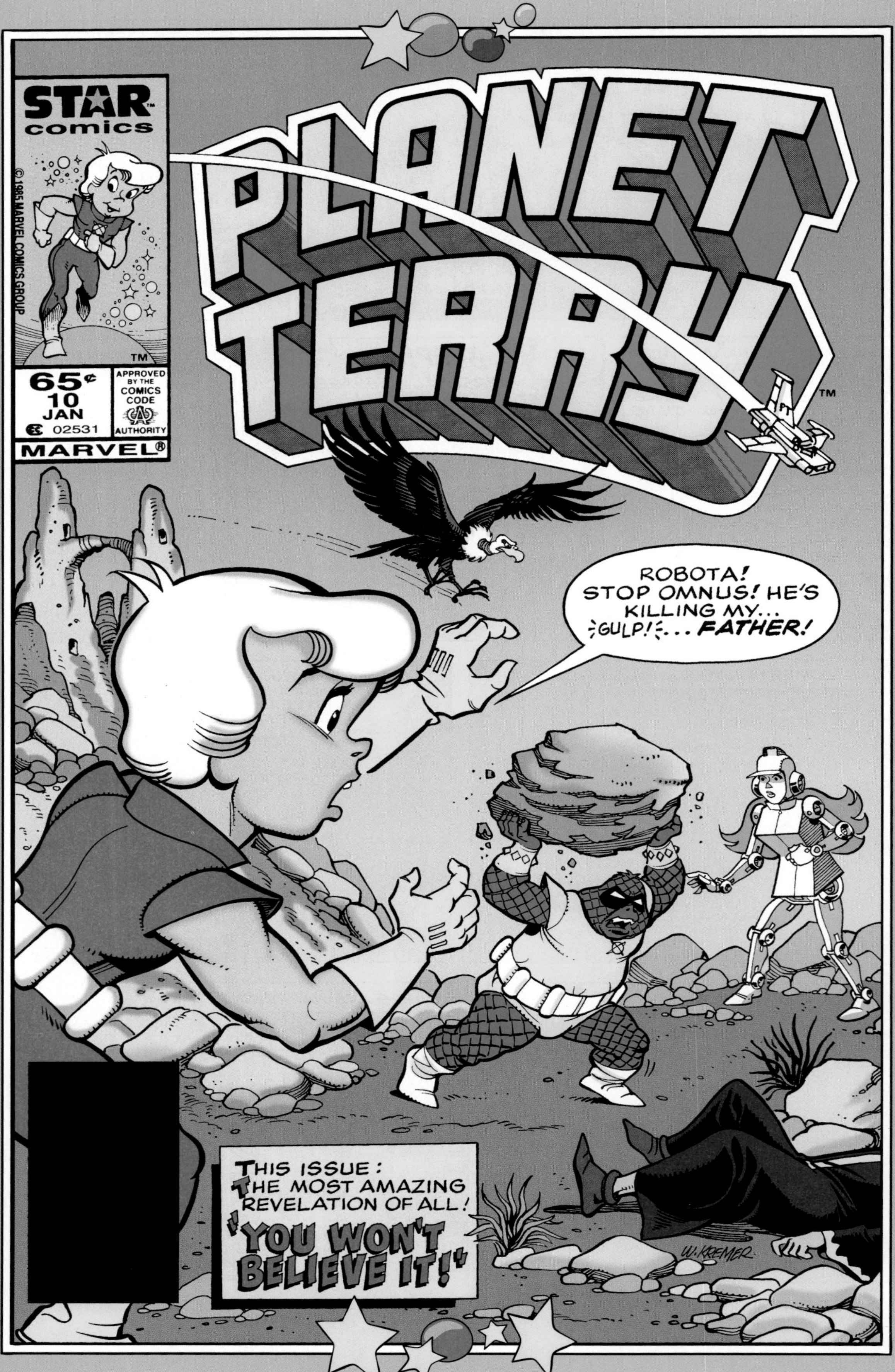
STAR comics
©1985 MARVEL COMICS GROUP
PLANET TERRY
65¢
10
JAN
02531
APPROVED BY THE COMICS CODE AUTHORITY
MARVEL®
ROBOTA! STOP OMNUS! HE'S KILLING MY... GULP! ... FATHER!
THIS ISSUE: THE MOST AMAZING REVELATION OF ALL! "YOU WON'T BELIEVE IT!"
W. KREMER

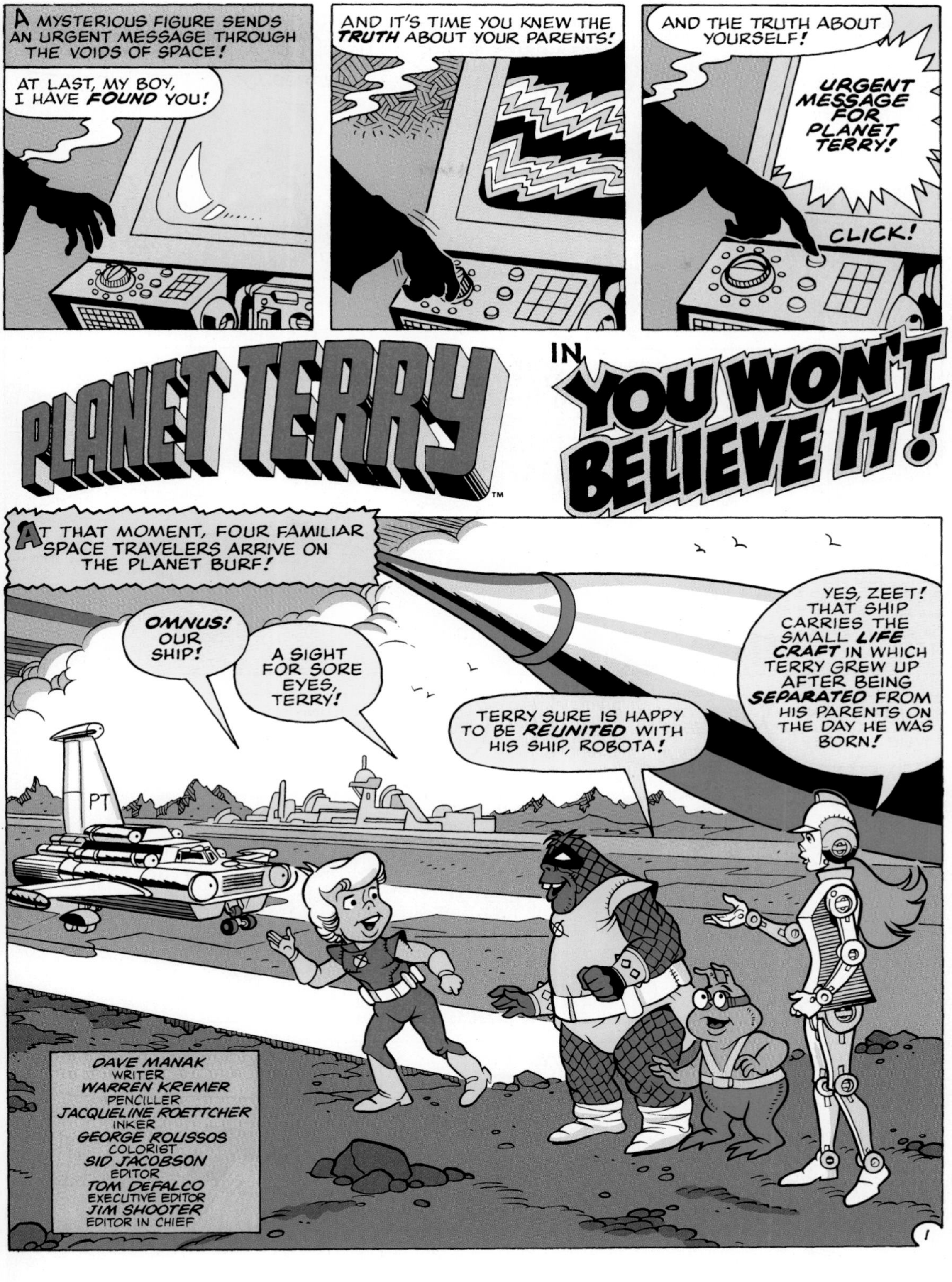
A MYSTERIOUS FIGURE SENDS AN URGENT MESSAGE THROUGH THE VOIDS OF SPACE!
AT LAST, MY BOY, I HAVE FOUND YOU!
AND IT'S TIME YOU KNEW THE TRUTH ABOUT YOUR PARENTS!
AND THE TRUTH ABOUT YOURSELF!
URGENT MESSAGE FOR PLANET TERRY!
CLICK!
PLANET TERRY™
IN
YOU WON'T BELIEVE IT!
AT THAT MOMENT, FOUR FAMILIAR SPACE TRAVELERS ARRIVE ON THE PLANET BURF!
OMNUS! OUR SHIP!
A SIGHT FOR SORE EYES, TERRY!
TERRY SURE IS HAPPY TO BE REUNITED WITH HIS SHIP, ROBOTA!
YES, ZEET! THAT SHIP CARRIES THE SMALL LIFE CRAFT IN WHICH TERRY GREW UP AFTER BEING SEPARATED FROM HIS PARENTS ON THE DAY HE WAS BORN!
PT
DAVE MANAK WRITER
WARREN KREMER PENCILLER
JACQUELINE ROETTCHER INKER
GEORGE ROUSSOS COLORIST
SID JACOBSON EDITOR
TOM DEFALCO EXECUTIVE EDITOR
JIM SHOOTER EDITOR IN CHIEF
1

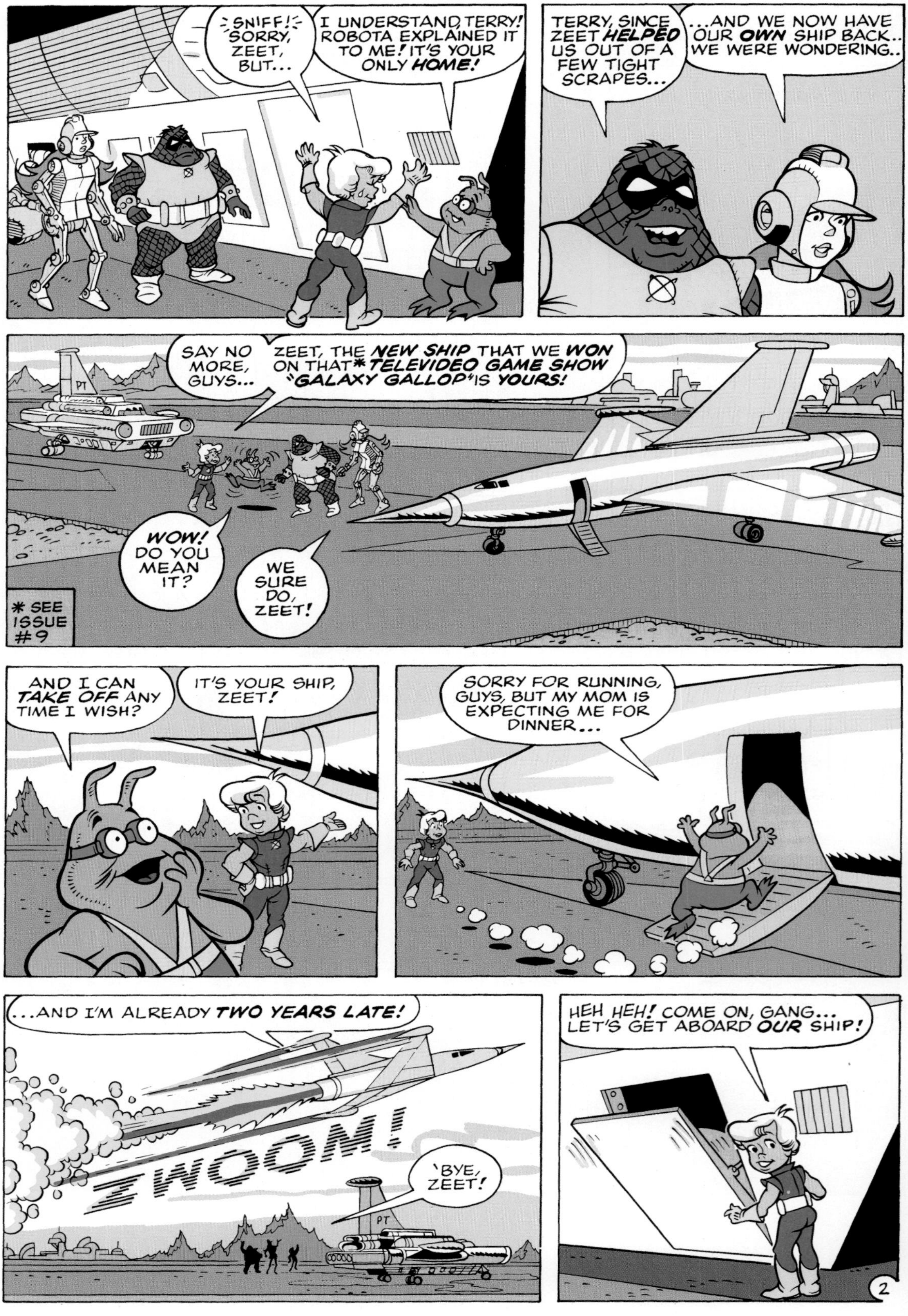
SNIFF! SORRY, ZEET, BUT...
I UNDERSTAND, TERRY! ROBOTA EXPLAINED IT TO ME! IT'S YOUR ONLY HOME!
TERRY, SINCE ZEET HELPED US OUT OF A FEW TIGHT SCRAPES...
...AND WE NOW HAVE OUR OWN SHIP BACK.. WE WERE WONDERING..
SAY NO MORE, GUYS...
ZEET, THE NEW SHIP THAT WE WON ON THAT* TELEVIDEO GAME SHOW "GALAXY GALLOP" IS YOURS!
WOW! DO YOU MEAN IT?
WE SURE DO, ZEET!
* SEE ISSUE #9
AND I CAN TAKE OFF ANY TIME I WISH?
IT'S YOUR SHIP, ZEET!
SORRY FOR RUNNING, GUYS, BUT MY MOM IS EXPECTING ME FOR DINNER...
...AND I'M ALREADY TWO YEARS LATE!
ZWOOM!
'BYE, ZEET!
HEH HEH! COME ON, GANG... LET'S GET ABOARD OUR SHIP!
2

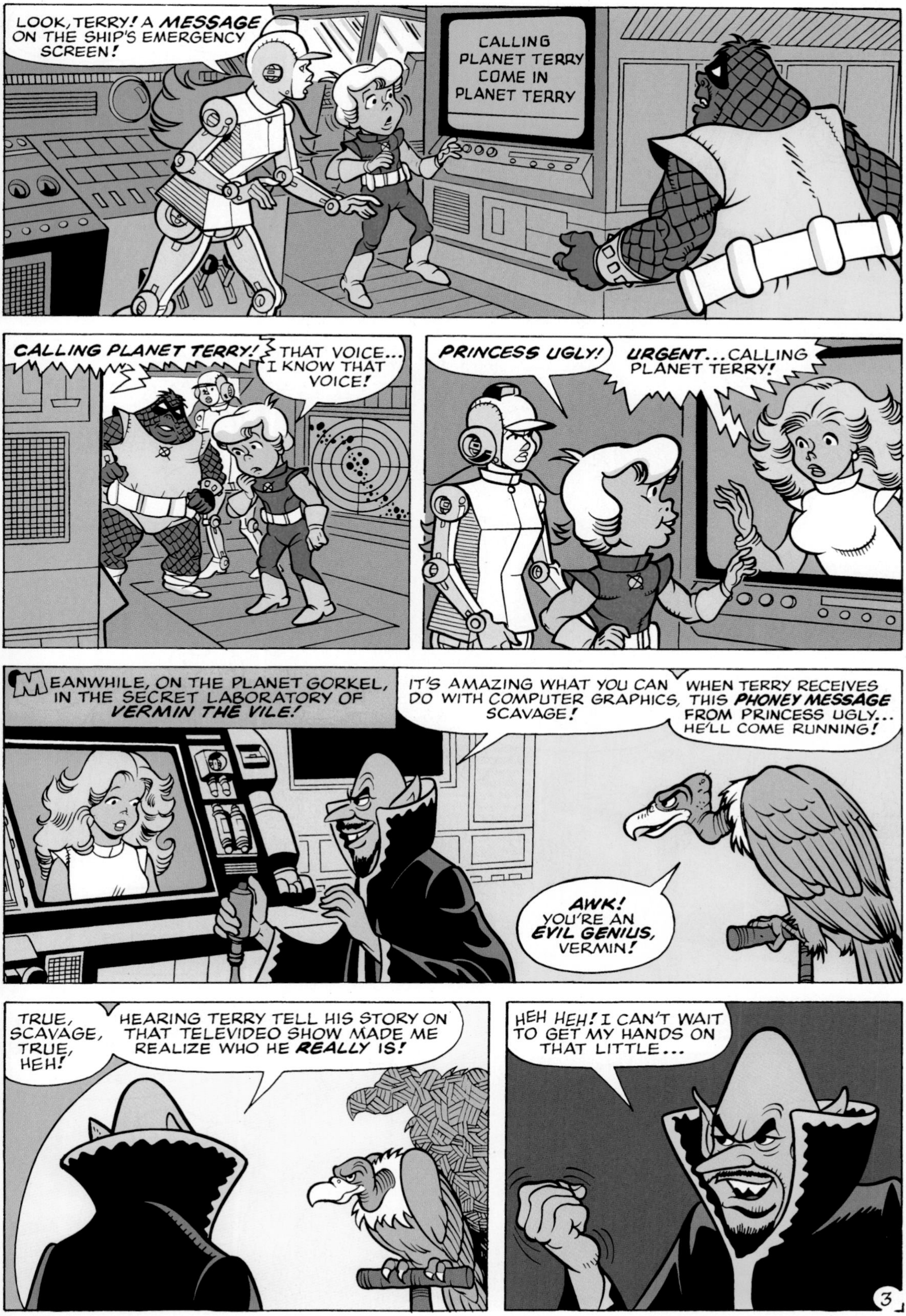
LOOK, TERRY! A MESSAGE ON THE SHIP'S EMERGENCY SCREEN!
CALLING PLANET TERRY COME IN PLANET TERRY
CALLING PLANET TERRY!
THAT VOICE... I KNOW THAT VOICE!
PRINCESS UGLY!
URGENT...CALLING PLANET TERRY!
MEANWHILE, ON THE PLANET GORKEL, IN THE SECRET LABORATORY OF VERMIN THE VILE!
IT'S AMAZING WHAT YOU CAN DO WITH COMPUTER GRAPHICS, SCAVAGE!
WHEN TERRY RECEIVES THIS PHONEY MESSAGE FROM PRINCESS UGLY... HE'LL COME RUNNING!
AWK! YOU'RE AN EVIL GENIUS, VERMIN!
TRUE, SCAVAGE, TRUE, HEH!
HEARING TERRY TELL HIS STORY ON THAT TELEVIDEO SHOW MADE ME REALIZE WHO HE REALLY IS!
HEH HEH! I CAN'T WAIT TO GET MY HANDS ON THAT LITTLE...
3

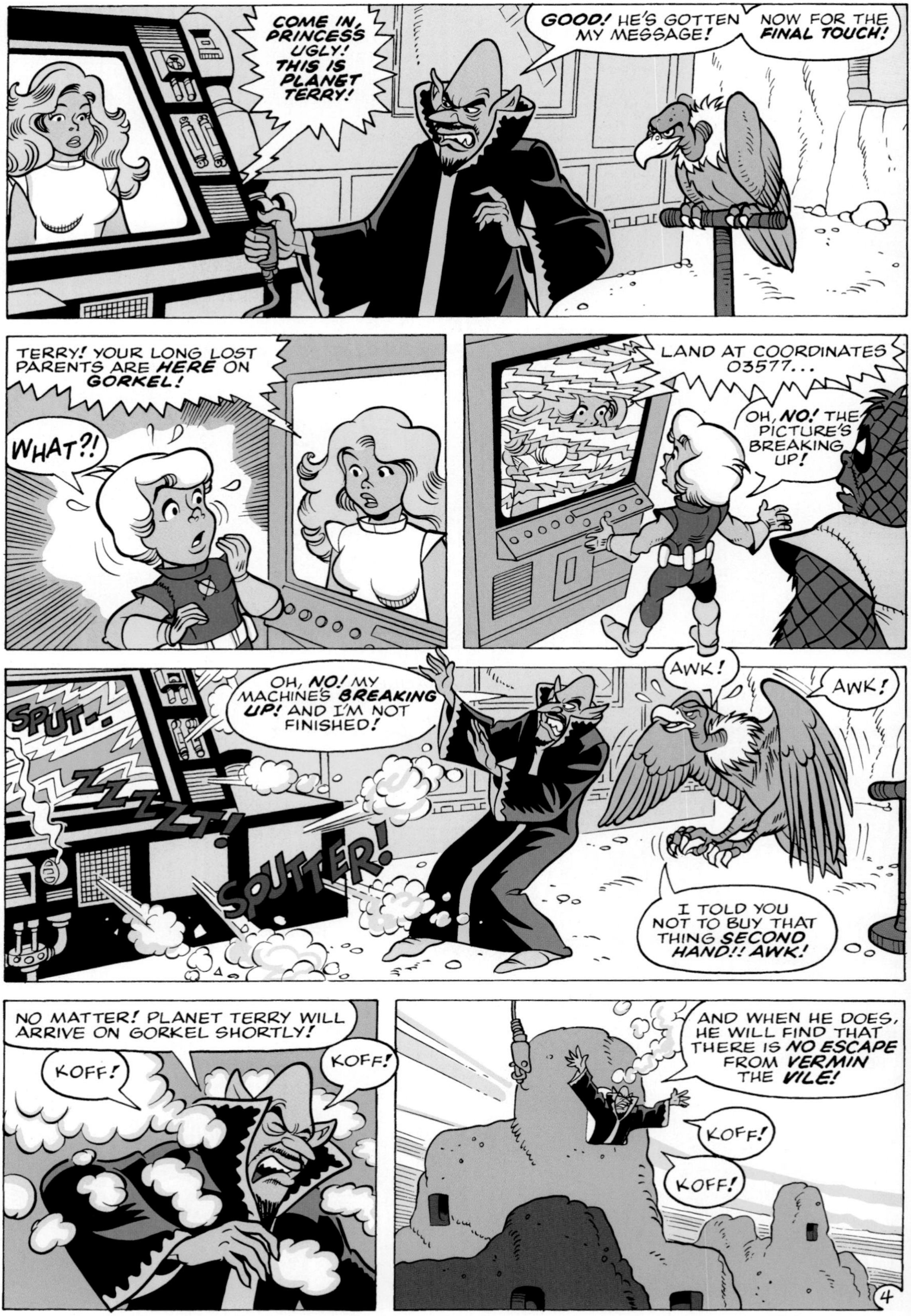
COME IN, PRINCESS UGLY! THIS IS PLANET TERRY!
GOOD! HE'S GOTTEN MY MESSAGE!
NOW FOR THE FINAL TOUCH!
TERRY! YOUR LONG LOST PARENTS ARE HERE ON GORKEL!
WHAT?!
LAND AT COORDINATES 03577...
OH, NO! THE PICTURE'S BREAKING UP!
SPUT-
ZZZZZT!
SPUTTER!
OH, NO! MY MACHINE'S BREAKING UP! AND I'M NOT FINISHED!
AWK!
AWK!
I TOLD YOU NOT TO BUY THAT THING SECOND HAND!! AWK!
NO MATTER! PLANET TERRY WILL ARRIVE ON GORKEL SHORTLY!
KOFF!
KOFF!
AND WHEN HE DOES, HE WILL FIND THAT THERE IS NO ESCAPE FROM VERMIN THE VILE!
KOFF!
KOFF!
4

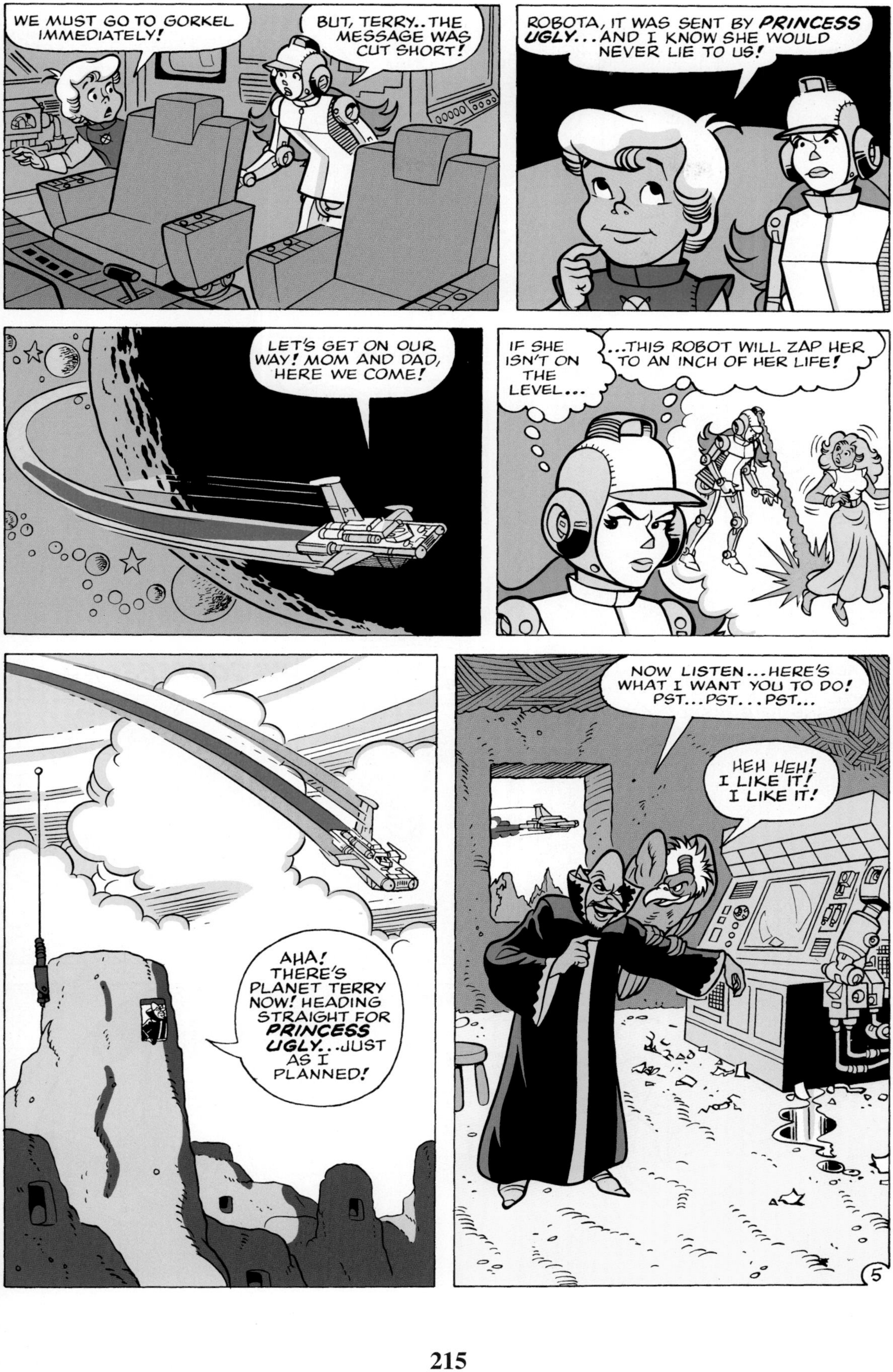

WE MUST GO TO GORKEL IMMEDIATELY!
BUT, TERRY.. THE MESSAGE WAS CUT SHORT!
ROBOTA, IT WAS SENT BY PRINCESS UGLY... AND I KNOW SHE WOULD NEVER LIE TO US!
LET'S GET ON OUR WAY! MOM AND DAD, HERE WE COME!
PT
IF SHE ISN'T ON THE LEVEL...
...THIS ROBOT WILL ZAP HER TO AN INCH OF HER LIFE!
AHA! THERE'S PLANET TERRY NOW! HEADING STRAIGHT FOR PRINCESS UGLY... JUST AS I PLANNED!
NOW LISTEN... HERE'S WHAT I WANT YOU TO DO! PST... PST... PST...
HEH HEH! I LIKE IT! I LIKE IT!
5

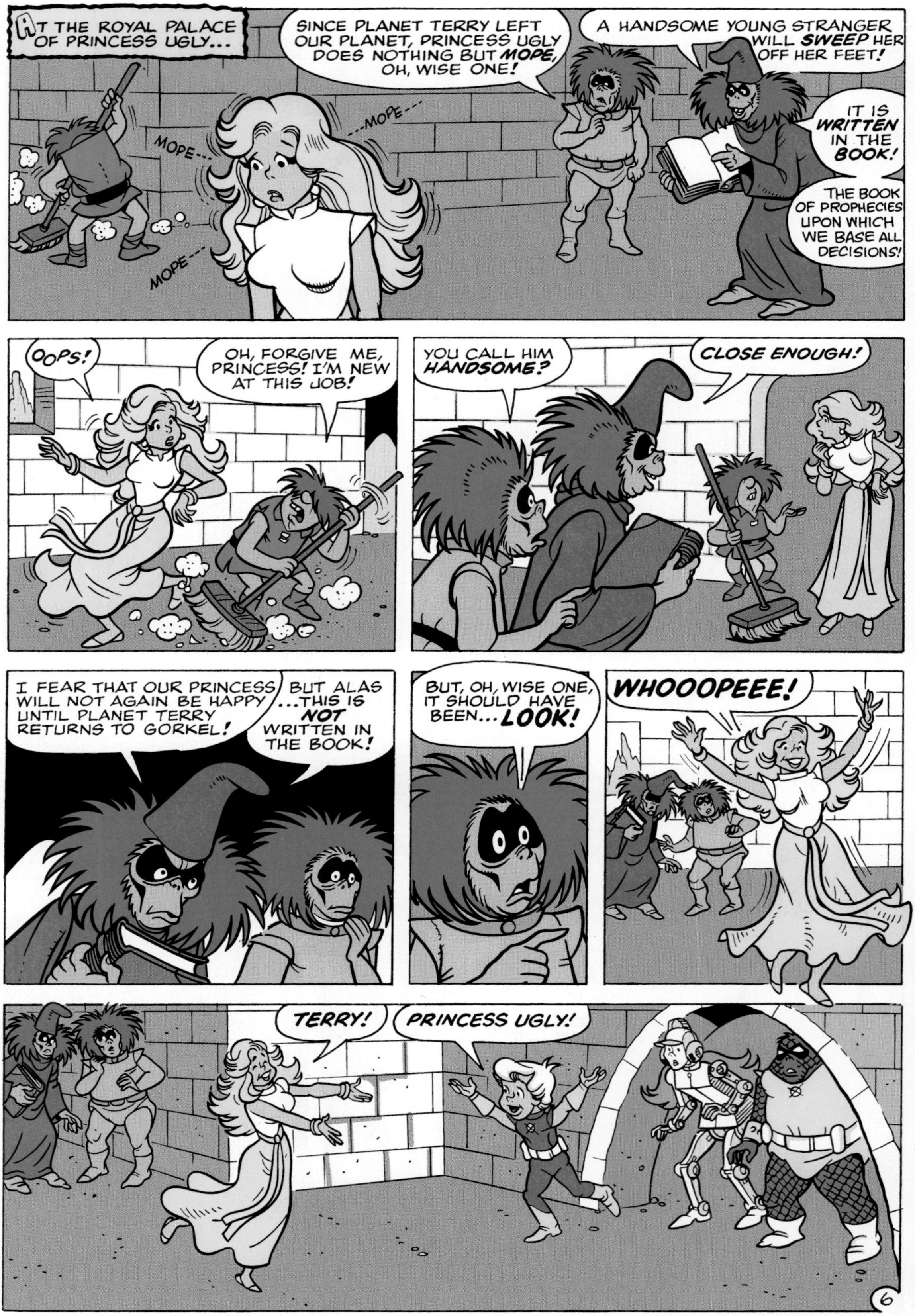
AT THE ROYAL PALACE OF PRINCESS UGLY...
SINCE PLANET TERRY LEFT OUR PLANET, PRINCESS UGLY DOES NOTHING BUT MOPE, OH, WISE ONE!
A HANDSOME YOUNG STRANGER WILL SWEEP HER OFF HER FEET!
IT IS WRITTEN IN THE BOOK!
THE BOOK OF PROPHECIES UPON WHICH WE BASE ALL DECISIONS!
MOPE---
---MOPE
MOPE---
OOPS!
OH, FORGIVE ME, PRINCESS! I'M NEW AT THIS JOB!
YOU CALL HIM HANDSOME?
CLOSE ENOUGH!
I FEAR THAT OUR PRINCESS WILL NOT AGAIN BE HAPPY UNTIL PLANET TERRY RETURNS TO GORKEL!
BUT ALAS ...THIS IS NOT WRITTEN IN THE BOOK!
BUT, OH, WISE ONE, IT SHOULD HAVE BEEN... LOOK!
WHOOOPEEE!
TERRY!
PRINCESS UGLY!
6

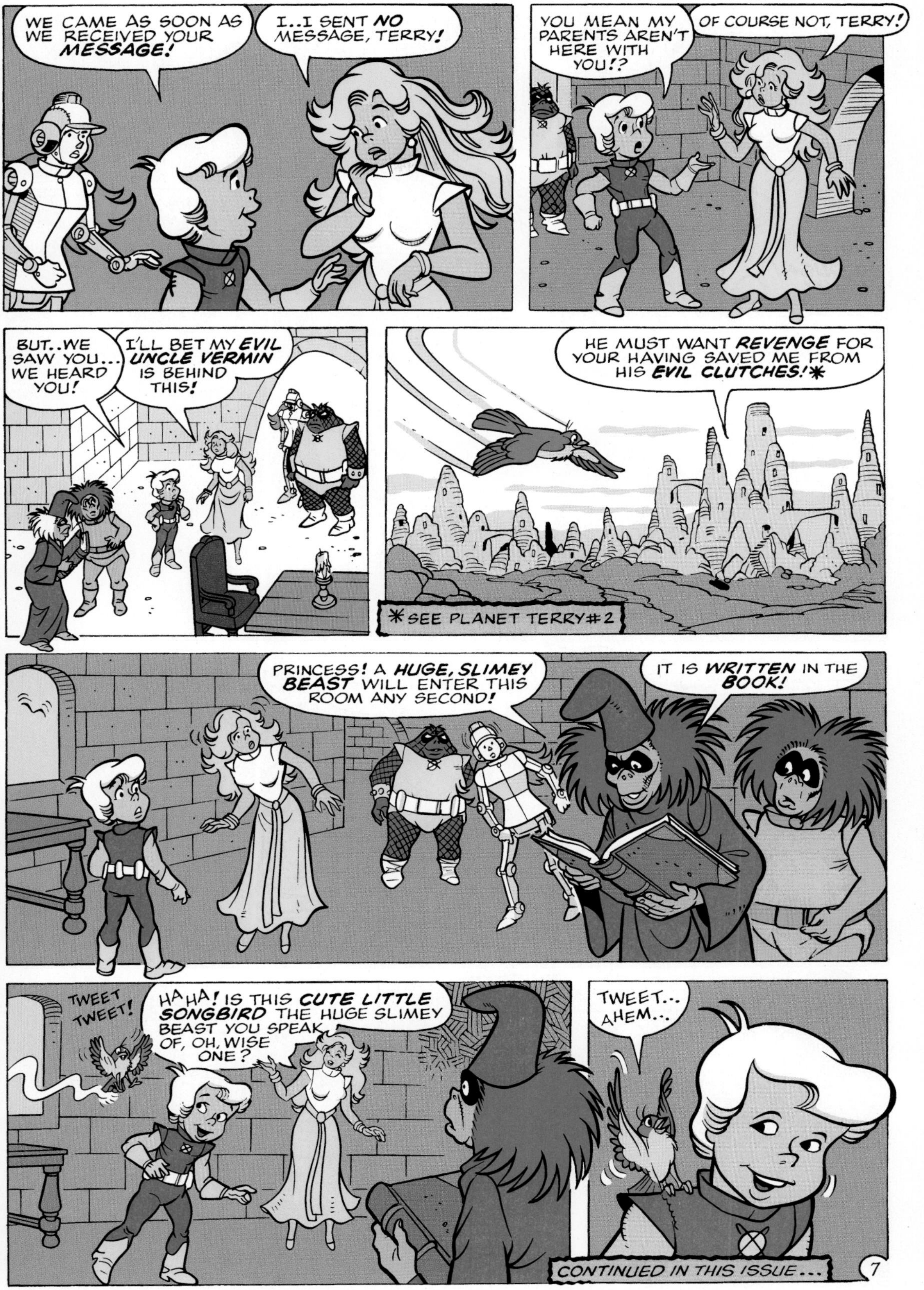
WE CAME AS SOON AS WE RECEIVED YOUR MESSAGE!
I..I SENT NO MESSAGE, TERRY!
YOU MEAN MY PARENTS AREN'T HERE WITH YOU!?
OF COURSE NOT, TERRY!
BUT..WE SAW YOU... WE HEARD YOU!
I'LL BET MY EVIL UNCLE VERMIN IS BEHIND THIS!
HE MUST WANT REVENGE FOR YOUR HAVING SAVED ME FROM HIS EVIL CLUTCHES!*
*SEE PLANET TERRY #2
PRINCESS! A HUGE, SLIMEY BEAST WILL ENTER THIS ROOM ANY SECOND!
IT IS WRITTEN IN THE BOOK!
TWEET TWEET!
HA HA! IS THIS CUTE LITTLE SONGBIRD THE HUGE SLIMEY BEAST YOU SPEAK OF, OH, WISE ONE?
TWEET... AHEM...
CONTINUED IN THIS ISSUE...
7

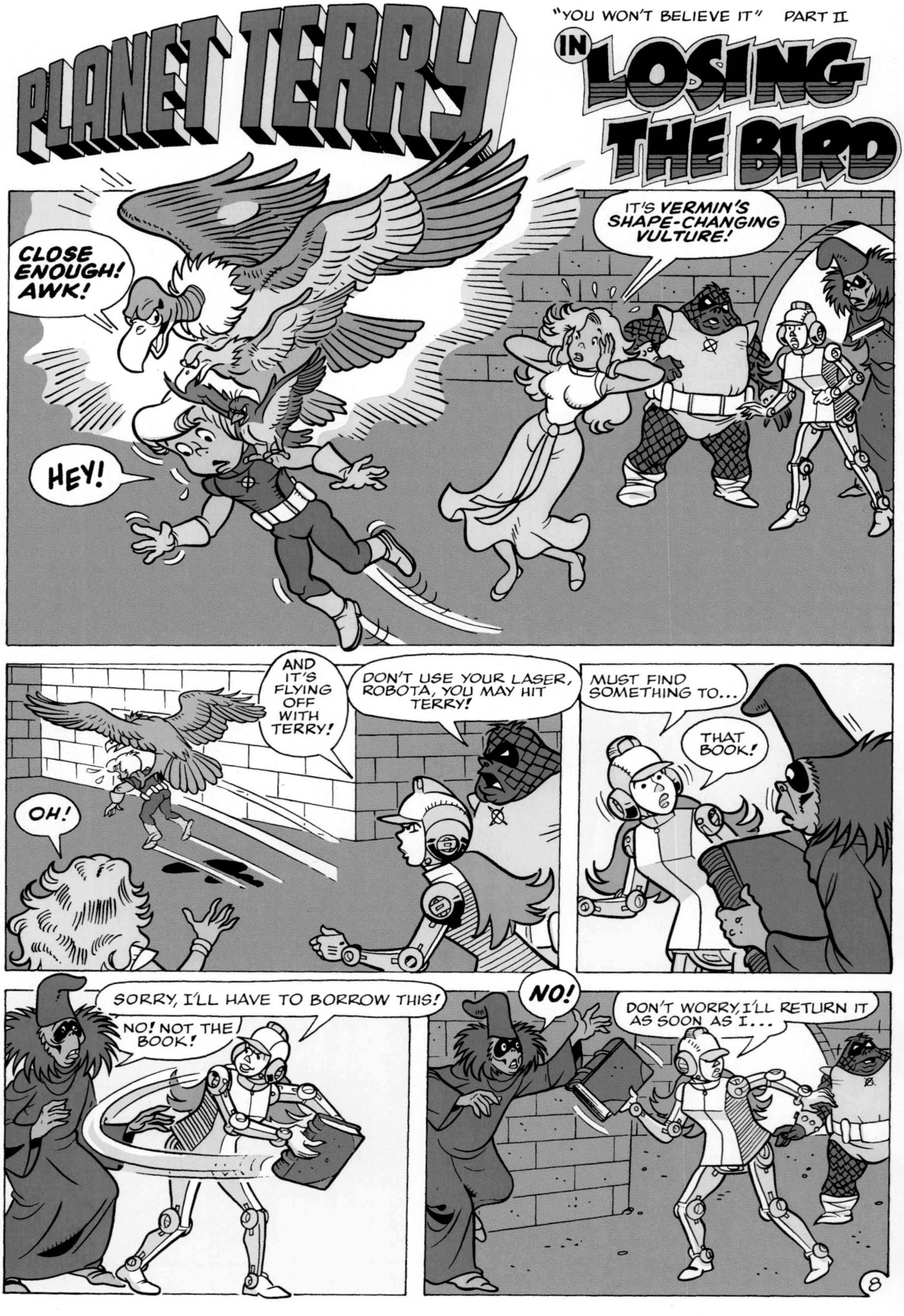
PLANET TERRY
"YOU WON'T BELIEVE IT" PART II
IN LOSING THE BIRD
CLOSE ENOUGH! AWK!
HEY!
IT'S VERMIN'S SHAPE-CHANGING VULTURE!
AND IT'S FLYING OFF WITH TERRY!
OH!
DON'T USE YOUR LASER, ROBOTA, YOU MAY HIT TERRY!
MUST FIND SOMETHING TO...
THAT BOOK!
SORRY, I'LL HAVE TO BORROW THIS!
NO! NOT THE BOOK!
NO!
DON'T WORRY, I'LL RETURN IT AS SOON AS I...
8

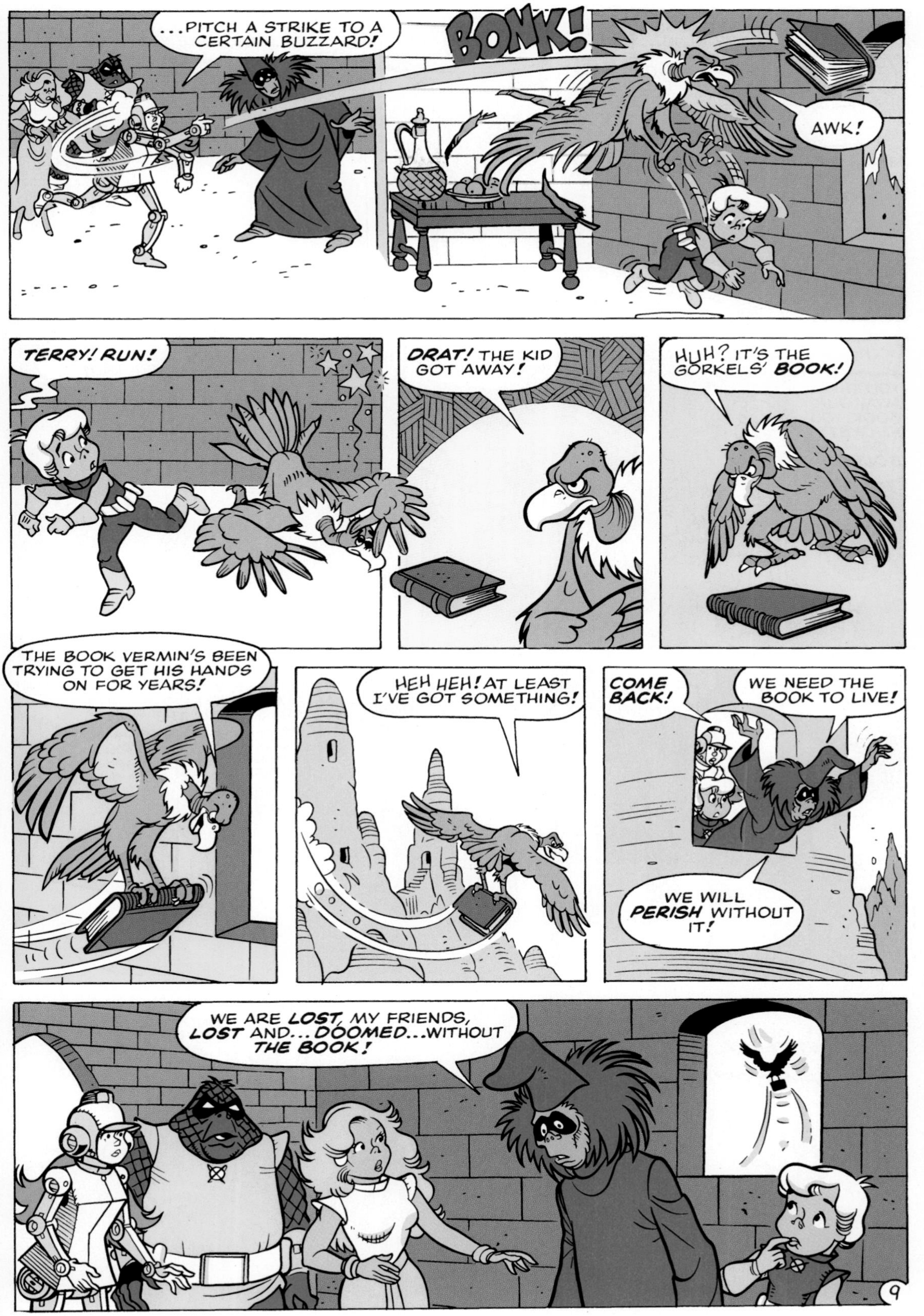
...PITCH A STRIKE TO A CERTAIN BUZZARD!
BONK!
AWK!
TERRY! RUN!
DRAT! THE KID GOT AWAY!
HUH? IT'S THE GORKELS' BOOK!
THE BOOK VERMIN'S BEEN TRYING TO GET HIS HANDS ON FOR YEARS!
HEH HEH! AT LEAST I'VE GOT SOMETHING!
COME BACK!
WE NEED THE BOOK TO LIVE!
WE WILL PERISH WITHOUT IT!
WE ARE LOST, MY FRIENDS, LOST AND...DOOMED...WITHOUT THE BOOK!
9

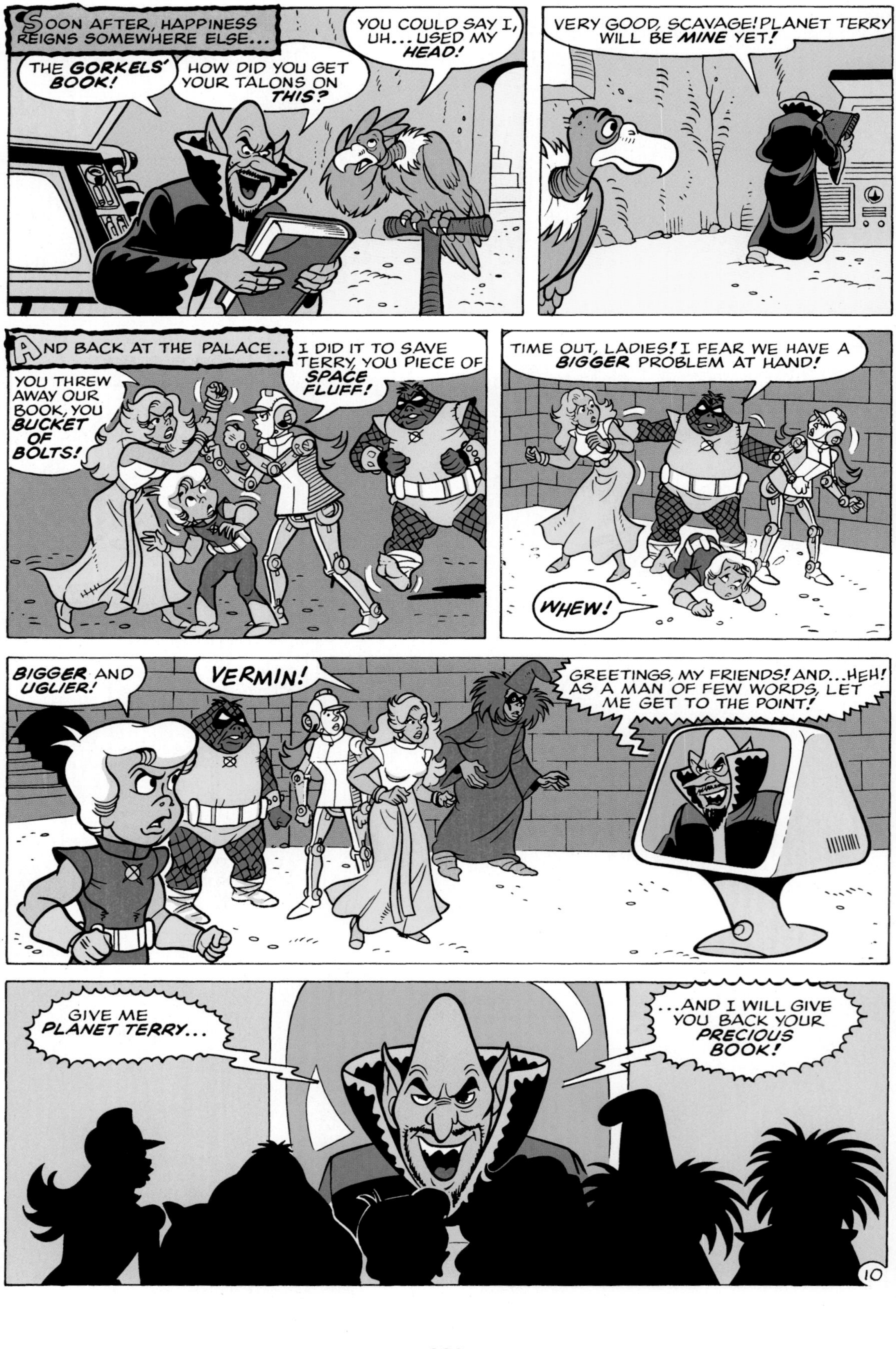

SOON AFTER, HAPPINESS REIGNS SOMEWHERE ELSE...
THE GORKELS' BOOK!
HOW DID YOU GET YOUR TALONS ON THIS?
YOU COULD SAY I, UH...USED MY HEAD!
VERY GOOD, SCAVAGE! PLANET TERRY WILL BE MINE YET!
AND BACK AT THE PALACE..
YOU THREW AWAY OUR BOOK, YOU BUCKET OF BOLTS!
I DID IT TO SAVE TERRY, YOU PIECE OF SPACE FLUFF!
TIME OUT, LADIES! I FEAR WE HAVE A BIGGER PROBLEM AT HAND!
WHEW!
BIGGER AND UGLIER!
VERMIN!
GREETINGS, MY FRIENDS! AND...HEH! AS A MAN OF FEW WORDS, LET ME GET TO THE POINT!
GIVE ME PLANET TERRY...
...AND I WILL GIVE YOU BACK YOUR PRECIOUS BOOK!
10

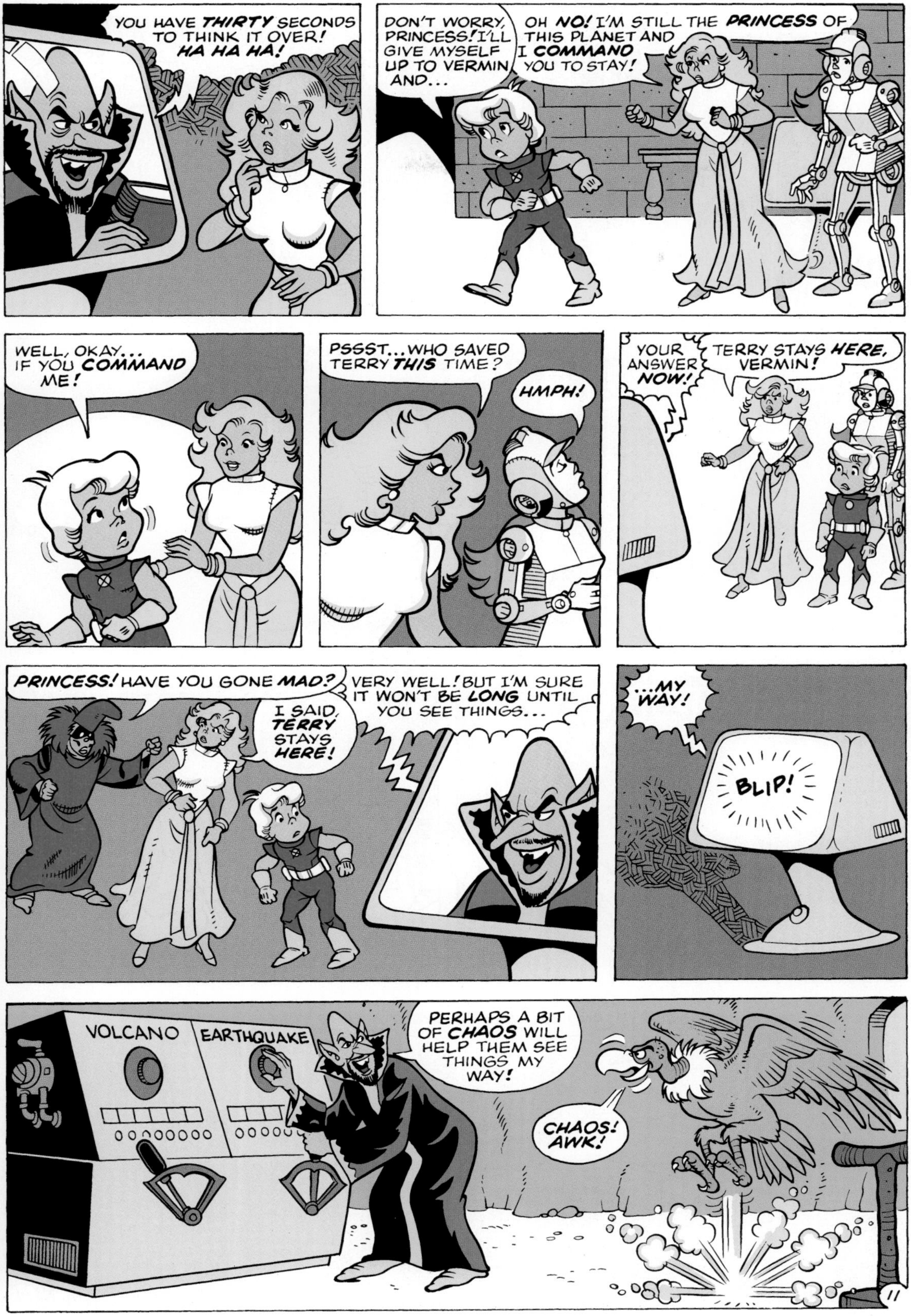
YOU HAVE THIRTY SECONDS TO THINK IT OVER! HA HA HA!
DON'T WORRY, PRINCESS! I'LL GIVE MYSELF UP TO VERMIN AND...
OH NO! I'M STILL THE PRINCESS OF THIS PLANET AND I COMMAND YOU TO STAY!
WELL, OKAY... IF YOU COMMAND ME!
PSSST...WHO SAVED TERRY THIS TIME?
HMPH!
YOUR ANSWER NOW!
TERRY STAYS HERE, VERMIN!
PRINCESS! HAVE YOU GONE MAD?
I SAID, TERRY STAYS HERE!
VERY WELL! BUT I'M SURE IT WON'T BE LONG UNTIL YOU SEE THINGS...
...MY WAY!
BLIP!
VOLCANO
EARTHQUAKE
PERHAPS A BIT OF CHAOS WILL HELP THEM SEE THINGS MY WAY!
CHAOS! AWK!
11

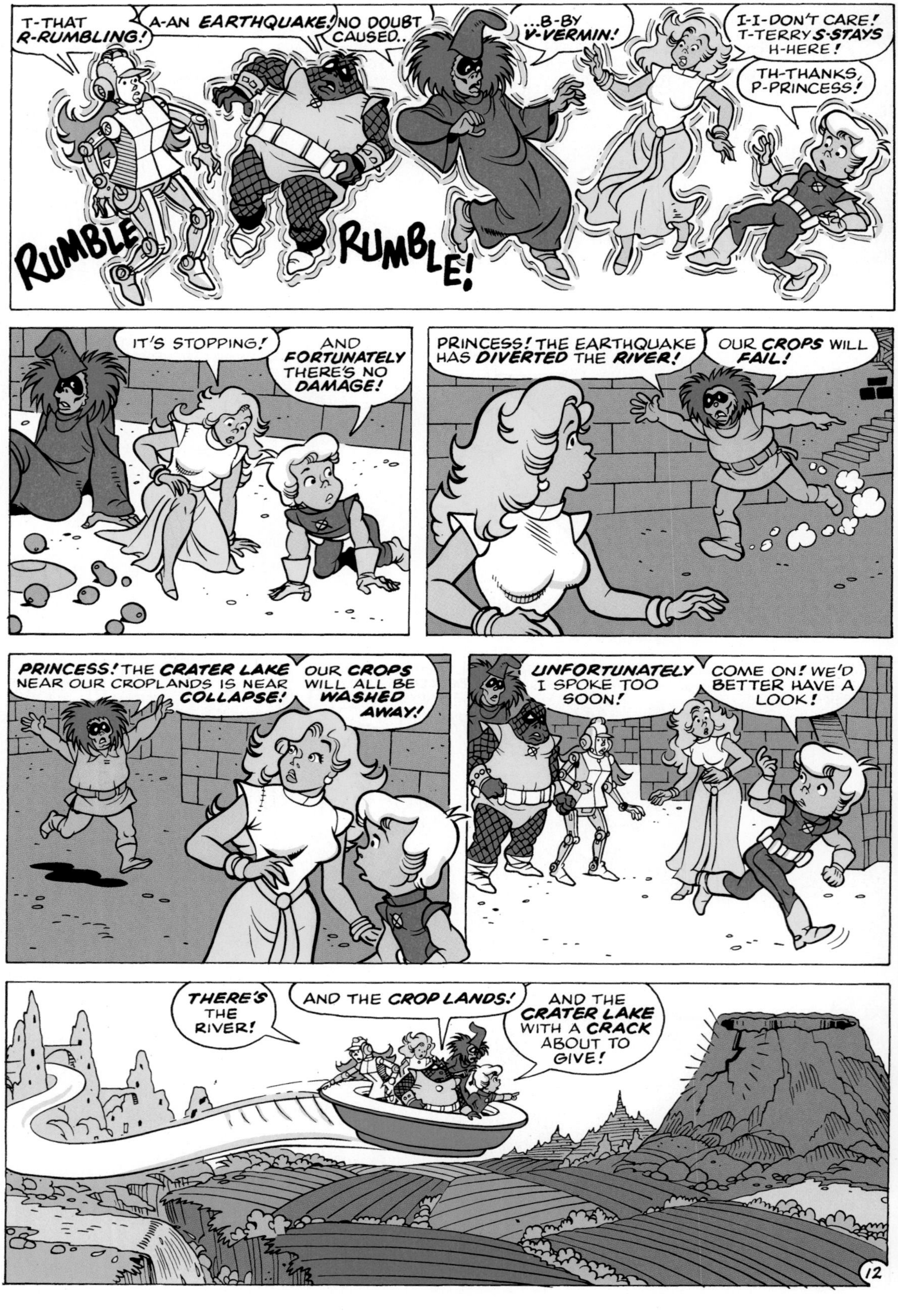

T-THAT R-RUMBLING!
A-AN EARTHQUAKE!
NO DOUBT CAUSED..
...B-BY V-VERMIN!
I-I-DON'T CARE! T-TERRY S-STAYS H-HERE!
TH-THANKS, P-PRINCESS!
RUMBLE
RUMBLE!
IT'S STOPPING!
AND FORTUNATELY THERE'S NO DAMAGE!
PRINCESS! THE EARTHQUAKE HAS DIVERTED THE RIVER!
OUR CROPS WILL FAIL!
PRINCESS! THE CRATER LAKE NEAR OUR CROPLANDS IS NEAR COLLAPSE!
OUR CROPS WILL ALL BE WASHED AWAY!
UNFORTUNATELY I SPOKE TOO SOON!
COME ON! WE'D BETTER HAVE A LOOK!
THERE'S THE RIVER!
AND THE CROP LANDS!
AND THE CRATER LAKE WITH A CRACK ABOUT TO GIVE!
12

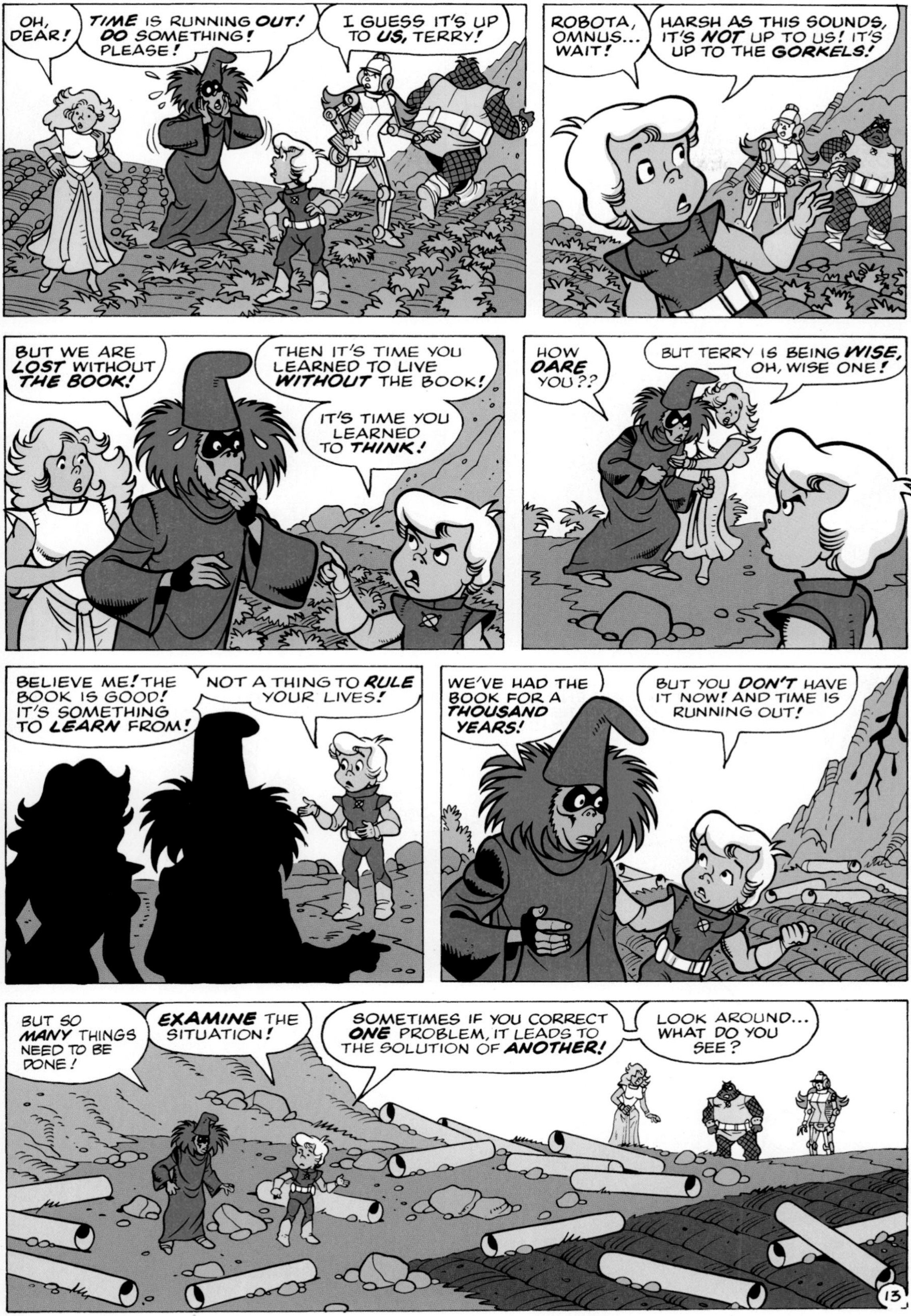
OH, DEAR!
TIME IS RUNNING OUT! DO SOMETHING! PLEASE!
I GUESS IT'S UP TO US, TERRY!
ROBOTA, OMNUS... WAIT!
HARSH AS THIS SOUNDS, IT'S NOT UP TO US! IT'S UP TO THE GORKELS!
BUT WE ARE LOST WITHOUT THE BOOK!
THEN IT'S TIME YOU LEARNED TO LIVE WITHOUT THE BOOK!
IT'S TIME YOU LEARNED TO THINK!
HOW DARE YOU??
BUT TERRY IS BEING WISE, OH, WISE ONE!
BELIEVE ME! THE BOOK IS GOOD! IT'S SOMETHING TO LEARN FROM!
NOT A THING TO RULE YOUR LIVES!
WE'VE HAD THE BOOK FOR A THOUSAND YEARS!
BUT YOU DON'T HAVE IT NOW! AND TIME IS RUNNING OUT!
BUT SO MANY THINGS NEED TO BE DONE!
EXAMINE THE SITUATION!
SOMETIMES IF YOU CORRECT ONE PROBLEM, IT LEADS TO THE SOLUTION OF ANOTHER!
LOOK AROUND... WHAT DO YOU SEE?
13

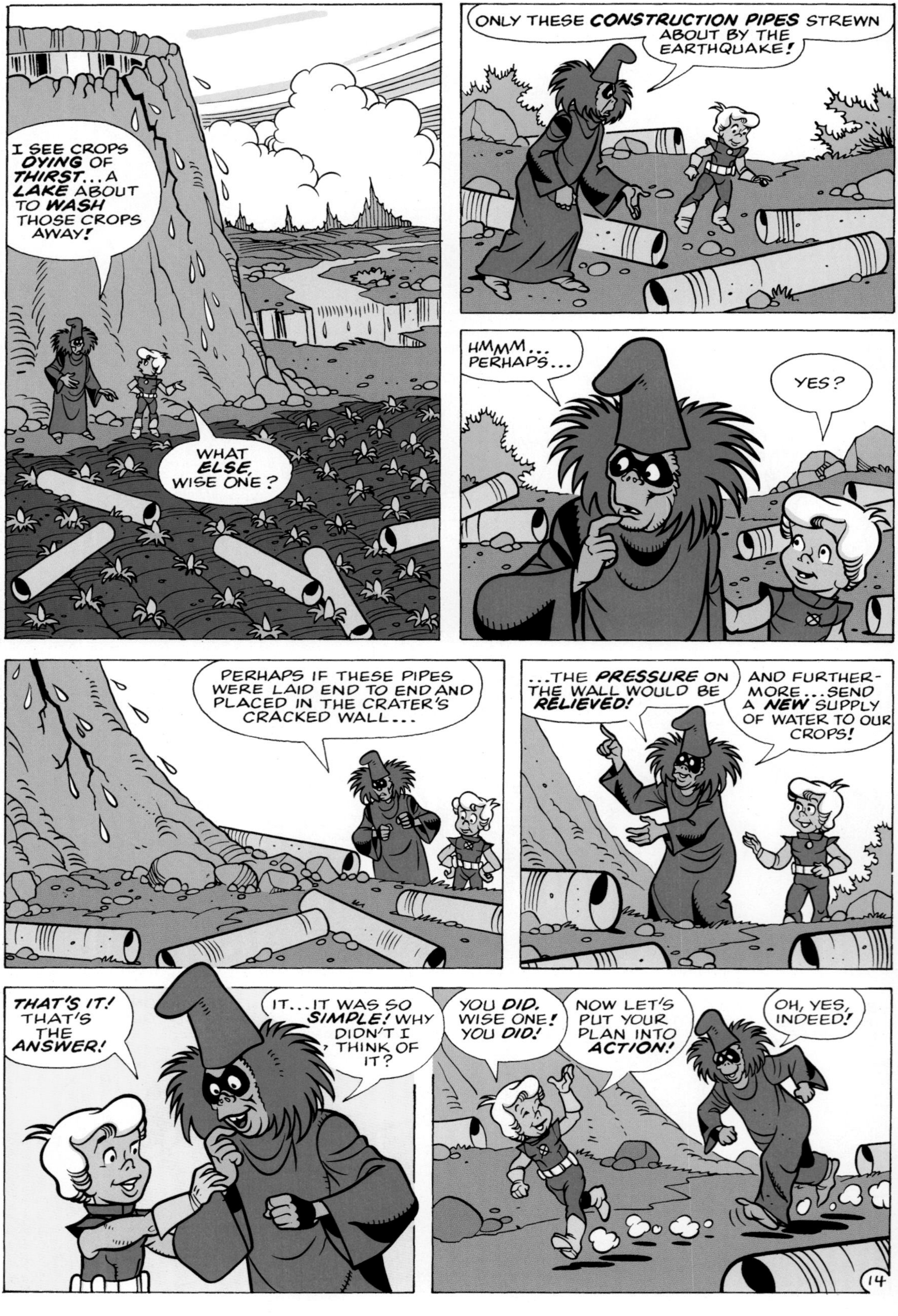
I SEE CROPS DYING OF THIRST... A LAKE ABOUT TO WASH THOSE CROPS AWAY!
WHAT ELSE, WISE ONE?
ONLY THESE CONSTRUCTION PIPES STREWN ABOUT BY THE EARTHQUAKE!
HMMM... PERHAPS...
YES?
PERHAPS IF THESE PIPES WERE LAID END TO END AND PLACED IN THE CRATER'S CRACKED WALL...
...THE PRESSURE ON THE WALL WOULD BE RELIEVED!
AND FURTHERMORE... SEND A NEW SUPPLY OF WATER TO OUR CROPS!
THAT'S IT! THAT'S THE ANSWER!
IT... IT WAS SO SIMPLE! WHY DIDN'T I THINK OF IT?
YOU DID, WISE ONE! YOU DID!
NOW LET'S PUT YOUR PLAN INTO ACTION!
OH, YES, INDEED!
14

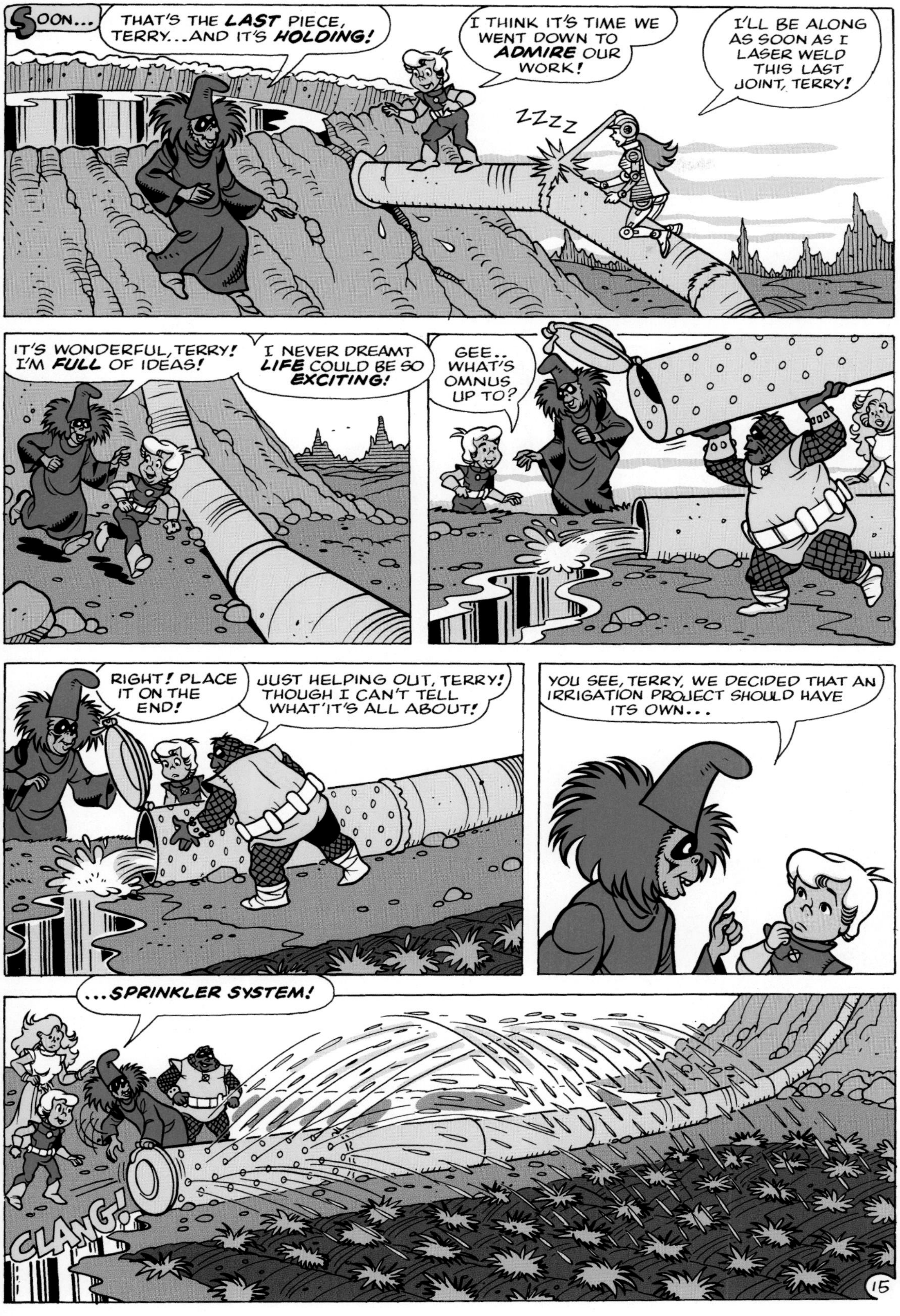
SOON...
THAT'S THE LAST PIECE, TERRY...AND IT'S HOLDING!
I THINK IT'S TIME WE WENT DOWN TO ADMIRE OUR WORK!
I'LL BE ALONG AS SOON AS I LASER WELD THIS LAST JOINT, TERRY!
ZZZZ
IT'S WONDERFUL, TERRY! I'M FULL OF IDEAS!
I NEVER DREAMT LIFE COULD BE SO EXCITING!
GEE.. WHAT'S OMNUS UP TO?
RIGHT! PLACE IT ON THE END!
JUST HELPING OUT, TERRY! THOUGH I CAN'T TELL WHAT'S IT'S ALL ABOUT!
YOU SEE, TERRY, WE DECIDED THAT AN IRRIGATION PROJECT SHOULD HAVE ITS OWN...
...SPRINKLER SYSTEM!
CLANG!
15

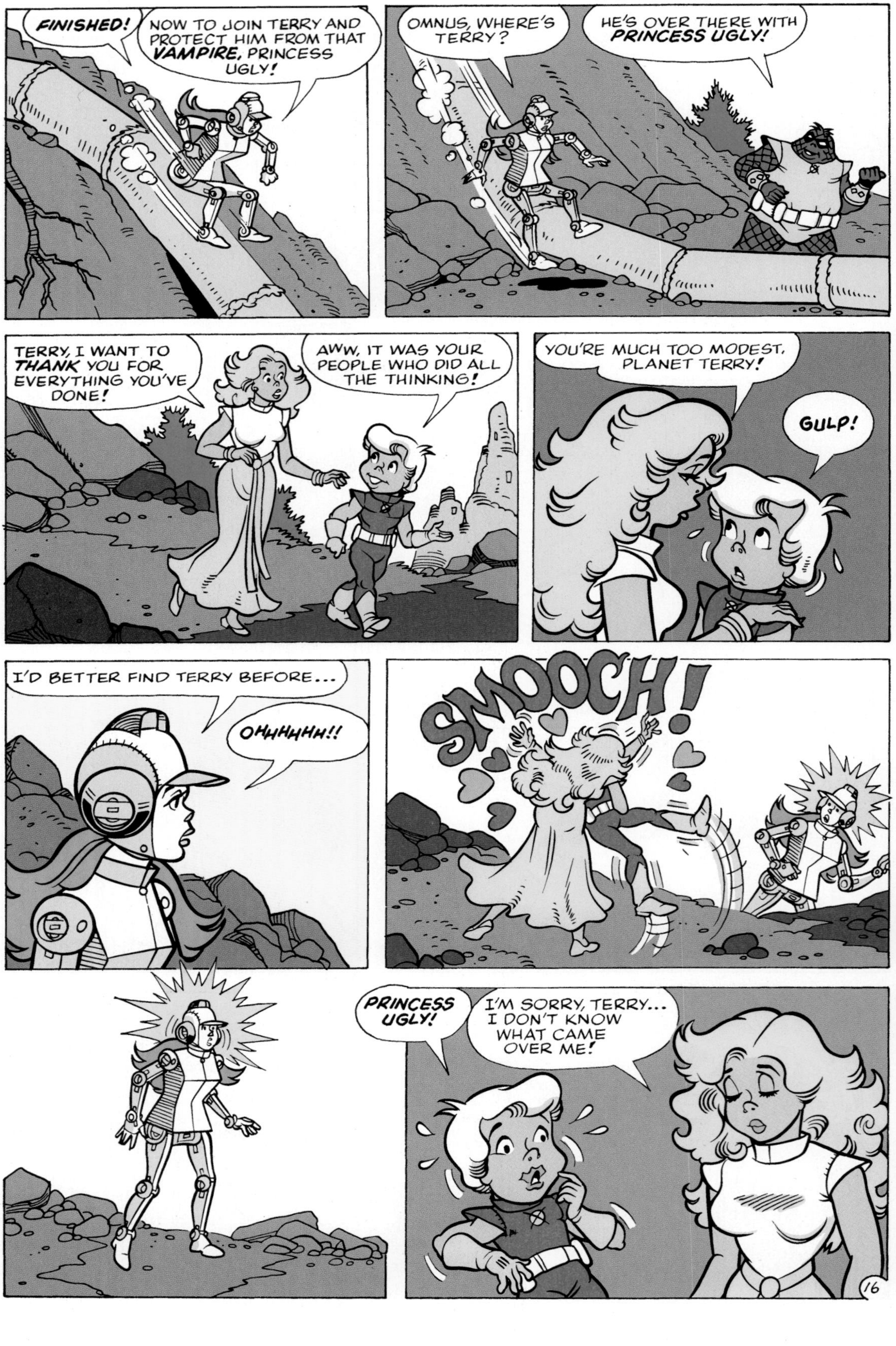
FINISHED!
NOW TO JOIN TERRY AND PROTECT HIM FROM THAT VAMPIRE, PRINCESS UGLY!
OMNUS, WHERE'S TERRY?
HE'S OVER THERE WITH PRINCESS UGLY!
TERRY, I WANT TO THANK YOU FOR EVERYTHING YOU'VE DONE!
AWW, IT WAS YOUR PEOPLE WHO DID ALL THE THINKING!
YOU'RE MUCH TOO MODEST, PLANET TERRY!
GULP!
I'D BETTER FIND TERRY BEFORE...
OHHHHHH!!
SMOOCH!
PRINCESS UGLY!
I'M SORRY, TERRY... I DON'T KNOW WHAT CAME OVER ME!
16

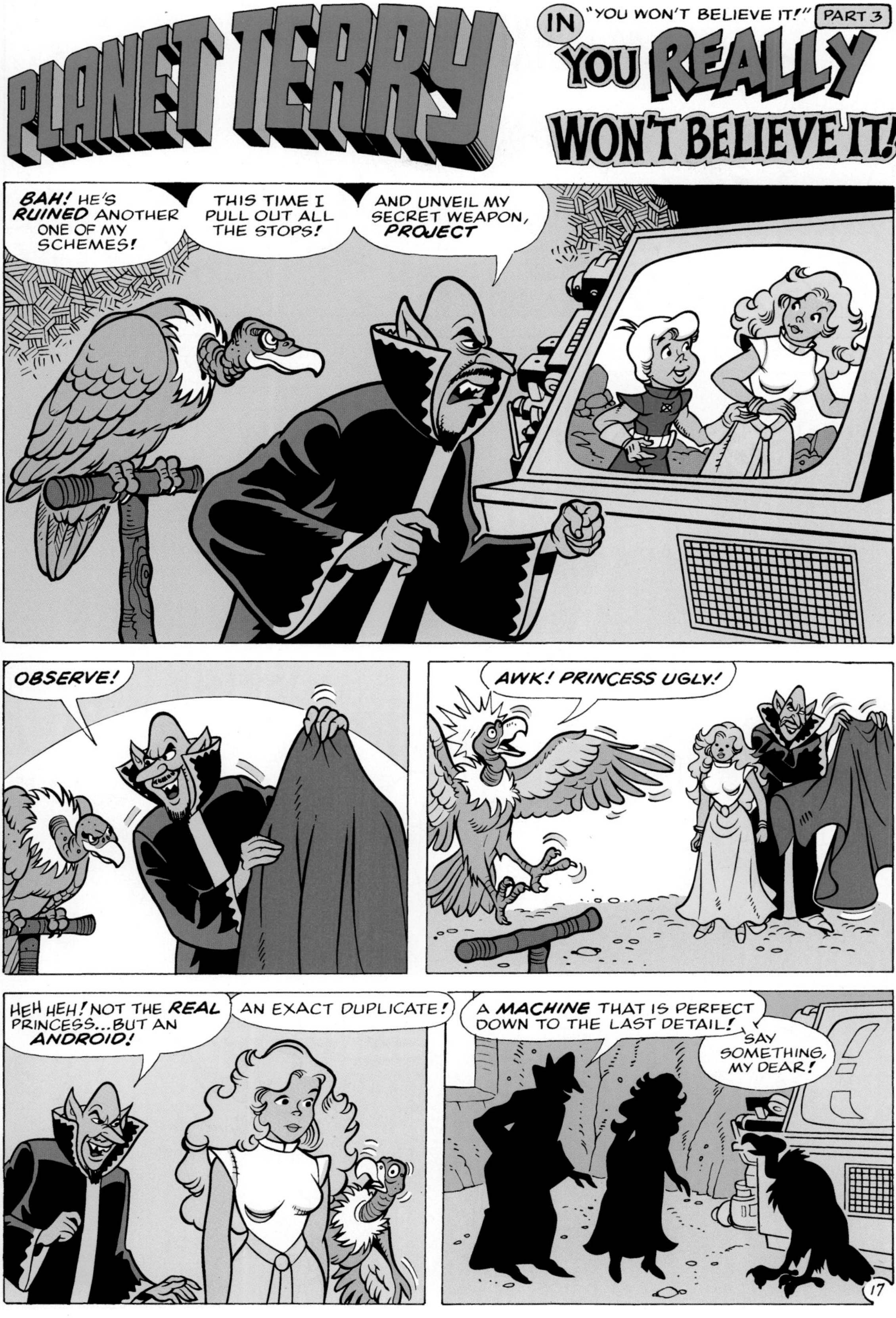
PLANET TERRY
IN "YOU WON'T BELIEVE IT!" PART 3
YOU REALLY WON'T BELIEVE IT!
BAH! HE'S RUINED ANOTHER ONE OF MY SCHEMES!
THIS TIME I PULL OUT ALL THE STOPS!
AND UNVEIL MY SECRET WEAPON, PROJECT
OBSERVE!
AWK! PRINCESS UGLY!
HEH HEH! NOT THE REAL PRINCESS...BUT AN ANDROID!
AN EXACT DUPLICATE!
A MACHINE THAT IS PERFECT DOWN TO THE LAST DETAIL!
SAY SOMETHING, MY DEAR!
17

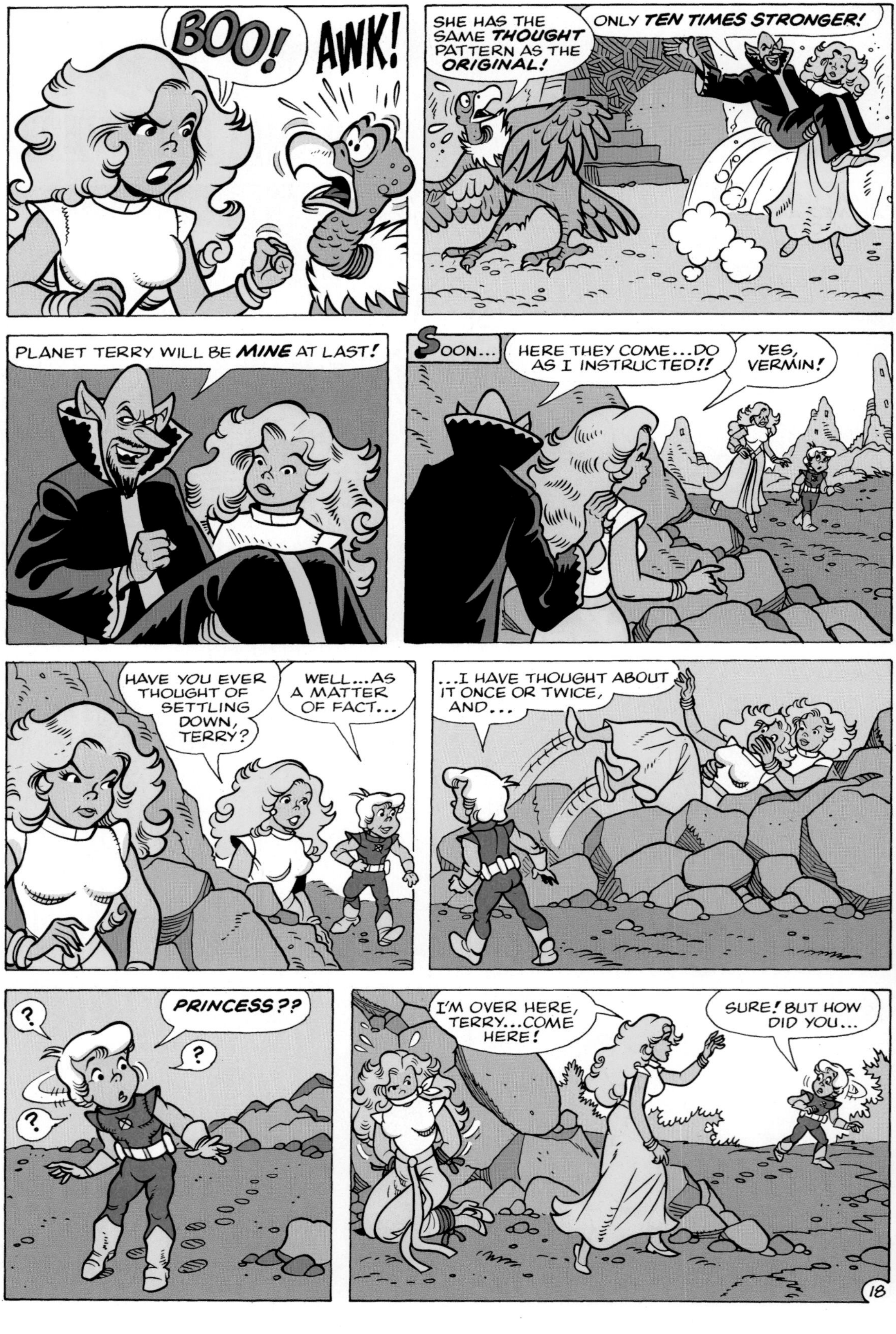
BOO!
AWK!
SHE HAS THE SAME THOUGHT PATTERN AS THE ORIGINAL!
ONLY TEN TIMES STRONGER!
PLANET TERRY WILL BE MINE AT LAST!
SOON...
HERE THEY COME...DO AS I INSTRUCTED!!
YES, VERMIN!
HAVE YOU EVER THOUGHT OF SETTLING DOWN, TERRY?
WELL...AS A MATTER OF FACT...
...I HAVE THOUGHT ABOUT IT ONCE OR TWICE, AND...
?
PRINCESS??
?
?
I'M OVER HERE, TERRY...COME HERE!
SURE! BUT HOW DID YOU...
18

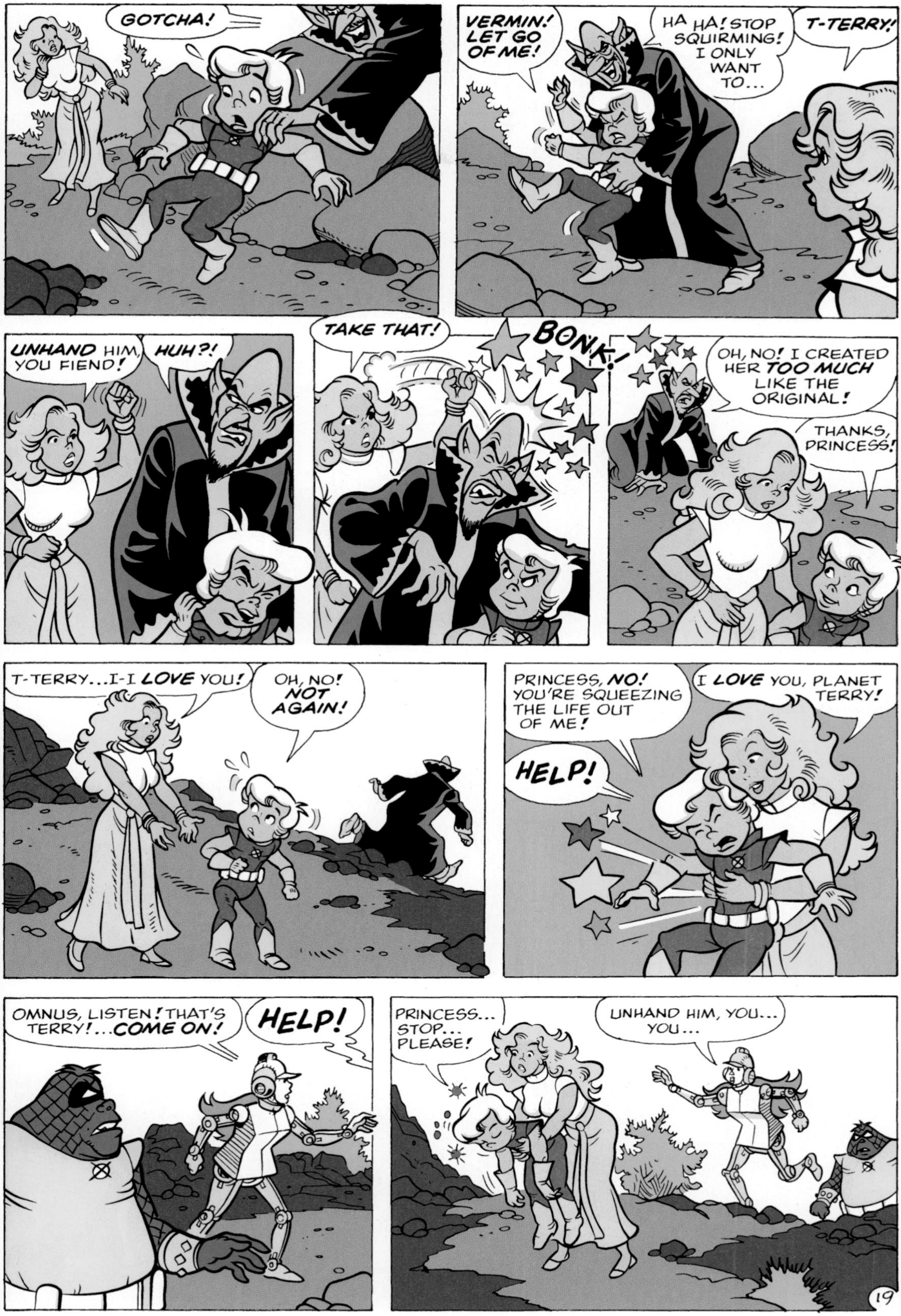

GOTCHA!
VERMIN! LET GO OF ME!
HA HA! STOP SQUIRMING! I ONLY WANT TO...
T-TERRY!
UNHAND HIM, YOU FIEND!
HUH?!
TAKE THAT!
BONK!
OH, NO! I CREATED HER TOO MUCH LIKE THE ORIGINAL!
THANKS, PRINCESS!
T-TERRY...I-I LOVE YOU!
OH, NO! NOT AGAIN!
PRINCESS, NO! YOU'RE SQUEEZING THE LIFE OUT OF ME!
I LOVE YOU, PLANET TERRY!
HELP!
OMNUS, LISTEN! THAT'S TERRY!...COME ON!
HELP!
PRINCESS... STOP... PLEASE!
UNHAND HIM, YOU... YOU...
19

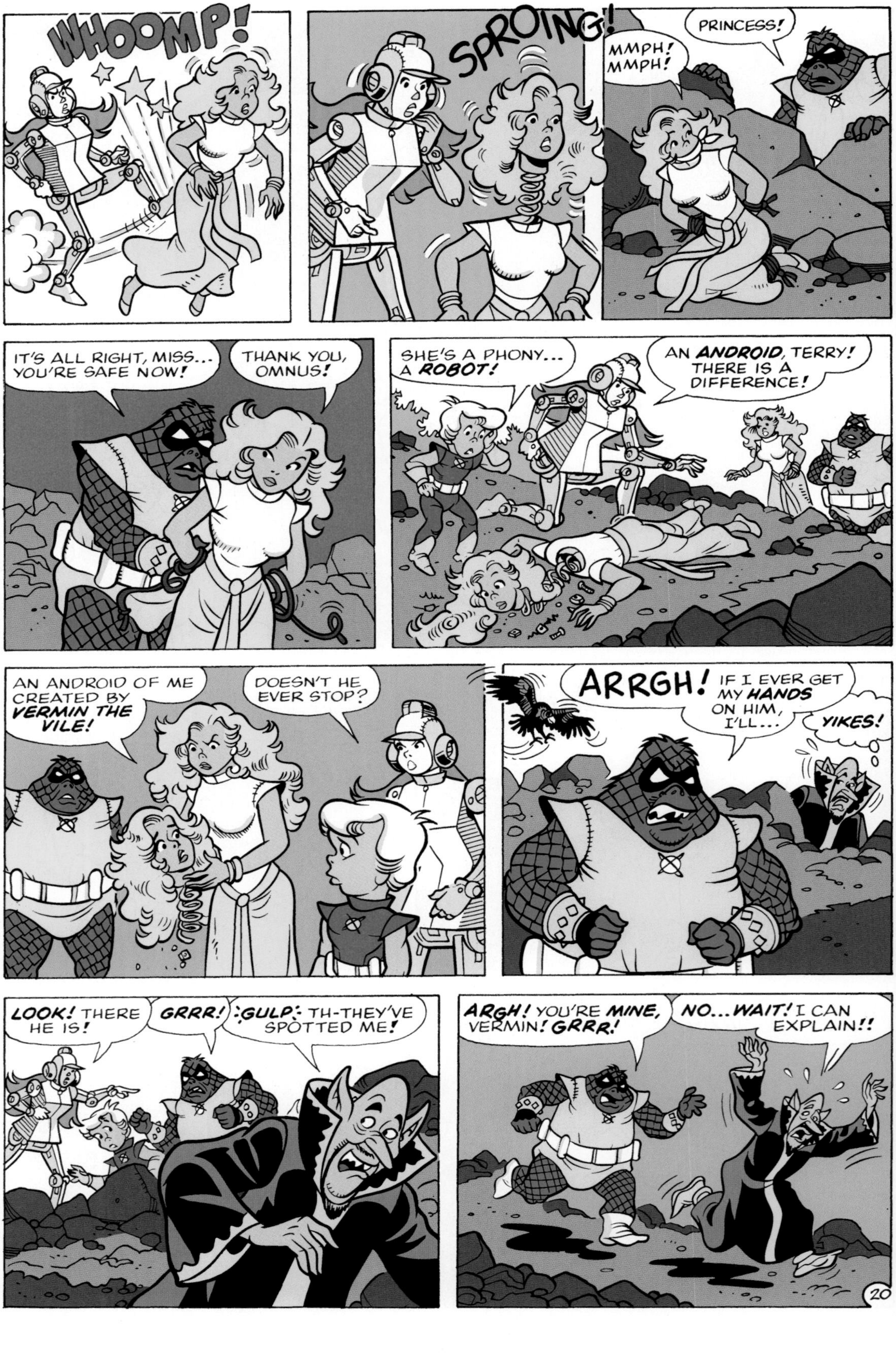
WHOOMP!
SPROING!
MMPH! MMPH!
PRINCESS!
IT'S ALL RIGHT, MISS... YOU'RE SAFE NOW!
THANK YOU, OMNUS!
SHE'S A PHONY... A ROBOT!
AN ANDROID, TERRY! THERE IS A DIFFERENCE!
AN ANDROID OF ME CREATED BY VERMIN THE VILE!
DOESN'T HE EVER STOP?
ARRGH! IF I EVER GET MY HANDS ON HIM, I'LL...
YIKES!
LOOK! THERE HE IS!
GRRR!
:GULP: TH-THEY'VE SPOTTED ME!
ARGH! YOU'RE MINE, VERMIN! GRRR!
NO...WAIT! I CAN EXPLAIN!!
20

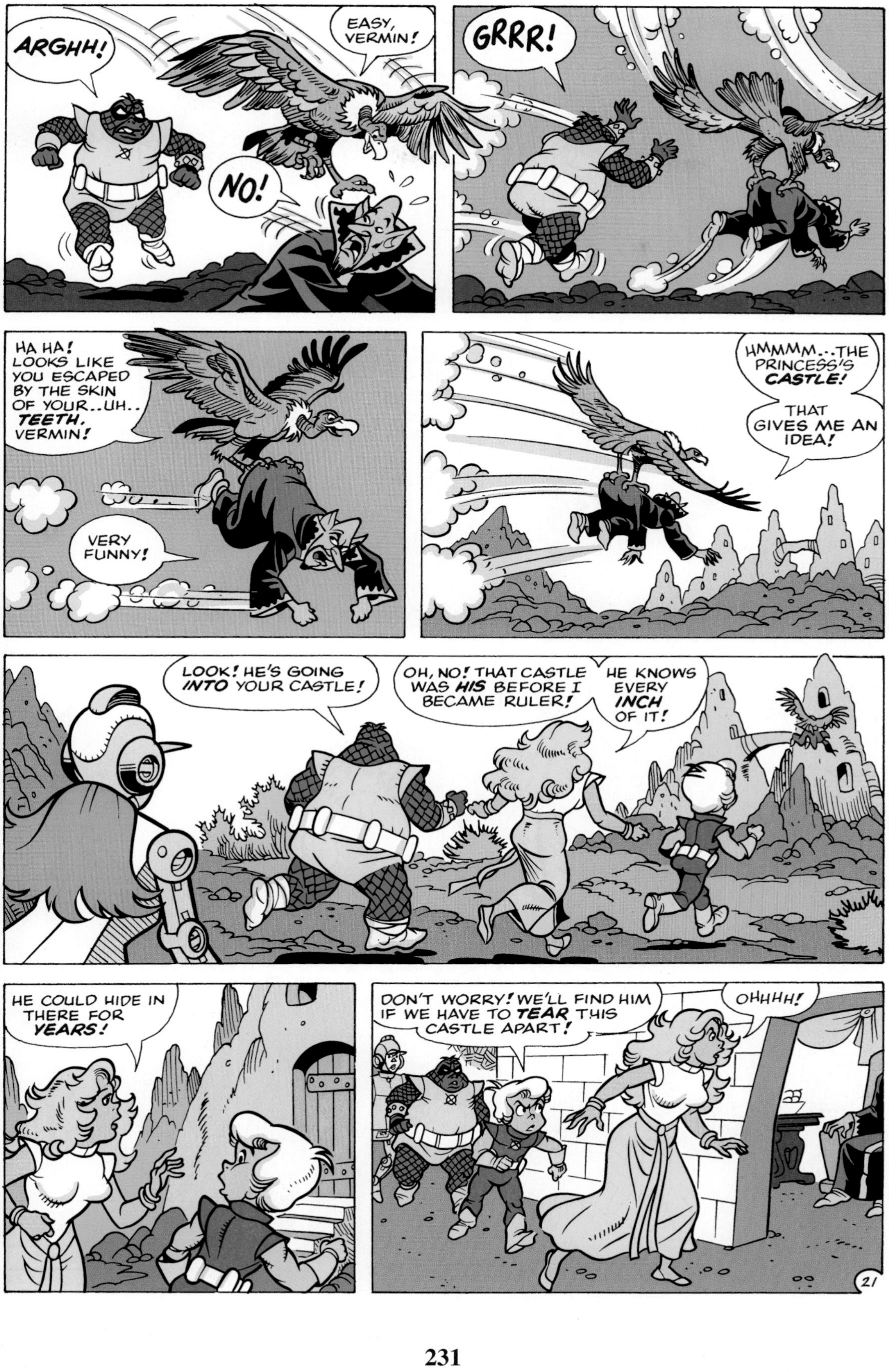
ARGHH!
EASY, VERMIN!
NO!
GRRR!
HA HA! LOOKS LIKE YOU ESCAPED BY THE SKIN OF YOUR..UH.. TEETH, VERMIN!
VERY FUNNY!
HMMMM...THE PRINCESS'S CASTLE!
THAT GIVES ME AN IDEA!
LOOK! HE'S GOING INTO YOUR CASTLE!
OH, NO! THAT CASTLE WAS HIS BEFORE I BECAME RULER!
HE KNOWS EVERY INCH OF IT!
HE COULD HIDE IN THERE FOR YEARS!
DON'T WORRY! WE'LL FIND HIM IF WE HAVE TO TEAR THIS CASTLE APART!
OHHHH!
21

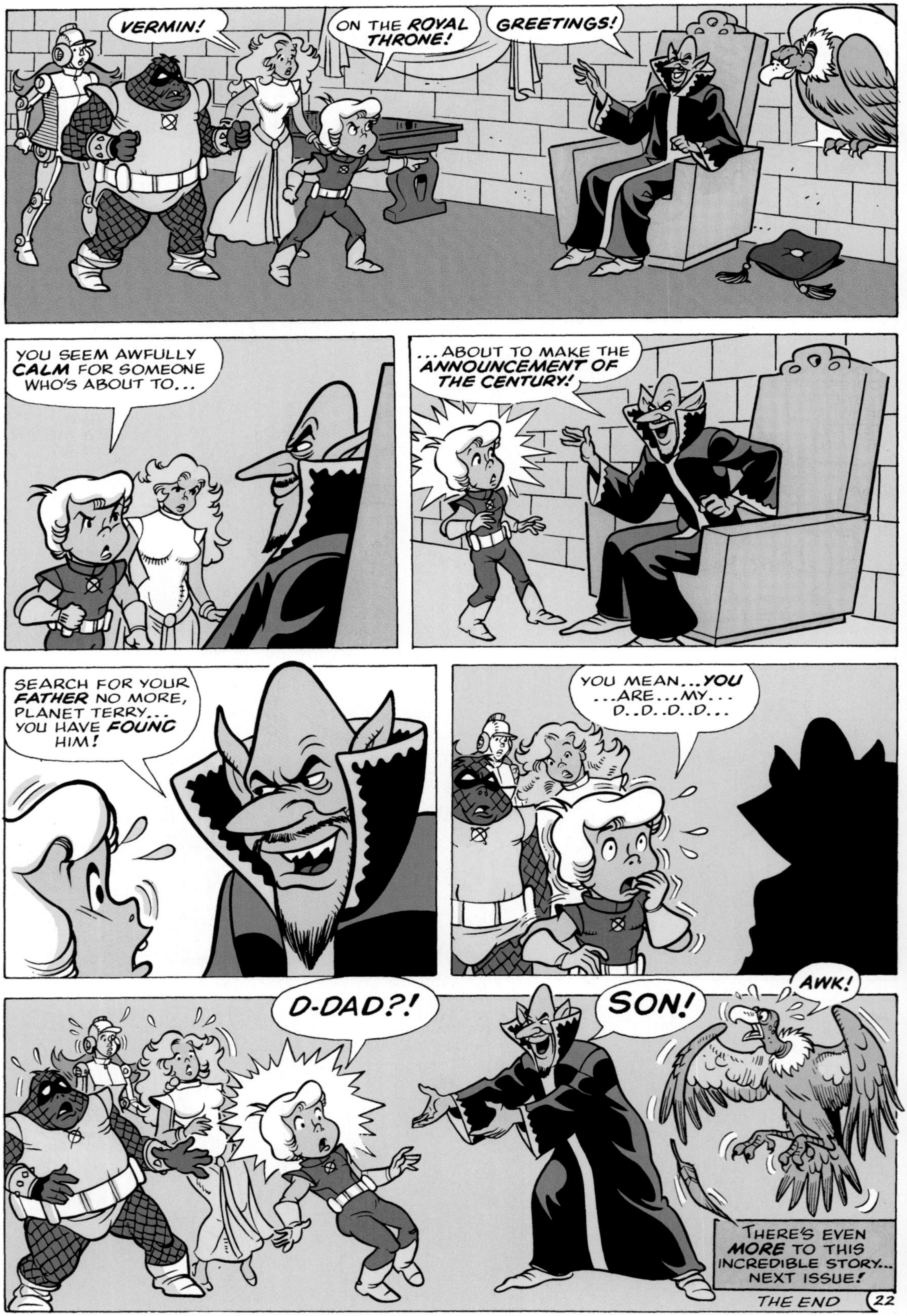
VERMIN!
ON THE ROYAL THRONE!
GREETINGS!
YOU SEEM AWFULLY CALM FOR SOMEONE WHO'S ABOUT TO...
...ABOUT TO MAKE THE ANNOUNCEMENT OF THE CENTURY!
SEARCH FOR YOUR FATHER NO MORE, PLANET TERRY... YOU HAVE FOUNC HIM!
YOU MEAN...YOU ...ARE...MY... D..D..D..D...
D-DAD?!
SON!
AWK!
THERE'S EVEN MORE TO THIS INCREDIBLE STORY... NEXT ISSUE!
THE END
22

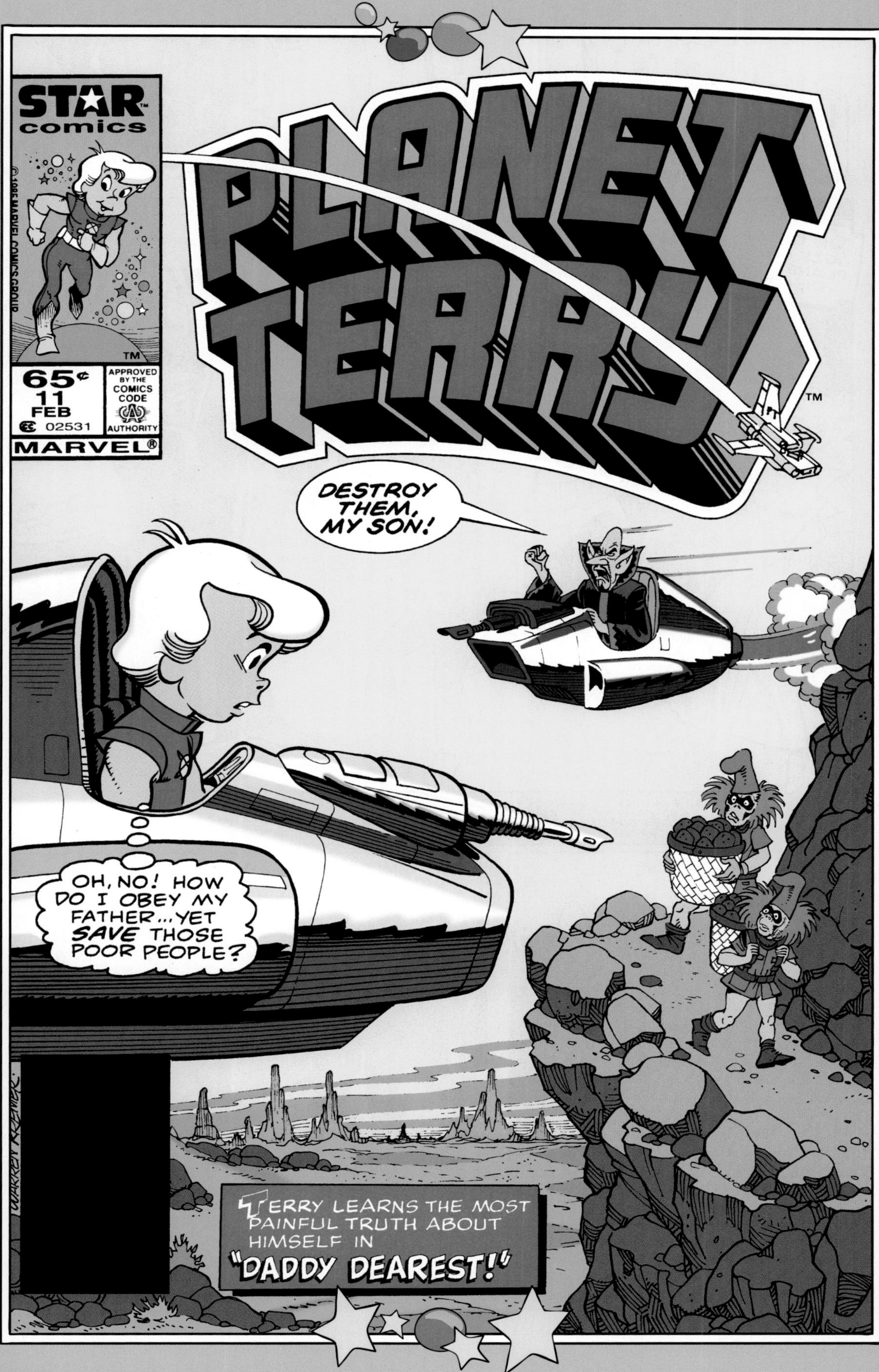
STAR comics
© 1985 MARVEL COMICS GROUP
PLANET TERRY
65¢
11
FEB
02531
APPROVED BY THE COMICS CODE AUTHORITY
MARVEL
DESTROY THEM, MY SON!
OH, NO! HOW DO I OBEY MY FATHER... YET SAVE THOSE POOR PEOPLE?
WARREN KREMER
TERRY LEARNS THE MOST PAINFUL TRUTH ABOUT HIMSELF IN
"DADDY DEAREST!"

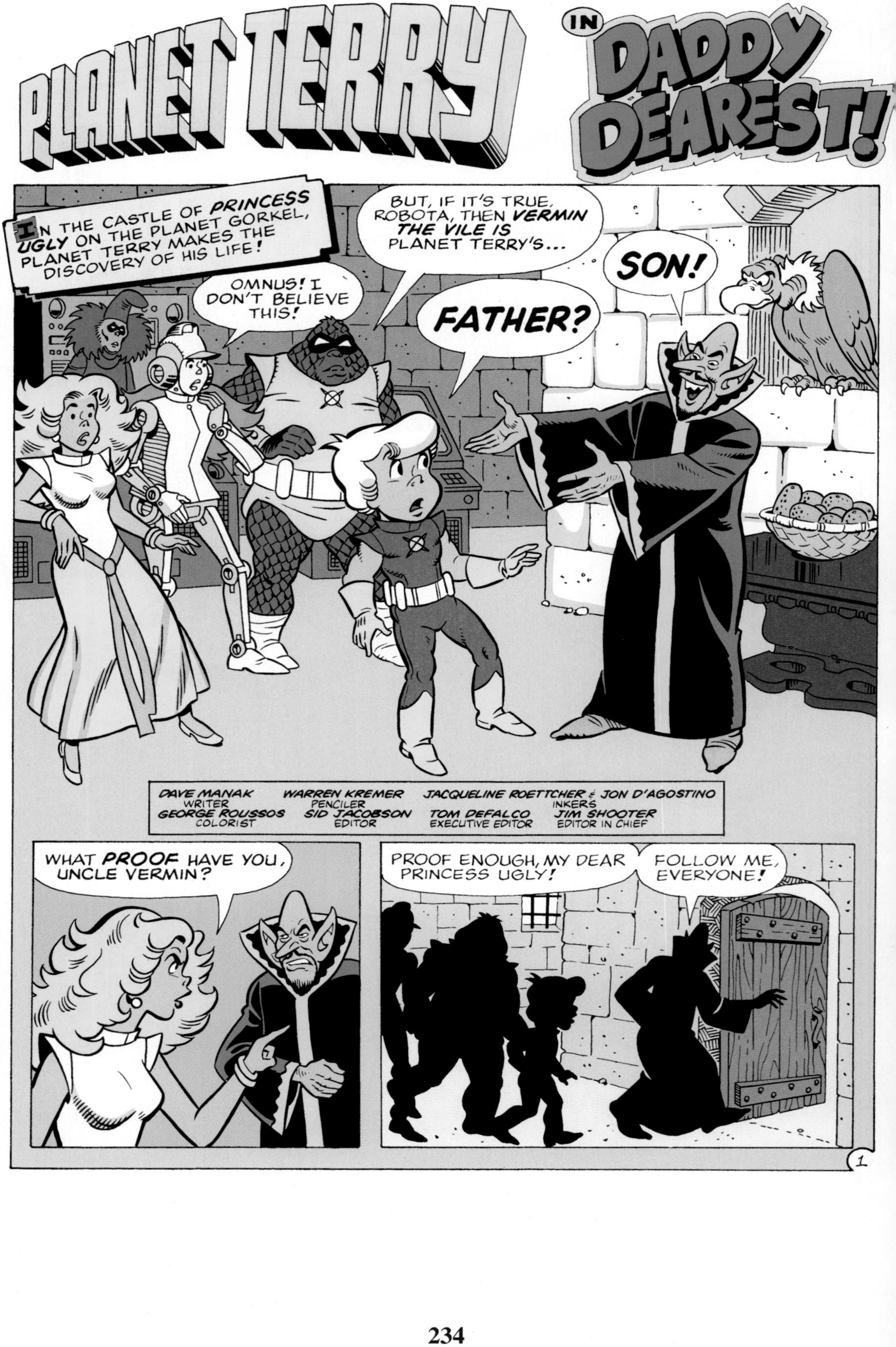
PLANET TERRY
IN
DADDY DEAREST!
IN THE CASTLE OF PRINCESS UGLY ON THE PLANET GORKEL, PLANET TERRY MAKES THE DISCOVERY OF HIS LIFE!
OMNUS! I DON'T BELIEVE THIS!
BUT, IF IT'S TRUE, ROBOTA, THEN VERMIN THE VILE IS PLANET TERRY'S...
FATHER?
SON!
DAVE MANAK WRITER
WARREN KREMER PENCILER
JACQUELINE ROETTCHER & JON D'AGOSTINO INKERS
GEORGE ROUSSOS COLORIST
SID JACOBSON EDITOR
TOM DEFALCO EXECUTIVE EDITOR
JIM SHOOTER EDITOR IN CHIEF
WHAT PROOF HAVE YOU, UNCLE VERMIN?
PROOF ENOUGH, MY DEAR PRINCESS UGLY!
FOLLOW ME, EVERYONE!
1

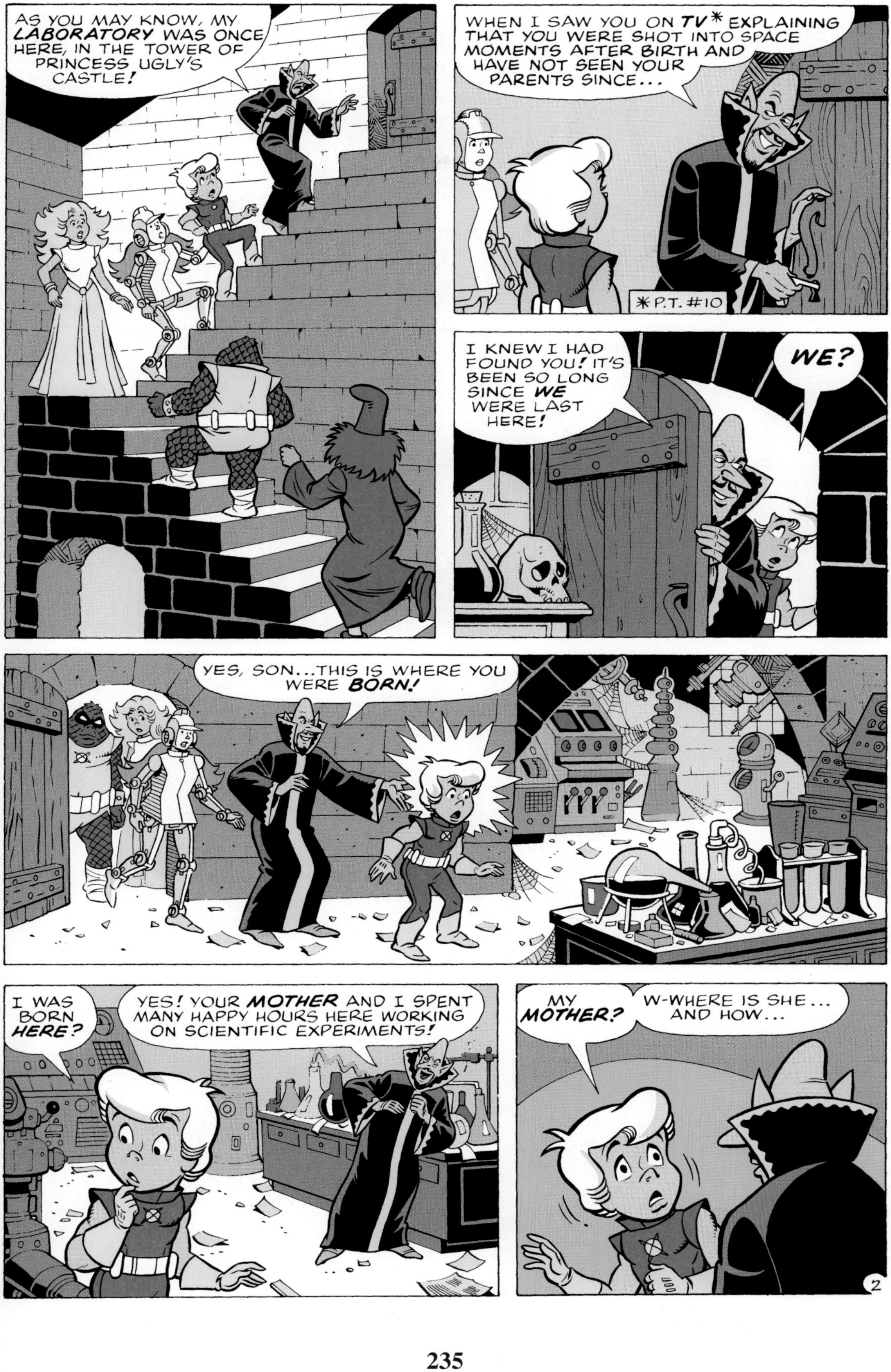
AS YOU MAY KNOW, MY LABORATORY WAS ONCE HERE, IN THE TOWER OF PRINCESS UGLY'S CASTLE!
WHEN I SAW YOU ON TV* EXPLAINING THAT YOU WERE SHOT INTO SPACE MOMENTS AFTER BIRTH AND HAVE NOT SEEN YOUR PARENTS SINCE...
*P.T. #10
I KNEW I HAD FOUND YOU! IT'S BEEN SO LONG SINCE WE WERE LAST HERE!
WE?
YES, SON...THIS IS WHERE YOU WERE BORN!
I WAS BORN HERE?
YES! YOUR MOTHER AND I SPENT MANY HAPPY HOURS HERE WORKING ON SCIENTIFIC EXPERIMENTS!
MY MOTHER?
W-WHERE IS SHE... AND HOW...
2

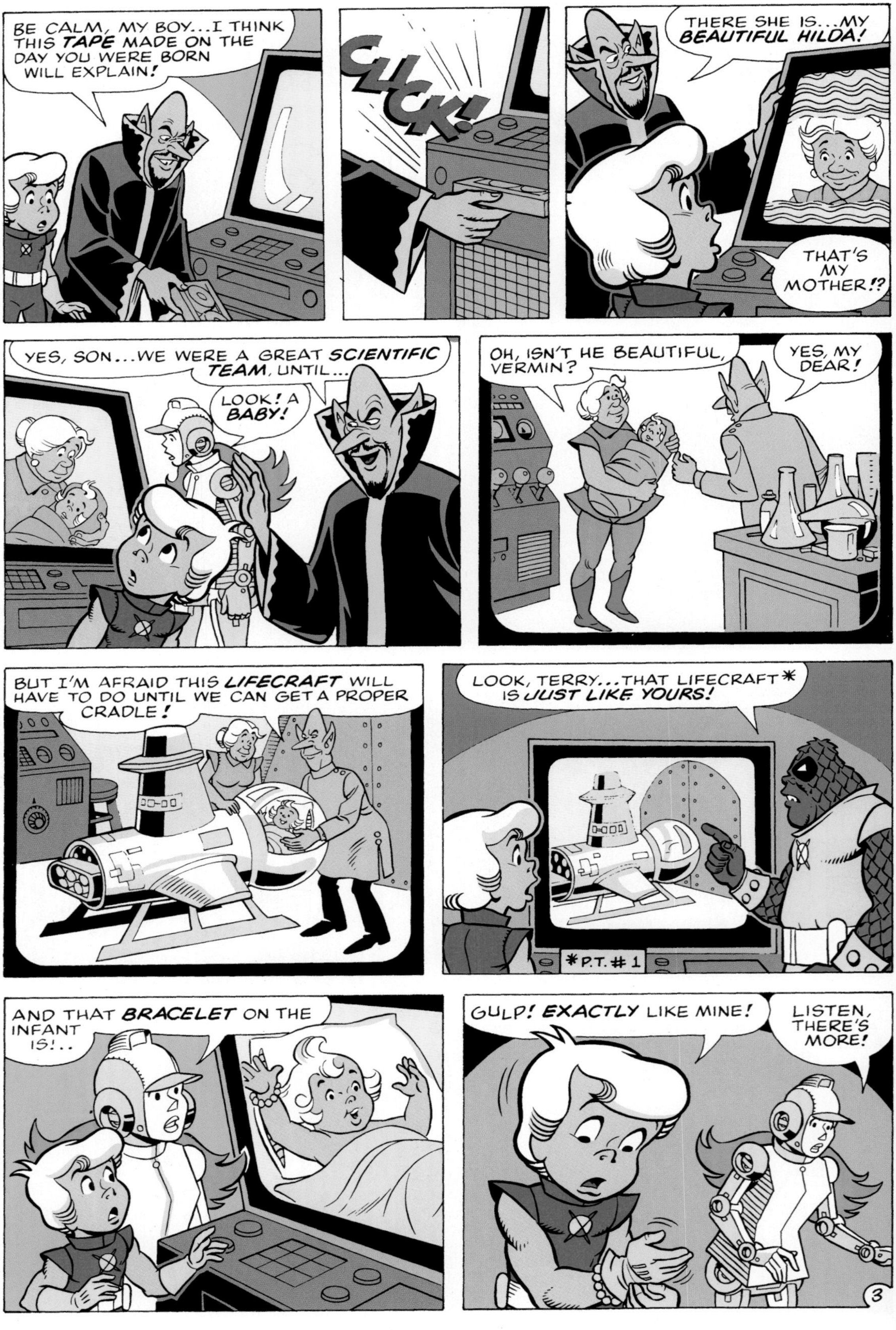

BE CALM, MY BOY...I THINK THIS TAPE MADE ON THE DAY YOU WERE BORN WILL EXPLAIN!
CLICK!
THERE SHE IS...MY BEAUTIFUL HILDA!
THAT'S MY MOTHER!?
YES, SON...WE WERE A GREAT SCIENTIFIC TEAM, UNTIL...
LOOK! A BABY!
OH, ISN'T HE BEAUTIFUL, VERMIN?
YES, MY DEAR!
BUT I'M AFRAID THIS LIFECRAFT WILL HAVE TO DO UNTIL WE CAN GET A PROPER CRADLE!
LOOK, TERRY...THAT LIFECRAFT* IS JUST LIKE YOURS!
*P.T. #1
AND THAT BRACELET ON THE INFANT IS!..
GULP! EXACTLY LIKE MINE!
LISTEN, THERE'S MORE!
3

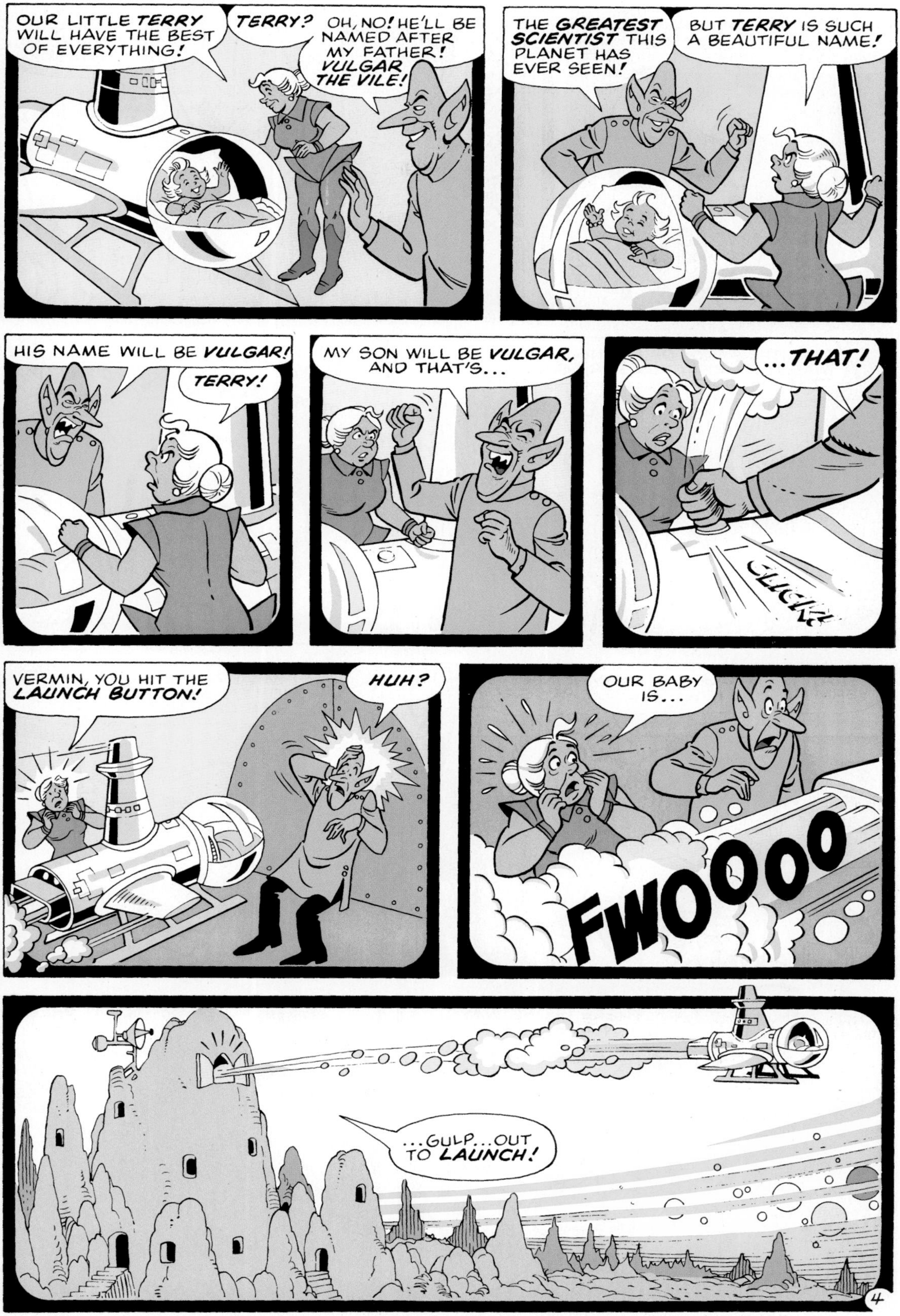
OUR LITTLE TERRY WILL HAVE THE BEST OF EVERYTHING!
TERRY?
OH, NO! HE'LL BE NAMED AFTER MY FATHER! VULGAR THE VILE!
THE GREATEST SCIENTIST THIS PLANET HAS EVER SEEN!
BUT TERRY IS SUCH A BEAUTIFUL NAME!
HIS NAME WILL BE VULGAR!
TERRY!
MY SON WILL BE VULGAR, AND THAT'S...
...THAT!
CLICK!
VERMIN, YOU HIT THE LAUNCH BUTTON!
HUH?
OUR BABY IS...
FWOOOO
...GULP...OUT TO LAUNCH!
4

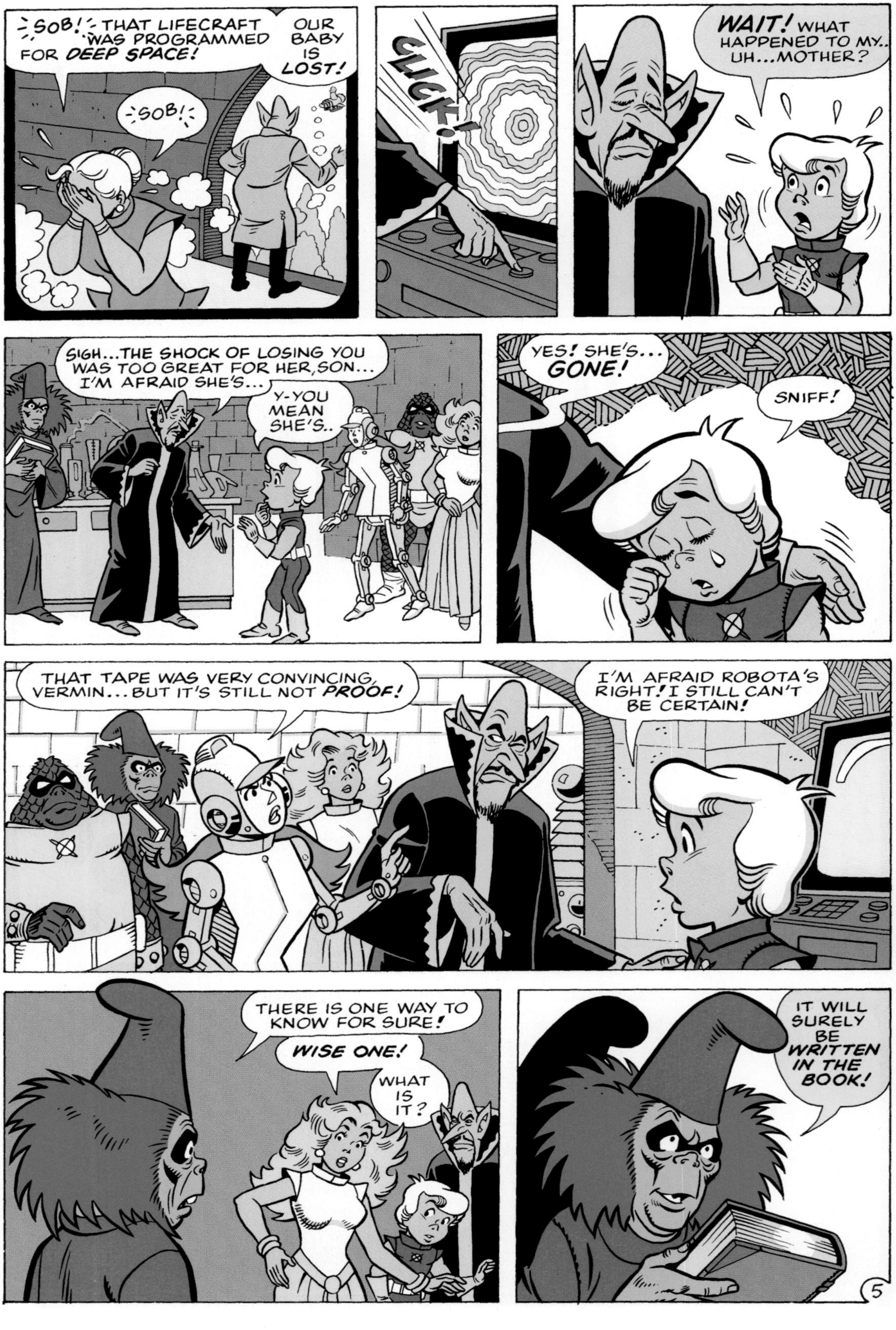

SOB! THAT LIFECRAFT WAS PROGRAMMED FOR DEEP SPACE!
OUR BABY IS LOST!
SOB!
CLICK!
WAIT! WHAT HAPPENED TO MY.. UH...MOTHER?
SIGH...THE SHOCK OF LOSING YOU WAS TOO GREAT FOR HER, SON... I'M AFRAID SHE'S...
Y-YOU MEAN SHE'S..
YES! SHE'S... GONE!
SNIFF!
THAT TAPE WAS VERY CONVINCING, VERMIN... BUT IT'S STILL NOT PROOF!
I'M AFRAID ROBOTA'S RIGHT! I STILL CAN'T BE CERTAIN!
THERE IS ONE WAY TO KNOW FOR SURE!
WISE ONE!
WHAT IS IT?
IT WILL SURELY BE WRITTEN IN THE BOOK!
5

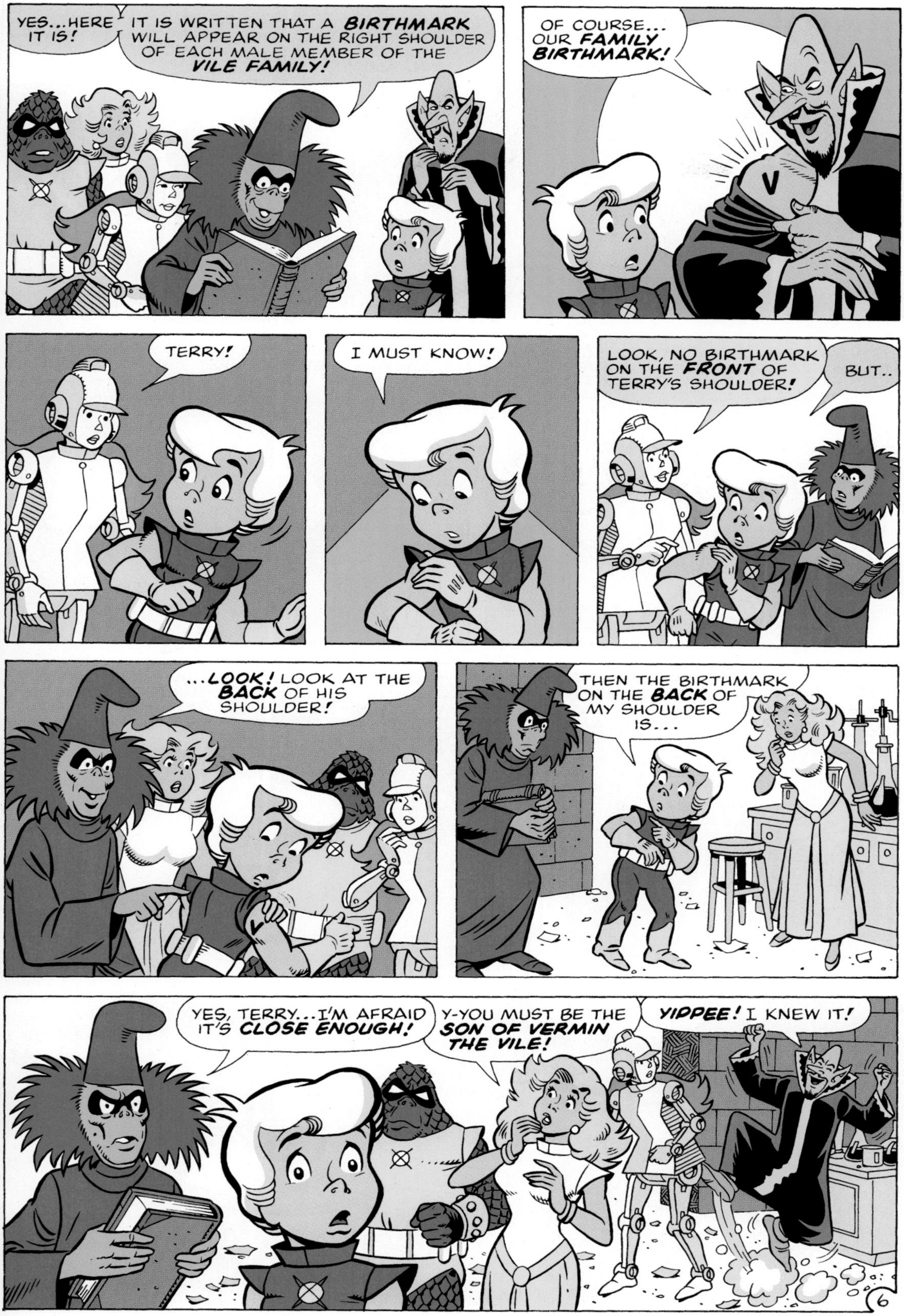
YES...HERE IT IS!
IT IS WRITTEN THAT A BIRTHMARK WILL APPEAR ON THE RIGHT SHOULDER OF EACH MALE MEMBER OF THE VILE FAMILY!
OF COURSE... OUR FAMILY BIRTHMARK!
V
TERRY!
I MUST KNOW!
LOOK, NO BIRTHMARK ON THE FRONT OF TERRY'S SHOULDER!
BUT..
...LOOK! LOOK AT THE BACK OF HIS SHOULDER!
V
THEN THE BIRTHMARK ON THE BACK OF MY SHOULDER IS...
YES, TERRY...I'M AFRAID IT'S CLOSE ENOUGH!
Y-YOU MUST BE THE SON OF VERMIN THE VILE!
YIPPEE! I KNEW IT!
6

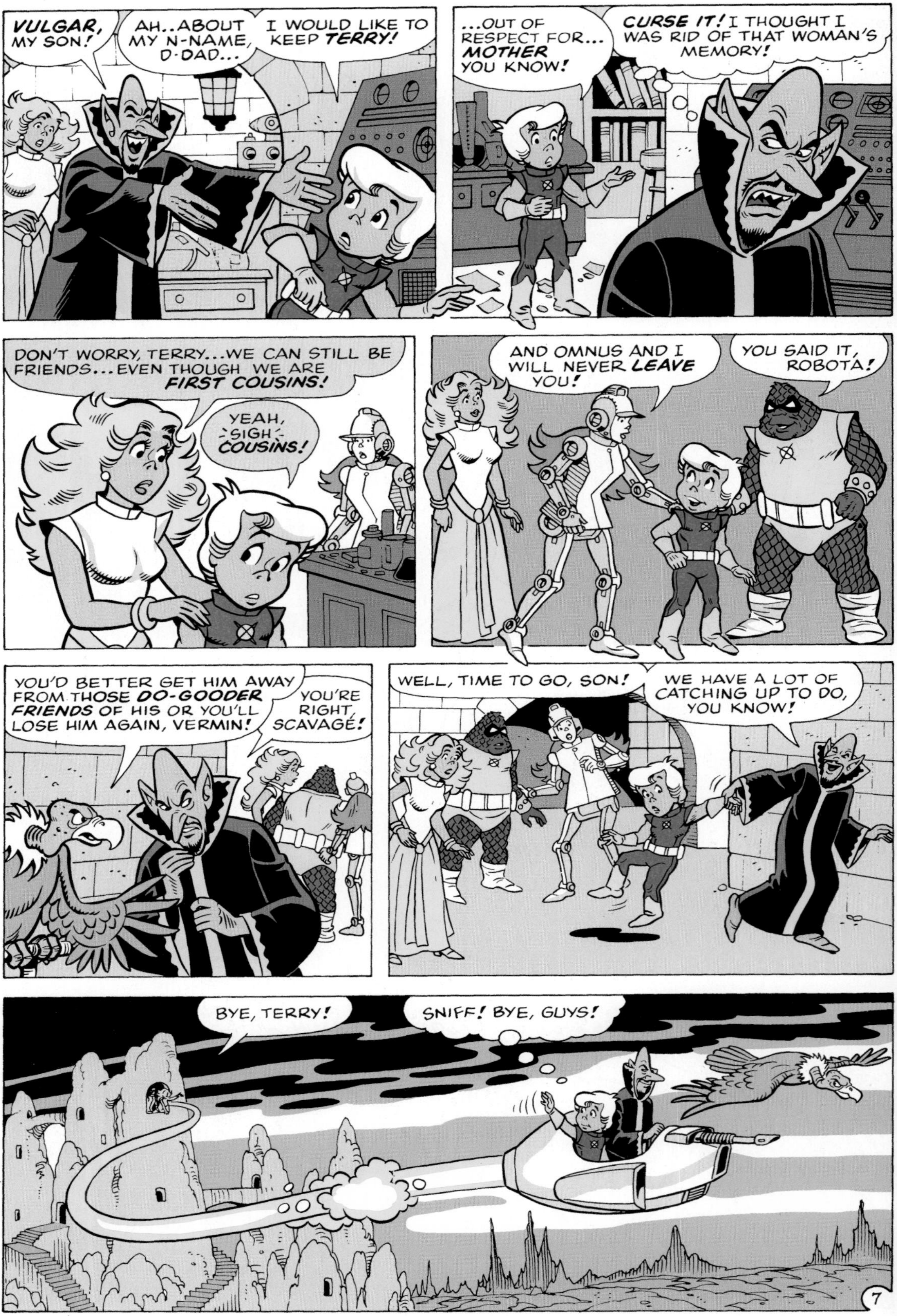
VULGAR, MY SON!
AH..ABOUT MY N-NAME, D-DAD...
I WOULD LIKE TO KEEP TERRY!
...OUT OF RESPECT FOR... MOTHER YOU KNOW!
CURSE IT! I THOUGHT I WAS RID OF THAT WOMAN'S MEMORY!
DON'T WORRY, TERRY...WE CAN STILL BE FRIENDS...EVEN THOUGH WE ARE FIRST COUSINS!
YEAH, SIGH COUSINS!
AND OMNUS AND I WILL NEVER LEAVE YOU!
YOU SAID IT, ROBOTA!
YOU'D BETTER GET HIM AWAY FROM THOSE DO-GOODER FRIENDS OF HIS OR YOU'LL LOSE HIM AGAIN, VERMIN!
YOU'RE RIGHT, SCAVAGÉ!
WELL, TIME TO GO, SON!
WE HAVE A LOT OF CATCHING UP TO DO, YOU KNOW!
BYE, TERRY!
SNIFF! BYE, GUYS!
7

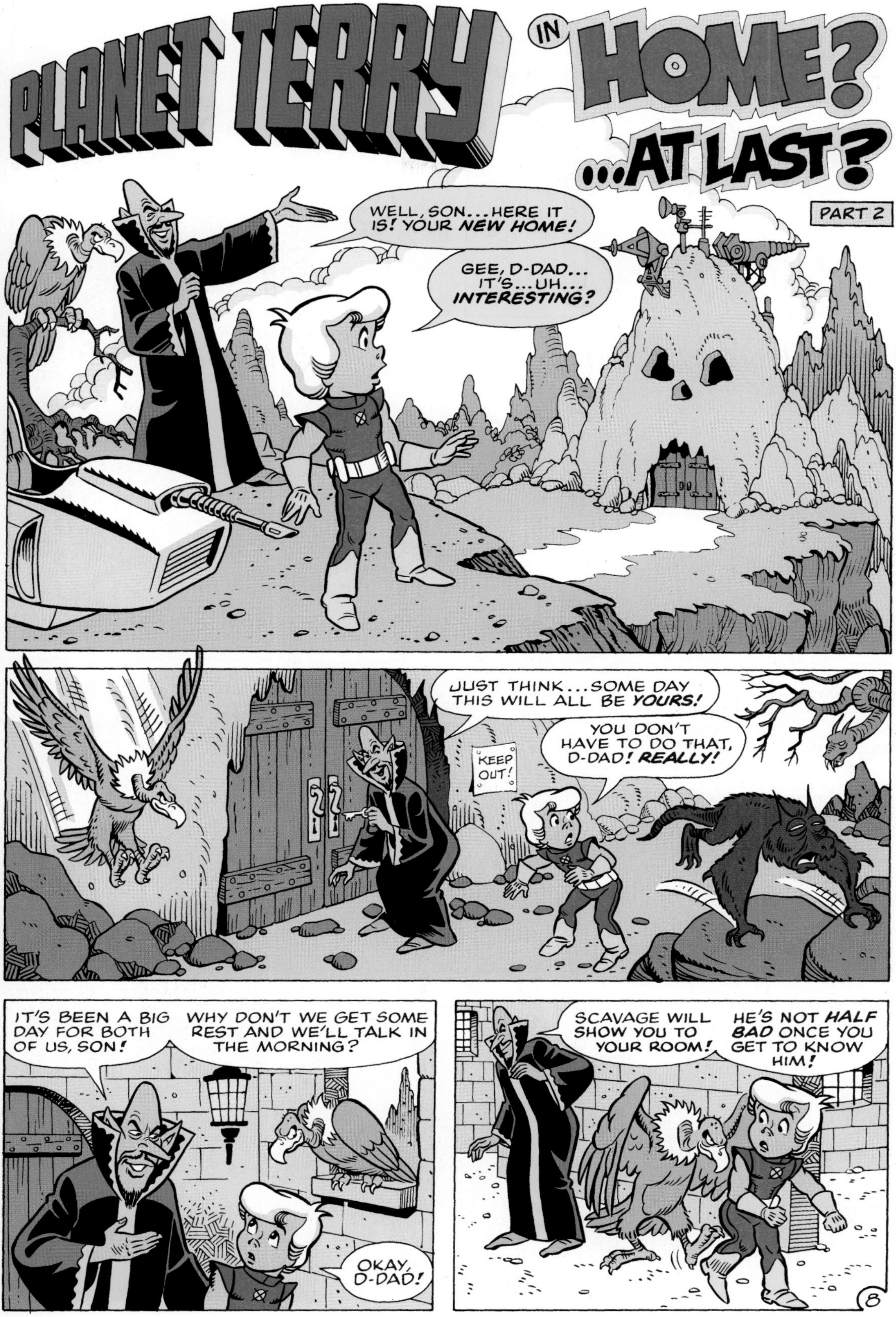
PLANET TERRY
IN
HOME? ...AT LAST?
PART 2
WELL, SON...HERE IT IS! YOUR NEW HOME!
GEE, D-DAD... IT'S...UH... INTERESTING?
JUST THINK...SOME DAY THIS WILL ALL BE YOURS!
YOU DON'T HAVE TO DO THAT, D-DAD! REALLY!
KEEP OUT!
IT'S BEEN A BIG DAY FOR BOTH OF US, SON!
WHY DON'T WE GET SOME REST AND WE'LL TALK IN THE MORNING?
OKAY, D-DAD!
SCAVAGE WILL SHOW YOU TO YOUR ROOM!
HE'S NOT HALF BAD ONCE YOU GET TO KNOW HIM!
8

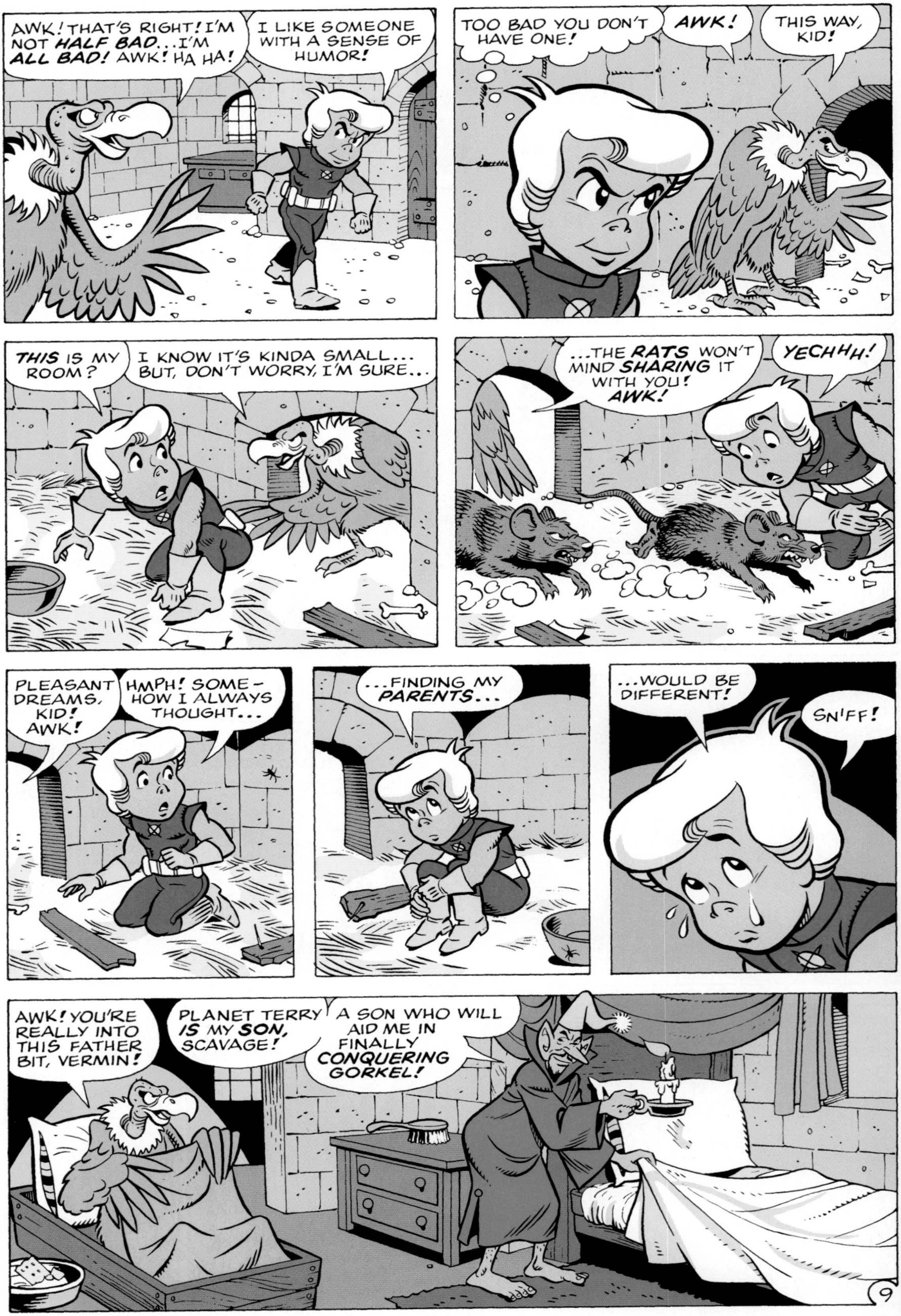
AWK! THAT'S RIGHT! I'M NOT **HALF BAD**...I'M **ALL BAD!** AWK! HA HA!
I LIKE SOMEONE WITH A SENSE OF HUMOR!
TOO BAD YOU DON'T HAVE ONE!
AWK!
THIS WAY, KID!
THIS IS MY ROOM?
I KNOW IT'S KINDA SMALL... BUT, DON'T WORRY, I'M SURE...
...THE **RATS** WON'T MIND **SHARING** IT WITH YOU! **AWK!**
YECHHH!
PLEASANT DREAMS, KID! AWK!
HMPH! SOME-HOW I ALWAYS THOUGHT...
...FINDING MY **PARENTS**...
...WOULD BE DIFFERENT!
SNIFF!
AWK! YOU'RE REALLY INTO THIS FATHER BIT, VERMIN!
PLANET TERRY **IS** MY **SON**, SCAVAGE!
A SON WHO WILL AID ME IN FINALLY **CONQUERING GORKEL!**
9

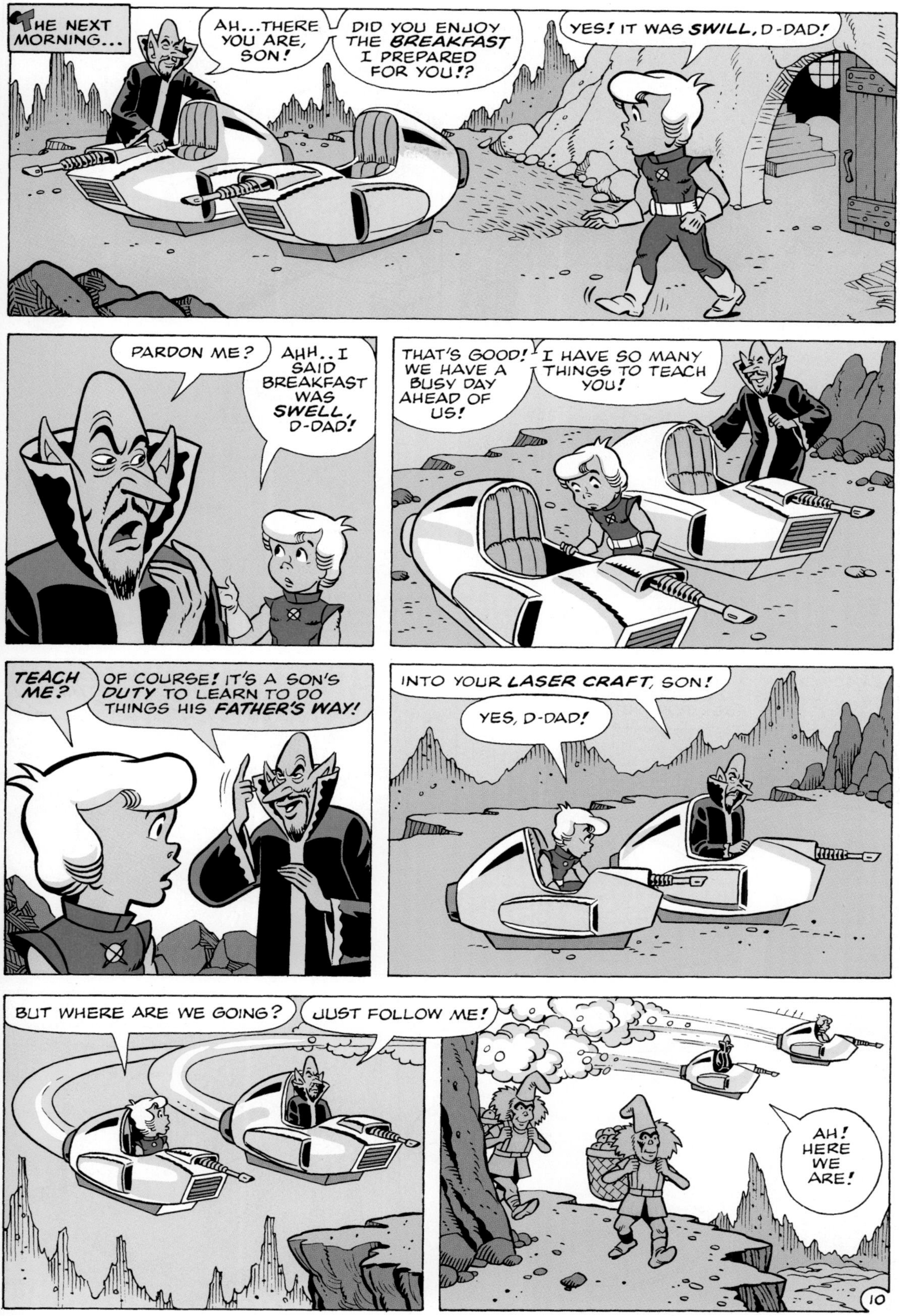
THE NEXT MORNING...
AH...THERE YOU ARE, SON!
DID YOU ENJOY THE BREAKFAST I PREPARED FOR YOU!?
YES! IT WAS SWILL, D-DAD!
PARDON ME?
AHH..I SAID BREAKFAST WAS SWELL, D-DAD!
THAT'S GOOD! WE HAVE A BUSY DAY AHEAD OF US!
I HAVE SO MANY THINGS TO TEACH YOU!
TEACH ME?
OF COURSE! IT'S A SON'S DUTY TO LEARN TO DO THINGS HIS FATHER'S WAY!
INTO YOUR LASER CRAFT, SON!
YES, D-DAD!
BUT WHERE ARE WE GOING?
JUST FOLLOW ME!
AH! HERE WE ARE!
10

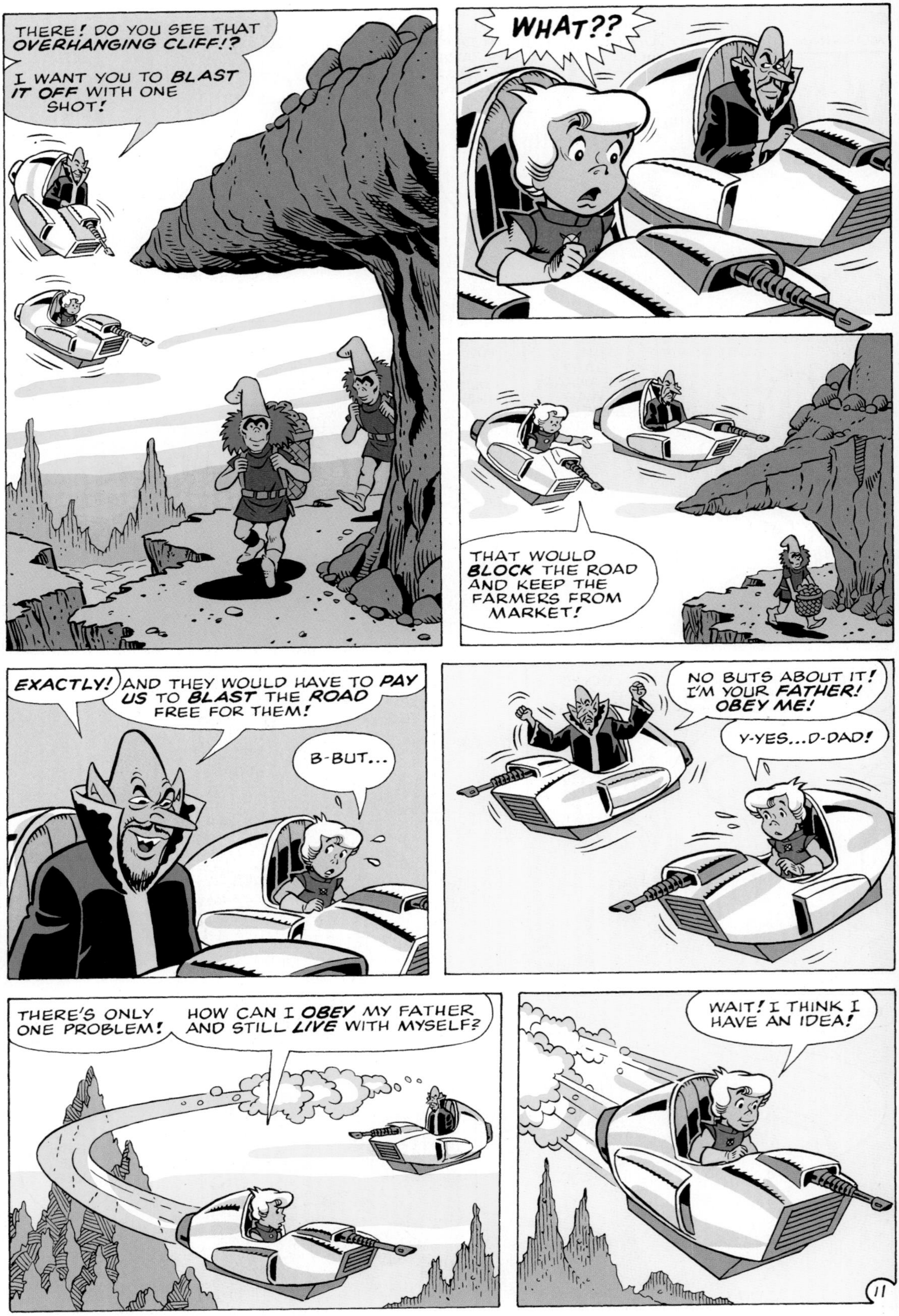
THERE! DO YOU SEE THAT OVERHANGING CLIFF!?
I WANT YOU TO BLAST IT OFF WITH ONE SHOT!
WHAT??
THAT WOULD BLOCK THE ROAD AND KEEP THE FARMERS FROM MARKET!
EXACTLY!
AND THEY WOULD HAVE TO PAY US TO BLAST THE ROAD FREE FOR THEM!
B-BUT...
NO BUTS ABOUT IT! I'M YOUR FATHER! OBEY ME!
Y-YES...D-DAD!
THERE'S ONLY ONE PROBLEM!
HOW CAN I OBEY MY FATHER AND STILL LIVE WITH MYSELF?
WAIT! I THINK I HAVE AN IDEA!
11

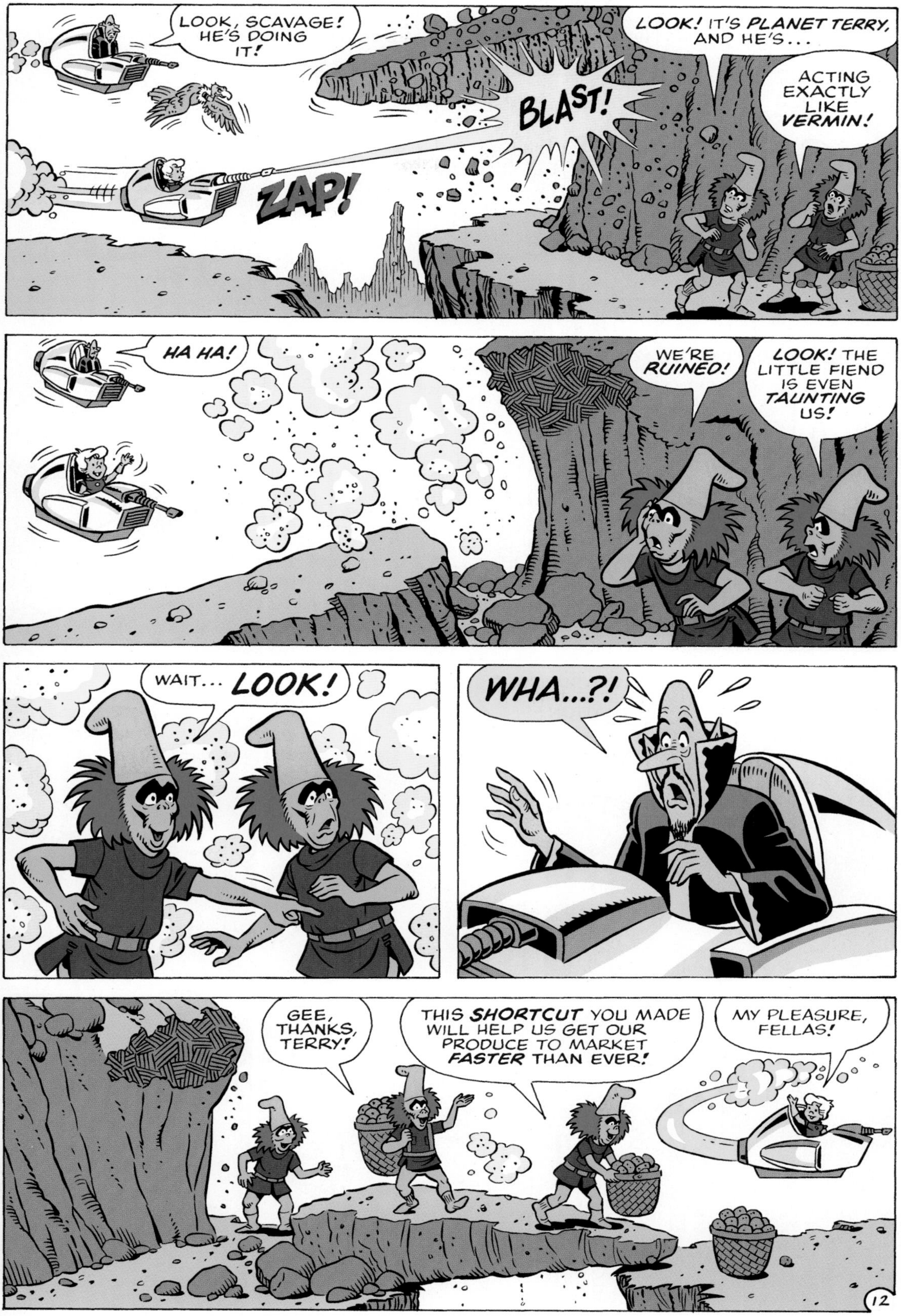
LOOK, SCAVAGE! HE'S DOING IT!
LOOK! IT'S PLANET TERRY, AND HE'S...
ACTING EXACTLY LIKE VERMIN!
BLAST!
ZAP!
HA HA!
WE'RE RUINED!
LOOK! THE LITTLE FIEND IS EVEN TAUNTING US!
WAIT... LOOK!
WHA...?!
GEE, THANKS, TERRY!
THIS SHORTCUT YOU MADE WILL HELP US GET OUR PRODUCE TO MARKET FASTER THAN EVER!
MY PLEASURE, FELLAS!
12

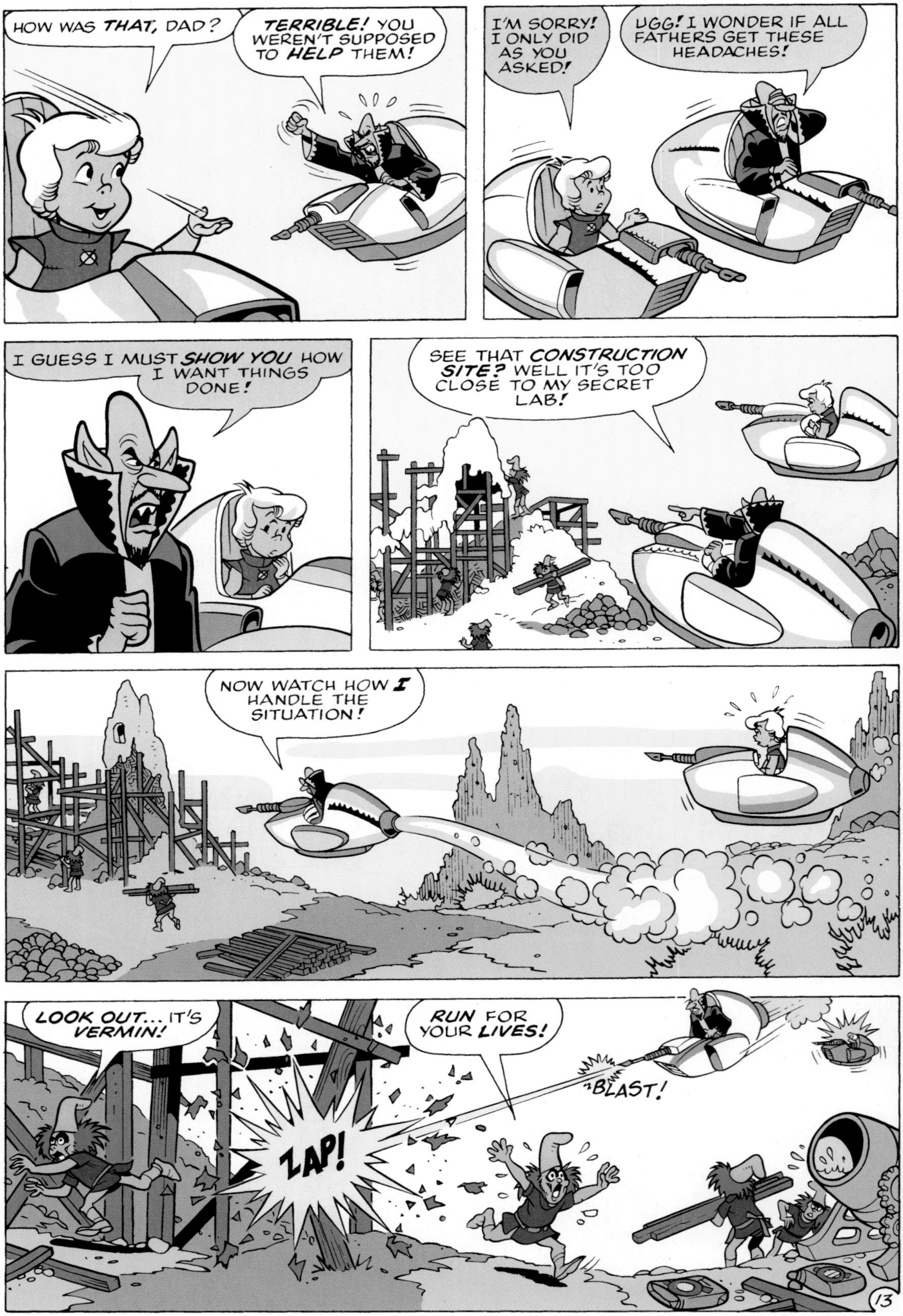
HOW WAS THAT, DAD?
TERRIBLE! YOU WEREN'T SUPPOSED TO HELP THEM!
I'M SORRY! I ONLY DID AS YOU ASKED!
UGG! I WONDER IF ALL FATHERS GET THESE HEADACHES!
I GUESS I MUST SHOW YOU HOW I WANT THINGS DONE!
SEE THAT CONSTRUCTION SITE? WELL IT'S TOO CLOSE TO MY SECRET LAB!
NOW WATCH HOW I HANDLE THE SITUATION!
LOOK OUT... IT'S VERMIN!
RUN FOR YOUR LIVES!
BLAST!
ZAP!
13

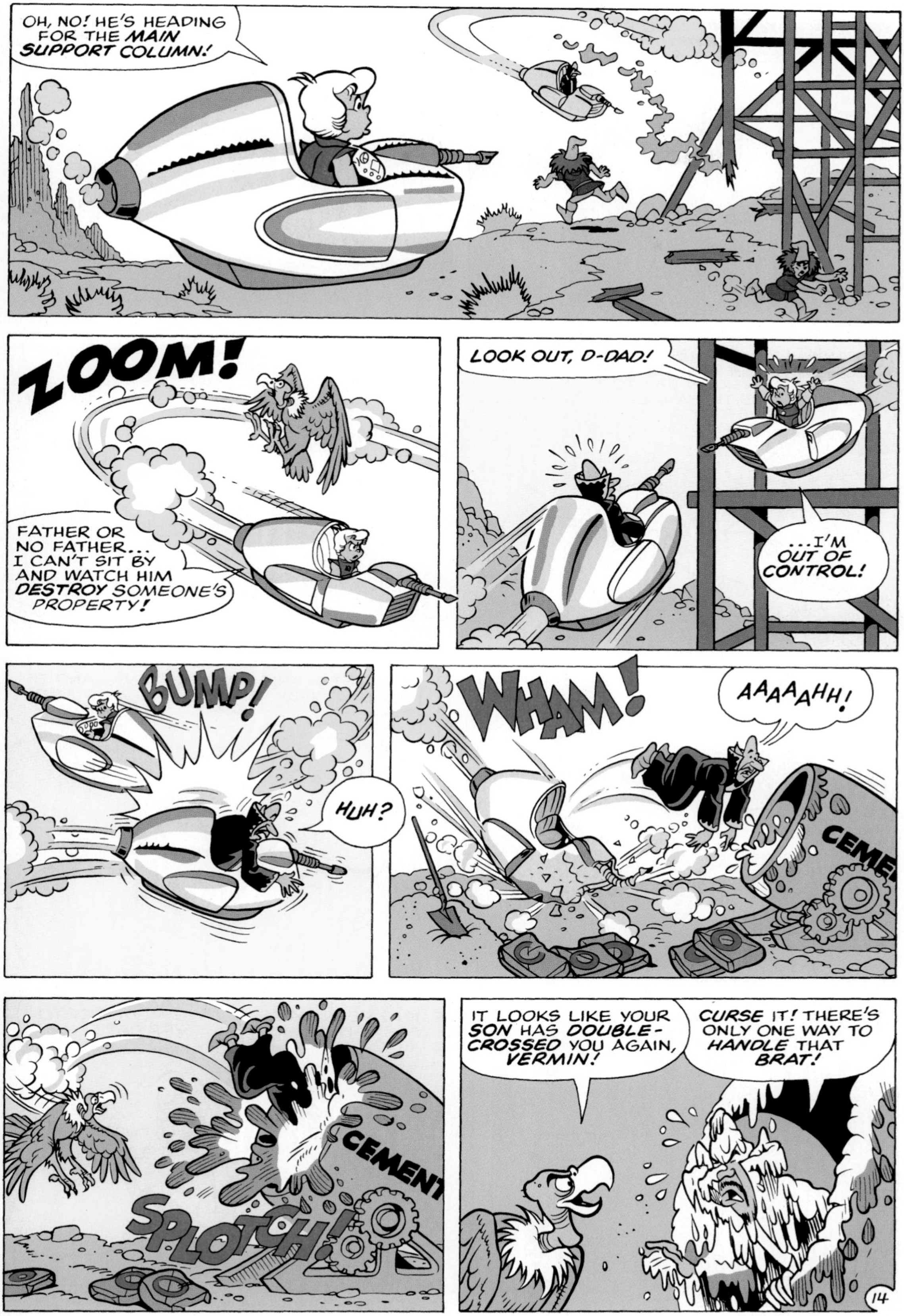
OH, NO! HE'S HEADING FOR THE MAIN SUPPORT COLUMN!
ZOOM!
FATHER OR NO FATHER... I CAN'T SIT BY AND WATCH HIM DESTROY SOMEONE'S PROPERTY!
LOOK OUT, D-DAD!
...I'M OUT OF CONTROL!
BUMP!
HUH?
WHAM!
AAAAAHH!
CEME
SPLOTCH!
CEMENT
IT LOOKS LIKE YOUR SON HAS DOUBLE-CROSSED YOU AGAIN, VERMIN!
CURSE IT! THERE'S ONLY ONE WAY TO HANDLE THAT BRAT!
14

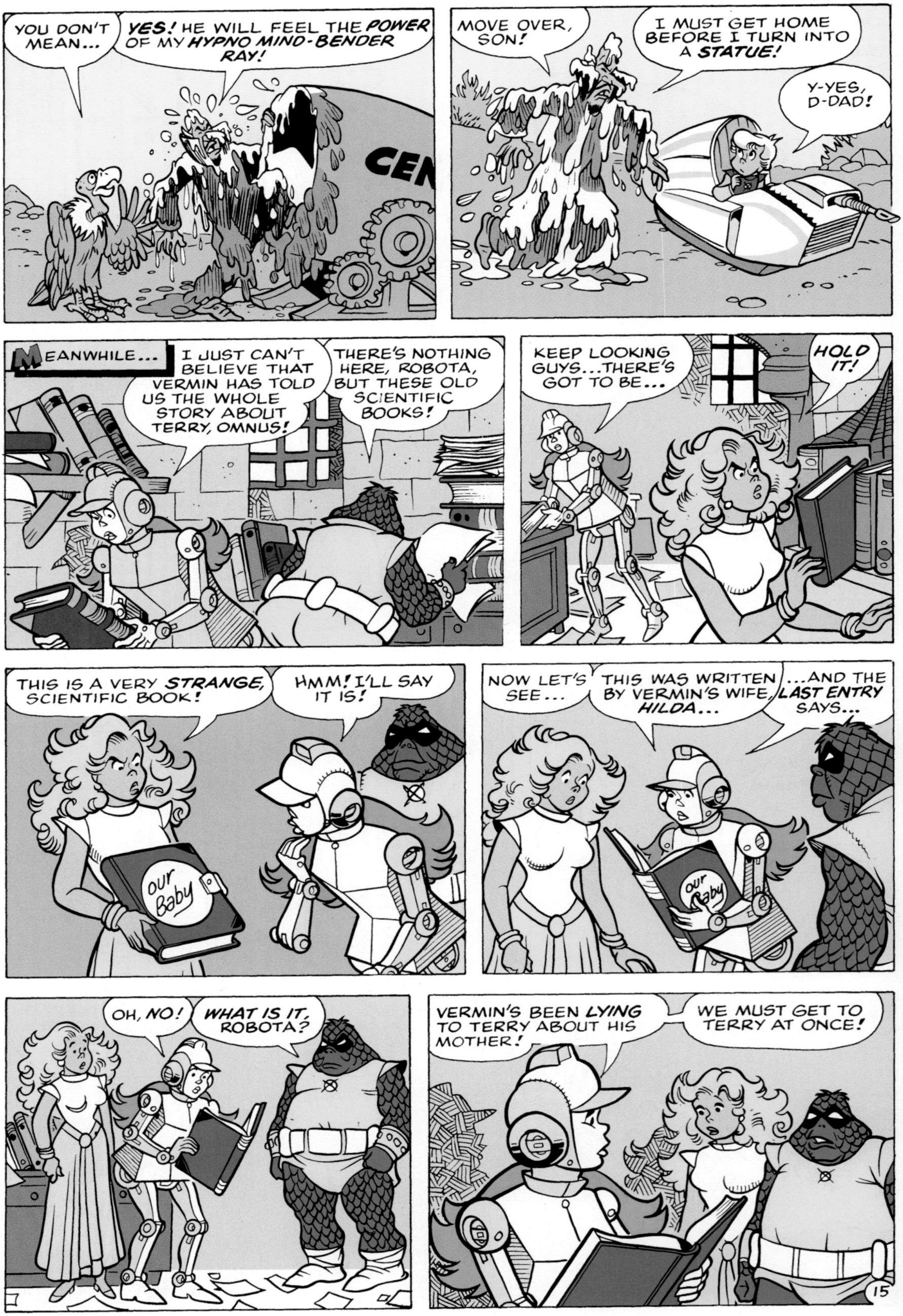

YOU DON'T MEAN...
YES! HE WILL FEEL THE POWER OF MY HYPNO MIND-BENDER RAY!
CEN
MOVE OVER, SON!
I MUST GET HOME BEFORE I TURN INTO A STATUE!
Y-YES, D-DAD!
MEANWHILE...
I JUST CAN'T BELIEVE THAT VERMIN HAS TOLD US THE WHOLE STORY ABOUT TERRY, OMNUS!
THERE'S NOTHING HERE, ROBOTA, BUT THESE OLD SCIENTIFIC BOOKS!
KEEP LOOKING GUYS...THERE'S GOT TO BE...
HOLD IT!
THIS IS A VERY STRANGE, SCIENTIFIC BOOK!
HMM! I'LL SAY IT IS!
Our Baby
NOW LET'S SEE...
THIS WAS WRITTEN BY VERMIN'S WIFE, HILDA...
...AND THE LAST ENTRY SAYS...
Our Baby
OH, NO!
WHAT IS IT, ROBOTA?
VERMIN'S BEEN LYING TO TERRY ABOUT HIS MOTHER!
WE MUST GET TO TERRY AT ONCE!
15

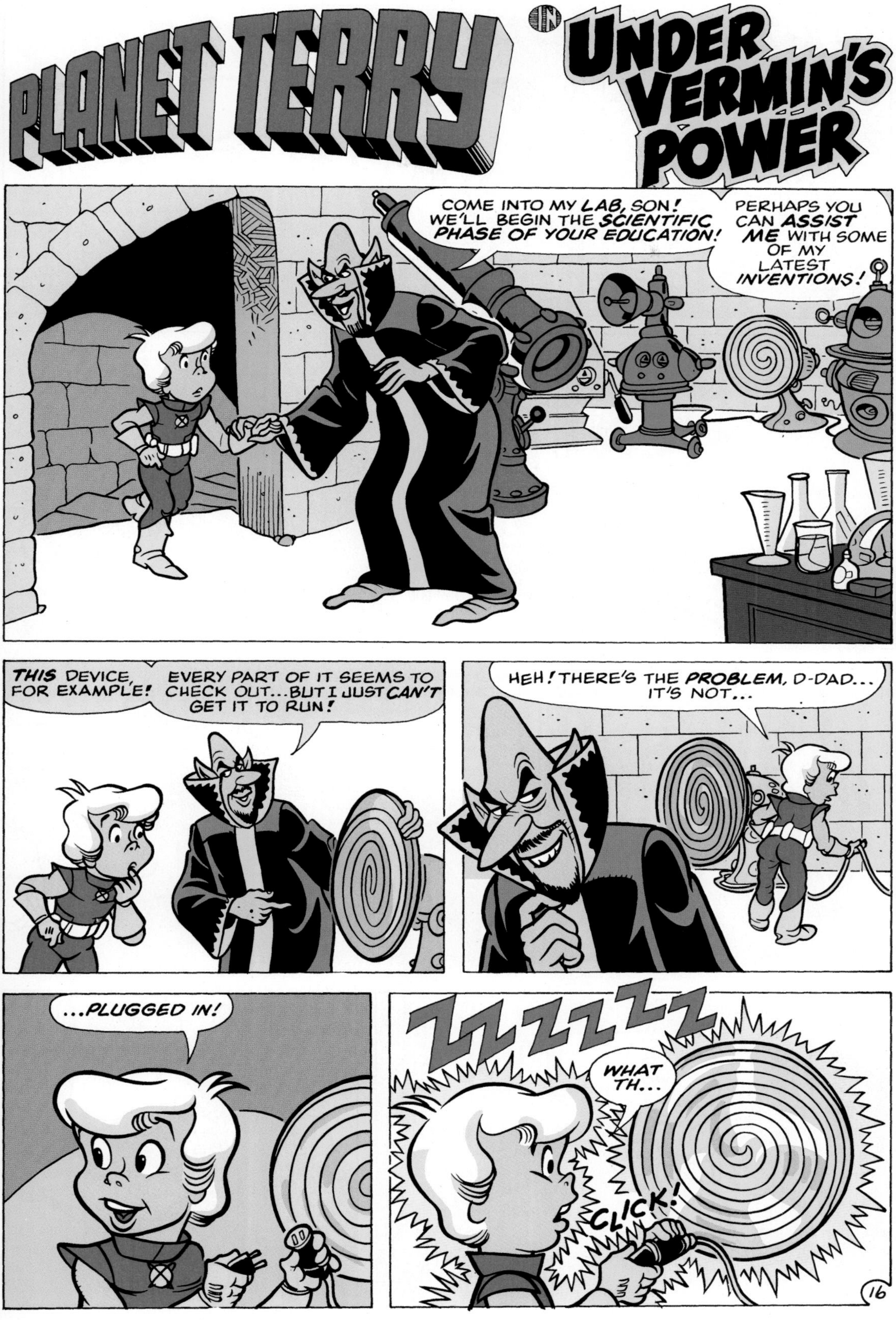
PLANET TERRY
IN
UNDER VERMIN'S POWER
COME INTO MY LAB, SON! WE'LL BEGIN THE SCIENTIFIC PHASE OF YOUR EDUCATION!
PERHAPS YOU CAN ASSIST ME WITH SOME OF MY LATEST INVENTIONS!
THIS DEVICE, FOR EXAMPLE!
EVERY PART OF IT SEEMS TO CHECK OUT...BUT I JUST CAN'T GET IT TO RUN!
HEH! THERE'S THE PROBLEM, D-DAD... IT'S NOT...
...PLUGGED IN!
ZZZZZZ
WHAT TH...
CLICK!
16

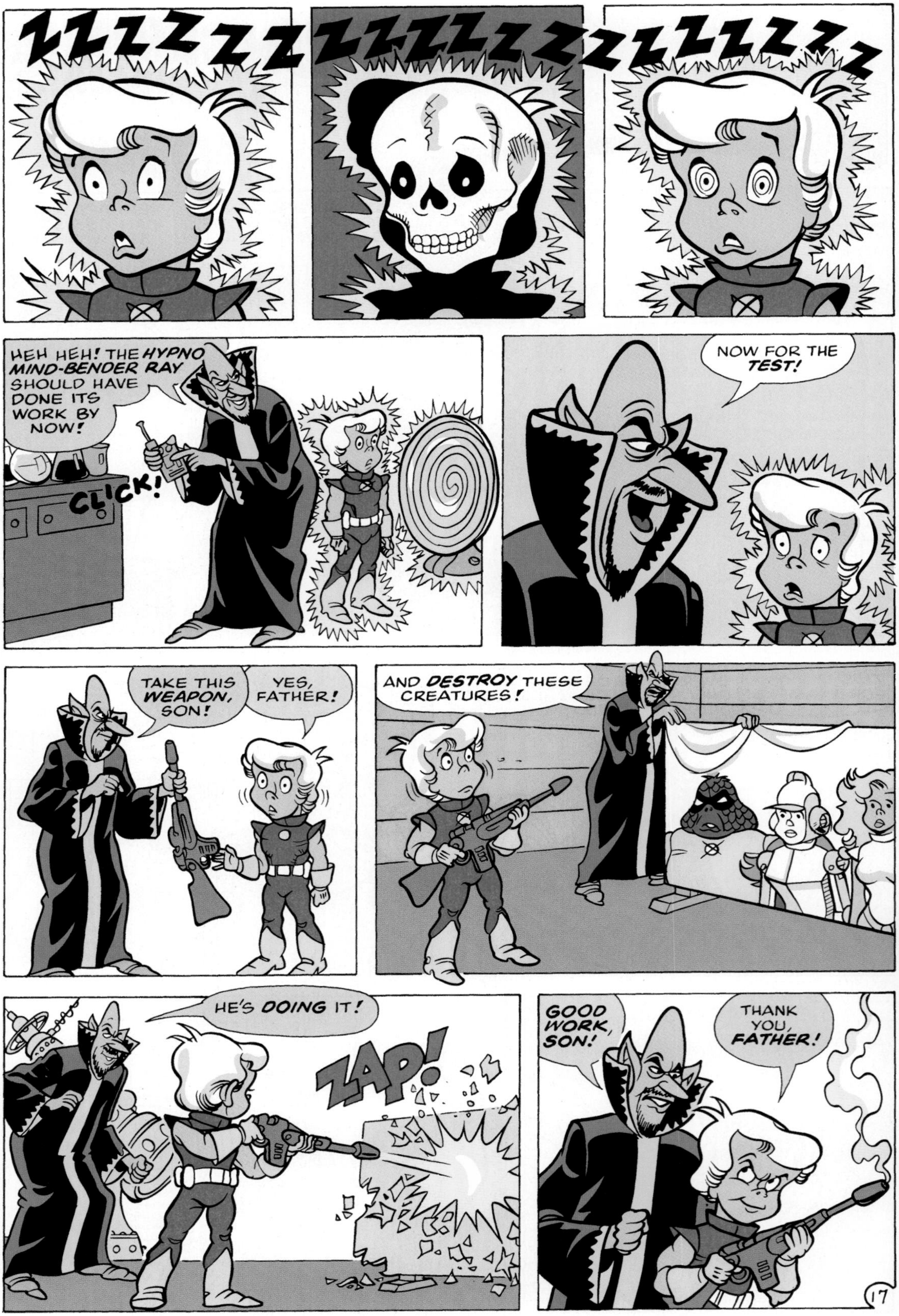
ZZZZZZZZZZZZZZZZZZZZZ
HEH HEH! THE HYPNO MIND-BENDER RAY SHOULD HAVE DONE ITS WORK BY NOW!
CLICK!
NOW FOR THE TEST!
TAKE THIS WEAPON, SON!
YES, FATHER!
AND DESTROY THESE CREATURES!
HE'S DOING IT!
ZAP!
GOOD WORK, SON!
THANK YOU, FATHER!
17

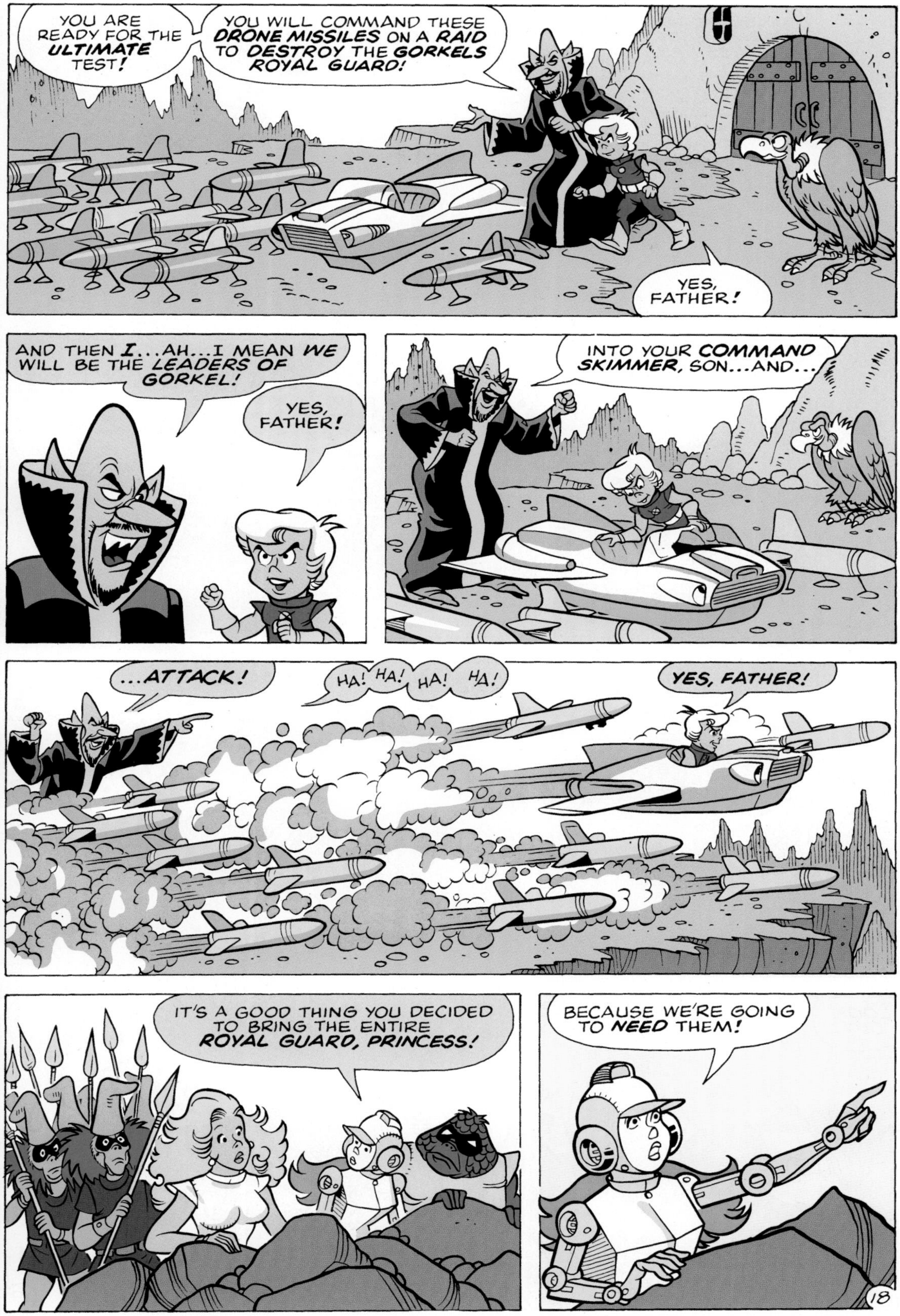
YOU ARE READY FOR THE ULTIMATE TEST!
YOU WILL COMMAND THESE DRONE MISSILES ON A RAID TO DESTROY THE GORKELS ROYAL GUARD!
YES, FATHER!
AND THEN I...AH...I MEAN WE WILL BE THE LEADERS OF GORKEL!
YES, FATHER!
INTO YOUR COMMAND SKIMMER, SON...AND...
...ATTACK!
HA! HA! HA! HA!
YES, FATHER!
IT'S A GOOD THING YOU DECIDED TO BRING THE ENTIRE ROYAL GUARD, PRINCESS!
BECAUSE WE'RE GOING TO NEED THEM!
18

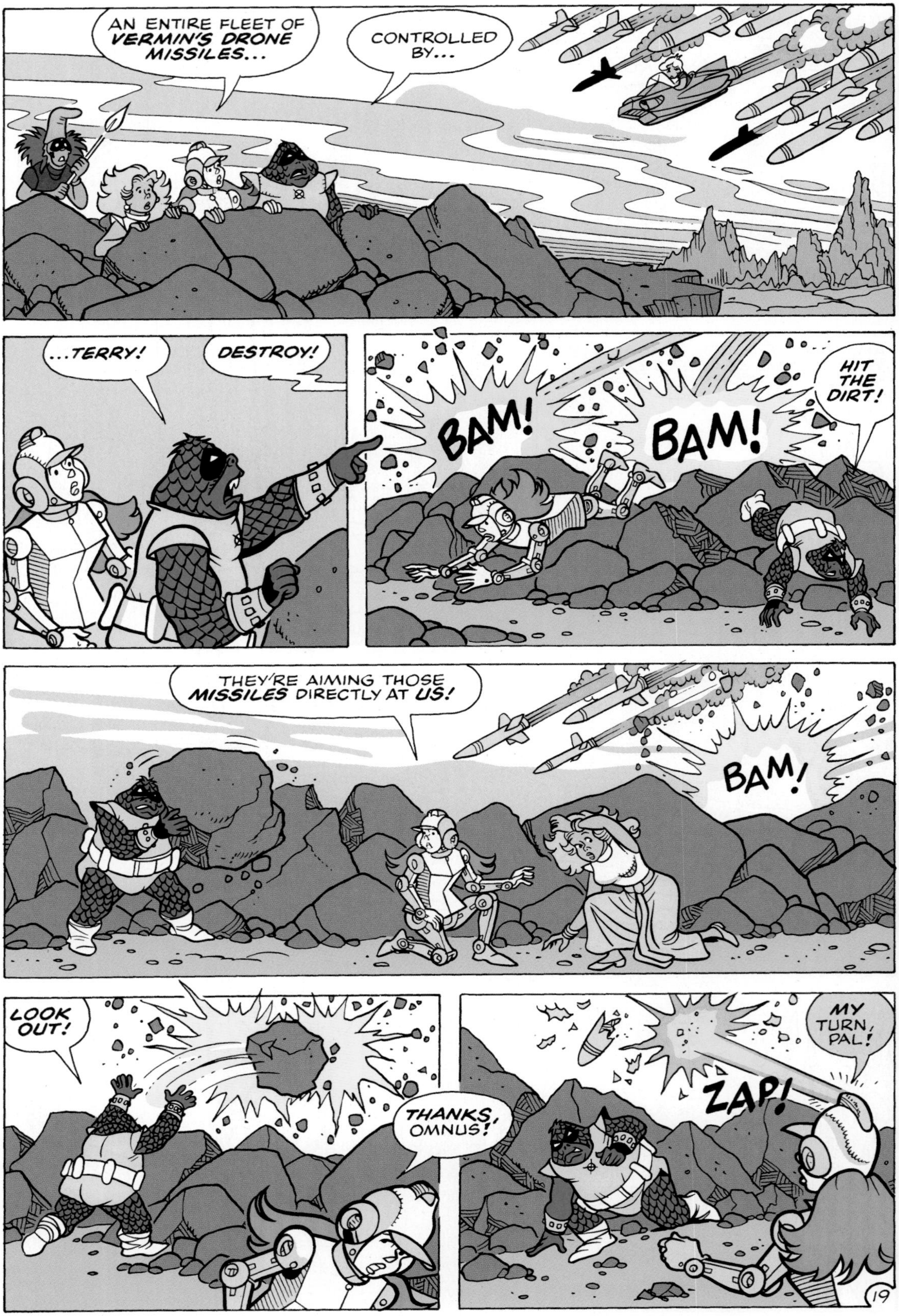

AN ENTIRE FLEET OF VERMIN'S DRONE MISSILES...
CONTROLLED BY...
...TERRY!
DESTROY!
BAM!
BAM!
HIT THE DIRT!
THEY'RE AIMING THOSE MISSILES DIRECTLY AT US!
BAM!
LOOK OUT!
THANKS, OMNUS!
MY TURN, PAL!
ZAP!
19

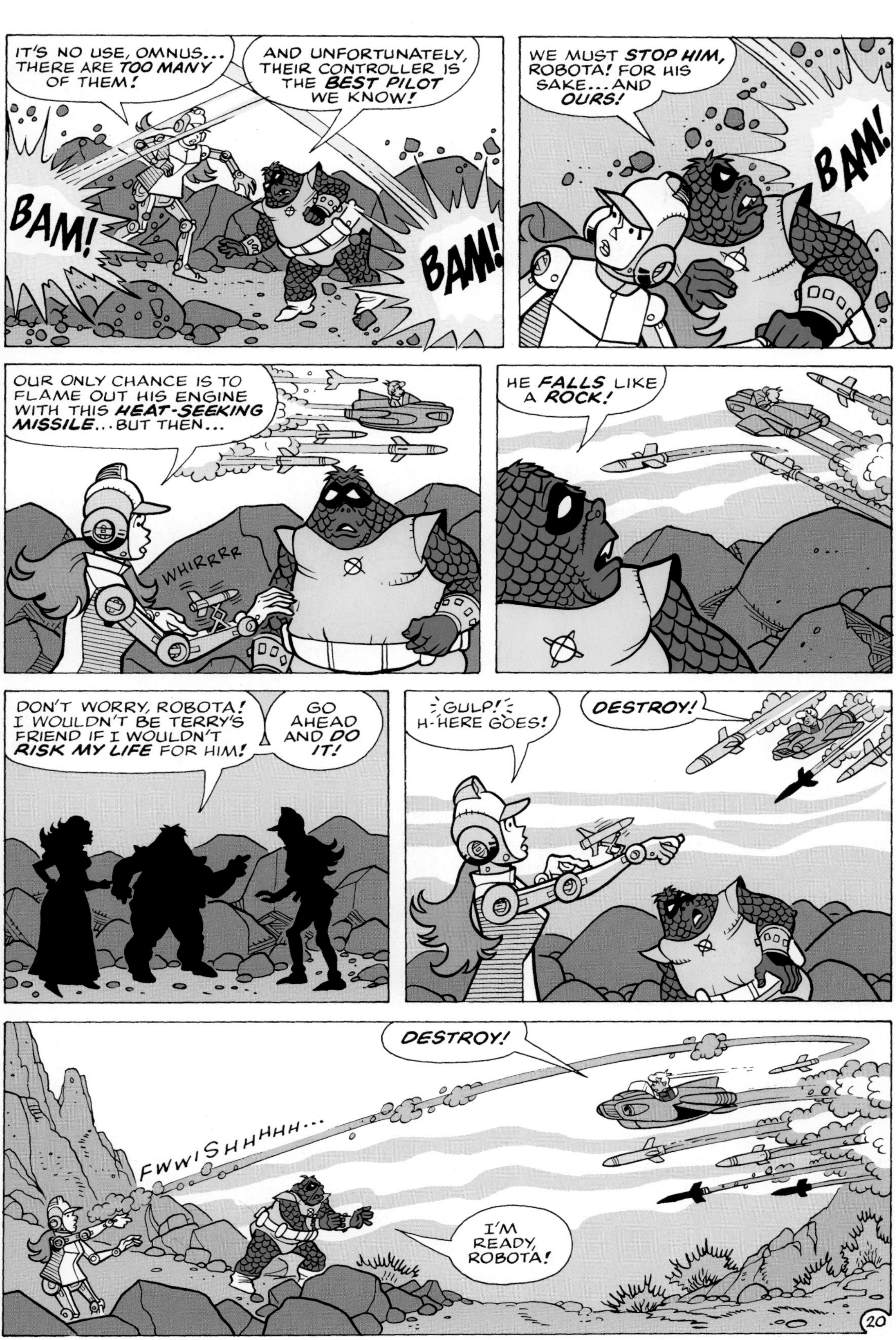
IT'S NO USE, OMNUS... THERE ARE TOO MANY OF THEM!
AND UNFORTUNATELY, THEIR CONTROLLER IS THE BEST PILOT WE KNOW!
BAM!
BAM!
WE MUST STOP HIM, ROBOTA! FOR HIS SAKE... AND OURS!
BAM!
OUR ONLY CHANCE IS TO FLAME OUT HIS ENGINE WITH THIS HEAT-SEEKING MISSILE... BUT THEN...
WHIRRRR
HE FALLS LIKE A ROCK!
...
DON'T WORRY, ROBOTA! I WOULDN'T BE TERRY'S FRIEND IF I WOULDN'T RISK MY LIFE FOR HIM!
GO AHEAD AND DO IT!
GULP! H-HERE GOES!
DESTROY!
DESTROY!
FWWISHHHHH...
I'M READY, ROBOTA!
20

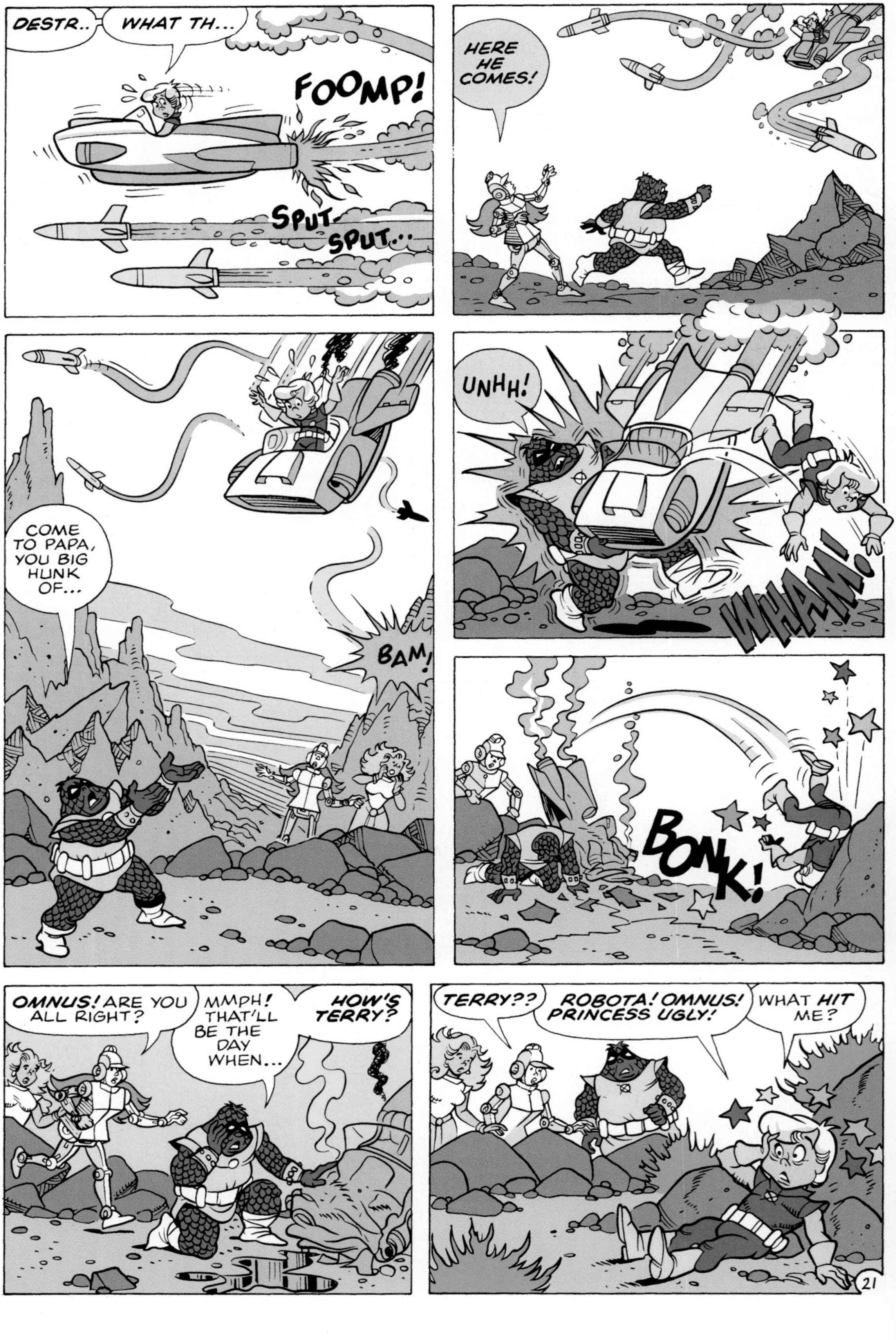
DESTR..
WHAT TH...
FOOMP!
SPUT-
SPUT...
HERE HE COMES!
COME TO PAPA, YOU BIG HUNK OF...
BAM!
UNHH!
WHAM!
BONK!
OMNUS! ARE YOU ALL RIGHT?
MMPH! THAT'LL BE THE DAY WHEN...
HOW'S TERRY?
TERRY??
ROBOTA! OMNUS! PRINCESS UGLY!
WHAT HIT ME?
21

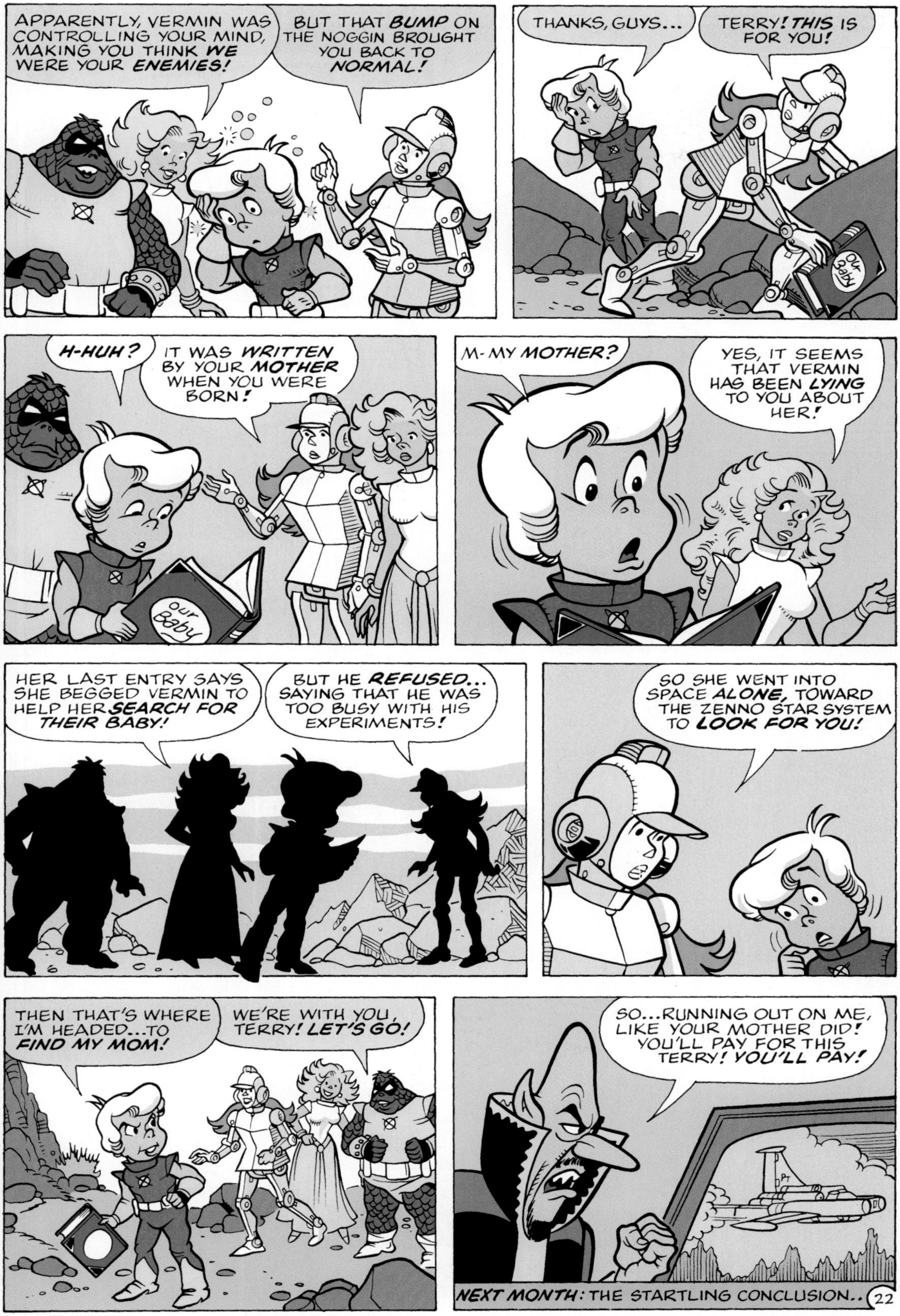
APPARENTLY, VERMIN WAS CONTROLLING YOUR MIND, MAKING YOU THINK WE WERE YOUR ENEMIES!
BUT THAT BUMP ON THE NOGGIN BROUGHT YOU BACK TO NORMAL!
THANKS, GUYS...
TERRY! THIS IS FOR YOU!
OUR BABY
H-HUH?
IT WAS WRITTEN BY YOUR MOTHER WHEN YOU WERE BORN!
OUR BABY
M-MY MOTHER?
YES, IT SEEMS THAT VERMIN HAS BEEN LYING TO YOU ABOUT HER!
HER LAST ENTRY SAYS SHE BEGGED VERMIN TO HELP HER SEARCH FOR THEIR BABY!
BUT HE REFUSED... SAYING THAT HE WAS TOO BUSY WITH HIS EXPERIMENTS!
SO SHE WENT INTO SPACE ALONE, TOWARD THE ZENNO STAR SYSTEM TO LOOK FOR YOU!
THEN THAT'S WHERE I'M HEADED...TO FIND MY MOM!
WE'RE WITH YOU, TERRY! LET'S GO!
SO...RUNNING OUT ON ME, LIKE YOUR MOTHER DID! YOU'LL PAY FOR THIS TERRY! YOU'LL PAY!
NEXT MONTH: THE STARTLING CONCLUSION..
22

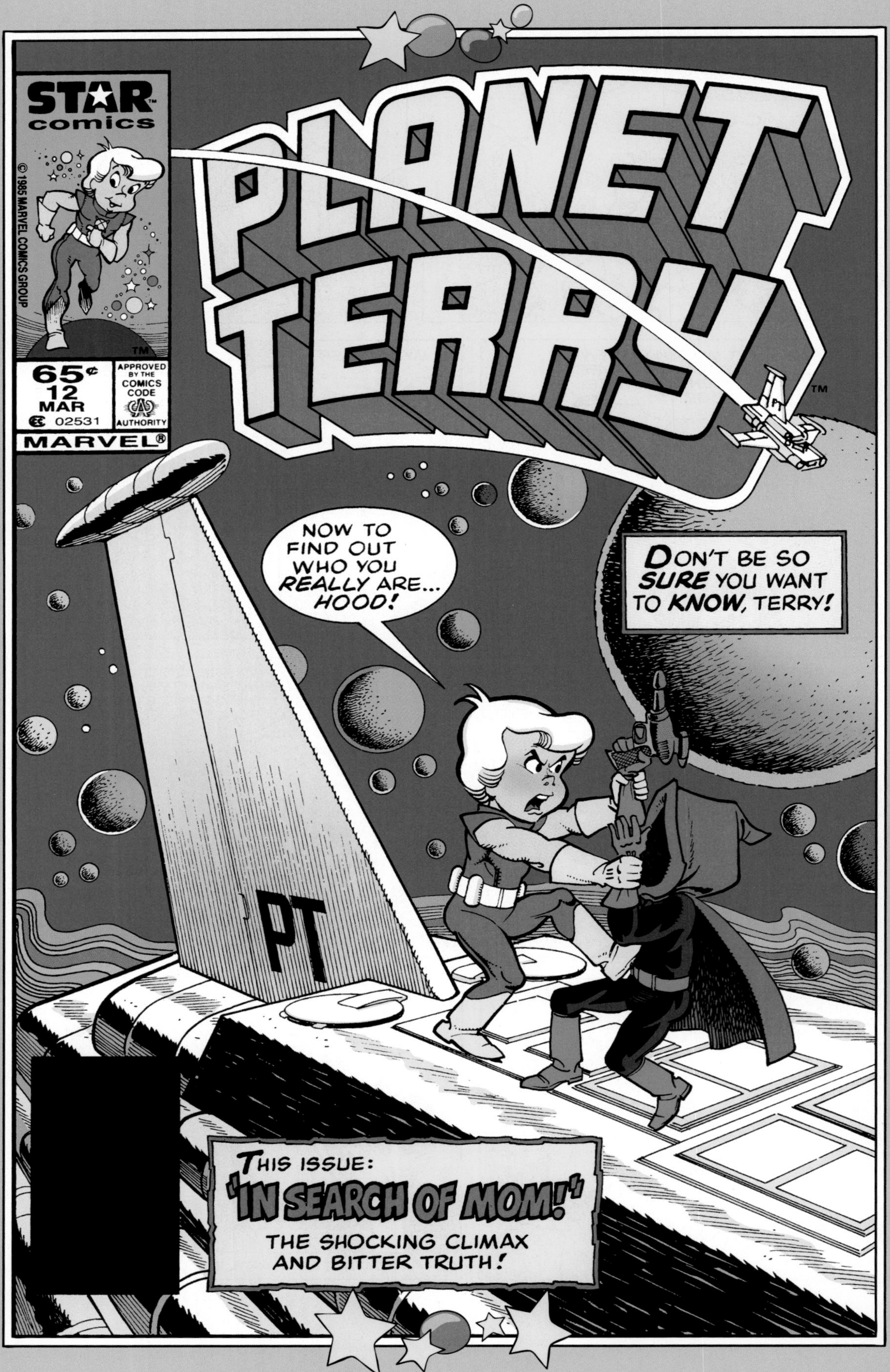
STAR comics
© 1985 MARVEL COMICS GROUP
PLANET TERRY
65¢ 12 MAR
02531
APPROVED BY THE COMICS CODE AUTHORITY
MARVEL®
NOW TO FIND OUT WHO YOU REALLY ARE... HOOD!
DON'T BE SO SURE YOU WANT TO KNOW, TERRY!
PT
THIS ISSUE:
"IN SEARCH OF MOM!"
THE SHOCKING CLIMAX AND BITTER TRUTH!

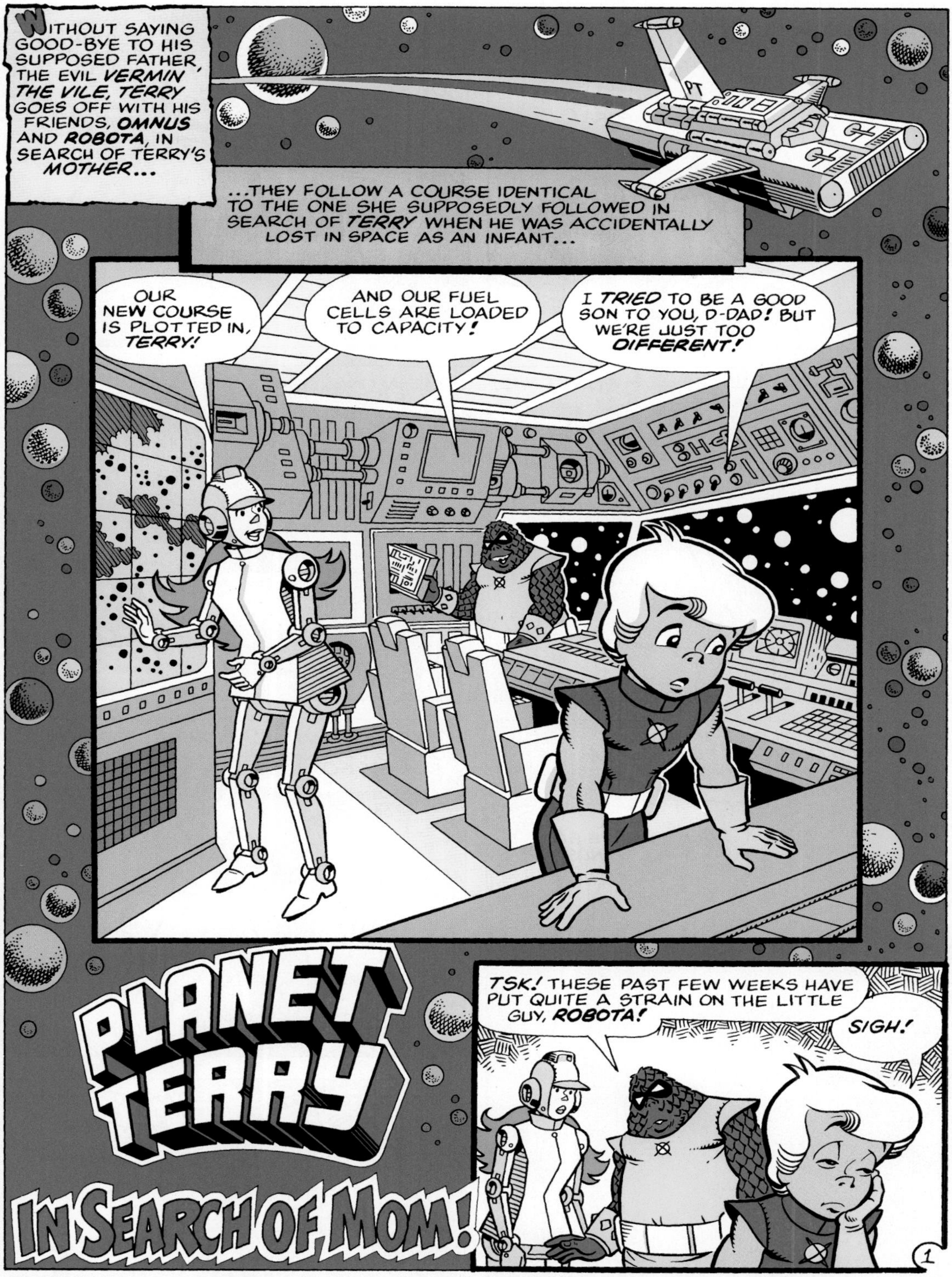
WITHOUT SAYING GOOD-BYE TO HIS SUPPOSED FATHER, THE EVIL VERMIN THE VILE, TERRY GOES OFF WITH HIS FRIENDS, OMNUS AND ROBOTA, IN SEARCH OF TERRY'S MOTHER...
...THEY FOLLOW A COURSE IDENTICAL TO THE ONE SHE SUPPOSEDLY FOLLOWED IN SEARCH OF TERRY WHEN HE WAS ACCIDENTALLY LOST IN SPACE AS AN INFANT...
OUR NEW COURSE IS PLOTTED IN, TERRY!
AND OUR FUEL CELLS ARE LOADED TO CAPACITY!
I TRIED TO BE A GOOD SON TO YOU, D-DAD! BUT WE'RE JUST TOO DIFFERENT!
PLANET TERRY
IN SEARCH OF MOM!
TSK! THESE PAST FEW WEEKS HAVE PUT QUITE A STRAIN ON THE LITTLE GUY, ROBOTA!
SIGH!
1

DAVE MANAK-- WRITER • WARREN KREMER-- PENCILER • D'AGOSTINO-ROETTCHER-- INKERS • GRACE KREMER-- LETTERER
GEORGE ROUSSOS-- COLORIST • SID JACOBSON-- EDITOR • TOM DEFALCO-- EXECUTIVE EDITOR • JIM SHOOTER-- ED. IN CHIEF

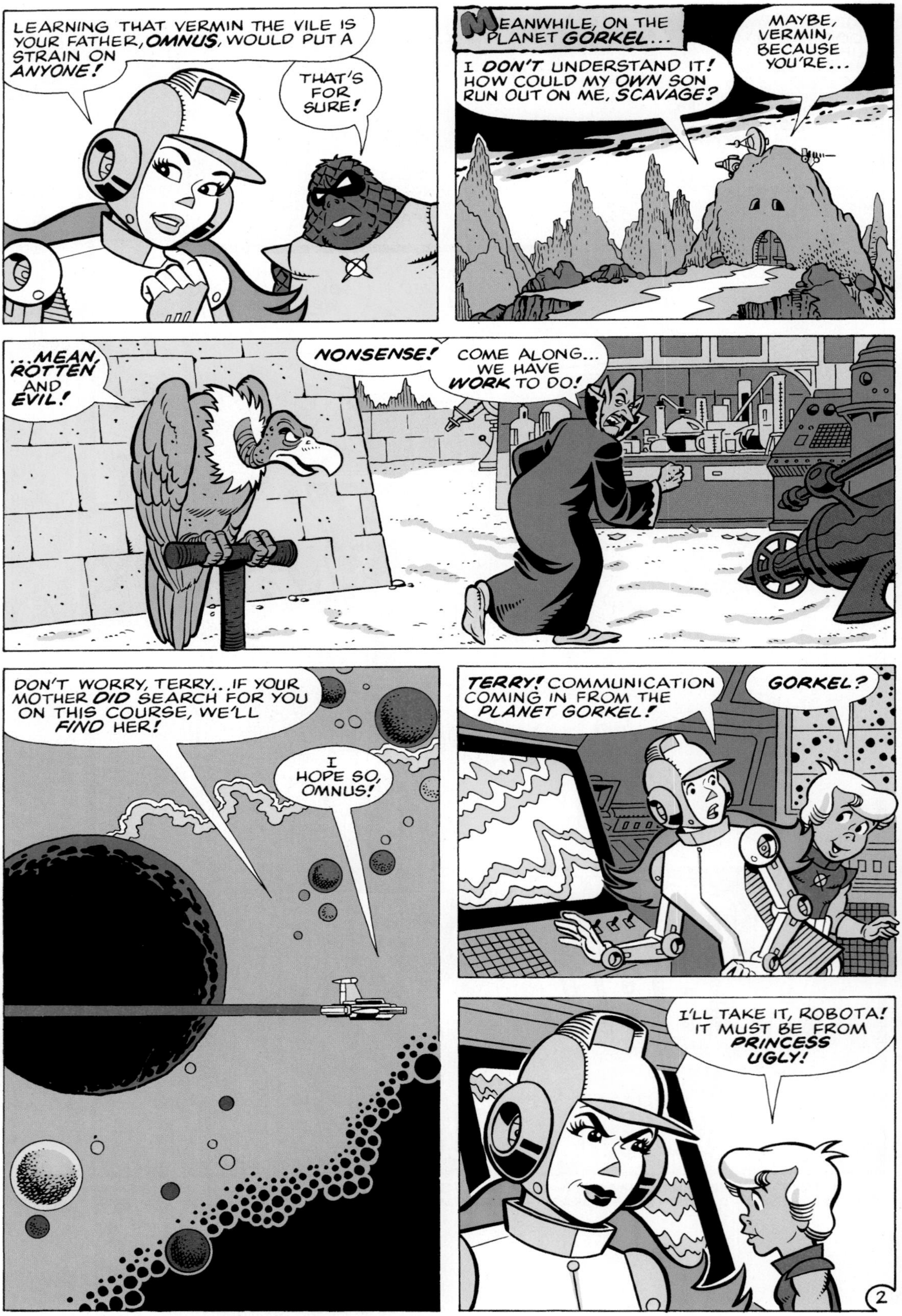

LEARNING THAT VERMIN THE VILE IS YOUR FATHER, OMNUS, WOULD PUT A STRAIN ON ANYONE!
THAT'S FOR SURE!
MEANWHILE, ON THE PLANET GORKEL...
I DON'T UNDERSTAND IT! HOW COULD MY OWN SON RUN OUT ON ME, SCAVAGE?
MAYBE, VERMIN, BECAUSE YOU'RE...
...MEAN, ROTTEN AND EVIL!
NONSENSE!
COME ALONG... WE HAVE WORK TO DO!
DON'T WORRY, TERRY... IF YOUR MOTHER DID SEARCH FOR YOU ON THIS COURSE, WE'LL FIND HER!
I HOPE SO, OMNUS!
TERRY! COMMUNICATION COMING IN FROM THE PLANET GORKEL!
GORKEL?
I'LL TAKE IT, ROBOTA! IT MUST BE FROM PRINCESS UGLY!
2

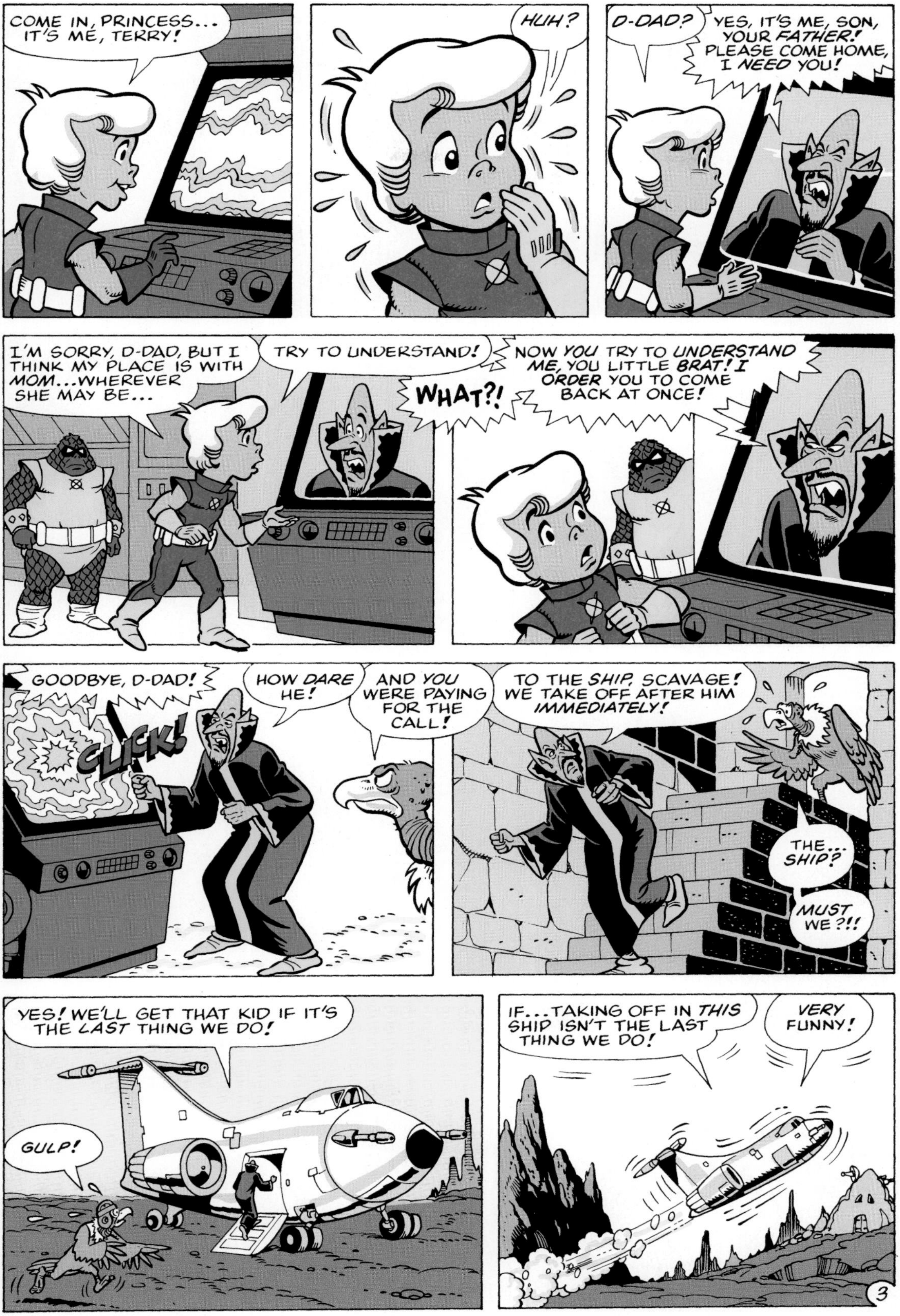
COME IN, PRINCESS... IT'S ME, TERRY!
HUH?
D-DAD?
YES, IT'S ME, SON, YOUR FATHER! PLEASE COME HOME, I NEED YOU!
I'M SORRY, D-DAD, BUT I THINK MY PLACE IS WITH MOM...WHEREVER SHE MAY BE...
TRY TO UNDERSTAND!
WHAT?!
NOW YOU TRY TO UNDERSTAND ME, YOU LITTLE BRAT! I ORDER YOU TO COME BACK AT ONCE!
GOODBYE, D-DAD!
CLICK!
HOW DARE HE!
AND YOU WERE PAYING FOR THE CALL!
TO THE SHIP, SCAVAGE! WE TAKE OFF AFTER HIM IMMEDIATELY!
THE... SHIP?
MUST WE?!!
YES! WE'LL GET THAT KID IF IT'S THE LAST THING WE DO!
GULP!
IF...TAKING OFF IN THIS SHIP ISN'T THE LAST THING WE DO!
VERY FUNNY!
3

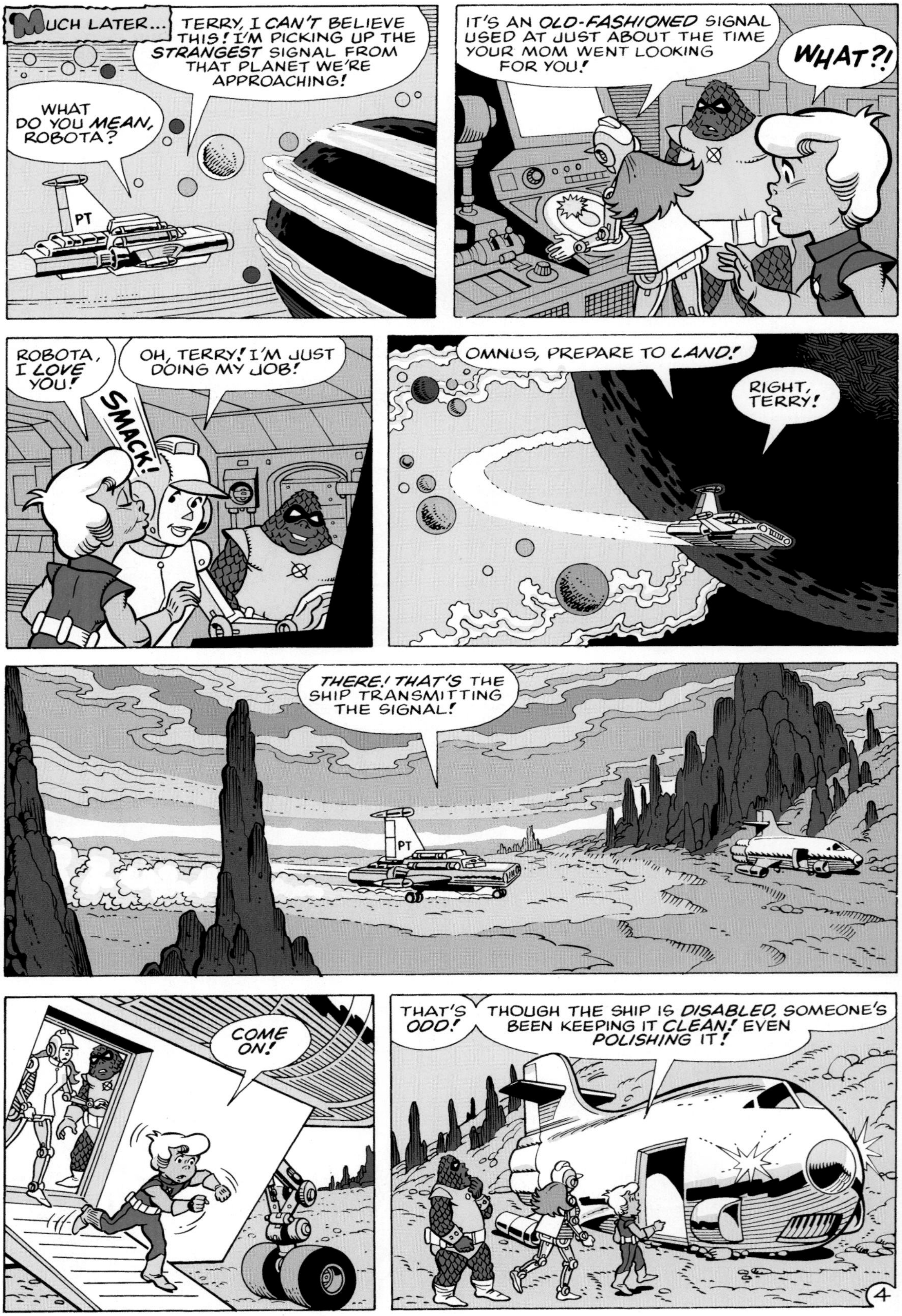
MUCH LATER...
TERRY, I CAN'T BELIEVE THIS! I'M PICKING UP THE STRANGEST SIGNAL FROM THAT PLANET WE'RE APPROACHING!
WHAT DO YOU MEAN, ROBOTA?
PT
IT'S AN OLD-FASHIONED SIGNAL USED AT JUST ABOUT THE TIME YOUR MOM WENT LOOKING FOR YOU!
WHAT?!
ROBOTA, I LOVE YOU!
OH, TERRY! I'M JUST DOING MY JOB!
SMACK!
OMNUS, PREPARE TO LAND!
RIGHT, TERRY!
THERE! THAT'S THE SHIP TRANSMITTING THE SIGNAL!
PT
COME ON!
THAT'S ODD!
THOUGH THE SHIP IS DISABLED, SOMEONE'S BEEN KEEPING IT CLEAN! EVEN POLISHING IT!
4

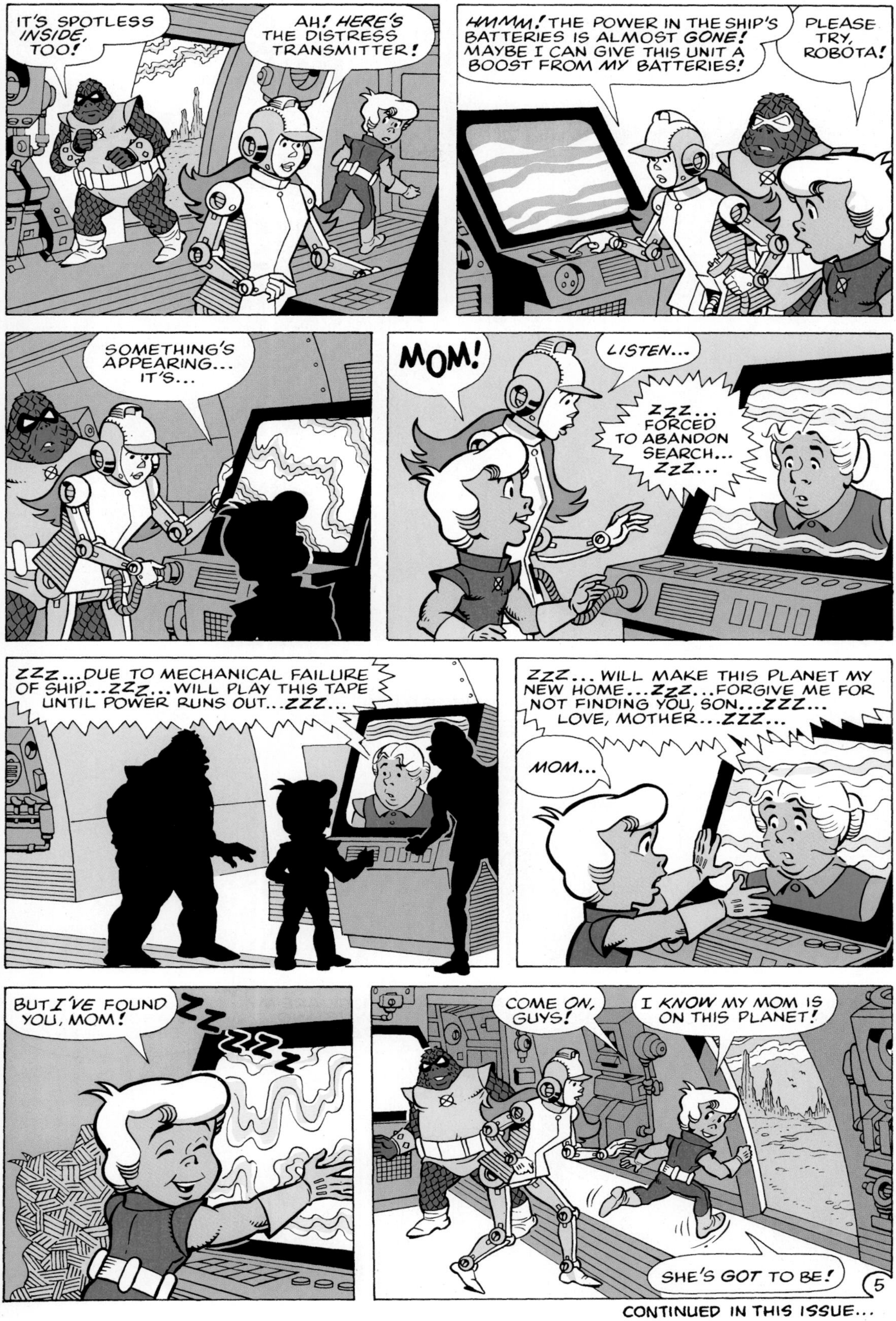

IT'S SPOTLESS INSIDE, TOO!
AH! HERE'S THE DISTRESS TRANSMITTER!
HMMM! THE POWER IN THE SHIP'S BATTERIES IS ALMOST GONE! MAYBE I CAN GIVE THIS UNIT A BOOST FROM MY BATTERIES!
PLEASE TRY, ROBOTA!
SOMETHING'S APPEARING... IT'S...
MOM!
LISTEN...
ZZZ... FORCED TO ABANDON SEARCH... ZZZ...
ZZZ...DUE TO MECHANICAL FAILURE OF SHIP...ZZZ...WILL PLAY THIS TAPE UNTIL POWER RUNS OUT...ZZZ...
ZZZ... WILL MAKE THIS PLANET MY NEW HOME...ZZZ...FORGIVE ME FOR NOT FINDING YOU, SON...ZZZ... LOVE, MOTHER...ZZZ...
MOM...
BUT I'VE FOUND YOU, MOM!
ZZZZZZ
COME ON, GUYS!
I KNOW MY MOM IS ON THIS PLANET!
SHE'S GOT TO BE!
5

CONTINUED IN THIS ISSUE...

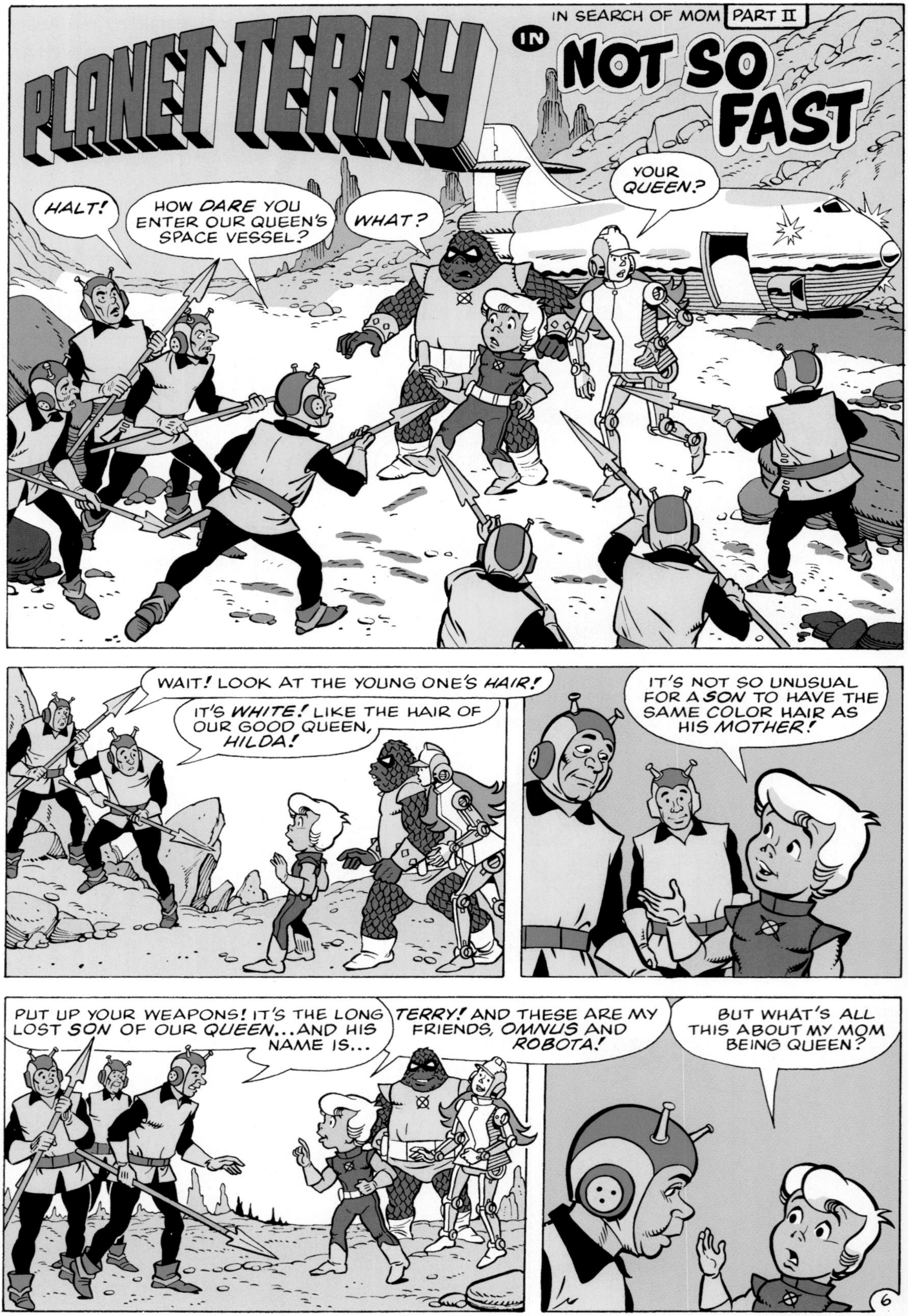

PLANET TERRY
IN
IN SEARCH OF MOM PART II
NOT SO FAST
HALT!
HOW DARE YOU ENTER OUR QUEEN'S SPACE VESSEL?
WHAT?
YOUR QUEEN?
WAIT! LOOK AT THE YOUNG ONE'S HAIR!
IT'S WHITE! LIKE THE HAIR OF OUR GOOD QUEEN, HILDA!
IT'S NOT SO UNUSUAL FOR A SON TO HAVE THE SAME COLOR HAIR AS HIS MOTHER!
PUT UP YOUR WEAPONS! IT'S THE LONG LOST SON OF OUR QUEEN...AND HIS NAME IS...
TERRY! AND THESE ARE MY FRIENDS, OMNUS AND ROBOTA!
BUT WHAT'S ALL THIS ABOUT MY MOM BEING QUEEN?
6

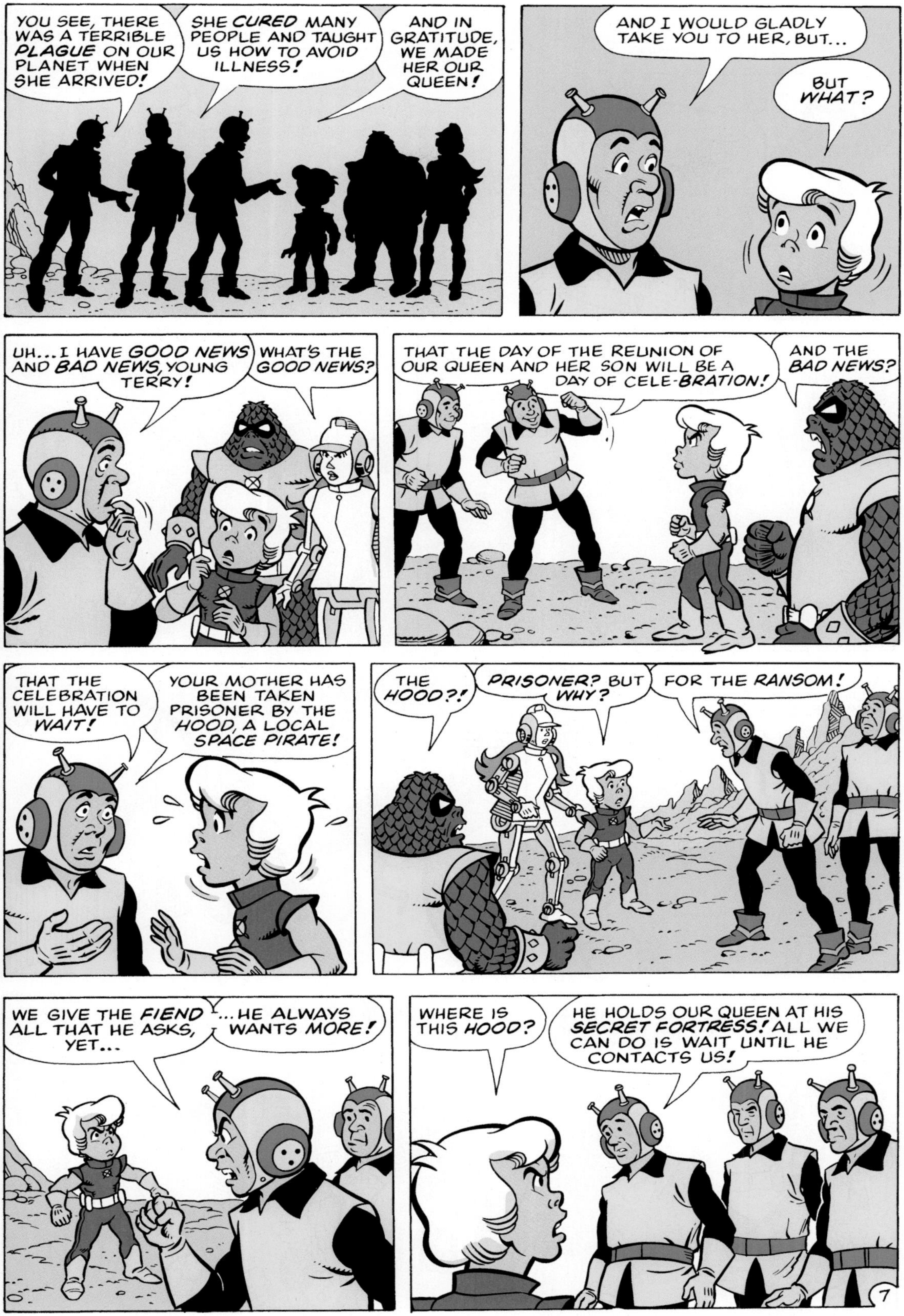
YOU SEE, THERE WAS A TERRIBLE PLAGUE ON OUR PLANET WHEN SHE ARRIVED!
SHE CURED MANY PEOPLE AND TAUGHT US HOW TO AVOID ILLNESS!
AND IN GRATITUDE, WE MADE HER OUR QUEEN!
AND I WOULD GLADLY TAKE YOU TO HER, BUT...
BUT WHAT?
UH... I HAVE GOOD NEWS AND BAD NEWS, YOUNG TERRY!
WHAT'S THE GOOD NEWS?
THAT THE DAY OF THE REUNION OF OUR QUEEN AND HER SON WILL BE A DAY OF CELE-BRATION!
AND THE BAD NEWS?
THAT THE CELEBRATION WILL HAVE TO WAIT!
YOUR MOTHER HAS BEEN TAKEN PRISONER BY THE HOOD, A LOCAL SPACE PIRATE!
THE HOOD?!
PRISONER? BUT WHY?
FOR THE RANSOM!
WE GIVE THE FIEND ALL THAT HE ASKS, YET...
...HE ALWAYS WANTS MORE!
WHERE IS THIS HOOD?
HE HOLDS OUR QUEEN AT HIS SECRET FORTRESS! ALL WE CAN DO IS WAIT UNTIL HE CONTACTS US!
7

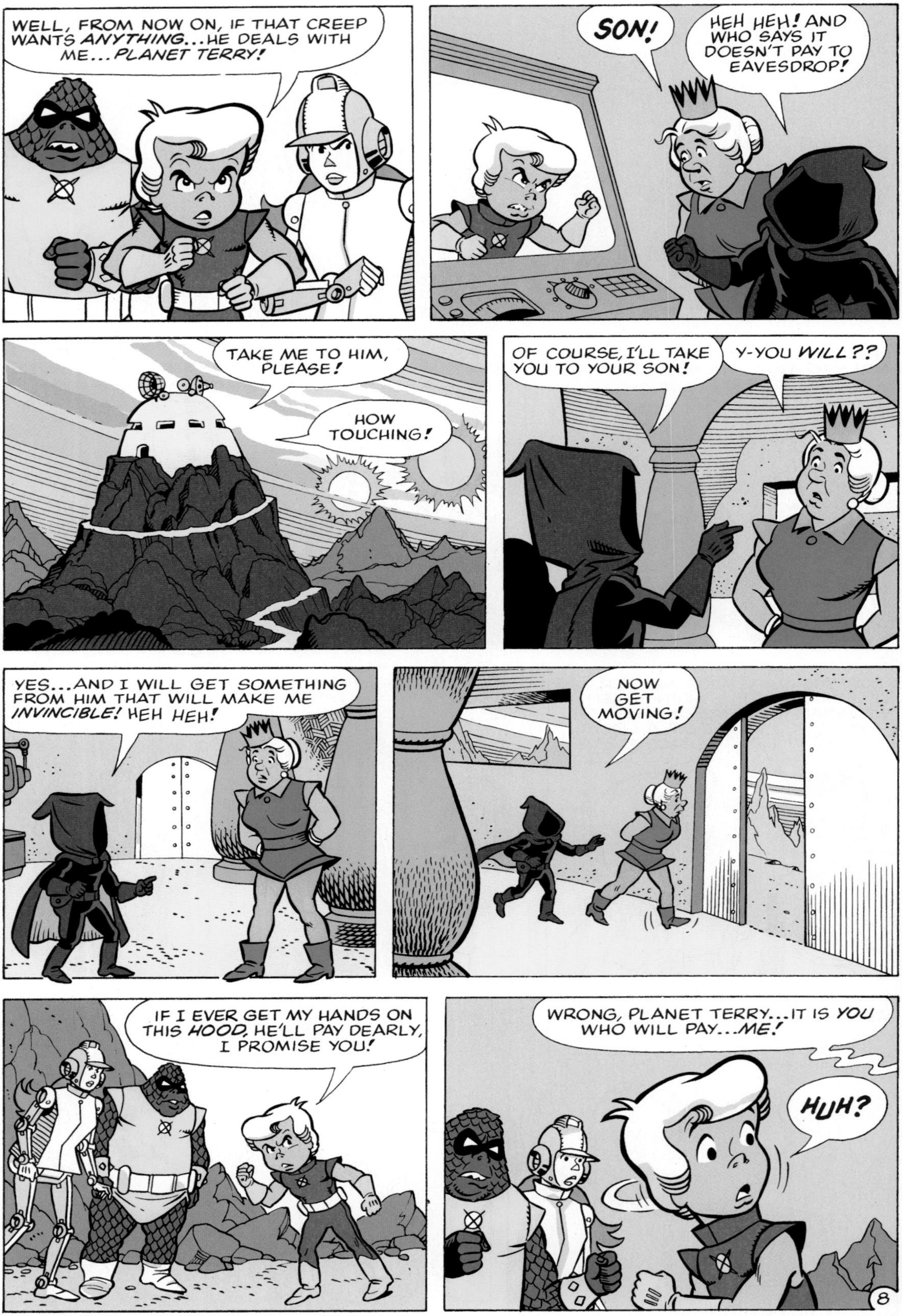
WELL, FROM NOW ON, IF THAT CREEP WANTS *ANYTHING*... HE DEALS WITH ME... *PLANET TERRY!*
SON!
HEH HEH! AND WHO SAYS IT DOESN'T PAY TO EAVESDROP!
TAKE ME TO HIM, PLEASE!
HOW TOUCHING!
OF COURSE, I'LL TAKE YOU TO YOUR SON!
Y-YOU *WILL??*
YES... AND I WILL GET SOMETHING FROM HIM THAT WILL MAKE ME *INVINCIBLE!* HEH HEH!
NOW GET MOVING!
IF I EVER GET MY HANDS ON THIS *HOOD*, HE'LL PAY DEARLY, I PROMISE YOU!
WRONG, PLANET TERRY... IT IS *YOU* WHO WILL PAY... *ME!*
HUH?
8

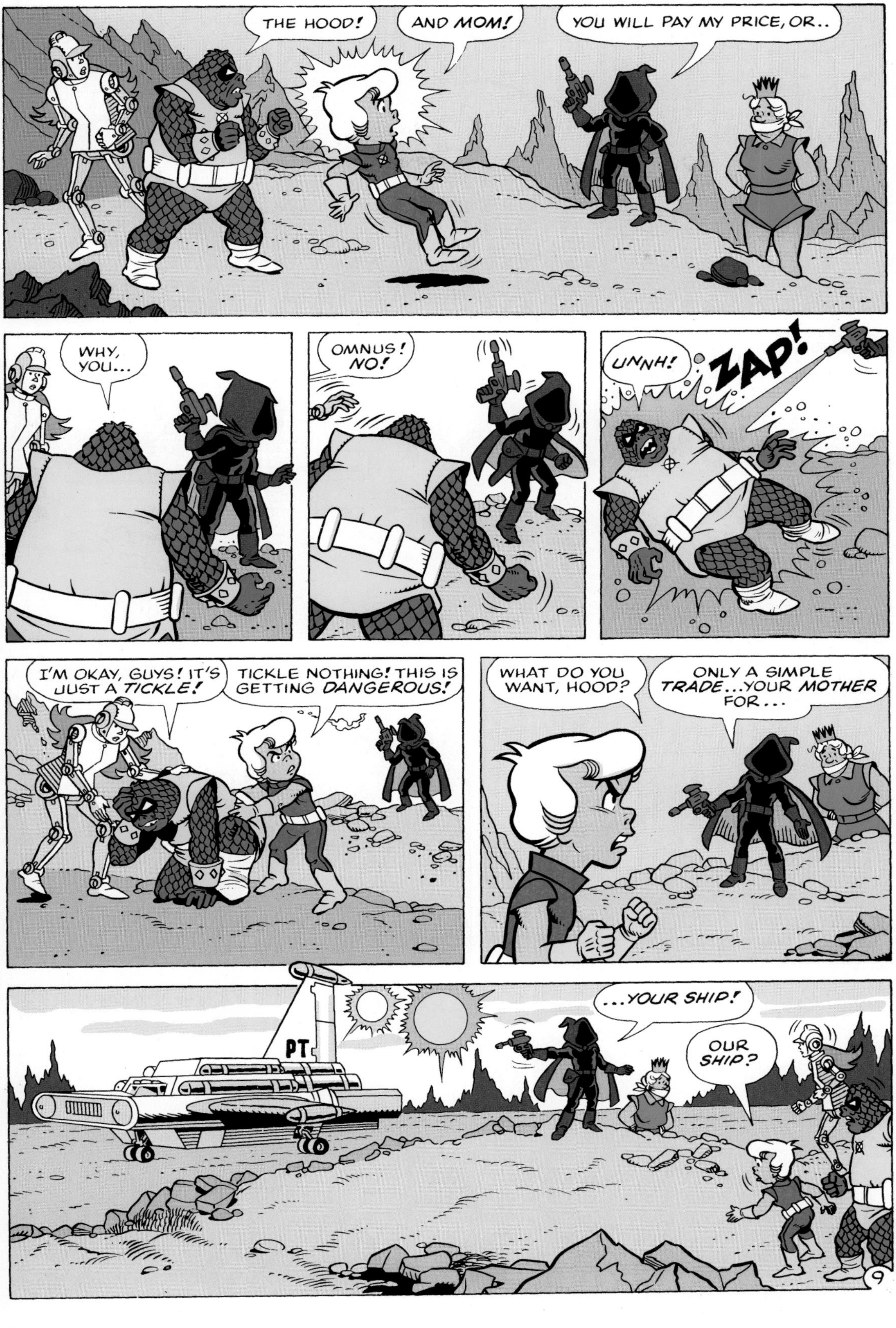
THE HOOD!
AND MOM!
YOU WILL PAY MY PRICE, OR..
WHY, YOU...
OMNUS! NO!
UNNH!
ZAP!
I'M OKAY, GUYS! IT'S JUST A TICKLE!
TICKLE NOTHING! THIS IS GETTING DANGEROUS!
WHAT DO YOU WANT, HOOD?
ONLY A SIMPLE TRADE...YOUR MOTHER FOR...
...YOUR SHIP!
OUR SHIP?
PT
9

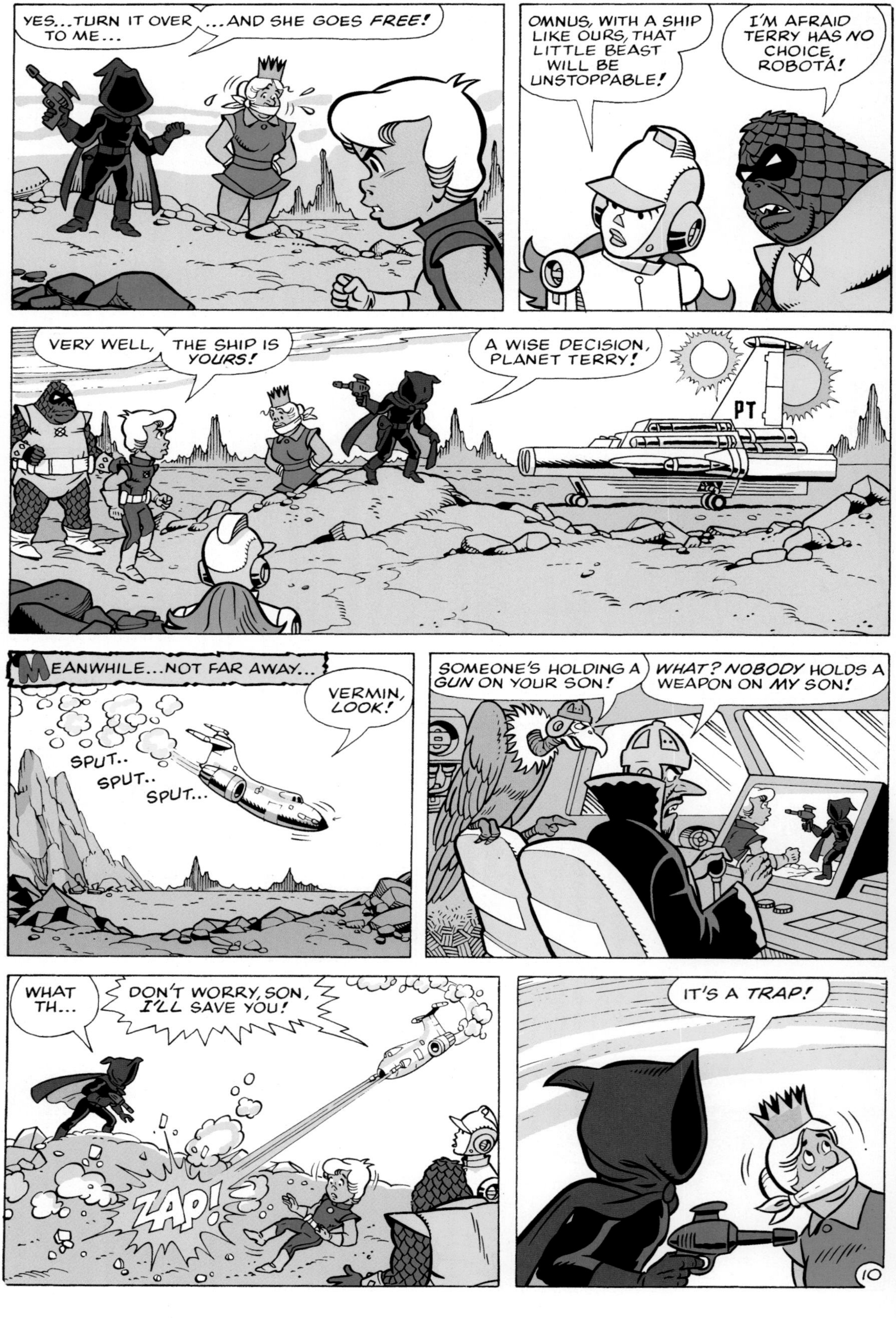

YES...TURN IT OVER TO ME...
...AND SHE GOES *FREE!*
OMNUS, WITH A SHIP LIKE OURS, THAT LITTLE BEAST WILL BE UNSTOPPABLE!
I'M AFRAID TERRY HAS *NO* CHOICE, ROBOTÁ!
VERY WELL,
THE SHIP IS *YOURS!*
A WISE DECISION, PLANET TERRY!
PT
MEANWHILE...NOT FAR AWAY...
VERMIN, LOOK!
SPUT..
SPUT..
SPUT...
SOMEONE'S HOLDING A *GUN* ON YOUR SON!
WHAT? *NOBODY* HOLDS A WEAPON ON *MY* SON!
WHAT TH...
DON'T WORRY, SON, *I'LL* SAVE YOU!
ZAP!
IT'S A *TRAP!*
10

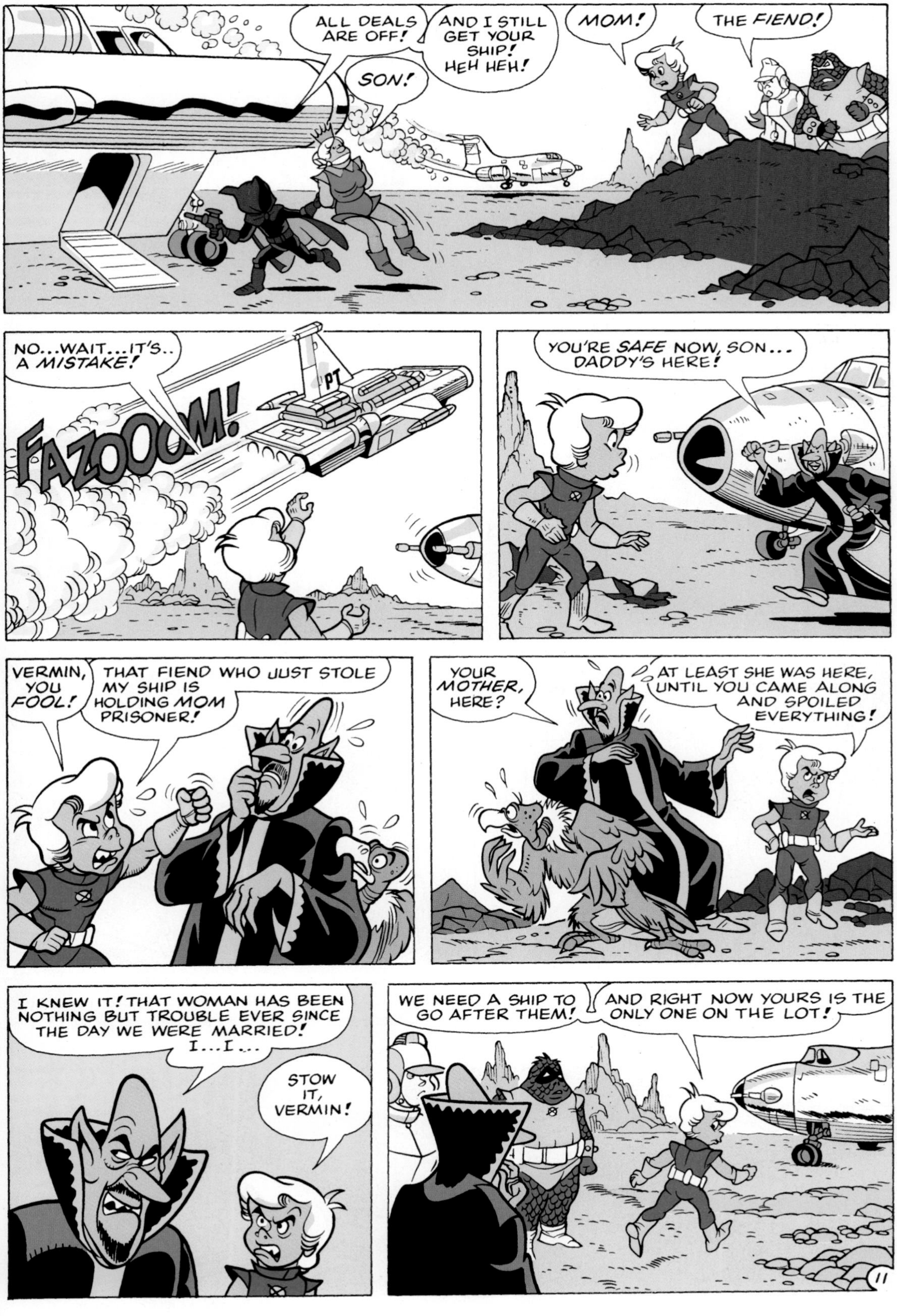
ALL DEALS ARE OFF!
AND I STILL GET YOUR SHIP! HEH HEH!
SON!
MOM!
THE FIEND!
NO...WAIT...IT'S.. A MISTAKE!
FAZOOOM!
PT
YOU'RE SAFE NOW, SON... DADDY'S HERE!
VERMIN, YOU FOOL!
THAT FIEND WHO JUST STOLE MY SHIP IS HOLDING MOM PRISONER!
YOUR MOTHER, HERE?
AT LEAST SHE WAS HERE, UNTIL YOU CAME ALONG AND SPOILED EVERYTHING!
I KNEW IT! THAT WOMAN HAS BEEN NOTHING BUT TROUBLE EVER SINCE THE DAY WE WERE MARRIED! I...I...
STOW IT, VERMIN!
WE NEED A SHIP TO GO AFTER THEM!
AND RIGHT NOW YOURS IS THE ONLY ONE ON THE LOT!
11

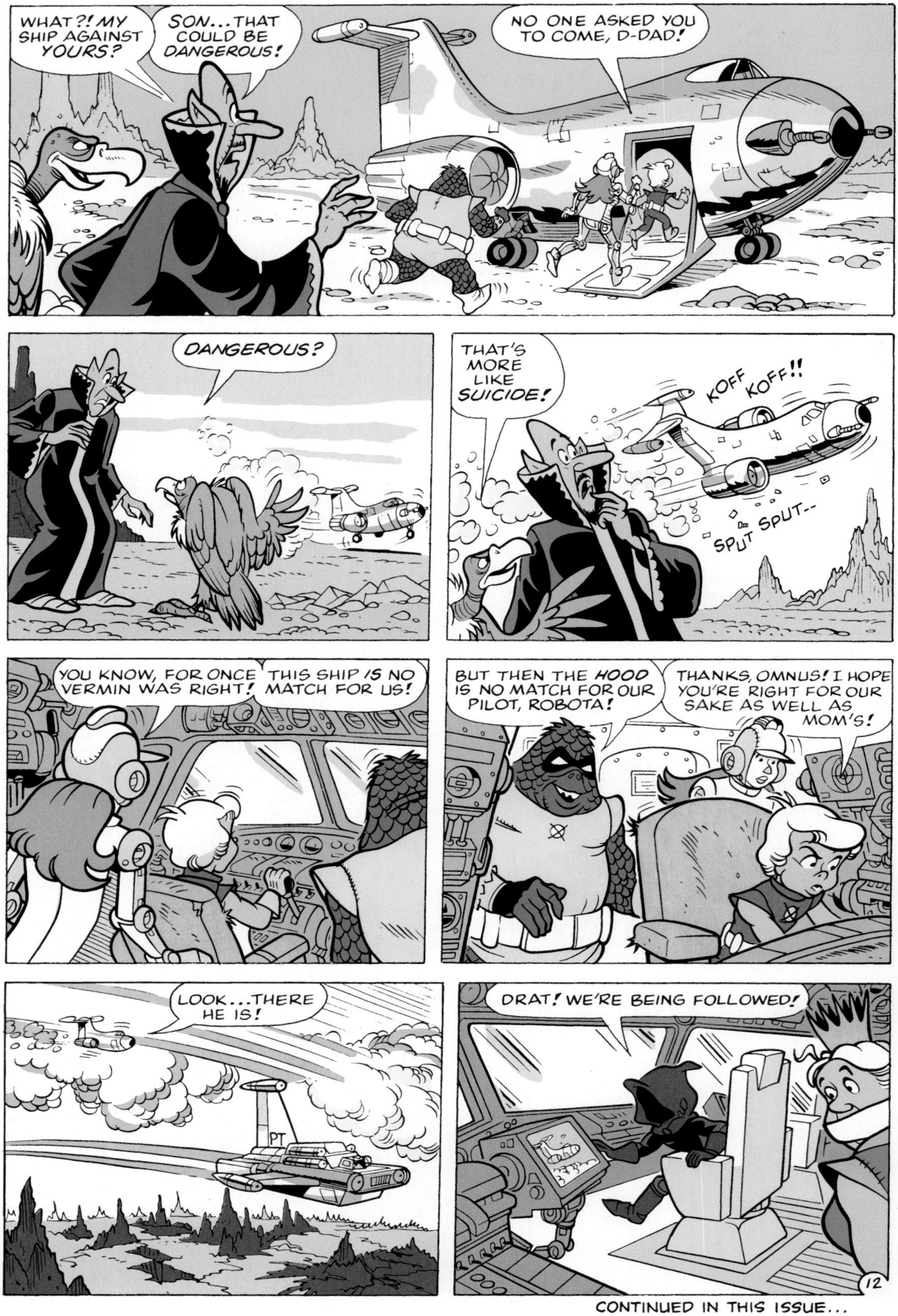
WHAT?! MY SHIP AGAINST YOURS?
SON...THAT COULD BE DANGEROUS!
NO ONE ASKED YOU TO COME, D-DAD!
DANGEROUS?
THAT'S MORE LIKE SUICIDE!
KOFF KOFF!!
SPUT SPUT--
YOU KNOW, FOR ONCE VERMIN WAS RIGHT!
THIS SHIP IS NO MATCH FOR US!
BUT THEN THE HOOD IS NO MATCH FOR OUR PILOT, ROBOTA!
THANKS, OMNUS! I HOPE YOU'RE RIGHT FOR OUR SAKE AS WELL AS MOM'S!
LOOK...THERE HE IS!
PT
DRAT! WE'RE BEING FOLLOWED!
12

CONTINUED IN THIS ISSUE...

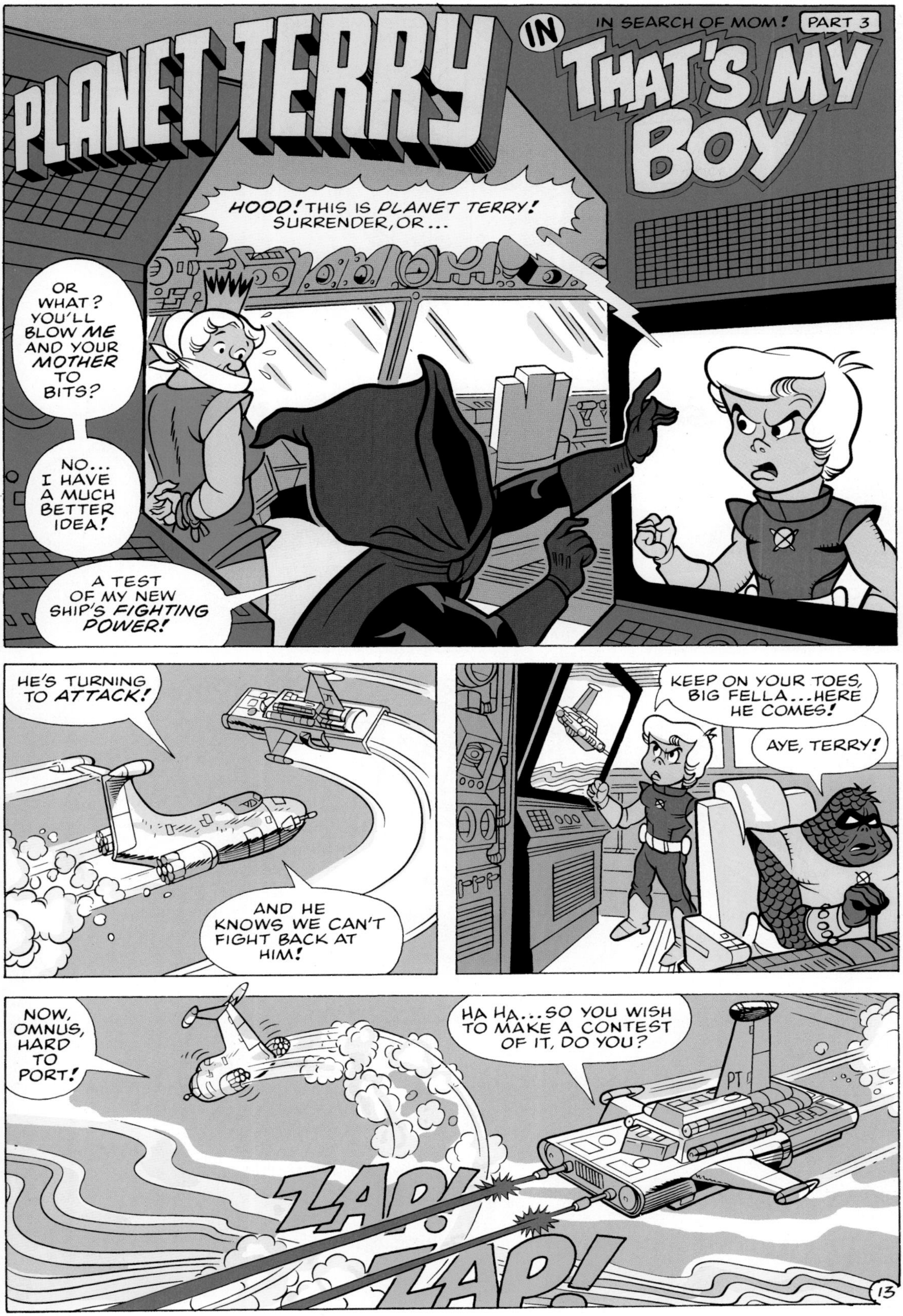

PLANET TERRY IN THAT'S MY BOY
IN SEARCH OF MOM! PART 3
HOOD! THIS IS PLANET TERRY! SURRENDER, OR...
OR WHAT? YOU'LL BLOW ME AND YOUR MOTHER TO BITS?
NO... I HAVE A MUCH BETTER IDEA!
A TEST OF MY NEW SHIP'S FIGHTING POWER!
HE'S TURNING TO ATTACK!
AND HE KNOWS WE CAN'T FIGHT BACK AT HIM!
KEEP ON YOUR TOES, BIG FELLA...HERE HE COMES!
AYE, TERRY!
NOW, OMNUS, HARD TO PORT!
HA HA...SO YOU WISH TO MAKE A CONTEST OF IT, DO YOU?
PT
ZAP!
ZAP!
13

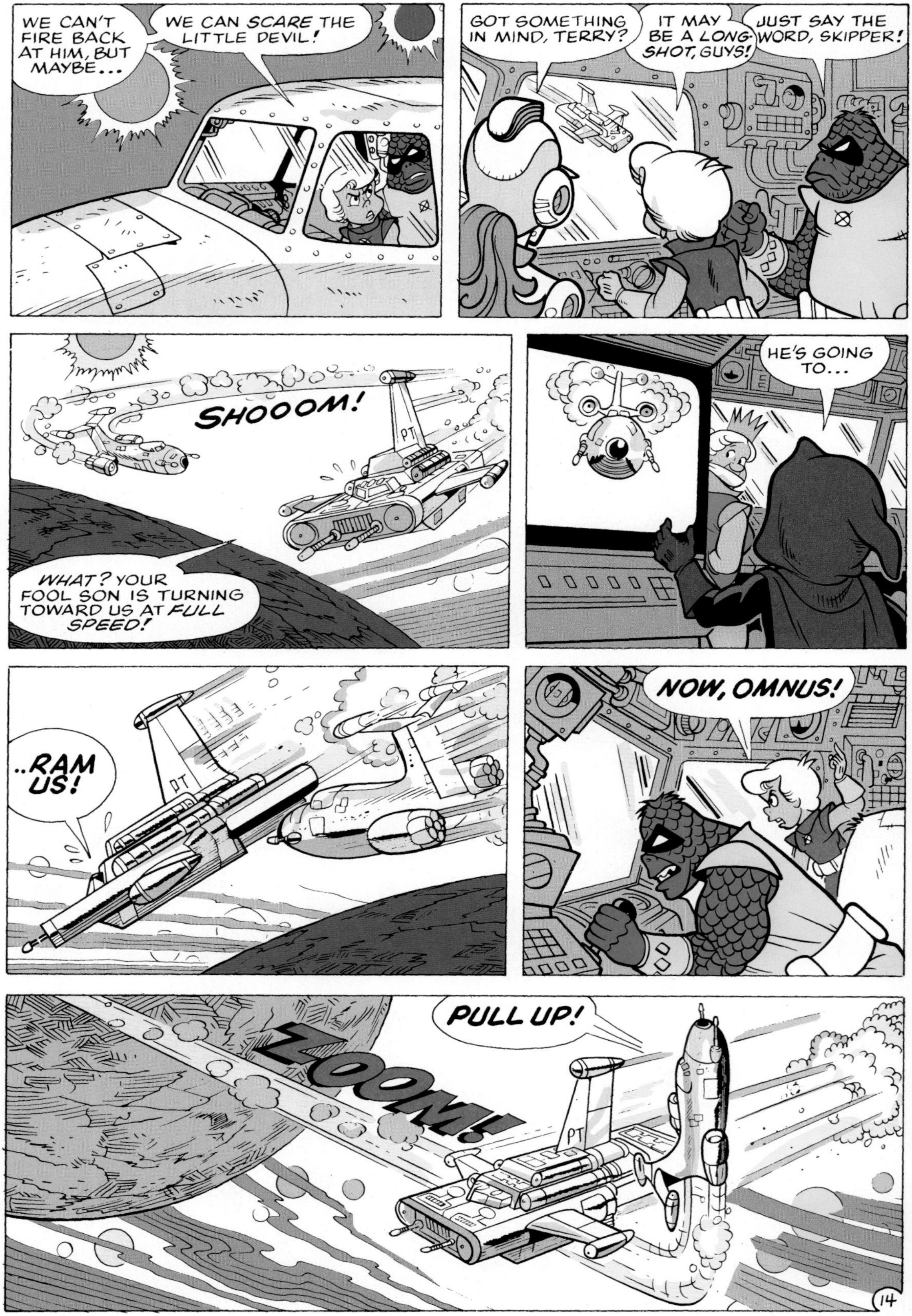

WE CAN'T FIRE BACK AT HIM, BUT MAYBE...
WE CAN SCARE THE LITTLE DEVIL!
GOT SOMETHING IN MIND, TERRY?
IT MAY BE A LONG-SHOT, GUYS!
JUST SAY THE WORD, SKIPPER!
SHOOOM!
WHAT? YOUR FOOL SON IS TURNING TOWARD US AT FULL SPEED!
HE'S GOING TO...
..RAM US!
NOW, OMNUS!
PULL UP!
ZOOM!
14

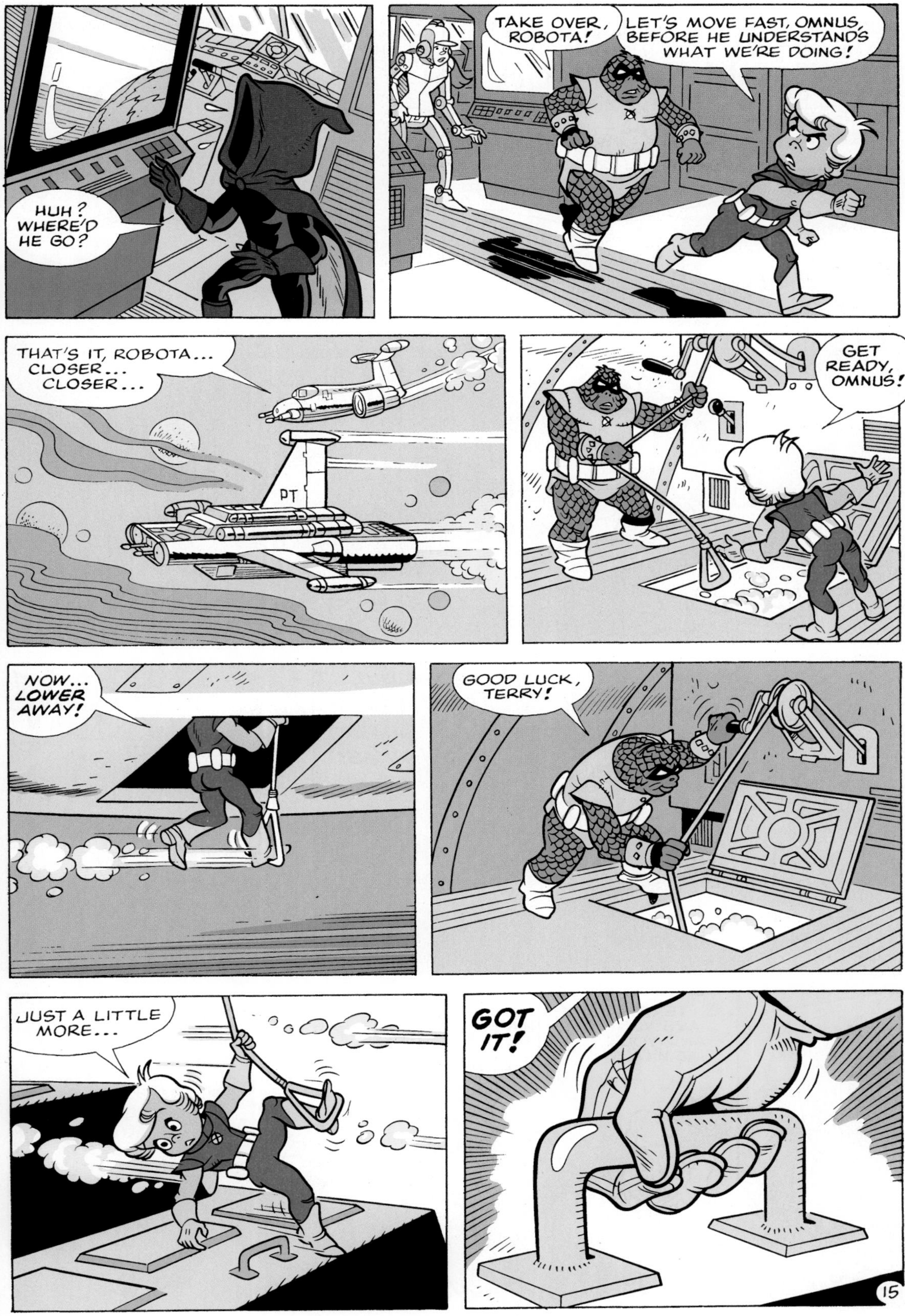
HUH? WHERE'D HE GO?
TAKE OVER, ROBOTA!
LET'S MOVE FAST, OMNUS, BEFORE HE UNDERSTANDS WHAT WE'RE DOING!
THAT'S IT, ROBOTA... CLOSER... CLOSER...
PT
GET READY, OMNUS!
NOW... LOWER AWAY!
GOOD LUCK, TERRY!
JUST A LITTLE MORE...
GOT IT!
15

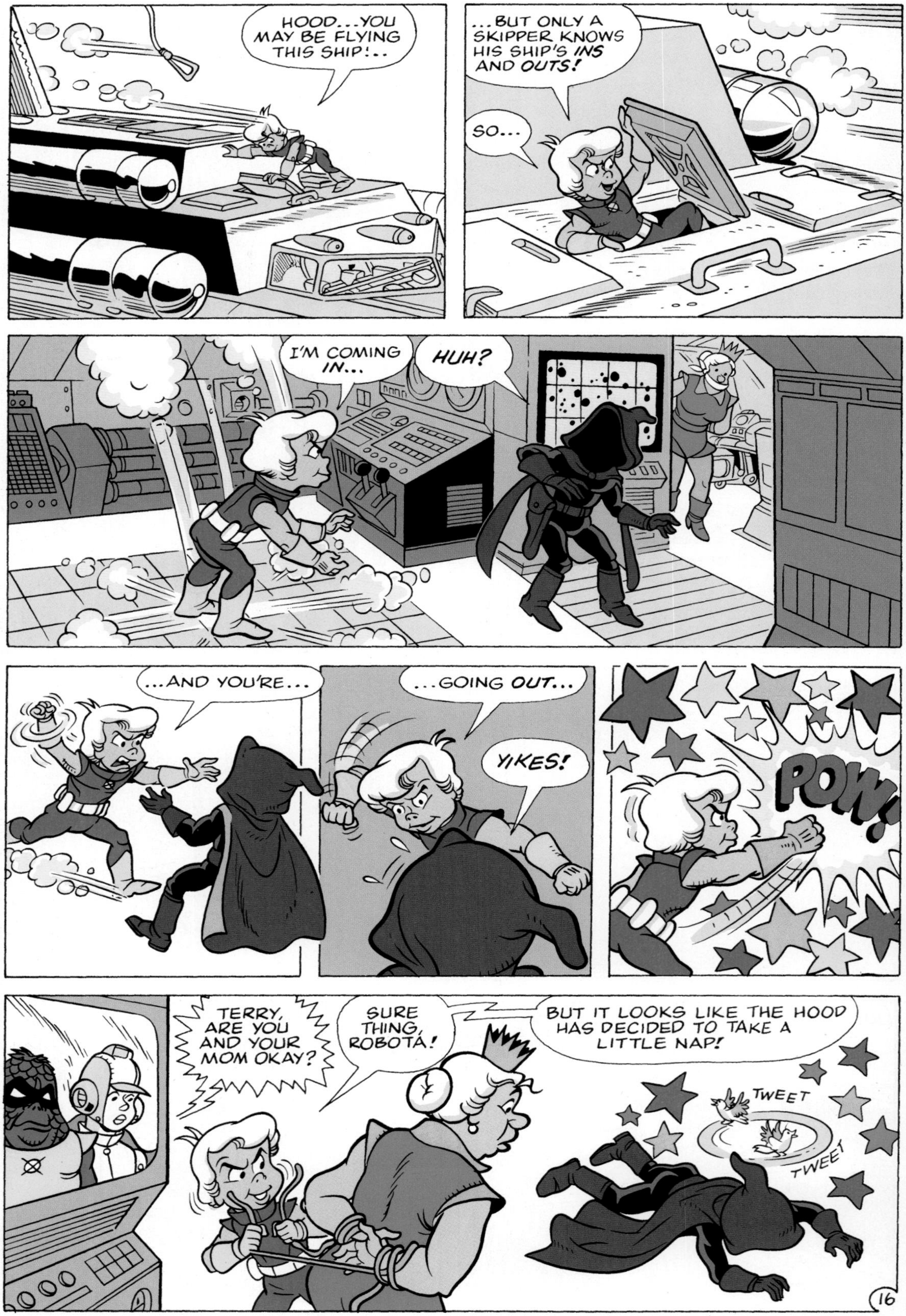
HOOD...YOU MAY BE FLYING THIS SHIP!..
...BUT ONLY A SKIPPER KNOWS HIS SHIP'S INS AND OUTS!
SO...
I'M COMING IN...
HUH?
...AND YOU'RE...
...GOING OUT...
YIKES!
POW!
TERRY, ARE YOU AND YOUR MOM OKAY?
SURE THING, ROBOTA!
BUT IT LOOKS LIKE THE HOOD HAS DECIDED TO TAKE A LITTLE NAP!
TWEET
TWEET
16

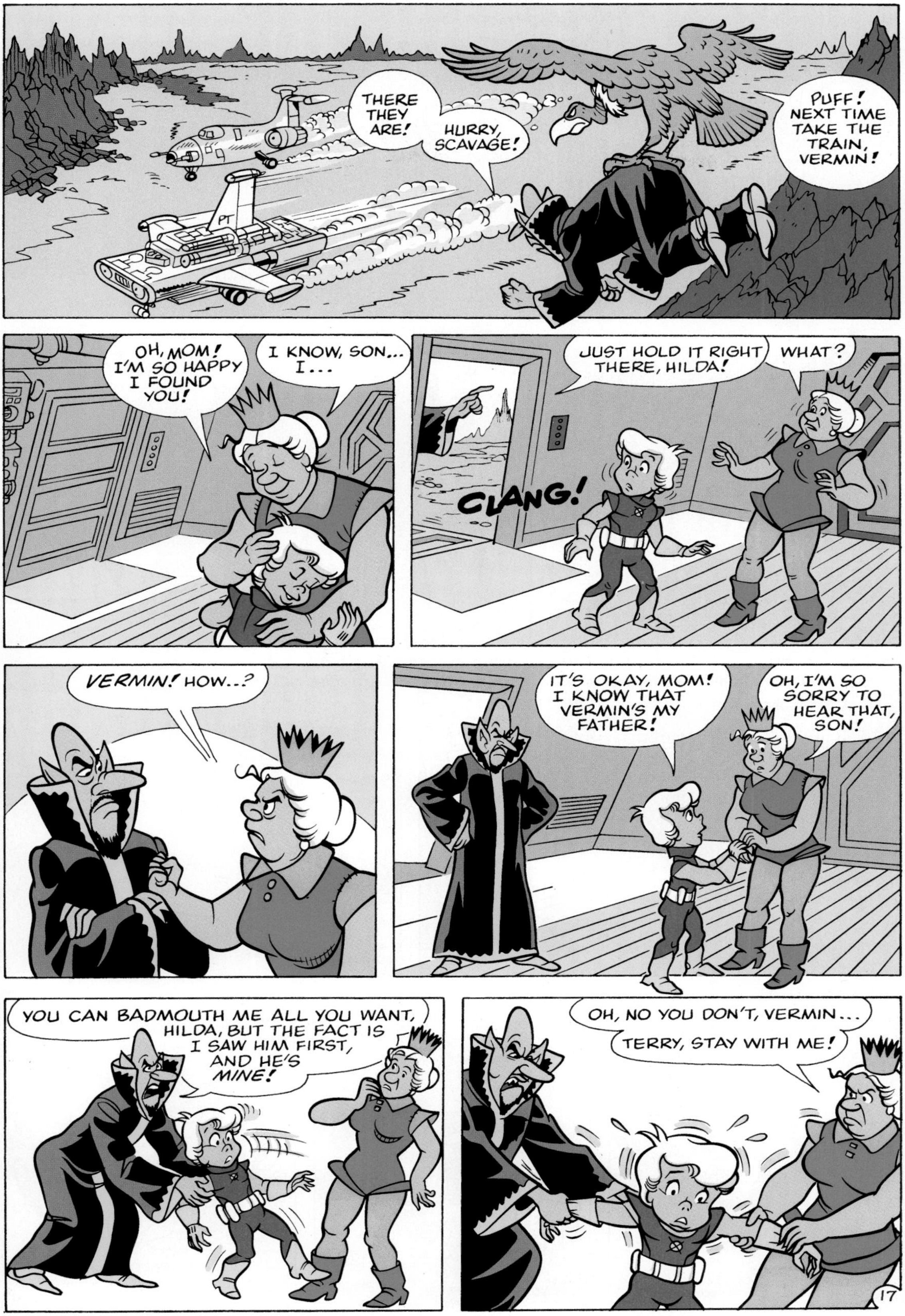
THERE THEY ARE!
HURRY, SCAVAGE!
PUFF! NEXT TIME TAKE THE TRAIN, VERMIN!
OH, MOM! I'M SO HAPPY I FOUND YOU!
I KNOW, SON... I...
JUST HOLD IT RIGHT THERE, HILDA!
WHAT?
CLANG!
VERMIN! HOW..?
IT'S OKAY, MOM! I KNOW THAT VERMIN'S MY FATHER!
OH, I'M SO SORRY TO HEAR THAT, SON!
YOU CAN BADMOUTH ME ALL YOU WANT, HILDA, BUT THE FACT IS I SAW HIM FIRST, AND HE'S MINE!
OH, NO YOU DON'T, VERMIN...
TERRY, STAY WITH ME!
17

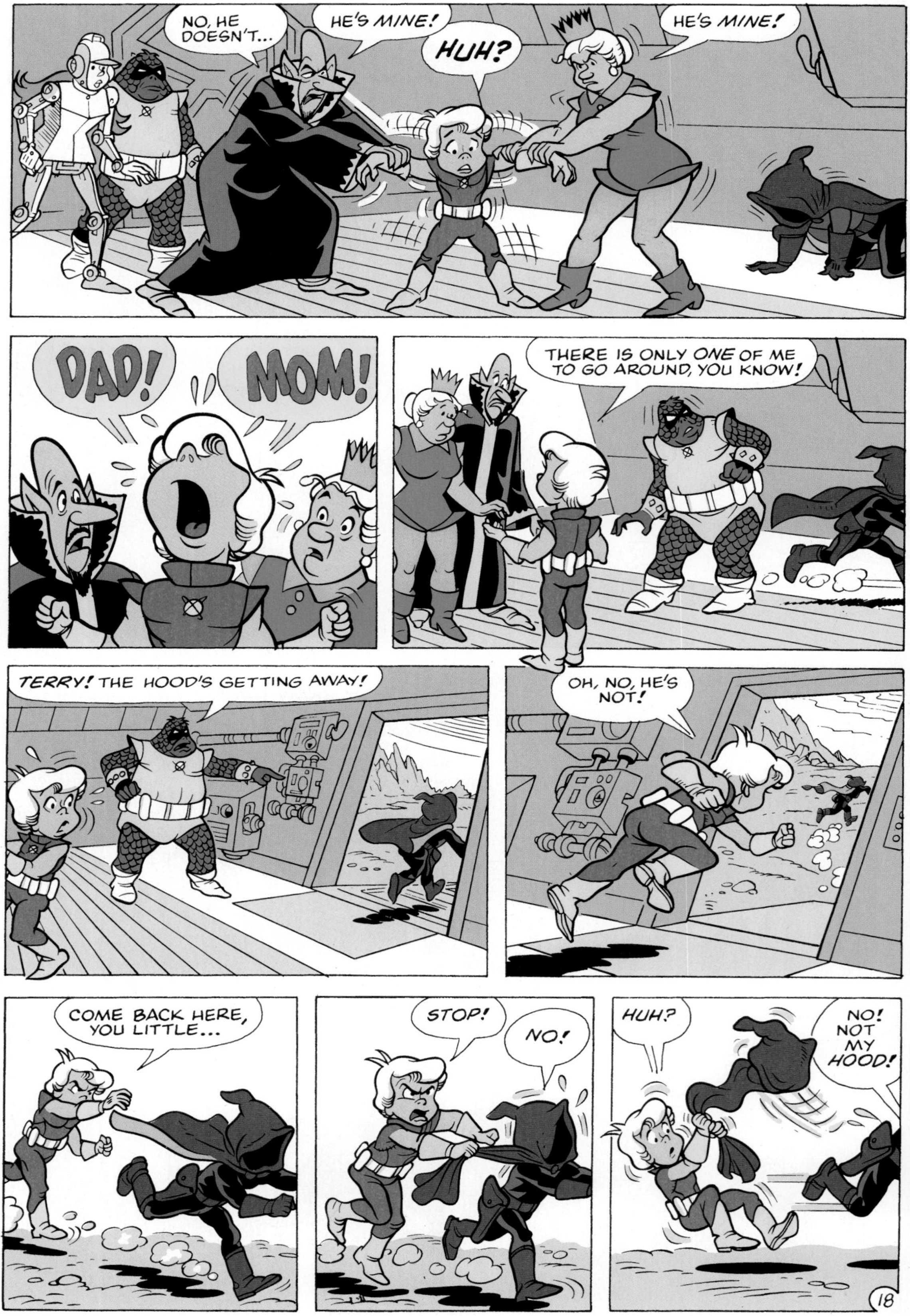
NO, HE DOESN'T...
HE'S MINE!
HUH?
HE'S MINE!
DAD!
MOM!
THERE IS ONLY ONE OF ME TO GO AROUND, YOU KNOW!
TERRY! THE HOOD'S GETTING AWAY!
OH, NO, HE'S NOT!
COME BACK HERE, YOU LITTLE...
STOP!
NO!
HUH?
NO! NOT MY HOOD!
18

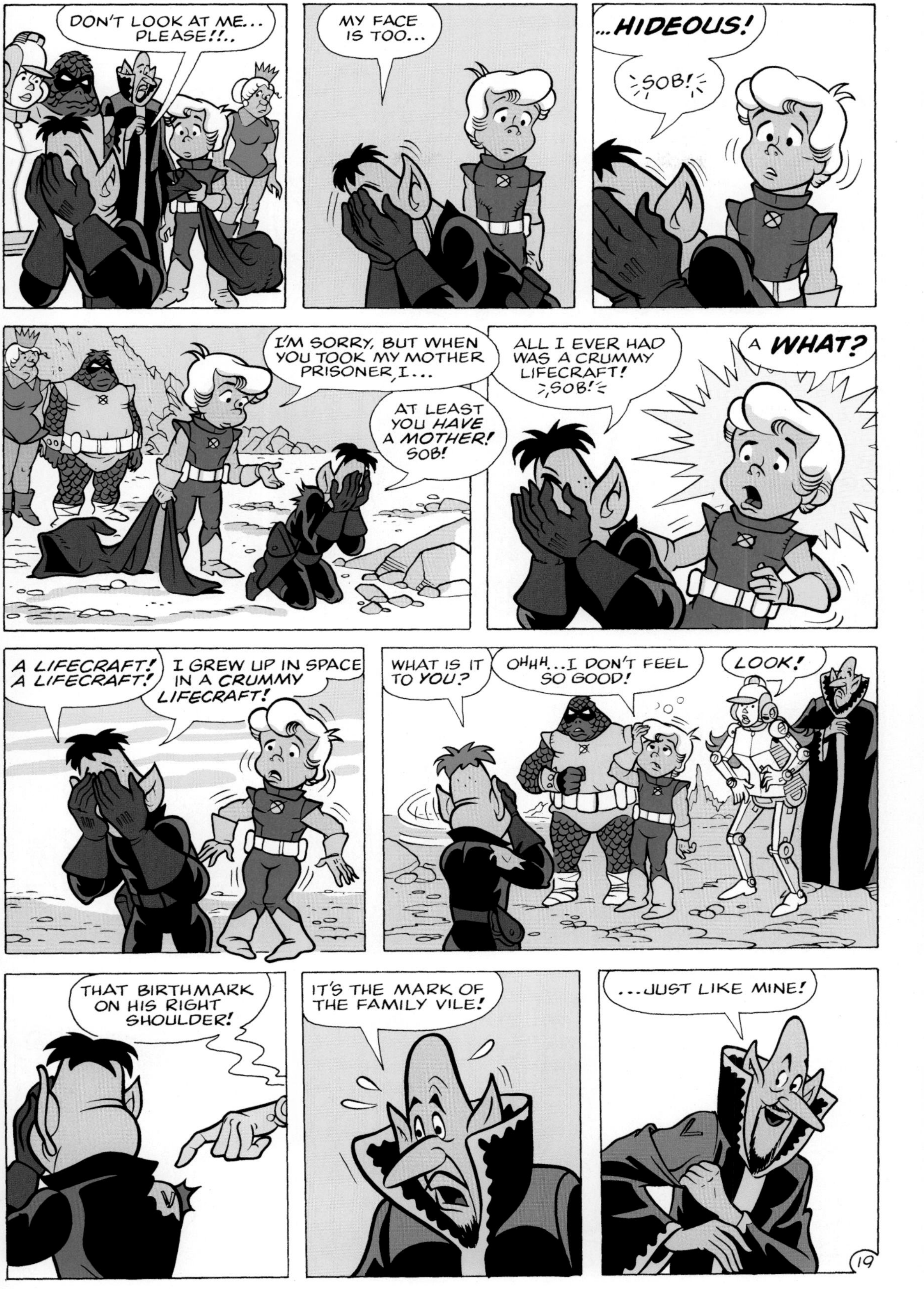
DON'T LOOK AT ME... PLEASE!!..
MY FACE IS TOO...
...HIDEOUS!
SOB!
I'M SORRY, BUT WHEN YOU TOOK MY MOTHER PRISONER, I...
AT LEAST YOU HAVE A MOTHER! SOB!
ALL I EVER HAD WAS A CRUMMY LIFECRAFT! SOB!
A WHAT?
A LIFECRAFT! A LIFECRAFT!
I GREW UP IN SPACE IN A CRUMMY LIFECRAFT!
WHAT IS IT TO YOU?
OHHH...I DON'T FEEL SO GOOD!
LOOK!
THAT BIRTHMARK ON HIS RIGHT SHOULDER!
IT'S THE MARK OF THE FAMILY VILE!
...JUST LIKE MINE!
19

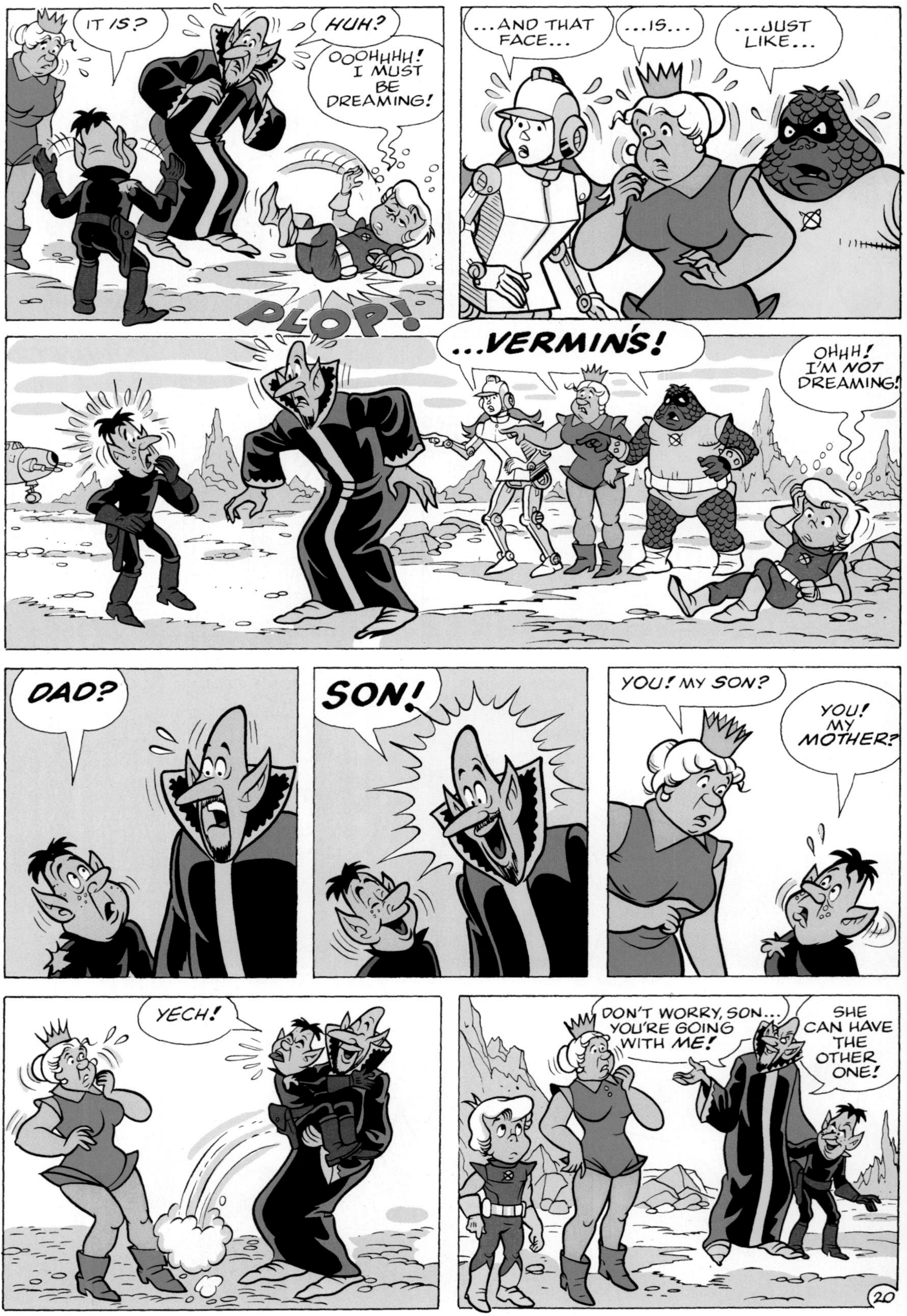
IT IS?
HUH?
OOOHHHH! I MUST BE DREAMING!
PLOP!
...AND THAT FACE...
...IS...
...JUST LIKE...
...VERMIN'S!
OHHH! I'M NOT DREAMING!
DAD?
SON!
YOU! MY SON?
YOU! MY MOTHER?
YECH!
DON'T WORRY, SON... YOU'RE GOING WITH ME!
SHE CAN HAVE THE OTHER ONE!
20

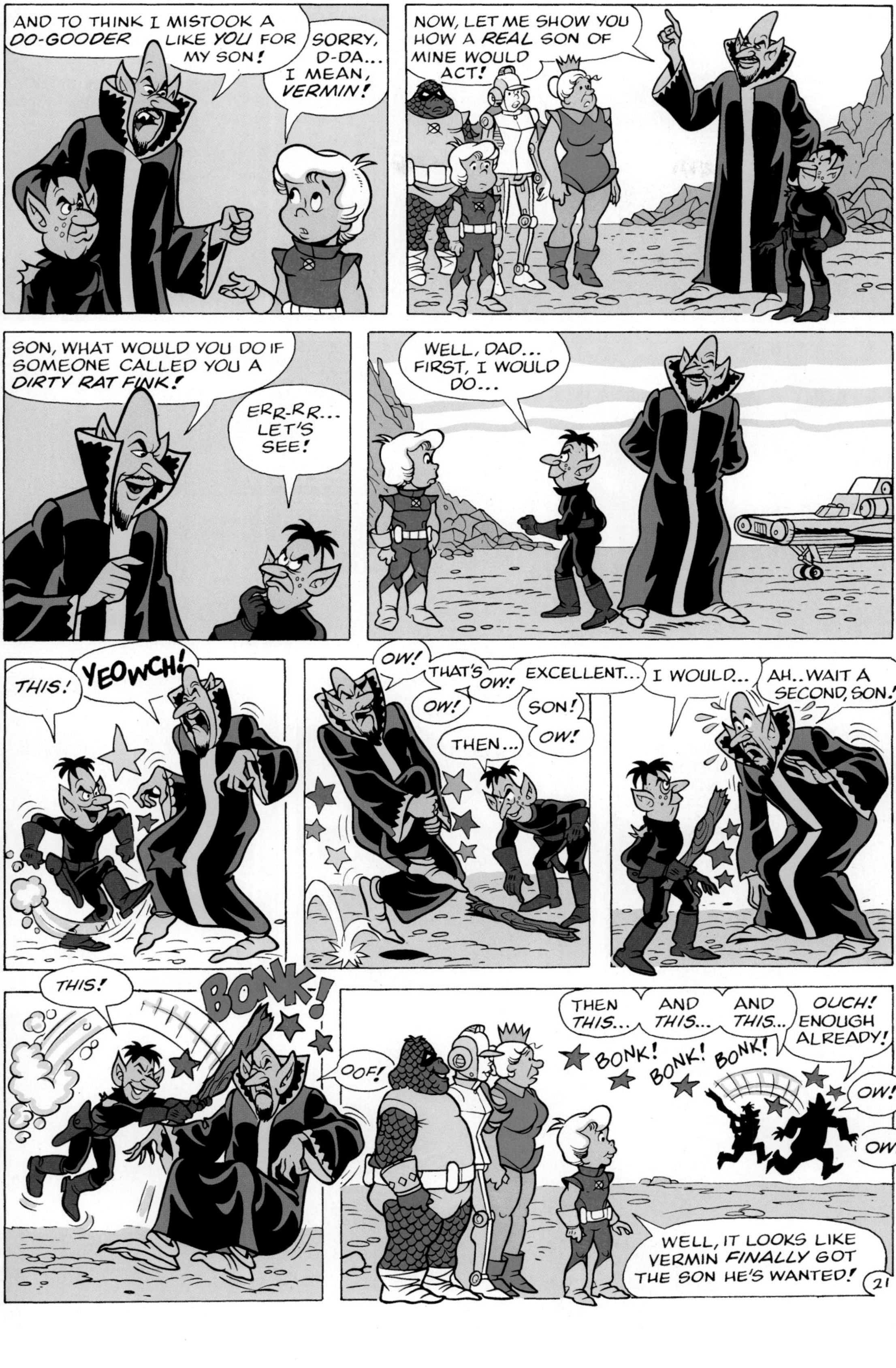
AND TO THINK I MISTOOK A DO-GOODER LIKE YOU FOR MY SON!
SORRY, D-DA... I MEAN, VERMIN!
NOW, LET ME SHOW YOU HOW A REAL SON OF MINE WOULD ACT!
SON, WHAT WOULD YOU DO IF SOMEONE CALLED YOU A DIRTY RAT FINK!
ERR-RR... LET'S SEE!
WELL, DAD... FIRST, I WOULD DO...
THIS!
YEOWCH!
OW!
THAT'S
OW!
OW!
EXCELLENT...
SON!
OW!
THEN...
I WOULD...
AH..WAIT A SECOND, SON!
THIS!
BONK!
OOF!
THEN THIS...
AND THIS...
AND THIS...
OUCH! ENOUGH ALREADY!
BONK!
BONK!
BONK!
OW!
OW!
WELL, IT LOOKS LIKE VERMIN FINALLY GOT THE SON HE'S WANTED!
21

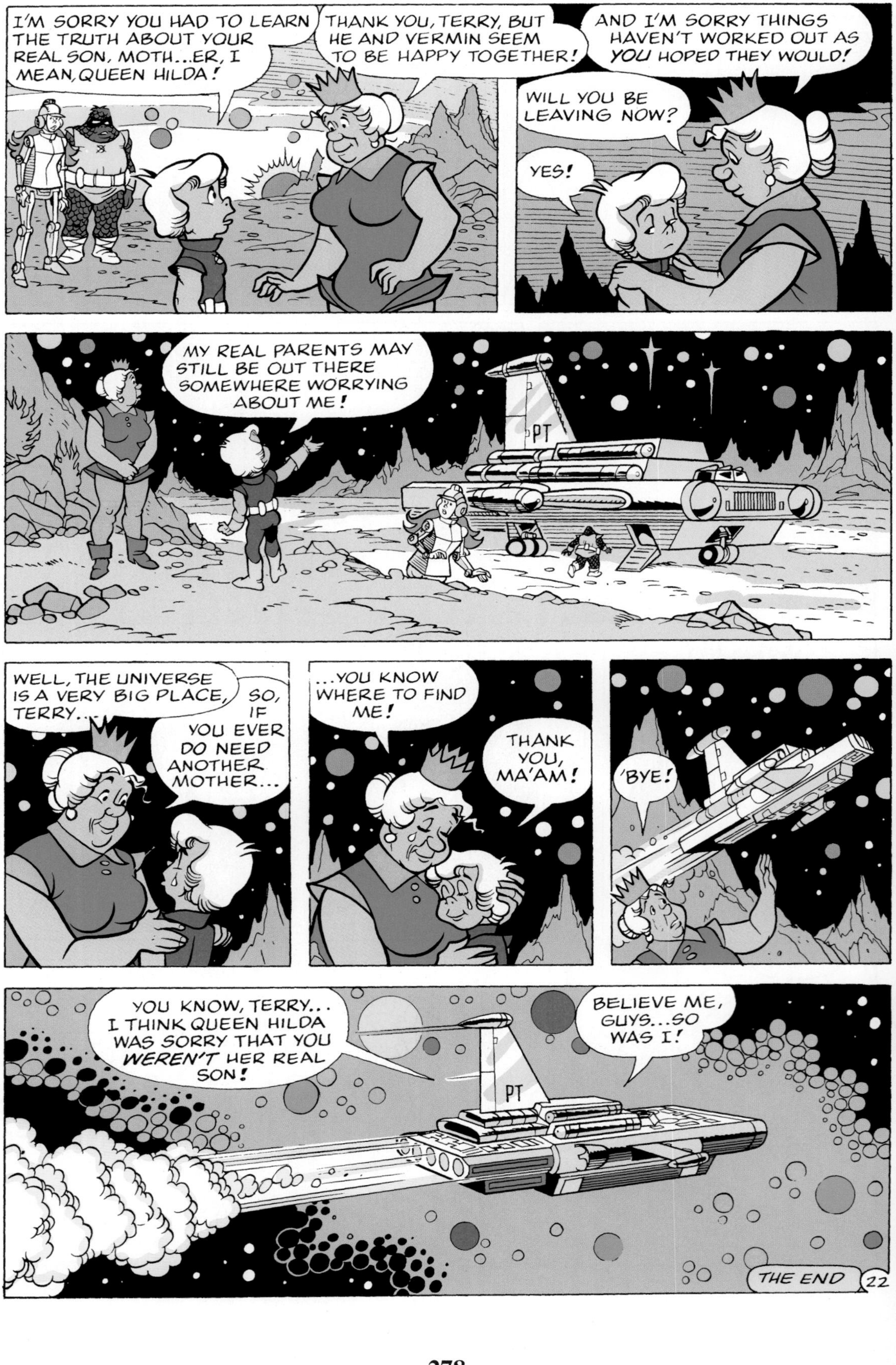
I'M SORRY YOU HAD TO LEARN THE TRUTH ABOUT YOUR REAL SON, MOTH...ER, I MEAN, QUEEN HILDA!
THANK YOU, TERRY, BUT HE AND VERMIN SEEM TO BE HAPPY TOGETHER!
AND I'M SORRY THINGS HAVEN'T WORKED OUT AS YOU HOPED THEY WOULD!
WILL YOU BE LEAVING NOW?
YES!
MY REAL PARENTS MAY STILL BE OUT THERE SOMEWHERE WORRYING ABOUT ME!
PT
WELL, THE UNIVERSE IS A VERY BIG PLACE, TERRY...
SO, IF YOU EVER DO NEED ANOTHER MOTHER...
...YOU KNOW WHERE TO FIND ME!
THANK YOU, MA'AM!
'BYE!
YOU KNOW, TERRY... I THINK QUEEN HILDA WAS SORRY THAT YOU WEREN'T HER REAL SON!
BELIEVE ME, GUYS...SO WAS I!
PT
THE END
22

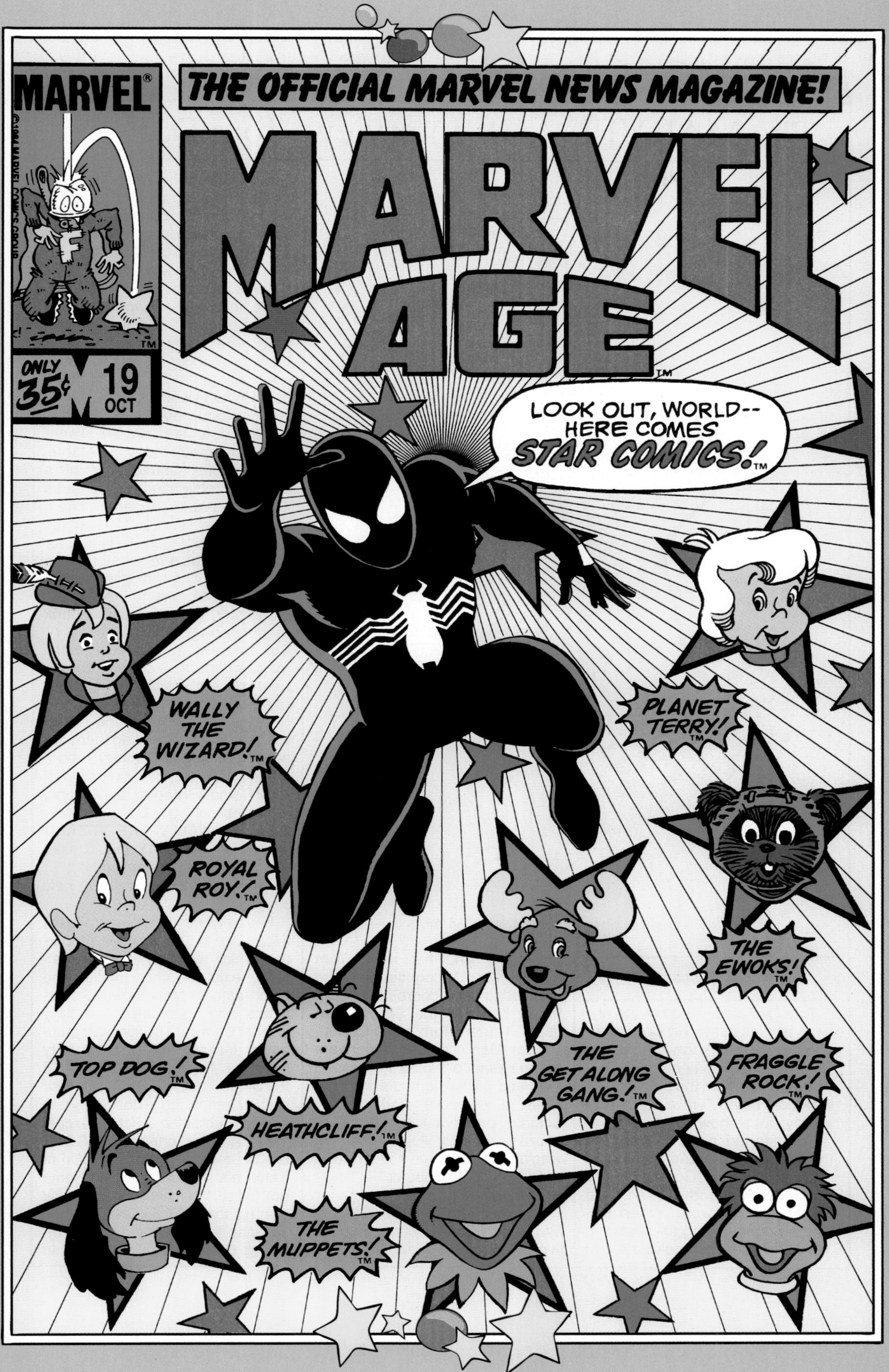

MARVEL®
©1984 MARVEL COMICS GROUP
ONLY 35¢
19 OCT
THE OFFICIAL MARVEL NEWS MAGAZINE!
MARVEL AGE™
LOOK OUT, WORLD-- HERE COMES STAR COMICS!™
WALLY THE WIZARD!™
PLANET TERRY!™
ROYAL ROY!™
THE EWOKS!™
TOP DOG!™
THE GET ALONG GANG!™
FRAGGLE ROCK!™
HEATHCLIFF!™
THE MUPPETS!™

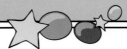

The MARVEL AGE Interview: Tom DeFalco

PLANET TERRY
WARREN KREMER 4-83

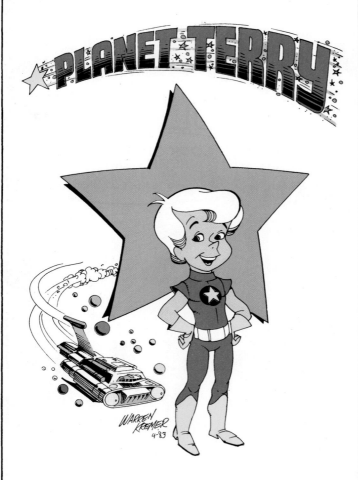

by **Jim Massara**

Tom DeFalco is one of the unsung heroes at Marvel Comics — and he'd just as soon keep it that way. "I'd prefer to keep myself invisible, away from the public eye," **DeFalco** says. "I'm a typewriter jockey, not a showman."

Tom started in the comics field in 1972 as a proofreader and later, a writer for Archie Comics, where until recently nobody was credited in print for his work. When **DeFalco** began writing for Marvel in 1979, readers first took notice of his name and his work. **Tom** gained wide recognition as the first editor to coordinate continuity between the **Spider-Man** titles. Under **Tom's** editorship, **Spider-Man's** career underwent a renaissance which impressed fans and professionals alike. "I'm given a lot more credit than I actually deserve for that," **Tom** characteristically disclaims. "It was the first time one editor had all of **Spider-Man's** books."

Last year, **Tom** left editing **Spider-Man's** books to become Executive Editor of the Marvel Comics Group. One of his many projects as second-in-command to Editor in Chief **Jim Shooter** was overseeing the creation of the newest line of comics, **Star Comics**.

Why was the new line of Star Comics created?

We've been looking at today's comics market, and we've seen that there really isn't much out there for younger readers. Children are really getting ripped off these days! When I was a kid, there was plenty of stuff out there for us to read and to see on TV. There really isn't much today. So Marvel created Star Comics out of a sense of obligation — because kids deserve to be entertained, too.

Also, Marvel Comics is in it for the long haul. We expect to be around twenty years from now. If we want to be around then, we've got to start grooming comic book readers now!

Are the new Star Comics strictly for kids, though — or can they appeal to both older and younger readers?

Oh, yeah. I'm sure the adults will look at them and find them appealing. Adults will easily recognize some of the titles, like **HEATHCLIFF**, who will appeal to everyone, regardless of age. Our new creations like **WALLY THE WIZARD** and **PLANET TERRY** should make good fun reading for anybody!

Give us a rundown on all the new titles.

Basically, we've got two groups of titles. One is the licensed properties, which star characters who already exist in other media. The other features Marvel-owned characters who we created especially for Star Comics. The licensed properties include those little furry creatures from *Star Wars* — **THE EWOKS**! They'll soon have their own TV series, too — the Star Wars tie-in has created a lot of excitement. Another one is **FRAGGLE ROCK**, featuring the cast of **Jim Henson's** new TV show on Home Box Office. We're working on a book starring the **GET ALONG GANG**. You may not have heard of **the Get Along Gang** yet, but I know that

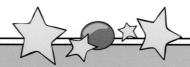

you'll know them by the end of this summer. They were created by the people at American Greetings, the people who gave us **the Care Bears** and **Strawberry Shortcake. The Get-Along Gang** will have a network TV show next fall. You won't be able to walk into a greeting card store without seeing these great new characters — and now we've got them as well. Another Star title, as I mentioned, is **HEATH-CLIFF**, whose strip is being syndicated in hundreds of newspapers. He's had his own network show, and he'll have a syndicated show next year that should be on every day of the week. You already know that we're putting **the Muppets** in comics, starting with our adaptation of *The Muppets Take Manhattan*. As if that weren't enough, we're working on plans for **Strawberry Shortcake** and the **Cabbage Patch** dolls!

These particular comics are titles that everybody — kid or adult — will recognize right away. People should know that their favorite characters will now have adventures published in Star Comics. And if any parents are reading this, they should know that we're out to appeal to them, too — Mom can now go to a newsstand and think, "My little boy or girl loves **Fraggle Rock** — and now there's a **FRAGGLE ROCK** comic book!"

We've also got a batch of original Star Comics creations. **PLANET TERRY**, Orphan of the Astros, will appear monthly. **Planet Terry** is a little kid who travels through space with a big monstrous creature named **Omnus** and a gorgeous female robot called **Robota**. When **Terry** was born out in space his parents accidentally ejected him from their spaceship — and they've been trying to find each other ever since. Just like a good old-fashioned Marvel comic, **PLANET TERRY** will have adventure, action, and suspense all the way to shocking cliff-hanger endings!

WALLY THE WIZARD, another monthly series, chronicles the adventures of an apprentice wizard growing up in the middle ages. Poor **Wally** has to deal with dragons, monsters, knights in shining armor, griffins, and who knows

what! It's guaranteed to be a lot of fun.

TOP DOG will start off as a bimonthly limited series. **Top Dog** is a genius dog who is a computer expert, a world-famous chef and a secret agent — and a number of other things — who decides that life at the top is too rough and that he should hide out. He meets a boy named **Joey Jordan** in the park one day, and they sort of adopt each other. So the boy's got this talking dog, but he can't let

anybody know about it!

But isn't the dog already world famous?

Yes — but only to the world's leaders. For example, the president of the United States is aware of him. The king of a foreign country knows about him, because **Top Dog** used to be his chef. Because it's known by heads of state that this genius talking dog is walking around, the wildest adventures take place for **Top Dog** and his friend. Some-

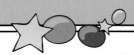

times he has to drag the kid along kicking and screaming!

Another bimonthly series will be **ROYAL ROY**, the adventures of a young kid who's the prince of a fantastically wealthy country. He can buy whatever he wants and do whatever he wants — he lives every kid's fantasy!

Last, but hardly least, we have **PETER PORKER, THE SPECTACULAR SPIDER-HAM**. Remember last year's **MARVEL TAILS**, with funny animal versions of our super heroes? It proved to be so popular that our distributor called us and demanded another issue! That's the first time that's ever happened to us! This is truly by popular demand. We had only planned on doing him as a one-shot!

Is that the entire line-up?

Hardly. We're constantly in the process of developing new and different kinds of books — for girls as well as boys. One such book is **MICKEY**, done by the incredible **Trina Robbins**. It's the exploits of a young high school girl who also works on a TV soap opera. She wants to be an actress and model — but she has problems with her father and family and all sorts of crazy things. It's really a nice, old-fashioned adventure-romance kind of book.

You know, girls are in worse shape than boys when it comes to entertainment they can enjoy these days. Star Comics is going to change all that!

It sounds like you've essentially built a comics line from scratch. How did you do it?

Lots of phone calls. **Sid Jacobson**, who will be Star Comics's major editor, editing all the comics except **PETER PORKER**, is a veteran professional in the field of children's comics with over thirty years experience. He called many of his old co-workers with the news that Marvel was starting a new comics line. I had worked at Archie Comics for a number of years before I came to Marvel, and I called up a lot of my old colleagues. And that's how we built the line.

As it became known that Marvel was entering the area of children's books, we started hearing from a lot of other people in the comics field who wanted to try out new ideas. That's how **Trina Robbins** came in. I'm sure that once the Star Comics appear, we'll find even more creative people anxious to join. No one has launched a major line of children's titles since the 1950's. That's why it took us such a long time to get the right creative people, because what we're doing — children's comics with heavy emphasis on story and characterization — hasn't been done in years.

Who are the creative people?

Warren Kremer was a top artist at Harvey Comics for many, many years. He was the main artist for **RICHIE RICH** and **CASPER**, and his style will be quickly recognizable. He's a fabulous penciler. He designed **Royal Roy**, **Top Dog**, and **Planet Terry**. We've also got **Bob Bolling**, a fan-favorite, who used to do classic **Little Archie** stuff. He's going to be doing some

HI, MOM! HE FOLLOWED ME HOME, CAN I KEEP HIM?
WHAT ARE YOU TALKING ABOUT, JOEY JORDAN?
NICE ORIGINAL DIALOGUE, KID!
OH, A DOG! WHAT'S HIS NAME?
HE CALLS HIMSELF TOP DOG!
WHOOPS! JOEY... YOU JUST BLEW IT!
OH, JOEY! DON'T TEASE YOUR MOM! HEH! SO YOU'VE ALREADY GIVEN HIM A NAME! WELL, TOP DOG IS CUTE!
YOU'RE NOT SO BAD YOURSELF, LADY!

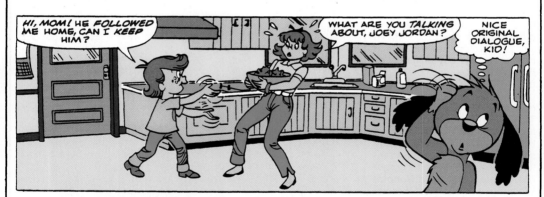

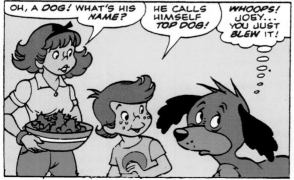

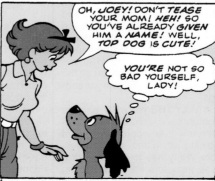

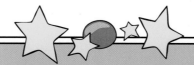

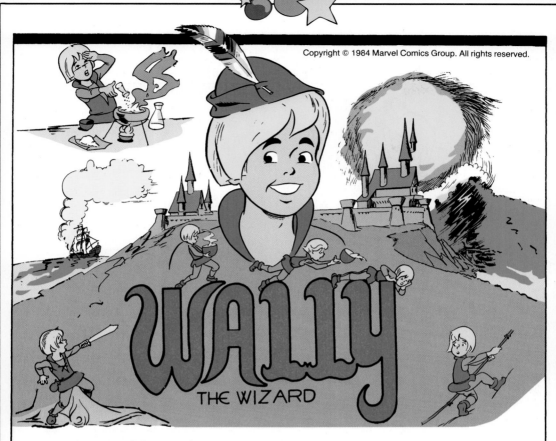

work on **WALLY THE WIZARD**. Then there's **Howie Post**, who did animation work for many years and ran the old Paramount cartoon studio for a term. **Don Christiansen** — who sometimes goes by the name "**Don Arr** —" is another well-known talent in the animation field who will be writing for Star Comics. **Stan Kaye**, a legend in the field, will be writing many of our projects. **Dave Manak** will be writing **HEATHCLIFF** and **THE EWOKS**. **Harold Smith** will be writing for **HEATHCLIFF** as well, and **Mort Gerberg**, a well-known *New Yorker* cartoonist, is doing some work on **ROYAL ROY**!

For inkers, we have **Jon D'Agostino**, who inked for Archie Comics for a long time, but whom you best know from **G.I. JOE**. **Jacqueline Roettcher**, who inked many of the old Harvey books, is with us, and so is **Vince Colletta**, who's inked just about *everything* at one time or another!

One of the greatest talents we had, though, died recently, before Star Comics would ever become known. **Lennie Herman** was instrumental in creating the Star Comics Line. He was just starting to produce the kind of great material we'd waited so long to publish when he died. We really had to start all over. He was a tremendous loss.

That brings up a point. Attention new talent — we desperately need writers. It's hard to get people who can do the kind of material that Star Comics is about. We want new writers who are as dedicated to stories for younger readers as they would be to doing an issue of the **X-Men**. It's hard to find people who have just the right attitude and who are completely dedicated to this line of work. If you're good enough — and willing to put sweat into it — we need you!

What are the greatest children's comics of the past?

The **Carl Barks Donald Duck** material is classic. **Barks** did a *lot* of great children's books. **Little Lulu** by **John Stanley** was great.

And I think the early **Spider-Man** by **Stan Lee** and **Steve Ditko** was great! You might not think of **Spider-Man** in the same category as **Carl Barks** because the character has gotten so much more sophisticated in the last twenty years, but when it started it caught on immediately with younger readers. Now the character appeals to both older and younger readers, just on different levels.

This isn't the first time Marvel has published childrens' comics. But it is the first time we've put so much energy and talent into it. What's going to make Star Comics Special?

Most of the other children's books we've published in our history were licensed to us, but produced outside the company. We just printed them. This time Marvel is going to be actually producing original material. We know how to make comics better than anyone, and I know they'll come out just beautifully. I'm betting my job on the fact that we *know* what we're doing! ●

THE ORIGIN OF STAR COMICS

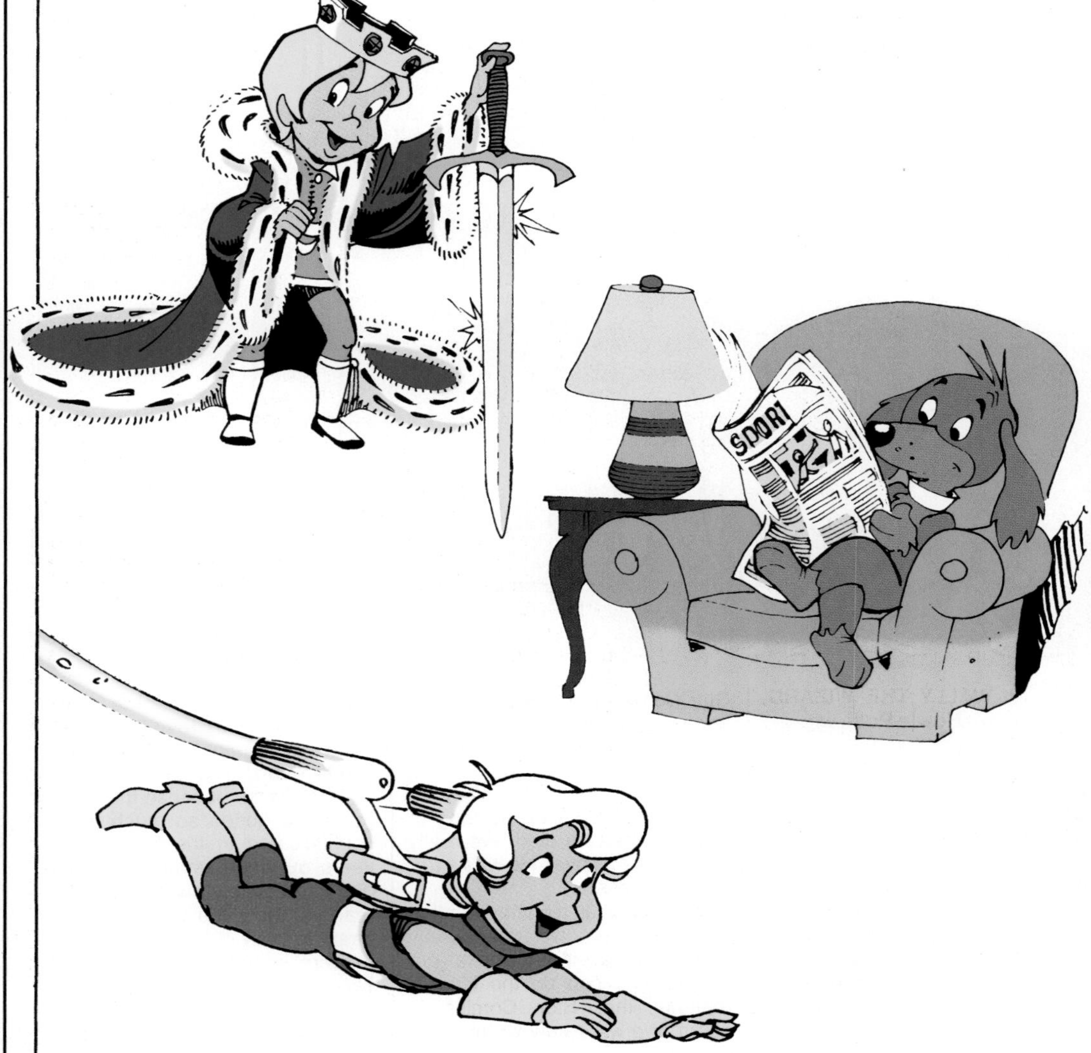

by **Jim Massara**

Building a line of comics from the ground up isn't easy. Just ask **Sid Jacobson**.

"It was step by step," says **Sid**. "It's hard. I mean I've . . ." He pauses, then lets go with a laugh. "I mean, I've never worked so hard in my life!"

There's a good reason of course. The new line of comics is Star Comics, Marvel's answer to the needs of the younger reader and the first launch of its kind in years. **Sid** is in the hot seat; the thirty-plus-year veteran editor from Harvey Comics not only created several of the new line's major characters, but will be editing them as well.

Sid's involvement with Marvel began early in 1983 when **Mike Hobson**, Vice President in charge of Publishing invited him to come up with some ideas for a new line of comics the company was developing. **Sid** brainstormed with writer **Lennie Herman** and **Warren Kremer**, both long-time associates at Harvey, to create the nucleus of the new line, **PLANET TERRY**, **ROYAL ROY**, and **TOP DOG**.

Which makes it all sound a lot easier than it really was. Along the way, the characters and ideas were constantly revised and re-

fined, with many creative suggestions from both Editor in Chief **Jim Shooter** and Executive Editor **Tom DeFalco**. For example, **Royal Roy** was originally conceived to be set in medieval times. Instead, it was decided that **ROYAL ROY** would take place in modern times, with **Tom DeFalco's** creation **WALLY THE WIZARD** taking place against the magic of the middle ages. **Omnus**, **Planet Terry's** monster sidekick, was redesigned to be less squat and more fierce-looking. **Jim** and **Tom** both contributed the emphasis on **Planet Terry's** search for his parents. **Top Dog's** ears were changed from brown to black for a crisper, more graphic look.

These were minor trials compared to the unexpected death of **Lennie Herman**, who had been slated to write many of the books. "The loss of **Lennie** was enormous," says **Jacobson**. "**Lennie** was the best writer of humor comics I ever met, and I think he was doing his best work here. It's been a tremendous job replacing that talent." **Herman** had only written a few scripts for the characters before he passed away, leaving practically no precedents from which new writers could work. Fortunatly, several talented new writers have stepped in to fill

the breach.

If a constant did remain after **Lennie Herman's** death, it was the approach to the characters. "We started with a background, a workable premise that's both fanciful and exciting," **Sid Jacobson** told **MARVEL AGE MAGAZINE**. "For example, science fiction forms the background for **PLANET TERRY**. We then thought of fantasy, a dream which every kid would like to come true. Who wouldn't want the kind of power **Royal Roy** has? This is the same sort of idea that inspires the creation of super heroes, except that this is for a slightly younger audience.

"It's important," **Sid** continued, "to develop positive characteristics in any character. Take **Heathcliff**, for instance. We're adapting him from a nationally syndicated newspaper gag panel, but we're going to focus on his personality. **Heathcliff** is mischievous, but he's really a positive force in the family. He does a lot of good things for his owner and for other characters in the strip. I mean, he does beat the stuffing out of bullies — but he also protects. He's a troublemaker, but he isn't **strictly** a troublemaker. He's a more sympathetic character than that. He has human qualities, if

you will."

Artist **Warren Kremer** concurs. "There's an honesty to our characters — a charm, a niceness, never a nastiness."

But, says **Sid**, that does not mean that the Star Comics Line will be saccharin. "The books do not pander. They're written with a great amount of sophistication and humor, and they're *full* stories with beginnings, middles, and ends — not just a run of gags or a premise to run gags around. Star Comics will work for any age level, adults, children, and in-between."

We *know* all of you must be wondering, so we'll tell you right now — all the charcters in the Star Comics Line *will* exist in the Marvel Universe. Does that mean **Royal Roy** may one day meet **Spider-Man**, or that **Top Dog** could team up with **the X-Men**? "Oh, certainly," answers **Sid**. "There aren't any plans yet, but it is a strong probability." In fact, **Joey Jordan**, **Top Dog's** boy owner, will appear in the first issue of **TOP DOG** wearing a **Spider-Man** t-shirt!

"I hope the fan market gives these new books as much of a chance as the kids do," **Sid** concludes. "I think they'll be pleasantly surprised. It's *not* just kiddie stuff!" ●

STAR COMICS COMING ATTRACTIONS

Here's the latest information on the first issue of each new Star Comics title. The shipping date refers to the date the comics leave the printer; you can expect to find the books in your favorite comics specialty shop a week to two weeks later. Following each title is the creative team, if known. All these books will be edited by **Sid Jacobson**.

Titles shipping September 11:

PLANET TERRY #1 — Written by **Lennie Herman**, penciled by **Warren Kremer** and inked by **Vince Colletta**.
FRAGGLE ROCK #1 — Written by **Stan Kaye**, penciled by **Martin Taras** and inked by **Jacqueline Roettcher**.
HEATHCLIFF #1 — Written by **Joe Edwards**, penciled by **Warren Kremer** and inked by **Jacqueline Roettcher**.

Titles shipping September 25.

WALLY THE WIZARD #1 — Written, penciled and inked by **Bob Bolling**.
TOP DOG #1 — Written by **Lennie Herman**, penciled by **Warren Kremer** and inked by **Jacqueline Roettcher**.
STRAWBERRY SHORTCAKE #1.

Titles shipping October 9:

THE MUPPET BABIES #1.
THE EWOKS #1.

Titles shipping October 23:

ROYAL ROY #1 — Written by **Lennie Herman**, penciled by **Warren Kremer** and inked by **Jon D'Agostino**.
GET ALONG GANG #1. ●

STAR-SPOTLIGHT ON . . .

PLANET TERRY ™

by **Sandy Hausler** and **Adam Philips**

"Go bother the Earthlings!" said one alien. Another said, "Enough already!" Who were they talking to? Young **Planet Terry**, of course, the space-travelling star of his very own Star Comics. And what were the aliens so annoyed about? Well, **Terry** wanted to ask (for the umpteenth time) if anyone had seen his parents.

You see, **Terry** was lost in the far reaches of space when merely an infant. Just after his birth he had been put in the star cruiser **Space Warp's** only sterile environment, a tiny lifeship — but as fate would have it, the lifeship was jettisoned accidentally, and **Planet Terry** was stranded in space.

In spite of his lack of parents, **Planet Terry** grew up a bright young boy. He was fed, cared for and educated by the lifeship. Now he searches the galaxy for the parents he has never known, accompanied by his friends **Robota** and **Omnus**. **Robota**, a Series III ser-

vant robot, was **Terry's** reward for having vanquished the dreaded **Yung-mun** on the planet Bznko. She had become obsolete when the new Series IV robot came out, and **Terry** found her in a garbage dump when he was given (quite literally) the "pick of the litter" by the Bznkoans. **Omnus** is a large, green, rowdy alien whom **Planet Terry** and **Robota** encountered on their way to the Milktoast Malt Shop. **Omnus** accompanied them as they followed up a lead on the whereabouts of **Terry's** parents. In a fight with the sleazy patrons of the bar, **Omnus** formed an alliance with **Planet Terry** and **Robota**, and joined them on their quest for **Terry's** parents.

The gentle humor and exciting science fiction of **PLANET TERRY** are the products of writer **Lennie Herman**, who, sadly, did not live to see his latest creations in print. **Herman**, also the guiding force behind **TOP DOG** and **ROYAL ROY** for Star Comics, had long been an important force in children's comics, including being a writer and editor for Harvey Comics. From 1972-1983 Herman scripted many Harvey titles, among them **RICHIE RICH**, **DOLLAR THE DOG** and **JACKIE JOKERS**, and was also a contributor to Marvel's **CRAZY MAGAZINE**.

Lennie was also the vice-president of the **Cartoonist Guild**, and was well known as a gag-panel cartoonist. His

cartoons appeared in **COLLIERS**, **THE SATURDAY EVENING POST**, and **READERS DIGEST**, among others.

Sid Jacobson, editor of the Star Comics line, remembers **Lennie** fondly. "**Lennie** was the funniest person I've ever known and the funniest writer I have ever worked with in comics. He made a tremendous impact on everyone he knew. He was everyone's friend." **Lennie's** work in children's humor comics will influence writers for years to come, and his creations for Star Comics show that children's comics need not be restricted to childish topics. The science fiction of **PLANET TERRY** is as convincing and enjoyable as any "down to earth" comic book.

Lennie Herman died of a heart attack on January 2, 1984. The three comics he created for Star Comics have just debuted, and although he wrote only a few issues of each title before his untimely death, his memory will live on, as new writers take on the rich series concepts that **Lennie** created, and continue them for years to come. And nowhere is this more apparent than in the pages of **PLANET TERRY**. If and when **Terry** finds his parents, his wandering star is sure to keep shining. He's destined to travel to worlds beyond our imagination, sure to find excitement, friendship and adventure wherever he goes.

For **PLANET TERRY**, not even the sky's the limit!

Planet Terry house ad by Warren Kremer

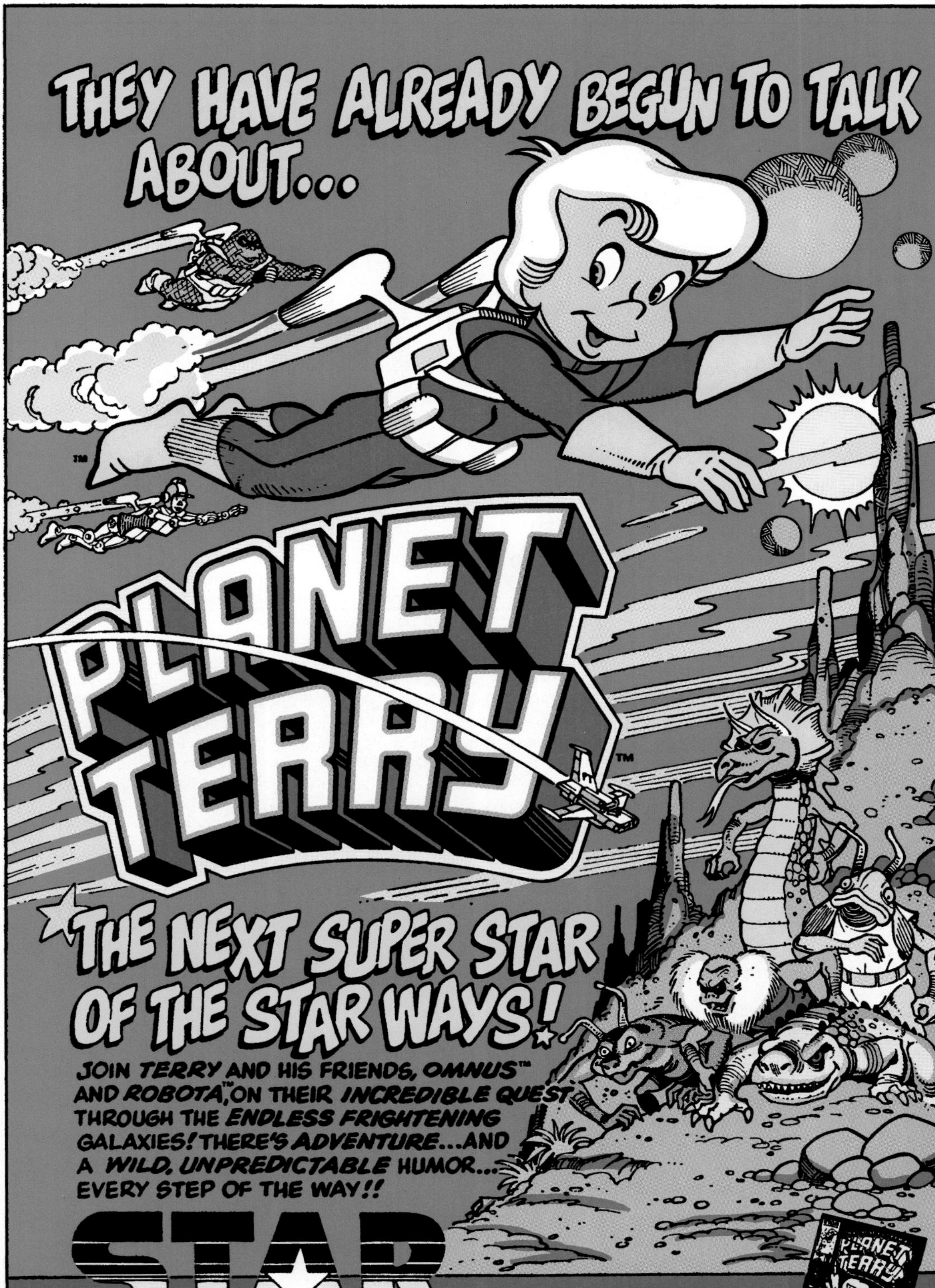
THEY HAVE ALREADY BEGUN TO TALK ABOUT...
PLANET TERRY™
THE NEXT SUPER STAR OF THE STAR WAYS!
JOIN TERRY AND HIS FRIENDS, OMNUS™ AND ROBOTA™, ON THEIR INCREDIBLE QUEST THROUGH THE ENDLESS FRIGHTENING GALAXIES! THERE'S ADVENTURE...AND A WILD, UNPREDICTABLE HUMOR... EVERY STEP OF THE WAY!!
STAR COMICS™
THE NEW WORLD IN THE MARVEL® UNIVERSE

Star Comics **promo poster by Warren Kremer** COURTESY OF HERITAGEAUCTIONS.COM

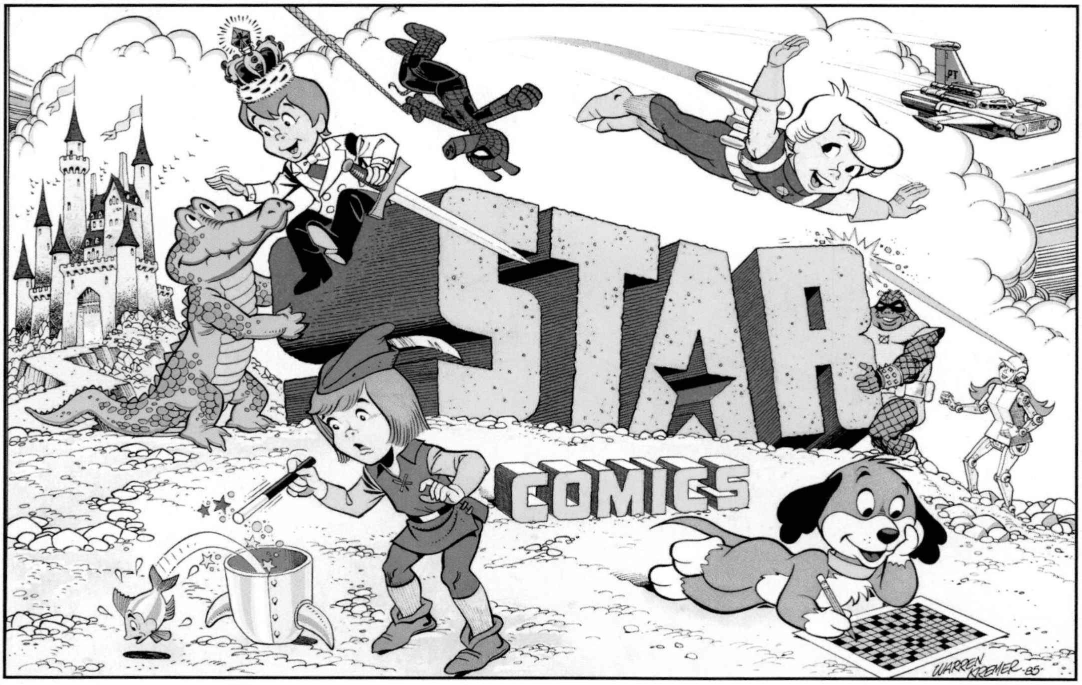
STAR
COMICS
WARREN KREMER '85

Star Comics: All-Star Collection Vol. 2 GN-TPB
cover art by Warren Kremer & Tom Smith

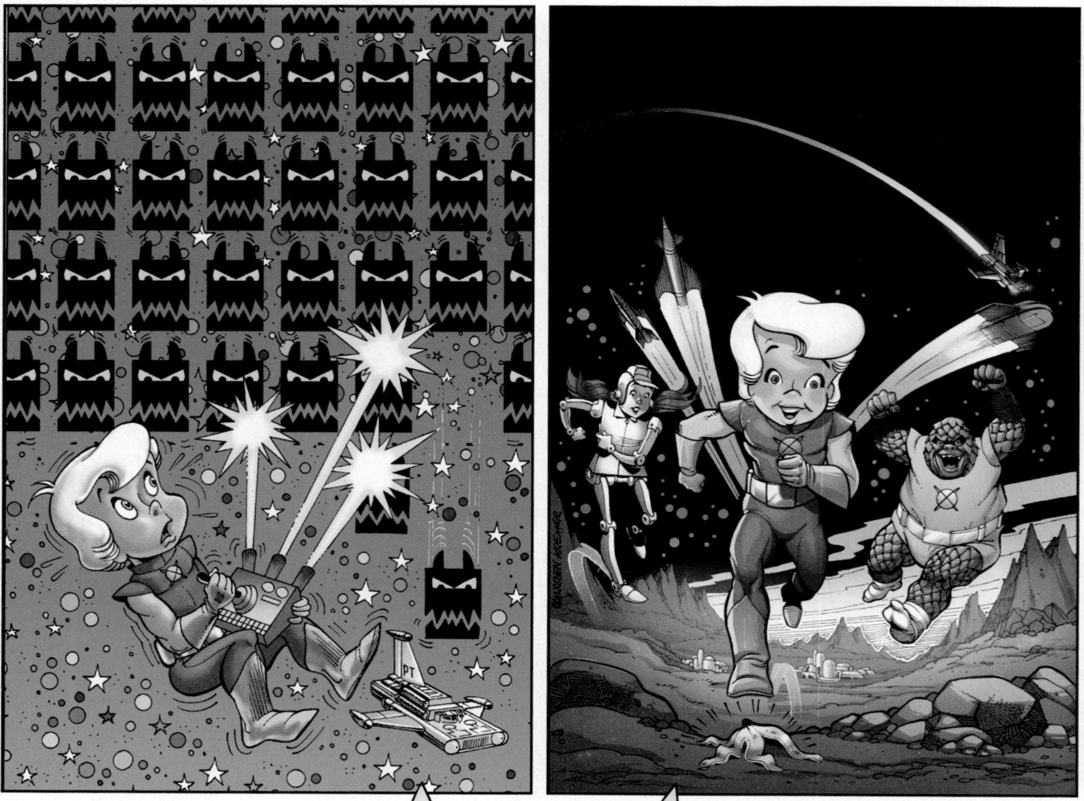